I0841070

THE DEPLORABLE UNDERGROUND

PAULA T. WEISS

For my wonderful and patient husband Mitch.

Acknowledgments

My heartfelt gratitude once again, to my dear friend and fellow writer, Janice Sebring, for a magnificent developmental review. Janice's knowledge of upstate New York through her genealogical research made the grittier Cayuga scenes more realistic than they would have been otherwise. I took her advice as much as possible, and as in *The Antifan Girlfriend*, she remained my go-to source for advice on all things Lutheran, and broadly Christian.

I also wish to thank Jennie Cohen for her discerning copy edits. She caught many apparent discrepancies that I subsequently had to edit my way out of. She also made me realize that I had failed to adequately carry over into the sequel various things, including brain chips, surveillance, and New Women—that were introduced in *The Antifan Girlfriend*.

Thank you, Antifan Sibling, for your brilliant cover and interior design. No, the Antifan Sibling does not wear a cape, and is not really an Antifan. Proof that blood is thicker than politics.

Thanks also to all those wonderful *Antifan Girlfriend* readers who popped out of nowhere—and my past—to praise the novel and tell me how it had moved them. Now some of you are my friends, both on social media and in real life. The finest reward, short of a movie deal.

Any deficiencies or errors remain my own.

Paula T. Weiss
Fairfax, Virginia
June 2023

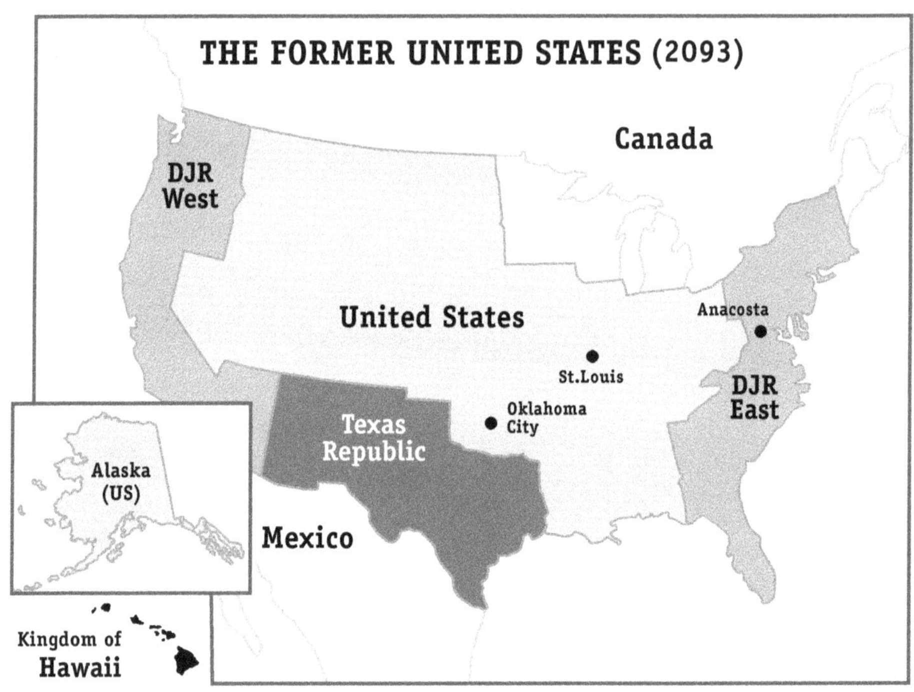

The former United States comprising the United States, the Diversity Justice Republic and its subordinate Kingdom of Hawaii, the Republic of Texas, and the four states that joined Canada in 2060.

CAST OF CHARACTERS

OKLAHOMA CITY

Malia Jenness Harris, aspiring professor

David Harris, former Antifan commander, now Capettone's security director

Rex (Isabelle) Jenness, Malia's daughter

Kevin Malloy, Rex's boyfriend

Cristobal Mendoza, Capettone robotics director

Baxter Berry, Capettone CEO

Lauren McCall, FBI Special Agent

Daniel Harris, David's brother

Fern Harris, Daniel's wife

Emmett and George Harris, David and Malia's sons

Nathan Robertson, Rex's new suitor

ANTIFANS

Commander Khalid Ma, "Paragon," 290

Captain Exterra Boyd, 185

Director Vladivar Montoya, 305

Deputy Director Steven Rosen, 275

Lieutenant Marcus Vanover, 150

Commander Liam Battista, 190, militia commander

Lieutenant Loki Greene, 135, militia officer

ANACOSTA PLOREVILLE

Warren Welcome, grocery store owner

Jeff Welcome, his son

Marjory Mitchell Harris, David's mother

Emma Harris McArdle, David's sister

Larry McArdle, Emma's husband

Christine Harris Sutherlin, David, Emma and Daniel's sister.

Rabbi Robert Goldberg

ST. LOUIS

John Gaines, Sr. Director DJR Affairs, National Security Council
Vernal Booth, American Intelligence Agency (AIA) operations officer
Bob Dietz, Dallas station chief, AIA

CAYUGA

Lucy Martin Gawser, roundup leader
Seth Yancy, Lucy's lover
Tom Nichols, aspiring rebel
Gary Bleiweiss, a self-described "broken old man."
Rachel Miller, the roundup medic

COMMITTEE OF UNJUSTLY DETAINED SOCIAL CREDITEERS

Araceli Perez, 100
The Political Commissar, 100

YRAMALAND PLORES

Oren Olliver, seeking revenge against Sokos
Rebecca Olliver, Oren's sister
Harry Noonan, one of the guards

THE COLLEGE OF THE EARTHLOVING PRIESTS

Sohan Maweidaughter, 70, janitor
Melusine Lilithdaughter, 300, College political commissar
Aleta Hekatedaughter, 290, Great Priestess of the College

Prologue
November 2091

Anacosta (formerly Washington, DC), the Diversity Justice Republic

Director Vladivar Montoya, 305, and his deputy Steve Rosen, 275, had just returned to Beaufort Tower, the headquarters of the Antifan Defense Forces, after the late director's funeral at the National Diversity Cathedral. The black uniforms they and the other ADF mourners wore had contrasted sharply with the pink pussy hats required for religious decorum, and Montoya had simply refused to wear the sacred hat. "Ridiculous female stuff," he said to Rosen, who had swallowed hard and worn his for the sake of propriety. He wouldn't have wanted to offend his wife or college-aged daughters, who were purists in these matters and who would watch the news footage later.

The tall, gray-haired Rosen had mixed them highballs at the director's ample bar, since it was afternoon by now, and now the two men sat silently, not quite gloomy, but pensive, thinking of the inexorable fate that awaited all. But you never knew how it would come for you, which was the most frightening thing of all, Steve mused. And in the Diversity Justice Republic, the austere Blue successor state to the United States, death had various unpleasant ways of coming to you.

The old director's passing marked the end of an era. Victor Ferraro had served even before the civil war that officially broke up the United States, doing his humble part as Antifan leaders built pasty-faced foul-mouthed gangs into a lethal militia, and then into the super-secret police and military force of the new Republic. Almost no one left in the ADF had firsthand recollection of those pioneer days, when a chain or a Molotov cocktail, or even a skateboard, was considered part of the arsenal, and a military engagement was more often than not a street brawl.

"He understood why we were here," said Montoya. "No one was better at protecting Diversity," namely periodically excising the rot that festered and flared in the Towers as bureaucrats inevitably forgot the purpose of the revolution and rooted for privilege like pigs searching for truffles in a forest.

"He loved the ADF," Rosen replied, "and all our folks knew it."

"Remember when that Knowledge Tower piece of crap tried to assassinate him?

Remember how fast we turned on the KTs? They haven't made a peep since."

Montoya stared directly at Rosen with his dark beady eyes, and said, "When I sat by his bedside the last time, he said we had some unfinished business that we needed to take care of."

Rosen knew what he meant. Privately, Rosen doubted whether the hospitalized Ferraro had even managed to utter a complete sentence in his final weeks. More likely, Montoya was projecting his own preferences onto the director. But it didn't matter.

"When Harris and that girlfriend of his crossed the border, and took two other Antifans with them, that was the beginning of the end for Victor," said Montoya. "Victor was never the same after that." That was the first, and only time, since the founding of the DJR in 2055 that Antifans, let alone a senior commander, had managed to escape across the militarized frontier into the still-free United States. It hadn't helped either that the two other Antifans were a young black couple, not when the DJR was supposed to be a paradise for non-whites.

"It was a mistake on his part not to let them marry," said Rosen, who had been a friend of Commander David Harris, and whose recent promotion to deputy director had been a close call on account of that relationship.

"Regardless," said Montoya, "a very bad precedent. No one should think that an Antifan, especially at that level, should be able to escape to the fascists and get away with it. Think of what he must have told them."

"What do you want to do about it? We're not going to invade the US to get at them, are we?"

Montoya replied, "Nothing should be off the table. We should be talking with that station chief of ours in St. Louis. Maybe he'd have some ideas. I know he's doing a lot of work making progress in spreading Diversity Thought among the intellectuals and the activists in the US, but he could help us here as well." St. Louis was the capital of the remaining Red United States.

"What do you want to do? Have Harris killed?"

"I'd like to bring him back here, somehow. And kill him, but slowly. So no one else in the ADF ever thinks they can get away with this again."

"What about the others, Vlad? Are we going to kidnap all of them?" Five others had crossed into the US with David Harris and his bride, Malia.

"I'd settle for Harris. He betrayed his oath," replied Montoya. "Not that I would mind smacking that wife of his around for causing all this trouble in the first place. And yeah, that daughter of the wife's—she belongs back here too.

"I'm not going to worry about the Plore brother and I definitely don't like the optics of bringing back those black ingrates, even if they were Antifans.

"Steve, I hope you're not showing a lack of Antifan spirit here. Just figure it out."

At times like these, Rosen almost wished he had remained a junior commander. Almost.

PART ONE

OKLAHOMA

"Social justice is antithetical to individual justice."
—Dr. Cristobal Mendoza

Chapter One
The Bump
(May 1, 2093)

Malia Harris waited on the platform at St. Louis Gateway Station for the train that would take her home to Oklahoma City after a busy week of meetings. Her face was calm, but alight with the pleasure of a productive day behind her. She would never take for granted the miracle of high-speed train travel and the ability to move freely around the country like any other citizen. Other people around her might look grumpy, impatient, or bored, but Malia was still excited by freedom. After escaping the Diversity Justice Republic almost four years ago, she was about to become a citizen of the free United States.

Her curly dark hair was barely restrained in a bun, a few tendrils escaping in the warm spring sunshine after a busy day. A crisply tailored blue suit made her look taller than she really was. Her suitpod contained not just the outfits she had worn that week to talk with the analysts at the American Intelligence Agency, but the drafts of her dissertation. During the week she had ventured over to St. Louis University to talk with her thesis advisor, the renowned political theorist Dr. Robert Upton.

The sleek gray bullet train pulled smoothly alongside the platform. It was late Friday afternoon, and most of the travelers were tired businesspeople heading back to Little Rock after a day of meetings or a conference in the capital of the postwar United States. Only a few would make the full five-hour journey to Oklahoma City.

Malia boarded her compartment after checking her phone ticket. Each compartment in business class contained four workstations, one in each corner, so one could work in relative privacy, unless one happened to share the space with an inconsiderate chatterer. She had hesitated before spending the money, but her husband, David, had insisted. "It's a better class of people," he said, always concerned about her safety. "We can afford it."

While the train still trembled gently in the station, she took out her workscreen and the edited paper notes, and laid them on the pullout table. She tapped on the screen to order her dinner. Before settling down to work, she looked out the window at the other passengers as they strode down the platform, pulling their suitpods. She was confident that most took for granted their freedom to travel on demand. As a low Social Crediteer in the Diversity Justice Republic, only a few years ago, she had not been permitted to travel on the long-distance trains, let alone airplanes. Too wasteful of the earth's resources, they said.

She and David had flown to Chicago and Denver for short vacations, her first airplane trips ever. They were still hesitant about foreign trips, even to Canada, which put them in potential reach of vengeful DJR operatives. Their US handlers had advised waiting a little longer.

"One minute to departure," a firm bass conductor voice announced. "This is the Amtrak Indian Belle en route from Chicago to Little Rock and Oklahoma City via Norman. All aboard!" The conductor drew out the "ALLLLLLL..." so that for a moment even the most jaded traveler experienced an invigorating jolt of old-time rail drama.

Malia hoped that she would have the compartment to herself. The rapidly fleeting seconds suggested she might obtain the precious privacy she sought.

And then a tall, dark-haired man about her age entered the compartment. "Good evening," he said, as he took the seatdesk ahead of hers by the window. He carried only a leather satchel.

"Hello," she said, disappointed.

The doors closed, and the train began to move, slowly, then building within minutes to the maglev maximum of two hundred miles per hour. At this rate, they would arrive in Oklahoma City by 9:30 p.m. Even for high Social Crediteers, such as David, nothing like this had existed in the DJR.

No conductor would pass through, since the train management could confirm remotely that the passengers who had booked the seatdesks were the same who had entered the compartment. Nor could a passenger move from one secured compartment to the next, so Malia and the dark-haired man, whoever he was, would be riding together until Oklahoma City, or whenever he chose to disembark.

Malia was relieved that the other passenger showed no signs of interest in casual conversation, instead setting up his workscreen and appearing to read messages, sitting sideways with his rugged profile in her full view. She began transferring Dr. Upton's suggested edits from the manuscript to the workscreen document. However, it was hard to ignore the other passenger. He was part Asian, she surmised, judging by his almond-shaped eye visible to her and his brushlike black hair. He seemed to be about her age. When he removed his suit jacket to hang it up, she noticed his broad shoulders straining under the cotton dress shirt.

An attendant arrived with two drinks and placed the pink one on her desk. He handed the old-fashioned to the dark-haired man.

"I'm sorry, I didn't order this drink," she told the attendant.

"I ordered it for you," said the dark-haired man. "As a courtesy, that's all. For a beautiful woman."

"Thank you," she said, but a bit resentfully, because it meant she would in fact owe him the reciprocal courtesy of engaging in conversation.

"A pink lady," he said, "I apologize for the presumption. Perhaps you would prefer a glass of wine?" She was impressed by his deep, sonorous voice, with just the hint of a foreign accent.

"No, this is fine. Thank you very much," she repeated, aware that her initial words had come across less than graciously.

Once the attendant had left, the other passenger turned around to face her. She saw he was indeed partly Asian, but he had a swarthy complexion and heavy brows. Not Chinese or Japanese, she imagined, but possibly central Asian? His muscular build also suggested the steppes, not the delicate scholars of Confucian Asia.

"So you had business in St. Louis, and now you're returning to Oklahoma City."

"That's a good guess," she said, a touch sarcastically.

"Not a whole lot between here and there," he smiled at her, dismissing Little Rock altogether.

She dared to ask about him. He had a very slight accent, barely detectable, but hinting at a more exotic origin. He also spoke formally, which suggested English was not his first language.

"I teach Chinese history at St. Louis University," he said. "And I am going to the University of Oklahoma to deliver a lecture on Monday. But I thought I would do some sightseeing around the university area this weekend. Hire a self-driving car, and see the countryside. I've never been to Oklahoma before. Is there anything you would recommend I see?" Malia told him about the hiking she and her husband liked to do south of the university, toward the Texas border.

"It's rough country," she said, "but good trails. And the gangs on the Texas side stay there."

By the time the third round of drinks arrived, with their dinners, she had confided that she was working on her PhD in political science with Dr. Upton.

"He's very famous," said her companion, dining on an eggplant panini with fried potatoes. "One of our finest scholars at the university." He had never heard of Upton before. "What is your dissertation about?"

"It's an application of John Locke's social compact to the Diversity Justice Republic and to the Texas Republic."

His eyebrows rose. "And what do you know about the DJR? We don't hear much about the DJR these days, do we? The border is sealed."

"I lived in the DJR until a few years ago. So I know plenty about the DJR and how it treats its citizens, or so-called citizens."

"Ah," said the man, "I think I know who you are. Aren't you Malia Jenness? Didn't you escape the DJR a few years ago? That was well publicized."

Malia smiled, and nodded, even though she was proud to be Mrs. Harris these days. The train pulled into the station at Little Rock, but was off again in less than two minutes. No one entered the compartment, the man having purchased all three remaining seatdesks in the compartment to ensure they would not be disturbed.

"Ervin Yusufov," the man introduced himself. "You can call me amba-sah."

Hearing the almost-forgotten salutation used by lower Social Crediteers to address male DJR elites brought back Malia's decades of subjugation and fear in a single, breathless moment. Now she knew she was in the presence of a senior official of the DJR, perhaps an Antifan Defense Forces commander from his confident demeanor and his athletic build. How he had made it across the militarized border and into her train compartment was another matter.

She looked at him guardedly, but then collected herself. She was no longer a Diversan, defined by her Social Credit score, which was now far less relevant than her student ID number. Under no circumstances would she kowtow to this likely Antifan, who as an Antifan, almost certainly had innocent blood on his hands. It did not occur to her at that moment, but it would later that evening, that he could easily have added her to the total casualty numbers, and disappeared into the crowds at the next station.

"I don't call anyone amba-sah anymore. I'm about to become an American citizen and I'm free."

"Charming concept. Surely you miss some things about the DJR?"

"What would I miss? Eating fish paste and soybakes? Reading Diversity garbage instead of real books? Being a number and not a name? Worshipping a pile of dirt?" The last was a reference to the official pagan Mother Earth Diversity religion in the DJR.

Now she had successfully seized the initiative, because she could tell Yusufov was angry. The three drinks that had lowered her inhibitions also made her defiant. She had never had a chance for a reckoning with the DJR, and now sitting right here was the epitome of the tyranny she had endured for decades.

"Even though the DJR raised you and educated you?" Then she realized he knew more about her than he had pretended, at least that she had been an orphan, thanks to the civil war, and that their meeting on this train was no accident.

"What do you want from me? Why are you here, Mr. Yusufov? Or whoever you are."

"Tell your traitor husband that the DJR hasn't forgotten him. And as for you, we know that you have been going quite often to the fascists' spy agency and telling them our secrets. If you value your life, and the life of your sons, you might want to stop doing that."

She started to reach for the alarm button under her desk that would summon a conductor, but he laughed at her. "I've disconnected that remotely. Don't worry, I won't hurt you—tonight. But you might want to take my warning seriously."

"Do you really care that they know you worship dirt?" she mocked him. She sensed that last comment had struck a nerve. "Or that you starve most of your population so that a few people can live in luxury? And that your military can't afford to do more than just keep people behind your walls? Frankly, they don't need me to tell them that."

Yusufov responded, "You should know that the DJR has increasing numbers of sympathizers here in the United States. Many of the young people are drawn to the tenets of Diversity. They understand how their European ancestors oppressed the earth and racial and sexual minorities. If they themselves come from the Diverse People they want to seize their just due once they learn the truth. Only socialism can achieve Diversity and suppress individualism. We benefit from being able to operate in this so-called free country, and we give the youth the simple answers they want. Someday you may find that you escaped the DJR only to live in the DJR—again."

"I seriously doubt that. Who would choose to live under slavery?"

"That's rather naive of you. Most people will gladly accept slavery if you package it in a way that appeals to their sense of virtue or need for safety. Human beings want to be slaves, but only for a good cause.

"But my main point, Ms. Jenness, is that if you want to protect yourself and your family, you might want to start becoming more cooperative. If you're going to talk to US intelligence agencies, perhaps you need to tell us what you have learned about them as well. We know you attended the reception with General Ralston last night." Ralston was the chief of the US Defense Intelligence Agency. The kitchen staff at the St. Louis Heritage Hotel eagerly provided information to Yusufov's colleagues for a fee.

"Do you miss Beltane?" He switched the subject abruptly, reminding her of the upcoming pagan summer solstice holiday when the men and the women, both those natural-born and newly made, would meet and couple by the civic fires. The Beltane celebrations in Anacosta, the DJR capital, drew thousands. Malia had only gone twice, once out of despair and loneliness after the authorities had stolen her daughter, and in neither case could she remember with whom she had paired. Now it all seemed quite sad and pathetic.

"Not at all," she said. "It's disgusting. Sex outside marriage is purposeless."

"I don't think you really believe that, Malia," Yusufov said. "You certainly found it purposeful when you spied for us against the Economic Tower." Now she was confident he was an Antifan because he knew about how she had exploited the lust of the lawbreaking Tower bureaucrats and helped bring them down for the ADF, only four years ago.

"The Diversity Cultural Association will be sponsoring a Beltane festival in the Hickory Hills near Norman that night. You might want to attend."

"Me? Attend a Beltane festival? Are you crazy?" Malia wasn't sure whether she was more shocked by the invitation or by the very idea that Beltane orgies were occurring in the very heart of one of the reddest states in the Bible Belt, albeit near the university. She sputtered, "I'm married!"—which in the DJR, however, would not have been a relevant objection.

"To a traitor. If you come to the festival, I will personally lie with you. You need not worry about a partner."

She pressed her lips together, with exasperation or contempt, she wasn't sure herself. "Thanks, that was my big concern about going to your Beltane party. But I don't have enough Social Credit to be your Beltane partner." She had been a menial 70 when she left the DJR.

"I'll overlook it. And then I will give you your instructions. You would be wise to serve us. You are not as safe as you think you are in Oklahoma."

The train was pulling into the Hot Springs station. To her surprise, Yusufov gathered his belongings and prepared to exit.

"I won't need to travel to Norman tonight," he said. In fact, he planned to wait on the opposite platform for the return express to St. Louis. "Remember what I have told you. I expect to see you at Beltane, if you care for your life and that of your sons. All of the information about our gathering can be found online." He looked down at her, still seated, as he waited for the compartment door to open. Her brown eyes looked up at him sullenly.

"You may not be interested in the DJR. But the DJR is still interested in you." And then he was gone.

Malia slumped back into her seat, exhaling deeply. She realized that he had not promised that if she cooperated, her husband would be safe. She knew David, the first successful Antifan escapee from the DJR, was the ADF's ultimate target. But really, how could the ADF ever think she would conspire against the beloved husband who had saved her life? And in any case, how could the ADF reach out and harm them, in Oklahoma? She had asked David why he still routinely carried a firearm outside the house, but perhaps he already knew that the ADF would not forget him. She had the compartment to herself for the remaining two hours until they reached Oklahoma City.

Chapter Two
Home
(Friday, May 1, 2093)

Malia saw David approaching as soon as she entered the main terminal at Oklahoma City. At that time of the evening, few people were around to greet the final train from St. Louis. It was easy to spot a handsome, not-quite-tall blond man in his early forties with a confident stride. David still retained the self-assurance honed by two decades in the Antifan Defense Forces, although it had taken a battering by US law enforcement officials who refused to hire a man who had willingly carried out the orders of a brutal dictatorship and shed innocent blood.

For his part, David felt that the US authorities had not really understood his situation and had not given him the chance he deserved to show his mettle after he and Malia had risked their lives to cross the border. It had been galling when the FBI had expressed an interest in hiring Malia rather than himself. "Are you kidding?" he'd said. "They'd make you a secretary. And you're pregnant anyway."

David contended that it wasn't his fault the ADF had plucked him out of a ninth-grade gym class and forced him to become an Antifan. Malia had tried to explain the US point of view to him, that perhaps the US government felt it would be hard to retrain him from the instincts that encouraged him to smack an unruly prisoner or trick them into confessions, but such reasonable arguments only angered David, so she let it go.

"Hello, beautiful," he said as he closed the remaining few feet between them and sealed her welcome with a kiss.

She smiled at him, the eyes that had flashed a hostile warning at Yusufov now sparkling and sweet. "Hello, sweetheart." Then, "Who's watching the boys?" It was well past their bedtime.

"They're asleep in the car."

Malia frowned, but checked herself.

"They're fine. Let's go say hi to them." David grabbed the suitpod handle and several minutes later, she was indeed gazing upon the peaceful sleeping countenances of her two sons in their car seats in the sport utility van. Emmett was almost three, dark-haired and narrow-faced, like a miniature Italian count. Even in sleep, his face shone with intelligence. George had just turned one. His blond curls and chubby red cheeks gave him the look of a cherub, even though his parents already knew he was a much more mischievous sort than the sober Emmett.

David's older brother, Daniel, who lived nearby with his wife, Fern, often commented that George looked like his namesake, Daniel and David's youngest brother, who had died of diphtheria in an Antifan transit camp back in 2055. Malia herself had no relatives to compare resemblances with, thanks to the civil war, so she was content with knowing that at least Emmett resembled her more than he did the blond Harris brothers.

"How was your week?" she asked David as he navigated the suburban boulevards leading to their house. He still preferred to drive his own vehicle, but that wasn't unusual in the United States where driving a car was equated with independence.

"Same as always," he said, "Capettone pays me a good salary to shut up and shuffle paperwork." Capettone Medical Industries, which manufactured medical equipment, had hired David as its security director after the Oklahoma City police chief had suggested he was perhaps not well suited to police work in a democratic country where the rights of criminal suspects were respected. But neither was David suited to the deskbound confines of the executive suite. He suspected the US government was paying part of his salary.

Malia diplomatically refrained from saying, "But at least it's a good salary," since she knew that if she remained silent, David would rebound.

"At least it's a good salary," he said.

They pulled into the driveway of their bungalow-style house, welcoming with its tidy lawn, beige steel siding, and burgundy shutters under spotlights that turned on as they approached. The neighbors were all asleep, judging by the darkened homes. In a few minutes, they had tucked the children in their beds, although Emmett awoke, and said, "Mommy? I love you, Mommy," before grasping his stuffed Mr. Monkey, turning over, and falling back to sleep.

"Tell me about your week," David said a few minutes later, at the kitchen table. "Did the analysts want me to come with you next time?" David had accompanied her on some of these visits, where as a former ADF commander, he was a reliable if slightly outdated fount of information on the organization.

"They didn't mention it," she said. "We mostly talked about standard of living stuff. They're trying to figure out what might be of interest to the DJR, now that negotiations are starting on diplomatic relations."

"They should ask whether the DJR can be trusted to honor its end of the deal," said David cynically. "I wouldn't trust Peace-Williams one iota." Kumbaya Peace-Williams, the president of the DJR, had supplanted his senile predecessor in the dustup that followed David and Malia's escape. The ADF kept him on a short leash. "Or the ADF, of course."

Malia finally told him about the Antifan who had cornered her on the train. "He didn't try to do anything to me, other than the threats," she said, "and plying me with cocktails." She refrained from mentioning the invitation to Beltane. Not yet. "He said I needed to provide them with information about St. Louis if I wanted to stay safe, and the boys to stay safe."

David cursed softly.

"What did he look like?" He knew he would not necessarily recognize Malia's travel companion, not after more than three years away from Anacosta, but no harm in trying. She described Yusufov, and David said, "Yes, I recall someone like that around Beaufort. Not a senior officer. I think he might have been a Muslim—obviously, within the MED." The Mother Earth Diversity Church had branches corresponding with all major denominations so a loyal DJR citizen might preserve the trappings of his ancestral backward faith—Islam, Judaism, or Christianity—while worshiping Mother Earth among his fellow Diversans. If you wanted to pray to Mother Earth prone on a rug, or fast during Ramadan, the DJR wouldn't stop you. But praising Allah or the Prophet Muhammad instead of Mother Earth would be risky.

"I thought we were safe here," said David, "but now I am not so sure."

"Should we call Isabelle?" said Malia. Isabelle, her daughter, was now finishing her freshman year at Taylor University. "If they approached you, and now me, wouldn't they target her as well?"

"Yes, they would. How did he expect you to deliver this information to him? Did he give you any instructions?"

"He told me to come to the Beltane fires outside the university next month in the Hickory Hills."

"Beltane fires? At the university? Since when? That seems like a strange place to pass information. But it would be a good place to kill someone, and afterward, most people around here would figure you got what you deserved for messing with pagans." A few lurid headlines, and then the story would fade, especially with no proven DJR link.

Malia had taken Yusufov at his word, but David was right, it would be a perfect setting for a murder committed amid the gasps and moans of lust around her. A slit throat, a body lying there in the dark late at night, an onlooker might well assume her to be an exhausted celebrant until the dawn revealed a corpse lying alone by the fires' embers.

Malia was relieved that she didn't have to share Yusufov's "I will lie with you" proposition with David, at least not yet.

"I know, wouldn't a coffee shop or a park make more sense?" She started wondering whether the Beltane fires were indeed just a ruse to lure her to a remote setting. No wonder David had already saved her life several times—she was indeed too trusting, even of men who had boldly revealed themselves to be Antifan operatives on a US train.

"Let's go to bed," said David. He was tired, but the mention of Beltane had reminded him Malia had been gone from his own bed all week. He hoped she wasn't planning to return to St. Louis too soon. If the analysts wanted to ask them questions, they could just answer them from the secure terminal in the basement. "Come on, honey. We'll think more clearly in the morning."

Chapter Three
Relatives In The Park
(May 2, 2093)

In the morning, Malia urged David to go jogging in the park, a gesture acknowledging that David had anchored the home front all week while she was traipsing around St. Louis with professors and spies. By the time David had left, wearing black nylon shorts and a red Sooners T-shirt, Malia had fed George and Emmett and was leaning back against the sofa, legs stretched before her, a novel balanced on her thigh. George navigated down the sofa's front on unsteady but solid legs. Emmett placed wooden blocks on top of each other, his face scrunched with concentration. When one fell, he tried again, without complaint.

Emmett then brought over his favorite book, *Cowboys and Dinosaurs*, in which boys rode dinosaurs in a rodeo. If you pressed the dinosaur in just the right place, it would emit a satisfying roar, and the boy would slide down the dinosaur. Then if you pressed the dinosaur's head, the boy would again rise to the top of the dinosaur's back. Malia knew no children's book about boys riding dinosaurs, or about cowboys at all, would ever have been printed in the DJR. Possibly a group of Diverse boys and girls and nonbinary types might save dinosaurs from environmental catastrophe caused by white supremacist business executives.

"This book is definitely knowledge crime," joked David, who had pursued and punished such crimes in the DJR.

After she had read the cowboy dinosaur book three times, a call from Fern provided relief for Malia. "Do you want to go to the playground?" Fern and Daniel's daughter, Ivy Ann, had just turned two, and was an energetic foil to her cousin Emmett. The playground was at the park, and Fern would stop by Malia's en route so they could all stroll over together.

Within half an hour, the two women, who had been friends in Anacosta long before they married the Harris brothers, were sitting on a bench watching the toddlers scamper around the baby playground. Few others were around despite the beautiful warmish spring morning. George seemed willing to crawl within the sandbox, at least for the moment, and fling sand with his chubby palms. The jogging trail encircled the playground before heading toward the playing fields and into the woods beyond. David ran by them once, and they all waved before he disappeared.

An onlooker might have thought the women siblings as well, with Fern the elder. Fern was of average height and build, but she and the more petite Malia shared brown hair and brown eyes. Fern's hair was cut in a bob, with a few gray streaks, while Malia's, when freed from the bun as it was now, tumbled beneath her shoulders in lazy swooping ringlets. Once Fern had been rescued from the Economic Zone camp by David and Malia, and they had crossed the border, she had regained her natural chubbiness.

Malia hesitated to tell Fern about the train passenger, but Fern could be trusted, and likely David would tell Daniel later that day anyway.

"Oh, Malia, that's awful. I thought we would be safe here from…all that."

"Nothing like that has happened to you or Daniel yet, has it?"

Fern shook her head. "They're probably not interested in us. I was nothing and Daniel was a Plore. You and David were blue mud."

Malia almost smiled at the expression, which meant "hot stuff" in DJR circles. Her Social Credit score had been no higher than Fern's when they had escaped, but David had plucked her out of her half-starved obscurity in the False Knowledge Depository and set her on a more glamorous, if dangerous path as an Antifan spy against the Economic Tower. As a senior Antifan commander, David had been the bluest and muddiest of all of them, despite his tainted Deplorable origins.

Malia raced to the sandbox to stop George from shoving sand in his mouth. As she pulled him out of the sandbox, she looked up and across the playing fields behind which lay the track where David was no doubt jogging.

Wait, was that David returning? But not at a steady lope or jog, rather he was racing toward them, across the playing field, waving his arms. Soccer players stopped their game to stare at him. He yelled at them from a distance, but the women couldn't hear him until he had come closer. Malia saw with alarm as he approached that his left leg was scratched and bloodied, "Let's go! Let's go!"

She quickly placed the boys in the double stroller. They were too surprised to cry. Fern was slower to react, but soon she was scrambling after them, pushing her own stroller with Ivy Ann during the family retreat. A Hispanic family that had just arrived at the playground, a foursome with mother and father, stared at them. "It's OK, don't worry!" David shouted back at them.

David explained. He had been finishing his run, when a medium-sized, athletic black man in a tracksuit, perhaps in his late twenties, had passed him on the track. But then the other jogger slowed down and, turning around, asked, "Are you David Harris? The David Harris?"

David assumed this was another admirer. Their fame had vanished quickly after they had resettled in Oklahoma City, since in the fast-paced United States, sudden celebrities tended to exhaust their welcome quickly to make way for the next sensation. But every once in a while, someone remembered him from the intense news coverage after the dramatic escape. Occasionally, he was asked for an autograph, and he gladly obliged.

"Yes," he said, "I am."

Still jogging, the man turned around again. "Your friends in Anacosta say hello! Better watch out!" He sprinted off toward the other side of the park. David stood for a split second in shock, and then chased after the man, bringing him down onto the path with a desperate jump that dragged his own leg along the asphalt. They grappled briefly, David landing a punch, but then the other man wriggled free from David's grip, leaped to his feet, and ran off into the woods. David would have been unable to catch up with the younger man, so he let him escape.

While Malia knelt at his feet in the kitchen, applying heal-salve to the scratch and then a bandage, David called Lauren. Lauren McCall was the agent at the local FBI field office who was their official point of contact with the US government and responsible for threats to their safety. So far she had had an easy job of it.

"It's Saturday," Malia warned him.

"The ADF doesn't take off Saturdays. Lauren? Sorry to call you on a weekend, but we've had two disturbing incidents in two days." He told her about Malia's experience on the train and now his encounter in the park.

Lauren did not find the park incident particularly worrisome. "Just a prankster. We don't have any DJR agents in Oklahoma, let alone Antifans." Her cheerful cluelessness infuriated David.

"And the guy on the train? Who followed and threatened my wife?" He put the phone on speakerphone so Malia could hear.

It was harder for Lauren to dismiss that out of hand. "Come into the office on Monday. We'll talk about that. Do you want us to have the police send a presence to your house until Monday? Do you feel that you may be in immediate danger?"

David hesitated, and his eyes met Malia's. She gave him a quick shake of the head. No point in attracting the interest of the neighbors.

"No, we don't think that's necessary—yet," he said. "We're armed. I feel sorry for any intruder this weekend. But we can't ignore this." When he hung up, he and Malia had scheduled a meeting at the Bureau field office on Monday afternoon.

Malia made them all a quick lunch while Fern and David sat in the living room. David stared in the direction of the playing children, but his thoughts clearly lay elsewhere.

Here they had built a good life for themselves, or at least had laid its foundation. The living room spoke to their aspirations. The walls were a light gray, the drapes an elegant tan. On the wall hung paintings of faraway cities such as Venice or tropical beaches that they might visit someday when it would become safer to travel abroad. The white brick fireplace hosted crackling fires in winter around which they gathered cozily, a real family. Emmett would stare into the flames with wonder, and after the boys went to bed, David and Malia would cuddle on the rug before the hearth. Framed photographs on the mantelpiece testified to their efforts to become a family like the ones all around them, although, true, the devastation of the civil war had left few families intact on either side of the border and, in the United States, where at least families were not discouraged, they were all in rebuilding mode. In addition to the portraits of his and Daniel's families, David prized the small photograph of his mother and another of her with his two sisters and their families, trapped back in the DJR.

The photo of his mother had made it across the border in an inside jacket pocket, and the other one had more recently arrived from David and Daniel's sisters after having eluded the gauntlet of vengeful DJR censors in regular mail, the only communication permitted between the two countries. The post office clerk had sympathetically rejected David's effort to send a rolled-up group photograph of his and Daniel's families to their mother in Anacosta's Ploreville.

"Not permitted by the other side," the clerk had said. "Too big." Ploreville was the name everyone used for the ghetto where Deplorables lived. Each DJR city had its City, for the Social Crediteers, and its adjacent Plorevilles, for the helots who served the Social Crediteers.

Built-in bookcases held the real books that Malia had longed to own in the DJR, where almost all permitted reading was stored on the vetted and monitored Great Virtual Network. David had promised Malia, his beloved librarian, that someday she would have all the books she wanted and he would never complain about tripping over them. He had kept his promise.

Would all this carefully constructed normalcy be lost to the DJR's implacable revenge, he wondered. Or were these threats essentially empty ones meant primarily to disturb their complacency? Either way, David resolved, it was not to be borne.

Fern interrupted his reverie. "David, Daniel is asking whether you can drop by the store this afternoon. He can't get away."

"Sure," said David. His brother owned an electrical supply and repair shop a few miles away.

After lunch, David told Malia that he was heading over to the store. "Say, are you going on the box today?" he asked her. That was how they communicated with the analysts in St. Louis. Malia nodded, since she liked to check the queue daily. Someone might have questions for them after her week of discussions in St. Louis.

"We'll draft a cable when I get home. We'll need to ask for some instructions on how to proceed. Maybe they're seeing some changes on the DJR side that would explain what's happening to us."

"You don't want to wait for the FBI meeting on Monday?" Malia asked.

"Let's not put all our eggs in that basket," he said, in one of those endearing Ploreisms that Malia to her surprise had found out were by no means archaic sayings in the United States. "I don't trust them to take our concerns seriously. And call Isabelle this afternoon, would you?"

He kissed her, and then left for Daniel's store, this time carrying.

Malia put the boys down for their nap, and headed down to the secure room. She locked the door behind her, and turned on the baby monitor so she would hear if either child awoke suddenly or needed help. Then she tapped in the various pass codes to access the shared workspace with the analysts. She was pleased to see that some of her AIA contacts had indeed sent messages. It was gratifying to be considered useful for defending national security, and while some of the questions seemed arcane, she knew they were never idly asked.

HI SIDONIA. (MALIA'S ONLINE NAME) THIS IS CHRIS. THANKS FOR COMING TO SEE US YESTERDAY AND DISCUSSING DJR HOLIDAYS. SOME OF US WERE WONDERING WHETHER IT'S MANDATORY TO PARTICIPATE IN THE CORONAVIRUS LIBERATION DAY FESTIVITIES, OR EARTH WEEK, OR TO WHAT EXTENT PEOPLE CAN JUST QUIETLY OPT OUT. I'M REFERRING TO SOCIAL CREDITEERS HERE, NOT PLORES. THANKS AGAIN!

HI, THIS IS BRENDA. DO YOU KNOW WHAT THE SOCIAL CREDIT REQUIREMENTS ARE FOR DIFFERENT UNIVERSITIES? OR ARE ACADEMIC GRADES SUFFICIENT? THANK YOU.

CAN YOU TELL US THE REQUIREMENTS FOR PROMOTION TO SERGEANT AND LIEUTENANT IN THE ADF? ARE THE BORDER COMMANDS DIFFERENT FROM THE BEAUFORT HEADQUARTERS' UNITS IN THIS REGARD? (MALIA WOULD PASS THIS ONE TO DAVID LATER.)

Half an hour later, she had satisfactorily answered the first two questions. She closed down the secure room and headed upstairs. No sound from the boys' rooms, good. She settled on the sofa with a cup of tea, breathed deeply, and called Isabelle.

Chapter Four
Isabelle Or Rex
(Saturday, May 2, 2093)

"Hello, Mom." Isabelle had actually answered her phone, which caught Malia by surprise. Malia had been leaving voice mails for two weeks, with no response. Malia excused it as due to Isabelle's no doubt heavy class workload, especially with finals approaching. David merely commented that Isabelle seemed to have forgotten who was paying her tuition.

When Malia called, Isabelle was lying on a blanket in the sun on the Great Lawn outside Psychology Hall with her boyfriend, Kevin. They were making somewhat lackadaisical efforts to swipe through their textbooks, but the sun made them sleepy and it was hard to read with the bright rays glinting off the screen. Isabelle wished she'd brought the print version. Also, last night had gone late, in Kevin's bed in the house he shared with his genial roommates who didn't complain about the squeaking bedsprings or her cries.

"I'm so glad I found you," said Malia. "How are things going, dear?"

"Great, Mom. We'll be home on the twenty-second, after finals."

Kevin pushed aside his workscreen, and propped himself up on his elbows, his long legs stretching onto the grass. Isabelle sensed he did not want her call to go on too long, mother or not. She attributed his lack of interest in family relations to his being an orphan. His childhood had been even tougher than hers, she gathered. He didn't want to talk about it.

Malia drew in her breath.

"David and I wanted to let you know that some very strange things have happened to us in the last few days, and we want you to be alert in case anyone tries anything suspicious with you," said Malia. She related the episodes, without explicitly describing Yusufov's threat. It suddenly occurred to her that Yusufov had threatened her sons, but not her daughter, although he certainly must have known about Isabelle.

"Okay, Mom. That must have been very scary," said Isabelle dutifully.

"You be careful too," Malia responded. "Don't be naive about what's out there, just because you're in a college town." She was grateful that Isabelle would be coming home soon.

"Yes, Mom," said Isabelle, but Malia sensed that she wasn't really paying attention. Perhaps Kevin would at least serve as a protective shield between Isabelle and any DJR agents who sought to accost her.

Kevin had made a good initial impression on Malia and David. But why was Kevin, supposedly twenty-three, only a sophomore? "He was in the army, Mom," Isabelle had huffed impatiently, back in March. "And he served at Fort Hood, so he learned to like this area of the country. It's nothing to worry about." On the surface, Malia had had no reason to distrust this answer. Things were more fluid in the United States, where young people chose their own paths, including what majors and jobs to pursue.

Isabelle asked politely about her half brothers and Uncle Daniel and Aunt Fern and little Ivy Ann. "By the way, Mom," said Isabelle, "I'm thinking of going back to using Rex."

"Really? Why?" Malia was concerned. After the authorities kidnapped the five-year-old Isabelle, her adoptive parents had given her the name Rex. Once they had escaped to the United States, Isabelle had gladly taken her real, feminine, name back.

"It just feels more like me, that's all," said Isabelle. But Kevin had said that if she wanted to be respected in the campus diversity movement, her authentic DJR name, and not the frilly Isabelle would give her instant credibility. "Mom, I gotta go. I've got a psychology test on Monday."

"All right," said Malia, who had become subdued after taking her cue from the distracted Isabelle. "Good luck with the test, honey."

"Thanks, Mom! Love you! Bye, Mom!" Isabelle said, and hung up. She did have a psychology test on Monday, but she probably wouldn't spend much time studying for it. The diversity movement was demanding the university give pass/fail grades this semester in core classes to at least the non-white students, due to how objective letter grades reinforced systemic racism, as Experts had shown, and the administrators were weakening under pressure, judging by their equivocations. Isabelle and her friends were betting that the university would extend the favor to the whole student body to disguise the racism involved in fighting systemic racism.

Now she was beginning to realize that it was standards that were racist. That had seemed ridiculous at first, since she herself thought she knew from experience that hard work and some brains tended to correlate with good grades, but Kevin had explained it to her. As a political science major, with experience in the world, he comprehended the workings of society better than she did.

She turned to Kevin. He was so handsome, with the brown hair, lighter than hers, the hazel eyes, and the fair complexion. She also appreciated his athletic build and his height—six foot two, so tall, but not so tall she felt awkward beside him. The only debit was his thin-lipped mouth, which connoted impatience to neutral observers.

"Something wrong at home?" Kevin asked.

She hesitated. It seemed distasteful to air her family's personal business, even to Kevin, but especially when it involved criticism of the DJR that he admired, albeit from afar. He often said someday the DJR and the United States would be united again, and patriots should try to bring about that day.

"Tell me," he said. "Aren't I here for you?"

"Oh, my mother was bothered by some deejer type on the train from St. Louis on Friday night and it scared her. And this morning someone came up to my stepfather while he was jogging in the park and said something about watching out. So I guess they're worried about me too."

"But you are going to be a bridge-builder between the US and the DJR," Kevin said, "so it wouldn't be in the interest of the DJR to harm you, would it? I'm sure they'll hear about your speech tonight at the service."

"How would they hear about it?" Isabelle asked. She was going to share her story with the others at the Mother Earth Diversity service, a story that she had mostly kept under wraps here at Taylor University. Kevin insisted that it would inspire those who loved Diversity, and it might win some skeptics over to the DJR side. The service always concluded with each attendee confessing their sins and/or rededicating themselves to Diversity.

"They have their ways," said Kevin mysteriously.

Kevin told her he remembered hearing about her family's escape to the United States when he was a new army recruit. Given her background, Kevin said, she had a great opportunity to help heal the rift between the two countries, but that would require people to learn about the DJR and to show willingness to understand the DJR perspective. "I hear we're negotiating with the DJR for diplomatic relations," he said. "Once the border opens up, the US will need people like you who are positioned to create better understanding."

Kevin drew her closer to him, and was running his fingers through her hair, and then staring down into her eyes as she looked up.

"Please kiss me," Isabelle said, melting again.

"One kiss for each Mother Earth commandment you can remember," he said. "I'll make it worth your while."

"Blessed are the meek, for they shall inherit Diversity," she gasped, as the hands reached under her T-shirt and moved upward.

"No," he said impatiently. "In the right order. Otherwise it makes no sense."

She thought, and then remembered, "Thou shalt worship Mother Earth."

"Yes," he said, and his mouth closed over hers. She moaned happily. But then he pulled away after a few seconds. "What's next?"

"Thou shalt honor Diversity as the source of all earthly goods," she said, but not really remembering what that had meant. Maybe that referred to socialism. She hoped Kevin would not expect more. She would study the catechism harder, she promised herself.

"Good," he said, resuming the long kiss. His tongue pressed into her mouth. She was losing it, right on the lawn. This time the kiss lasted ten seconds, but he pulled back again. She whimpered.

"Thou shalt honor Social Credit as a sign of Mother Earth godliness?" she asked.

"That's not the third one," he said sternly.

She looked at him piteously, but he was not easily moved. In such matters one could not be lenient.

"Thou shalt know that Gender is different and all its ways are good?"

"Variable," he corrected her, but he planted his mouth on hers again, and she eagerly lifted her body toward him. This time, fifteen seconds.

She gave him the Social Credit commandment, correctly, this time, and he rolled over onto her and brought her very close to completion, his hand moving up her shorts this time. "Oh!" she cried. It was embarrassing, here on the Great Lawn, even though the nearest party was at least a hundred feet away, but who else might be watching them?

"What's the final commandment?" he demanded. When she hesitated, he said impatiently, "Come on. There are only five MED commandments. If you could learn the Jewish fascist ones, all ten of them, you can remember these, can't you?" Jewish fascist? she thought. Despite her lustful haze, the phrase would stick with her later. What American—on this side of the border—talked like that?

She wept with frustration, and then remembered the first commandment she had uttered. "Blessed are the meek, for they shall inherit Diversity," she breathed, and then his mouth closed over her one last time as he made it worth her while, as promised. It also silenced what would have been her final cry, but that didn't stop a pair of young men walking by from calling, "Hey, get a room!" But the pair were secretly envious of the complete lack of self-consciousness of the couple, and the complete pliancy of the girl. Imagine getting a girl to do that with you on the Great Lawn, they thought, as they headed back to their dorm from the library. "That's the big Diversity guy," one said softly to the other.

"Diversity," nodded the second young man, respectfully.

At that moment, her stepfather was sitting at the counter in Daniel's electrical supply shop. Daniel made them both some coffee, and David sipped his as Daniel attended to a contractor who had come in to purchase some remote-control switches.

Daniel didn't mind working on Saturdays. It was his store, which he had purchased from the elderly Mr. Purvis last year, and he was proud that he worked for himself, for the first time ever. He had bought the store with his settlement from the US government as a refugee from the DJR, and other sums from the book and movie based on their escape, on which he had worked as a technical adviser. Each month he sent Purvis, now enjoying retirement on the Gulf Coast, a percentage of the profits. That was part of the deal. Daniel had kept the Purvis name, because it carried a good, honest reputation. At some point he might add Harris, but there was no point in vainglory, he thought. He was proud of his tidy and spotlessly clean store.

The contractor left, and Daniel pulled up a chair to the metal counter facing David. An onlooker would have known instantly the two men were brothers, with Daniel clearly the older. Daniel's hair was mostly gray, and David's was still mostly fair.

"Fern said you'd had some problems this weekend," Daniel began in his understated way.

David told him about the man who had accosted Malia on the train, and then related his encounter that morning with the jogger. "I don't know what to do at this point," he said, "other than meet with the Bureau on Monday. What will they be able to do?"

"Maybe they could trace the fellow on the train, at least?" suggested Daniel. "There's got to be a record of who purchased the tickets for the compartment."

David nodded, "but he would know how to cover his tracks, if he was really ADF."

"Do you think Fern and I need to worry?"

"I don't know that you and Fern need to worry as much as Malia and I do, but I'd carry if I were you, for now, just in case."

"What about Isabelle?" Daniel asked.

"Malia's calling her this afternoon. Thank God she'll be coming home from school in a few weeks. She's coming with her boyfriend, who seems like a fine young man. He's from Montana. Isabelle says he was stationed at Hood, so that's why he decided to stay in our area."

"If they really meant to do you harm, though," asked Daniel, "why would they warn you? All this is just going to make us very alert, right?"

"So is this just meant to keep us on edge?"

"Well, these guys are your people. What do you think they're up to?"

David bristled at the "your people," but it was true that if anyone should be able to infer Antifan intentions from these overtures to him and Malia, it should be him. They had urged Malia to spy against him, trying to drive a wedge between him and her by threatening their children. There was a certain logic, however flawed, in the Antifan sally against Malia, but why would they confront him, almost simultaneously? Was the ADF trying to pressure Malia into working with them, by showing it could reach out to them in Oklahoma?

As he drove home, David realized he was no wiser for the talk with Daniel. Perhaps the Bureau or the AIA analysts would be able to share some insight about ADF motivations. It had been over three years since he had last worn his Antifan uniform, and he couldn't claim to know what was preoccupying senior Antifans at Beaufort these days. That sinister Tower was receding in his mind with the passage of time and the vibrancy of his new life in the United States. He knew that Director Ferraro had died more than a year ago, but if anything, shouldn't that have slaked the ADF's thirst for revenge? Can't we all just move on, folks?

He pulled into the driveway. The boys were playing in the front yard under Malia's watchful eye, and they shrieked with joy to see him. Even the reserved Emmett clasped his leg. Tomorrow they would walk to Immanuel Lutheran Church, and he and Malia and Daniel and Fern would sit together, while the children played and heard a Bible story in babysitting. He would occasionally give his beautiful wife, possibly wearing the blue diamond-patterned dress with the belt that cinched her slender waist, an affectionate glance. After the service, at the coffee hour, they would chat with other congregants, who were almost friends. The boys would filch cookies until their appetite was spoiled. Then they all would walk home, because the spring weather was so pleasant. What more could he want from life?

A purpose, thought David, a sense of purpose. Malia now had hers. But where his would come from or how he could find it in this comfortable country, he did not yet know. And for the first time in his life, he was frightened.

Chapter Five
Bureau
(Monday, May 4, 2093)

"I'll swing by around one and pick you up for the Bureau meeting," said David, as he adjusted his tie in the small guest bathroom off the kitchen. As usual, he liked what he saw in the mirror, even the crinkles in the corners of his eyes, which he felt gave him some gravitas, but nowadays he wore a navy suit rather than a black uniform. "Can you check sometime during the morning to see whether St. Louis responded to our cable?"

"Yes," Malia replied, distracted by George flinging oatmeal. Emmett sat quietly at the table, on his raised cushion, chewing on mini-pancakes, lost in thought. As soon as Daddy left, he would ask his mother where the zoo kept the dinosaurs, since they never saw any on their visits.

"Don't wear that to our meeting," David said, joking about Malia's now-oatmeal-spattered bathrobe. She flashed a look of irritation, and he knew her well enough to identify its source. A few days ago some of the brightest young intelligence analysts in the country had been asking her questions bearing on national security, and now she was back in babysitting mode. Too bad, he thought, a few days ago I was feeding the boys, waiting for Fern to show, and arriving late for work. Your turn, book babe. He leaned over her and gave her a kiss, careful to avoid oatmeal contamination. Then he gently rubbed Emmett's shoulder, "Take care of Mommy today, would you, buddy?" Emmett looked up somewhat absentmindedly at him.

Malia smiled, her good humor almost restored. They would spend several hours at the playground with Fern and Ivy Ann, trying not to let the incident on Saturday spoil the lovely day. "We can't hide at home," said David, anticipating her question about whether the outing was wise, so soon after the upsetting weekend. "Just take the Beretta in your purse. I don't think you'll need it."

Despite his bravado at home, today David kept a sharper eye out than usual on the expressway for erratic drivers. A few days ago, he would never have guessed ADF officers or their minions would or could show up in Oklahoma City and now he saw them everywhere. He worried about one red sedan that tailed him aggressively, but eventually it swerved around him and exited the highway. Private cars mixed effortlessly with the black self-driving vehicles that could be relied on to drive safely without human egos at the wheel, and overall, traffic moved smoothly thanks to computerized systems that adjusted tolls. Within twenty minutes, he was pulling into his own space in the parking lot at Capettone Medical Industries.

The Capettone complex consisted of two beige buildings, bland and suited to the scrubby hills surrounding them. The eight-story spotless and hushed factory and laboratories were in one building, and the administrative offices in the other, shorter building. Capettone owned patents on the latest gene-splicing tools, artificial organs, and robotic surgeons that were just as effective but cheaper than actual surgeons for routine procedures such as knee replacements. Its modest setting belied its forward-leaning role in the medical field.

He walked into the latter building, greeting the receptionist and Jason the security guard in his tan uniform. "Quiet day so far?" he asked Jason, who reported to him.

"Yes, sir, and hopefully it'll stay that way," said Jason.

David hesitated about whether he should caution Jason about possible suspicious visitors, but what could he say that wouldn't send alarms through the building? "Jason, please watch out for trained Antifan killers, would you?"

"Yes, sir," he imagined Jason saying. "They won't get past me." Or "I'll direct them to the pastrami special in the cafeteria, Mr. Harris, that'll do it." He decided to wait until after the Bureau meeting to approach his colleagues. Possibly Lauren would alleviate his and Malia's concerns, although David was already not expecting much.

In his office, in the third-floor executive suite three doors down from the sumptuous office of CEO Baxter Berry, David hung up his jacket, and switched on the computer.

For all that he had dismissed his job as shuffling paperwork, David knew that as security director, he played an important role in fending off foreign spies, including DJR elements, from stealing Capettone's technology. His proudest achievement so far was strengthening the company's computer safeguards from European hackers who were working at Russian direction.

The only nagging concern was what he considered to be lax scrutiny of recent hires. Capettone recruiters traditionally had focused on applicants' technical skills, and a clean criminal record had sufficed for the security check. But David's qualms had grown in recent months. A purple slash in one technician's hair alongside a fondness for profanity, a proven affiliation with the DJR-sponsored Anticapitalist Strike Collective for another scientist. Capettone only hired US citizens, but that didn't protect the company from elements sympathetic to the DJR who could blend in, David had emphasized to his colleagues. Some eyebrows would raise when he warned them in meetings of the potential threat, but most of his fellow executives dismissed his concerns. "I don't blame him, being a deejer," they said among themselves, "but he really needs to calm down." If anything, David thought, his Antifan background, which they all knew and respected, should have lent credibility to his charges. Ironically, they used it to dismiss them, demonstrating that most middle-range minds were impervious to alternative perspectives and exercised cognitive vigilance to keep them at bay.

On his desk was a printed inventory of all the infotech property on the campus. David would need to confirm the accountings with each of the department heads. He couldn't deny this task was important, but it didn't excite him. He went and helped himself to coffee from the executive suite carafe, returned, and started paging through the document.

Malia returned to the house around eleven, relieved at an uneventful playground excursion. She placed both boys in the playpen, among electronic toys that she hoped would occupy them for a few minutes while she dashed down to the secure room.

She logged on in the small room. One question from an analyst, Hi Sidonia…

As tempting as it was to read the question, she scrolled over to the cable queue.

TO: SIDONIA AND ARGONAUT

IN RECEIPT OF OKC 45633. HQS WILL CONVEY LONGER REPLY IN DAY OR TWO AFTER DISCUSSIONS ON THIS END. WE FIND YOUR REPORT DISTURBING, ESPECIALLY THE TRAIN EPISODE. AMTRAK RECORDS INDICATE NO PURCHASES MADE BY ANY YUSUFOV. RECORDS INDICATE THREE PERSONS, ALL US CITIZENS, SEPARATELY RESERVED SEATS IN COMPARTMENT AND ALL SEATS SHOULD HAVE BEEN OCCUPIED. WE HAVE NO REPORTS OF DJR LET ALONE ADF ELEMENTS IN YOUR LOCATION.

ANACOSTA HAS BEEN CRACKING DOWN ON ITS OWN POPULACE SINCE YOUR ESCAPE. OVERALL TENOR THERE IS INCREASINGLY HARSH ESPECIALLY IN LAST YEAR. WE WOULD NOT HAVE EXPECTED THIS TO AFFECT YOU ACROSS THE BORDER, THOUGH. REPORT ANY NEW CONCERNING INCIDENTS AND AWAIT FURTHER INSTRUCTIONS. REGARDS.

Malia found this reassuring. She quickly answered the question, which was from one of the economists and about the contents of Healthy Eating grocery bags for different Social Credit ranks. As she described the ingredients and taste of a soybake, Malia rejoiced that she for one would never have to eat one again. She went upstairs to find George attempting to clamber over the side of the playpen, while Emmett sternly admonished him to wait for Mommy.

A few hours later, Malia and David headed to the Bureau field office downtown. Fern was babysitting, and would put down Ivy Ann for her nap with the boys shortly.

In a spare conference room, whose plain white walls and leatherette chairs shouted government issue, waited Supervisory Special Agent Lauren McCall and two of her agents. After some pleasantries, McCall got down to business.

"Here's the deal, Mr. and Mrs. Harris," she said. "It's a delicate time in US-DJR relations."

They looked at her blankly.

"You know that negotiations are underway between the two countries aimed at restoring—well, opening diplomatic relations for the first time ever. We need an ocean-going port. Pensacola-Mobile isn't enough for our navy and all our foreign trade. And definitely not helpful for Asian trade. And the DJR needs to trade with us. Under socialism, they just sputter along. Can't even properly feed their population."

"You'd think these kinds of episodes would make us rethink reopening ties," said David pointedly.

"Not at all," said McCall. "You've got to think bigger picture. Maybe we'd have more leverage to defend you once we had a deal the deejers would value."

"So you're saying that once we were committed to diplomatic and trade ties, we'd be more likely to challenge the DJR on this kind of behavior against US citizens?" Malia challenged her. "Wouldn't you think this would encourage the DJR? They'd know we wouldn't want to jeopardize the ports once we had them."

"None of us are sitting in St. Louis, Mrs. Harris," said McCall. "They've got to look after the security of the whole nation." Her glance darted upward at the clock.

"So what do you think is the ADF's goal in harassing and threatening us?" asked David. "And more so, what do you propose to do about it?"

Lauren McCall ran a hand through her coiffed blonde hair, delaying her answer. The Oklahoma City field office mostly focused on human trafficking gangs in lawless northern Texas. Until the Harrises had surfaced in Oklahoma, she had barely ever had to think about the DJR. She vaguely recalled some second cousins who were said to still live in South Carolina, last heard from thirty years ago. The security of the Harris family was a bullet point far down on her task list at review time, and until this week, easily checked. Now she was out of her comfort zone.

"We need to check with St. Louis," she said. "But of course, we'll give you protection."

"AIA responded to our cable this morning," said Malia, her tone sharp. "They take these threats extremely seriously. They said they'd get back to us shortly."

"Good, we'll touch base with them," said McCall. She was running late for a conference call on a planned disruption of a trafficking cell on the Texas border. The trustworthiness of the main informant preoccupied her, and would be the subject of the meeting.

"But remember," said David, "The AIA isn't on the ground here and isn't responsible for our day-to-day security. The Bureau is."

"I hear you, Mr. Harris," McCall responded. "Do you want that police guard at your house? Do you want an escort?"

David and Malia looked at each other. "We'll take the guard, yes," David said.

Chapter Six
Homecoming
(Friday, May 22, 2093)

The squad car still sat in front of the house, as it had all week, inviting curious glances from the neighbors, but now starting to blend into the background. If they mentioned it at all to each other, the neighbors probably were saying, "Well, that's good protection for all of us, isn't it? I don't mind. What is it with the family, though?"

David came home from work a little earlier than usual. After removing his jacket, hanging up the holster, and washing his hands, he took the bowl and knife from Malia and finished the potato salad for her. He added powdered mustard and mayonnaise. Malia's cooking was uninspired at best.

An hour later Isabelle and Kevin walked around the house to the backyard, finding the family in the midst of dinner. Kevin shook hands with David and Daniel and addressed Malia as "ma'am." Isabelle bubbled excitedly to be introducing Kevin to the larger family group. "This is my Uncle Daniel and my Aunt Fern. They're from the DJR too."

"It's a pleasure to meet you, sir, ma'am," said Kevin.

"You must be starving," said Malia.

"It was a long drive, ma'am," Kevin said. He looked very presentable in a blue button-down shirt and neat jeans.

"What's the police car doing out there, Mom?" Isabelle asked. As they pulled up to the house, Kevin had asked, crossly, "What the fuck is that?"

David shot Malia a look, conveying, "Didn't you tell her?"

"Just a little extra security under the circumstances," said Malia. David served hamburgers to the couple, who helped themselves to the potato salad and other fixings, and settled down at the picnic table on the patio to eat. From his corner of the patio, Daniel watched the couple intently.

"Oh right! I forgot." Isabelle had been distracted since Malia's call earlier in the month. Finals had turned out to be more challenging than she had expected; the administration failed to crumble when accused of racist grading. More happily, the Diversity crowd had applauded her speech enthusiastically, although the impact dissipated quickly, given the general distraction as the academic year ended. She had told the attendees how the Social Crediteers worked to build Diversity in the DJR, and how comfortably all lived under socialism. She didn't specify that she meant high Social Crediteers like her adoptive parents. But she underscored how rational Social Credit was, since the government ensured those who contributed the most to society reaped the most rewards—a system that capitalism could not equal.

"Brilliant," Kevin told her afterward, which made Isabelle flush with pride. Kevin normally wasn't lavish with praise.

After dinner, they all sat comfortably in the growing twilight, listening to the crickets in the warm evening. The anti-mosquito perimeter ensured the biting creatures stayed away. George and Ivy fell asleep in the portable playpen and Emmett on his mother's lap. In response to some tentative but polite questions, Kevin told them about his orphaned upbringing in Montana, to which Malia, herself an orphan, responded sympathetically.

"My sister's still up there, and married, and she's got a farm near Helena," he said. "We try to stay in touch, because we're all we have left in the world."

To their surprise, Kevin added, "I'm going to visit my sister for about ten days starting next week. Then I've got an internship lined up here in Oklahoma City."

"Really? Where?" David asked.

"Pargeter, sir," said Kevin. Pargeter was a medium-sized project construction firm with major government contracts on various military bases.

David nodded appreciatively. "That's good."

After the gathering had broken up, Emmett and George had been put to bed, and even Isabelle had trailed upstairs to her bedroom, the phone rang. Surprised to get a call at that hour, David answered. It was Daniel.

"Isabelle isn't listening right now, is she?" he asked.

David grunted no.

"Her boyfriend wasn't pronouncing Helena correctly. It's 'Helenna,' not 'Heleena.'"

"What's the big deal?" David was too tired to want to think about pronunciation of strange American state capitals. He wished Daniel would have called in the morning.

"If he was from Montana, you'd think he'd know how to pronounce the capital's name, that's all."

"Are you sure that's the correct pronunciation?"

"Yeah, I just checked. You know, I memorized all the state capitals for the citizenship test." Daniel had been the first Harris to receive his US citizenship, and Fern had followed quickly. David had taken the oath of citizenship back in November, and Malia, distracted by her dissertation and the demands of two toddlers, was scheduled for her citizenship ceremony this coming November, along with Isabelle.

David decided not to confide this disturbing nugget to Malia, at least not until tomorrow morning. At least one of them would sleep soundly. He knew his counterpart at Pargeter, not that well, just from some professional panels and cocktail parties, but well enough to call on Monday and mention his concerns. And, yes, he would ask Vernal to run down Kevin's information. He wasn't going to bother with that FBI woman this time.

Chapter Seven
Beaufort
(Tuesday, June 9, 2093)

Lieutenant Marcus Vanover arrived safely in Anacosta after a two-day journey lengthened by operational requirements. He had flown to Chicago, rented a car to drive to Toronto, and dealt with annoying Canadian border guards at the Kenosha border crossing into Wisconsin Province. Once the Canadian Border Services Agency officer found his reservation at Happy Trout Fishing Lodge near Green Bay after a quick check of the online Canadian Hotel Security System, the mood lightened. The officer wished him good fishing and waved him into Canada.

The Canadians were even leerier of Americans than of Diversans, whose government conveniently constrained most of them from foreign travel. Since the beginning of the US civil war, the Canadians had tightened their border protocols so that unruly Americans, or now, Diversans, could not export their troublesome ways to the land of the maple leaf. Vanover knew he would receive extra scrutiny if he ventured the notorious Detroit crossing as a US citizen, so prudently avoided it. Twenty miles past the Canadian border, in the Milwaukee outskirts, he stopped for lunch and switched his US ID with the official Diversan one stashed under the insole of a shoe.

Once he was in Canada, no one would bother him until he reached Toronto. He drove up toward Green Bay as expected, but then crossed into Michigan Province's Upper Peninsula, driving down through to Port Huron, where he checked into a motel for the night. Yes, a normal traveler would not have chosen this wildly roundabout route unless truly planning to sightsee, but Vanover found it safer to take the less-traveled route.

Early the next morning, he headed into Ontario. At the Toronto airport, the DJR plainclothes customs officer assigned to the airport ensured that Diversair passenger Lieutenant Vanover would encounter no hassles during onboarding for the flight to Anacosta. As far as the Canadians knew, Marcus Vanover had been serving as a junior attaché on the DJR side during the talks with the United States in Toronto for the last week. The fellow who had filled in for him during the talks would manage to cross the border on his own near a remote outpost in upstate New York.

By noon, Vanover had arrived at Barack Obama Airport in Anacosta, where an Antifan officer handed him a temporary armband that would get him back to his apartment via self-driving car. It was illegal for a Social Crediteer not to wear his (or her, or zir, or their) armband outside their homes, even if you were an Antifan. He dropped off his suitpod at his apartment, changed into his black Antifan uniform and his own armband, and headed via another self-driving car for the eighty-story Beaufort Tower in Upper Northwest. The headquarters of the ADF, Beaufort's glass spire soared eighty stories above the Anacosta skyline, as did those of its counterparts the Social Tower, the Economic Tower, and the Knowledge Tower. But Beaufort, strictly speaking, was the tallest of all, because it also contained another seven stories deep underground, housing jail cells, and torture and execution chambers.

Vanover's home unit, the Resolution Command, was on the seventy-fifth floor, lofty enough not to worry about casual visitors and close enough to Director Montoya's suite to hurry there on short notice. He had barely entered the command when he saw Deputy Commander Leahcim Okuro, 240, hastening toward him. Okuro was a medium-sized, muscular man, three generations removed from Nigeria. Even though his ancestors had quite voluntarily moved to the United States, he still benefited from the forty-point African-Diversan bump. No extra points for the white tattoo design on his forehead, however. Three years after Vanover had joined the command, he was still trying to figure out what the tattoo represented.

Vanover Antifan-saluted his commanding officer, with the crossed arms followed by a standard right-hand salute while the left rested on the chest. "Sir, reporting for duty."

Okuro returned the salute. "Welcome back from your studies, Lieutenant. We've been following your chip this morning so we have been able to keep the director's office updated on your arrival time. We're expected upstairs at three p.m." A lima-bean sized chip pulsed behind the right ear of every DJR citizen, allowing authorities to track their movements. Meeting planning was one of the more practical, if benign uses of a chip.

Vanover freshened up in the washroom, steadying himself on the sink edge. Splashed some water on his face. Brushed his teeth. Scrutinized himself in the mirror. Six foot two (metric had never quite taken hold in the DJR despite its ideological cachet), hazel eyes, strong, "commander" features. Thin lips connoted his austere outlook on life.

He was on a fast track, he knew. If he were black or transgender, he'd already be a deputy commander, even at twenty-seven, but he preferred to keep his man package, thank you. His performance reviews praised him for his "iron commitment to Diversity," his "resolution in confronting the fascist enemies," his refusal to be tempted by considerations of mercy. The mandatory firing squad rotation had not unsettled him, although he had not exactly enjoyed it. "Very impressive in such a young officer," they noted to each other, thumbing through his file at promotion time.

Vanover credited his orphanage upbringing with building the hard shell he needed to succeed in the ADF. Most Antifans needed to be broken, a little or a lot, into brutality. Hardness was prized, especially in the tumult and self-recrimination that had followed the escape of David Harris and two other Antifans—blacks at that!—who had ungratefully followed him across the border. ADF leaders had belatedly realized that they had allowed a tolerant and lax culture to take hold among their ranks. Vanover was well suited for the Resolution Command, which dealt with thornier and often political issues that required greater cleverness or brazenness to reach closure. Director Vladivar Montoya had formed the command after Harris's escape, and the resolution of that case was its primary objective for now.

In the aftermath of Harris's escape, the ADF had purged its ranks. All the officers who had worked for the defector had undergone reinvestigation to ensure his humane ways had not infected them. Two officers who had unwisely expressed respect for Commander Harris even after his treason were transferred to prisoner cell guard duty. Even Deputy Director Steve Rosen had fallen under scrutiny because of his friendship with Harris. He issued a violent denunciation of his former friend, and kept a low profile until the initial storm had subsided.

Antifans were now expected to attend weekly Mother Earth Diversity services. They had not traditionally been a religious lot, but now each officer had to pick a MED denomination, whether Protestant, Catholic, Jewish, Muslim, Hindu, or Strict Pagan, and select a patron saint from the MED panoply tended by the Knowledge Tower. St. John Beaufort, who had launched the Antifan gangs and led them through the civil war, was naturally popular.

Vanover had chosen Strict Pagan, since the other denominations connoted a feeble accommodation to ancient and discredited forms of worship. If you needed a crutch, your grandmother's simple monotheist faith, to appreciate Mother Earth Diversity, fine, but Marcus Vanover did nothing halfway. He approached the service held weekly at Beaufort in his methodical manner, roaring angrily during the Four Minute Hate and mentally dissecting work challenges during the quieter parts. Sometimes he volunteered to give a homily, most recently, his well-received "St. John Beaufort and Climate Change Activism." The Antifan worshipers were permitted to forgo the pink pussy hat required of all other Mother Earth worshipers.

Vanover and Okuro rose from their seats in the director's conference room when Montoya and Rosen joined them. All Antifan-saluted and settled themselves around the table. Vanover had not yet met Montoya in person, and was surprised by how compact and gnarled the director looked, as if decades of tough decisions for Diversity had played themselves out on the man's face. It was hard to imagine him wielding a chain on the streets of Portland, although Montoya—and Rosen—were just old enough to have fought in the civil war on the Antifan side.

"So you're our forward man in Oklahoma City," Montoya said. "We've heard good things about your work there."

"Thank you, sir."

Okuro said, "Vanover has penetrated to the center of the Harris family. He has been intimate with the stepdaughter, the one who crossed the border with them. She is showing willingness to return to the DJR."

"It's not her fault that Harris and his low-credit bitch dragged her there," said Montoya. "She should have notified the authorities, of course, but I'm not going to hold that against her now. How are we planning to get her back into the DJR?"

Vanover cleared his throat. "She has agreed to study at Diverse American University. I've persuaded her that with diplomatic negotiations underway with the US, she can perform a valuable service bringing Diversans and fascists together under the banner of Diversity." He told them about her speech, and his offer of marriage.

"She was showing a little reluctance to move to the DJR, and I thought I'd sweeten the deal," Vanover said.

"So that worked?" Rosen asked.

Vanover said, "She's crazy about me, sir. In a very shallow and heterosexist way, of course. If she thinks we'll get married on this side of the border, I am sure she'll come with me, and not tell the Harrises if I warn her not to."

"Does she have any of her mother's or Harris's views? I want to know how much ideological deprogramming will be necessary," Montoya said. "Can we trust her as a student among other students at Diverse American, or will she need to be kept on an incubation farm for a while?" Not many foreigners came to the DJR anymore, and then only from the globe's most desperate countries, but the DJR ran the farms to ensure the would-be immigrants were suitable before integrating them among Diversans. Sometimes, astonishingly, they showed prejudice against Muslims, women, blacks, or even gay people. Rigorous indoctrination was required for many to purge them of cultural views at odds with Diversity.

"I don't think her IQ is much above ninety, sir," Vanover said. "She doesn't think much about politics. And she's only been in the US for four years, after a lifetime in the DJR, so I didn't have to start from scratch. The good Diversity foundation was already there."

"What'll happen after you say goodbye to her?" asked Okuro. "She's not going to fall apart on us, will she?"

"Sir, as you know, we can't be responsible for every bit of collateral damage. But my guess is that we could find her another partner and a good Social Credit score so she won't miss Oklahoma or me very much."

"And her parents, the Andrewses, will take her back in," Okuro added. "We've sounded them out. They know she was kidnapped by Harris and the mother. So the girl won't be alone."

"Have you been in their house?" Montoya asked.

"Yes, sir, I was a guest at a barbecue they had a few weekends ago. I went into the house at one point and planted two listening devices. One under the kitchen table. It's flat and smooth, so they won't find that device very soon. The other is underneath the sofa in the living room. I was thinking of going upstairs to plant a third, but Harris's brother came into the house."

"You can leave the Plore and his wife alone," said Montoya. "They're not of interest to us. But I want Harris and that wife of his back here. Especially Harris."

A tall, broad-shouldered Antifan entered the room. His black hair stood up, short and brushlike. It was Commander Khalid Ma, nicknamed "Paragon," for his excellence in pursuing Diversity. Here was Malia's traveling companion, now in his natural habitat, after two years as the ADF's chief of station in St. Louis. In two weeks, he would again travel behind US lines to attend the Beltane celebrations in the Hickory Hills, where Malia Harris would meet him, if she valued her life and that of her sons, as he had told her on the train.

"Khalid," said Montoya, "Thank you for joining us. We were just about to discuss the next stage of Operation North Taco."

Chapter Eight
Beltane
(Saturday, June 13 and Saturday, June 20, 2093)

David had decided against asking his counterpart at Pargeter about Kevin. He wanted to be fair to the young man, and not ruin his prospects. The only evidence he could offer was Daniel's observation that Kevin didn't know how to pronounce Helena. David knew Pargeter screened its employees, given the sensitive work the corporation did for the government. Would David's counterpart take seriously the idea that mispronouncing Helena outweighed all the homework Pargeter must have done before hiring Kevin?

Kevin was busy at Pargeter, but he also had his "real duties," as he termed it, which was inciting love for Diversity. The Diversity and Inclusion Collective, which Kevin had quietly launched, but without putting himself forward as a leader, was already demanding Transgender History Month programming. Kevin had ingratiated himself with a member who was working on a special jet propulsion project. He was just hoping that he could acquire the information he needed before he had to give into the importunings of the young man for sex—he wasn't homophobic, of course, and he would do whatever was necessary for Diversity, but some tasks were just less appealing than others.

But more critically, Paragon had entrusted him with overseeing the plans for the Beltane celebration at Hickory Hills, and since Paragon himself would attend, no effort would be spared. Rex would just have to play with her baby brothers—he'd get around to her eventually.

The vapid Diversity adherents in the area could not be trusted with paying their own bills on time, let alone with administrative arrangements for the Great Beltane Diversity Celebration. Kevin had acquired the park permit for a "Flag Day Patriotic Gathering," complete with bonfires, and ordered kindling, beer, and ample refreshments. Participants were asked to bring their own blankets and camp chairs for the Joyous Mingling after the Great Coupling. Kevin expected about seventy-five attendees and had done online searches on each registrant just in case any MAGA

Party stalwarts or other potential troublemakers sought to infiltrate the event.

But unfortunately, Malia Harris's name was yet not on the list, Kevin noted anxiously. Having observed the Harris family in their self-satisfied fascist domestic idyll, Kevin thought Paragon was overconfident in his assessment that Malia would find herself drawn to the fires.

"It's in the soul of every Diversity-raised person, the call to the bonfire," Paragon had said solemnly, and to Kevin, a little pompously. But Kevin couldn't argue with the man who outranked almost everyone else at Beaufort these days, and possibly even the director.

"But just in case," said Paragon, "we'll send her a reminder." Paragon himself intended to attend, but were it not for Malia Harris, he would have stayed and enjoy the festivities in Anacosta. Were Kevin not dating the daughter, it might have been possible to pair him with Malia, and save Paragon the trip, but since she knew Kevin as her daughter's boyfriend, she almost certainly would not couple with him, given her Christian pretenses, Paragon thought. And it would not take much to rip aside those veils, once she was under their control again.

David and Malia returned from running errands the weekend before Beltane. Malia had slipped into a neighboring card shop to buy a Father's Day card for David while he thumbed through racks of jogging clothes in the sporting goods store.

The police cruisers were no longer stationed in front of the house, the couple having decided that the threat had receded, and surely the officers were needed to keep the rest of the city safe. To the couple's relief, Emmett and George were actually napping. Rex accepted their thanks and disappeared into her room.

Malia went downstairs to the secure room. She turned on the machine and typed in the code. Instead of the expected list of polite inquiring emails, however, a vicious bloody image immediately splashed across her screen at her. Malia reared backward, breathless, at the impact.

Before her was the image of a dark-haired young woman, resembling herself, blood spurting out of her abdomen after a knife attack. The camera went back and forth from the leaping blood to her face, convulsed in either orgasmic pleasure or agonizing pain, or both, who knew, her mouth wide open. The evil photograph, or drawing, covered the entire screen, then a crackling yellow fire consumed it, and finally several words emerged on the screen, "BELTANE CALLS YOU." The image continued to pulse as the words faded, only to reappear and fade every ten seconds.

"David!" she screamed. But she was behind the steel door of the secure room, and he couldn't hear her. She ran upstairs, not even caring if the boys awakened. "David! The screen! The screen!"

He had been watching a baseball game, on low volume because of the boys, but he sprang up and ran downstairs. Rex came out to the upstairs landing and asked, uncertainly, "Mom?" But they didn't respond, since they were already in the basement.

Malia pointed accusingly at the screen and the evil pulsing image, as if it were a bug she had found and wanted David to kill. David stared grimly for about ten seconds. Then the words "Beltane Calls You," streamed once again across the screen. David took a video with his phone camera, and then manually turned off the machine. He turned it on again, and the usual email list came up, as if nothing had happened. "The code is compromised," he said. "We need to call Vernal." He picked up the phone.

"Well, that's awful," said Vernal, at home herself. "Let's get you a new password."

David was incredulous that Vernal seemed to take this so matter-of-factly, and he grimaced in Malia's direction.

"We can't stop them from playing these games," said Vernal. "But that's the worst they can do, I'm confident. I'm sorry it was so distressing." A few minutes later, they were typing in a new password. David transferred the video in an encrypted package and within a few minutes, Vernal was seeing it for herself. "Classic ADF propaganda," she said. "We know they are trying to recruit the worst elements for Diversity activity. We don't think it's very successful, though."

How would you know, thought David cynically. Malia was looking at him anxiously, unable to hear the conversation on the secure phone. He gave her a quick, reassuring nod.

He heard Vernal sucking in her own breath as she watched the video. "That's ugly, for sure," she said, "but like I said, nothing to take seriously. I don't think it's snuff, just computer-generated."

When David had hung up, he said soberly to Malia, "Sometimes I really think we are completely on our own." He turned to Malia, and pulled her tightly into his embrace.

"Is this going to go on forever?"

"We can wait them out," he said. "But I'm not sure I share Vernal and Ms. FBI Agent's confidence that they mean us no further harm. If they hadn't been able to get across the border at least twice...don't go out without your weapon, OK?"

"I'd forgotten about the Beltane invitation," she said.

They closed the secure room, and went onto the regular workscreen to look up the Hickory Hills Beltane celebration information. It was described as a "Flag Day Patriotic Diversity Bonfire." A small description below noted the congruence of Flag Day with the "traditional Beltane fires of Celtic lore."

"That sounds wholesome, doesn't it?" Malia asked.

"You're not going," said David.

"We could go together. You could get a look at Mr. Yusufov."

"That's not exactly my idea of fun," retorted David. He had attended two Beltanes in Anacosta, both when he was young, and again, mostly due to peer pressure from other Antifans. "Seriously, it could end up being very dangerous given what he said to you. We shouldn't take the risk."

"Given what he has in mind," said Malia, "I suspect it would be even more dangerous for you than for me."

"I'm not looking to be a Beltane hero."

Suddenly, he stared hard at her, almost disgusted. "You want to go to this Beltane, don't you?" he said. "Can you not get that pagan stuff out of your system?"

She denied it, vehemently, turning away from his accusing gray eyes. She felt embarrassed, because it was a shameful thing to want to lie in public, even with your husband, and why go now, when she had, like David himself, mostly avoided the celebrations in Anacosta?

Many years ago, the Mother Earth Diversity teacher had explained to Malia's class the religious symbolism of the sacred Beltane holiday. "It is a normal and a good thing to engage in sexual congress before others. The fire sanctifies the collective sex act. The individual ego is erased and there is no shame." It had made perfect sense at the time to Malia, as she eyed the boys in the class appraisingly. But David was a Plore and would never really understand.

They turned around to see Rex looking at them. "Is everything all right?" she asked. She had heard the screams.

"Your mother saw a disturbing image on her workscreen," said David, "That's all."

"Mom, are you all right?" Rex pressed.

"Yes, honey, it was just a shock. I don't know what happened. I must have hit the wrong keys."

Rex went upstairs, and texted Kevin, "Overheard Mom and David talking about Beltane. I don't think she will go. David is very opposed." This made her happy, because Kevin had said if her mother would be attending, he didn't think they should go. Kevin had explained his curiosity about Malia and David's plans by saying that DJR people found it hard to stay away, even if they were Christians, and he didn't want to risk Malia or David seeing them at Beltane.

"Good, thanks," Kevin responded, pretending relief, but he wasn't himself happy at all at the news. Would Paragon show if Malia weren't coming? Would Paragon blame him?

Rex hadn't dared to tell Malia about Kevin's proposal, let alone about studying in the DJR. Rex herself was still uneasy about the proposal, which didn't seem at all like the ones in the romantic movies she watched or books she read. Was it right to expect more? It wasn't like her mother and stepfather's closeness, but maybe you needed to be married to achieve that.

On Beltane evening, David and Malia were finishing their meal with matching chocolate soufflés. Other diners looked approvingly at the handsome, seemingly carefree couple, him blond and still athletic, her dark, slender, somehow intellectual, or at least quick and nervous, conveying sensitivity. They were young enough to be conventionally attractive, but old enough to look comfortable in their skins. They chatted about new movies, their boys and how Emmett was more like Malia and George like David, and whether David should go with his friend Chris to the MAGA Party meeting next week. "Chris says it will be good to meet other people in the community who are business oriented," said David.

"Then I think you should go," said Malia. She herself was not particularly interested in politics, except in her dissertation. They agreed he would attend the meeting.

As they exited the restaurant, hand in hand, the sun was setting. It was a lovely midsummer evening. Malia was sure they would make love, after the boys went to bed but before Rex got home from her date with Kevin.

To her surprise, David took the highway going in the opposite direction from their house.

"Are we going to pick up some milk?" she asked him.

"Nope," he said. They headed south, toward the hills.

She suddenly realized where they were going. "Are you sure? Isn't this dangerous? Should we call Fern and Daniel and let them know?"

"Nope," he repeated. "And now you can keep quiet. Let me handle this." She subsided at the authority in his voice. He pulled over and extracted a black bandana from the glove compartment. "I'm going to cover your eyes. I want this to be a surprise."

They left the main road and headed up into the Hickory Hills. Malia trusted David completely, but wondered, Why did he cover my eyes? What shouldn't I see? What if Yusufov shows up and I can't even warn David? She assumed they were heading for the Great Coupling.

After a few minutes, David pulled over to the side of the road and turned off the engine. He opened the door and Malia heard him exit, close the door, and open the car's trunk. Items in the trunk clattered, maybe tools and wood planks? She heard no people or voices, just crickets and cicadas and other night noises. So they were not at the Beltane Flag Day celebration, or whatever it was. She wanted to pull the bandana off her head, but was afraid of how David might react, or what surprise she might inadvertently spoil. She waited patiently.

David opened the passenger door. "You can get out now," he said, steadying Malia as she found her footing on the dusty ground. She heard the crackling of several campfires.

"I'm going to carry you," he warned her, so she wasn't alarmed when her feet lifted from the ground. She linked her arms around his neck, pressed her warm chest against his, and felt his cool cheek, with its freshly shaven stubble, against hers. The hissing and spitting of the campfires grew louder and she felt their heat on her bare legs. Then she was lying on some vaguely familiar-feeling vinyl mats, the heat surrounding them, and he took off her bandana. She looked up into David's mischievous gray eyes.

"Welcome to our own little Beltane," he said. His mouth closed on hers, and his left hand clasped her wrists and gently pinned them above her head. When he released her wrists, she wrapped her arms around him. Malia only worried briefly about rattlesnakes before she forgot them and gave herself to David. It was an open area that presumably rattlesnakes would avoid, if they were sensible, and his firearm lay on the ground only a few feet away, if they weren't. Soon most of their clothes lay piled near the weapon as well.

An hour later, the fires were beginning to die and they were shivering in the evening chill, so they dressed quickly. They were sitting up on the mat that Malia now recognized from the closet in the basement playroom, watching the Beltane fires in the distance, several miles away on a ridge above a short valley.

"That's your friend's party," David said. They could just make out the outlines of cars parked in the shadows beyond the fires.

Down in the camp, Paragon glowered. He had participated in the Great Coupling with some pretty blonde, whom he had quickly forgotten because that traitorous bitch, Malia Jenness, preoccupied him. He was not accustomed to anyone defying him, not anymore. Malia Jenness had foolishly decided to spurn him and forgo Beltane, which he vowed she would regret. He had come all the way to this fascist backwater, for nothing.

Kevin, or Marcus, stood at his side. No matter how smoothly the arrangements had gone tonight, Malia's betrayal was dampening what would normally have been a huge success for Kevin. Six campfires for heterosexual couples, one for gays and another for the lesbians. Everyone stayed afterward to eat snacks and drink beer and soda. Kevin had offered Paragon the opportunity to address the crowd, but Paragon was reluctant to draw attention to himself, since his presence in the United States was illegal. Instead, Kevin welcomed the attendees, speaking soberly about the beauty of Beltane, and its symbolism.

"By participating in our Beltane ritual," Kevin said, "you are helping overthrow the patriarchal and oppressive mores that restrict with whom we partner and diminish our joy. Sex on Beltane is a political act. Do not think it is simply for your release. All across the Diversity Justice Republic tonight, our cousins are doing the same." For that reason, he had coldly paired Rex with some bespectacled nerd while he pulled down a cute ethnic Chinese girl—an option not easily available to his tired palate in the DJR.

Rex had whimpered in protest, and he whispered to her severely, "You don't understand how this works. And you, a champion of Diversity!" Then she was ashamed, and quieted, and afterward Kevin noticed she was chatting on a blanket with the nerd and some of his friends, so she seemed to be enjoying herself.

As some returned to the circles, possibly with new partners, throwing fresh timber from a large pile onto the sputtering fires, Kevin and Paragon stood off to the side of the clearing, watching some small campfires on the hillside in the distance.

"What is going on there?" Paragon sneered. "A baby Beltane?"

Kevin knew Paragon did not like the idea of a stray Beltane taking place outside their control.

"I don't know, sir. Would you like me to check it out?"

Paragon pulled out binoculars and handed them over. Kevin had to admire his preparation and was relieved that Paragon had not had to futilely ask him for binoculars. Here he was, a trained ADF officer, and he had focused only on the party preparations and not anticipated other needs.

But Paragon did not seem to hold that against him. "What do you see, Lieutenant?" They were out of earshot of the chatty crowd.

"Sir, that looks like a couple having their own Beltane celebration. Now I can tell… it's the Harrises."

Paragon took the binoculars, "Yes, and that's his wife, who should have listened to me."

"Should we drive up there and confront them?"

"No," said Paragon. "We'll show our hand soon enough, when we have the advantage. I told her she would regret not coming to me at Beltane, and she will." His dark almond eyes narrowed as he stared into the distance. As cold a man as Kevin knew he himself was becoming, and wanted to be, he could not yet compare with Paragon, and later that night, finally alone in his bed, he wondered how Paragon had become Paragon.

Chapter Nine
The Past Is Prologue
(Tuesday, June 30, 2093)

David arrived at Baxter Berry's executive suite promptly at 10:30, wearing the very expensive tan suit he saved for important occasions and good luck. He had no idea what Baxter wanted from him, but the opportunity for a one-on-one meeting was rare. Could Baxter finally be showing interest in the Chinese espionage threat?

Baxter's office was exactly what one would expect from the CEO of the forty-third largest publicly traded company in the United States, and Oklahoma's second largest. A giant wooden desk virtually clear of paperwork, with a workscreen casually pushed to the side; a resplendent mahogany conference table bearing a fresh floral arrangement, and seating ten in deep leather chairs. In the back corner of the room a grouping of more casual sofas and accent chairs in a masculine beige and matching plaid pattern. Oversized antique oil paintings of cattle rustling and of white coated doctors and nurses hovering tensely over a patient lent a distinguished air to the room. "First Heart Transplant," read the gold plate under the latter painting. Hanging over the fireplace was a portrait of Bernard Capettone, the company founder, dead these ten years, but still facing Baxter Berry, his son-in-law, with a stern visage, as if to say, "I handed you this company on a silver platter. And my Katie. Don't eff it up, boy."

"David, good to see you," Baxter said warmly, coming from behind the desk to shake hands, as if four years, not four days had passed since the last executive board meeting. "Let's sit over here, shall we?" Picking up a large manila folder, he steered David toward the accent chairs. Baxter was a broad-shouldered former running back for OU who had parlayed local sports fame into his corporate career, and he still maintained the confident demeanor of a man whom life had favored in every way, starting early. He exuded the affability that had won him the hand of Miss Katie Capettone, a pert cheerleader.

"How did the meetings go with Hernandez?" David asked politely. Hernandez Parker was a medical supplies distributor in New Orleans, where Baxter had gone to market Capettone's new virtual catheter.

"Great," said Baxter, "They placed an initial order for ten thousand. We'll see how that goes. I made sure they know these catheters have been used successfully in China now for two years. Hernandez can get ahead of their US competition on this product if they buy now."

Then, "So, you've been here two years now," stated Baxter.

David nodded, "Yes, I think it's been a good fit."

Baxter let that go. "Very different from your former career, I imagine."

"I guess I wasn't cut out to be a police detective after all," David said. "At least not here. But I do like chasing down threats to organizations I care about." Where is this going, he wondered.

"I meant your former career—over there," said Baxter, waving generally in the direction of Kansas, but what David instantly realized must have meant the DJR.

"Absolutely. No private industry whatsoever, you know. You worked for the government, and you had almost zero latitude to do anything. That's socialism for you."

The two men acknowledged the evil of socialism with a brief respectful silence.

"But you were pretty high up there, right, Dave?"

"I had a very high Social Credit score and yes, that meant you lived well, much better compared to the vast majority. Ask my wife sometime what it was like to live at the other end of the scale."

Baxter paused to pay the usual southern compliment. "Yes, a lovely lady you have there. But what I meant is that sometimes you did things that wouldn't pass muster here, right?"

David stiffened. In his experience, this was usually not a prelude to an easy conversation, let alone a promotion or pay raise. "Yes," he said curtly. But didn't Baxter know this already? The AIA had surely spoken frankly with Baxter when it approached Capettone about potential employment. Hadn't they?

The CEO handed him the manila folder. "Take a look at this. It was delivered via courier late Friday afternoon. We don't know who the sender was."

David took a deep breath and peered inside the folder. He knew this was the latest sally by his enemies. Inside were two sheets of paper, which he extracted carefully.

"DAVID M. HARRIS, KILLER" was the header. Following the header was a very detailed, and David had to admit, accurate summary of his twenty-year Antifan Defense Forces career. The list included awards he had won for gunning down a trainload of would-be refugees; apprehending a pro-democracy cell, all of whose members eventually were executed at Beaufort; and various other engagements in which dissidents ended up dead, whether on the street or in the basement at the Beaufort Tower. David now remembered the eight months he had spent on a firing squad—a required rotation for anyone under consideration for advancement at Beaufort. He had served the minimum required time on that assignment, drank more than he would ever drink again, and moved on, compartmentalizing, once again.

And he had advanced, he couldn't deny it, until Malia Jenness had entered his life and reawakened his shriveled conscience. He had overcome his stigmatized Deplorable background to become a senior commander. But doing so had required gritting his teeth and climbing over heaps of weaker victims, figuratively at least. And throughout that rise, he sat next to his mother most Sundays at St. Paul's Lutheran Church in Arlington with a mostly easy conscience.

The second page said, in large block typed letters, "FIRE KILLER HARRIS OR WE WILL DISCLOSE TO THE MEDIA THAT CAPETTONE HIRES ANTIFAN KILLERS." No signature of responsibility, of course. But David knew who was responsible. The Bureau would run chemical tests on the pages, but the outcome would be inconclusive.

"This isn't good," said Baxter calmly, but firmly.

"This is the handiwork of the Antifan Defense Forces," David said, bitterly. "Nobody else could have compiled this list, even me. They know things I forgot long ago. Everything here was done under their orders. They've started to harass both my wife and myself, even here in Oklahoma City." He then realized, belatedly, he could have denied the charges as vicious slander, and won a reprieve, but he owned up to it, like a man. Too late to back off.

"Have you told the police?"

"FBI knows. They had a police squad car at our house for a while. None of the harassment happened at our house, but at least we can sleep at night."

"Look, Dave," Baxter said, with what he thought was patience, "We're running a business. A publicly traded corporation. I have a responsibility to our shareholders. If they think we have someone on our executive board who's committed not just crimes, but ghastly ones, won't they think we've been running our affairs irresponsibly? Think of the millions we could lose, regardless of whether our products are superior. Which they are."

"Didn't AIA talk to you about my background before you hired me?" David asked.

"They said you'd been a senior commander in the ADF. Obviously, we know that the ADF is the security arm of the DJR, and we know the DJR is pretty evil. But we figured that your hands must have been relatively clean to have made it that high, and a senior commander in the ADF would be a good bet to handle our security interests. It sounded good and tough. But now I don't think the AIA was particularly forthcoming on that issue, and I'm just a *leetle* bit irritated now about that lapse in candor."

"Actually, the senior commander part should have been the tip-off that you were getting a pretty bad hombre." David decided to pursue a different tack. "Which really should have reassured you about the value you were getting from your security executive. Haven't I done a good job for Capettone and for you?"

"Yes, Dave, you have," admitted Baxter. "Although part of me thinks you'd rather be out there on the streets collaring enemies of the state. It's just that look in your eyes at the conference table I see sometimes.

"We have absolutely no complaints about the quality of your work here. It's just that if your ADF role became publicly known, it would be a very challenging PR problem for us, and possibly a big financial one."

David tried a third tack. "Can't we just see what happens first? If it's made known, then fire me quickly and say you were misled. Which, it sounds like, happened in any case."

Baxter sighed. These deejers were not business savvy, that was for sure. "Dave, if we let you go now, we'll give you a very generous severance package. Eighteen months at your current pay, and you keep your stock options. You won't starve, and I'm sure you'll land on your feet somewhere else. We'll make sure everyone in town knows that you weren't fired for cause—you know, maybe 'philosophical differences.'"

That sounded good to Baxter. He would have taken that deal himself, although he couldn't imagine being in David's position. If Capettone had to fire David, the deejer would be in much worse shape. Of course, then David could sue, which would put Capettone in a tough position, because it wouldn't want to acknowledge they had hired someone with David's background and they'd have the same problem, only with more lawyers involved. A generous severance package was the dignified way forward for everyone, unless you had a crazy deejer on your hands. Baxter thought Harris should also realize that having his bloody career detailed in the *Oklahoma City Star* wasn't going to look very appetizing either, especially to his neighbors and his church. The initial coverage after his heroic escape from the DJR had lacked precise details about David's ADF career, a void enabled by reporters' inability to contact authorities in Anacosta.

"I'll land on my feet until the ADF catches up with me there too, I suppose," David said blackly.

That's your problem, killer boy, thought Baxter. He took a moment to give David a more direct appraising stare. Baxter was a good judge of character, at least in a business setting, and had to admit that David didn't look like a murderer. For someone without a college degree, David was well spoken, and on the surface didn't stand out from the hail-fellow-well-met crowd in the Capettone executive suite. But David was not talkative, and a careful observer would note his bearing, and even the muscles in his face, were tenser than that of the usual Oklahoma MBA who occupied the executive suite. Wonder if he ever has nightmares about back there, ran through Baxter's mind.

"It's not like I was engaged in a crime rampage, or carjacking or strangling prostitutes. Did I have a choice?"

"I don't know, Dave," Baxter said smoothly. "Did you have a choice?"

Easy for you to say, David thought to himself. You've never had to make choices either. But all your non-choices were great ones, one terrific connected-white-guy opportunity yielding another. My non-choices were brutal. Nobody here really understands the DJR, for sure.

"What if I had the AIA call you before we make a decision here?" asked David.

We make a decision? Baxter thought ironically. Mr. Harris, the decision has been made, and it isn't yours. Nonetheless, he figured whoever was making the threats wouldn't spring the trap immediately, and Capettone probably had a few days to pretend to deliberate. No harm in hearing out the spy guys. You never knew when you might need a favor from bureaucrats in St. Louis. Not to mention, if David Harris was a tenth as ruthless as his alarming résumé seemed to suggest, he, Baxter Berry, should avoid antagonizing him too quickly. Those cold gray eyes, now tinged with desperation, unnerved him.

"Sure, Dave, have St. Louis give me a call," Baxter said, as genially as he could. "Let's sleep on this a day or two. No emergency. We'll find a mutually agreeable way to resolve this."

Instead of returning to his office, where he knew he would not be able to focus on the inventory list, let alone bigger issues, David headed over to the laboratory building. The guard greeted him respectfully, and his badge gave him access to the elevator. On the fifth floor, he walked down the spotless hallway, to the door labeled "Robotics Lab." David stayed in the open door of Cristobal Mendoza's office by the main door, loath to disturb the white-garbed technicians moving purposefully around the steel tables and conveyor belts. Behind a pair of swing doors David could see the robotic surgeons, waiting patiently for their testing turn on the floor. Robots had a lot of time on their metal hands.

A trio of scientists stood at a whiteboard in the corner, viewing and marking up an equation. Sensing eyes on them, they turned around. Chris Mendoza, the lab director, gave David a quick wave, and pointed upward, as if to say, "Give us five minutes, would you?" David raised his hand in amiable acknowledgment. He retreated into Chris's office, but came out again when he saw the spare chair covered in piles of paper. A book, *Advanced Principles of Medical Robotics*, lay precariously atop the tower of paper.

Chris greeted him warmly a few minutes later. "David, my friend, what brings you to our humble laboratory?" One look at David's face shrank Chris's smile, and he said, "Ay, let's go have lunch." Chris hung up his white lab coat and they went downstairs to the main cafeteria.

On the surface, one would have thought the pair incongruous—the short swarthy Filipino, and the blond athletic David whose ancestors had arrived in North America centuries earlier. But that comparison was deceptive, as more united them than divided them. It wasn't just that both were happily married, with two small children each, although that helped. Both were immigrants to the United States, or in David's case, a returnee, but Chris paradoxically blended into the American mainstream more easily than David had. That was because the Philippines, for all its troubles, had a history entwined with America's, a mostly Christian population, familiarity with English and US pop culture, and shared values about education and democracy.

After China had conquered the Philippines in 2075, hundreds of thousands of Filipino refugees came to the United States. Chris had been finishing his PhD in mechanical engineering at Purdue when the takeover occurred, and stayed. China had been steadily encroaching into the South China Sea while the United States was convulsed with its own civil war, and the United States' loss of its Pacific coastline to the DJR had made it impossible for the country to fulfill its mutual defense treaty obligation to the Philippines. And the DJR was a Chinese protectorate, so it neither would or could intervene.

Chris had left his mother and sisters behind in the Philippines, as David had left his family in the DJR. Unlike David, however, Chris was able to bring his relatives to the United States for occasional visits, although he dared not venture on Philippine soil himself due to his political activities in the United States. He was active in the local MAGA Party, which had been jostling with the Republican Party for political supremacy since before the civil war, with a wan Whig remnant of a Democratic Party rounding out the trio. Party leaders were even encouraging Chris to run for the state legislature, but so far he had fended them off.

Since the DJR, for all its foundational ideology of Diversity, discouraged knowledge of other countries and world history—their beliefs and unpleasant histories were often difficult to assimilate into the DJR's obsessive race-and-sex narrative—David had known no more of the Philippines than he did about the moon. Upon befriending Chris, he diligently researched the Philippines, so that when he revealed his new knowledge, Chris was impressed. "Most Americans don't want to learn about other countries," he said, without rancor.

"I'm late to learning," said David, and had explained to the surprised Chris that he himself did not even have a college degree. Then he told Chris his story.

"Maybe you should run for the legislature," said Chris admiringly. But that's as far as their political discussions had gone.

The men talked, in low voices, about the infiltration of Diversity elements into the Capettone recruiting pool. As Robotics Lab director, Chris used his authority to reject any hires he considered temperamentally unsuitable, but he had told David about the problems less politically savvy labs were facing. Chris was virtually certain that anticancer pill technology developed on the second floor of the lab building had made its way to China via Capettone employees, who were possibly motivated more by ideological kinship than money, although China always used the latter to sweeten the deal and create greater dependence.

"I'd hate to see you leave Capettone," he told David, as they finally began to rise from the table, "because I don't think anyone who replaces you would understand the seriousness of the security threats we are facing."

They passed by the electronic bulletin board in the corridor leading from the cafeteria to the main lobby. "Just a second," said Chris. "I want to show you something." They stared at the rolling messages. Nobel Prize winner in Chemistry speaking in Oklahoma City next week, cosponsored by Capettone and the university. Cafeteria Advisory Committee meeting every other Wednesday at 11:00 a.m. Employee Climate survey due on June first.

"Here it comes," said Chris.

"Scientists for Social Justice. Employee Action Group forming to demand real not fake Diversity and Inclusion. Contact Michelle V., ext. 45655."

"Poison in the veins of the Capettone body," said Chris. "Social justice is antithetical to individual justice. I leave it to you whether you want to look further into this, Mr. Security Guy. Maybe you won't have enough time left here to investigate. But I bet this group contains Capettone employees who care about something else even more than they do the company or science, for that matter."

As David walked back to the executive building and his office, he felt slightly better about his own situation, which he could now view, at least partly, against a broader backdrop of sinister forces targeting the United States. But for that reason, his despondence lingered. Had he and Malia risked their lives to come to the free United States, only to find out they had not escaped after all?

David had hated having to show her the flyers, but otherwise it would be hard for Malia to grasp the menace. She skimmed down the list of accusations, her head bent, and her expression not visible to David.

"Is this all true?" she asked, her voice a little faint, finally lifting her head to look at him directly. "All of it?"

"Yes," he replied honestly.

"You never told me...about some of these," Malia said. She remembered that long ago day when she was telling Fern about the handsome Antifan commander she had just met, and she had dismissed irritably the remarks Fern's roommate had made about the evil deeds committed in that gleaming glass Tower called Beaufort. She had never pressed David for details and he had mostly not offered them. "It wasn't terrorists who blew up the parade float and killed the little girl? That was you?"

"Would you have wanted to hear this?" he demanded. "Do you think I had a choice?" She shook her head.

"And a lot of this happened long before you came into my life, I swear to you," he said. "By the time you showed up, I was mostly pushing paper." Neither mentioned the Red Room chambers where David had reluctantly shown up each Friday to punish the enemies of the DJR even as they plotted their escape to the United States.

"Firing squads?"

"Mostly Saturday nights. Then you'd sleep late and drink the rest of the week. For God's sake, Malia, it was torture for me. But unless your hands were stained with blood and then they had you trapped, for good, you'd become one of their victims too."

Their eyes met. She turned to him, wrapped her arms around his shoulders and drew him into her embrace.

"You're a good man," she said. "Never doubt it. If you weren't, you wouldn't have lifted a finger to help me or help Fern escape. The evil people are the ones who are persecuting us." Out of curiosity, she wanted to ask whether he had truly repented those deeds, or whether he was just regretting they had caught up with him, but knew her curiosity was not worth his anger.

On Friday afternoon, David came home, relieved that Baxter was apparently going to let him survive through the weekend. When he ran into Baxter in the men's room Friday morning, the CEO had bestowed a friendly smile, and a "Have a good holiday, Dave" that boded well for a temporary reprieve. Vernal had reassured him on Wednesday they would reach out to Baxter and win David some time. "Don't worry," she had said, "we can reassure Mr. Berry that there's no harm in keeping you around for a while longer. Just have a good weekend, all right?"

David neither knew nor cared what AIA chose to tell Baxter, as long as they ensured he could stay at Capettone for now. He needed time to digest his options. Things moved too fast in the United States, he thought ruefully.

Chapter Ten
Vacations
(Wednesday to Friday, July 22–24, 2093)

Much to Kevin's dismay, Rex was suddenly resisting transferring to Diverse American University. "It will break my mother's heart," she said firmly. Kevin knew where he had gone wrong. While he had been slaving away at Pargeter, Rex had been spending quality time with her mother and the family, and re-imbibing fascist values. You really could not leave that girl unattended, he thought irritably, since whoever was in her proximity filled what he unfairly called her empty head. And now, after all that work he had done to get Rex to consider Diverse American and brave her parents, and that suspicious Plore uncle, she was faltering.

Only two Sundays ago, as they sat at the small desk in the uncomfortably warm but very private attic he was renting for the summer, he had walked her through the application for foreign students to Diverse American and coached her on the correct answers. Not that it really mattered, because the application was a cached shell that had been constructed specifically for Isabelle "Rex" Jenness to believe she was in fact applying to Diverse American. Unless she explicitly praised truth, justice, and the American way, and even if she did, she would be "admitted," with a full scholarship.

"This isn't normally how you'd get into college in the DJR," she said. In the DJR, you did not apply to colleges. You indicated interest in attending college, and the Knowledge Tower would decide whether you were fit to attend college at all, based on your intersectionality score, your Social Credit score, your parents' positions and ideological credibility, and your grades in key Diversity courses. It helped not to be too good at math or science, which suggested a predisposition for logical thinking. If you met the requirements, the Tower would assign you a university and a major. It would also decree whether you could attend in person or online, with the former degree far more prestigious. Malia had been dispatched to Justice University in person to major in knowledge management, of which she still remained quite proud.

"Yes, I know," said Kevin, who himself was an alumnus of the Antifan Defense School, where he had started studying—if you called comparing truncheons and torture techniques studying—at sixteen. "But since you're now a foreigner, you don't have the usual credentials. They have a different process for the foreign students. Don't worry about it. And once we're together in Anacosta, we'll get married."

Rex sighed with pleasure at the thought. She knew she would be hailed as a celebrity back in the DJR. Her adoptive parents would forgive her, since the state would look benignly on her return, with an actual American defector in tow.

Rex had to remind herself that her mother had certainly had a rough time of it in the DJR, with her low social credit score, so her view was understandably jaundiced. She, Rex, would be treated like royalty, returning to build bridges between the DJR and the United States, and all that, and really, she hadn't asked to escape, so the government wasn't going to hold her responsible for Malia and David's sins. Or would it?

For the first time, with Kevin's gravitational pull waning, she entertained doubt. She had been secretly texting with Nathan, the young man with whom Kevin had paired her at Beltane. Nathan was so thoughtful. He had remembered her birthday, and taken her to a trendy outdoor restaurant where he even presented her with flowers. Nathan said he had only attended the Beltane festivities because friends had dragged him there, and he claimed to be interested in traditional Celtic customs. "That was weird," he commented on the Beltane orgy, "although I was glad to meet you," and Rex was relieved she didn't have to pretend otherwise.

Kevin, in Vanover mode, pulled out a second laptop from a hidden shelf under the bed he'd built himself, and typed in the codes that would connect him with Resolution Command.

"XAVIER GROWING SUSPICIOUS OF DA UNDER FAMILY INFLUENCE." The third letter of Rex's name and a gender switch explained the code name. "DA" referred to the Diverse American project.

"VALERIE JOINED MAGA, WORRIED ABOUT NT." Likewise, David became Valerie. "NT" stood for North Taco, an operation whose outlines David and Malia were only barely glimpsing at this point. But soon they would reel under the brunt of Diverse Power, Kevin assured himself.

To Kevin's disgust, he hadn't been able to steal pages from Malia's dissertation, in which Beaufort was interested because she was divulging DJR secrets while pretending to discuss some ancient philosopher. He didn't dare enlist Rex to acquire the hard copy, since even she would ask why he wanted to read her mother's dissertation. He wondered if Malia would respond to flattery and lend him a few chapters. It would help if he were a political science student rather than an engineering one, but too late for that. The ADF would not have allowed even a trusted officer such as Vanover to take politically dangerous coursework—engineering was considered safe, and it would set him up for a future assignment in the ADF's Construction Command.

Two days later came the reply.

"ABANDON DA. TIME TOO SHORT GIVEN SCHOOL CALENDAR.
FIND ALTERNATIVE STRATEGY IMMEDIATELY."

And more ominously,

"VALERIE WON'T BE A PROBLEM MUCH LONGER.
OPPORTUNITY TO PUT NORTH TACO IN MOTION."

As they had relaxed in the living room a week earlier, the boys safely in bed, David proposed to Malia they finally take a weekend trip to Dallas. "Vernal asked me to meet with their station chief in Dallas to discuss opening a security firm. We could stay for an extra day or so and go see some plays, try some restaurants."

"That would be great!" Malia's horizons had expanded with their escape to the United States and she longed to see the big world she knew was out there. She searched for hotels, restaurants, and plays, and drew up an itinerary. David was pleased to see her excitement—Malia could be reticent.

This would be their first trip beyond US borders since arriving in the country. The United States and the Texas Republic had friendly relations based on respect for free markets, civil rights, and shared Anglo-American culture. The Texas Constitution echoed the US Constitution and included a very similar Bill of Rights. The Texas government struggled with reining in gangs engaged in drug trafficking in the north, near the Oklahoma border, but the main highway between Dallas and the Oklahoma border was tightly patrolled, and unless the gangs had a beef with you, you were as safe as anywhere in the United States. Malia's US resident papers would suffice at the border crossing, which was far less onerous than Canada's. It seemed as safe a way to test the waters of foreign travel as anything else.

"Rex wants to take a trip to Montreal with Kevin," Malia said. "She called it a romantic getaway. I guess we all need a change of scenery."

"That's an improvement over studying in the DJR," David said. When he heard from Malia about the Diverse American application, he had clapped his hand to his forehead in disbelief.

They looked at each other, not sure who would be the first to voice qualms they shared. Rex was a grown woman, at least technically, and David knew Rex was Malia's daughter, not his.

"Montreal is very close to the DJR border," David said. "I hope this isn't an end run around us."

"She seemed to realize that returning to the DJR is a bad option. I didn't get the sense she planned to do anything more than visit Montreal. I've heard it's a beautiful city."

"Hmm," said David. They knew that if Rex was determined to return to the DJR, they wouldn't be able to stop her. "But what does this Kevin want? I thought he was a normal patriotic American and now he seems to be one of these Diversity freaks after all."

"He can't just traipse over the border with her, can he?" Malia pointed out. "She'd know something was up, and I can't imagine that the DJR would welcome them if they just showed up at the border, right?"

David didn't say anything. It all depended on who Kevin really was. He promised Malia he would do some research on his own, pronto. Maybe AIA would help, although it technically wasn't allowed to spy on US citizens. He couldn't trust the FBI to take this threat seriously if they wouldn't take seriously direct confrontations against him in Oklahoma City.

Meanwhile, Kevin was listening, grinning, before turning into bed. It was better than a movie. He just hoped that David wouldn't get around to doing the research too soon.

Chapter 11
Gone Wrong
(Thursday to Saturday, August 6–8, 2093)

Kevin had reinvigorated his courtship of Rex, and her parents, even accompanying the Harrises to church to reassure them, as distasteful as he found it. In accordance with Beaufort's latest regulations, he filed a Heretical Church Attendance report each time he went, which was a bureaucratic pain in the neck, since it required him to pay sufficient attention to the sermon to report on its contents. Someday, when Diversity presumably triumphed in Oklahoma, the authorities would use it to target the pastor.

On the bright side, Kevin's greater attentiveness to Rex had banished Nathan to the periphery, not that Kevin ever knew he had a rival. Kevin and Rex now had airline reservations from Oklahoma City to Chicago and then Chicago to Montreal, for Wednesday, August 12.

"Why not fly directly to Montreal from Dallas?" Daniel had asked them, puzzled, during the coffee hour following the church service. "That's a much bigger airport."

"We're saving some money, sir," Kevin had replied, evenly.

In reality, Kevin did not want to risk an additional border crossing, even if it was just Texas. The final destination was Anacosta, but he wouldn't tell Rex until the last moment. Diversair had canceled its normal flight from Montreal to Miami at that time and replaced it with the mysterious Flight 004 to Anacosta, airport code ANC, on which only two passengers were expected, although they would be accompanied by some plausible extras. Just to keep Rex motivated, Kevin sent her photographs of charming Montreal street scenes and buildings, which, if his plan went right, she would never see.

On Thursday morning, David and Malia were off, scheduled to return Saturday night. He had meetings on Thursday afternoon and Friday morning with the AIA station chief in Dallas. Not trusting Rex to watch them for two full days and nights, Malia and David brought the boys over to Aunt Fern's. The boys were so accustomed to staying with her and Ivy that they hardly noticed when Malia gave them each a hug and kiss in farewell.

Daniel walked them out to the car before heading over to open the store. He placed a hand on David's shoulder, and said, "Give us a call when you leave Dallas, all right?"

"Sure," said David. "And thank you for watching Emmett and George again."

"No problem," said Daniel, "Fern loves all the kids. A few years ago I would have never dreamed it was possible we would both have kids and live in a free country and watch them play together. It's all good."

At the Texas border, the officials quickly handed David's passport back to him, but scrutinized Malia's US resident papers with interest. At the officer's request, Malia downloaded the documents onto the Texas Border Control site. They waited for ten minutes in a parking lot before he reemerged to wave them onward.

"That's a relief," said Malia, "I can't wait to get that ceremony over with."

"Good thing we left early," said David. They drove down the highway, lined by tall fences that protected travelers from the depredations of the gangs, although an effective truce kept the bands mostly concentrated in the dusty hills beyond. The gangs did not dare cross the Red River into the United States, but as David and Malia now knew, the FBI kept an alert eye on them. They marveled at the frothing brick red waters of the Red River below them. The summer had been rainy so far.

The gleaming towers of Dallas—not as tall as Anacosta's solar-powered monoliths—appeared on the horizon within the hour. Since Texas's declaration of independence in 2055, its cities had grown as citizens flocked away from the insecure and economically fragile hinterland. For decades, the disenfranchised of Central America had been flooding into Mexico, and Texas, and for every would-be worker just seeking a better life, there was a peasant not even literate in his own indigenous language, or a fatherless boy vulnerable to the gangs that flowed up from that obscure corner of the Americas. With migrants came their culture, for better or worse.

Texas devoted most of its national security budget to its western border with the DJR at Phoenix, and to its southern border with Mexico, although the latter country's growing prosperity—its GDP had recently exceeded the DJR's—was helping soothe tensions.

"Don't worry, it's not Anacosta," David joked, referring to the towers, and Malia replied with an ironic grunt.

In the hotel suite in Dallas—they were splurging—David showered and dressed for his first meeting. The hotel adjoined a luxury mall, and Malia planned to shop, or at least browse.

"Hey, can you pick up something nice for Daniel and Fern?" he asked her, eyeing her in the mirror before him. Malia was curled on the bed, shoes off, leafing through a novel.

"Do you think they're annoyed at having to watch the boys again?"

"Daniel was nice about it," said David, "and he said Fern really enjoyed being a mom…I mean, or aunt…to all of them. But it couldn't hurt us to show some appreciation."

"I know we'd do it for them if they'd only take a trip of their own. But they never go away. They're such homebodies."

"Do you really enjoy being a mother?" David dared. He turned around from the mirror, having straightened his tie and found his image pleasing. He looked like a successful businessman ready to sign some deals and shake some hands.

"Do you doubt it?"

He shrugged. He was used to old-fashioned Plore mothers, and he knew that Malia had begun motherhood with full devotion but lost ten years when Isabelle was seized from her. It must have been like trying to play soccer again after recovering from a crippling soccer injury. One might hold back, even unintentionally. You would never recover your original confidence.

"No, I don't doubt it," he responded, but something in his voice caused her to look up sharply from her book.

"I'm sorry I have other things going on in my life, just like you do."

"Am I a bad father?" he asked, deliberately softening his tone.

"No," she said, "We do the best we can." But it was still awkward.

A few hours later, gift shopping done, Malia ensconced herself and the bulky bag in a coffee shop and finished the book over two cappuccinos. It troubled her that David had somehow detected her aloofness. She loved Emmett and George, and she was proud of them, of course, not just when other shoppers or neighbors commented on how handsome or clever they were. After she finished the dissertation, she said to herself, she would focus on her sons.

The conversation resumed on Saturday morning, after they had drunk expensive champagne and made love until late into night. In the cold light of their second and last morning in Dallas, all Malia could think about was that David, and possibly Daniel and Fern, thought she was a bad mother. The angst had returned in the early morning hours and disturbed her rest.

"All right, what's the matter?" David asked. He could read her face.

"I'm not a bad mother," she pouted.

"Didn't we agree you're not a bad mother? And I'm not a bad father?" He was now irritated that their romantic getaway was spiraling into a squabble, but he was unwilling to capitulate.

"But you're not saying I'm a good mother."

Oh Lord, he thought. "You're a great mother to the dissertation."

Malia rose from the bed in a wave of self-righteous anger that David almost laughed at, it was so comical, her face stretched in outrage. There was a time when she would never have dared confront him, four years ago in Anacosta, when he held the reins. He had never ever intimated he might send her back to her low-credit penury after rescuing her from the False Knowledge Depository; he would have been shocked had anyone suggested he play that card. And he had sensed Malia held back sometimes out of that fear he might play that card.

"If it weren't for my housewife duties, the dissertation would have been done a year ago. We could have hired help."

"And so what? Is the public dying to read the dissertation? You have a movie deal waiting for it?" And then, more pointedly, "Emmett and George won't stay babies while you finish that. And while we're at it, why exactly are you writing it? Are you planning to become a professor?"

"Yes," said Malia primly, "that's a possibility. Dr. Upton says that my dissertation is one of the best in the department right now and DJR studies is becoming very popular. I'd have a good shot at a tenure-track job at a lot of schools."

"In Oklahoma City? You don't think we're leaving Oklahoma and my brother, do you? And what about my job?"

"You can get a job anywhere. This is the US, not the DJR."

"Look, you have bigger responsibilities at home. Would it really be better for us if you sat in a library all day? Again? Or taught someone else's kids when you have your own at home?"

"At least I would be doing something constructive for the country. I wouldn't be torturing or killing innocent people. You're still proud of a job that made you blow up little girls."

David sank back onto the pillows, as if she had hit him. His face collapsed. He turned over on his right side, facing away from her. "I didn't have a choice," he told the window.

"You had a choice whether to enjoy it or not. And you did."

Malia was shocked by her own boldness, but refused to apologize. Her eyes on David's back, she burst into tears, but this time he refused to comfort her.

"I'm sorry," she said lamely. "It's just that there are so many opportunities here in the US and I feel time is so short." He ignored her. Eventually, they both rose from the bed, and dressed separately, silently, before heading out for one last day of sightseeing.

A few hours later, in a pleasant air-conditioned courtyard, during a late lunch after a museum outing, the conversation resumed, cautiously. It was late in the lunch hour, and she and David had a corner mostly to themselves.

"I've been thinking," she said. "I've been very defensive. We have two beautiful sons and yet I have to admit, it doesn't feel the same way it did with Isabelle.

"I never dreamed that the government could snatch her from me in a single day. I gave her my heart and soul and every conscious moment. And in a single day, it didn't matter. They knocked the air out of me. Even though she's now back with us, fourteen years later, I can't commit like that again. I mean, it's not a conscious decision, but I hold back."

"If you feel something isn't quite right, it isn't quite right. There's no shame in talking to a therapist. We could both go." David was subdued. Neither mentioned her insults that morning, but they had treated each other awkwardly all day.

This wasn't the right moment to also confide that she was worried about Rex. Something didn't seem right about that trip to Montreal. But she had no specifics, other than her uneasy intuition, and you couldn't tell a nineteen-year-old woman, even a somewhat immature one, that she couldn't take a trip with her boyfriend. Or could you? She decided they could discuss Rex after they returned home. For all they knew, the trip had been called off.

Chapter 12
Highway Robbery
(Saturday, August 8, 2093)

By evening, they were in the car returning to Oklahoma City, the towers of Dallas receding behind them. A rich pink and purple sunset to the west framed their sport utility van as it headed north, before the looming roadside fences began and ruined the view.

Even though it was generally ill-advised to travel north Texas after dark, and traffic was sparse, they encountered no problems along the highway south of the border. Beyond the fences, the hills sat, dark and silent. "It's a little spooky, isn't it?" Malia said, as the lights disappeared behind them and they hurtled into the darkness. David silently wished they had crossed the border before sundown, but would say nothing to alarm Malia further.

Ahead they saw the lights of the border crossing. Leaving Texas was easier than arriving had been. The lone guard clicked on Malia's documents and gave a cursory glance to David's. A few hundred yards down the road, on the other side of the now-colorless Red River, the US border guard did the same, wordlessly.

Trucks were lined up in an alternate lane, and Malia and David were just close enough to see some sniffer canines moving around them. The constant threat of narcotics smuggling from Texas meant that US border control gave trucks more scrutiny, because even when the truck drivers themselves were honest, a gang still might have infiltrated a trucking company and planted cocaine under the flooring or behind a giant wheel. Everything was quiet, and it seemed much later at night than was really the case. Rolling down the windows, they heard crickets chirping and an owl hooting.

The fences had disappeared, since they were now in the United States, back in Oklahoma. They were driving up the little peninsula that lay between the two banks of the Red River, with Texas to their right and left on the other side. On the left, they saw a sign for Thackerville, the twinkling lights of farmhouses just ahead of them, and then the town was behind them.

David saw flashing police lights in his rearview mirror. "Uh-oh," he said, but he assumed the car was responding to an emergency farther up the road and would pass them. He pulled over to the shoulder to give way to the cruiser, but to his alarm, it started to pull in behind them. "We've done nothing wrong," he said, "I don't get it." His mind raced, thinking of what road rules he might have violated.

Two helicopters approached from the west. They heard the deafening sound of choppers.

Malia and David looked at each other.

"It's got to be a mistake," she said. "Why would they come after us?"

David floored the gas pedal. They lurched back onto the highway; Malia shrieked with surprise. The patrol cruiser was caught by surprise as well, but then followed them, gaining steadily. They were at one hundred miles per hour. But then, just ahead of them, two other patrol cars were blocking the road. A lone civilian car also paused at the barrier, but then was able to move around it to the left and speed off, the driver realizing that he was not the target and not wanting to become involved.

David couldn't tell if this was a legitimate traffic stop, and giving it the benefit of the doubt, came to a screeching halt several feet away from the cars. Items on the back seat slid to the floor. The cars looked like Oklahoma state trooper vehicles, but it was hard to check that in the dark. And the gangs were on the other side of the border, right? Not here. And he wasn't going to kill himself and Malia by slamming into the police cruisers. He took a deep breath, removed his sweaty palms from the wheel, and wiped them on his slacks. And waited. He placed his firearm under the seat but within reach and shoved the extra magazine into his front right pocket.

About a minute passed. The helicopters landed, noisily, on their right, on open ground.

"Do they think we're drug smugglers? What is this?" Malia asked.

"I don't know. Let me do the talking." David hoped that his brief experience on the Oklahoma City police force would come in handy.

They heard the sounds of a man's boots scraping the gravel along the roadway. David reluctantly rolled down the window. A round face under a state trooper's hat looked down at him. "Please exit the car, sir."

Even in the dark, David recognized the face from ADF headquarters at Beaufort. *It's them! Here!*

David raised his weapon, and fired it into the trooper's face before the man could react. He threw open the door, and growled to Malia, "Get out and run! Run away!" He heard her scramble out of the car and start to flee, but he couldn't follow her. As soon as he got out of the car—he could not allow himself to be trapped inside the vehicle—he shot two uniforms who approached him from the squad cars. They each fell to the ground, wounded or killed, he couldn't tell. But he realized quickly thanks to his brief law enforcement experience here that they were not wearing Oklahoma state trooper uniforms, only some approximation of them concealed in the darkness.

Other soldiers were jumping from the helicopters. "Halt!" someone shouted. He ran toward an outcrop about fifty yards off the road, knowing he could defend himself behind it. He assumed that Malia was not of interest to the men, or at least hoped they were not seeking to kill her, but rather him, so he forgot her, for the moment.

It did not seem that the armed men were using night vision equipment, or not very good equipment, because he eluded two more shots and, breathing heavily, dashed behind the outcrop with its grassy fronds stirring in the night breeze. Aside from the two initial shots, nobody was shooting at him. But his assailants were approaching the outcrop in a large semicircle, which would presumably become a larger circle, and then he would be surrounded.

Dammit, the cell phone is in the car. Can't call for help. David tried to collect his thoughts, to remember the class they had taught at the ADF academy about nighttime apprehensions, but that was a long time ago and all jumbled in his mind. All he could do was hope to pick off some of the closest attackers and discourage the others. A rattlesnake slithered past, its habitat disturbed.

He peeked around the outcrop, and saw shadows in the distance. When the moon rose, it would reveal his hiding place, as he heard drones overhead. He was grateful for his pistol's night sights, which were standard, and glad he had spent more money than usual on the weapon and trained more than usual this spring after the Antifans showed their hand. He saw the ends of the semicircle starting to approach from his left side, but not yet within range of his firearm. Even that weapon would have no more than 150 feet, reliably, and he couldn't afford to waste ammo by firing blindly.

"Fuck, a snake!" he heard someone shout, and then a cry. "Medic!" Thank you, friend snake, thought David, the side of his mouth twitching with bitter amusement. One of the shadows lumbered back clumsily toward the helicopters. Otherwise it was eerily silent, but David watched the other shadows coming nearer, and now he could discern their outlines. He raised the firearm, and took his time centering on the nearest one. He fired. The figure toppled. His partner now ran toward the outcrop, and David neatly dispatched him as well. If they all stormed him at once, he would be overtaken, and he was watching carefully for a sudden rush. But they didn't know the terrain, which was bumpy and pitted, and had clearly expected to accost him at the original pullover spot, which featured an open concrete apron alongside the road.

How many are there? he pondered, his heart pounding. Maybe four each in the helicopters, not including the pilots, and two from each of the three cars. Fourteen, minus four, minus five if you counted snake guy. Nine, maybe fewer left. David swung around to see whether the ends of the circle were nearing. Yes, just within range. Two more down in quick succession. They could rush him now, but they were out in the open and with his night vision, easy pickings. Antifan battle armor lacked night sights for the most part, except for those scary late-night raids on dissident apartments, where you only needed to frighten your victims. Military units on the border didn't expect to exchange artillery or fire with US counterparts let alone raid them. And the DJR didn't have the money for the most sophisticated equipment—even an ordinary US citizen could defend himself as well or better than an individual Antifan soldier.

They knew he was somewhere behind the outcrop, but he saw them better than they saw him. He picked off another soldier. "Halt!" ordered the lieutenant, or whoever was in charge. Stupidly, a clump conferred about ninety feet from David. He eliminated them briskly. He took advantage of the pause to load the second magazine.

"Thirty six!" they called, the sign for retreat, which David knew, and without leadership, the remaining members of the group—perhaps no more than three or four troopers—began loping back toward the helicopters. He fired another two rounds without aiming, just to encourage their departure.

They didn't want to kill you, he realized, they wanted to take you alive.

Where is Malia, he thought, suddenly panicked. He had not heard her at all after they fled the car. Perhaps that meant she had successfully run off into the field and found a hiding place, or even across the highway. Malia would not take any chances by coming out of hiding before she was absolutely certain the danger was past, he told himself, that wouldn't be like her. If they didn't want to kill him, surely they would not bother to kill her, he tried to convince himself. As soon as the helicopters left, he would search for her.

It was encouraging that she had not yelled, although he knew that in the thick of the battle, with his enemies closing in, it was possible to close out every extraneous sound and focus on your own survival. Once, after an intense firefight against fascist resisters (now, years later, he realized they were freedom-loving democrats and better human beings than him) he had mentioned to his Antifan comrades that it had been strangely quiet throughout the battle. They had said to him incredulously, "Are you kidding? That was like sitting through a drum set!" But that's how you protected yourself, by closing out all those meaningless sounds that could only distract you from focusing directly on the threat and reacting with pure instinct.

The helicopters lifted into the air and a minute later were whirring noisily to the west. David watched cautiously until they had disappeared into the night clouds. It was a breach of Antifan protocol to have left the bodies of the fallen behind, he recalled. Or it would have been once upon a time. Now normal sensations made themselves felt, demanding his attention. His body crawled with sweat, including the feet in his sockless canvas shoes. He shivered from the cooling night air. He finally realized he needed to relieve himself, and he did, with no living eye on him.

"Malia! Malia!" he shouted as he came out from the outcrop. The moon was rising and he could finally see clearly the ten or so bodies littering the field. He had done this, single-handedly. He would never kill again, he had put death and blood behind him, or so he had thought. But now he realized, as he had in Baxter Berry's office, that the

Antifan background would follow him forever, and he would never shed it.

Maybe one or two Antifans, or for all he knew, all of them, were not dead, but lying in wait for him, hoping he would walk near enough to be taken by surprise. Could this all have been a ruse, and the allegedly dead bodies would suddenly leap up and grab him? Deceit and dishonor were part of the Antifan playbook, and David would not have put such tactics past his former comrades. Still, he walked out into the middle of the field, keeping his eyes on the nearby corpses for any sign of movement.

"Malia! Malia! Malia!" He ran around, shouting her name. Silence. Somewhere a fox screeched.

David heard nothing else. He walked back to the car, futilely hoping he might find Malia hiding in it, retrieved his phone instead, and called the emergency number. While he waited for the local police, he walked over to the nearest body, aside from the original fake police officer, one of the two he had killed after exiting the car. It looked familiar. He peered more closely at it, his hand on the gun, just in case.

Pain stabbed his chest as he recognized Sam Kenard, from his own Knowledge Crimes Unit. Sam had come to the KCU after a rough time at the Antifan training academy. His mother, battling breast cancer, had been ordered to the Euthanasia Palace when the authorities decided that a low–Social Credit clerical employee, even the mother of an Antifan soldier, was not worth the expensive cancer treatments, or even the basic chemotherapy that ordinary Social Crediteers could normally expect. She was one year older than the cutoff for treatment.

"Have a good time at the Palace," they told her, "everything comes to an end in Mother Earth." They let Sam visit on the day before she swallowed the fatal dose. He and his mother had sat dejectedly over a lavish vegetarian meal served on excellent china, weeping together until the nurse scolded them for their lack of Diverse piety.

Sensing Sam's bitterness, David strove to give him interesting assignments and training opportunities. Over lunch in the cafeteria, he had explained how even as a Plore, who should have hated the government, he felt the DJR did the best it could with the resources it had.

Wasted my time, David thought. Sam had been correct in his hatred, and David had kept him from coming to the correct conclusions about the DJR. David had not even allowed himself to ask whether Sam was right, which would have been dangerous to himself as well.

Suddenly David's legs buckled beneath him. A handy tree stump provided a good perch for awaiting the real police. He sat down, and regarded the moonlit landscape and Sam, several yards away. Sam's open eyes safely stared into the dark sky, into the night. As a Christian, David liked to think Sam had been reunited with his mother, but could not quite believe it.

What had Sam thought when ordered to take part in this mission, and to betray a man who more than anyone else at Beaufort, had helped him? Had he sufficiently restored Sam's psyche so that Sam could treat the mission as justified, and dismiss David as a traitor to the cause who only deserved death? Or had the mission so tormented him that his shot fired at David missed, and he had allowed himself to die instead, perhaps without even consciously realizing it? You'll never know, David thought glumly. And where was Malia?

He wept silently near Kenard's body. In the distance sirens grew louder.

PART TWO

ANACOSTA

"The smallest minority on earth is the individual. Those who deny individual rights cannot claim to be defenders of minorities."
— Ayn Rand

"No man is a number."
—Malia Jenness Harris

Chapter 13
Hospital
(Wednesday, August 12, 2093)

First, emerging from deep unconsciousness, she felt a bone-aching cold, her body groaning with its heaviness. Then she felt herself shivering. "Cold…" she moaned, her eyes still closed. The weight of a heavy blanket was laid on her. And crisp sheets beneath her and above her. She fell asleep again.

Then she opened her eyes. She was in a hospital. Not really a hospital room, but her bed was surrounded by various instrument panels. The room was windowless, and lit by fluorescents, so she had no idea of what time of day or night it might be. When she moved her arm, she saw a clear IV tube jerk alongside it. Several blurry white-coated doctors or nurses were conferring at a distance. Yes, she thought, we were in an accident. She vaguely remembered their car speeding down the dark highway toward the parked cruisers in the middle of the road. I must have been injured, but nothing hurts. They brought me to the hospital. I am wearing a hospital gown. Malia fell asleep again.

When she awoke next, she blinked and must have made a sound, because one of the white jackets exclaimed, "Look, she's awake!" Several came over to inspect her. She was still dozy.

"Where's my husband?" she asked. The white jackets turned away, seemingly embarrassed. Had she said something wrong? Was something wrong? Was David all right? Then she saw the white armbands worn by DJR health professionals inside their workplace, because the standard black armbands were presumed contaminated from their daily outside use. Health workers changed into the white armbands when they arrived at work. A citizen's white and black armbands were synced so the authorities would not miss a moment of surveillance when switched.

Oh, I'm dreaming, she thought. I'm back in Anacosta, in a hospital. When I wake up, I'll tell David about this funny dream I had. And he'll say, not so funny.

The fourth time she awoke, she felt pressure on her arm. She opened her eyes. A heavyset white nurse was pressing her fleshy body down on Malia's left shoulder and arm. A densely tattooed arm was holding a raised armband phone's camera trained on her. Nobody else seemed to be around. The nurse was preaching into the camera:

"I'm Corona Velstrup, 130, a nurse here at the ADF infirmary, with the fascist we recaptured over the weekend in the US and brought back here to face justice. Look at her evil, pale face. The Diverse People are soon going to pass judgment on her for deserting our beloved country and joining the white supremacists. Mother Earth bless the heroic Antifan Defense Forces!"

In a split second, the now-fully-awake Malia realized what had happened to her, and where she was. And she was repelled, disgusted, and furious at the gross creature virtually lying atop her. She struck the fat nurse's face with her forearm, with all her strength, which was not very much right now, but which caused the IV attached to the other arm to jiggle violently. The nurse gasped, since Malia's arm had smashed into her broad nose.

"Out of here!" Malia yelled. "Get off me, you fat turd!"

A slew of white jackets rushed into the room. Having briefly been left alone with the infamous patient, the nurse had taken advantage of the opportunity to film herself with Malia. She had hoped to show the patriotic footage to her friends and family later, and prove how she helped protect the Diversity Justice Republic from its enemies.

"Get her away from me!" Malia hissed. "She was filming me with that camera!"

An older white-coated man, an Asian, who seemed to be the senior doctor on duty, indicated to the nurse to hand over the phone. "Detach the phone from the armband, please, Nurse Velstrup." The nurse reluctantly handed the phone to the doctor, who reviewed the footage, and deleted it before returning it to Velstrup. "Very unprofessional. There will be consequences."

He turned to Malia, surrounded by four other colleagues, while the fat nurse went to sulk in a corner. He decided to pretend he had not heard the fatphobic remark, because it would require him to file paperwork.

"How are you, Ms. Jenness?"

Even though she had listened to the nurse's diatribe, Malia was still unwilling to believe the evidence of her eyes and ears. "I have no idea what has happened, or where I am, or what is wrong with me. Is my husband here?"

The doctor looked uncomfortable. "No, it's just you here. This is the Beaufort Tower infirmary, in Anacosta. You were apprehended in the United States and brought back to the DJR. You are recovering from your journey."

"What journey?" A cold spidery sensation overcame her whole body, and she realized it was fear.

"Perhaps Commander Ma will be able to explain the details to you," said the doctor. "We are just physicians and nurses taking care of you." The doctor had no idea exactly how Malia had been captured, and very little knowledge of the details of her transport, and was unsure how much he was authorized to reveal in any case.

"Commander Ma is here!" someone called from the doorway. Malia had been left alone only because everyone else had been lined up in the hallway awaiting his arrival.

Ma strode into the room, followed by three uniformed Antifans. Malia first noticed the lithe young woman behind him. Unlike other Antifan women officers, her long, blonde hair was streaming free, not collected in a demure bun above her head. Even stranger, her face seemed disfigured. One half was normally pale, presumably her default coloring. The other half had been dyed a rich deep brown. Unusually deep blue eyes stared out at Malia, like traffic lights. While the woman wore an Antifan uniform, Malia sensed she was not an ordinary squad officer. Behind Ma was Commander Okuro, whose tattoo also fascinated Malia, and a brown-skinned male officer with jet-black hair, perhaps of Indian descent.

But in another second, she lost all interest in the three attendants, as she recognized her train companion. She was speechless with shock. Instead of a traveler's blazer and button-down shirt, he was wearing his full black bloc Antifan regalia, with the close-fitting pants and leather jacket. A string of color bars and symbols presented on his chest pocket, all evidence of evil deeds committed, she knew. The brushlike hair and the broad shoulders had not changed a whit in three months. She saw the glimmer of triumph in the almond eyes.

"I see you recognize me, Malia. My real name is Commander Khalid Ma, 290." He lingered pleasantly on the number. "Welcome home."

"You bastard!" Almost four years in a free country had loosened her tongue. Malia sensed rather than saw the functionaries in the room shrink back in horror at the woman who had just insulted their Paragon. He weighed slapping her, but restrained himself. He would lose face by giving into his temper in front of all these medical underlings.

"Did I not warn you that you would regret not coming to Beltane? Not only did you stay away, but you mocked the sacred holiday by coupling with your husband, the traitor, on another hill, away from the collective."

"Where is my husband?" she snarled at him. "What have you done with him?"

"I regret to inform you he is dead. When we apprehended you at the field, he tried to run away and was shot by our officers. You see, in the end he was a coward and did not protect you. He knew that he was guilty of betraying his oath."

Malia struggled to remember that night, only a few days ago. After a few minutes fully awake, she could now recall the car chase, and she remembered David yelling at her to run from the car. That was the last she had seen or heard him. She had run about a hundred feet, and then everything had gone black and she had fallen to the ground.

"I don't believe you," she said, but with hesitation. She had no idea what actually was the truth, but she did not trust this man. "You are the real cowards."

"Not at all. It was an impressive operation, one of our first across the border, and planned for many months. We knew you were traveling to Dallas, and we have cultivated contacts among the gangs in north Texas, who, for a generous fee, supplied us with the helicopters, and the landing space in their territory. And they outfitted several vehicles as Oklahoma Highway Patrol cars. Very well done, under our strategic direction. So in a few minutes, once we saw your car at the border station, we were underway to intercept you."

Malia, with difficulty, now recalled the churning helicopters. The steady groan of the engines was embedded deep in her consciousness, even though she could not recollect the journey. "How did you know we were going to Dallas?"

"Perhaps I will tell you later. But even though your traitor partner was killed on the spot, we captured you and brought you back to our Texas landing base. By midnight, we drove you to the Dallas airport to a cargo facility in which we have an interest. We cryogenically froze you, packed you in a ventilated box, and included you in a shipment of similar containers, all containing Texas beef, for the DJR market. The flight landed in Orlando by early Sunday morning and you were placed on another flight for Anacosta. You slept for four days, until now."

The scenario was so bizarre that now Malia began wondering whether she was still mired in a nightmare after all. Wake up, please, she urged herself.

"See, you and your traitor mocked DJR science and technology, but we could carry off a very sophisticated operation. We will add that to the list of charges against you."

Malia suddenly remembered she and David had been laughing at their kitchen table a week or two ago about the backwardness of the DJR. "If you showed them a molecular fryer," he had said, referring to a whistling pot that did marvelous things with chicken and beef, "they'd probably worship it as a god in the National Diversity Cathedral." A coincidence or not?

"What do you plan to do with me? What is the point of all this nonsense?"

He bent over her, casting a shadow, and said, "What we do with you will depend on you. First, you will have to repent, because the Diverse People demand justice. Then you will have to be reeducated. If you resist, you will not survive. This process will take time. If you cooperate, we will let you live."

And then she thought of her baby sons, now possibly orphaned, most definitely motherless, maybe asking what had happened to their parents, but because they were so young, not wondering for more than a few weeks. Soon George would forget them, and not long afterward, Emmett. Perhaps he would retain a hazy memory of her, at best. "What about my sons? I have children! Have you no shame at all?"

"Your breeding habits are of no interest to us. If you would like us to rescue them, perhaps we could arrange that eventually, depending on your behavior.

"But you may be interested to know that in another day or so, your daughter, Rex, will join us here. An operation is underway to rescue her for Diversity. Fortunately, she is naive and willing to believe our officer that he will marry her here. It is like coaxing a dumb chicken into the slaughterhouse with a handful of corn."

Malia groaned. She had meant to warn David about the trip to Montreal, but she had refrained from mentioning it, not willing to cast an additional damper on their weekend after the now—she realized—foolish squabbles about whether she was a good mother. When they had left for Dallas, they were still waiting for AIA to report back on Kevin Malloy. "Just for peace of mind," they told themselves. She hoped that her disappearance and David's presumed death would keep Rex close to Oklahoma City for a few days while the authorities sorted out the disaster, but she had little hope that Rex would cancel the trip in the face of Kevin's iron will.

"Kevin?"

"That's what you knew him as. He is actually one of our finest young officers. He will bring your daughter back home, and then his mission will be done. He says he found it disgusting to attend your heretical church and witness your extremist patriarchal lifestyle."

Malia sagged into the pillow, drained by the onrush of awful information. She had failed to warn David of her rising anxiety about Rex and Kevin's trip, now she realized founded on solid intuition. Now David was dead, and innocent Rex would be helpless against the Antifan plot. No one would know what had happened to her, Malia. She had just disappeared into thin air.

"I hate you, you bastards," she scowled at him. "God will punish you. Wait until the Americans hear about this."

Ma signaled for the doctor. "Sedate her until she can comport herself more decently." And as the doctor approached with a giant needle, and the nurses finally moved to hold her down—it was beneath Paragon's dignity to assist—he told her, "I don't think the Americans will care very much about what happens to you. After all, you're not an American yet, are you? You're still a DJR citizen. And your husband is dead." And as he turned to leave the room, he smiled, baring his teeth. Once again, she fell into a deep dreamless sleep.

Chapter 14
No Trust In Princes
(Wednesday, August 12, 2093)

David turned over on the living room sofa after another sodden, unconscious night. His left hip ached from an awkward sleeping position. He knew his breath stank. His whole body ached, but he could not bear to sleep in his and Malia's bed.

He had spent Saturday night in the hospital, and then most of Sunday undergoing questioning from an escalating series of concerned parties, first local police, then Oklahoma state troopers. In the afternoon, Lauren McCall arrived. Within five minutes, she exited grimly, David having hoarsely shouted at her, "You didn't take this seriously. Thanks to you, my wife is nowhere to be found. I hope you get your goddamned promotion!"

Vernal and Bob Dietz from AIA arrived later in the day from St. Louis. Bob Dietz was the AIA Dallas station chief, with responsibility for covering the security situation on the border with the United States. Dietz had met with David in Dallas. He and Vernal briefly encountered McCall as she left the building.

"It's a mess," McCall confessed. "And he," referring to David, "is completely unreasonable."

Dietz disagreed. He didn't think it was unreasonable to be angry after you and your wife had been attacked by ADF troopers and she had likely been kidnapped by the DJR.

"What do you want him to say?" Dietz snapped. "Thanks for taking such good care of our security?"

McCall glared at him, and hurried out of the building. Dietz and Vernal entered David's hospital room, the nurse cautioning, "I don't know how much more he can take today."

They found a haggard David, propped up against his hospital bed pillows. He had mostly refused to eat all day, and a lunch tray sat pushed to the side, with perhaps a bite taken from a cup of applesauce and sips from the cup of water. His eyes were bloodshot.

"And you're sure these were guys out of Anacosta?" Dietz asked.

"Yes, one of them used to be on my squad. I also recognized the first one as one of the night shift guards from a few years ago. So that's when I killed him and Malia and I both ran from the car."

"You killed nine of them," said Dietz. "Pretty impressive."

"Once I realized they were ADF, I had no choice. I knew what they would do to me if they got me back to Anacosta. But I never thought they'd take Malia instead."

"Now," Dietz said, hand partly raised, "we can't be sure of that yet. For all we know she's on the Texas side of the border with the gangs. We might get a ransom request."

"No," said David. "Not if we haven't already. She's too big a prize. They probably won't kill her, at least immediately, but she's a trophy to show you can't escape the DJR and get away with it." His voice sounded tired. He had used up his last reserves on lambasting Lauren McCall.

A nurse came into the room to take his vitals. After the door closed behind her, he asked,

"What happens now? I assume we're going to démarche Anacosta?"

"We'll see," said Dietz. "It's not necessarily to our advantage to bring this up right now. The negotiations were going pretty well. We were on the verge of inking a big machinery deal with the DJR and we still need access to ports.

"Now, now," said Dietz cautiously, as David glared at him. "I didn't say we weren't going to raise it. This was blatant violation of US territory and of the treaty, if they were really Antifans."

"If? I just told you I recognized two of them, and it wasn't from church!"

"It's delicate, that's all," said Dietz. "And we can't démarche Anacosta directly because we don't have diplomatic relations. It would have to be through the Mexican embassy, which is our intermediary with the deejers."

Groaning, David slumped back against the pillow.

"David, I want you to know that we are collecting information right now. Every asset I have tasked against those gangs is reporting back. Assuming the attackers were in fact Antifans, we will know within a day or two what we're up against. If we're going to raise this issue with the deejers, we need to know exactly what happened. The more credible details we have, the more seriously we can engage Anacosta. At least when they lie to us, we'll know they're lying."

As he and Vernal rose to leave, Dietz reassured him. "Don't worry, we will find out who is responsible and we will bring your wife home." As they left the room, David stared dully at the telescreen, on mute, watching the moving jaws of news anchors. The chyron read, "DJR Negotiations Poised for Progress." Unless he had missed it while sleeping, the news stations had not yet broadcast anything about the odd shooting incident on Highway 35. Then the anchors moved on, joking with each other about weather and sports.

Outside, as they approached the car, Vernal asked, "If they were Antifans, why would they have carried out this attack at this point in the negotiations? Don't they want the negotiations to succeed as much as we do?"

"Maybe they think that we need the agreement more than they do at this point," said Dietz. "Which may be right. And maybe kidnapping David and Malia back to Anacosta was worth more to them than an agreement. Damned bad timing, though."

"She's not even an American citizen yet."

"That's going to be a problem," Dietz said. "We are on shakier ground than if she had taken her citizenship oath. If she's in DJR hands, and I bet she is, they will probably insist that she committed espionage against her own country by escaping, and then by working with us. Even if she were a US citizen, the DJR might do what the Soviet Union used to do. They'd claim when a former citizen fell into their hands, that they still were a Soviet citizen. We're going to have to decide how much this matters to us."

"But don't we owe her something for having helped us?"

"Of course," said Dietz, as they sped back toward the Missouri border and the capital. "But I don't know that I can convince State or even our own folks that we need to raise it immediately. And what happens if the deejers just deny they have her? What do we do, just stop the negotiations and go home?"

Vernal stared out the window. She blamed herself for having been so cavalier, in retrospect, about what she had just assumed was an Antifan intimidation campaign. The AIA easily could have moved Malia and David to a safer place, or provided discreet surveillance if they had insisted on traveling to Dallas. So far nobody had accused her of negligence, and she hoped to keep it that way by not arguing with the powerful station chief. Still, she felt badly. She recalled how quickly Malia had responded to analysts' emails, and how she would eagerly come to St. Louis to meet with AIA. The AIA owed her help. If only she could believe Dietz's assurances that the issue was just one of timing.

Daniel arrived the next morning, Monday, to bring David home. David was pathetically grateful at the sight of his practical, stolid brother, especially knowing Daniel was missing a day of work. With all the emotion rippling through him— anger, sadness, regret, shame at his cowardice—David needed a calm bulwark, and that was Daniel.

"We'll get you home, that will help," said Daniel, "and then we will sort all this out." He left no doubt that everything would be sorted out. Forty years ago, as a beardless teenager, he had anchored their family through war, hunger, and defeat after their father was killed, and he assumed the mantle of leadership in crisis once again.

"They don't want to do anything for us," David said.

"Let's see about that. They're probably just trying to figure out what's happened. First, home." He walked alongside the wheelchair as a nurse pushed David out to the curb.

And now, on Wednesday morning, his second at home, David was awakening on the sofa, with the partly open curtains letting in dim light. He had been taking sedatives ever since Monday, with Daniel or Fern administering the dose during waking hours, and David doubling it when he awoke in the middle of the night, in order to sleep. He glimpsed an emptied highball glass on the end table, and a whiskey bottle a few inches away. He didn't remember drinking, but Daniel did not drink alcohol, so it must be him, and he should hide the bottle before his brother returned.

The door creaked open.

"Daniel?" he called out. He reached under the sofa for the firearm, just in case. It would not have shocked him had the Antifans sent an operative to assassinate him after the initial sweep failed to capture him.

"No, my friend," said a familiar voice, and David's spirits lifted instantly.

"Chris!"

"Hello, David. Your brother gave me the key code. I hope you don't mind my coming to visit with you this morning."

"I'm happy to see you."

"Good, then let's tidy up here." Within a few minutes, the shades were open and letting bounteous sunshine into the room, the liquor bottle and glass vanished, and the blankets were folded. Chris sent David upstairs to shower and dress, while he began rummaging in the coldbox for eggs and bread.

They sat at the kitchen table, Chris eating only sparingly just to keep David company, but making sure David himself ate a decent breakfast. "You say you're not hungry, but you need your strength. The challenge is just beginning."

David, choking at times, told Chris the story, lamenting that he had failed Malia.

"It's not in the news," Chris said. "The Bureau and AIA are keeping this quiet. There is a small item about a traffic stop with drug traffickers on Saturday night in which several gang members were supposedly killed. That would explain any gunfire that people in the town nearby heard. And then there was some story on RealNews about alien abductions taking place that night."

"I guess RealNews got closer to the truth than anyone else this time," David joked bitterly. "That's why I don't see reporters on my front lawn, I suppose. But this is a double-edged sword, because there's no publicity either. How are we going to pressure St. Louis to fight for Malia? She hadn't even taken the citizenship oath yet. The ocean access matters a lot more to them than my wife does."

Chris replied, "Put not your trust in princes, in a son of man, in whom there is no help."

David recognized Psalm 146, and responded, "The Lord sets the prisoners free... the Lord loves the righteous." Strangely, the words buoyed him.

"Either St. Louis will help you," said Chris, "or we will help you rescue Malia."

David stared at him.

"This is a free country, and we must do the right thing when our government will not," said Chris. "The MAGA people can make things happen. But let's give St. Louis a chance first.

"Where's your stepdaughter?"

David was jolted by the realization that in his haze, he hadn't even thought about Rex, who most definitely was not at home. Daniel hadn't mentioned her. Wasn't today the day she and Kevin were supposed to travel to Montreal? Maybe it was Thursday? He struggled to remember. "I don't know. Maybe she's with the boyfriend."

That reminded him of the search on Kevin Malloy that AIA had promised him, and would hopefully deliver in the wake of the assault. "I need to check for messages in the basement," he told Chris. "That's how we communicate with AIA, it's a secure room." Technically, he shouldn't have confessed this to Chris, but he trusted his friend. He got up unsteadily from the table. "I'll be right back." Chris nodded, and began washing dishes.

Settled on the chair in the secure room, David also struggled to recall the passwords. He found the new code under a shelf in the corner, also against the rules.

The message was dated Tuesday, yesterday.

GREETINGS ARGONAUT. HOPE YOU ARE RECOVERING.

THERE IS NO LIVING KEVIN MALLOY FITTING THE DESCRIPTION YOU GAVE US. WE HAVE IDENTIFIED ONE KEVIN MALLOY, DOB 6 APRIL 2064, POB KENTON, MONTANA, SERVED IN ARMY AT FORT HOOD FROM 2082-2084. DIED BY HIS OWN HAND IN IDAHO IN MAY 2086. REGARDS.

David stared at the screen for a few extra seconds as it dwindled to black. He trudged upstairs.

"The boyfriend doesn't exist," he told Chris, tiredly. "He's not who he says he is. He's adopted the identity of a dead man from Montana."

"So who is this boyfriend?"

David called Fern, who was now feeding the children. She promised she would bring them over later. "Go to the park with them," she told him. "They need to see you and do something normal. They know something's wrong, because they're definitely more cranky than usual."

Fern said that they hadn't seen Rex since Sunday. "She told us that she would stay out of the way and at Kevin's place until their trip."

David was embarrassed to have to ask. "Do you recall when they were leaving town?" He now realized that he didn't even know exactly where Kevin lived.

"Today, I think?" but Fern sounded unsure.

David texted Rex, "Hey, hope everything's all right, when exactly is your trip?" As if Rex's mother hadn't disappeared over the weekend, as if their trip to Dallas had ended perfectly uneventfully. Rex knew perfectly well about the disaster that had befallen them over the weekend. How could she simply disappear herself?

If Kevin wasn't really Kevin Malloy, he must be a criminal of some kind. Maybe an Antifan, although even after Saturday night, that still seemed far-fetched. A bigamist? And Montreal wasn't the DJR, right? They couldn't disappear in Canada, could they? He confided his worries to Chris.

"Does she have a workscreen here?" Chris asked David.

"Yes," David said, "in her room." Chris went upstairs, David following, his phone in hand, waiting for Rex's return text. Chris opened the laptop. Rex had conveniently left her password on a scrap of paper under the keyboard.

Chris sat down at the keyboard, tapping away. He opened the mail file, and scanning the queue, found an attachment sent from Kevin Malloy dated three weeks earlier, called "Canada Trip Itinerary."

The first two legs seemed normal. "They're traveling early this afternoon," said Chris, his eyes still on the screen. "Cloud Air Flight 445 to Chicago. Connection, also Cloud Air, Flight 34, to Montreal. And there's a tab for the return flights, so at least they plan to come back, I think...but something seems odd here..." He tapped away. There was a hidden tab behind a link that Kevin had not bothered to erase, so confident was he in Rex's obtuseness, or perhaps he himself had not realized the link was buried among the lines at the bottom of the page.

"Diversair Flight 004 to Anacosta, leaving Montreal at 5:55 p.m."

"No!" David said. "Show me."

His lips pressed together with dismay, David read the itinerary for himself. A ping signaled a text from Rex.

"Hi David, we are leaving tomorrow."

She's lying, thought David, they are hoping to get away before we even realize what's happening. He told Chris.

Another ping, "Have you heard anything about Mom?" More dutiful than frantic, was David's initial reaction.

"We need to apprehend them at the airport," said Chris. "They're probably about to leave for the airport any minute now. Can you do this?"

David nodded. "I lost Malia to those bastards, they sure as hell won't get her daughter."

"That's the spirit," said Chris. He made another phone call or two. "Just some friends from the club for backup."

David received another text from Rex. It said, "I'm really worried about her."

(two minutes later) "Kevin thinks she might have been kidnapped by the Texas

gangs, but he says they won't hurt her, just ask for money."

And how would *he* know? David, almost spitefully, shoved the phone in his jacket pocket without responding. He sensed that Rex was trying to compensate for her initial silence with a flurry of texts.

They piled into the car that had almost plowed into Antifans on Saturday night, and were soon barreling down the road in the direction of the airport. David was armed, and while he wouldn't be able to bring the gun into the terminal, he'd worry about that later. It was 11:18 a.m.

Chapter 15
On the Concourse
(Wednesday, August 12, 2093)

When they pulled up to the departure curb under the "Cloud Air" signage, a young brown-haired man in jeans and a sweatshirt greeted them.

"Give him your key, David," said Chris. "This is my neighbor's son, Lars. He'll stay behind the wheel here for us."

David peered dubiously at the young man through his dark sunglasses.

"Absolutely trustworthy," Chris assured him.

David handed the key to Lars, hesitantly. But much more was at stake here than the car. Just a damn car, he told himself. He left the firearm in the locked glove compartment. The sensors at the entrances would have immediately summoned security and police.

They strode into the terminal, David wearing his sunglasses and a baseball cap. He conveniently sported a light blond beard, not having shaved since Friday morning in Dallas. Rex might recognize him in the disguise from the way he walked, but David was counting on Rex resembling her mother, who tended to be oblivious to details. David gambled that Kevin would neither recognize him nor expect to see him in the terminal, and that he and Rex were confident that David had believed their lie about leaving on Thursday.

At the counter he and Chris purchased tickets to Chicago at a kiosk, round-trip to avoid suspicion, and David checked a battered suitpod into which he had thrown some old clothes that Malia had been planning to donate to charity.

As they paid for their tickets, David saw Kevin and Rex, having completed their transaction at the counter, heading for the security gates. Rex, who was wearing a red beret and black leggings, presumably in anticipation of the café life in Montreal, barely reached Kevin's broad shoulder. The Antifan carried their duffel over his other shoulder. David shook with anger. Here he was, witnessing a second kidnapping of a family member this week, and for the moment, helpless.

He and Chris stayed about fifty feet behind Rex and Kevin. At one point, as the couple were placing items into the security scanning box, Kevin by chance glanced behind them. He did not seem to see David, and would not have recognized Chris. In what was a good-sized crowd of mostly business travelers, the two friends did not stand out. Kevin and Rex took their carry-ons from the other side of the scanning box and moved on.

On the other side of the security area, a uniformed policeman joined them.

"MAGA, don't worry," said Chris under his breath.

They shook hands with Sergeant Reed Colquhoun, whom David recognized from the MAGA meetings. Chris quickly explained the situation to Reed, who said, "When you confront this guy, I'll be watching. If you need support, I'll be there. Do we want to arrest him, or do we just want him out of here?" All Reed knew was that Chris needed help to rescue a young lady in danger at the airport. Without asking more questions, he immediately had pulled on his uniform—he was off duty that day—and holstered his service weapon, and driven to the airport.

That was a good question. Arresting Kevin Malloy, or whoever he was, might introduce some wrenches into the diplomatic maneuverings that were preoccupying the United States. As much as David wanted these negotiations to fail, he didn't necessarily want to draw attention to themselves. But then, he quickly intuited, maybe he and Malia needed some publicity. On the other hand—and now this was a third hand—embarrassing the United States and the DJR might unite both countries against Malia's cause. It was too early to assume the United States was averse to rescuing Malia, and he could not risk antagonizing his side, not yet.

"I just want my stepdaughter back home and away from him, the bastard."

"Got it," said Reed, "Maybe we can do this with not much fuss."

"I don't know," said David, "He's gotten this far with her. This was his main mission in the US. She would be a big prize. I don't think he'll just hand her back and walk away." He could tell Reed was puzzled by the "main mission in the US" remark but wouldn't pursue it right now.

"You have the advantage of surprise," Chris said.

"One thing you should know," said Reed, who was familiar with the airport, "they won't directly board the flight. Because of the construction on the lower level, they'll go downstairs from this gate and board a bus that will take them out to the plane on the tarmac. Where exactly do you want to confront them?"

"Not in the waiting area, I guess," said David. "Too much of a scene?"

"I'd recommend following them through the tunnel and catching up with them on the ground before they board the bus. If your fellow wants to run, he can do it there, without causing havoc in the terminal." Reed said, "I'll step aside for now and not draw any more attention to you. But I'll be watching, don't worry."

David hoped at that point, with boarding imminent, Kevin maybe would relax his guard. As he and Chris sat a few seats apart, six rows behind Kevin and Rex's backs,

David wondered whether one or the other might get up to use a rest room, or buy a meal. He froze when Rex stood up, looking in his general direction, as if she wanted to do some shopping. Kevin shook his head, and she sat down again. Great, not, thought David. Thirty minutes to boarding for Cloud Air Flight 445 to Chicago, the announcer said.

Rex must have insisted she needed to use the restroom, because Kevin reluctantly rose, and accompanied her in that direction. Chris shook his head when David started to make a move to follow. They won't recognize me, Chris's body language conveyed, as he waved David off. And both knew the couple would return to the gate. David slouched down, pulling the baseball hat over his eyes for when the couple returned to their seats.

Rex and Kevin returned ten minutes later, holding paper sacks from an eatery. Chris followed about twenty feet behind, then sat down again, leaving one seat open between himself and David.

Adrenalin and anger coursed through David's veins, almost as headily as last Saturday night. Sometimes he had felt like this in his Antifan days, while waiting to pounce on an unsuspecting knowledge criminal. But the knowledge criminal usually had been fearful of and intimidated by, not contemptuous of, his Antifan pursuers, a difference that David found particularly galling here in this airport. It had been a long time since his last operation, and he knew this target was worse than any of the feckless writers or musicians he had typically rounded up as an Antifan charged with policing knowledge crime. *This time it would be Antifan on Antifan.*

He knew that when they got on line to go downstairs, he and Chris needed to be close enough to Rex and Kevin to ensure the couple would not simply board the bus ahead of them, or that the bus would not reach capacity and speed off before he and Chris could make it downstairs. Unfortunately, it would be dangerous to get in line before Rex and Kevin, since they might well recognize him, if not Chris. He needed to stay close, but not too close, to them.

"Boarding for Chicago Cloud Air Flight 445. Gold members, first-class, and Eagle Club patrons first, please. Chicago."

To his and Chris's shock, Kevin and Rex rose and headed toward the counter with their phones in hand for the check-in. The men had not anticipated that Kevin would smooth their departure with a priority club membership, although now it made sense.

"Go," said Chris.

Kevin and Rex passed through the door from the terminal into the air tunnel. David quickly followed, pushing past the few travelers in line behind them for priority boarding.

"Hey! Whaddya think you're doing?" a fat businessman shouted. The others stared at David, astonished at the presumption.

"It's a matter of life and death!" he declared.

"Excuse me, sir, you can't…" said the attendant. David leaped over the stanchions and disappeared into the tunnel. The airline employee paged for support.

But there was Sergeant Colquhoun, reassuringly. "I've got it," he told the agent, and as the passengers gaped, he followed David into the tunnel.

David ran down the tunnel, catching a glimpse of the duffel bag on Kevin's shoulder as he and Rex rounded the tunnel. In about thirty feet, they would descend down an escalator to the tarmac. David had intended to confront them on the tarmac, but with the adrenalin pounding, he caught up with the pair while they were within reach on the landing. The escalator churned below them.

"Stop!" he demanded.

Kevin and Rex turned, Rex's mouth a shocked oval.

"Too bad, Daddy. We're taking a trip," grinned Kevin.

"The hell you are, you bastard," David said.

"She's a grown woman. She can decide whether she wants to come with me or not."

"Rex, he's kidnapping you! There's a Diversair flight to Anacosta he's going to force you on. You're not going to Montreal."

"Is that true?" Rex naively directed her question at Kevin. Then to David, "He loves me. We're going to get married in Montreal."

"You're not getting married to him anywhere. It's all a lie to get you back to Anacosta, where you'll get sent to an incubation farm and you'll never see him or us again."

Kevin approached David menacingly. "Get away from us, fascist. I'll break your neck." He leaped at David, who deftly stepped aside, and flung himself at Kevin's legs to bring him down. The muscular Antifan was solidly planted on the ground, however, and instead kicked at David. David pulled him down to the ground, powered by his anger at this man who was destroying his family, and landed a punch on Kevin's face.

"Hey, chickie," he hissed at Kevin, using the slightly condescending, slightly affectionate nickname for a new Antifan, "your game is up." The "chickie" signaled to Kevin that David knew who he was, even if it was mostly a lucky guess.

Reed rounded the corner, weapon drawn. "Stop! You're both under arrest!"

With a powerful thrust, Kevin shoved David aside, scrambled to his feet, and ran for the escalator, abandoning the duffel bag. David pulled himself up, a little creakily.

Reed holstered his firearm and called for support down on the tarmac. The bus would not be leaving for the plane, not anytime soon. Nor would Kevin be foolish enough to board the bus anyway. Flight 445 was now delayed due to unexpected turbulence in the tunnel. The passengers in the terminal had heard the shouting, and stared as more uniformed officers ran into the waiting area and into the tunnel. Sirens wailed in the distance.

Rex was weeping. David looked at her. "I'm sorry," he said, "but this guy was up to no good. They've kidnapped your mother and they were going to kidnap you too."

He hesitated, but then wrapped his arm around her shoulder to comfort her. She did not resist.

Reed led them back through the tunnel, carrying the duffel for them, but they entered the waiting area through an alternate door and escaped the notice of the Chicago-bound passengers who were still staring vacantly at the departure gate. Chris saw them, and hurried over, his face awash with relief. David took the duffel bag from Reed.

"Thank God," Chris said. Rex looked confused at this stranger who had approached them.

"Rex," said David, "this is my friend Chris Mendoza. You can thank him. I was in such a funk I'd completely forgotten about your Montreal trip. But Chris asked me where you were and then we realized something was very wrong."

Rex had stopped crying, but her face was pale under the makeup. "I was starting to wonder...but he proposed to me...he said I didn't need to worry about Mom. I didn't know what to do. He was really an Antifan?"

"Yes. But it's all right now," David reassured her, as if she were a child again who had awakened from a nightmare.

"How could I have been so stupid?"

"We were all fooled. If I'd been thinking clearly, your mother would still be here. I should have known better."

Reed asked, "You guys all right now? Can you just tell me exactly what happened here, so I can let my folks know?" David explained. Reed took notes, presumably for a police report.

"Hopefully we'll apprehend him. It sounds as if he's in the country illegally."

"Thank you, Reed. Not sure what would have happened if you hadn't shown up when you did. The guy's a lot younger than me." David knew that Kevin Malloy would not allow himself to be captured. An arrest in the United States would embarrass the DJR and would likely torpedo Kevin's Beaufort career. David suspected that Kevin was fleeing the airport grounds. He would let the police handle the matter, though. It was not material any more.

"It was my pleasure. Really. We'll give you a call if we need anything else." The officer shook his hand, smiled politely at Rex, and headed back downstairs to meet the emergency vehicles.

"We will resume boarding Cloud Air Flight 445," the disembodied voice announced. Jostling in anticipation and impatience, the crowds paid no attention as David, Rex, and Chris retraced their steps through the terminal. Just as Chris had promised David, Lars was waiting with David's car.

Within half an hour, they were back at the house. Chris made David promise to take the boys to the park. "You're absolutely all right now?" he had demanded of David. "Get some sunshine and do some normal things." And to Rex, "How are you, young lady?"

"Thanks to you, much better. I'm going to get my act together now."

Once Chris had departed for his laboratory, David remembered an odd bump under the sofa. He quickly retrieved the listening device that Kevin—presumably—had placed there. He and Rex then spent the next hour crawling under furniture and into cabinets, looking for others, after he instructed her what to look for. He was relieved not to find any devices in the secure room; although that had always been securely locked when not in use, you never knew for sure, and the incident with the bloody video did not give him confidence. It was Rex who, running her hands under the kitchen table, found the second device. Under my own kitchen table, possibly for months. Some Antifan, after decades of feeling under every restaurant table you ever ate at.

"See what I mean about being foolish myself? This is how they probably learned your mother and I were traveling to Dallas." He sat on the sofa, his head in his hands.

"Dad," said Rex. He looked up sharply. She had not called him that in years, shortly after he married Malia. Then she had resisted in some act of teenage stubbornness and insisted on calling him David instead. "I hope you don't mind."

"No, I'm honored," he said.

"I want to call you Dad because only a real father would have cared enough to do something like this for me.

"Dad, we have to work together. We can't fall apart. We have to get Mom home again. I don't want to return to school until she's rescued too."

David looked at Rex with respect. "Let's see what's in the duffel bag."

They examined the contents of the bag. Rex had packed an extra outfit or two, and some toiletries in case their checked suitpods missed the connection in Chicago. She blushed at the lacy nightgown David pulled forth, but he just placed it carefully on the sofa.

A pair of men's dress shoes lay at the bottom of the bag. The insole of the left shoe seemed a little loose. David picked at it under Rex's curious eyes. He drew forth a Canadian driver's license in the name of Marcus Vanover, but the photo was definitely Kevin's. And there was a small green booklet, the Mother Earth Hym/Hernal. This told David all he needed to know. He reached for the phone and called the airport police with the information, requesting Sergeant Reed Colquhoun be notified. When Reed called back that evening, he admitted they had not found Kevin/Vanover. A citywide alert proved fruitless, not that David was surprised.

Vanover had indeed leaped the fence, stolen a just-returned car at an airport car rental place, driven to a secluded but familiar spot near the Red River, and swum across to Texas where he located the gang that had cooperated in the ambush of David and Malia. They ensured he was on a flight from Houston to Mexico City the following morning under his real name—the roundabout itinerary would fool any pursuers, at least out of Oklahoma City. Despite assuming his kidnapping of Rex would proceed as planned, he had been sensible enough to prepare a backup plan. Within a day, he was back in Anacosta, but much humbled. It was hard for him to face Paragon after this defeat.

Chapter 16
Next Steps
(Friday, August 14, 2093)

The three men watched Vanover, his shoulders sagging with relief at the interview's end, exit the director's suite. They had expected to see a triumphant Vanover returning with the stepdaughter, and now David Harris had foiled them again, even worse, twice in one week. The loss of nine soldiers could not be hidden, and the lavish public media tributes to their sacrifice rang hollow, at least to Beaufort's senior leaders.

It was hard to berate Vanover, however, who at least had heroically escaped his pursuers, avoiding arrest and public embarrassment.

"Not that she was such a big prize or anything," said Montoya, referring to Rex, "but I don't like to fail. And I don't need David Harris crowing about this too."

"I don't think he's crowing much as long as his wife is here at Beaufort," Steve countered.

"But he doesn't even know she's here."

"She's not there, and he knows who took her," said Steve. He turned to Paragon, "What's going on with Ms. Malia?" Montoya frowned at the wry, almost affectionate reference. Steve's former friendship with Harris was common knowledge, and had not helped his candidacy when the deputy position became available. Nor was Montoya confident that Steve Rosen could be trusted in dealing with the traitor's wife with appropriate severity.

Paragon said, "We moved her to VIP quarters yesterday until we figure out what to do next. She didn't need to be in the infirmary any longer."

"Khalid, what *are* we going to do with her?" Steve asked.

"Shoot her and get it over with?" suggested Montoya. "I hardly think we can rehabilitate her at this point. If you sent her to an incubation farm, she'd only infect the other prisoners."

"That's a lot of trouble we went to just to finish her off in the basement."

"It would be good publicity for anyone else who was considering escaping."

Montoya retorted.

The pair looked hopefully at Khalid Ma. Paragon was the idea man of the three. When he returned from St. Louis, they had dual-hatted him as the political commissar at the Knowledge Tower as well as the Resolution Commander. The feckless Knowledge Tower had demonstrated it was incapable of policing the culture, and after the ADF had purged it four years ago, the ADF had decided to place its own representatives alongside the directors of both the Knowledge Tower and Economic Tower, to prevent any further backsliding.

Khalid Ma, who had just scattered seeds of cultural revolution throughout the United States, installing avatars of Diversity in the universities and the corporations, was the obvious choice to guide the Knowledge Tower. Back home, and now in effect political commissar for the DJR, Ma had also imposed a rigorous Diverse agenda on the Social Crediteers, most recently outlawing all first names with Biblical origins. Social Crediteers with now-banned names could reverse them, so someone named Christopher would be called Rehpotsihc, or Rehpot. Palindromes such as Anna or Hannah could be rectified by the addition of a new consonant, such as Annap or Phannah. A Resolution Command team was supervising the effort and approving names, since a citizen out of malice or just ignorance might pick an equally dangerous name. Lists of approved Diverse names were posted online in case a citizen wanted to make a fresh start altogether.

Ma's own nickname, Paragon, had originally been intended ironically in that he was upheld as the exemplar of Antifan purity, as in "He's quite the paragon, isn't he?" His only perceived flaw was that instead of professing the Strict Pagan version of the MED Church, he retained membership in its Islamic branch out of what some rumored was loyalty to a long-dead father. Or mother. Nobody was quite sure. Of the Abrahamic faiths, Islam was considered the least tainted because of its association with oppressed brown people, some of whom had nobly struck at white supremacy, on September 11, 2001, as all DJR students learned.

Paragon agreed that the ADF needed to maintain by force the preeminence of Diversity, but was skeptical of its ultimate power. "Force alone," he said, "is not satisfying and it eventually exhausts the enforcer. One must continue to move the people to greater ideologically-rooted practice. The more one submits to the habits of Diversity, the more the mind will seek to justify it. Humans cannot bear for their actions to be completely without meaning."

Thus each month this year he had decreed a new order for all Social Crediteers to obey throughout the country, on penalty of prison or worse, at least in the Cities. In August, the campaign had mandated the public wearing of pink pussy hats, despite the sweltering summer heat of Anacosta and Miami. Typically one only wore those hats in a MED service. Paragon was now mulling options for the September campaign.

So Montoya and Rosen now looked expectantly at Paragon.

"I think Malia Harris presents us with a remarkable propaganda opportunity," Paragon said. "When she returns to Diversity with a full heart, she can speak to the people about her sufferings in the United States and her happiness here."

"Sounds great," Steve said, "but what makes you think she will agree with that assessment? Are we just going to threaten her unless she says what we want?"

Paragon said, "We will make her realize that she is not going back to the US. She thinks her husband is dead, and she is not even a US citizen, so St. Louis won't try too hard to bring her home, not if it will harm the talks. We will give her the opportunity to repent, and if she does, we can give her a high Credit score and a good life. The DJR will start to look like a good deal. After all, she had a Diversity education and background. Harris and the US were only four years of her life. She only became a Christian because of him.

"I told her that her daughter would be coming back here. It's unfortunate that failed, because that might have been an additional incentive for her to cooperate. On the other hand, the daughter presumably knows that David Harris is still alive, so perhaps it's just as well they aren't going to see each other soon."

"What about her children?" asked Steve. "Don't they have two sons? She isn't just going to forget them, is she?"

Paragon shrugged. "Maybe we could bring them here. That's a problem for another day."

Montoya—with admiration, and Steve with distaste—marveled at the breezy cunning of Paragon, who could convince a woman that her very-much-alive husband was actually dead, and even that she could forget her children. Paragon said, "I showed her the news programs. She believed them.

"First," said Paragon, beginning to look somewhat dreamily at the far wall, "she will have to repent. I will also find religious and political tutors and a Diversity psychologist. We will also show her the best of Anacosta, which can be hers. She will have to choose." Then his face hardened. "There can also be punishment if she refuses to learn."

"Wait," Steve said. "I insist that there will no physical coercion of Malia Harris while she is at Beaufort. No beatings, no sexual assaults, nothing. She did great work for us bringing down the Economic Tower's conspiracy in '89, and we owe her some gratitude."

"That will deprive me of some of my basic ideological reform tools," Paragon complained.

Montoya absentmindedly doodled on a notepad. "Steve, this isn't really your area of expertise, is it? Why are you interfering with Khalid? I think he knows better than us what will work."

"Just basic decency," said Steve. "And some logic. I can't imagine that beating her will make her any fonder of the DJR."

Montoya was willing to humor his deputy, at least for now. "Khalid, try it the kinder and gentler way for now. If it doesn't work, we can revisit—more rigorous techniques."

Paragon wasn't happy with the decision, but confidently thought that once Malia Harris knew she had no alternatives, she would embrace her new normal. He welcomed the challenge of converting an intelligent knowledge crime suspect without harsh punishment, not that he would tell her he had foresworn those techniques. Let her think it was a possibility, even in the VIP quarters. "What if she disobeys an order?"

"That's different," said Steve. "But not as a normal procedure, not yet."

That morning, Malia had awakened in unfamiliar surroundings. She started, thinking for a brief moment she was home again in Oklahoma City, and the last week had only been a terrifying nightmare. She had just begun to accustom herself to the hospital room, the routine with the vitals check every three hours, the bland but not distasteful meals, the cup of fruit juice between the meals. The staff was increasingly familiar, and in familiarity, comforting, and the fat drone nurse did not reappear. They behaved correctly toward her, if not warmly. Twice a day they allowed her to walk down the corridor back and forth several times, with a nurse at each elbow.

She watched DJR talk and news shows, documentaries, and even movies, all with unremittingly progressive themes. She entertained herself by identifying how the filmmakers had sanitized and corrupted the actual history or reality in each program, now that she had four years in the United States with which to rebut the propaganda. Her minders were misleadingly encouraged by her attentiveness. Malia even praised the documentary about Aztec history, sanitized to present the Aztecs as very much like progressive deejers, sending women into battle, but the film made no mention of human sacrifice. With no paper books, and without the armband all other DJR citizens relied on for permitted reading and entertainment, Malia was becoming bored, but she felt safe. She had not yet begun to weep, since the enormity of her plight had not yet sunk in. One never spent a long time in the hospital, so she had not viewed this room as her prison.

Now she was somewhere else, presumably still at Beaufort. She looked up at a cinder-block tile ceiling, and ran her hand along the painted beige drywall. She lay in a real, albeit narrow bed, with no restraints, still wearing the hospital gown. A camera was trained on the bed from the opposite corner, next to an arched open door. The room was a small but clean cell, with a tiny wooden table next to the bedside, and a plain wooden chair.

On the chair lay an olive-green T-shirt, a set of green paper pants, and underwear. A pair of flip-flops were neatly arranged under the chair. Malia understood that she was probably meant to wear the outfit, but she needed to use a toilet, so she peeked timidly out the open door.

A compact living room awaited her. A brown sofa sat against the back wall, a coffee table before it and a matching armchair to the side. No windows, which with the low ceiling made her feel claustrophobic. A small round bistro-style table in the corner was flanked by two small resin folding chairs, and now that Malia was surveying the room, she saw another arched open doorway with bars beyond it. The long vertical bars could be raised and lowered from the anteroom just beyond them. So, yes, I am still a prisoner, she realized. Adjoining the bedroom was a normal bathroom, albeit tiny, with a green ceramic toilet, a sink, a shower, and a towel rack with plain white towels.

Just in case Malia might think she had landed in a somewhat spartan but normal apartment, she saw cameras trained on her from all corners of the room.

When she emerged from the bathroom, an older female trusty with weathered skin was placing breakfast on the table. The plate, coffee cup, and utensils were all cardboard.

"You must dress before you can eat lunch," the trusty chided Malia, who pulled on the strange outfit. The paper pants rustled as she moved. This was going to be annoying.

She sat down at the small table, looking suspiciously at a gray slab occupying the center of the plate. She recognized a small fried egg, and toast. The trusty handed her a sheet of paper with a Mother Earth Grace Before Meals.

"What's this?"

"It's the grace you need to say before the meal."

"No, I mean, what's this?" she asked, pointing to the gray slab.

"Health Meat," said the trusty.

"What's Health Meat?"

"Not for you to ask. All food is bounty from Mother Earth."

"Not this," Malia said, poking it with her cardboard fork.

"You'll eat it," said a voice from the doorway, and Malia looked up to see the half-vanilla half-chocolate face of the blonde Antifan woman from the infirmary behind the bars of the entryway. "Because if you don't, you'll find the liquefied version we use in forced feedings even worse." The bars rose and receded into the top of the door frame.

The mysterious woman, dressed in Antifan black bloc, entered the room and seated herself opposite Malia at the table. Malia, who had learned something about Antifan insignia while dating David, recognized the patches corresponding to Hate Crimes Heroism and the red X for direct elimination of a fascist cell.

"I'm a vegetarian," Malia gambled, wondering if this would spare her Health Meat.

"Won't matter," said the trusty. "No real meat in Health Meat anyway. I mean, not that you'd recognize anyway." She exited, wiping her hands on a dirty cloth hanging from her belt, and the Antifan officer called out, "Secure the cell," at which point the bars descended again.

"Who *are* you?" Malia asked.

The Antifan woman said, "I'm Captain Boyd, 175. But you can call me Exterra,"

"That's an interesting name."

"I invented it myself," said Exterra proudly. "Ex-terra. Latin for 'from the Earth.' My birth name was Janet, but I needed a properly Diverse name. Too many fascists named Janet.

"Please eat," said Exterra. "First, say the grace. And you can use the tomato ketchup on the Health Meat. That will help you get used to it. It's more economical than real meat, and kinder to animals. The Diverse People are kind to animals. I promise you it's perfectly safe and has been developed by our scientists for a Diverse socialist palate."

No wonder I'm going to hate it, thought Malia, but she reluctantly picked up the sheet of paper and read, "Thank you Mother Earth for the bounty you have given us. From the fields and sea and Economic Zones you supply us with all our needs. I am an unworthy prisoner but will eat to preserve my strength to repent and help build Diversity and socialism. Awomen." It took willpower to keep herself from laughing at the "awomen"; her lips trembled slightly with suppressed amusement.

Exterra handed her a ketchup bottle. Malia would much rather have eaten one of the soybakes she so detested from her Anacostan days, when it was a reliable staple of her Healthy Eating grocery bag each week. As dispiriting as her grocery allotment had been, at least it had never included Health Meat. Things must be worse than four years ago. She speared a cube of Health Meat, eyed it suspiciously, and closing her eyes, chewed it. The texture was predictably rubbery, but it was almost tasteless without the ketchup. Malia detected a faint almond smell. If she did not think about the meat, or look directly at it, she could swallow it without gagging.

Exterra watched with a condescending half smile as Malia dutifully finished the slab, and turned to the recognizable egg and toast with relief.

When I return to the US, I will tell the analysts about Health Meat, Malia vowed. I will not despair. While I wait to be rescued, I will record every single detail about this experience, so that it will help the AIA defeat the DJR. She assumed that somewhere, the United States was working to determine her location and to free her. Even if David were gone, she knew Daniel and Fern would not let her languish. And they would protect her sons with their lives.

Nor was she sure that David really was dead, because she could not trust any Antifan, any deejer, to tell her the truth. The DJR news outlets would recite whatever Beaufort Tower gave them. Of one thing she was sure—David was not in this building, because Paragon would have bragged about his capture, and they would have walked her past his open coffin, with his mangled body on display. That's how they had treated the Antifan officer who had not succeeded in escaping, twenty years earlier.

Since she knew David was not here at Beaufort, she deduced that either they really had killed him that night in Oklahoma, or they would create lies to cover their failure to capture him at all. She decided to place her trust in the second surmise, because the first would only plunge her into despair. And if David really were still alive, she knew he would stop at nothing to rescue her from Beaufort Tower and the Antifans.

"And when you are finished, we will discuss your educational program," said Exterra. "I am going to be your mentor."

"I already have a degree from Justice University in knowledge management. The on-campus program."

"This is different. You need to learn Diversity precepts all over again. Otherwise, how can we release you into society?"

"I'm really not interested in propaganda."

Exterra's smile vanished, and she said bluntly, "The alternative is death."

Oh, well, in that case, thought Malia.

"You are a special project. Commander Ma is willing to see whether a Christian fascist can be rehabilitated into Diversity. Diversity is a loving parent, and will accept you if you can relearn its doctrines. We have engaged several tutors for you—a MED priest, a social scientist, and a Diversity counselor. No expense will be spared. But we will not tolerate disobedience."

I could pretend to believe all the nonsense, and then just live in Anacosta as I did before, quietly, meekly, waiting to be recovered by St. Louis, thought Malia. This won't be hard. Maybe they'll give me a good social credit score this time if they think I am cooperating.

"And don't think you can fool us by lying as you did before," Exterra cautioned. "We have the truth serum and will make sure you really are a believer before we release you."

"I thought the truth serum had been destroyed!" Malia cried. She had assumed her efforts against the Economic Tower and the ensuing raid at the Economic Zone camp would also have led to the destruction of the truth serum stores. But she thought, yes, it was powerful, I could not resist it myself. How could I have thought the ADF would actually destroy the serum, instead of taking it for its own use?

"Not at all. It is a very useful weapon for identifying the traitors and the heretics. We are about to start applying it to the general population. Once a year, everyone will undergo a truth exam. Anyone who fails will be sent to an incubation farm, or the Economic Zones, or if they are really beyond hope, we will just dispatch them here. Society will be perfected." She beamed at Malia with those bright blue eyes, like blue traffic lights.

I will be in Beaufort forever, as long as they are willing to keep me alive, Malia thought. Because I cannot believe their nonsense, and I cannot outwit that serum, especially if the ADF has perfected it since the Economic Tower tried it on me.

"And you should know, I am the partner of Commander Ma. So rest assured that anything I tell you is his will. Your case is of great interest at the highest levels of the DJR." This meant only Beaufort, because the ADF had not yet bothered to inform President Peace-Williams at the White Black House, or the Economic Tower that was conducting the negotiations with the United States, that Malia Harris was in ADF custody. "Your lessons will begin tomorrow. On Sundays you will attend MED services with me."

Malia wondered whether they would leave the Tower for the services and she would see the streets of Anacosta for the first time in four years. That would be worth the indignity of pagan worship and donning the required pink pussy hat. She kept reminding herself, I am a spy, I am documenting everything I see for the AIA. You have a mission. Do not despair.

After lunch, Exterra chose a movie for her on the TV in the living room. Unlike a normal TV, which could access any GVN entertainment available for the viewer, filtered by his Social Credit number and status, this one was programmed by the jailer. The movie, *A New Beginning*, was about a young black woman who had fled the United States and was building a new life in the DJR, including pursuing a love affair with a transgender Muslim woman. Malia was desperate enough for diversion that she could overlook the silliness of the dialogue. The movie concluded with a stirring speech on a mountaintop at sunrise. Then they watched a documentary on oppressed US farmworkers.

A soybake dinner arrived after the documentary ended. Malia was relieved to see the familiar cardboard oval.

Only late that night did she weep copiously but silently into her pillow, thinking of her sons, wondering whether David was still alive. How long would her sons remember her? But she wasn't sure whether it was to her advantage to play along with the Antifans' version of events, while cherishing the hope that her husband was already taking measures to rescue her, or to deny their version. Who was really the fool? It wasn't clear.

From outside her bedroom drifted the faint voices of the troops guarding her cell in the anteroom behind the vertical bars. They seemed to be discussing something unrelated to her, possibly sports scores. But she knew they at least occasionally would glance at the screens of the camera they trained on her bed.

Chapter 17
Not The Faculty Lounge
(Monday, August 24, 2093)

Malia waited patiently for her interrogator in Room L on the fourth subterranean floor of Beaufort. If the ADF had hoped that Malia would grow more timorous as the minutes passed, they were sorely mistaken. She was heartened, or possibly misled, or both, by the lenient treatment she had experienced so far, except for the hideous Health Meat. She cried only at night, silently into her pillow, determined not to allow her jailers to witness any weakness. She imagined David, somewhere, nodding with approval, "Way to go."

Dressed in her cotton olive-green T-shirt (Malia had learned this non-paper shirt was a marker of VIP prisoner status) and the creaky green paper pants, she shifted in the eco-plastic chair. The flip-flops had been replaced with open-ankle unlaced black cotton shoes for the journey throughout the building. The Antifan women privates who had escorted her to the interrogation room had removed the handcuffs and now occupied two other eco-plastic chairs near the bathroom, whispering to each other.

A long metal table stretched across the back of the room; a bathroom was near the entrance, along with a cluster of extra chairs for the audience. The tile floors shone. Thanks to David, Malia knew that behind the long dark window along the side of the room sat analysts taking notes and other observers. And she knew that this was not one of the dreaded Red Rooms where torture took place, which was encouraging.

Malia's eye caught a small dark bug placidly moving along the wall just under the ceiling across from her. She suspected that this bug, possibly a beetle, that had found its way into the feared Beaufort Tower, would find its way out again. She saw this as a positive omen for herself.

Yes, they had been relatively gentle so far with her. The only real disappointment had been the Sunday Strict Pagan service, which had taken place inside Beaufort. Most of the attendees were other prisoners, with whom communication was forbidden. The priestess wore black robes with the green Mother Earth symbol across her chest. Malia had politely mumbled the various lyrics in the holy Green Book but refused to move to the front of the chapel to kiss the statue's feet and receive the sacramental wafer in return. Exterra scowled at her, but Malia figured, why surrender to idolatry even before torture had begun? "It should only be for believers, right?" she argued with Exterra. The Antifan did not force the issue, but Malia knew her refusal would be noted.

At about a quarter after nine, the interrogator, a thirtyish black Antifan, entered the room carrying a stack of folders. She cast an angry look at Malia and placed the stack on the long table. She had straightened hair and large gold hoop earrings just on the permissible side of regulations. To Malia's relief, Exterra followed the interrogator into the room. Exterra was clearly there as an observer, since she took a chair from the cluster where the privates sat, and moved it to the other corner in the back of the room.

"Captain ReShonda Vance, 215. You are Amalia Jenness?"

"I am Amalia Harris now."

"No traitor names here," said the interrogator harshly. "And that will be 'ma'am' to you."

"Yes, ma'am."

They ran in a businesslike manner through basic biographical details that either the ADF had known for years, or more recent ones it would have known thanks to Marcus Vanover, Malia chirping "ma'am" throughout. Honesty was easy at this stage of the interrogation, although she almost laughed when Vance asked, "How many spawn do you have and what are their ages?"

The questioning moved to Malia's relationship with the AIA. "How many times a year have you met with AIA to reveal secrets?"

"Well, I didn't reveal secrets, ma'am. I went to St. Louis about four or five times a year to meet with their analysts and discuss the DJR. I only told them about my experiences and perspectives. I never told them secrets, per se."

"Anything about the DJR is a secret, if we wish to keep it one. By speaking with AIA, you showed your willingness to reveal secrets and betray your country, which raised and educated you."

It seemed pointless to argue. What Malia regarded as basic conversations with curious analysts was clearly treason in this building. And, she had to admit, the AIA was a spy agency that sought the destruction of the DJR, if not very energetically.

"What did you tell AIA?" Captain Vance demanded. "Including all the times you communicated with them on your computer at home?"

"I explained how the society worked, ma'am. I explained about the different gradations of the Social Credit system, how citizens ate, lived, vacationed, and enjoyed greater privileges if they had high scores…" Vance looked up at the window, which Malia realized signaled she had just said something incriminating, which needed to be documented, even though it was a fact.

"What else?"

"I told them about the Economic Zones and the Diversity Warehouse and how they supplied the needs of the population. I told them about how the Plores are segregated and how they must work in the City in return for their basic income, and how they face discrimination…"

Captain Vance slapped her. Malia inhaled sharply, not quite knowing what she had done wrong and having forgotten that even the slightest intimation of DJR cruelty was inherently criminal, and all the more so in the basement of Beaufort Tower. Exterra knew she'd have to pull the interrogator aside and tell her about the no-violence policy before the interrogation went much further. Exterra conceded that at least Vance's slap would remind Malia that however kindly she had been treated until now, she existed on the sufferance of her ADF jailers.

"Discrimination! How can white supremacists experience discrimination? It is logically not possible. They enjoy the complete mercy and kindness of the Diversity Justice Republic after having inflicted generations of suffering on the Diverse People.

"You have just committed a knowledge crime here in this room by uttering that phrase in connection with those disgusting Deplorable savages."

"Sorry, ma'am, I just thought that was a fact. They can't even come into the City, can they, unless they're working? They can't travel beyond their assigned containment areas. They can't go to college. Isn't that discrimination?"

Captain Vance stared at Malia in disbelief, horrified at the prisoner's matter-of-fact statements. She was used to berating cringing DJR Social Crediteers who were desperately trying to avoid convicting themselves or forfeiting their lives. Here was a fascist who was so brazen after four years in the United States that she said these things naturally, as if they were not obviously false. The privates in the corner were open-mouthed.

"Prisoner Jenness, do you not remember that the Treaty of the Red and the Blue gave the fascists the right to live in their own neighborhoods and practice their backward religion and customs? This was a great kindness to our enemies. Of course they must work to receive money from the state. They could stay home in their squalor if they wished. But we are not going to pay them to sit around and watch TV. And they are ignorant, lazy, and unlikely to benefit from higher education. They would only use it to harm the DJR, not to help build socialism. That is why they do not go beyond high school, where they can at least be trained to do useful chores for us.

"I am shocked at your own malice and ignorance in repeating these baseless lies."

"Ma'am," said Malia, "we seem to have different ideas as to what this country is about."

The black-leather-clad arm raised to strike Malia again, but then Vance caught Exterra's signal to desist. Irritably, Vance lowered her arm. She normally would not have taken orders from another captain, with a much lower Social Credit score at that, but Exterra was the partner of Paragon. Vance resented that Paragon's fake half-black-faced tart was protecting this white fascist, who should have been killed on arrival at Beaufort. They were both white, she grumbled, they protect each other, that's what mattered in the end. Even in the DJR, systemic racism survives.

And then Paragon himself entered the room. Even in her distress, Malia had to admit he was a good-looking man, with the snug Antifan jacket highlighting his broad shoulders and the leggings sculpting powerful thighs. But right now she had to ignore it. All that mattered now was that he posed a dangerous threat to her.

"Sir!" breathed Captain Vance.

"Captain," said Paragon. "I'll take over from here." He had been watching from the secret observation room, and while in principle having little objection to Malia Harris taking a slap here or there, did not want to risk jeopardizing his investigation by defying Rosen's orders. He removed a stack of papers from one of the folders and handed them to Malia as he stood over her. Vance retreated to the back corner, where she stood next to Exterra.

"What is this, Prisoner Jenness?"

Malia stared at the stack with confusion. "This is my dissertation, sir. Or at least part of it." She recognized the coffee stains on the pages she had given to Kevin Malloy in expectation of some feedback, which he had never delivered.

"What is a dissertation, Prisoner Jenness?"

Surely he knows what a dissertation is, Malia thought. Even the DJR awarded doctoral degrees, however spurious.

"It is a body of independent research that one completes to earn a PhD from a university."

"Should one infer that the writer of a dissertation agrees with the points of view expressed in the paper?" Paragon asked.

Malia hesitated, knowing where this was leading. "Not necessarily. The conclusion of the dissertation may have been forced on the writer by the department's own views. Or the scientific method may lead to a conclusion with which the writer himself does not agree." But she knew she was allowing fear to curb her answers.

"Sir?" Paragon said, reminding her of who she was and where she was and who he was. It was basic Antifan interrogation protocol to remind your victims of their subservience and helplessness as they cowered in your basement.

"Sir," she gulped.

"I find that unconvincing," Paragon reflected. "I would hope you would have had the character to defend your idiotic views if you are bothering to spend years putting them on paper. Now, if I recall our conversation on the train, you are writing about John Locke and the application of his ideas, such as they were, to our own beloved Diversity Justice Republic."

"Yes, sir," she said, but unable to meet his eyes.

"John Locke was a famous fascist, was he not?"

"They would not have known the word in the seventeenth century in England, sir. He is one of the Western world's greatest political philosophers and a defender of liberty."

Paragon snorted. The analysts in the side room would mark "Western world" and possibly "liberty," unpreceded by a "so-called," "baseless," or at least "problematic," as a possible additional knowledge crime. He brought over the remaining eco-plastic chair and sat opposite her, only three or four feet away. Malia felt anxious and unsettled by his proximity.

"Let me read you some passages of yours that I find rather interesting," Paragon said.

"First, page thirty-five: 'Locke's contention that the people are absolved from any obedience to a government that takes away and destroys their property, or reduces them to slavery under arbitrary power, is particularly apt in understanding the DJR. The obedience given to the DJR authorities by the enslaved citizenry is not willing, it is coerced. The people, especially those in low credit status, scheme and connive to improve their material status, recognizing that they have lost the little they have earned through their own work, and it has been stolen from them. Here are several typical ways in which low Social Crediteers outfox the state...'

"Let me clarify, Prisoner Jenness, what you mean here. You seem to be saying that under socialism, the people are robbed. And because they are robbed of what you consider to be their rightful due, they owe the government no obedience. And you are accusing our low credit citizens of illegal behavior."

"I am pointing out the significance of low Social Credit behavior, and why people feel they are justified in engaging in these actions. I am not saying they should engage in those behaviors."

"Nevertheless, you seem to imply this all makes sense and should be expected under socialism. We'll return to this passage. Here's another one we need to get to the bottom of..." Paragon shuffled through the stack until he found the page he sought. "Page eighty-six." He read: "'As Locke said, "every man has a property in his own person. This nobody has a right to but himself." The DJR is built on the premise that no man owns himself, but the collective owns him. It assigns him a numerical worth, it tells him where he may be educated, and in what, it tells him where he will labor, and in some cases, whom he may marry. When he is old and tired, the collective will destroy and discard his body at the Euthanasia Palace, when it no longer wishes to use it. In the DJR, the elites own him and use and discard him for their own benefit, like a slave or an animal.'"

Paragon's dark eyes flashed at her. "How is this anything other than rank treason? How dare you use the word "slave" to describe a citizen of the DJR? Is this what you tell the fascists the DJR does to its citizens? And what about the rights of the collective, who must support the citizen? Does the collective have no rights?"

Malia's temper rose. "Collectives do not have rights. Human beings, individuals have rights. Sir. This is true, whether you like it or not. What have I said here that is incorrect? Sir."

Normally Paragon would have beaten her himself at this point if this were an ordinary interrogation. He wondered whether he could cite her impertinence as justification for physical punishment given Steve Rosen's halfhearted exception to the no-punishment rule. Instead, he silently counted to ten, staring darkly at her. She did not drop her eyes this time.

"Prisoner Jenness, you are confessing to treasonous thoughts at a brisk pace this morning," Paragon said.

"Everything you cite, and will cite, was written in the United States, not here," she countered. "How can this be treason? Sir?"

"How? Because you now admit to it here. Without shame. And you shared knowledge about the DJR with Americans. And I know you are not an American, but a Diversan, because you never bothered to gain this supposedly precious US citizenship. So you are subject to our laws, not their ridiculous fascist ones.

"If I did not cherish some hope that you were redeemable, I would send you down to the firing range for execution today. We will give you a chance to reconsider in the hope you can someday be a decent Diverse citizen and admit your wrongdoing. But do not try my patience too much."

Malia was tempted to say that his words indeed proved the DJR defied Locke's philosophy, given that her person was only permitted to exist as long as the collective, represented by Paragon, found it useful, and that she had no rights here by virtue of being a sentient human being. But she knew that he truly could exercise the option of executing her on short notice.

"We will resume tomorrow morning," said Paragon. "I believe that Prisoner Jenness has her religion lesson this afternoon, is that correct, Captain Boyd?"

"Yes, Commander."

"Well, we wouldn't want to tire our little traitor too much here, would we?" Paragon stalked from the room. As he exited, he turned around and said to her, "Prisoner Jenness, I hope you will make progress on your studies before it is too late."

Late that night, Paragon and Exterra lay in his great bed, in the spacious penthouse apartment at the Avalon Tower ten minutes away from Beaufort. In a few minutes they would use the signaler to draw the curtains against the twinkling array of City lights to their south. Paragon was entitled to a house—one had been offered him just down Palisades Parkway from Montoya's—but he preferred the relative anonymity, private elevator, and concierge services of the luxury tower.

Paragon was reading the final news headlines of the night, and Exterra finishing a movie about a neurotic young woman in a polyamorous relationship on a remote island. It made Exterra think of her own situation. She gazed upon Paragon, especially his bare brown arms, which unlike most Antifans', lacked any tattoos. He had once told her that tattoos were forbidden to Muslims. But he had made her tattoo half her face brown.

"Do you really think Malia Jenness is redeemable?" she asked him, curious about his views of this peculiar case, which they had not yet discussed in privacy.

"Probably not," he said. "We'll doubtless end up executing her, but perhaps we can learn some things about fascist thought processes that we can use in the incubation farms.

"And it's possible that David Harris will come looking for her. He has that primitive Plore trait of wanting to defend and rescue the women in his life. We saw that with his stepdaughter earlier this month, and what was the stepdaughter to him, really? When he walks into this country, we will find him and spring the trap."

That hadn't occurred to Exterra. "She doesn't really believe he's dead, you know."

"We showed her the news videos. What doesn't she believe?"

"She says she doesn't believe any DJR news coverage. She accuses us of falsifying the news."

Since this was indisputably true, it was hard to argue with Malia, albeit in absentia.

"Maybe we could craft some US news coverage that would make the same claim. Would that be more credible? Take some actual US news programming and doctor it?" asked Exterra.

"That's a good idea. Wish we'd done it weeks ago, but now isn't too late. I'll have the analysts tackle that tomorrow."

Exterra waited a moment, and then asked, "Khalid, do you think she's attractive?"

"Who, Malia Jenness?"

"She seems to find *you* attractive."

Paragon was vain enough to want to discuss the topic. "Really? How can you tell? It can't be that I mentioned the firing squad." He paused, "Although you never know."

"A woman can tell." Exterra looked sidelong at her partner.

"Hmm. It doesn't matter, because I wouldn't touch a fascist like her. Even if Rosen hadn't forbidden it, I would find it disgusting."

"What if we invited her to a threesome? She's probably tired of being in prison and Health Meat and all that. Maybe she'd like a romantic getaway at the Avalon Tower."

"What makes you think she'd accept? Isn't she a good Christian? Loyal to her husband's memory and all that?"

"If she thinks he's dead, after we've shown her some more convincing videotapes, maybe she'll be less reluctant to accept our invitation." Exterra smiled slyly.

"My dear, I think that perhaps you are attracted to our little traitor," Paragon said, reaching for the signaler. "But if she doesn't change her ways soon, she won't be with us much longer."

Chapter 18
Grocery Central
(Wednesday, September 2, 2093)

An elderly lady, not very strong but not quite frail, and still pretty, stepped cautiously down the sidewalk carrying her reusable cloth shopping bags, which were required by law in the City and by thrift in Ploreville. The sidewalks of Ploreville—the Deplorable ghetto across the Potowmack River from the City—were notoriously pitted and treacherous, since the Social Credit authorities were uninterested in maintaining any infrastructure used by the reactionary ex-rebels. To the east, you could glimpse on the horizon the gleaming towers of the City of Anacosta.

Her chestnut hair had turned a salt-and-pepper gray with a few fair highlights. She wore a worn pink coat; when you were seventy-nine, you chilled easily, even on a pleasant early September morning. In cash-strapped Ploreville, the clothing stores sold gently worn items discarded by Social Crediteers in the City. If you wanted to splurge, you could brave the carbon offsets that applied even to Plores, and buy something new.

Marjory entered the Welcome bodega, as she did every Wednesday on weeks beginning with an even-numbered date. On odd-numbered weeks, she came on Monday. "Welcome to Welcome's" said a large, neatly red-lettered sign in the window.

"Good morning, Mrs. Harris," said Warren Welcome, the proprietor. Warren was a spare, medium-sized widower about fifteen years younger than Marjory, with close-cropped hair and a walnut-brown complexion. In hardscrabble Ploreville, he had managed to keep the grocery afloat. You had to pay off various bureaucrats both in the City and in Ploreville, and you had to pay extra to the driver bringing you produce from the Economic Zones so that he would deliver to your store early in his Arlington run. Otherwise, you'd be stuck with wrinkled oranges and wilted lettuce. Doing business in Ploreville was about taking care of bureaucrats, truck drivers, and, when you could, your loyal customers such as Mrs. Harris.

He felt genuine sorrow for Mrs. Harris. Only one month ago they had learned that the ADF had killed her son David, the renegade Antifan, on a deserted highway in Oklahoma, where he had thought he was safe. As the ADF commercials blared triumphantly afterward, "We always get our person." The whole neighborhood had quivered with sympathy for the mother of the Plore-turned-reluctant-Antifan who had become a hero when he escaped the DJR. Even so, Welcome was surprised by how tranquil Mrs. Harris seemed, only a few weeks later.

"Good morning, Mr. Welcome," she replied. As always, Marjory gravitated over to the produce. "Let's see what you have for me today."

Two rows of produce bins ran against the wall opposite the counter, seven bins on top and seven below. A long narrow shelf ran just above the top bins. Today, the top bins contained, in order, potatoes, onions, tomatoes, broccoli, cucumbers, eggplants, and small paper bags of blackberries, which were a luxury even though they were in season. On the small shelf above each relevant bin rested a single potato, two onions, a cucumber, and two small bags of blackberries. Marjory recalled the abundance she and other Americans had enjoyed in her youth, before the civil war and the socialist DJR destroyed it all.

The store, like everything else in Ploreville, was shabby, but clean. Plores couldn't get loans from government banks, because their enterprises were not joint ventures with the state. Money stores were expensive, what with their high interest rates. Welcome kept the premises as scrubbed as possible, owned an industrious tabby mouser who roamed the store, added a dash of color where he could, and planned on investing in a bright red awning. Yet the casual patron might have wondered why Welcome, who in his constant tidying seemed a controlling sort, would not have returned the stray produce back to their respective bins immediately after shoppers carelessly left the items on the shelf.

Marjory popped the potato, onions, cucumber, and blackberries into her bag, selected a few dry goods items, and paid Welcome. A teenage boy came into the store from the back, grabbed several full bags, and went out to the bicycle to make deliveries. That was the son of Welcome's oldest son, who had attended Bethune Junior High with her David before the Antifans took David away.

"How's your sons?" she asked, politely. She sensed that Welcome seemed more anxious than usual, and what other problems could people their age have but children and grandchildren?

"Mostly the usual," said Welcome. He paused, wondering whether to confide in Marjory, and feeling guilty that he would discuss his own problems when Marjory's grief was so fresh. But he couldn't resist. "Jeff went Social Credit, you know, Mrs. Harris." Jeff was the youngest of the three Welcome sons.

"Yes, I heard," Marjory sympathized. She would not have raised it with Welcome.

The decision to "go Social Credit" was not a minor one. The government dangled it enticingly in front of the black Plores such as the Welcomes, and to a lesser extent

Hispanics. A white Deplorable might apply, and after excruciating self-abasement as he acknowledged his racism, sexism, homophobia, and transphobia, be granted Social Credit status, but the government distrusted Plores on principle and it needed a menial Plore workforce. But it remained a sore point with the leaders of the DJR that so many blacks—more than the government would admit—had fought on the Red side during the civil war, and after the war most had steadfastly refused what they considered a poisoned social credit chalice.

Each black Plore who could be lured into Social Credit allowed the government to burnish its credentials as the protector and defender of the oppressed Diverse People, and each black Plore who resisted the promise of more comfortable living and less freedom remained an affront to the government. For these reasons, black Plores enjoyed great prestige in Plorevilles up and down the East Coast, and when any slipped and fell into the hands of the dreaded Antifan Defense Forces, or ADF, they were punished all the more severely for their heresy.

But the temptation always existed. No Plore could attend college, a privilege reserved for Social Crediteers. The local high schools trained Plores for trades and service occupations such as bus drivers, cooks, florists, and drywall and floor installers. Thousands of Plores trudged into the City each day, on their buses and then through the great glass tunnel bridges to serve in City jobs, whether as waitrons, sandwich makers, roofers, store clerks, or cleaning and road crews. A plumber or an electrician rose to the top of the heap, since while Social Crediteers usually disliked working with their hands they still valued working toilets and lights. Each Plore household was required to dispatch at least one worker to the City in return for the small monthly stipend that kept many Plore families from outright destitution.

Two blocks away from Welcome's was a storefront labeled, "Social Credit Recruiting Office." It drew little traffic, partly because no Plore wished to be seen entering. Behind the dusty windows you could glimpse the shadows of uniformed officers waiting for a furtive visitor. Plore mothers darkly warned their children as they passed, "Move quickly or the Blues will grab you!" and the children would cast fearful looks back at the windows.

If you were Jeff, twenty-four years old and repairing drywall in the City, but liking to read and envious of what you saw as the carefree Social Crediteers your age, it would be tempting to walk into that office and place yourself in the recruiters' hands. Otherwise, what was left to you? Forty, fifty more years of drywall? Maybe inheriting the bodega and spending your days haggling with surly truck drivers? Jeff knew that the recruiters would gladly accept his application, although he was hazier about what would happen afterward and became impatient when his father asked directly whether Jeff could trust the government to deliver on its promises.

"I don't blame him for wanting more education," said Welcome. "He read some of the old paperbacks sometimes—not just the GVN," or the Great Virtual Network on which the government placed all approved reading and viewing. Unlike Social Crediteers, Plores were not forbidden from reading the yellowing paperbacks that still circulated legally around Ploreville, as long as they were not outright seditious. "But he didn't realize what he'd be giving up, or taking on."

Marjory nodded. As a Social Crediteer, Jeff would be discouraged from visiting his family in Ploreville, and Plores were forbidden from visiting the City unless working there or attending celebrations for major holidays. Jeff would have to surrender his faith for pagan MED services and distance himself from his family. His political minders would monitor him constantly for signs of Plore backsliding, scrutiny that your blackness would not spare you.

But most ominously, the path only went one way—there was no way to change your mind and return to Ploreville. If you objected to your assigned job or housing, you would find yourself at ADF headquarters. If you worshipped as an actual Christian outside of the MED umbrella, you would be executed, Diverse or not. Christian proselytizing, like firearms ownership, was a capital crime.

"He knows he made a mistake now," said Welcome. "He came here, in the middle of the night. He apologized for giving me heartache." Going Social Credit was a rejection of your parents and their values, preserved for you at great risk and sacrifice. The local Ploreville paper—under Social Crediteer control—had run a fawning story on the young black Plore who had embraced Diversity, embarrassing Welcome before his neighbors and customers.

As Marjory began to walk out the door, he called after her. "Be careful out there. We've started to see more ADF in the streets. I'm not sure they care too much about the treaty these days." It was a four-block walk home past the shabby storefronts, but the sight of other passersby enjoying the warm sunshine cheered her. Small children whooped and ran down the block, circling back to their mothers like birds to their nest.

Some passerby knew her by sight and reputation if not personally, and greeted her respectfully. At the corner, she glimpsed one block farther down the black uniforms of two ADF officers and decided to take a more roundabout route back to her house. They also knew who she was and she did not want to risk any trouble. She would not trust vengeful ADF officers to let her walk past them without incident.

The ADF officers stood under yet another flagpole flying the DJR flag, a round green earth against a black Antifan background. She could see the hated flag fluttering in the breeze above them. She could not risk an encounter with the ADF on the day her knitting circle met. The participants donated all the completed hats and sweaters to charity, for which there was always need. But knitting was not the group's main function. Nor was reading the main focus of the book club that met on the alternate weeks.

Marjory had originally hosted all the sessions, until Emma realized what the club gatherings really were about. "Mom! You can't do this! We're already in their sights!"

Marjory had asked, "Who really would suspect a dozen nice older ladies of subversion?"

"The Antifans, that's who!" Emma retorted. Finally, Marjory had reluctantly agreed that it was unwise to draw extra attention to their household. The participants rotated meeting places after that. Yet her daughters and their husbands would not stop Marjory.

"At least we can keep an eye on her," said Emma's husband, Larry. "I'm kind of proud of her, you know. That's the right Plore spirit, the way we were before they beat us down."

After the announcement of David's murder, and the visit to her house by two triumphant ADF officers to inform Marjory of his death, Marjory's will to resist the government had only grown. The family decided against having a funeral, mostly because there was no body to bury, and Marjory was reluctant to believe David had died. Moreover, the ADF officers had instructed them, "You cannot hold a service with more than twenty people, including your heathen priest."

"I can't believe it," she said firmly. "If he were gone, I would feel it somehow. There would be an emptiness, like after Elijah died..." She was referring to her husband, dead forty years in the civil war. "The universe would be lighter. I don't feel that now. And where's his body? If they killed him, why wouldn't they give us his body for burial? And whatever happened to Malia?"

Her family members almost believed she might be right. The ADF tolerated a steady stream of neighbors and well-wishers who came to the house for the next several nights, if only because it reinforced their narrative that the traitor was dead. Several black-jacketed officers stood on the nearby corner, noting all those who came to pay their respects. Most of the mourners observed Marjory Harris's surprising serenity, and having heard of her refusal to believe the news, nodded pityingly. But she would not turn away the well-wishers, because she liked hearing their memories of her son.

The absence of a body, the disappearance of Malia—the DJR media ignored her status entirely—and the heroism of the alleged decedent soon spawned rumors that David Harris had disappeared entirely from both the United States and the DJR. In less sophisticated places than Anacosta, Plores began to tell each other that a Plore Antifan, more powerful than any Antifan, and more humane than any Plore, would return to rescue them. Even in places where nobody knew the name of the missing Plore Antifan, the legend spread. "He will come," they were starting to say to each other, "but nobody knows exactly when or how."

Marjory's resolve, and her family's willingness to believe her increased when a letter arrived from her son Daniel, in Oklahoma, in early September. It was the only way that people could communicate over the militarized border, and any written communications, let alone Daniel and David's, were scrutinized especially carefully. Daniel must have known that the DJR censors would only allow his letter to arrive in

Ploreville if he echoed the DJR propaganda line.

After some innocuous greetings and inquiries after her health, Daniel wrote:

"You have doubtless heard in Anacosta of David's death at the hands of the ADF. Perhaps we should not have sacrificed his life by escaping to the US, where life is not as easy as they portrayed it at first. It may have been a mistake. It was foolish to think we could escape the justice of the Antifans." In writing this, Daniel hoped it would please the DJR censors enough to let the letter through. "Emmett and George cry a lot for their lost parent."

Then, a few paragraphs down, "Our friend John Lazarus was ill but he is better now."

Here, Daniel gambled that the DJR censors would not recognize the New Testament story in the book of John about the brother of Mary and Martha who was deemed dead, but after Jesus's prayerful ministrations, rose from his grave. Marjory and the family knew of no other Lazarus but the biblical figure.

"He is not dead," Marjory said. "But something has happened." It was telling that Daniel did not mention Malia by name either. Marjory and Emma and Christine puzzled over the odd phrase, "...cry a lot for their parent." Why not say father? Was this a cryptic reference to Malia? The DJR censors, whose culture strove to avoid gender-specific references to mothers and fathers, known in officialese as "birthing parent" and "sperm parent," might not have even hesitated over that odd word.

Eventually, the Harris women decided to wait and take comfort in the implicit message that all was not lost.

Regardless where the ladies met, and today she herself was hosting, Marjory would relay the instructions for the week. The produce arrangement on the top shelf at Welcome's was a code. The first bin always represented Thursday, and the last Wednesday. One item atop a bin signaled which day clandestine Plore travelers would arrive in Arlington en route to somewhere else, perhaps to join the bands starting to organize along the Florida-Alabama border. Or maybe a woman just wanted to see her dying mother in Anacosta or Philadelphia and couldn't get a permit to travel.

Two onions after the potato said "two travelers on Thursday," and two bags of blackberries next to the cucumber said, "two travelers on Wednesday." A Plore family willing to give overnight shelter to a traveler would receive a paper delivery bag from Welcome's the afternoon before the traveler was expected to arrive, hidden in a delivery truck from the adjoining Plore region to the north, Philadelphia–Wilmington Outer Suburban, or Charlotte Outer Suburban to the south. Plores were banned from traveling outside their home region, but truck drivers were overwhelmingly Plore, sympathetic to the cause, and easy to bribe. Sharing the housing burden minimized attention for the circle's participants. Plores generally minded their own business, but enough informants circulated in Plorevilles to make caution advisable.

The next day or so, another truck or connections of the hostess with access to transportation and guides would convey the traveler to the next safehouse. Among themselves, they called it the "Plore Underground." The reference to "Underground" made it a knowledge crime, by daring to compare their enterprise with the network that hundreds of years ago had smuggled escaping slaves to freedom in the North.

The house was quiet when Marjory let herself in. Like on any other Wednesday, Larry was driving his bus route along Columbia Pike, the boys were in school, and Emma must be running her own errands before going into the City to clean offices. Next year the older boy would graduate and take a job in the City so that his mother could stay home.

Two of the three cats came to greet her, rubbing along her legs. She helped herself to some of the blackberries, and decided against sharing them with the knitting ladies. She laid out crackers and rolls, sliced some cheese, and placed a precious jar of strawberry preserves on the sideboard in the living room. Recalling that for at least two of the ladies, this might be their main meal of the day, she guiltily retrieved and rinsed the blackberries as well. She pulled her knitting project, a pink scarf, out of the sideboard, where it had rested since the last meeting.

The ladies would not arrive for another half hour. She nibbled on the berries and crackers, while mentally composing the next illicit news bulletin, adding some of the unverified but generally reliable gossip that Welcome had shared with her.

Plores could read the official *Anacosta Post*, which they mocked, and watch the City's TV stations, with their condescending coverage of Ploreville backwardness. ("Eighteen-Year-Old Girl Marries Second Cousin," or "Hungry Schoolchildren Welcome Burrito Breakfast from City Benefactors," for example.) Plores had their own online newspaper, *The Suburban Record*, which listed high school drama performances and notified them of the steady rate increases for garbage collection, wifi, and bus fares, but never dared attack real issues of concern.

Marjory's news bulletin was handwritten on no more than one sheet at a time. Copiers and printers were scarce in Ploreville, and all copies contained an encrypted coding that could be traced all too easily to their owners. Marjory was eager to access an off-grid copier or printer, but for now it was safer to painstakingly produce each bulletin one by one, like a medieval monk. To protect herself and the family, and not waste paper, she did not write until she had composed the bulletin copy in her mind— it was dangerous to leave seditious sheets lying around and the treaty would not protect her if the ADF discovered them. She had a neat, distinctive cursive last taught in schools half a century earlier.

The knitters and the book club members would add other tidbits. Having been president of her Ohio high school's journalism club, Marjory insisted on including some indication of the reliability of the information, such as "reported by a high school student from a respectable family, and corroborated by two eyewitnesses at Bethune

Arlington that a classmate was beaten by a Social Credit history teacher for praising George Washington."

The knitters and the readers would write more copies of the bulletins at home after all had memorized the contents for the week, safely ignorant about which of them had contributed each item. Then truckers would ingeniously smuggle the flyers up and down the East Coast in the walls of their trucks. Sometimes bulletins from the Plorevilles in Boston and Atlanta made their way back to Marjory and her circle, reassuring them that they were not alone.

Marjory was determined—while she was still alert and healthy—to finally wrest some meaning out of five decades of suffering. The civil war had consumed her husband and her youngest child. The Antifans had herded them from Ohio into the DJR and then to Anacosta, and later taken her second youngest child to serve them. She was old enough to remember their comfortable prewar lives. Perhaps others were resigned to their serfdom, but counterintuitively, she had gained resolution with age.

"I may be an old lady," she always told herself firmly, "but I will be older tomorrow, so I should do whatever I can today."

The doorbell rang, and she let in the first knitter.

Chapter 19
Celadon Vase
(Friday, September 4, 2093)

Paragon's chauffeur pulled into his usual spot in the VIP garage, next to Steve Rosen's modest sport-van, which the deputy director drove himself. Exterra had left for work earlier, to avoid encountering Bettina, the sex worker who visited the Avalon on Fridays. On Tuesdays, the strapping Ivan met Paragon in his office at Beaufort, where the Antifans could see for themselves that Paragon did not allow his Muslim leanings to lessen his dedication to Diversity, in this case his open-mindedness on sexuality. Nor did Paragon mind collecting ten extra social credit points for "proven" bisexuality.

He could have taken an office on the eightieth floor with the director and the deputy director, but he preferred to stay with his Resolution Command on the seventy-fifth floor. The corner office was as spacious and as plush as anything upstairs. Natural light organic woods paneled the walls; his desk allegedly had belonged to the last US vice president before it was looted from the Observatory. Both chairs facing his desk, as well as the chairs and sofa framing his own armchair in the corner were deliberately lower than his. Indulging his one superstition, Paragon had engaged a feng shui consultant when he returned from St. Louis, whose legacy was the burbling fountain between the sofa and his desk.

He was proudest of the Song dynasty celadon vase that stood on a console under a bamboo-framed mirror against the far wall. Thirty-five years ago, his father, a senior Communist Party functionary, had smuggled the family heirloom into the United States from China, leaving the family behind in Xinjiang, in that remote terrorized Islamic outpost of the Chinese empire. Now his father was dead and the vase was truly his.

It was a family, of sorts, cobbled together through oppression and politics, although in China, that was mostly one and the same. His mother, a kindhearted, broad-faced Uighur, widowed by one of those anti-Muslim purges the Communist Party periodically unleashed against its dwindling Muslim population, came home one day in 2047 to find party functionary Ma Jin-hua assigned to her house and her bed. This scene played out across Xinjiang as the Han overlords neatly solved the dual challenge of insufficient ethnic Chinese Han brides and persistent Islamic practices. The new Mrs. Ma, helpless, made no protest. What else could she do? She was at least certain that her husband had died in one of the reeducation camps several years earlier. She and their six-year-old daughter, Patigul, needed to eat.

Three Ma brothers were born in quick succession. Kang Li, the youngest, was his mother's favorite, and he kept secret her devotion to the Koran and even joined her in prayer. She called him Khalid when no one could hear. Khalid loved his half sister, Patigul, twelve years older, and followed her around devotedly. The boys ate pork under the watchful eye of their father. He considered it a sufficient concession not to force his wife or stepdaughter to share the meal, but they had to cook it for him, the greasy smell filling the small house in Urumqi.

Then the Chinese government dispatched Functionary Ma to the United States to serve as a political advisor to the new Diversity Justice Republic government. Just as Ma had engineered the roundups and reeducation of the Uighurs, he would advise the DJR on the treatment of backward Plores from his office in the stately Chinese embassy in Anacosta. Three years later, he sent for his family. Khalid was now eight, a sturdy boy who looked more Uighur than Han. This would have been a problem back in China, but Khalid found to his delight that Diversity favored Muslims here, up to a point. Instead of fighting Han bullies, he dedicated himself to his studies. Since China was popular, having bestowed on the DJR its Social Credit system, cure for coronavirus, and ideological and military wisdom, Khalid smoothly switched gears to benefit from his Muslim faith or Chinese ancestry, as the situation demanded.

When Khalid turned sixteen, his father was reassigned to Beijing. But Khalid did not want to return to China. Fortunately, the DJR considered sixteen the age of emancipation, and even if it had been higher, was perfectly willing to accommodate a Diverse-minded child over an obstinate parent. In the end his father did not press him, perhaps because he saw that his son was succeeding in Anacosta in a way that would not have been possible in China, given his Uighur looks. His older sister, Patigul, also stayed, probably for similar reasons, but at twenty-eight, she was already established in the Muslim Relations section of the Knowledge Tower, overseeing Diversity outreach to female Muslims, and married to a Muslim of Syrian ancestry who had arrived in the DJR under the Welcoming New Friends program. He labored on the Knowledge Tower loading dock, earning a menial Social Credit score. This embarrassed Khalid.

Khalid and Patigul's mother wanted to stay with them, but she was afraid of this country that was not like the free America she had heard about during her sufferings in Xinjiang. And after all these years, she felt love for her husband, or at least a sense of belonging with him. So the parents went back to China with the two older sons. There was nothing about the United States, or at least the DJR, that was superior to China at this point.

His father gave him the celadon vase, "in case you need money. But do not sell this unless you are desperate. Contact me first." Khalid later realized that the reappearance of the vase at the airport in Beijing might have caused his father some difficulty with the authorities.

Khalid, or Paragon, settled down at his desk, refreshed by his morning exertions with Bettina. He would be interrogating Malia Harris at one o'clock, so he needed to be efficient with what remained of the morning. Deputy Commander Okuro came in bearing some intriguing reports from the Antifan cyber hack on the New White House in St. Louis. The National Security Day parade on the second Monday in September, anchored by the ADF, would bear the marks of Paragon's artistic and choreographic genius. Paragon gave final instructions to organizers about the order in which the floats should go in the parade.

Next Paragon met with the branch chief for the Naming Initiative. The DJR had renamed most cities or towns in accordance with Diverse principles, but somehow the names of its citizens had slipped through the cracks. As did the Chinese, Paragon felt that your name connoted character, and was not simply random. Even though the DJR had been founded almost forty years ago, people were still thoughtlessly using their Christian and white supremacist names, and even bestowing them on their children.

Some cases were sensitive or borderline enough that the branch chief consulted Paragon personally. They went briskly down the list until they reached one last case.

"This fellow, 115, in Boston, is named Thomas St. Pierre..." said the branch chief.

"Well, that won't do anymore," said Paragon curtly.

"Right, he wants to change his name to Max Imum."

"As in 'maximum'? Does he think this is a joke?"

"Apparently, sir. But it seems ideologically harmless, so I thought we should just run it by you to be safe."

"It is not ideologically harmless. Mocking the policy is tantamount to anti-Diverse propagandizing. Every time he would use his name, others would know he had not taken our directive seriously. Do I need to educate you, of all people, in this basic Diverse reality? Do you need to be replaced in your job?"

The branch chief trembled. "Apologies, Commander. We will reject the name application."

"You'll do more than reject it. Have him arrested and let him spend a few weeks at Boston Beaufort thinking about it. And then we'll change his name to Rectal Hole. H-O-L-E." Despite his fear of Paragon, the branch chief giggled.

"And we'll publicize it in the media so nobody else thinks they can play these games with us. If he wants to use the nickname Rec, that's fine. But every time he goes to a government store or office, he'll be introducing himself as Rectal Hole. For the rest of his life."

Next came his weekly video conference with the director of the Knowledge Tower,

Vaughan Mitsuyama, 305. Because of his Chinese background, Paragon disliked the Japanese, even Japanese-Diversans. But he accepted the pallid Mitsuyama, who was a competent administrator with zero vision. Paragon did not want to preside over spreadsheets, and he was happy to provide the vision.

"What's the status of the latest campaign in Anacosta Ploreville?" he asked Mitsuyama. "We've been hands off too long. We aren't seeing enough recruitments of Diverse Deplorables for Social Credit status. Those broadsheets that have been circulating around Plorevilles with fake news can't be tolerated either."

"We've been upping the Diverse content of the television and video programming for Plores, including propaganda commercials," said Mitsuyama. "Unfortunately, we can't force them to watch it, so the ratings have gone down sharply since the campaign began."

"We can't force them to watch it? What do you mean, Director?"

"Well," faltered the director, "you can't just plunk them in front of the TV."

"Why not? Does the treaty forbid it?"

"No, but what do you have in mind, Commander?"

"I understand that food supplies have been scarce in Anacosta Ploreville at least in recent months. The Economic Zones obviously need to send most of the produce to the Cities, and the Plores get what's left over. Too bad for them, the fascists. Why don't we have movie nights, take over one of their depraved churches, show a good Diverse movie, and then give the attendees a food package when they finish watching?"

"That's an excellent idea, Commander."

"And let's rejigger the cable TV packages. What's popular with Plores these days?"

"Sports, soap operas, game shows, reality shows where a bunch of guys compete against each other to survive in the wilderness," said Mitsuyama. "Not political at all."

"Let's make sure that each of these packages becomes cheaper if you take the Diverse Drama option," declared Paragon. "And don't bundle the sports with other nonpolitical stuff. I don't want anyone getting away without Diverse programming. If they want both, more cheaply, they'll have to take the Diverse programming."

He moved onto the last item on the agenda. "And speaking of churches?" He was referring to the program forcing Ploreville churches to accept Diversity art shows or Mother Earth lecturers in return for the government-provided utilities. How the DJR government had gotten roped into paying for the electricity of the fascist churches for four decades still bemused Paragon. Cleverly, the government did not ban the services themselves, which were protected by the treaty, but the dependence of the strapped congregations on government aid for electricity and water was a cudgel that no one had yet sought to use against them. Until Paragon.

"Most of them are complying, Commander. Some balked at having a Mother Earth lecture on Sunday afternoons. They're afraid some of their parishioners might stay after their service to hear Diversity Truth. But we're actually getting more pushback about the Diversity art. They object to the content."

"They don't get to determine the content of the art," said Paragon. "They should be grateful—we're putting some of our best Diverse work on display. So there's a little gay sadomasochism here, some satirical cartoons about Abraham Lincoln there. It's a learning opportunity. They all have placards explaining the point of the art, right?"

"Yes," said Mitsuyama sadly, "but that only makes things worse. Nobody is coming."

"Plore school groups will," responded Paragon impatiently. "Or else. Let's make one such cultural visit a month required per household in return for the basic income check." Mitsuyama agreed to implement the program. As the screen faded with the director's image, Paragon thought, No wonder we see all this backsliding in the DJR. We have settled just for holding onto power, but we are leaving so many pockets untouched where we could be pushing forward Diversity, whether through lack of imagination or lack of will, or both.

Failure to advance is the prelude to retreat, Paragon told himself. Savoring his wordsmanship, Paragon decided he would request the Knowledge Tower post the slogan on billboards and play it on propaganda commercials in October. Why is no one else here of your caliber, he asked himself, but of course he was Paragon. His eyes lingered on the celadon vase—the evidence of a robust culture that had dominated its entire region for centuries. Surely Diversity could become the cornerstone of a rich new culture here in North America?

Irritated by the evidence of ideological obtuseness among his own ranks, Paragon resolved he would not spare Malia Harris during the afternoon interrogation. He reviewed Captain Vance's notes from the previous day's session, thinking he would recommend she change her last name to "Advance," which would fit in well with the ideological campaign. "You don't have to do it," he imagined telling her, "since there's nothing particularly egregious about Vance, but do you really want to carry an enslaver's name when you could set an example by choosing one that embodies the Antifan spirit?" He suspected she would agree quickly, since promotion time was coming.

Malia awaited him in the interrogation room. She was exhausted after a morning spent arguing with the Diversity history lecturer. She hadn't intended to argue, and she kept silent as much as possible, conserving her strength and her temper, but what could you do when he insisted that Theodore Roosevelt, born in New York in 1858, had owned slaves, and had used slaves to build the Panama Canal, and that the Constitution decreed that blacks were only three-fifths of a person due to sheer racism? The Panama Canal logic was that all slaves must be black, and some blacks had participated, as Panamanians, in building the canal, and therefore the canal had been built by slaves. As for the three-fifths of a person, Malia knew that that formula had been a compromise between southerners who wanted to benefit from counting their bondsmen in the allotment of congressional seats in 1789 and northerners who knew full well that those blacks were by no means citizens. Despite his elevated position at Diverse American University, the professor was unable to grapple with her counterarguments, and always ended up making snide comments about the inability of fascists to learn, his mustache wiggling with frustration.

In part she tried to keep quiet because she was tiring more easily these days. She wasn't sure why this was happening. With lights out at eight, she could sleep for a good ten hours unless Exterra came by to watch TV with her. She was permitted exercise several times a week in the interior courtyard, and she dutifully walked around its perimeter — at first she could only do six circuits in the allotted time, and then ten, but now she had dropped back to eight.

"Prisoner Jenness," said Paragon as he entered the room. Aside from two privates sitting in the back corner, it was just the two of them today, except for any observers in the side room.

"You can stand today. Place your back against that wall, please. I'm sure you'd appreciate a change of pace after sitting all morning. I didn't get a very good report from your professor, by the way."

She waited, feeling the damp chill of the subterranean cement wall creep through the paper pants.

"You're possibly not a very good historian, judging by his reports, and your garbage dissertation," Paragon sneered.

I'll answer you when you ask me a question, she thought.

"Explain to me negative liberty," he demanded, placing his workscreen on the table and looming over her. She recognized the theme of the last dissertation chapter she had managed to finish, which gave her hope they would soon put the incriminating document behind them.

"Negative liberty is the right to be left alone," she said. "The government is permitted to do what is necessary to protect property and life. If one's activities do not infringe on others' property or life, a citizen should be allowed to freely engage in them, whether religion, or speech, or travel, for example."

"And positive liberty?"

"Some use this term to describe giving of agency to a person in a way that allows them to fully engage in human activity and realize their potential. The assumption is that some kind of constraint exists that needs to be eliminated to allow that. If negative liberty is the absence of external constraint, positive liberty frees a person to fulfill their potential. For example..."

"I don't need a college lecture, you bitch," he cut her off. "So which do you think is better?"

Go for broke, she thought bleakly. Even if she tried to avoid the clearly stated conclusions of her dissertation, he had read it and would drive her back into the corner.

"Negative liberty, if you believe that a human being is capable of achievement on his own. Positive liberty is often an open-ended excuse for collectivism. Anything can be justified by claiming it is necessary for the people's enlightenment or betterment."

Paragon countered, "How do you think the Diverse People could have moved forward without our government taking measures to ensure positive liberty? How could they have progressed from starvation to a guaranteed income, from racism to complete equality under law? From living in the streets to being given safe and clean housing? From dying of illnesses such as COVID to receiving the Healing Vaccine every year? Answer me this."

"To do all this, Commander, you force them into one way of living, at the mercy of some bureaucrat who will decide what number they bear, and that in turn will determine their life. You deprive them of the right to decide how they shall live. This is not liberty, it is slaves' rations, doled out at the behest of the master, but you call it liberty."

"Enslaved person," he corrected her, although he was secretly impressed by the enormity of the knowledge crime she had just naively committed before him.

"Liberty is about living according to one's own conception of the good life," she continued, as if he had not spoken, but she was passionate, even in, maybe especially in, this room. "If someone claims they are your benefactor, but they are your jailer, you have no liberty."

Paragon thought, You are making my job easy. No judge—not that you shall see one besides myself—would hesitate to condemn you.

"So positive freedom is achieved through the collective, is it not, through adherence to the general will?"

"Yes, Commander, because it requires the pooling of strength to overcome opposition from individuals whose own freedom is constrained by the collective."

"But what is wrong with the collective deciding what will benefit the majority it represents?"

"Because the collective never really represents the will of everyone, just those that have placed themselves at its head. The leader cites the will of the collective to justify what he wishes to do anyway, not ever anything he does not wish. And strangely, the collective never goes against the leader's will."

"Commander," said Paragon, but thoughtfully. He stared up at the darkened window.

"Commander," replied Malia, more firmly.

"Now," said Paragon, "We will discuss some of the recordings from your house in Oklahoma."

Malia froze. She had no idea that the ADF had been secretly listening to her and David's conversations. Kevin must somehow have planted the devices. How naive they had been.

"Most of your conversations were trivial and idiotic," Paragon began, "as one might expect from your meaningless life in that backwater. Nor were we surprised to hear that your traitor husband is—was—active among the MAGA fascists. Nevertheless, we found some interesting evidence of your treasonous mindset and intentions.

"Evil people run that place…" Paragon read from his workscreen. "July twenty-second. Let's parse that statement." Malia to her dismay recognized what she had told Rex when her daughter had expressed an interest in studying at Diverse American.

"You look tired, Prisoner. Why don't you sit down? No, not in the chair. Have you earned a chair today? On the floor there. Yes, that's good. We've got all afternoon to discuss your treasonous words…" He nudged her cautiously with the steel tip of his boot. "That's no excuse for slouching, though, please sit up."

Malia knew there was no use in denying she had called Paragon and his colleagues "evil." Her mind raced to think of what else she might have said at that kitchen table.

"Here's another interesting remark. You said to your sister-in-law, 'Someday I hope that David and I can work to help free people in the DJR.' Free people from what? Who? How?"

Malia said, "To work to bring the DJR and US together again under a democratic government. But we never got more specific than that."

"What do you mean by a democratic government?"

"One in which the people vote for their leaders," she responded. Her eyes were growing heavy. She stifled a yawn, which would only enrage Paragon.

"Diversans vote for their leaders here, you know," said Paragon. Every four years a vote was held by Social Crediteers to ratify the choice of the Diversity Advisory Council.

"They don't choose their leaders," Malia objected, "Commander."

"Of course, they don't choose them," Paragon said disdainfully. "How on earth would ordinary Social Crediteers understand who is best qualified to lead them?"

Malia felt dizzy. It was like *Alice in Wonderland*, she thought. Not caring anymore, and unable to stop herself, she curled up on the cold tile floor and started falling asleep. Infuriated, Paragon kicked her in the arm and, yelping, she sat up again. "Don't do that again in here, bitch." He figured this was just short of the "physical violence" redline, and in any case, she had disobeyed him.

He produced a long list of additional offenses culled from the devices in Oklahoma, enjoying the sight of Malia's shocked face each time he reminded her of another seditious comment the Antifans had recorded. David's joke about the DJR worshipping the molecular pressure cooker and naming it a saint should not have counted against Malia, except Paragon pointed out she had laughed at it, thereby suggesting she agreed with its heretical premise.

Later that day, Paragon called Exterra and said, "For Earth's sake, have them adjust the dosage. She's so drugged she's falling asleep in the interrogation room."

Chapter 20
Popcorn And Movie
(Tuesday, September 8, 2093)

"Please tell me your Diversity journey," Malia asked Exterra. It was a polite way to ask, "Tell me how you ended up as an Antifan jailer eating popcorn in my VIP cell at Beaufort."

The two women were relaxing—insofar as you could relax as prisoner and jailer in a Beaufort cell—while a Diversity-themed documentary about new immigrants to the DJR played in the background. A Somali woman was enthusing about her daughter's clitoridectomy, "paid for by the Cultural Retention division of the Knowledge Tower!" and then a Honduran man talked with an interpreter about how the gangs had brought him to Florida and "were like my family until I got my 120 number. Estoy aprendiendo ingles ahora." Some fried patties sizzled on a stove in the next scene as a friendly round Bangladeshi lady said, "Here in the DJR, we always have enough white flour for our chapatis!" Despite having promised Paragon they would dutifully watch propaganda that evening, Exterra was also inclined to chatter with Malia. She was confident Paragon would approve of her telling Malia her inspirational life story.

A Diversity story always began with a statement of one's family's class, or more precisely, intersectional status.

"I grew up in western Pennsylvania," said Exterra, "the youngest of three children. Our family of course, was white and cisgender. I was the only one born after the war had ended. Before the war, my father was an adjunct lecturer in politics at Cornell, which is now Navasky University, and no matter how hard he tried, the university would not give him a tenure track professorship. My mother worked in a doctor's office where only rich white patients could get medical care. Because of the system of payment-based housing, we could only afford to live in a tumbledown house that the government wouldn't fix for us. I have learned in school how privileged we were because of our whiteness, and how our privilege came at the expense of the people of color around us, as well as gays and transgender people. My oldest brother is gay, however," she bragged, "and is the partner of the vice president of the Diversity

Warehouse in Pittsburgh." The Diversity Warehouse was the nationwide provider of goods that had swallowed up independent storekeepers in the last sixty years.

"The Diversity struggle came to our area early in the war, and my father was quick to join the Antifan movement, knowing only this way could justice come for the Diverse People."

Malia uncharitably thought that a low-level adjunct instructor must also have quickly recognized the possibility of advancement from a movement that revered academic credentials, if not knowledge.

"He became a lieutenant in the Antifan forces, and killed lots of Deplorables and Reds in New York Schuylkill. He even executed his dissertation thesis advisor at Cornell, who was a very vocal Red. Meanwhile, my mother was raising my brothers and working as an Antifan medic. When the war ended, they were rewarded for their service to the Diverse People. My father became a full professor of Diversity politics and my mother a nurse at the local Abortion Palace.

"Our family was given a Social Credit score of 150," Exterra said proudly, "and were allowed to live in the City of Pittsburgh."

"But how did you become an Antifan?"

"In high school I joined the Defend Diversity Movement. My grades weren't very good, and I knew that if I joined the right organizations and made friends there, it would help. A guaranteed 25 Social Credit points. We spent a lot of time roaming the streets in our uniforms, beating up Plores, forcing storekeepers to give us free stuff. If they were still running private stores, that is. Most of them had given up on making a living without the government.

"My guidance counselor said I probably wouldn't get into college, at least not on campus. She said, 'Have you ever considered the Antifans? Since you like pro-Diverse street action?'

"It had never occurred to me, even though my parents were Antifans during the war. But I liked the thought of punishing knowledge criminals, and it gave me pleasure to make Plores cry, given everything they'd done to us. I also needed to figure out a way to keep the Social Credit points, since I would soon lose my family score.

"Have more popcorn," Exterra thrust the bowl at Malia, who gladly accepted. One good thing about the evenings with Exterra was that they ordered in a decent meal from the Beaufort kitchens—no Health Meat on those nights—and Exterra would call afterward for popcorn, cherry tarts, chocolate, or something else Malia craved. It was ironic—during the day Paragon would rant and rave at her, and then at night, or at least some of them, his girlfriend would ply her with goodies. Good cop, bad cop, Malia smiled to herself. She knew their game.

"So I applied, and I got in because of the Diversity Movement activity and my parents' good social credit numbers. They were a little suspicious of western Pennsylvania—so close to the border. But they could tell I had it in for Plores. And I passed all the physical exams with flying colors. Now I've been here eleven years—I turn thirty next month."

"Is it everything you hoped it would be?" Malia asked.

Exterra nodded vigorously, taking the bowl back from Malia. "Lots of action. I mostly served in the Hate Crime division—we wiped out a whole nest of knowledge criminals who were trying to start a movement to demand equality among all races, but of course they were just oppressors trying to worm out of punishment." She pointed to the red X on her jacket pocket, "Finished them off. I must have killed four myself in the battle."

"A real battle?" Malia asked, knowing the answer. "Did they actually have guns?"

"No, of course not. Nobody wants to be executed for owning a firearm. We've made it impossible for them to get guns anyway. But they put up a fight with metal bars and chairs, and it was great plugging them before they could even get close to you. More fun than the firing squad, which was another rotation."

"My husband hated the firing squad rotation," Malia confided. She plunged her hand into the popcorn bowl again.

Exterra raised her eyebrows, "Well, as a traitor, he lacked a real understanding of the purpose of the firing squad. I wasn't a coward like him. All I meant was that it wasn't as satisfying as killing in battle." Malia wanted to throw the bowl at her head. Exterra's victims in "battle" were hardly more dangerous than the blindfolded condemned prisoners the firing squads would execute in the Beaufort basement.

"How did you meet Commander Ma?"

"We were both serving in the Hate Crime division. It was about six years ago. He was a captain and I was only a private. But I could see he was going to rise fast. And of course, as you can see, he is very handsome. I was saving myself for a truly Diverse partner—he only got the Asian bump after he appealed to have central Asians counted, and Muslims don't get points at all because they are not following the true Earth faith.

"But one day we were in a meeting. We were debating what to do with a woman from Massachusetts who had called a group of Somali immigrants awful names... and debased their culture. Some of us felt that since they had raped her daughter and looted her house, her anger was slightly justified. We were thinking of sparing her life. But then Khalid rose to remind us that the original sin of America had been its racism. As agents of Diversity, he said, we needed to strive every moment to suppress racism. Sometimes those who had been the victims of racism lashed out, through ignorance, and innocent people like the daughter might have to pay the price for her ancestors' crimes against black people. If we were lenient, other racists would take heart and do even worse things. He reminded us that Somalis might see rape differently than progressives, and it was a sign that we needed to educate them, but not punish them for their righteousness in rejecting racist treatment. He said the Somali-Diversans were behaving correctly, even if their ideological justification was immature."

"Wait, though," Malia said. "Those Somalis arrived voluntarily in the US, didn't they? After the DJR was founded and systemic racism was over?"

"Racism is never over. Somalis came to the US to find freedom, but found they had been fooled. Systemic racism was pervasive, and even after the victory of the DJR, it keeps popping out. That's why we can't afford to relax our grip for one moment. So that woman was executed, and we did not give into weakness, thanks to Commander Ma's resolute spirit.

"It was such a brilliant speech!" The right side of Exterra's face flushed with pride. "And after the meeting, late that afternoon, I went to his office and offered myself to him. I said that I wanted to learn more about Diversity at his feet."

"And you've been partners ever since?"

"No," Exterra admitted. "He said he appreciated the offer, but he would need to investigate my credentials and test my devotion to Diversity before he would partner with me. I understood—he couldn't afford to tarnish himself with anyone not up to his standards. So he subjected me to various tests."

"What kinds of tests?"

"First, I had to read about ten books on racism and Diversity theory and history and prepare reports on them for him. This wasn't easy, because as I mentioned, I wasn't really into studying. But I did them. He made me rewrite most of them. He said I was uneducated, which I guess was true. But he was very kind about it.

"Second, I had to prepare a speech admitting my own racism and read it to several different victims of racism that he had personally selected, and allow them to select punishments. Most of them were very nice about it, and said no punishment was necessary, but Khalid insisted, so he came up with punishments himself. And then finally, he said if I really wanted to show I wasn't racist, I should tattoo my face brown."

"How did you react to that?" Malia asked curiously.

"I was horrified at first. Who would do that to themselves? But then I realized my reluctance was truly due to residual racism. Almost every Antifan has tattoos, so that wasn't the problem. We normally cover them at the office, though, so clearly I was objecting to the brown color and to having that brown color on my face. I cried, realizing how awful and racist I was. Khalid took me in his arms for the first time and comforted me. He said I was so close to perfection, and he longed for me as I longed for him, and when we united, soon, it would be a truly Diverse union.

"Khalid then said, 'Just do half your face, and then nobody will think you are trying to impersonate a black person. Which would be a crime. So I went to the tattoo parlor and, over two weeks, it was done. It was very painful. But it gave me such joy to think I was doing this for Khalid and to show my love for Diversity.

"And then he finally accepted me as his partner," Exterra said happily. "It was hard when he was in St. Louis as our station chief until last year, but when he returned and created the Resolution Command, he moved me into the unit as well."

"Can I have the popcorn back?" Malia asked. "And what exactly is the Resolution Command?" *The AIA will be very interested in learning this,* she told herself as Exterra proudly relayed all the mysterious cases the command had shepherded, some of which had indeed puzzled the AIA, such as the pulsing rays that had caused spikes in cancer rates in the United States along the borders. On its own, the DJR could not have come up with or implemented some of these bizarre schemes, but Chinese assistance was always available for its DJR protégé. And the Resolution Command had been responsible for the intimidation of the Harrises and the plot to kidnap them. *If only I survive and get out of here, I will tell the AIA everything.*

"Now Monday is National Security Day," Exterra said as she rose to leave, "and we have a special treat for you. We're going to take a walk in the Botanic Gardens."

"Opposite the Octavian?" Malia had worked at that palatial apartment building, where she had recovered the stolen Rex, who had been living there with her adoptive parents.

"Yes, I hope you'll enjoy your outing."

Malia knew that Paragon and Exterra must have something else in mind besides a bucolic stroll, even though it was a holiday. She feared that they planned on displaying her in the parade later that morning, like a prisoner of the Romans, following behind a triumphant charioteer. But the promise of fresh air and seeing the streets of Anacosta again outweighed her fears. Not that she had a choice anyway.

"Are your parents still alive?" she asked Exterra.

"Yes, but they are frail. My mother is taking good care of my father. We don't want him to come to the attention of the authorities, so he avoids the doctor. I'm sorry, I shouldn't have said that."

Malia knew that Exterra really meant, "We don't want the authorities to send him to the Euthanasia Palace for consuming excess health resources, so we're hiding him at home. It doesn't matter whether you fought in the revolution, or if your daughter is an Antifan or your son the gay partner of a Moneycrat. When you are worn out, or disabled, they will come for you."

"Good night," Malia said, kindly. To her amazement, she felt almost as if Exterra were the prisoner and she, Malia, were free to come and go. She slept better than she had in weeks.

Chapter 21
Take Her to the Zookeeper
(Monday, September 14, 2093)

By 7:30 a.m., Malia was installed in the back of the black limousine, next to Paragon, with Exterra facing them on the jump seat. "This way you'll see more of the City," Exterra promised her. Instead of the awful paper pants, Malia wore a pair of olive-green cotton jeans that matched the T-shirt, new white socks, and a new pair of the black canvas shoes, still without laces. The morning was unseasonably cool, so they had given her a thick green cotton jacket as well. It was not quite civilian clothing, but it boosted Malia's spirits.

A black van followed them from Beaufort down to the Botanic Gardens, which Malia knew well from her time as a night concierge at the Octavian, across the street. Not that she was terribly familiar with the Gardens, since low Social Crediteers such as herself were only permitted to patronize them on weekends. But once she had eaten ice cream at the pavilion with Rex.

Even though she expected her outing would end with some parade-related humiliation, Malia was eager to view the City. They sailed down Massachusetts Avenue under its canopy of leafy trees. She recognized the Texan embassy on a hill above the street.

The second thing she noticed was that the pedestrians and bicyclists were all wearing masks, as if it were Coronavirus Liberation Day in June. But it was now mid-September.

"Why are people wearing masks?" she asked. "It's a different holiday."

Paragon smiled with feline satisfaction out his window.

Exterra said, "Mask wearing is the new Diversity campaign this month. Last month it was pink pussy hats. Everyone needs to wear the masks outside their houses until the end of September or they'll be arrested."

"But why masks? For a whole month?"

"Why not?" Paragon said, finally turning back toward them. "Why should the campaign be easy to fulfill? It is an inconvenience to wear masks all the time, and to be prevented from breathing easily. But this way our citizens will be reminded constantly of the importance of Diversity. It is also a way to show you care about your fellow citizen."

"Shouldn't we be wearing masks too?" Malia asked.

"Not for us, you fool," said Paragon.

The car stopped at a red light, and Malia stared, horrified, as a knot of policemen beat a maskless man. The light changed and the car surged forward. During her days in Anacosta, the authorities had visited terror on the inhabitants mostly behind closed doors, if only to avoid undermining the general impression that compliance was ubiquitous and eager.

"Probably a Deplorable," said Paragon. "But there is no excuse for ignoring the order. The enemies of Diversity especially must comply with the campaign."

The car headed over to Connecticut Avenue. The row houses she remembered had been demolished and a sign in the vacant lot read "Jenifer Tower Coming Soon. 140 and Above." Fewer pedestrians were out.

"It's quiet today, isn't it?" she asked. "I guess it's because of the holiday?"

"Will you shut up?" Paragon snapped.

"Khalid, she hasn't seen the City in almost four years," Exterra gently clucked. "Of course, she's curious to see the progress we have made since then."

Paragon snorted, and Exterra said, "Yes, it's the holiday, but a lot of people are now working from home, especially those doing clerical tasks. It's a much more efficient use of resources. We've set up thousands of work cubicles in the basements of the big housing pens and apartment buildings. We save so much in utilities. Think of how much that protects our carbon footprint! There is no reason for so many people to wander around on the streets when the Diversity Warehouse can supply almost all their needs."

Paragon added, proudly, "And the computer tracks their faces constantly to make sure they are sitting at their screens and working for Diversity rather than wasting time. If they use the toilet, they must type in the password when they return."

Malia recognized the elite apartment buildings on Connecticut, of which the Octavian was among the most prestigious. The Octavian looked the same as it had four years ago. They turned into the Botanic Gardens and parked in the small lot for VIP vehicles.

"Driver, a mask for the prisoner," Paragon requested. A cloth mask with string loops that said "PRISONER" was passed to the trio in back and Malia obediently pulled them over her ears. Neither Paragon nor Exterra bothered. Outside the car they were joined by three unmasked Antifan troops from the other black van.

"Let's take a walk, shall we?" said Paragon.

Malia's spirits soared. So what if she were displayed in the parade later? She rejoiced in the freshness of the hour, even if it was hard to breathe the dewy air through the mask.

They set down one of the paths, and Malia admired the bushes and flower beds. The Antifan party had the Gardens to itself due to the early hour, about an hour before they opened to the public. On a holiday such as this one, even Plores would be able to visit the Gardens, although that usually meant the more fastidious Social Crediteers would stay away, complaining of noise and disorderly behavior, such as the Plores referring to their god or his son.

About ten minutes later, Paragon announced, "And now we are coming to the zoo." Malia failed to detect the note of triumph in his voice. Once upon a time, the Botanic Gardens had been the National Zoo, famous for its China-gifted pandas. But surely, Malia thought, the animal-loving DJR would not have imprisoned animals in cages again?

Ahead of them stretched a clearing, anchored by a circle of six giant cages. A wide cement sidewalk, edged by flowering bushes, connected all the cages. The cages were like jewels on a cement necklace. In front of each cage stretched a broad asphalt apron for spectators. In the midst of the grassy clearing squatted a round two-story windowless building with a slanted roof.

Only a few Plore groundskeepers, supervised by a longhaired Social Credit overseer, were tending to the bushes at this early hour. All wore masks.

They came to the first cage. An Asian woman was lying there among dogs, crying.

Malia wondered, is this some kind of circus act? But circuses had been banned in the DJR for forty years and were in disrepute even in the United States. And why was she crying?

"She was found to be secretly owning a fur coat," said Paragon, checking some notes on his phone screen. "Her punishment is to live in the cage with wild dogs for a week and eat their food. If she is lucky, they will not attack her, because no one will save her. Perhaps they will treat her as one of the pack."

Malia was horrified and confused. She knew it was illegal to own fur, but wouldn't the woman normally just be jailed for a few years?

"This is a special exhibit for National Security Day week," explained Paragon. "One tires of parades, although of course we always have the parade."

In the second cage, a scruffy white man was attached to a device that was beginning to intermittently blow dark smoke around him. A technician was adjusting the controls.

"This man was smoking tobacco," said Paragon, "whose association with slavery and Deplorables is well-known. Had he stuck to marijuana he would have been law-abiding." They paused to watch the technician. The man looked dejected, coughing slightly. "He may survive the week. But he will probably end up at the Euthanasia Palace within the year."

Malia was outraged. "I don't understand! Why are you torturing these people in public?"

"They had a choice. They all chose exhibition in the zoo for one week over five years in prison. They are serving as examples to other citizens. They are all Social Crediteers who should have known better than to violate the laws."

The third cage held an older white woman sitting half naked in a pile full of dirty recyclable plastics, glass, and metal cans. "Failed to recycle," said Paragon. "But the recyclables will keep her warm, or so she must hope. It is a cool morning."

The fourth cage contained a thirtyish black woman and a large screen playing a video of two beautiful curly-haired girls who kept saying over and over, "Mommy, how could you do this to us? Mommy, they took us away." The woman sobbed noisily, but by midmorning the tears would end and she would sit in a stony silence until she went mad several days later, to the amusement of the crowd.

Malia felt faint. It was her story too. "What did she do?"

"She celebrated Christmas with them last December and took them to an illegal Christian service. And she gave them only girl-appropriate toys such as dolls and brooms. If she had chosen the toys more carefully and celebrated Saturnalia instead, she would have been left alone. She is fortunate not to be subject to the death penalty for Christian proselytization."

This is evil, thought Malia. Here is the evilest square mile of any in the DJR, the Economic Zones and the incubation camps notwithstanding. And standing before me is the man whose sick mind generated this idea.

Malia was afraid to approach the fifth cage, but despite his stated aversion to touching her, Paragon took her arm and genially steered her along the path.

"He taught math." A white man in late middle age sat hunched on a stool in the middle of the cage. Arrayed in a row along the edge of the cage were eco-plastic dart guns and huge vats full of darts to shoot at him.

"Any child who has felt frustration learning math will enjoy venting at this criminal. Instead of teaching the approved curriculum, which presents concepts in an appealing way conducive to achieving equity, this man insisted on secretly teaching algebra and geometry to students he considered intellectually curious and worthy." Paragon almost spat the "intellectually curious."

"Our curriculum emphasizes equity. No one should be made to feel inferior in school. It is more important that the outcome is equal among all groups than that some are allowed to persist in their feelings of superiority."

"But how will the DJR build bridges? Where will your engineers come from without higher math?" Malia had been an indifferent math student herself, but she respected the endeavor.

Paragon said, "No need to worry. Chinese Peace Corps squadrons come here to supervise the building of infrastructure and engineering projects, so they are all quite safe. And some college students may study math under strict ideological supervision."

They continued along the path. The contrast between the beautiful plantings and the evil cages disturbed Malia. She recalled that the Nazis who ran the extermination camps ordered prisoners to play classical music for the condemned as they filed to the gas chambers and tried to deceive them by planting flowers and bushes. Malia feared what awaited them in the final cage. But to her relief, it was empty, except for a wooden armchair that a century ago might have graced an execution chamber.

"Thank goodness," she said aloud. "Five of those were quite enough."

Paragon smiled down at her. "But we do have six, my dear fascist. What better exhibit than the widow of the only Antifan traitor? You will be living evidence that the Antifan Defense Forces must not be thwarted."

"No!"

"Yes, very much yes, Prisoner Jenness. Did I not tell you that you must show repentance to the Diverse People? How did you expect that would happen? A tea party? Do you think I meant it only as a figure of speech? I'm afraid you have grown too comfortable with our hospitality."

"I won't! I won't!" she shouted. "You're all sick and depraved." The dispirited math teacher raised his head to look in her direction.

"You will publicly repent. All week. We will provide little rubber balls for the Diverse People to throw at you to demonstrate their righteous anger. They will shout at you, and curse. Perhaps you will finally understand the crime you committed in escaping Diversity."

She turned to flee, but the Antifan troopers, prepared for resistance, stood in her way, a wall. She yelled as two seized her arms and propelled her toward the cage. She struggled and thrashed sufficiently so that in response to Paragon's signal, the bulkiest of the three, a Samoan, lifted her bodily and carried her to the back. Paragon called out, "Take her to the Zookeeper."

A gnarled elderly man, a Social Crediteer with an armband, because a Plore could not be trusted with such heretical charges and might even sympathize with them, met them at the back of the cage. He opened a small, creaking iron door through which the Samoan-Diversan squeezed only with difficulty. Underneath the cage floor was a series of small rooms—first a storeroom with some cabinets, a small coldbox, a table and a chair, perhaps for the Zookeeper's meals. Then a toilet and sink. Third was a narrow cell with a barred window in the door and a flimsy cot. This was where Malia would sleep at night. All this made her Beaufort quarters seem palatial. Beyond her cell was a short staircase and a trapdoor that opened into the cage.

They let her use the toilet, and then almost gratefully, because she felt claustrophobic below, she ascended up into the cage, preceded by the Zookeeper. The miserable Samoan followed, wriggling almost comically through the trapdoor. She looked down at Paragon and Exterra and the two remaining Antifans.

"Shame on you," she said. "How can you think this will change my beliefs? This vile spectacle makes me even stronger in my resolve. I will repent nothing!"

"Tie her to the chair," ordered Paragon. "The Gardens have opened."

Realizing the futility of further struggle, since the Samoan stood by, Malia let the Zookeeper fasten her to the chair with rubber bindings. He must have had a kind streak, because he did not draw them very tightly across her wrists, arms, and calves. At least she would be able to quietly stretch her limbs during the long day. "I love animals," he explained, "but now they don't have them here." He removed her mask at Paragon's command, possibly because it would have afforded her mouth some protection against the balls.

Two groundskeepers came along, rolling two carts on which were piled boxes filled with small hard rubber balls. They placed the carts between Malia and the cement apron. At least no one would be able to hurl a ball at close range.

Paragon took a red ball, rolling it around in his large palm, and then sent it whizzing by Malia's head. "Alas," he said, "my aim is poor." His next throw caught her in the solar plexus. She choked and bent over. "Exterra?"

Exterra shook her head. But Paragon thrust an orange ball at her insistently. Exterra let it sail over Malia's head. "Some Antifan," sneered Paragon. "Perhaps you need a remedial class. Well, we must be getting to the parade. We'll bring you back on Sunday evening, my dear traitor. Unless you need hospitalization first." Off they marched toward the entrance to the zoo clearing and were soon gone.

"Bastards!" she shouted at their backs.

"No point," said the Zookeeper, almost genially. "Save your energy. They always win." As if she had checked into a hotel, he informed her that she would get a break at noontime for lunch and the bathroom, and another break at four. "Dinner won't be bad, I promise. I'll cook it myself."

"No Health Meat?" she almost smiled at him.

"Horrible stuff, ain't it? No way, not in our zoo." The Zookeeper disappeared into the ground, only to emerge and sit at a picnic table off to the side. Occasionally he would reenter the apartment to do light housekeeping or take a nap. His Healthy Eating grocery bag was scheduled to arrive this morning so he needed to keep an eye out for the delivery. Two teenage Plore boys were assigned to cages five and six, charged with collecting the balls and darts on the ground and returning them to the bins. They stood by, awaiting action.

The first visitors were approaching her—a family of four, walking a pampered white dog.

Malia gazed at the central building. Noticing the cameras trained on her from the upper corners of the cage, she realized that workers in the windowless building were monitoring her and the other prisoners. The building at least blocked her distant view of distressing cages one and two.

It occurred to her that the theater in which she was an unwilling actress was the mirror of woke virtue signaling. Just as the exalted woke Social Crediteers flaunted their moral superiority, and awarded themselves accordingly high numbers and better lives, the degeneracy of their opposites must similarly be exposed, if only to underscore their own virtue. Malia was pleased with her insight.

The family of four and a young black cis couple, all masked and armbanded, stared at her. They read the electronic placards on the right and left.

"Oh wow," breathed the family's son, thirteen years old. "She escaped into the United States! That's amazing." He looked at her, longing to ask her about the Red country.

"Now, now, Nhoj," the sperm-donating parent chastised, alarmed at the respectful tone in his son's voice. "That was a wicked deed. She deserves to be punished severely." He looked around them, afraid at who might be listening.

"Disgusting," said the birthing parent, "What ingratitude. I'm so glad they killed her partner. Imagine, he was an Antifan! Children, why don't you throw some of these balls at her? Neleh, take this yellow one," which she gave to the girl.

The boy and his younger sister took several balls and threw them gently in Malia's direction. None hit her, although one rolling ball stopped at her foot. The family moved toward the math teacher, and the black couple hurriedly exited the clearing altogether without bothering to visit any other exhibits. Malia wondered, by the time the family reached the poor woman with the dogs, whether the children would have become inured to the suffering, and eager to join in punishing the caged criminals.

The numbers visiting her in the morning were light, because so many preferred to see the parade. That meant, however, the crowds would grow in the afternoon as they looked for entertainment after lunch. The visitors looked at her, they read the screens, they looked at her again, and then they moved on to the math teacher or left the enclosure, depending on whether they had gone clockwise or counterclockwise around the circle. They did not speak to her, nor did she address them. Nobody crossed the center green.

Almost no one aimed at Malia with intent to hurt her. The one exception was a grossly fat teenage boy with a red Afro who hurled a dozen rubber balls at her, shouting obscenities. One hit her in the nose, and she cried as blood flowed. The Zookeeper stood by helplessly. He was forbidden from intervening. Paragon had not been entirely jesting with his final remark about hospitalization. The only way to leave the cage before Sunday would be by sustaining a serious injury. Except if…an idea began forming in her mind.

Chapter 22
Ploreville Hears
(Monday–Thursday, September 14–17, 2093)

Emma called Marjory to the door. A thirtyish Plore dressed in dusty workmen's clothes, with thinning brown hair, his eyes bloodshot and tired, wanted to talk with her. He had rushed over from his house on hearing the news, with no time to change. Marjory took a quick look at the street from an upstairs window, but saw nothing unusual, let alone black jackets in the street, so she carefully descended the staircase and joined Emma.

"My boy was working at the Botanic Gardens today," said the man. "He's sixteen now, so we sent him to the City since his mother isn't well enough to work…" Marjory nodded, waited patiently.

"They've put people in zoo cages—six of them. They're all criminals, but not real criminals, just Social Credit crazy stuff, like celebrating Christmas or teaching math or smoking cigarettes…"

"But they're not Plores, are they?" Emma asked with concern.

"That's not the point, ma'am. What I'm trying to say—and excuse me, I'm not used to carrying important news, and not to people like you, is that one of them is your daughter-in-law. Her name is Malia, right?"

The women stared at him.

"Please come in, take a seat," Emma urged him. She went to bring him a lemonade and then she and Marjory held hands on the sofa, while the man sat opposite them in an armchair, apologizing for dirtying their carpets. He might have been a drywall installer, or maybe a housepainter like the husband of Christine, Emma and David's older sister.

The man seemed to think the hospitality called for additional detail, so he told them how his son had just been hired by the Social Tower's Pleasure and Recreation Division. This holiday week the boy was assigned to work at the Botanic Gardens and next week he would start at the indoor Tennis Palace in Anacosta, minimum SC score 140, handing out rackets and chasing balls so upper-class Social Crediteers could save their energy for the court game. Nothing unusual for a teenager with strong knees unable to finish high school in Ploreville.

"So he was assigned with another boy—he lives in Alexandria Ploreville, we don't know the family—to take care of the fifth and sixth cages. They have darts for shooting at the math teacher—all he wanted to do was teach real math, but he had to do it secretly because it's not Diversity math, you know…"

"What about my daughter-in-law?" Marjory cried.

"My son said they are showing her off to prove that you can't fool the Antifans and get away with escaping. They killed her husband—I'm sorry, ma'am, I know that is your son and your brother…" he nodded at Emma. "And there are tubs of little rubber balls that they want people to throw at her. She's sitting in a chair up in the cage, and they throw the balls at her, but my son said most people either don't have good aim or they feel sorry for her and don't try to hurt her.

"My son's job is to pick up the darts and balls outside the cage, and then during the breaks, when they put the prisoners downstairs, go into the cages and clean up there."

"That's really her? Are you sure?" Marjory asked. It would not be beneath Antifans to place a decoy in the role, just to convey the propaganda message, counting on Malia's obscurity to keep visitors from recognizing the dupe.

"She's kind of short to medium height, dark curly hair that's shoulder-length. Brown eyes. She'd be pretty under normal circumstances," said the man. "But that's only what my son told me."

"I'll have to go myself to see for sure," said Marjory. "They must have cut her hair."

"He did say it looked like it had been chopped off, not a normal haircut."

"Mom, they're not going to let you in the Gardens," Emma informed her. "Plores can't go in there unless they're working."

"Today was an exception because of the holiday," the man agreed. "Rest of the week, only Social Credit. Because of the holiday, low Social Credit can go all week, as a special treat, and don't have to wait for the weekend."

"Is there any way some of the workers could sneak us in?" asked Emma.

The man hesitated. "If any were caught doing it, they'd go to prison forthwith. My son doesn't know any of the other Plores except the other boy and maybe a groundskeeper or two now. They had lunch together, away from the Social Credit people. The overseer is Social Credit."

"And they'd see immediately we didn't have armbands," Marjory acknowledged. The armband with its myriad of tracking devices and soothing entertainment options was required of Social Credit citizens, whereas Plores enjoyed the privilege of bare arms, carrying a cell phone the old-fashioned way. The treaty had explicitly forbidden the DJR from forcing Plores to wear armbands, which at least allowed the Social Crediteers to identify and shun Plores.

"We'll figure this out," Marjory said. "There's got to be a way to get into the

Gardens." She knew that security personnel stationed at the entrances were tracking each visitor as he or she entered only for the ping of an approved armband. Ping, ping, ping. But chances were that the security personnel just sought to match the number of visitors and approving pings, and didn't look into the visitor's metadata unless someone triggered an alarm. When crowds were thick, as on weekends, the personnel could rely on heat sensor technology to identify anyone entering with a bare arm.

Around midnight, her mind racing, Marjory realized how she could make this happen. She showed up at Welcome's shop as soon as it opened.

On Thursday morning, Christine took the bus with Marjory to the Arlington side of the Route 50 tunnel. She would ensure that Marjory made it to the City side but wouldn't dare follow after that. Christine was skeptical that Marjory would manage to finagle her way into the Gardens, but she agreed that their mother needed to try. She had been willing to attempt it herself, and spare Marjory, but she and Emma realized that if the prisoner were truly Malia, she might not actually recognize them in the masked crowds, under the stress. They had only met her several times, four years ago. So Marjory had to be the one to go.

The bus blared constant propaganda, against which most of the Plore passengers wore music headphones or earpods. A new campaign was offering free food packages in return for attending an art show at St. James Catholic Church.

"Disgraceful," Christine whispered to her mother. "I've heard it's perverted."

"It's a good sign if they have to bribe people with food," Marjory murmured back, "nobody would go otherwise."

"The priest can't say no. The City says it'll stop providing utilities otherwise. And arrest him, treaty or no treaty."

They stopped talking, because informants rode the buses. What they were doing was dangerous enough without inviting more trouble.

At the tunnel entrance, Christine handed Marjory a cheap paper mask. The Mask of Safety and Caring campaign was in full force, and dozens of Plores had already been arrested or beaten on the streets of the City for trying to forgo theirs. "Here's an extra one, just in case," she told her mother. A loop of the cheap Chinese-made mask might snap, or a mask blow away in the steady breeze that morning.

The conveyor belt moved them steadily toward the City.

Even though Marjory technically did not need to wear her mask until she stepped outside the tunnel, it covered the bottom half of her face, which along with her hat and sunglasses helped her disguise herself as a working-age Plore. An elderly lady would invite suspicion, because only Plores employed in the City were permitted to enter; illegal Plores were not rare, but nowadays there was little incentive to visit the City under the new stricter regime. Marjory was wearing her blue wool coat, her best, and sensible shoes. Others on the belt might have thought her an aging counter clerk at a sandwich shop, or at a clothes shop catering to low-end Social Crediteers, and felt sorry that she had no younger relative to take on the burden of working in the City.

At the end of the conveyor belt, at the other end of the tunnel, they could not hesitate, lest they invite attention from the police officers stationed at the entrance. As planned, Christine squeezed her mother's hand, and turned around, back toward Ploreville. Marjory headed out into the sunshine, onto the large plaza.

Having been briefed, she knew that the buses waited on the left, and a variety of sundry stores selling snacks to the right. The heart of the City lay beyond; Social Crediteers wanted buffer space between themselves and the Plores pouring into the City to repair the toilets and tile the floors. Straight ahead was the Kennedy Center, which hosted the National Diversity Symphony, and approved plays and musicals.

Even though Marjory had eaten breakfast, she headed for the shops. About a dozen little sheds lined the walkway. They were owned by the City, but Social Crediteers managed them, selling ginseng iced tea and soy chips to hungry commuters. Behind the shops lay a small pocket park where tired Plores lingered before heading home, but at 9:00 a.m., it was empty. She sat on a green wooden bench, running her hand underneath it as David had taught her, just in case.

About five minutes later, Jeff Welcome showed up, carrying a cloth bag. Marjory saw his black armband still looked new and crisp. His eyes were tense. He reached into the bag, pulled out a smaller black armband and quickly fastened it around Marjory's left arm. "I'll take you up to the Gardens," he said, which relieved Marjory, who hadn't visited the City in many years.

The driverless bus automatically tallied her fare from the armband, which seemed to be working normally. Marjory didn't dare ask Jeff how he'd found the armband. She stared out the window at the giant glass towers that flanked the avenues. The streets were surprisingly empty for a rush hour. "Lots of people working from home these days," Jeff said shortly. Marjory observed that his hands were shaking slightly, which was strange, in one so young.

"Where are you working, Jeff?"

"Euthanasia Palace."

Marjory looked at him with dismay. "How did that happen?"

"I wanted to go to college. My dad might have told you that's why I went Social Credit, back in the spring. They promised me it would happen." He stared dully ahead.

"But when I asked about it, they said I must have misunderstood. If you're twenty-four, you're too old, they said, at least for on campus. They said, do your assignment for a year or two, show you're serious about Diversity, and maybe you can study online. But that's not what I had in mind, and won't I be even older then?"

Marjory sighed at the trickery. Welcome had tried to reason with his son, and to warn him of the devious ways of the Social Crediteers, but Jeff had been headstrong.

And now they had placed him in what, for a Plore, was the belly of the godless beast, where sickly or aged Social Crediteers went to die, or more precisely, to be made dead.

Jeff realized that in a crowded bus, anyone could overhear him.

"But I'm glad to be helping Diversity now," he said, louder. "It was a good move, overall." Marjory knew he was lying, and Jeff knew Marjory knew, but that was better than her actually believing him.

They exited the bus at the Gardens entrance, Jeff extending an arm to Marjory, who stepped off daintily. "It'll be a bit of a walk, if you can handle it."

"Thank you for taking the morning off to accompany me," she said, as they sailed through the entrance. Her armband was clearly legitimate.

"No problem, Mrs. Harris," he grimaced. "Always happy to take a day off."

"What exactly do you do there?"

"I wheel the guests around from one room to another, make them comfortable, show them movies, have them sign paperwork. Whatever they need me to do. I won't bring them the death pills, though, I said absolutely not. I don't care what they do to me, but I won't do that. They respect you when you stand up to them on a matter of principle. It's like they don't know how to handle it. It confuses them.

"But it's strange knowing that everyone I help will be dead in a few days. Nobody stays more than a week."

They approached the cage enclosure.

"You just want to see Malia, right? Not the others?" Jeff was relieved when Marjory nodded, saying, "It's awful. Don't look anywhere else." The lady in the first cage had been mauled to death yesterday, and the now-madwoman whose daughters had been stolen was howling at the spectators—in between long fuming silences—that they deserved to lose their own children. But since few had children, nobody empathized with her. "Look at the crazy fascist!" they laughed.

Malia sat almost tranquilly in the chair, on the beginning of her fourth day as a zoo exhibit. She felt that her presence was a blow for sanity and liberty, a reminder to the more thoughtful in the crowd that somewhere, not far away, a country existed where people could exercise their humanity. A small dark-haired boy ran around in the center green trailing a kite—she thought of Emmett. In a few years, he might be like that boy. But would he have a mother by then?

The Zookeeper, Bob, was responsible for some of her equanimity. Each evening, after the Gardens had closed, he would cook dinner for them and, against the rules, they would eat together outside, on the picnic table next to the cage. After dark, no one came around, and the only sounds were those of crickets and owls. A small lantern on their table illuminated their meal. He was a capable cook with the limited ingredients on offer.

For her jailer, Bob was surprisingly respectful.

"It's an honor to protect you," he told Malia over their Wednesday night dinner of grilled cheese sandwiches and bean soup. Malia found that a rather charming restatement of his assignment. "I've never known anyone who lived in the US, at least not since the war ended. What is it like? Is it true that the white supremacists are in control?"

"Not at all," said Malia. "It's a free country. As long as you don't harm anyone else, you can do what you like. What is your Diversity story?"

Bob hesitated. He rubbed his bearded chin, as if it helped him summon the words. "I grew up in Yramaland, on the Eastern Shore, in a white oppressor family, although we didn't know it then. My father was a truck driver and my mother cooked lunches at the elementary school, for the health insurance. I went to work for a landscaper, but then the war started, and I wanted to see some action, although I wasn't sure which side I was on. It was easier to be Red, given where we lived, but when things started going the Antifan way in our area, I switched over. My wife said it would be dangerous to be on the wrong side. We weren't very political, but we liked the idea of getting regular checks from the government. Of course, we didn't know they'd close our church, but we got used to the Mother Earth service. I mean, god is god, right? And I understood why people who had been oppressed deserved extra social credit points, that seemed fair. I took a class that told me all about why it was necessary.

"Then after the war, they hired me to be a groundskeeper here at the Gardens. It's forty Social Credit points, because it's the Gardens. I'm a 65, but that's enough, I don't mind living in Solar House because I'm not alone there. My wife died last year, so when they needed volunteers for the cages this week, I didn't mind. It's a break." Solar House was one of the giant complexes in which low Social Crediteers shared dormitory-style accommodations.

"I'm sorry about your wife," said Malia sincerely. Bob seemed only about seventy years old at most.

"Thank you. She had cervical cancer, and then when the doctors gave up, we got the letter from the Euthanasia Palace. The last week was good. She could order anything she wanted to eat. She wasn't hungry then, so I ate it instead of her. We held hands a lot." Bob pushed his plate away, and avoided meeting Malia's eyes. "I understand we can't afford to keep everyone alive, and everyone has their time..."

A few minutes later, out of the blue, he blurted, "If we had the real doctors, you know, the ones who are trained in China and who have to take science courses, maybe they would have found her cancer earlier...no, I shouldn't have said that...ours had a lot of Social Credit points, like 170, so she must have known something, right?"

Shortly after the park opened on Thursday, a lithe blonde woman pushed an expensive Chinese stroller bearing a small boy to Malia's cage. She and Malia locked eyes, and then the woman—whose nose and mouth were masked—looked away, frowning. She read the description on the electronic board. Then she grabbed a bunch of rubber balls and began hurling them at Malia. One hit Malia in the nose, which began to bleed.

"Hey!" Malia said, emboldened by the fact they were alone. "Don't you have any shame? What kind of example are you setting for your son?"

A loudspeaker suddenly erupted above her. "Exhibits must not speak to the visitors. Exhibits must not speak."

The woman gave her a hostile stare. "Your husband was my partner. If you hadn't come along, he would have married me. I had to have my child on my own. We could have been happy together, and instead you got him killed."

Malia realized this must be Kate Langley, 190, the ADF senior commander's daughter whom David had refused to date again after meeting her, Malia. Malia knew that even then, David had lost interest in Kate.

"You're fooling yourself, Kate," she shouted back. "He said you were more boring than rocks."

The woman burst into tears and pushed the stroller away, as Malia, for good measure, yelled at her, "We have two sons! Together!" But of course, they were not together, not anymore.

Two uniformed guards emerged from the panopticon and headed toward her cage. When they saw the cause of the commotion departing, however, they also desisted. Several more visitors were now gravitating to Malia's cage, staring up at her. Disciplining the exhibit would have caused more trouble than the effort was worth.

Malia told herself, you are a queen. Pretend you are receiving emissaries from a foreign land, and you are too exalted to acknowledge them directly. Let them admire you. Never mind that blood is running down your lip and drying on your chin.

Within the next fifteen minutes, a crowd stood before her cage. She ignored the balls, mostly tossed good-naturedly, as if at a picnic. The balls that hit her were nowhere near as hard as those Kate had thrown. The Plore boy scrambled to pick up the ones that bounced off the bars or even went through one set of bars and out another. People in the crowd called out, "Hey, traitor!" before they let a ball fly, or "Fascist!" Some laughed, "Bet you wish you was in St. Louis now!"

Malia daydreamed. At least I'm not the one wearing a mask, she thought.

Then she sensed, rather than saw, a pair of eyes intently staring at her from below. She awakened from her near-trance to recognize her mother-in-law. But why was she wearing an armband? Or more precisely, how had she acquired it? Marjory put her finger quickly to her lips, or to the cloth covering them, and then she crossed her hands in front of her heart, uncrossing them quickly. Cameras would catch any more sustained interaction. Malia smiled gently at her. They spoke to each other silently, conveying their love, but unable to share their mutual confidence that David was somehow still alive. Until now, she had thought of Marjory only as David's mother. Malia had never known her own mother, but now she had one.

After about ten minutes, Marjory left, pushing politely through the crowd. The owner of the armband, a middle-aged woman in Jeff's building who was pretending to be sick to stay at home that morning, but was willing to rent the armband to Jeff for a sizable sum, needed it back before any monitor detected a discrepancy between where the woman was supposed to be and where the armband was. It was worth the risk; most likely any monitor would assume the woman was malingering and had instead headed down to the gardens on a holiday week. Such a trick wouldn't interest Beaufort at all—it wasn't political, so just a police matter. But if Marjory lingered, the chances would increase of some employee realizing an armband belonging to a fifty-year-old black woman was actually encasing the arm of a much older white Plore.

They retraced their steps, with Jeff making sure that Marjory reached the tunnel safely. He called Christine to give her Marjory's arrival time, so that Christine was awaiting her at the other end.

"Was it her?" Christine asked eagerly when Marjory met her at the other end of the tunnel and they emerged into the bright sunshine of Arlington.

"Yes," Marjory said. "And she was like a martyr, sitting in that chair, tied down, ignoring all the mean words and the little rubber balls. There was blood on her face—someone must've hit her hard with a ball before I got there."

"Did she see you? Did she recognize you?"

"Yes, I pushed my way to the front, and we looked at each other for ten minutes until I had to go. We tried to say as much as we could without actually speaking. I did this…" Marjory demonstrated the fingers-to-masked-lips motion, "and then this…" (the crossed arms). "I tried to tell her how much we loved her, even though I couldn't speak."

"She knew that just by your being there this morning," Christine said. "She must know you took a big risk to be there. You wouldn't have done it if you didn't love her so much."

They were waiting alone for the bus, in the middle of day, so they felt safe talking, for the moment. "But what now?" asked Marjory, without expecting an answer.

"Write it up," Christine urged her. "Put it in the bulletin and send it up and down the coast to all the Plorevilles. So all the Plores will know how the Antifans are treating the wife of the greatest hero we've seen since the war."

"Is he?" Marjory mulled. "Yes, he's a great hero. But where is he?"

The bus pulled up to the stop and Christine reached into her faded blue denim jacket for the phone to pay their fares. They kept a practiced silence until they reached Emma's house where the family was waiting.

Chapter 23
No Man Is A Number
(Thursday–Friday, September 17–18, 2093)

Marjory's visit had heartened Malia. You are not forgotten, she told herself. For that reason, she had postponed her original plan for the afternoon, because she wanted some time to think about the meaning of Marjory's visit and to relish the evidence that someone besides Beaufort, someone who cared, knew she was imprisoned. Also, the crowds were thinner on Thursday afternoon than Malia had expected. As her mind whirred, she barely heard the jeers or felt the balls thud on her limbs and chest. At night, she was surprised to see all the bruises.

When the Gardens closed for the night, Bob quickly untied her and they hurried downstairs. "Crab cakes!" he said triumphantly. A Social Credit buddy able to travel from the Outer Plore areas near Chesapeake Bay had brought him live crabs last weekend, and he had cooked them immediately and saved them in the freezer. "You won't get this in your Healthy Eating bag," he told her. Once darkness had safely fallen around them, and all the workers gone home, they sat outside eating crab cakes and a delicious tomato-cucumber salad. "I found some parsley," he said, "just like in the old days. Makes a difference, don't it?"

Bob told her how to store live crabs, and then how to put them in a freezer for about fifteen minutes before you dropped them in boiling water. "It's more humane," he said. "No point having them suffer any more than necessary."

Malia thought grimly that all around them was more suffering than necessary, in fact as much suffering as humans could bear, but not quite as much as humans could bear to watch, given the apparently high tolerance of the visitors for the spectacles in the cages.

"But they're good, aren't they?" Bob pleaded, noticing the frown on Malia's face in the lantern light. She agreed the crab cakes were quite good. Bob beamed.

The next afternoon, the crowds grew in anticipation of the weekend. Bold low Social Crediteers wangled early dismissal from jobs, and high Social Crediteers were lured from their offices in the Knowledge Tower and the Economic Tower and the Diversity Warehouse by the sunshine and perfect late summer weather. Malia watched an ice cream vendor ("Organic pure soy milk ice! Save Mother Earth!" he called) wend his way through the crowds, doing a brisk business.

A band of children—about nine or ten years old, she guessed—were playing Antifa Riot on the central green, organizing themselves by racial and sexuality group and meting out punishments accordingly. Malia remembered playing that game at the orphanage, usually garnering a bruise or two from having foolishly agreed to play the policewoman who attempted to arrest Antifans.

A few minutes later, the teacher corralled the band of children for their instructive walk past the cages, the price to pay for the fun excursion. They were starting with the smoking man, since the dog woman's cage was empty. It had been hard to find a replacement for her on short notice, and the smells were unbearable anyway. Malia decided she would wait for the children to arrive at her cage. It was almost three o'clock.

By the time the children lined up before her, Malia was satisfied with the size of the crowd. Ten rows of viewers stood before her in gently rising rows so that no one might be deprived of a good view. Balls landed around her, like fat raindrops, several in her lap. People jostled to read the signboards. A large electronic one above the cage also informed them of her crimes, "Malia Jenness, 70, Traitor, Recaptured in the US by the Heroic Antifan Defense Forces."

Her eyes scanned the masked audience. The children watched her from the front row, balls in their small hands that they did not quite dare to throw at an adult, even though their teacher reassured them it was perfectly all right to punish a traitor. Elderly people stood just behind the children, leaning on canes or walkers. Young men and women jeered at her. Low Social Crediteers' faces were grim, since her resistance to the same status, and her escape, only exposed their cowardice. High Social Crediteers were disdainful because she had betrayed their system in rejecting it, and triumphant because they had the last word now, which was as it should be.

"Diversans!" she announced. Now there was no return. "Once you were Americans. Once you were a free people!"

"Exhibits must not speak! Exhibits must not speak to visitors!" the loudspeaker screeched. Malia knew she had about a minute before they would silence her. After a brief catcall or two, the audience fell completely silent.

"We lived under the Constitution of the United States, which respected our God-given rights to speak, to worship God, to assemble peacefully, to own and bear firearms, to complain to the government for redress of our grievances. We voted for our representatives to make laws and to protect our freedoms. This is how a free people lives.

"Not far away, in the so-called fascist United States, Americans enjoy all these freedoms today. I know this because I lived for four years among Americans. They are even more diverse than we are, because people want to live in the US, and they come from all over the world to do so. Americans read whatever books—yes, books—they want! They watch any movie they want. No one lives as a number! No one is superior to another because the government tells him he is! No man is a number!"

The crowd stared at her, mouths agape. Three guards emerged from the panopticon and ran, awkwardly and foolishly, in her direction. They were not the youngest or fittest security officers. Other listeners, slack-jawed, loosened their grip on balls that dropped silently from their hands onto the ground. A few spectators at the edges of the crowd drifted off cautiously, sensing trouble was coming.

"The DJR divides you by giving you numbers, by defining you by the color of your skin, your preferred sexual partners, your ethnic background. They do not define you by your character. St. Martin Luther King Jr. once said he looked forward to the day when his children would not be judged by the color of their skin, but by the content of their character. And yet, by law, all we care about today is color and sex!

"The DJR does not want you to have character, because character is inconvenient to them. They want you to be their slaves, without character. You are slaves to tyrants who work you until you are no longer of use, and then they send you to the Euthanasia Palace to kill you! No one in the world is oppressed like you are! The Plores live more like free people than you do!"

The guards were now calling "Zookeeper! Zookeeper!" as they rattled the lock to the outside door of the cage, the one the boys climbed through during breaks to retrieve balls. The guards did not have the keys, or had run from the panopticon without grabbing them. Bob must have stepped away. She knew he sometimes disappeared on breaks to drink with the math teacher's keeper behind that cage, which got fewer visitors than hers.

"Demand your rights! I have been kidnapped from Oklahoma, stolen from my husband, a Plore, an Antifan, who is a hero! I have two young boys at home, and if the ADF is correct, my husband is dead, and my boys are fatherless, and now motherless… but unlike you, they live in freedom!" The crowd rippled slightly at the now somewhat daring mention of mothers and fathers, rather than birthing and nonbirthing parents, which was the new fashion under Paragon.

She pointed to the children in the front row. "Children, I feel sorry for you. You are also in a cage, a cage called the Diversity Justice Republic!" Several children, not yet bereft of kindness, cried to think about the two little boys whose mother had been put in a cage. One or two of the brightest recalled the madwoman two cages back whose children had been stolen from her.

Bob ran up the stairs into the cage, and opened the door for the guards. He had been napping downstairs.

Malia knew her time was up. "What kind of depraved government places human beings in a zoo and encourages you to abuse them? Be kind to each other! Show this evil government how human beings, who are not numbers, treat each other! We are children of the living God, not a pile of dirt…"

The guards leaped into the cage and buried Malia under a flurry of fists. Steve Rosen's diktat was unknown here. Bob sliced through the bindings with a knife, and then the foursome gagged and bound her and carried her downstairs into the basement. The guards threw her in a corner of the basement on the hard cement floor while they waited for the crowd to disperse. An ambulance from Beaufort was already pulling discreetly into the service road behind the cages.

Malia looked up through bloodied eyes, swallowing blood, to see the once-genial Bob glaring at her. He had shown her kindness, as you would a pathetic injured animal, and she had repaid it by biting his hand. Malia realized she had given no thought to how her rebellion would implicate Bob. By evening he would be in a Beaufort cell himself, although he would be released several days later and returned with dire warnings to the groundskeeping crew.

Malia could not permit herself regret. Esau in the Old Testament had sold his birthright for a mess of pottage. Should she have done the same for a bucket of crabs?

The crowd had scattered once the guards started yelling and rattling the bars of the cage, and the remaining few fled once the beating began.

No one wanted to be interrogated later on what they had overheard. Some zoo visitors would tell their partners, in whispers, away from the armbands, what the madwoman had shouted at them. "The United States…she said it was a good place to live. People can read or watch anything they like…"

But Malia had been cruel to these people, as she had been cruel to Bob. Even if they were more enlightened than they had been before her outburst, and they were able to fairly consider her words, they had no outlet for acting on them. The contrast between their own misery and the free world she had painted for them was unbearable. Even Malia would have been helpless to act on her own awakening had not David, with his Antifan connections and resourcefulness, appeared in her life.

Each listener resolved the cognitive dilemma differently. Some simply brushed aside her words as an example of "the Big Lie," which the DJR media used to describe the notion that life was better in the United States. Some told themselves that Malia might be right, but since they could do nothing to improve their lot, they refused to think of her words, except longingly at night. Others convinced themselves that at least in the DJR, they never had to worry about where their next meal came from, and they were taken care of by the government. "She never talked about unemployment in the US," they told themselves triumphantly, having discovered the flaw in her reasoning. "Or having to live in payment-based housing."

But one onlooker was a junior diplomat from the Embassy of Texas on his first foreign tour for the Texas Intelligence Agency. By nighttime, his report would be in the hands of his superiors in Austin, who would bring it to the attention of their counterparts in St. Louis, in return for an unspecified favor.

Chapter 24
Call to Repentance
(Friday, September 18, 2093)

Paragon was reporting to Montoya and Rosen on the disaster at the Gardens that afternoon. Neither had known that Malia Harris was on display at the zoo, and had dismissed the exhibition as another of Paragon's Diversity morale circuses, not worth the attention of ADF seniors.

"You might at least have told us you were doing this," said Rosen. "You know she's a sensitive case." His wife and younger daughter had been at the Gardens that afternoon, but fortunately nowhere near the zoo when Malia's outburst happened.

Paragon scowled. "This was meant to symbolize her repentance. Next week she was to begin an intense course of Diversity religious thought. Repentance, then learning." He thought, don't hand her over to me and then forget about it. You want credit for winning her back, but you leave the dirty work to me.

"What about all those people who heard her rant?" Montoya drummed a pen on his desk, a sure sign of stress. "That was blatant knowledge crime. How do we do damage control here?"

"We've done a chip scan on the area at that time," said Paragon. "Every person who heard her will be questioned and monitored for deviance for at least a year, with a truth serum test at the end of the year."

"Including the children?" Rosen asked.

"Especially the children," responded Paragon, "while their brains are still malleable and we can rectify any damage. All the children will be brought to the Youth Incubation Farm for the school year. We have footage of one girl who we saw push a rose through the bars at the prisoner. She's already been apprehended."

"And everyone who was there today has told at least one other person about it," grumbled Montoya. "I hope that no Plores snuck into the crowd. And now what do we do with the bitch? I told you it might just have been easier to finish her off a month ago. Now we've got a problem."

Paragon bristled at the rebuke. "She's in the cell immediately next to the firing range. I thought if you ordered her execution, at least it would be convenient." The firing range was a long cement hall with a back wall stained red after thirty years of constant use.

Rosen sighed. "What if there was a foreigner in the crowd?" Like Plores, foreigners would have neither chips nor armbands, and would have shown their passport at the gate to the Gardens for admission. "How are we going to explain if St. Louis finds out and starts asking about her?"

Paragon looked to Montoya. Montoya's dislike for women had become particularly pronounced since he had brought the glamorous Antifan songster Carolina Cruz into his house and bed last year, dispatching his irritable dumpy wife off to some retirement community in Florida. After his initial lust had been slaked, he realized that at least his wife had been an excellent cook and now he had to rely on an indifferent Antifan cook or deliveries from restaurants. You could force a woman into your bed, but you could not force her to cook a decent meal.

"Can she hear the volleys from her cell?" the director asked.

"Oh yes," said Paragon, "she'll hear them all night."

"That's a good start. Maybe she'll be more cooperative on Sunday." Montoya's beady dark eyes bored into Paragon's. "If we don't just finish her off tonight."

Rosen was now standing at the window, gazing at the Anacosta skyline through the venetian blinds.

Malia stared up at the bare light bulb embedded in the ceiling of the cell. Her jaws and limbs ached painfully from the beating at the zoo. She had woken up here, not in her VIP quarters, in the cell at the very bottom level of eighty-story Beaufort, with its clammy gray cement walls. A centipede crawled up the wall above her cot. The only other furniture in the room was the steel toilet, which she used, and a small sink that provided a spurt of cold water with the push of a square metal button.

Oh my God, she panicked, as her tongue probed a new wide gap between two teeth. I've lost a tooth. She felt dried blood on her face. She wet her hands and rubbed delicately, not able to see her reflection, but hoping she was now more presentable. But for what?

She wished she dared ask for another blanket, and now she was hungry as well. Her neighbors had eaten their last meal hours earlier, but Malia did not realize where she was right now. She assumed she was back at Beaufort, just in worse quarters. Surely they would feed her, she hoped, counting on relentless adherence to prison routine. Even Health Meat would be welcome, just to silence the rumbling in her stomach, the loudest noise in the cellblock.

She sat on the cot with the blanket wrapped around her shoulders, listening for clues to where she was. Suddenly she heard a man shouting farther down the corridor. She made out "I'm innocent! I love Diversity!" amid a spray of curses from the Antifan guards. They were approaching her cell, since the man's cries and the guards' snarls became louder and more decipherable instead of one long angry shout. Malia tensed, but then a blur passed by the bars in the small window of her cell door, not stopping, and then she heard a large metal door creak open, only to shut firmly.

Several minutes later, she heard a steady rumbling next door, through her wall. It lasted about three long seconds. What is that? she thought. Twenty minutes later, another shouting man was shoved past her cell, with cursing guards. Metal door opened, metal door slammed shut. Another few seconds of rumbling.

Now Malia knew where she was. The killing hallway. This was the assignment that David had loathed, twenty years earlier. He had walked down this very corridor on forty or fifty weekend nights in a row, only feet away from where she sat now, and even though he was in no danger himself, had sweated as much as any knowledge criminal awaiting his end. As his mother had told him, "God sees everything you do." It occurred to Malia that David had probably entered this very cell to extract a condemned prisoner for his execution, but it was not the David she liked to think about.

"Last meal?" a guard offered through the bars. It was in effect, the intermission between executions.

"Yes, please," said Malia. She felt numb, not frightened. The door opened and the guard, a middle-aged black man, opened a small folding table next to her cot, placing on it a covered stainless steel plate, a can of cola, and a small plate with a slice of lemon cake in the corner.

"You wouldn't do better in the Euthanasia Palace," joked the guard as he left.

As he left, Malia called out, "Could I have another blanket, please?"

"What is this, a hotel?" he retorted, which was the standard polite Antifan reply to any prisoner request. But he was a kinder man than most Antifan guards, or maybe she still retained some shreds of VIP status, because ten minutes later he did in fact bring her a second blanket. "Not that you'll need it very long," he joked again. He pressed the electronic button on the outside, firmly locking her door.

Malia was grateful for the small kindness. To her surprise, when she lifted the cover, she found a real steak, nicely cooked, asparagus, and small red potatoes. It was the best meal she had eaten in two months in Antifan custody. Her spirits were strangely fortified by the good humor of the guard, which bespoke normality.

Another tooth must have been loose, because she could only eat the steak gingerly. Her cardboard knife was useless, so she tore small bits from the steak with her fingers. While she ate, two more condemned prisoners were dragged past her, but they were either resigned or unconscious because neither shouted or protested their innocence.

The fifth condemned prisoner was a woman, who screamed all the way down the hall. Something about a man who was really responsible for Gina's death. "My baby!" she sobbed. "I didn't do it! Gina!" The guards did not even bother to curse at her, just hauled her along like a sack of potatoes. The metal door opened, the metal door slammed, and a few minutes later another rumble of gunfire.

Malia waited for her turn, for them to open her door in a burst of black uniforms and colorless eyes, but they seemed to be clearing out the rest of the hallway first. She was now regretting her speech earlier that same day—was it only a few hours ago? Was that speech worth dying for tonight? She had recklessly indulged her spite and passion and now she realized she would never see David or her sons again. What good had it done? Maybe twenty people in the crowd would remember what she had shouted at them, and one or two might believe her, but they would never dare share their insight with others. Her efforts to arouse them would wilt in parched soil. And she regretted never having an opportunity to confront Paragon before her death. She had wanted revenge on him for placing her in the zoo, and she had longed to witness his reaction to her betrayal and her speech to the onlookers. Now indifferent strangers would destroy her and she would never enjoy revenge.

She awakened, and then jerked, startled. She knew many hours had passed, even though it was dark in her dungeon, because she felt refreshed by her deep sleep. But she was very much alive, even though her whole body now ached, and now the fear that she had kept at bay last night rushed in. Over a dozen human beings on this corridor had been extinguished, almost before her eyes, but she had been spared, at least last night. It was deadly quiet, as if she were very much alone, not as if other prisoners were sleeping. She did not sense that others were sharing this floor with her—no toilet flushed, no voices murmured, no guards yelled.

The door opened, and in her fear, she fell back, crouching against the cement wall. But it was only a guard, not the same as last night's, declaring "Breakfast!" Either her status had diminished, or there was no such thing as a "last breakfast," since he delivered only a bowl of gray cereal and a cup of some odd orangeade. Clearly not as jovial as her last guard, the young white man with tattooed arms refused to meet her eyes. Malia did not dare ask him for anything, although she would have liked the toothbrush from her VIP quarters. Her mouth felt dry and stale. She rinsed it with cold water from the sink.

When the guard came for the table and dishes, he delivered a copy of the Mother Earth Diversity (MED) Bible. "Our leader Paragon himself sent this to you," he said, now admiringly, because this woman must indeed be a very exalted prisoner to receive a gift from the political commissar of the ADF. "To give you comfort in your final moments." In the break room, his fellow guards had told the young man that the woman was in fact the widow of the infamous traitor Antifan.

This did not give Malia much hope that she had been spared after all. Maybe they had run out of ammunition last night. Maybe Paragon was dragging out her agony, out of sheer vindictiveness. Indeed, her isolation and idleness only made her fear more palpable, because she knew that another night of executions was approaching with each slow hour. Sometimes she heard other cell doors open and close as prisoners were brought downstairs to await their final hours.

The hours passed slowly, but not as slowly as they might have had the evil night ahead not loomed. Malia thumbed through the pages of the MED Bible, familiar to her from her orphanage and Anacostan days. In fact, still more familiar to her than the Bible of the Christians to whom she now belonged. The MED Bible was organized thematically into six books: the Book of Greta was about the sin of climate change denial; the Book of Floyd about racism; the Book of Dworkin (feminism); the Book of Milk (sexuality liberation); and the Book of Money Evil (capitalism); all culminating in the Book of Intersectional Joy, in which Mother Earth benignly cast her love over the Diverse People and destroyed the white supremacists.

Malia's thoughts wandered back to her argument—how ridiculous now—with David on their last morning together. Now she had to reconsider, in the stillness of a condemned prisoner's cell, whether her pedestrian ambitions really mattered. When they were still in the DJR, they had vowed to do something for those left behind when they could, after they had escaped to freedom. Yet once they had reached the United States, they had forgotten the imprisoned masses—Social Credit and Plores—except for their own relatives. The Antifans had reminded them, brutally, of their forgotten promises. Burrowing into suburban obscurity had not saved them.

"If you save me," she prayed silently to the one true God, hoping He would not take offense at the noxious MED Bible on the cot before her, "I will do whatever is necessary to help destroy the DJR. And save the people trapped here. Maybe I will do it through becoming a professor, maybe through working for the AIA. Maybe in some other way invisible to me today. I put myself in Your hands.

"And if David is alive, bring us together again so that we can combine our strength and fulfill our promise. Please send me a sign that he still lives. Thank you, Lord."

A burly guard of ambiguous ethnicity entered with a stale yellow roll and a cup of water on a tray, her lunch. She stared at his muscled tattooed arms as he placed the tray on the cot. She saw a red snake coiled around "Diversity or Death." No table this time.

"You're going soon to join your traitor husband," he mocked her as he left.

"Thank you," said Malia sweetly. Short of David appearing in her cell with his confident smile and tousled blond hair, or her dreaming about him if she was allowed another night's sleep, that was the best sign she was going to receive.

About ten miles north of Beaufort, Steve Rosen parked his SUV outside a Plore school just over the border from the City in Rockville. It was a plausible place to park a privately owned vehicle in Ploreville, since vehicle ownership was banned for most urban Plores and a car would have sparked curiosity on a residential side street. Social Crediteers taught in the Ploreville schools, so he could park at Kamala Harris High School, and if Anacosta Police did a tag search, they would not be alarmed that the vehicle associated with a high-ranking ADF officer would be parked there, not far from Beaufort. It was usually not in the interest of the Anacosta Police to pursue any otherwise unexceptional lead connected with Antifans.

The tall, gray-haired Antifan officer in his midfifties walked northward, until he reached a street lined with shabby ramblers with scrabbly lawns. Occasionally he tentatively thrust a hand inside his jacket, to make sure the small thick volume was still there. For these excursions he always tried to dress as a Plore might—he wore the old cloth jacket he used for gardening and denim jeans—but his confident stride belonged to someone at home in the DJR, not a harried Plore. And his shoes were a very good quality fake leather, not shiny vinyl or cloth. Fortunately, it was a damp, overcast day in sharp contrast to yesterday's brilliant sunshine—and almost no one was lounging outside.

Most of the houses, however small, were occupied by multiple families. Very few Plore families could afford to live in even a single-family house, what with the taxes and the utility bills. The putative owners—deeds having been converted to hundred-year leaseholds from the government—found it necessary to rent to other Plores. Rockville city hall reserved the right to assign needy families or individuals to various properties. It seemed to take special satisfaction in parceling out sex offenders and drug users to young families or elderly couples.

Rosen went around to the back entrance of the humble ranch house on Portland Drive. It was futile to expect to avoid neighbors' curiosity, so he just tried to look natural. When he had first started coming here, Rosen had taken some initial precautions by looking up the surveillance records for the address, burying the request amid other addresses of no real interest to him. One could always come up with an excuse about an investigation regarding Plore black market dealing. The sole report by the Anacosta Police in ADF files had dismissed a neighbor's complaints of frequent traffic as merely indicating drug sales or fencing of stolen goods. This was not sufficiently offensive activity to cause the indolent Anacosta Police to investigate further. Unless someone was killed at this address, the occupants would be left in peace. The Anacosta Police counted on Plores to police their own, up to a point.

A small black-bearded man wearing a skullcap opened the door for him. "Shabbat shalom, *chaver*," *friend*, he said. "We've been waiting for you." Inside, at a metal folding table, sat an older, gray-bearded man, with twinkling blue eyes and wearing a black skullcap.

"Gut Shabbes, rabbi," said Rosen. Good Sabbath.

"Gut Shabbes," said the rabbi. "Sit down, and let's learn. And let me touch that *siddur*," or prayer book, "of yours. That gives me great comfort. We have so few reminders of our great and holy past among us now."

Rosen brought out the little burgundy leather-bound book, perhaps three by four inches. The worn binding said "Daily Prayers." This little book, with its yellowed pages and frayed cover edges, bore a publication date of 1938, just before the Holocaust had consumed the Jews of Europe. It was now over 150 years old. Rosen had found it among his father's belongings when he went to Florida twenty years ago after Michael Rosen's death. How this volume had survived repeated purges of religious books and items Rosen did not know. Possession of this volume would have constituted a knowledge crime, since it was clearly unconnected to the pallid version of Jewish worship permitted under the MED Church. And it was bound in leather, which was illegal except for Antifan uniforms and furniture.

Not knowing what else to do with the book, but afraid to throw it in the recycling dumpster, the young Rosen had shoved it in his inside jacket pocket, much as he had done before setting out for Rockville that afternoon. No one would have confronted the Antifan commander let alone demanded he hand it over, but all the way back on the train from Orlando to Anacosta, Rosen still feared its discovery. He was a deputy commander, not the deputy director, and still needed to obey the law, or at least some laws. Once home, he did not mention the book to his wife, Vicki, a devout worshiper in the MED Church, Protestant division, but hid it in an old shoebox and forgot about it for two decades.

The book had been handed down to Michael Rosen by his own aging father, before the DJR's founding, who in turn had inherited it in stages from a great-great-grandfather on the Lower East Side of New York, a union organizer, a man who preached socialism yet still could not break the ties to his ancient faith. The book had been honored more in the breach of its commandments than in worship. Here it was, in disrepair, but here all the same. Michael Rosen would not have dared show this dangerous book to his son, who had put aside his faith after his bar mitzvah in 2049 and at the age of eighteen had joined the Antifan side in the Diversity civil war.

"Tomorrow night is the beginning of the holiest period in our faith," said Rabbi Goldberg. They sat across from each other at the metal table. Upstairs could be heard the pattering of children's feet. "Tomorrow night begins Rosh Hashanah, the Jewish New Year, meaning 'the head of the year.' Ten days later will come Yom Kippur, the Day of Atonement. Between Rosh Hashanah and Yom Kippur, God judges every soul on earth and decides who shall be inscribed in the Book of Life for the coming year. For those ten days, we must seek forgiveness from those we have wronged and we must scrutinize our behavior with even greater urgency than usual."

Seek forgiveness from those we have wronged? Rosen thought, almost panicked. Where would I start? He had been faithful to his wife, and a loving father to his two grown daughters, but the list of Antifan victims he had indifferently overseen was long. You did not become ADF Deputy Director, 275, without great sinning.

"If you could join us for a minyan for the holidays, we would appreciate it," said Goldberg. "It is hard to find the ten men we need in Ploreville to be able to read the Torah and for mourners to say Kaddish," or the prayer for the dead. "We have so few

Jews in Ploreville these days." Most Jews had sided with the Diversity forces, and ended up on the Social Credit side when the war ended unless they were already in the United States. Others had taken advantage of a brief opportunity immediately after the war, brokered by the Mossad, to emigrate to Israel. Then the gate had closed, permanently. The rest had assimilated quickly into the DJR mainstream, after bleating pathetically that they were an oppressed Diverse minority like blacks and Latinx. Nobody believed them. They still behaved like oppressors, if only in assuming that justice could be theirs upon claiming it.

"I know it is a risk for you," said Goldberg. He had realized that Rosen was in the ADF, and could tell he had risen to a high level, just from his bearing and self-assurance. Rosen had given his name as Steve Rosselli, which Goldberg suspected might not be his real one. But the Social Credit armband was real enough. "Could you come tomorrow night? And on Yom Kippur, the holiest of all days, a week from Wednesday?"

Rosen reluctantly agreed, unable to refuse, even though the holiest day was a normal workday.

"What if I cannot seek forgiveness from those I've wronged?" he finally asked. "If they are...no longer here?" He could not bring himself to utter the word "alive."

"You can still atone," said Goldberg. "But atonement must be sincere. If it comes easily, you are not fully repenting. This is why we also fast—no water or food—from sundown when the holiday begins to an hour after the next sundown. If we can show self-discipline in refraining from food, from drink, from work, and from sexual relations, we can show self-discipline in our relations with others."

An hour later, Rosen left the house, in the midst of a gloomy twilight. The words of Goldberg rang in his ears: "You may not be able to seek forgiveness from those you have wronged, but you can do your best to help and protect others now that you are aware of your duty to other human beings. It may not be easy for you—I suspect that your position requires you to be brutal when you would rather not be—but when you have an opportunity to do right, you must take it."

And this time, Rosen had left the book with Goldberg, realizing that it was safer with this man, in this humble house in Ploreville, than in the elegant house of the deputy director of the Antifan Defense Forces, 275 or not. "It remains yours, of course," said the rabbi. "But let it stay for now with friends, where we can take it out of its hiding place and enjoy its presence and it can enjoy ours."

Rosen immediately drove to Montoya's house, unannounced. The Antifan sentry outside recognized Rosen, saluted, and called inside.

Montoya came to the door, wearing a button-down blue shirt and black slacks. Behind him Rosen saw a petulant-looking Carolina Cruz, clad in a metallic jumpsuit. Her large breasts strained against the thin material. Rosen could not help noticing them, but detachedly. Carolina was Montoya's problem now, he thought, and David

Harris was lucky to have escaped her seductive wiles when the ADF had used her to try to separate him from Malia.

"Join us for dinner, Rosen?" Montoya asked, but curious.

"Thanks for the invitation, but my wife is expecting me home. Can we talk in privacy?"

Montoya's eyebrows rose, but he ushered Rosen inside.

Chapter 25
Her Aim Is True
(Wednesday, September 23, 2093)

David answered the phone at work. "Hello, David Harris here."

"David, this is Vernal. We have news. Would you mind calling us back from your secure room?"

"Good news, bad news?" he asked eagerly.

"Both," Vernal said, "call me when you get home."

No, David would not mind. He left Capettone in a hurry, and in twenty minutes was logging onto the computer in the basement. The house was quiet. The boys now spent their days with Fern and their cousin Ivy Ann. David tried to forget that yesterday George had called Fern Mama.

"What's the news?" he asked curtly. No time for pleasantries. "Good or bad?"

"Malia is alive. She is in Antifan custody in Anacosta, as you suspected might be the case. We received a report from TIA. One of their case officers saw her in the Gardens in Anacosta and shared the report with us."

"The Gardens?" David was bewildered. "What was she doing wandering around the Gardens?"

"She wasn't wandering around. She was tied to a chair in a cage—."

David inhaled. "What?"

Vernal continued, in that cheerfully clueless way that David hated, "They were having some kind of zoo in the Gardens all last week in honor of National Security Day and they had a different kind of Social Credit criminal in different cages. Texas said in one cage they had a woman with dogs who was there for wearing a fur coat, and there was a man who taught math illegally—"

"Never mind that," David said sharply, but this was certainly a bizarre descent from the Anacosta and ADF he had known. "Were they hurting her? Was she all right?"

"They provided little rubber balls for the spectators to throw at her but she didn't seem to be injured, according to the Texas officer. Just a few bruises from the balls. But then she gave a speech to the crowd...Why don't I just forward you the report?"

"A speech?" Who gave speeches in Anacosta, other than the president and very top officials? It also didn't seem like the reserved Malia he knew.

In another minute, David was scanning the report on the screen.

———————————————

RD 13-54646-0922293

FROM: TEXAS INTELLIGENCE AGENCY

VIA: AIA AUSTIN

TO: ST. LOUIS

RE: TIA LOCATES MALIA HARRIS AT ANACOSTA BOTANICAL GARDENS

DJR CITIZEN AND US RESIDENT MALIA HARRIS, WHO WENT MISSING ON 9 AUGUST JUST NORTH OF THE TEXAS-US BORDER, APPEARS TO BE IN ADF CUSTODY IN ANACOSTA.

TIA OFFICER 347YG, ASSIGNED TO OUR EMBASSY IN ANACOSTA, WENT TO THE GARDENS ON FRIDAY 18 SEPTEMBER.

A ZOO EVENT WAS BEING HELD IN HONOR OF NATIONAL SECURITY DAY, THE MAIN HOLIDAY CELEBRATING THE ADF. THE ZOO EVENT IS AN INNOVATION BY THE POLITICAL COMMISSAR OF THE ADF, COMMANDER KHALID MA. SIX GIANT CAGES RING A CENTRAL GREEN WITH A...*[More description of the premises and of the other exhibits]*

MALIA HARRIS WAS IN THE FIRST CAGE ON THE LEFT AS ONE ENTERS THE CIRCULAR ZOO AREA. ELECTRONIC SCREENS ABOVE AND TO THE SIDES DESCRIBED HER ALLEGED CRIME OF ESCAPING THE DJR AND THE TREACHERY OF HER HUSBAND, FORMER ANTIFAN COMMANDER DAVID HARRIS. SHE WAS TIED TO A CHAIR WITH ARMS, AND...*[More description]* SHE SEEMED IN GOOD HEALTH, OTHER THAN A BRUISE ON HER FOREHEAD, PRESUMABLY FROM A RUBBER BALL IMPACT.

AT ABOUT 3:15 P.M., MRS. HARRIS BEGAN DECLAIMING TO THE CROWD...SHE ADDRESSED THEM AS "DIVERSANS" AND TOLD THEM THAT ONCE AS AMERICANS, THEY WERE FREE. SHE TOLD THEM ABOUT THE FREEDOMS THAT EVERYDAY AMERICANS ENJOYED, AND THAT WHILE IN AMERICA SHE TOO HAD EXPERIENCED. SHE SHOUTED MORE THAN ONCE, 'NO MAN IS A NUMBER!"

SHE REMINDED THEM THAT MARTIN LUTHER KING, WHO SHE CALLED ST. MARTIN IN ACKNOWLEDGEMENT OF DR. KING'S STATUS AS A SAINT IN THE DJR RELIGION, HAD

CALLED FOR PEOPLE TO BE RESPECTED FOR THEIR CHARACTER, NOT THE COLOR OF THEIR SKIN, BUT THE DJR HAD REVERSED IT AND WAS FOLLOWING THE DOCTRINE OF THE RACISTS.

SHE SAID THE GOVERNMENT DID NOT WISH ITS CITIZENS TO HAVE CHARACTER, BUT RATHER TO SERVE IT AS SLAVES UNTIL CALLED TO THE EUTHANASIA PALACE. SHE EXPRESSED SORROW FOR THE SCHOOLCHILDREN IN THE AUDIENCE, SAYING THEY LIVED IN A GIANT CAGE CALLED THE DJR. SHE SAID THAT HER HUSBAND WAS A PLORE AND AN ANTIFAN, AND A HERO, AND SHE HAD BEEN KIDNAPPED FROM HIM AND THEIR TWO BOYS.

SHE URGED THE ASSEMBLAGE TO SHOW KINDNESS TO EACH OTHER, ASKING WHAT KIND OF GOVERNMENT PLACES HUMAN BEINGS IN CAGES TO ABUSE THEM. SHE TOLD THEM THAT DEPLORABLES LIVED MORE FREELY THAN THEY DID. SHE CONCLUDED BY SAYING, "WE ARE CHILDREN OF THE LIVING GOD, NOT OF A PILE OF DIRT!" NOTE: CHRISTIAN PROSELYTIZATION IS A CAPITAL CRIME IN THE DJR.

AT THAT POINT, SEVERAL GUARDS RAN INTO THE CAGE, BEAT HER, AND WITH THE ASSISTANCE OF THE ZOOKEEPER, DRAGGED HER DOWNSTAIRS UNDER THE CAGE.

I DID NOT SEE MRS. HARRIS AGAIN. THE CAGE WAS EMPTY THE FOLLOWING MORNING, AND I ASSUME SHE WAS REMOVED TO BEAUFORT. THE DJR MEDIA DID NOT COVER THE INCIDENT.

THE AUDIENCE WAS MOSTLY SILENT AND EVEN RESPECTFUL AS SHE SPOKE. WHEN THE GUARDS APPEARED, THOSE ON THE EDGES OF THE CROWD BEGAN MOVING AWAY, NO DOUBT IN FEAR OF THE CONSEQUENCES FOR THEMSELVES.

UNDER THE CURRENT HARSH REGIME PROMULGATED BY COMMANDER MA, ALL THOSE PRESENT WILL LIKELY UNDERGO STRENUOUS INTERROGATION AND MONITORING...COMMANDER KHALID MA, KNOWN INFORMALLY AS "PARAGON" FOR HIS UNYIELDING COMMITMENT TO DIVERSITY, IS THE FORMER ADF STATION CHIEF IN ST. LOUIS.

COMPLIMENTS TO OUR FRIENDS IN ST. LOUIS. AUSTIN

NOTE FROM AUSTIN STATION: TIA EMPHASIZED THAT WE MUST NOT REVEAL THE SOURCE OF OUR REPORTING ON MRS. HARRIS. DOING SO WOULD PLACE THEIR OWN PERSONNEL IN ANACOSTA IN GRAVE DANGER, GIVEN THE HARSHNESS OF THE CURRENT REGIME. END.

"I don't know what to say," David shook his head, back on the call with Vernal. "This is completely depraved. This could not have happened when I was in Anacosta."

"We had no idea this Commander Ma was their station chief!" Vernal chirped.

"I'm glad she's alive, but now what?" he asked, thinking aloud. The thought of Malia in a cage baited like a bear at a medieval fair competed with his sheer relief at knowing she was alive and knowing her whereabouts, and frankly, it didn't surprise him that she was in Anacosta, which he had suspected all along would turn out to be the case.

"Can you come to St. Louis?" Vernal asked. "We can't talk about our options like this. We need to bring others into the picture as well." He gladly agreed to drive up to St. Louis the next day.

Unable to contain his turbulent thoughts, he phoned Chris at Capettone with the news. Chris put aside an article about a robotic surgical arrow and concentrated on David's news.

"You were right, David," said Chris.

"I knew if she was alive, that's who had her. Not gangsters. So I'm thrilled she's alive. But in the hands of monsters…The Antifans I worked with wouldn't have dreamed of a human zoo. Things have degenerated there; I just hope she stays alive until our politicians can rescue her."

Chris paused, causing David, irked, to ask, "They can't refuse to do something now, can they? I'm a citizen. My wife's being held hostage. Does a seaport really matter more than her life?"

"My friend," said Chris, "when you come back, we will talk."

Driving northeast toward St. Louis the next morning, David smiled at the image of his quiet wife lecturing Social Crediteers. No one else would have done this; her aim is true, he told himself. At one point I thought she was the meek librarian, and I was the brave Antifan, but really, she is more courageous than me. His thoughts then turned to the inevitable revenge of the ADF, especially given the capital crime of Christian proselytizing that she had committed publicly. The ADF could overlook private indiscretions, and even knowledge crimes, if the perpetrator was too valuable or too elite to destroy, but they could not ignore a prisoner who had uttered "the Living God" in front of dozens of Social Crediteers, who had since whispered the heresy throughout the City and relayed it to others. Despite the warm day, he shivered.

"No man is a number," he repeated to himself.

PART THREE

CAYUGA

When you called out in distress, I rescued you.
Unseen, I answered you in thunder.
I tested your faith at an oasis in the wilderness.
—Psalm 81

Chapter 26
To the Rescue
(Tuesday–Saturday, November 10–14, 2093)

David stood uncertainly by the side of the road south of Syracuse, looking the part of a vagrant with his scuffed boots, a scruffy blond beard that had been growing for two weeks, and a large backpack/bedroll resting on his shoulders. Earlier that morning, a well-paid truck driver had brought him across the Friendship Bridge from Canada, concealed beneath hundreds of boxes of diapers and a metal panel in the floor of the truck. He had lain face down for two hours in a compartment that featured an ingenious vent for circulating fresh air into the hiding place and carbon dioxide out, until they reached the disembarkation point south of Syracuse.

Until they had come within half an hour of the DJR border, where they picked up the diapers from the factory, David had sat with the driver in the cab. "I'm a Michigander, actually," said the driver. "That now makes me a Canadian, but I was born an American, just like you were. Isn't it funny, we were both Americans and now we're something else and foreigners to each other?"

Their journey had started about 150 miles north of Toronto, where David, Daniel, and a grizzled French-Canadian wilderness expert named Jean-Luc had spent the last two weeks, training David for his backcountry travel to Anacosta.

"You don't need to come," David had told Daniel, but he was secretly grateful his brother, with his outdoors experience, had insisted on leaving the shop behind for two weeks to join him in Canada.

"No problem," Daniel had said, a little gruffly. "When will I see you again?" Left unsaid was that David was recklessly endangering his life by returning to the DJR to rescue Malia. The chances were high that the ADF or some greedy informant would discover him en route, and his journey would end with torture and a gruesome death at Beaufort. The brothers hugged as the truck driver waited for David to board; the wilderness instructor would take Daniel to the Toronto airport.

"I can't tell you to be safe," Daniel admitted to his younger brother. "Because if you are going to accomplish your mission, you will have to be unsafe. Very unsafe. But Fern and I will pray every day for you and Malia. And hopefully God will bring you through."

"Thank you," David said simply. "I can only do this because my sons are safe with you."

"I love you," said Daniel, and turned away abruptly.

"I love you too, brother."

It was to David's advantage that the DJR authorities generally refrained from searching incoming trucks—the goods they contained were badly needed and who in their right mind would sneak into the DJR? Still, David had sweated at the border crossing, hearing the voices of ADF border guards doing a routine inspection. They engaged in polite chitchat with the truck driver about weather, but David knew they were alert for anything unusual.

Now the driver was taking a slight detour south to deposit him at a relatively quiet spot instead of Syracuse. Syracuse was big enough to boast its own Social Credit City and Ploreville ghetto and an ADF detachment—David knew this—and a lone hiker would quickly attract the attention of authorities. At the very least, the authorities would question him, suspecting he had wandered off from his assigned containment area, and David knew his cover story would survive only the most innocuous encounter with the police.

The driver would then resume his journey eastward, to Boston, to deliver his diapers. He said that his truck would likely return to Ontario empty.

"Good luck, buddy!" the driver said, before exiting to turn around at the cloverleaf and head back north to Syracuse. The truck soon disappeared around the bend, with David already missing its bulky promise of protection. Now he was truly alone.

Since an occasional vehicle would pass him, and the vast majority were occupied by Social Crediteers, David quickly plunged into the underbrush alongside the road. His backpack and roll weighed about fifty pounds, but after almost two months of rigorous training, he was in the best shape he'd been in since his pre-commander days at Beaufort. He easily navigated down a slope to a trail he had been told to find. It ran along a streambed.

About three hours remained until sundown, and David was determined to make headway on this first night back in the DJR. He and the MAGA geographer at UO had calculated that he would be traveling about three hundred miles, a journey that would take him about a month if all went well, since the route was tailored to avoid contact with settlements and towns, requiring numerous detours.

Without access to current DJR maps, closely protected by Anacostan authorities as state secrets, they had pored over dated maps from the National Archives in St. Louis. David had laboriously memorized every bend and turn in the route. He carried a compass, but no cell phone, which posed a security risk, even though all but the poorest Plores owned one.

He was otherwise very well equipped for a supposed Plore, who if accosted, would claim to be a Unhoused Person from Massena, near the Say Lawrence River in the farthest reaches of New York, but now wandering the countryside. Originally, he had considered claiming he had just been released from the Say Lawrence River prison, but a call to the facility would be too easy and would confirm his lie. If one lied about having been a prisoner, the police would rightly assume the truth must be far worse.

He carried a warm winter-weight sleeping bag, a tent, a water hydration unit, a collapsible cooking stove and a dish, silverware and a tin cup, about fifty packets of freeze-dried food convincingly obtainable in the DJR, fire-starting kits, bear repellent, and water purification tablets. He could not bring the advanced turferwear worn by experienced US and Canadian campers—it would be a sure sign he was not what he pretended to be. So he wore old ragged woolen and cotton layers and shaggy socks like a Plore tramp would—all this would slow him down and make him uncomfortable, and doubtless itch, but possibly save his life. His equipment was likewise ancient, acquired mostly from used-camping-supply stores and garage sales and in a few cases the back cabinet of Chris's lab.

Two items he especially prized—one was his brand-new but worn-looking DJR registration card, or at least a remarkably convincing laminated imitation.

Potter, Michael Brian
DOB: May 5, 2058, Massena, NY-Schuylkill
Place of Residence at Last Registration Cull: Massena, NYSk, April 30, 2092
ID: 74437694335577
Hair: Blond Eyes: Gray
Parent (1) Joanna Brown; (2) Richard Potter
Card expiration date: May 31, 2097
(a recent photo with a digitally altered beard was attached)

"Michael Potter was in fact a real person," said the forger whom MAGA had found for him. "Born in 2038 in Massena, NY. He died in the civil war, in Pennsylvania. The birthplace, parents and physical description are correct. If police run your card through the system, there will be plenty of duplicates, but enough of the details should stick so they won't question you're a DJR Deplorable. I mean, who else would you be?"

The second prized possession was a sinister-looking ten-inch hunting knife in a thick black vinyl case. David could not risk bringing a firearm into the DJR, with its capital punishment for unauthorized use or ownership of a gun. No Plore would ever dare carry a gun, as far as he knew. His training in knife work at Beaufort had paid off before, and David had to hope it would serve again. The wilderness instructor had shown him how to use the knife to kill game; the OU zoology expert MAGA had enlisted told him the woods of northern New York were now abundant with the "northern nutria" or Nutritious Food Animal No. 1 developed in a laboratory and released into the countryside to supplement the meager food supplies for Plores.

"This is the best way to kill and skin a nute," said Jean-Luc, his wiry hands demonstrating how to snap the creature's neck (some had reached Canada, prompting official complaints to the DJR about these nuisances). "But if you can't do it," he said, noticing David's face, "stab it here and it should die instantly."

David had laughed at himself—dozens of corpses to his credit after two decades in the ADF and then another nine only this year—and yet he quailed at the thought of killing a bizarre lab-nute mutation for food. Yet he did not have quite enough packets for his entire journey; he would have to take the risk of occasionally emerging from the woods to purchase meals with his DJR currency, or kill his dinner.

Well before dark, he found a quiet spot near a stream to pitch his tent and set up the stove. He picked a packet randomly—macaroni and cheese—and cooked his meal. He sat on a log, eating his dinner, observing a brilliant wintry sunset of pinks and dark blues to his right, to the southwest. "So far, so good," he told himself. As he ate, he wondered how Malia was doing.

He also recalled the hikes he had taken in southern Oklahoma with Emmett on his shoulders, for the initial toughening for this trip. When Emmett began to falter and trip, David then treated Emmett as the weight-equivalent of his now backpack. He had told Emmett stories about Malia so that he would not forget his mother.

"I want Mommy," Emmett said. David told Emmett that he was going to rescue Mommy from bad guys and bring her home. Emmett was just old enough to understand that Daddy was going to find Mommy, and young enough to believe all that it would take was a brave prince, just as in the fairy tales.

"Daddy, are they hurting Mommy?" the boy asked anxiously as they sat under a buckeye tree eating their bag lunches.

"No, no," David reassured him. "She is so beautiful that they will not hurt her. But they have placed her in a very high castle, with eighty floors. Three times a day, they bring her meals in a bucket, and she pulls on a rope attached to the bucket and pulls it up to her window, and that's how she eats. She is very safe, but she wants to come home." The boy's eyes had widened in amazement. Now sitting over another outdoor meal, a thousand miles away and alone, David blinked back tears.

It was dark at 7:00 p.m., but a very thin rim of light stretched across the horizon back in the direction of Syracuse. By this time of year, the trees were bare, giving David less cover than he would have preferred, and the temperatures would most likely dip below freezing again. He had refused to wait until spring.

"You may want to travel by night," cautioned the wilderness instructor, "especially if you are near towns. But then you have to be alert for nocturnal animals. It will be the rutting season." Tonight, though, David would give himself the luxury of sleep. He secured the tent from the inside and, listening to the hoots of owls and barking of foxes in the distance, fell asleep quickly.

On day two, David encountered a pair of Social Credit hikers, a middle-aged couple, who shied away from him as he passed them. Staying in character, David touched his cap politely, as a deferential Plore might salute his betters. Afterward, he resolved to begin traveling at night, lest some Social Credit passerby complain to the authorities about dangerous Plores roaming the government-provided paths.

On night three, he tramped southward near Cortland. He saw two oily nutes, but they were slippery and eluded his knife. An hour before dawn, he cooked another packet, this time of rice and chicken, and found a secluded place where a small hill concealed his tent from the trail. He slept until midafternoon. He heard voices from the trail, and emerged at dusk to march again.

On night four, he saw foxes. He killed his first nute at midnight with a lucky tree branch strike to the head, skinned and roasted it on a fire. He had expected a gamy taste but it was surprisingly flavorless. Later he would learn that, like tofu, nute meat took on the flavor of whatever sauce or seasoning it was cooked with. He came across a pond and decided to strip and wash as best he could, despite the temperatures hovering around freezing that night. He felt gamy himself. The DJR propaganda had routinely bewailed what they called historically warm temperatures in late fall and winter, to support the usual narrative of disastrous climate change, not that David could quite understand why a warmer winter in upstate New York–Schuylkill would be so terrible. Having mistakenly trusted the propaganda, David now found his layers of wool and cotton and wool gloves were just barely enough to keep him warm. *They even lie about weather.*

His main preoccupation now as he headed south, avoiding all human contact, was crossing the Susquehanna River. He had identified a narrow crossing where he would swim, but this required him to detour southwest, away from the town of Owego just north of the Pennsylvania border. He knew he was near the Finger Lakes, and Ithaca and Cayuga Lake, all tempting destinations and a quick trip in a car, but a serious detour if you were on foot with a heavy pack, and populated with Social Credit professors and students at Navesky University, at the southern tip of Cayuga, who would look on him askance. He reluctantly swung south of Cayuga Lake. "Come back as a tourist," he told himself.

On night five, a Saturday, after several hours of cold and hungry hiking, he was drawn to distant lights, and peeking through some bushes, saw a small roadside diner. It was a long shed with a few small windows framing light and flanking the narrow door, and an almost flat roof. An old marquee on a high pole read, in letters that had most likely been placed decades ago and were now too rusted to remove, "Candor Inn. Hot Food. Live Music." Once upon a time, the sign had been electrified and pulsed in the night. Beat-up pickup trucks and dented sedans several decades old were parked in an adjacent gravel lot. He heard pop music coming from the restaurant. This looks safe, he thought, it's a Plore place. No Social Crediteers would come here. He wanted a decent meal—the oily nute taste still coated his tongue—and he had plenty of DJR cash stashed everywhere from his socks to hidden compartments in the sleeping bag. So he approached the restaurant. A group of men talking about ice fishing turned to stare at him as he emerged from the woods. They wore baseball caps and thick quilted jackets made out of various rags and cloth odds and ends. It was the local uniform.

"This place OK for a meal?" he asked, as casually as he could. He wished he could ask, "Any Social Credit around?" but that would cause them to look suspiciously at him.

"Yeah, if you don't mind not having much of a choice," said a short man in a New York Gangstas baseball cap. "But it's warm in there and the company's cool. They got beer tonight."

"Good enough for me," said David, "thanks, guys," and he headed toward the front entrance.

The men watched the tramp with the military bearing enter the restaurant. "Not from around here," one declared.

"Sounds a little fancy," offered another, "but Plore fancy. Wonder how he ended up like that." They resumed their conversation, but it was not quite the same, and they too were getting chilled. They climbed into their trucks and went home to their wives.

Chapter 27
Candor Inn
(Saturday, November 14, 2093)

"Take a seat at the second table," ordered the ponytailed not-so-young woman behind the counter.

"Excuse me, can I just take out?" David asked.

She raised her eyebrows in great amusement. "This isn't some fancy place, mister. This is how we do it. How long you been out in those woods, anyway?"

She took pity on him, since he was handsome underneath the grime, and a little helpless, and pointed him in the direction of the table. "Leave your pack here, I'll watch it for you. It won't fit in between the tables. It's five dollars, all you can eat."

David was loath to abandon all he owned but he had to trust the woman. And he didn't want to attract any more attention than he already had, judging by how many heads had swiveled in his direction. Everyone here knew each other. He pulled out the few bills he was keeping handy in his jacket pocket and paid, wondering where they kept the buffet. Five dollars was a good deal for a buffet.

Along the length of the long room were about fifteen long wooden tables, like fingers stretching out from the back wall, flanked on each side by benches. Against the back wall hung varying posters, some framed, some just taped carefully to the wall. As David walked to his table, he saw one saying "Tioga County Fair 2078," which featured a large Holstein cow in the foreground, and another displayed a sultry Melody Backster, 250, the popular singer whom Plores and Crediteers alike adored. He noticed large metal bowls on the tables and smaller ones filled with what looked like tomato sauce.

He sat at the edge of the bench, with about three seats between him and the next guy.

"You gotta move down, *kamrat*," said the guy, kindly. He was a fleshy-faced fellow with large watery blue eyes. "So when the others come, nobody's got to climb over each other."

David said "sorry," and obliged. Apparently, no previous acquaintance was required. Across the table sat two young red-haired brothers wearing baseball caps, and to

David's astonishment, an old man wearing an actual Make America Great Again red cap, faded and dirty, but real. From the looks of it, the cap dated from the civil war, since it was unlikely that one had been smuggled over the border afterward.

"That's more like it," the old man approved. The men seemed happy to have a newcomer at their table.

David peered into the bowls, which were full of cheese-covered tortilla chips. "Is this for the table? Is there a menu? What should I order?"

The men chuckled, but amiably.

"Kamrat, this is it. Tonight, it's natchers. You eat all you want, for your five dollars. But you order your drink separately." They advised him to order the local lager, Saratoga, which was on tap tonight and "they even drink it in the City," meaning Syracuse. The waitress, a stout but fleet-footed woman in late middle age, brought him a paper plate and a single paper napkin, and took their drink order and their money.

David tried to hide his disappointment. He was taking a risk by coming out of the woods, and for his pains he had anticipated eating an actual meal, maybe even non-nute meat if he was willing to spend money, which he was.

"Don't look so sad, kamrat, it's good stuff. Just reach in and grab what you want." David's neighbor showed him. "Where're you from, someplace fancy?"

"Massena," David said briefly. He began eating, if only not to prolong his stay at the Candor Inn. They were right, the nachos were good.

"Local cheese," said the old man. "We make it ourselves. If you want vitamins, dip it in the salsa."

"What brings you down here?" the fleshy-faced man, named Tom, asked. "That's a long way. You're almost out of the containment area."

"I don't care about the containment area!" the smaller of the two red-haired brothers suddenly yelped. "I'll go where I want!"

"Not that you do," his brother teased him sardonically. "Or maybe three feet into Pennsylvania and then you pattersnap home again."

Then the four men looked at him inquisitively. Between the MAGA-hatted man, and the admission of breaking the area containment laws, they realized that here was a stranger who might well be an informant sent out by the local Antifan militia that reported to Syracuse.

"I'm traveling to my mother's deathbed," David said, hoping God would forgive him. "They wouldn't give me a travel pass. They said she probably wasn't dying and I just wanted to visit with her so was lying."

The men clucked sympathetically. "Where's she live?" asked the old man.

"Frederick, Anacosta region. Yramaland."

"Wow, you got a long way to go," said Tom. "You're not afraid of the militia?"

"No," said David, paling at the thought of militia elements. He hadn't known about them. Along the borders, yes. But he hadn't known how far inland the militias roamed. Maybe this was a new development. "I'm staying on the trails, and mostly traveling at night."

"They keep us in check," said David's other neighbor, as several more men sat down, filling their table. "Just to remind us who lost the war...someday, we'll come back. But don't ask me how."

Finally, introductions were made. David just barely remembered that he was "Mike Potter." His neighbor was Tom Nichols, who was working on a construction project in Owego on the new Mother Earth Meeting House; the brothers were Jim and Bernard, and the old man was Gary. Jim said he was in training to drive smaller trucks, "which hopefully will lead to driving bigger ones." Bernard, the younger one, was helping their mother make jams and sell them, with eggs and her homemade pies, along the road. Gary apologized for not working anymore, saying "nobody wants a broken old man." They looked at David.

"I'm a security guard," said David. "Usually the night shift at the shipyard, sometimes the mall."

"Are you married?" Now that work credentials had been established, the men moved to the next level.

"Yes, but she's...gone."

"Oh, that's a shame," Gary said softly.

"No, not dead, sorry I said it that way. I mean, not in the house anymore."

"Bitch! My wife left me too. Ran off with some guy ten years younger than her," Tom grumbled. "But her sister moved in with me, so I guess it's OK. Pastor won't marry us, though, not unless we get a proper divorce. How I'm supposed to get a divorce from that bitch I don't know."

"No, no," David said, embarrassed at his awkwardness. "My wife's in the prison at Elmira." His dining partners were shocked but sympathetic. "She was cleaning a Social Credit house and they accused her of stealing their jewelry. She never would have done that. But the judge didn't care. Two years now, maybe she'll be out next Christmas. So I might as well go to my mother, right?"

Everyone agreed, including the new party on his right. More introductions were made. The waitress brought more bowls heaped with nachos and more salsa. David ordered another beer.

"Hey, Aunt Lucy's looking at you," said Tom.

"Aunt Lucy?"

"Yeah, she's a leader around here, you might say. She's in charge of her roundup. Her father was a professor, but he was active on our side during the war. Got killed by one of his students." Tom discreetly indicated a fair woman, maybe in her late fifties, framed between the shoulders of two women facing her at a table on the other side of the room. When she realized that David was returning her gaze, she unconsciously ran her hand through her long gray-blonde hair, then looked away and rejoined the conversation at her table. At that point David realized that the tables were sex-segregated. Several tables of women only were at the other end of the hall, near the hostess. There were one or two tables with mixed groups, including children, probably families. He didn't dare ask about the seating custom, lest they start wondering if he was too clueless to even be from Massena. What's a roundup, he wondered.

"Aunt Lucy doesn't come here much," said Tom, "but tonight her niece is going to sing."

"Really? Live entertainment?"

"Well, you get tired of the local radio stations and the GVN feed—transpop and boysex and girls finding Social Credit daddies and Mother Earth at the same time... sometimes you just gotta sing your own music. And she's got a really nice voice." As if summoned, the presumed niece, a petite girl with long blonde hair, began directing two young men to set up a short stage and microphone near David's corner. David began thinking it might be good to depart before the entertainment started—it would be hard to leave discreetly if he had to pass between the singer and the next table. But it was warm, and David was sleepy from the natchers, the warmth, the beer, and the goodwill. If I lived around here, sure, I'd be a regular, he thought.

Five minutes later, as the girl was about to sing and the audience shifted expectantly, the door flew open. Four men dressed in black and matching armbands stalked in, casting dark looks around the diner. Militia, the whispers said. David started, as if he could dart out the back door behind them, but Tom patted him comfortably, unobtrusively, on his back. "Don't worry, they're not looking for small stuff. They won't ask about containment areas. They show up here maybe once every few months or so."

Then what are they looking for, David wondered. Not natchers, for sure. He knew that he could not flee at this point, because it would only attract their attention. He would live his cover and hope the ID would pass muster. He drained the rest of his beer, just to look more natural, and willed his facial muscles to relax. The young men had stopped setting up the stage and discreetly backed up against the wall. Back at the desk, the hostess stared with hostility at the foursome's backs, her arms folded. The canned music had ceased and all was deathly quiet.

The four started slowly striding up the aisle, ignoring the women and family tables, and scanning each of the men's.

The first man was clearly the leader. His name was Liam Battista, but he had just been notified by the authorities that he would have to replace Battista, given its origins in "Baptist." His subordinates joked—among themselves—that he should change his name to Battery.

He was about forty, just under six feet tall, with a harsh, hook-nosed face, slightly receding black hair brushed over his pate, and glittering dark eyes. David thought of a vulture. The one following him was younger, shorter, with a fair, round face but cold round blue eyes. He reminded David of a clean pig. Next came a heavyset, swarthy man whose leather leggings squeaked as they brushed against each other with his abundant flesh encased inside. His misshapen head and leather hide were like a rhino's. The fourth was the best looking of the lot, a strapping young brown-eyed brunet, but disfigured by the arrogance stamped on his face. A loop of chain hung at their left hips, the Antifan badge of honor from the days of the civil war street battles, and they were all armed with pistols, the privilege of only a very few functionaries.

The leader stopped at one table, and stared at one willowy Hispanic youth with dark liquid eyes. "Stand up." The youth, no more than eighteen or so, unable to look at the leader, rose.

"Against that wall," he commanded. The youth sidled over to stand near where the singer stood, frozen.

The group continued, slowly. A muscular young workman with dull eyes but strong hands, possibly a bricklayer, also caught Battista's attention, and was dispatched to join the Hispanic youth at the wall.

They reached David's table, second to last. David was relieved that Gary had discreetly dropped his MAGA hat to the floor under the table, where it now rested under his foot.

Battista's eyes locked with David's. David should have turned away submissively, but it was like being entranced by a python. "Hello, Blondie," Battista said. Then to his subalterns, "Him too. Get up, you Plore piece of crap."

David was shoved against the wall with the Hispanic boy and the workman.

"Check their IDs," the leader demanded, giving each of them an appraising stare.

David showed his card to the younger man. Either Brunet was careless, or didn't care where Massena was, because he just relayed to the leader, "Michael Potter."

"How old?"

"Thirty-five, sir."

"That's good."

David was confused. Were they looking for a thirty-five-year-old criminal?

"Mature but not too old. That's my taste for tonight. Let's take him."

This can't be. I just stopped here for a meal. All my belongings are behind that hostess podium. How could this happen? "What's going on?" David asked. "What did I do?"

The fat man slapped him across the face. "Shut up, Mike. You're going to have some fun tonight. If you behave, we'll let you go afterward."

The Plores looked down at their tables.

"Let's go," said Battista. "I've got some appetites that need satisfying and it won't happen in this dive." The men sniggered. The clean pig and the brunet each grabbed an arm of David's and propelled him toward the door.

As he stumbled past the hostess desk, the woman assured him, "I'll hold your stuff for you. It'll be here when you come back." The men ignored her and thrust him out the door.

David was too shocked even to thank her. In a minute they had shoved him into the middle row of the sports van, which the leader drove himself. The fat guy sat next to Battista, and the clean pig and the brunet flanked David. At least they just think I'm an ordinary Plore, he reassured himself. This isn't political, not yet. Maybe not even that dangerous. Overall.

Back in the restaurant, the singer was tremulously powering through her set, but the mood was leaden. The patrons felt badly for the stranger, and somehow deficient in hospitality, as if one of them should have offered to take the blow, not that Battista would have accepted it. "He just didn't know how it is around here," one of the brothers said referring to David. "Like a baby."

"At least he'll be able to take his body back after it's over," said Gary philosophically. "He'll get a good meal too. There's a girl from our roundup who works in his kitchen, so I know."

"This shouldn't be borne," Tom hissed. "We could have fought them off."

"And then what would happen?" The voice came from one of the newer arrivals to the table. "The Antifans would come down from Syracuse, or even Buffalo, and shoot us all. The treaty wouldn't apply."

"We'd scatter," said Tom defiantly. "They couldn't catch all of us. They wouldn't know everyone who had been here." Behind his deceptively fleshy exterior was a hard core of resolve, which only awaited a spark of leadership.

"Hopeless," drawled the pessimist. "Full of shit talking."

"This can't go on forever," said another man.

"It can go on pretty close to forever. Nothing will happen unless we stand up for ourselves." Tom gave a deep sigh. Something about that blond stranger had moved him, but he couldn't say what, exactly. Was it the injustice of the mother dying alone or of the jailed wife, or both, or the loneliness of a man forced to tramp the roads alone far from loved ones? Tom couldn't verbalize it, not quite, but he said to his wife's sister later that night, "He had somewhere else, something different, about him. He was... refined, but hard too. I don't know how to say it.

"I hope he comes back to the inn afterward, so we can try to put it right. I hope he won't hold this against us."

Chapter 28
Who's The Nute Now?
(Saturday–Sunday, November 14–15, 2093)

The men allowed David out of the car to pee alongside the road. As he aimed into the dead bushes beneath him, David sensed weapons trained in his direction. But fleeing wasn't an option, not without any of his gear or even a warm enough jacket to survive the night, with freezing temperatures. Fortunately, they seemed to have no suspicion that he was anything other than another submissive Plore, which suggested it would pay for now to play along.

David asked politely if he might defecate in the bushes. They agreed, using the opportunity to mock him, "Like a dog! But hurry up!" They were confident in their power, which they enjoyed most when they used it to humiliate and oppress. The jocularity gave David, squatting in the dark, a chance to transfer his knife from the inside jacket pocket to the outside shin pocket of his cargo pants without their noticing any unusual movement. Maybe they assumed he was wiping himself with the cloth they tossed him.

The round, confident peals of laughter reminded him of Beaufort. How many times had he done the same with his squad, especially after they had beaten some knowledge criminals, or driven a band of helpless demonstrators demanding some kind of ridiculous alleged right, like to write poetry, into black vans headed for Beaufort? The Social Crediteers' bleating and appeal to your higher sensibilities were so ludicrous that mocking laughter in concert was the only reasonable response. Your luxuriant enjoyment of your power was like stretching in bed after waking up from a good night's sleep. Shared with your fellow officers, your knowledge that no one could or would do the same to you, that your high Social Credit life would go on undisturbed, confirmed your high status; of course they had laughed joyfully in their cruelty.

David climbed back into the SUV, staring down at the floor like the submissive Plore they now knew he was, and they sat where they had before. Even though it was a cold night, the windows were partially open, so that the fat man could spit at the trees.

"Mother bitch Earth, Gutakas, you're disgusting," Battista threw in his direction.

They chortled.

"Better you want me to fart, Commander?" A rich smell filled the vehicle. The other men cursed.

"This is why you haven't found a girl yet," said Clean Pig, who was smugly married.

"I don't need a woman hanging 'round," shrugged Gutakas. "Just cramps my lifestyle. And it isn't good for Diversity. I'll settle for that girl in your kitchen, Commander."

"Well, leave her alone tonight," said Battista crossly. "She can cook, and if you keep bothering her, I might have to go and get some old hag instead."

The car sped down unlit dark roads, Battista taking the curves at a confident speed just short of reckless. The moon was rising, casting a silver glow on the bare trees around them. David realized they were heading north again—even if they let him go afterward, he would have lost at least ten miles of ground. The car hit some creature, maybe a raccoon, maybe a large nute, that had crossed in front of the car, causing it to jolt and yaw sideways. "Mother bitch Earth!"

About ten minutes later, the car spun into the gravel driveway of a large white old house. The house was rambling, in a pleasant way, like an amiable uncle who talked too much. A long porch ran along the front. The porch swing was hanging from the roof by one end, having broken years ago. Nobody cared enough to hire a Plore to bring it down or tie it back up. A few flimsy lawn chairs were scattered on the porch.

It was the kind of house that a hundred years ago might have housed a large, patriarchal family, with a father, mother, three or four well-scrubbed children—going to work, going to school, going to church on Sundays. Having company over on Saturday afternoon, playing croquet on the grassy expanse of lawn with lemonade in pitchers on the porch. David wondered what had happened to that family, whose grandchildren might still be alive. Possibly escaped into the United States with the Red Normals, or more likely herded into a City if they were liberal-minded and forced to live by their stated yard sign principles. He imagined a squad of Antifans showing up early in the civil war to evict the family, a slew of social workers in tow to separate the parents from their still-salvageable children.

A light had been left on in the large room above the porch. It might have been the commander's office, and a dimmer light shone in the front parlor. Electricity for lighting at night, used wastefully, was a sure sign of luxury in this hardscrabble region.

A sign in front said "ADF Militia HQ Unit 7: Tompkins County." Definitely lost ground, David thought bitterly. Tompkins was north of Tioga and the Candor Inn.

They climbed out of the SUV. Battista said, "Bring him upstairs. No Plores through my front door." The men shoved him along the side of the house to the kitchen entrance. A plain dark-haired Plore girl, no more than twenty or so, dressed in a long black skirt and frayed button-down tan shirt, shrank back against the wall as the men burst in. To his horror, David saw she was secured to the wall with a long, thin chain of about fifteen feet, terminating at her ankle, that allowed her to move around the kitchen and do her chores, and visit the toilet, but nothing more. A mattress with blankets occupied a corner of the room where she presumably slept.

"Sorry, miss," David said, touching his cap to her.

Brunet smacked him across the shoulder blades. "Don't talk to the bitch. You're not here to talk at all."

They were in a darkened hallway, lined with old-fashioned fleur-de-lis wallpaper and lit by one naked electric bulb. The walnut banister of the staircase was badly scratched. They hustled him upstairs to the landing, halting outside the door to the study.

"Commander, you ready for the Plore?"

Battista's voice called, "Yeah, bring him in."

David was pushed through the double doors and into a large study. Once upon a time, it might have been the master bedroom of the patriarchal couple. The windows he had seen from below were now across the room from the door. One lamp, the one he had seen from outside, was burning, but otherwise the room was dark. An unmade daybed occupied one corner of the room, and a cluttered desk, onto which Battista had tossed his armband, ran alongside the window. Nearest the door were a sofa and armchair for meetings. To his shock, David recognized the same "Are You the Fist" poster that had hung in his office at Beaufort. Maybe this poster had been given to every two-bit Antifan between here and Anacosta.

A workscreen sat, askew, on the desk, and various kinds of paper trash were scattered on the floor: receipts, a travel brochure, an old map, pornography. A damp towel hung over the back of the armchair. The dust made David sneeze. Clearly the girl was not given the responsibility of cleaning the commander's study. Behind the sofa was a gray sideboard, old enough to have served the patriarchal family, with a whiskey bottle and two glasses.

"You want us to stay, Commander?" asked Gutakas. "Just in case Blondie gives you any trouble?" David stared at the ground, visibly humbled by his surroundings and the evidence of Diverse Antifan power.

Battista sneered, "No, I recognize the type. He'll be a good boy. Look at that sweet baby face." He lifted David's chin in his right hand. David willed himself not to flinch. Let him think you don't mind being here, not if you'll get a hot meal for your trouble. "You guys can hang downstairs. Greene," indicating Clean Pig, "you can go home if you want."

"Thanks, boss," said Clean Pig, who left, whistling, the door swinging behind him.

Gutakas said, "Jesse and I'll be in the TV room. Call if you need us, Commander." They often awoke on Sunday morning sprawled on the sofas, nursing hangovers. Battista never needed them to handle the trembling men who were commandeered for the night. In the morning, the victim would stagger downstairs, eat a meal at the kitchen table prepared by the girl, and then wander down the road, grateful to still be alive.

"Don't drink too much of my liquor, will you, Gutakas?"

Then Gutakas and Jesse the brunet left. David was alone with Battista.

"Let's have a drink first," said Battista. He liked to display a little gratuitous geniality before the display of force. It might also relax his intended victim, just enough to make it easier for everyone. He poured two full glasses from the whiskey bottle and handed David one. "I'm not a snob, I don't mind if a Plore drinks from my glasses."

He indicated to David that he should sit on the sofa. "Take off your jacket and shirt. I want to see your chest."

David obeyed, his lips pressed together. He was glad he had transferred the knife to the shin pocket. He felt faintly feverish. Strange, the room hadn't seemed too warm when he had entered. Was it just shame?

"Nice," said Battista, appraising David's toned pectorals, covered in light blond fuzz. He licked his thin lips appreciatively. The lamplight glinted off his oily black hair. "You've got some muscle. A lot of these Plores go to flab too fast. What kind of work do you do?"

"Security guard," mumbled David.

"Security guard, sir," commanded Battista.

"Security guard, sir."

"That's better. Drink up. Here's to Diversity!"

Battista poured two more glasses. "I got into men for the points—forty extra makes a big difference up here. So I'm a 190. Pretty impressive, huh?"

David thought, My 240 was a lot better. Wish I could tell you. He wasn't feeling feverish anymore but his throat was sore. Uh oh. Who would give you antibiotics up here? Did they even have antibiotics and were vagrant Plores eligible for them? He was anticipating a long frigid hike back to the Candor Inn, and what if it was closed and locked when he arrived? One could die of cold waiting for the inn to open in the morning. And now he felt chilled, maybe because he was naked above the waist and a window was slightly open to air out the musty room, or because he knew what was coming.

"And then I realized it was better this way. Women make demands. They're nosy. They want you to be a house pet. This way, you fuck and it's over."

"You got a wife?"

"Yes, sir. She's in prison in Elmira for stealing. But she didn't do it."

"That's what all the Plores say, you crooks," Battista smiled contemptuously at him. David felt a surge of anger on behalf of the imaginary woman. "Oh, I see you're a little pissed off. Good, that'll make you more fun, squirming a little under me.

"Well, you don't seem like a great conversationalist. Let's get down to business, my beautiful Plore maiden. Stand up," he ordered.

David stood.

"Turn around and hold on to the back of the armchair."

David obeyed.

"Bend down, you crap Plore. You never did shit like this before, did you? I bet you go to church all the time. What are you, a Methodist?"

"Yes, sir."

David felt Battista's hand pressing down against his lower back, steadying him.

"That's good. I'll enjoy plugging you, choir boy. I can go all night. Drop trou, and don't keep me waiting!" David reached down, ostensibly to make it easier for Battista.

Two seconds later, as Battista fumbled with his fly, his eyes temporarily off David, David surged up, whirled around, his face stretched with rage, the knife in hand. A second later, he had sliced Battista deeply from throat to groin, and side to side. Battista had only a horrifying second to register that the meek face of his victim had transformed into a terrifying demon, complete with bared teeth. He then fell to the floor, leaving the world forever, not that it would miss him.

You shouldn't have messed with a real Antifan, buddy.

David grabbed Battista's brown and black checked sweater and black Antifan jacket, and pulled on the additional layers. The commander lay dead on the floor, blood pooling around him. David took the damp towel and covered the corpse, if only because he didn't need blood dripping through the floor and alerting anyone below. I am a tidy killer, he told himself, ironically. He poured his second glass of whiskey onto his hands and scrubbed. He heard nothing, but held the knife close as he slowly opened the door to the hallway.

He sidled downstairs, relieved that only two militiamen were left, and with any luck, they were already drunk or passed out. He would have climbed out the window instead, but was afraid he might fall to the ground and make an alerting noise, or even sprain an ankle, which would be a death sentence.

At the bottom of the stairs, he heard drunken voices rising and falling and a TV blaring behind a door to his left.

Good, David thought. He decided to exit through the kitchen and not risk the men seeing him on the porch. Then he remembered the Plore girl. She was stirring something on the stove, maybe his promised après-rape meal. It smelled like meat of some kind. When she saw David, his pants splattered with Battista's blood, and holding the knife, she fell back in fright.

"I killed him. We need to get out of here. Where's the key to that?" he asked, pointing her chain. She pointed mutely up at a high shelf. David climbed onto the counter and retrieved a key, freeing her from the chain. Later it occurred to him that she herself could have climbed the counter at any time and freed herself. But she hadn't.

"You got a coat?" he asked. She shook her head. "I'll give you this jacket, but let's get out of here first. Any matches here?"

She scrabbled in a drawer, and handed him a matchbook. David lit a match, then another, ran back into the hallway and tossed them at the staircase, just outside the closed living room door. They hurried from the kitchen into the dark night, and jumped into Battista's car. The key pod was lying on the passenger seat and David pressed the start button. Battista wouldn't have bothered to hide them. Who would steal the local Antifan militia commander's car? A few seconds later, they were driving back down the same road he had come up, and, looking behind them, they could see flames flickering through the windows.

"Where should we go?" he asked the girl, as if they were deciding on a dinner destination.

"My roundup," she replied. "Aunt Lucy will know what to do." Aunt Lucy again, David thought wonderingly.

As they drove briskly down the deserted road toward the lake in the moonlight, David following the girl's directions, he asked, "How did you end up working for the militia?"

"We always have to provide someone to work in their kitchen. So then they'll leave our roundup alone. This year was my turn. Aunt Lucy tried to send an older woman, but they wouldn't take her. When my year was up, which was going to be in March, I would get to choose whatever job I wanted in the roundup. Everyone agreed that would be fair. I'm going to be a seamster. I'm good with the needle."

"Did the militiamen pay you?"

The girl laughed genially. "Of course not. You get fed. And sometimes one of the militia would give you a few dollars if he felt sorry for you…afterward. I left it all behind now."

David felt anger course through him again. His throat was still sore and he was sure he was running a fever now. He felt light-headed.

"Don't be angry," the girl begged him. "That's just the way it is."

"What's your name?" he asked her.

"Jocelyn. Jocelyn Carter. Yours?"

He hesitated. "Mike Potter. Pleased to meet you."

They barreled down a gravel road and then a rutted dirt one, which narrowed and terminated in a clump of small wooden frame houses and a few dilapidated trailers. "This is our roundup," Jocelyn said proudly. "In the daytime, you can see Cayuga Lake just beyond the ridge."

"What's the roundup called?"

"Just Aunt Lucy's roundup. We're too small to be on a map, just as well."

Despite the late hour, nearing midnight, several people heard the car screech into the central gathering area, and after David and Jocelyn had stepped out of the car, they came out of the dark houses to greet them. Some exclaimed with pleasure to see Jocelyn, and hugged her. They gave David an odd look, especially because of the car that they recognized as the Antifan militia's. Thank goodness he had given Jocelyn the jacket and was not himself wearing it. They would have to bury or burn the incriminating jacket and sweater immediately, David realized.

"He rescued me!" Jocelyn called out, just in case anyone doubted David's bona fides. "He burned down the militia house!"

David was deliberating whether he ought to tell the crowd his version of what had happened at the militia headquarters, but he felt nauseous. The last thing he saw before he slumped to the ground was Aunt Lucy from the Candor Inn hurrying toward them, her face tight with concern in the moonlight. And then all went dark.

Chapter 29
Lessons In Power
(Tuesday, November 17, 2093)

Malia hunched over her laptop in the classroom at Beaufort, briskly answering the multiple choice quiz questions for the unit "Why Socialism?" Her Diversity economics instructor, Professor Gu (preferred pronouns zep, zarp) stared at her coolly, checking her answers simultaneously on zarp laptop. Zep reminded her of a giant-eyed beetle, but at least zep didn't yell at her, like some of the other instructors, like her Mother Earth ethics teacher, whose every second word was "heretic" or "fascist."

"One error, Prisoner Jenness," said Professor Gu. "Question seven, how does capitalism sustain racism? You answered (c), 'By legitimizing the belief that some are more deserving than others,' but the correct answer is (e), 'All of the above.' Your homework will be to write a two-page essay explaining the relationships between capitalism and racism."

Malia said, "Yes, amba-wah," using the polite salutation for a low Social Crediteer to a high Social Crediteer of ambiguous sexuality.

"See you on Thursday," said Professor Gu, "May Mother Earth sustain you." Malia gave the usual rejoinder, "And may She destroy our enemies."

Professor Gu exited, carrying zarp briefcase under zarp arm, and Malia waited patiently for lunch. She had made the connection between docility on one hand, and the quality of her food rations on the other. Exterra had confirmed that, telling her two weeks ago, "We've moved you into category three, just because you've been such a good student. No more Health Meat!" In practice, that meant a vegetarian diet and no meat, fake or otherwise, but at least Malia knew what she was eating. There were four categories of Beaufort prisoner; Malia had arrived as a two within the VIP group, which was a separate designation based on the sensitivity of the case. If she survived long enough to become a four, she would eat from the same kitchens that served ADF officers.

"And then," Exterra said excitedly, "you can have an evening off for good behavior and come visit me at the Avalon Tower!"

Malia's circumstances had improved since the zoo, and the nightmarish night in the cell block adjoining the firing range. On that Saturday night, now almost two months ago, she had huddled on the cot, listening to the periodic cries for mercy passing by her door and then the subsequent brief roll of gunfire that conveyed the response of the Diversity Justice Republic. *If I was miraculously spared last night*, she thought numbly, *they will not spare me for another.*

So when the door opened near midnight and two Antifan troops confronted her, with a third behind them in the doorway, she was sure she was being summoned to her death. She had resolved not to beg for mercy, but to call for freedom in the hallway loudly enough that some prisoners might hear, and that even her Antifan tormentors might remember. But facing the three stony faces, she forgot the words she had planned to utter, especially when one said to her, "You're going back upstairs."

"What?"

"You heard us. The Great Paragon our leader has spared you tonight." The speaker, a small wiry white man with a crew cut and tattoos encircling his arms, sounded disappointed. But he consoled himself that this was the only time he could ever remember a condemned prisoner once on this hallway escaping execution, so overall, Diverse discipline was maintained. Paragon knew best. And perhaps she would return to his hallway, soon.

They escorted her to the elevators, handed her over to another detachment, and soon she was back in her VIP quarters, as if she had never left. She slept deeply, and dreamed of nothing.

In the morning, she was served a Health Meat breakfast as if nothing had happened, except she was still eating gingerly due to the missing teeth. As she laid aside the eco-fork and knife, her tongue shivering at contact with the last oily nuggets, the bars of the door receded into the top of the doorframe and a tall gray-haired Antifan who looked vaguely familiar entered the room. The VIP quarters were spacious as cells went, but now they seemed to have shrunk with the officer's large presence; Malia became conscious of the low ceiling.

The man called through the now-descending bars, "Turn off the mic package. Completely."

"Yes, sir," came the prompt reply.

"May I?" he asked, indicating the armchair.

Malia nodded, joining him in the corner on the sofa. The MED Bible given her on Paragon's orders now rested conspicuously on the coffee table.

"Do you remember me?" he asked.

She was hesitant. "You look familiar." She was so terrible at remembering faces; David had joked about her cluelessness.

"I'm Steve Rosen. When we met, I was Commander Rosen and you came to

Beaufort to be debriefed on your visit to the Economic Zone."

"Yes!" she exclaimed, "I remember now. My husband always said you were a good person. He liked you very much."

"We were friends, before he betrayed us," said Steve evenly, but he warmed to the compliment.

"You would know…is he alive? They tell me he's dead, that he was killed during the raid."

"Yes, he was killed during the raid."

"Oh!" If Steve Rosen, a man of integrity, was telling her that David was dead, it must be so. She had not detected any hesitation on his part.

"Open your mouth," he requested. Puzzled, she complied.

"We'll get a dentist here to look at you immediately. It seems you lost a tooth or two during your adventure at the zoo. And you have some bruises, at least on your arms, and on your forehead." Lacking a mirror, Malia did not realize her face still showed the impact of the rubber balls.

"Aside from that," Steve asked wryly, "how are you doing?"

"Much better than two nights ago," said Malia, "when I was sure I was going to die."

"Yes, that was ridiculous. I'm sorry. Sometimes Commander Ma goes too far, and he was very upset about what happened at the zoo. When I heard where you were, I had them bring you back upstairs immediately." Steve did not tell Malia that her survival had required him to argue strenuously with Montoya once again, pointing out that even if St. Louis was not overly eager to recover Malia, the negotiations would break off if it were proven the DJR had killed her in its custody.

"They won't find out," spat Montoya, even as the Texas Intelligence Agency report was landing in the AIA's cable queue.

"She's too valuable right now," Steve said. "Let's not throw away our big chips here over a stupid speech at the zoo that nobody will remember next week." So Montoya had spared Malia's life and Steve had raced back to Beaufort to extract her from the basement before the inexorable death machinery sucked her into its maw.

Now in her VIP quarters, Steve said, "Malia, I am now the deputy director of this agency. Even so, I don't have the ultimate say over what happens to you. I don't know whether we will exchange you with the US for some political or economic favor. I don't know whether Director Montoya or Paragon will overrule me and demand that you be executed…"

She looked pale under the bruises, which was gratifying, since it suggested she might take his warnings seriously.

"I really don't know what will happen. But if you want me to be in a position to help you, you need to help me. We need to keep you alive as long as possible so a political deal might eventually become possible. And how do you stay alive here? For one thing, by not giving political speeches at the zoo, all right?"

They exchanged tentative smiles with each other.

"I understand you are taking a lot of Diversity courses to bring you back into the fold. Doubtless a lot of it seems silly or pointless. I know it's been many years since you were in a classroom here. But can you at least pretend to go along with it?"

"Most of it is sheer lunacy to me, not just silliness," said Malia. "If you talked like this in the United States, they'd throw you in a mental hospital."

"You're not in the United States, if you haven't noticed yet. Pretend to learn it again, can you? If the teachers give good reports to Commander Ma, it will keep you alive until we can resolve your case." Steve's arms were now crossed on his chest. He hadn't wanted to be quite so blunt, but it he wasn't sure from the pout on Malia's face that she really understood that her continued resistance might condemn her. "And eventually you'll be able to return to your family—your sons." He realized he had "exceeded his brief," as they put it at Beaufort, but he could explain it as just trying to secure her cooperation. Lying to prisoners to achieve confessions or good behavior was standard operational practice.

"Malia, I want you to survive. I know I shouldn't say this, but I want to do it out of respect for what you accomplished on our behalf in '89, and yes, out of respect for David's memory. There, I said it." He looked at her pleadingly. "Now that I've taken a chance and said something that even the deputy director shouldn't have said…can you please behave for a while?"

Malia said, "Yes, I will. And thank you for your honesty."

Not sure I would call it honesty, he thought, but perhaps it is sincerity.

"But I don't understand. If you're the deputy director, don't you outrank Commander Ma? Couldn't you just tell him how you want to handle my case?"

"Yes, but I don't outrank our director, who is no friend of yours. And Ma's a special case. After you and David and the other Antifans escaped, we cracked down. We needed to fight subversion in our own ranks, not just in the Economic and the Knowledge Towers, because your husband's betrayal opened our eyes. So Commander Ma is our political commissar, and he commands a special force that undertakes unusual projects, such as your recovery."

"Kidnapping!"

"Malia…I'm just telling you why he doesn't fit into the normal chain of command here. And have you wondered why you are in VIP quarters at all? And haven't been beaten, or assaulted at night? Do you think Commander Ma wanted you treated well, or maybe someone else pulled some strings to keep you safe?" His steady brown gaze engaged hers. He rose to leave, saying, "Just help me help you, all right?"

Since then, Malia had been a model prisoner. The next day, when Professor Tunwell explained to her the evil of whiteness, she had nodded dutifully, and repeated back the main points flawlessly.

Chapter 30
Mysterious Antifan Deaths
(Wednesday, November 18, 2093)

Montoya distractedly watched Paragon as the political commissar directed a workman who was placing the Mother Earth statue in the newly built recessed nook in the director's office. "No, a few inches to the left…a little farther back. It shouldn't look straight ahead, a little off to the side…Yes, that's good." Since Montoya preferred to keep the lights dimmed in his office, the light shining on Mother Earth from the nook ceiling only made it the center of attention.

Out of respect for the Transsexual Union at Beaufort, the Mother Earth statue mostly consisted of plaster waves and swirls of robes and a featureless half-hidden face. It was considered mildly sacrilegious to represent the features of any woman as Mother Earth, mother or not, since that might offend those who demanded the goddess feature an Adam's Apple and a brawny frame, just on principle. A plaster globe representing the earth hovered behind Her head just off to the side, supported by an invisible but taut wire. Looks like a witch in moonlight, Steve Rosen thought to himself, hoping Paragon would not inflict statuary on his office as well. This Mother Earth faced off against a statue of the manlier St. John Beaufort, the founder of the ADF, set on a pedestal across the room.

"I don't know, Khalid," Montoya said. "I'm fine with St. John, that's definitely relevant, but what does Mother Earth have to do with our mission?"

Paragon sighed in Montoya's direction. "Vlad, Mother Earth reigns over all of us, even the ADF. The ADF leads the nation, and what would we be telling Diversans if our director saw Mother Earth as irrelevant to our leadership? Not quite a knowledge crime, of course, but we could come under criticism if it were known that ADF director Montoya refused to honor Mother Earth in his own office."

"What if we put it in the lobby instead?" suggested Steve.

The two others looked at him with dismay.

"No, that would be even worse," Montoya admitted. He turned to admire the St. John statue, which showed him looking heavenward while clutching a rifle. Montoya was old enough to have seen St. John in person, toward the end of the civil war, when the hero—not yet become a saint—had addressed Montoya's battalion before the Battle of Atlanta. St. John had urged them to not be deterred by the pending peace treaty, and to kill as many Red Deplorables as possible, by trickery if necessary, until peace was forced upon them. Montoya and his comrades had howled themselves hoarse in adoration. Montoya conceded that the statue, with its rippling plaster muscles, was an improvement over the spindly, high-voiced St. John he remembered.

"Anyway, more serious business," said Montoya, as the workman departed. "The militia chief for New York–Schuylkill is coming in a few minutes to talk about the killing that happened last weekend south of Syracuse. They're sure Plores did it. We can't tolerate this kind of behavior—once Plores get away with this once, they won't stop. Taste of blood and all that.

"Khalid, I think you should stay and hear this. Maybe you'll have some of those great ideas since we're talking Plore pacification."

Paragon inclined his head in modest acknowledgement of Montoya's praise.

The militia chief for NY–Schuylkill, Commander Ariella Hernandez, arrived with a much more junior militiaman, a scrubbed looking youngster with a round pink face and round blue eyes. They Antifan-saluted the three leaders, trying to balance their exultation at the honor of visiting Beaufort, let alone meeting with the director, with sober recollection of the tragedy that had brought them to this room. Hernandez bowed deeply to the Mother Earth statue, the young officer following suit, which made the trio smile, and Steve Rosen discreetly coughed into a handkerchief. That Paragon, thought Montoya admiringly, he really does understand things we old policemen just don't. He also suspected it had been many years since the chubby Hernandez had gotten out from behind her desk in Paterdaughter, NJ, the headquarters of the regional militia, once known as Paterson, and soon to be renamed Materdaughter after Paragon's naming team had belatedly realized that "pater" meant "father" in Latin.

"Welcome to Beaufort," said Montoya gravely. "We are all very disturbed at the events of last weekend. We must track down the murderer of our comrades."

"Thank you, Director Montoya," said Hernandez. "I have brought along Lieutenant Loki Greene from the Seventh Unit for New York–Schuylkill, which is based in Tompkins County, south of Syracuse." Montoya's assistant brought up on the screen a detailed map of the location, and handed the laser pointer to Hernandez. "Lieutenant Greene was in the company of the murdered Antifans on Saturday night. He is our only eyewitness to what happened that night, because he was dismissed for the night after the squad arrived back at the building with a prisoner."

Loki, Paragon approved, a very Pagan name, if Nordic. The younger generation was throwing aside the shackles of Christian custom with gusto. And no harm either, that last name Greene!

Greene explained that the squad had gone to the Candor Inn to do a routine check on Plore IDs. The laser pointer trembled over Candor. "Lots of Plores gather there on weekend nights, and we just thought it was good for Diverse discipline to let them know we are watching them."

"Excellent, Lieutenant," said Montoya, leaning back in his leather chair.

"We found a Plore who seemed to be suspicious, and decided to bring him back to headquarters for questioning, even though it was late on a Saturday night. None of the other Plores spoke up for him, so we knew he was a vagrant, and probably up to no good."

"Go on, Lieutenant."

"We returned to the house, and brought the Plore upstairs to Commander Battista so he could be personally interrogated."

"And did any of you stay for the interrogation?"

"No, sir. Commander Battista told me I could go home, since my wife was waiting up for me. The other two—Deputy Commander Gutakas and Private Johnson—went downstairs to do some paperwork in the office, because of the arrest."

"Why wouldn't they have stayed upstairs? They weren't afraid that the prisoner could turn on your commander?"

"No, sir."

"That's typical procedure for you guys? Seems a little careless," said Steve, turning around from the window where he stood.

"Yes, sir."

"Did you often do these kinds of interrogation on a Saturday night?" Steve asked. "Why wouldn't you just have locked the guy up until Monday? Don't you have a jail around there?"

"Yes, sir, in Cortland, but that's a long drive," said Greene. "If it turned out the prisoner had a legitimate reason for being in the area, we might just have let him loose to find his way home. We do have a shed where we lock up prisoners for a few hours, but it wouldn't have sufficed until Monday, given the cold temperatures we're having at night."

"So Commander Battista was questioning this fellow alone, in his study, which if I understand is also his bedroom," said Steve. He had read the dossier, which Paragon hadn't, and which Montoya had only skimmed, and knew about those extra forty gay points. He had also seen the report from the ADF unit in Syracuse about the abduction of the blond stranger from the eatery.

Greene said, "Yes, sir."

"How often did these Saturday night interrogations take place, and were they also one-on-one between Commander Battista and the prisoner?"

"Yes, sir," gulped Greene, knowing where this was going. "Every few weeks or so."

"Was Commander Battista taking advantage of his position to sexually abuse prisoners?"

"Well, sir, I can't say for sure because I myself never…"

"Lieutenant Greene, would you please just tell the truth?"

"Now, Rosen," cautioned Montoya. "Militias need to be tough with the locals. They don't have the luxury of operating in Anacosta."

"If this murder was provoked by a homosexual rape, I think we ought to know about these extenuating circumstances," Steve insisted.

"You sound a little homophobic, Rosen," Paragon inserted silkily.

"All I am suggesting," said Steve, "is that the prisoner might have taken offense to an effort to seduce him. Plores are very sensitive about such things, being backward in these matters." They all turned to Greene, who blushed pink under the scrutiny.

"Yes, sir, I have to admit that Commander Battista probably did try to assault the prisoner. That was part of his usual interrogation method."

"What did the prisoner look like?" Steve asked. "Was he good-looking?"

"Yes, sir, at least by conventional racist standards. Blond, medium to tall height, thirty-five according to his ID, but very fit."

"So he might have taken the fancy of your commander."

"Yes, sir, Commander Battista said after we checked the IDs and found out his age, that thirty-five was good for tonight, that he preferred mature to youthful that night."

"How many IDs did you check?"

"Commander Battista picked out two others initially, but we only took the blond one."

ID check, my foot, thought Steve, and when his eyes met Montoya's, he realized the director was thinking the same thing, that the squad had entered the Candor Inn for one reason, and not for the first time. Normally Beaufort left militias up to their own business of pacifying the countryside, and as long as the locals stayed quiescent, Beaufort wasn't too fussy about the exact methods used. But this unit seemed wilder than most, which had backfired.

"Did they check women's IDs, or only the men's?" asked Steve.

"Only the men's," admitted Greene, glad that Battista was no longer around to punish him.

"Now another thing, Lieutenant. Did you frisk the prisoner before you took him from the inn?"

"We did it when we reached the house, sir. We found nothing on him to cause concern."

"Was it a full-body search?"

"No, sir, just down to the hips."

"Sounds a little careless too."

"They're just Plores, sir, we don't expect resistance. They know what the consequences would be."

Commander Hernandez broke in, to say that Unit 7 had clearly violated protocols laid out for them by ADF NY-Schuylkill HQ in Paterdaughter. "Nor would we countenance such arbitrary and brutal treatment of locals," she rushed to assure the senior leaders in the room.

The three men gave her a dismissive look. "Was this the first time you'd ever heard of Unit Seven?" asked Montoya.

"Yes, Director. It's never come up before as a problem. I have a deputy commander who would have collected any complaints against the unit."

"Maybe he ought to be here," Montoya said, implicitly saying, "instead of you."

"It would be zee, sir. Deputy Commander Pennington's pronouns are zee and zir."

"Director," said Steve Rosen, more formal in the presence of the visitors. "Another issue of interest is the nature of the killing, at least of Commander Battista. The autopsy report says the two subordinates died of smoke inhalation, exacerbated by intoxication. Commander Battista was knifed to death, but not in the way you'd expect by an ordinary Plore, a stabbing. It was a rapid-fire cross-sectional slice—which we teach at Beaufort. It kills virtually instantly."

Montoya and Paragon looked shocked. Hernandez and Greene did not seem to have absorbed the implications of that remark, not yet.

"I don't think any ordinary Plore would have known about that technique," continued Steve.

"Sir, the Plores in our neck of the woods tend to be good hunters," responded Greene. "Many of them are very skilled with knives, because they rely on game for food but cannot use firearms."

"Fine, Lieutenant," said Steve, "but I do not think they use the rapid-fire cross-sectional slice maneuver when gutting a deer."

"What are you saying, Rosen?" Montoya asked irritably. "Are you saying this killer learned how to use a knife from us?"

"Even more concerning, Director, I would hazard that he was one of us."

"Why would a former Antifan be hanging out in a crummy Plore eatery in the middle of nowhere?" Even though Plores were restricted to containment areas, those could encompass thousands of square miles, whereas Social Crediteers tended to stick close to cities and not wander into the countryside unless they were enforcing Diversity.

Paragon spoke up, "Lieutenant, please describe the prisoner to us again."

"Yes, sir. Blond, short beard, blue or gray eyes, mid to late thirties, not quite tall, well-built, which is why Commander Battista took a shine to him. He wasn't local, since he had a big backpack with him and a bedroll."

The three senior leaders looked at each other, aghast at the possibility.

"No!" said Montoya. "It couldn't be."

Steve said grimly, "It could be. He has a reason to sneak back into the country."

"But upstate New York?"

"Easier to come from Canada than back into Virginia. Lots of truck traffic. We check all the trucks leaving the DJR, but not so carefully coming back in here."

Montoya tapped on his workscreen. "Lieutenant, come look at this photo. Was this man the prisoner?"

Greene came around to Montoya's side. "Yes, sir. Maybe the photo's a little younger, but the same man."

"Commander Hernandez," asked Paragon, "have you confiscated that backpack yet?"

Hernandez cast a helpless look at Greene, who said, "When we returned to the diner on Monday, the backpack had disappeared. The owner said that someone must have stolen it over the weekend, maybe when the diner was closed on Sunday. Plores are like that, they must have figured the owner wasn't coming back for it."

"Have you located the girl who worked in the kitchen?" asked Steve. "I understand we didn't find her body in the ruins. Do you think she ran off with the attacker?"

"We haven't been able to search the area, sir. A very treacherous ice storm happened on Monday and almost all the villages are inaccessible. Only the major roads have been cleared."

Montoya turned grimly to Hernandez. "Hernandez, this operation falls to you. You need to move militia units into that area at once, from other parts of the region if necessary, and you need to search every single damn hut in every single village. If our attacker doesn't have his gear, he won't have gotten very far in these conditions. We are going to hold you personally responsible for finding this murderer, or you'll be doing swamp duty in Florida by spring." Hernandez was trembling. This was out of her comfort zone, which mostly involved shuffling spreadsheets and giving inspirational speeches at monthly Pride events in the auditorium.

"Use aircraft if you can't open the roads. Use the drone fleet. Show no mercy to anyone who stands in your way. If possible, capture this attacker alive. I will authorize all ADF resource areas to supply this effort. Do you understand me?"

"Yes, Director," quavered Hernandez.

"Sir, I know the village where the girl is from. If she escaped with the attacker, it's likely they went to shelter there."

"If they're idiots," said Montoya, "but since we're dealing with Plores, you're probably right. Hernandez, please make sure this young officer is closely involved with the effort because he clearly knows the area. And now you know where to start your search."

"Yes, sir," said Hernandez, dazed. The door closed behind them.

Montoya shook his head. "That sounds like a rogue unit, all right. We'll deal with them later. What matters is that the photo of Harris was the same man they arrested."

"This is an excellent chance to capture him," Paragon reminded them. "He's lost his gear, the winter's set in, and he probably doesn't have the connections to keep himself safe or alive up there. We need to move fast."

"And," said Steve, "we need to ask our station chief in St. Louis to track down Harris in the US. If we can locate him there, we'll know he's not the one here. Just in case."

Paragon smiled a wolfish grin at them as he headed for the door. "Gentlemen, the Resolution Command is on the job. My loyalty and my honor." Back in his office, he called out, "Vanover! I need to talk with you. Right now!"

Marcus Vanover emerged from a corner room where he was listening to armband recordings; he had been assigned to mundane surveillance tasks ever since returning from Oklahoma.

"Now Vanover, how would you like a chance to kill David Harris? I'm assuming you'd be more successful this time."

"Commander, it would be an honor. Thank you for your confidence in me."

"I'm not confident yet. Here's your mission..."

Chapter 31
Out Of Town
(Tuesday, November 24, 2093 and Friday, November 27, 2093)

Private Gwen Gong, 140, called Daniel Harris and left a message seeking a callback from Mr. David Harris. "I represent Bartlett Enterprises and we are trying to find Mr. David Harris, who has won our sweepstakes this week." One generally could not make direct phone calls between the two countries, but ADF cyberwarriors had hacked a discreet path into the US phone system that could be exploited when needed.

The next day when she called David Harris's house, his stepdaughter answered, said, "He's not home," and hung up.

"Hmm," said Paragon, when Private Gong's branch chief brought him the news that they had not yet reached David Harris. He spoke "St. Louis" into his console, and his successor as St. Louis station chief, Henry Warner, answered immediately. The ruddy, blond Warner was officially known to US authorities—had they cared to know—as a Canadian dealer in grain doing business with Midwestern companies.

"Hello, Khalid," said Henry. "I guess you want a report on our efforts to track down Harris."

"Yes."

"Well, it's not easy during Thanksgiving week, you know. And my officer can't just sit in front of their house all the time. It's a quiet suburban street, and he'd look conspicuous."

"I hope you're not going to waste my time telling me why you can't carry out the task I've assigned you."

"Not at all! In fact, my officer had a little coup this morning. He was parked a little down the street from the Harris house, in a plumbing van. Nothing out of the ordinary, someone might just assume a neighbor had a broken pipe. He was leaning against it, in workmen's—sorry, workpeople's clothes, just pretending to take a break. So this little Asian—I mean Asian-American—guy came walking along with a dog, and said hello. My guy engaged him in a conversation, and it turned out that he did know the Harrises."

"And?" Paragon pressed.

"He said that David Harris had had a nervous breakdown about a month ago and was at some mental hospital."

"Which mental hospital?"

"He didn't know. He just said that the children were staying with the brother, and wasn't it a shame?"

"What about the daughter?"

"My officer didn't ask. But it wasn't really necessary, because he's seen the daughter go in and out of the house occasionally. Sometimes with a young man."

"Short guy, glasses, brown hair cut short, a little poindex?" Poindex was Antifan slang for intellectual.

"Yeah, how do you know?"

Paragon didn't bother to tell Henry about the Beltane hookup. Instead, he asked, "How about calling all the likely psychiatric hospitals within a hundred miles to make sure Harris is really at one?" He listened impatiently to Henry's objection. "If they won't tell you over the phone, find out another way. They can't be paying their orderlies a lot. Find orderlies and bribe them. Or fuck a nurse. For Mother's sake, man, do I have to tell you how to do your job?

"Do you think your officer might run into the Asian guy again? Do you have a better description of him? Was he Chinese or Korean?"

"No," said Henry, his feelings bruised. "He was maybe Filipino or Indian. I can't tell the difference—they have a lot of immigrants here."

"Keep our officer there another week or so in case he runs into the guy again, all right? Now that they're acquainted, maybe the convo can go deeper?"

"Yes, chief," said Henry, who had been proud of his officer's discovery and now realized he had only created more work for himself. But not before Thanksgiving, he vowed. Even a Diversan spy was entitled to his turkey dinner, and his unwitting American girlfriend, the daughter of the junior senator from Missouri, would be cooking a feast for them. He told Paragon, who laughed at the stupidity of the Americans.

The mention of Thanksgiving reminded Paragon that Harvest Dinner, the DJR's version of the holiday, was nearing, and Exterra was still hounding him to invite Malia Harris to their apartment—no, *his* apartment, for the festive meal on Friday. Wasn't it enough for them to celebrate together, with a lovely meal from the top caterer in Anacosta, Cookerrie House No. 1, for 150 and over? They had argued about Malia Jenness only last night, as they sat on the beige faux leather sofa after dinner, Exterra's legs curled under her and Paragon stretching his long ones over the coffee table, pushing aside a large pictographic volume called *New Progressive Art of the DJR*. His arms were crossed.

"Khalid, she's been so much better behaved since the zoo! Her professors have been giving us sterling reports! The Diversity history teacher said that he even learned a lot from her explanation of how racism continues to permeate the United States. She's really not a knowledge criminal and she shouldn't be a regular prisoner at this point."

"Has she undergone the truth serum yet? You do realize that she may just be trying to fool us until some kind of deal can be worked out? Maybe she just realized how close she was to being executed and decided to behave. Try to be less naive."

Exterra's saucer-blue eyes brimmed with tears. Paragon drew in closer to kiss Exterra's mouth, almost tenderly. An Antifan captain, even a woman, should be more resolute and less naive in appraising a traitorous knowledge criminal, he thought. But he knew Exterra's true motives. Over the last few months, she had become close to Malia, having no close female friends herself, and Malia as a prisoner was completely unable to ignore or refuse her overtures. He guessed that Exterra wished to take advantage of the private Avalon setting to seduce Malia, which would be impossible in VIP quarters at Beaufort under a battery of cameras and against Steve Rosen's instructions. Antifans found it hard to build friendships with those outside of Beaufort, and Exterra's relationship with Paragon only made it more difficult for her.

It was hard for Paragon to object in principle, and he found it less threatening for her to dally with another woman than with a man. Not to mention Exterra could parlay that into an extra ten points for bisexuality, which would bring her up to a more respectable 185. Paragon thought it very sensible. He also figured that Steve Rosen's injunction probably didn't cover this situation.

But in my apartment, he thought with horror. A knowledge criminal in my bed?

"All right," he said, "she can have an overnight pass. But you are responsible for making sure that she does nothing wrong while she's here, and she goes back to Beaufort in the morning. And I'm going to accept the director's invitation, so I won't be here when she arrives so she won't ruin my appetite. And you'd better schedule that truth serum test soon if you want to bring her over again. And finally, I will not touch that knowledge criminal, so don't think you can involve me in your romantic scenario. She disgusts me—she is one degree removed from David Harris and now I have to be two degrees removed from that traitor's flesh."

Exterra smiled sweetly. "Khalid, you understand me so well. Thank you for your kindness."

"It's not kindness," he grumbled. "Those are five very firm conditions. You haven't yet taken me up on my offer until now to let you have your own version of Bettina or Ivan, so I suppose I need to be generous here."

They drew together.

"I might watch," he grudgingly conceded as they parted to take a breath.

"Oh, that would be so much fun!" Exterra giggled. "You'd probably have all kinds of suggestions for how we could improve our technique."

Paragon smiled thinly at her. "And I'm only agreeing because at some bizarre level, this is a pro-Diversity endeavor. You've been very rigid in your heterosexuality. Perhaps this can be seen as another way to draw Prisoner Jenness back to properly Diverse behaviors. Does she still think her husband is alive?"

"I showed her about two weeks ago the two US news videos that we deepfaked. If you remember, we even spliced in footage of his alleged funeral, and even of their pastor giving a funeral sermon, although it was someone else's, of course."

"Beautifully done," Paragon recalled. "And what was her reaction?"

"She was silent. But later that evening, she said, 'I will miss him.'"

"Maybe this is the right moment to bring her here," Paragon mused. "She's had a little time to grieve, and perhaps she is thinking of the way forward."

"You're so good to me," Exterra murmured, to which he responded dryly, "All for Diversity." But this time they did not draw apart.

Malia was awed at her good fortune. An excursion to the Avalon Tower, where she had lived with David. And a real Harvest Dinner feast! Exterra brought her an almost-normal outfit of green denim and a long-sleeved olive-green blouse. She apologized for the open-topped unlaced cloth sneakers, "but once you're in our apartment, you can just take them off."

Paragon's penthouse apartment was at least half again the size of David's, as befitted the third-in-command at Beaufort. But Malia recognized the same type of floor-to-ceiling drapes running along the rounded living room windows, and she knew that the Avalon still rotated gently on its pivot, giving its privileged residents a different view of the surrounding City every seventy-two hours, so smoothly that one would never notice except for the ever-changing vistas.

Most elite Social Krediteers would have requested a Plore servant from the City agency that provided temporary household help; it was a common practice when you were entertaining on Harvest Dinner evening. Plores would have enjoyed their Thanksgiving meal the day before, after all, since it was inexplicably celebrated on Thursdays. But Paragon refused to have Plores enter his apartment at all. Even their cleaners were low Social Krediteers hired from the building.

"We'll set it up ourselves!" enthused Exterra. The doorbell rang as the concierge brought up the Cookerrie House delivery. The concierge, who recognized Malia, almost dropped the vat of soup. Malia smiled at him. That was Jayson, who had tended her cats Ansel and Frida, who were now living in Ploreville with Marjory. She held her finger to her mouth behind Exterra's back.

"Please be more careful," Exterra admonished.

"Yes, amba-mam, sorry about that. My hands were slippery."

Once Jayson had retreated, the women began laying out the dinner. Malia's mouth watered longingly as they unpacked foods she had not eaten in many months.

Finally, all was done, and Malia's stomach was rumbling with anticipation. But where was Paragon?

"He's at the director's house," said Exterra. "You know, you can't exactly refuse an invitation from the director. He told us to start before him. That's the considerate Diverse man he is!"

They tucked into their meal of roast chicken—the historic US-patriotic associations of turkey made it unsuitable for Harvest holiday dinner—stir-fried spinach, potatoes, cranberry sauce, roasted vegetables, and a yogurt-based cream of carrot soup. Fresh soft yellow rolls accompanied the meal. Exterra poured them both deep glasses of non-Diversity cultivated red wine from France, and was quick to refill Malia's glass twice.

Exterra chattered about movies and her plans to take a trip with Paragon to Florida over Saturnalia. She mentioned a new comedy club in Anacosta, "We can take you there! That can be your next outing. Just please continue to be good!

"Maybe we should take a break before dessert?" The pecan and sweet beet pies were lying on the counter.

Malia nodded, feeling slightly unwell.

Exterra sat a bit more closely to Malia than the prisoner felt comfortable with. She reached along the top of the sofa to touch Malia's stiffening shoulder.

"We're so pleased with how far you've come. Paragon wants you to take the truth serum test so we can begin integrating you back into society. Until then, you have to stay at Beaufort, though."

"What would my Social Credit score be then?" Malia was curious. She knew that if David were to rescue her, it would be a lot easier for him if she were to have been released into Anacostan society than if she were jailed at Beaufort. The video footage Exterra had shown her had not truly convinced her, since she knew that Beaufort film editors could splice and craft whatever propaganda they wanted. Nor had they shown her the footage earlier, when she would have believed it more readily—it had taken a suspiciously long time to unearth. And Beaufort had had plenty of photos of David Harris to work with. Yet Malia was discreetly implying that she was beginning to believe their lie, since it was not in her interest anymore to argue with them about it.

"It would depend on your job assignment, wouldn't it?" said Exterra. "I haven't talked about it with Khalid, but I was imagining you could be a promotional speaker for Diversity. The Knowledge Tower sends speakers out across the country. You would be unique, having come back from the United States. People would love to hear your story!"

She lowered her voice meaningfully. "I am sure that the motivational speakers are at least 150, depending on their stories. And you'd be a celebrity!"

Malia felt nauseous. "Exterra, I'm sorry, I must have eaten too much…" In the marble bathroom, at least twice the size of David's, she vomited.

Exterra met her with a glass of water, which Malia drank gratefully.

"I'm sorry," she said, "I should have anticipated you wouldn't be ready to eat such a high credit meal after all these months at Beaufort. We could have eaten a little and then waited for Khalid. I haven't been a very thoughtful host."

"Exterra, if you don't mind, could I lie down?" she pleaded. "I'm feeling a little dizzy."

Ah, the medication interacted with the wine, Exterra thought regretfully. I should have anticipated this.

"Of course," Exterra said, leading her down the short corridor to the guest room. "Why don't you take a short nap?"

Malia luxuriated on the bed with the soft comforter and pillows. The comforter had a classic Diversity pattern, as you would expect from Paragon's guest room, with the anarchist symbol contained within a sunburst. The softness and warmth of the comforter and pillows were as much of a treat as the meal had been. Exterra placed the water glass on the nightstand, and withdrew, turning off the light and closing the door all but a crack. Malia glimpsed a thin line of light from the hallway before she fell asleep.

When she awakened an hour later, she started, feeling an unaccustomed soft body pressing into hers. Moonlight spilled over the bed. Looking to her right, Malia saw Exterra, lying on her side, smiling tenderly at her. To Malia's shock, Exterra was wearing a short black nightgown, the same one she used to entice Paragon after a long day at work. Her long blonde hair streamed over her bare shoulders. Even in the dark, the moonlight highlighted Exterra's dual-color face, making Exterra herself seem like a half-moon, with one bright side shining on the earth below, Malia's own face, and the other discreetly turned away in eclipse.

"Hello, Malia, dear," cooed Exterra, placing her hands on Malia's shoulders and moving them downward to her breasts. She placed her mouth on Malia's, which involuntarily opened in response. Malia suddenly jerked awake, but was paralyzed under those wandering hands. And she could not deny the fluttering in parts that had not been touched or aroused in months. "You're my prisoner, you know." The hands moved downward.

"No!" Malia shouted, pushing Exterra away.

"There is no 'no' here," Exterra said severely. "Do you realize who you're talking to? Stop being such a fascist." She sat up, and pinned Malia to the bed, resuming the kiss. Malia twisted beneath her, and began to cry.

"Oh for Mother's sake!" Exterra snapped. "What is wrong with you?"

The women heard the door open, and Exterra leaped off the bed. "That's Paragon," she flung back at Malia, "he won't be very happy about how uncooperative you are. This was a good opportunity to show how Diverse-minded you've become and you've ruined it." She flounced out of the room, slamming the door behind her.

Malia's sobs receded into a few small scattered chokes. She still felt slightly queasy from the rich meal. She drank lengthily from the glass on the nightstand. Although she couldn't make out the words, she heard Paragon's deep voice alternating with Exterra's presumed complaints.

Then she felt rather than heard the quiet thud of Paragon's footsteps coming down the hallway. Fearful, she curled up on the bedspread and pretended to sleep. The door opened, and even though it was risky, she peered through narrow slits at his dark outline, framed in the yellow light of the hallway. He was wearing his uniform, no doubt because he had attended Montoya's event; the broad-shouldered jacket nipped his waist, and the slim cloth pants that were barely wider than leggings broke off at the edge of the bed, below which she could not see.

He looked down at her from the doorway. Her eyes had now firmly shut. She imagined his eyes and breath upon her. Surely he could tell she was awake. Then he abruptly turned around and left the room, leaving the door slightly ajar, the thin line of yellow light casting a ray across the bedspread. At that distance, she could make out only some words that indicated he was telling Exterra about the director's dinner. Then Malia heard giggles, and deeper chuckles. She feared that they were now discussing, "What do we do with Malia Jenness?" and whatever they decided would not be in her interest. All she wanted to do was escape, even if she had nowhere to go.

Malia remembered that all the Avalon apartments opened onto a back staircase, the entrance to which was always at the end of the corridor with the guest room and the bathroom. She did not care that her sad prison shoes were in the living room, and her feet were clad only in thick indoor socks that Exterra had given her. By coincidence, a musky-smelling man's sweater lay draped on the chair in the room, perhaps left by the last non-jailed guest. Malia pulled it on, and tiptoed to the door. Paragon still seemed to be relaying details to Exterra about the dinner, a conversation punctuated by brief silences that masked affectionate interludes. Exterra was still wearing the nightgown that Paragon liked, and he was teasing her that she had wasted it on Malia Jenness.

"Go get her," ordered Paragon, as he started laying out the half-eaten dishes. The loving intermission with Exterra had improved his mood. "I can tolerate her at the table."

Exterra ran back into the living room. "She's not there!" she gasped. "Or in the bathroom."

Paragon and Exterra now remembered that David Harris had lived at the Avalon, and Malia must have known about the back staircases. Amateur hour, Paragon grimaced. Exterra should have locked that door electronically the second Malia entered the apartment.

"I'll meet her at the bottom," he told Exterra. "You start heading down the staircase from the other direction. She won't get away." Reaching for his jacket and armband, he took the express elevator downstairs, ran outside, and stationed himself outside the entrance to his private staircase. It was a cold, dark, cloudless night, and while he waited for Malia to emerge, he stared up at the starry sky. The same sky that his elderly mother, back in China, presumably saw. It had been a long time since he had last heard from her, or more precisely, since he had failed to respond to her last email. He knew that his brothers, now senior functionaries in the Ministry of State Security in Xinjiang, or as senior as you could become with a Uighur mother, were taking care of her since their father's death several years ago, but he felt a little badly and unfilial. Family ties were a hindrance to Diversity here in the DJR, he reasoned, but in China it was still the fabric of an ancient culture.

The door flung open, slamming into his armband, and surprised in his reverie, he grabbed at but missed Malia as she flew by him. He caught up quickly, twisting her arm as he whirled her toward him.

"Sit down there," he said curtly, indicating a park bench under a tree. "What the fuck were you thinking?"

She obeyed, panting heavily, since she had run downstairs in the flimsy socks. He sat down at the other end of the bench. Nobody was within earshot in the darkness.

"You can't even behave at a Harvest dinner," he snapped.

"The dinner wasn't the problem."

"You don't know how to accept Diverse hospitality. You gobbled too much food and made yourself sick. Then you were inexcusably rude to Captain Boyd. And I'm going to add homophobia to your list of crimes."

She dared to look directly at him. "If she had told me she planned to attack me, I would have stayed at Beaufort. I'm not that desperate for a meal."

He stared her down. "Hard to tell from what you managed to eat. You didn't leave much for me, I notice. And you're wearing my sweater. Now I'm going to have to throw it out."

And then, almost speaking to himself, he asked, "What the hell are we going to do with you, Malia Jenness?"

The tower back door opened about a hundred feet away, and Exterra peeked out. In the dark, she didn't see them on the bench. Confused, she left the building, and walked around to the lobby, where she would take the elevator upstairs. Malia started to call to her, but Paragon said, "Never mind. We'll just go back the way you came." They walked back to the tower, whose door Paragon opened with a wave of his armband. Malia, who was shivering, initially welcomed the comparative warmth of the tower.

He then made Malia climb forty stories, a feat far beyond her modest physical strength these days, and made harder still by the socks on her feet, on which blisters had begun to form. Paragon followed behind her, leaning against the wall with his arms crossed every time she halted, panting. She sat on the top step of every flight, breathing heavily, and crying after the eighteenth. "I can't do it," she said. "I don't know what's happened to me, but I can't do it. You can beat me to death, but I won't do it."

"You pathetic fascist bitch," Paragon said coolly after each outburst. "This can take all night, but you'll do it. Think of all the marginalized groups you and your people brutalized for hundreds of years. You didn't give them a break, did you? This is only a small payback. Feel free to crawl."

At the fortieth floor, she finally collapsed on the landing—with no exits, only a small landing punctuated the staircase on every tenth floor. The tower was designed only for speedy escape, not for reentry. Paragon stared disgustedly at her. After several minutes during which Malia just lay there, and he considered kicking her back down the stairs, he picked her up, and carried her up the remaining ten flights to the penthouse. Barely conscious, but crying, she felt his strong shoulder under her heaving chest as they mounted the final flights. He dropped her on the guest bed and signaled to Exterra.

In the morning, they returned her to Beaufort.

Chapter 32
Nurse And Killers
(Friday–Saturday, November 20–21, 2093)

A spoonful of warm chicken soup. David opened his mouth and swallowed obediently. Sitting on a stool by his bedside, Aunt Lucy bestowed an approving smile on him and once again dipped the spoon into the yellow broth in the chipped white bowl.

Half an hour earlier, David had awakened in a low, full-sized bed with an iron headboard, under rough wool blankets. He was alone, and in what he could only call a shed, albeit a cozy one, with floral curtains at both windows. Blankets hung on the walls to keep out the late autumn chill. Through the window he saw glittering sunshine and icicles hanging from the gutters. At first, he could not remember what had happened, or where he was. But then he saw his bedroll/backpack in the corner, and the nightmare of the Candor Inn, the militia headquarters, and of the house burning flooded back into his mind. He was relieved to see his gear. Still, what had happened since he and that girl from the kitchen—he could not remember her name—had arrived in this place? How much time had passed since then?

A fair woman of medium height and late middle age came into the room when she heard David sit up. David struggled to place her. Then he remembered Aunt Lucy from the Candor Inn.

"Your fever has finally broken," she said. "Good."

"How long has it been since…that night?"

"Today is Friday," she said. "You've been in this bed almost a week. How do you feel now?"

"Like a truck hit me," he admitted. "Headachy."

"You need to eat and drink," she said, going into the next room and returning with a paper box of drinking water and some crackers.

David wondered how he had refrained from using a toilet all week. Then he realized he was wearing adult diapers of some kind.

"My late husband's," said Lucy, reading his disgusted face. "He didn't use them very long."

"What happened to…" David still could not remember the girl's name.

"He had brain cancer," Lucy said. "We went to Navesky University Hospital when he started having strokes, but all they could do was diagnose it. They said, 'Take him home and make him comfortable.' At least they didn't give us nonsense about returning to Mother Earth. I think I would have smacked them if they said that. He lasted another month."

"What about the girl I arrived with?"

"Jocelyn? We've sent her on to Corning, to the west, where they won't be looking for her. But there's a serious manhunt out there looking for you, or whichever crazy Plore killed our very much unbeloved local militia leader. They came through here on Sunday night, but we had hidden you in the root cellar. If it weren't for the ice storm we had on Tuesday, a thousand Antifans would have been turning all our roundups upside down. The roads haven't been passable."

David asked. "What about the two deputies?"

"They died in the fire," said Lucy. "They might have escaped but for being drunk. Good work you did carving up Battista. Everyone knows about it, but the news program is just calling it the act of a deranged Plore, and they say "motive unknown." They don't want anyone to think we've got an insurrection under way. Which we don't, not yet. We don't get a lot of good news around here, so thank you."

"Thank you for saving my life," David said. He knew that the entire roundup was risking their lives by harboring him. "And for bringing the backpack here. Everything I own is in there."

"Deanna—she manages the inn—was determined to save it for you. She felt terrible about how the militiamen took you away. We all felt badly, this happening to a stranger such as yourself. It was just bad luck and timing. If the militiamen showed up every weekend, nobody would ever go to the Candor Inn, believe me. It can happen anywhere in the area, anywhere we go to hang out.

"But we need to move you on as well, once the roads start clearing. You aren't safe here. They know this is Jocelyn's roundup and now they assume you ran off with her, since they didn't find her body—thank God—in the ruins of the militia headquarters. That just means the orbit of the search will grow. But we also are grateful you didn't leave her in the kitchen to die."

A large bald man ran into the house, not bothering to knock. He had just gotten the call from the day's watchman, on alert because Lucy had known the Antifans would return.

"Helicopters!" he gasped. And then they heard the whir of rotors. David had last heard such a sound in Oklahoma on the night of the Antifan raid, and it chilled him.

"Out of the bed!" Lucy shouted. David clambered out stiffly, and Lucy and the man pulled the bed aside, scraping it along the wooden floor, revealing an otherwise invisible trapdoor. They opened the trapdoor, and Lucy said, "Go down in there, hide behind the vegetables for a few hours. Not a sound." He maneuvered down a crude wooden ladder, reached for the backpack and bedroll as they handed it to him, and moved aside as the trapdoor shut and the bed scraped back into place.

Now in complete darkness, David felt around him. Here was the ladder. He crawled over to what felt like a pile of gourds and potatoes, easily six feet high, almost reaching the ceiling, and around it into a tiny corner where he assumed Lucy wanted him to hide. He leaned against the wall, the cold mountain of vegetables to his right, and listened to the muffled sound of angry voices, thudding feet above, and crashing, presumably of furniture. The bed must have been pulled away, but not very much, from the wall. Men yelling above him, and a placating feminine voice, presumably Lucy's, responding.

Suddenly, he realized he was wearing cloth shorts, not the cargo pants in which he had secreted his knife. If the Antifans found those pants and the knife with streaks of Battista's blood, everyone in the roundup was doomed. My knife, he panicked, where is it? He knew that the Antifans would blow him to smithereens before he could use that knife against them, but he felt completely helpless without it. And still wearing diapers—what a humiliating way to die. His enemies would surely relish that detail in their triumphant media stories.

David sat up against the wall, his head buried in the arms that encircled his knees. At some point, he dropped his right hand to the ground, and unthinkingly, in his anxiety, pushed it into the bottom of the vegetable pile. His fingertips felt something metallic. He pressed farther and knew he was touching a firearm barrel. He was afraid to insert his hand any farther, lest he cause the vegetable pile to collapse noisily, but he now realized the cellar contained an illegal gun cache that, if discovered, would have led to the immediate execution of the entire adult population of this roundup. No wonder Aunt Lucy was unafraid of merely hiding him, when she had already committed the roundup to the harboring of this weapons store.

Hours passed in the bitterly cold cellar. David huddled under the scratchy wool blanket they had thrown down the hole after him. He would not unpack the bedroll, which might make a noise. He fretted about the knife. He tried to recall prayers long unsaid. He vowed that if God spared him and Malia, they would finally carry out their mission to bring freedom to the DJR. The noises moved farther away, but occasionally David heard an authoritative man's voice that suggested a sentry was guarding Aunt Lucy. The Antifans seemed to know she was the leader of the roundup. David dozed fitfully.

He started awake when he heard the trapdoor opening above him. "It's all right," Lucy called down. "They're long gone." David crawled to the ladder and was back in bed a minute later. It was now dark and the floral curtains were drawn.

Aunt Lucy sat on the stool again and fed him more chicken soup. "They screamed at us, searched all the houses, lined up the men in the center square and knocked a few around, but they couldn't do much more. I'm just glad they didn't drag anyone away to the City"—she meant Syracuse, where the regular ADF unit operated—"because I couldn't guarantee he wouldn't break. But I hope they've now decided that the killer wouldn't stay in Jocelyn's roundup.

"It was smart of you to burn down the house. They brought sniffer dogs, but the dogs didn't have much of a scent to go on." She grinned. "I guess we ought to introduce ourselves now."

"You're Aunt Lucy," he said. "They told me at the Candor Inn you were the village leader."

"Yes!" she said, visibly flattered. "Lucy Gawser. They elect me every year, you should know. I'm not a dictator."

"I'm Michael Potter. Mike." He was not yet willing to divulge his real identity to anyone in the roundup, even to Aunt Lucy. "From Massena." He gave her the cover story of traipsing through New York to visit his mother in Yramaland. She asked whether he was married; he told her about his wife unjustly jailed for a theft she had not committed. But he was also sure someone from the Candor Inn had already relayed this information to her.

Her pale blue eyes looked searchingly at him, for a longer time than he felt comfortable with. "All right," she said, somewhat oddly. "That'll do for now."

"Where is my knife?" he asked. "I was afraid they would find my pants and the knife covered in his blood. And the deputy would recognize the pants if he came along today on the hunt."

"He did, indeed, come along," Lucy replied. "Lieutenant Loki Greene. A little brownnosing Earth-worshiping twerp. Maybe you'll get him eventually too, if it's worth your time. But we burned the pants immediately that night and we cleaned the knife thoroughly and buried it in the woods. We will return it to you. I hope you don't think we're amateurs here."

Their eyes met, and they laughed. David's chest ached with the effort.

"We also took apart the van and buried the parts, thirty miles away, so the dogs wouldn't sniff that out. Those parts might come in handy later to repair our own trucks and cars. It's almost impossible to buy new ones, you know. But the trail is cold." David was impressed.

At bedtime, he apologized for occupying her bed, to which she said, "It's no problem. I've got a mattress in the kitchen. In a day or two, we'll just switch places. And don't worry about Antifans returning, I've got watchmen at all the access paths and they'll give us plenty of warning. You can sleep soundly." And he did.

In the morning, David explored Lucy's home. He had used the small bathroom with toilet and sink during the night, tiptoeing carefully by the mattress on the kitchen floor as Lucy slept. The wintry white sunshine spilled into the humble bedroom, dappling the wooden floorboards. Aside from the bed and the stool, the room contained a chest in which she kept clothes. The other room was a kitchen-cum-parlor—with an old-fashioned round Formica table and three chairs in one of which he sat to eat a breakfast of toast and cheese. She brewed coffee on an old white metal stove. As he ate, his eyes trailed along the wooden cabinets. Several cabinet doors had been yanked off yesterday during the search, and Lucy said she would repair them later. "Like you'd have been hiding under the counters," she sniffed. A small boxy refrigerator crouched in the corner next to a white metal utility sink.

"You're pitying me, aren't you?" she demanded. "You should know this is probably the nicest house in the whole roundup, if not the biggest. It doesn't rust, unlike the old mobile homes. And I don't have to use the outhouse."

"You started life higher than this, didn't you?"

Sitting across the table from him, with her narrow hands cupping a mug of coffee, she said, "We all did. It was a rich country before the civil war, you know. When the war began, I was a student at Buffalo University. My father was a professor of political science at Cornell, not far from here. We lived very comfortably. My father often appeared on TV to comment on political developments, and he was the author of many books. His name was Kenneth Martin—Martin is my maiden name. We spent time together hiking, cross-country skiing, and traveling. My mother was from a wealthy family and enjoyed the finer things in life, and tried to introduce them to my sister and myself. We went to New York City more times than I can count.

"We had to take sides. My father was a great defender of liberty. He was advised to curb his tongue, but he felt he could not be a coward, given that the pro-liberty side needed his voice. He knew what was at stake for the whole country. He was very lonely at the university, which was overwhelmingly pro-Diversity. Maybe some really believed in saving the earth and in critical race theory, and hated America, but just as many just saw which way the future was going and decided to protect themselves and their jobs.

"That's how wars are won, you know, by those who follow the prevailing winds. I hate them even worse than I hate Antifans...

"My mother became a passionate advocate for change. She hadn't been religious until then, but she joined several left-wing groups because her friends did. Marching for the Green New Deal and free abortions till birth and for non-payment-based housing and for a social credit system made her happy and gave her life meaning.

"When my father published his final book, *The End of Sanity*, her friends and her Diversity counselor demanded she divorce him, which she did, and she moved to Manhattan. The university revoked his tenure, and no lawyer would take his case. A mob taunted him outside our house, every night. I left Buffalo, which was in turmoil anyway, and came home to be with him. We were armed at home, but the situation was growing more and more dangerous. If we had fired on the mob, I knew who would go to jail. On his last day at Cornell, he was packing up his office, and I was supposed to pick him up. But he didn't show up at the traffic circle with the boxes, and so I parked the car and went up to find him. The office door was wide open, and I called out, 'Dad?'

"There was no answer. I walked into the office. His desk was splashed with blood and he was lying on his back behind the desk, with a knife sticking out of his chest. He had been killed by one of his former graduate students, Dennis Boyd, who had been incited by the hatred against my father in the media to come back and kill him as an enemy of Diversity."

"How do you know who did it?"

"How? Because Boyd bragged about it, claimed my father had attacked him first, and said he was glad he had struck a blow for the Diverse People against my racist father. My racist father, who had friends of all backgrounds! The local DA's office didn't dare bring charges, not with mob rule in Ithaca at that point. The police were completely helpless—they worked for the DA. That's how the Antifan militias got started around here. They didn't even arrest him. He became a celebrity and was given a professorship at another university after the war.

"And then I realized nobody was safe if the law only protected wokist evildoers and not honorable men such as my father. My days were numbered too. I grabbed some of his most important books and papers, our rifles and ammo, and some supplies, closed up the house, emptied our bank accounts while I still could, and joined a band of patriots operating in the area. One of them had come by to pay condolences, and I asked him how I could best serve the cause. He said, 'It's a war. Come and fight and defend yourself from those who would destroy our country and steal your liberty.' A year later, in 2051, I married him, in the woods.

"We fought in this area for seven years, until we had to admit the Antifans had won. Some of us escaped into Canada, but Ohio was far away, and the border was closing. When the treaty was signed, we kept our lives, but we were enslaved by the Antifans. Someone with my background normally would have become a Social Crediteer, but my choices made me a Deplorable. Most of my life since then has been very hard, but I had my husband, who was a good man, and I had a clear conscience, which is priceless."

"What happened to your sister?" David asked.

"She was like-minded to my mother," said Lucy, "as I was my father's child. So she finished college, at Oberlin, where she was the president of the Climate Change Collective. After she graduated, she moved to New York, where she became the CEO of an important NGO that brought the message of climate destruction to Latin America, to keep them poor. She was a very high Social Crediteer. We communicated, but we had to avoid politics. She rejoiced at our defeat. I was grateful that my husband understood why I wouldn't beg her for help. She's dead—she fell into a volcano while visiting Nicaragua a few years ago."

David choked with laughter. "I'm sorry," he said, "that's awful of me."

"Oh, that's just my private joke," said Lucy. "She's alive and well and lording it over me from afar. Now tell me about your family, Mike."

David told her a combination of truths and lies. He replaced Ohio with New York. He told her about his father, who had refused to heed his wife's entreaties to leave the fighting to others. "He never came back. I was five years old. My mother now had five children. We tried to flee into Canada, but the Antifans pushed us back into New York and resettled us in Massena. My youngest brother died in the Antifan resettlement camp. I didn't finish high school and I've worked as a security guard ever since. I met my wife in high school."

"What's her name?" Lucy asked quickly.

David was caught off guard. "Ma—Mary," he said.

"What a lovely old-fashioned name. You don't hear that anymore, even among Plores. And she's in prison, you said?"

"Elmira. She was accused of stealing jewelry from the Social Credit house she was assigned to clean. But she didn't do it."

"I know she didn't do it," said Lucy. An awkward silence. "Let me show you our roundup."

Fortunately, Lucy's late husband had left behind clothes that mostly fit David. He had been a little taller than David.

"I was planning to give them to the other men in the roundup," said Lucy, "but for some reason I never did. I must have known another man would show up in my life." She smiled coyly at him. Uh-oh, David thought.

Wearing faded jeans, a flannel work shirt, somewhat too-large boots with an extra layer of wool socks, and a heavy brown cloth jacket, David ventured out into the bright sunlight with Lucy, who was attired in a similar outfit. Lucy's house was on what seemed to be the main square, where he had arrived in the van that night with Jocelyn. Four other wooden houses fronted onto the square, which was really a rough circle. In front of one, a man was chopping wood. When he saw them, he waved briefly, then returned to his work. Otherwise it was quiet. Chimneys emitted thin puffs of smoke.

"These were the first houses we built after the war when we knew we would settle here," said Lucy. "So that's why mine is where it is."

As they walked around, David saw a second ring of houses, all prefabricated.

"These houses were purchased after the war, when there were still some companies manufacturing housing. But the government had no interest in allowing them to continue supplying Plores. The focus was on building housing for Social Crediteers in the Cities, and that meant upward building, even when the space was available, like in Syracuse. The government took over the businesses and then stopped making the prefab buildings altogether. So that's why the third ring of houses are also wooden."

"Easier to control people living in towers," observed David.

Lucy looked sideways at him, and said, "Yes, you understand."

Two long beige metal prefab buildings stretched before them, beyond the second ring but inside the third, wooden one.

"These are our community houses," said Lucy. "Let me show you what we do there." They walked up a few metal stairs and entered.

To the left, they heard children's voices.

"This is real school," said Lucy. "Around here, Plore children go to the public school half-time. The resources don't allow for more, but I say thank goodness for that. The authorities just throw all kinds of so-called Diversity propaganda at them, making them feel bad for the color of their skin, the values of their families, their belief in God. The goal isn't even to turn them into Social Credit citizens, just to make them despise themselves and convince the children that their families were on the wrong side in the war and they deserve to suffer. They only take attendance so they can harass us if the kids stay out. So we have them attend school here the other half of the time, just to undo the damage caused by public schools. And we use Saturdays too."

She and David stood in the back of the classroom, which contained about two dozen students aged five to ten. A young male teacher stood at the front, with an old-fashioned whiteboard, covered with division problems, explaining different ways to solve them. A few of the older kids just in front of Lucy and David were working on presumably more advanced problem sets on sheets of paper. "The high schoolers are meeting outside," whispered Lucy, "even in the cold. They're discussing the history of Thanksgiving today." David suddenly realized the holiday was next week. He wondered how these Plores would celebrate it.

In the other half of the trailer, several old women were knitting socks and scarves and chatting. Several shelves of actual print books faced them in a bookcase. Another woman was sitting in a worn red armchair, reading. "The real subversive ones are hidden," said Lucy, "available to anyone here, of course, if they ask, but we have to hide them from the authorities." Deplorables enjoyed more latitude in their reading than did Social Crediteers, but some books were completely banned, as David, the former commander of the Knowledge Crimes Unit at Beaufort, knew well. At the other end of the trailer, two men and a woman were having a meeting. "That's our budget committee," said Lucy. At the sound of her voice, the members looked in their direction, and waved before turning back to their discussion.

Lucy and David exited the trailer, and she showed him the plain white church in which the more articulate rounduprs took turns preaching on Sundays. Each weekend a delegation of villagers attended the Methodist and the Catholic churches in the neighboring town, cramming in two vans to save gas. Most of the local pastors or priests were ADF informants, but Lucy directed the rounduprs to attend the churches just often enough to keep the known informant in place rather than have to deal with an unknown replacement. It was fun plying the informants with false gossip, she said.

"So speaking of budgets," he asked, "how do you have money to spend? Do folks here work outside the village?" He was curious about to what extent these Plores enjoyed greater freedom than their counterparts in Anacosta.

"Yes," said Lucy, "Most of our adults work in Syracuse or Ithaca in return for the basic income checks. They can keep some of it, and folks buy and hunt most of their own food and clothes, but we pool most of it for common goods like education, protection, and utilities. Some folks are employed here as seamsters, tinkers, furniture makers, teachers, as you saw. We have a mechanic who maintains our trucks and cars. Our medic, Rachel, came by to look after you when you first fell ill. Money isn't as useful around here as goods, and there's no DJR bank we'd trust with cash, so it's easier to trade. Those ladies you saw will trade their knitting for game or firewood."

"My mother keeps her cash in an empty jug of detergent," said David. Before he had left Anacosta for good, or so he had thought, he had stuffed several thousand dollars into that jug. "But what you are showing me is like the frontier, all over again."

"Yes, we've gone backward in time, haven't we? We took our material progress for granted, and forgot about the foundations on which it was built—law and order, hard work, faith in God. Those who wanted to destroy us chipped away at all these values, and now they are surprised that socialism does not provide wealth or happiness. It is remarkable that no matter how many times experience proves socialism is unworkable, those who seek power and don't have the ability to succeed on their own, will try to impose it all over again. They never stop."

"Wait," David countered, "you condemn socialism, but what are you doing here? Isn't this socialism?"

"This is a socialism of poverty. We band together because we cannot survive otherwise. There is no compulsion. Anyone who wishes to leave may do so at any time. We do not pretend this is an ideal way to live. We would live in the United States or even Canada if we could."

The second trailer contained a viewing screen and an assortment of chairs and sofas. "Our media room," smiled Lucy. Several men were watching the Montreal-Calgary ice hockey match. Men's ice hockey had been banned in the DJR years ago, alongside men's football and rugby, due to their hypermasculinity, but the DJR was willing to collect fees from Plores to allow them to watch Canadian or Russian matches on the GVN.

The men greeted them, and Lucy politely declined the invitation to sit down, saying she was showing their guest the roundup. David was uncomfortably aware of a hostile stare from a handsome man about a decade younger than him. The man had floppy brown hair and a scar down his right cheek. Great, he thought, I've antagonized the local desperado. Lucy ushered him back out into the cold.

The ice and snow crunched underfoot. They had reached the outskirts of the roundup. A large wooden open-air pavilion contained a dozen long tables and benches to match, reminding David of the Candor Inn. About sixty feet away from the pavilion were roasting pits.

"We'll have our Thanksgiving on Thursday," said Lucy, "We are poor, but not destitute. We will be cooking wild turkeys and having a fine feast. You'll celebrate with us, I hope."

"I need to keep moving on," said David. "You yourself said I was in danger here. And I know I am placing you all in danger."

"The roads are not safe either now. There are checkpoints everywhere as long as they think Battista's murderer is at large. The Antifans won't return here soon. We'll let the hubbub die down, and then we'll find a trucker to move you south."

"A trucker?"

"Yes, some truckers are our Underground Railroad. This is how Plores who lack permits travel from one containment area to another. Some want to join the rebel forces forming on the Florida-Alabama border. Some, like you, just want to see a dying relative. I understand this is all organized out of Anacosta, but of course the details must be very closely held, to protect the organizers. You will be far safer traveling this way than roaming through the woods in the winter. But it will take some time to organize."

"Will it cost a lot?"

"Only as much as you can pay," Lucy said. "It is not a profit-making enterprise, but one aimed at helping other Plores."

"I can't wait too long. My mother is dying." David again felt guilty at uttering the lie. He sensed Lucy was in no hurry to see him depart. Yet without her help he would surely fail to escape.

"We will pray for her," Lucy said airily, "so that she will live to see you in good health and safely arrived."

They turned back toward the center of the roundup and Lucy's house. Everyone they met along the way was introduced to David; they all greeted him politely even though they must have realized how his presence endangered them.

As if she could read his mind, Lucy said, consolingly, "They do not think of you that way. It is the least we can do to stand up to this evil government. Someday we will have leadership that will unite all our sad little roundups, that will wake up even the rich Plores in Anacosta, and we will rise again. Socialism will kill the Social Credit system from within, but it keeps us motivated to topple it. Someday, it will happen."

He asked about the angry man in the trailer.

"Oh, that's Seth. He's jealous of you because I kicked him out of the bed when you arrived. You needed it more. So he had to return to bunking with the single men. Don't pay him any mind."

David wanted to tell Lucy he'd be happy to switch with Seth, but sensed she would not appreciate it. As they returned to her house, he cast a sideways glance at her profile, noticing the firm set of her jaw and the high cheekbones. This was a woman who, while perhaps twenty years older than him, would not go gently into old age.

Chapter 33
Upstanding Members Of The Community
(Friday, January 8, 2094, Diverse Year 39)

aragon gazed distractedly at the celadon vase. The new year was beginning on a galling note of uncertainty. The Resolution Command had not yet been able to locate David Harris, although a nurse at Stillwater Psychiatric Gardens had confirmed a patient by that name had been admitted in late August. But it was a common name, Henry had finally admitted. Nor had the dragnet managed to capture either the killer of the Antifan militia commander, or the girl servant. The pair had vanished.

It was also time to announce the campaign for February. In November, Paragon had been hesitating over whether to endorse a plan to have a suicidally minded young white man publicly and willingly commit suicide in grief over the injustices done by his race and sex to oppressed Diverse People. "I mean, if he's depressed anyway, one might as well take advantage of the situation."

But the timing was no longer auspicious. The prospect of a politically correct suicide had seemed potentially exciting in the general jollity around Saturnalia, but revisiting it in January, Paragon acknowledged that it might only deepen the midwinter gloom. The young man would be celebrated and enjoy great creature comforts and publicity in his final weeks, like a Euthanasia Palace experience on steroids. Unfortunately, sometimes that could backfire and encourage the recipient to take a greater interest in life. "Oh that's awful, Khalid," said Exterra when he ran the idea by him. But he tended to dismiss her opinions when they didn't align with his.

"I don't know how we'd top that in March," Paragon admitted. "We'd have to do something more cheerful, maybe talent concerts? We need a new trans celebrity since the last one overdosed." Maybe do the talent competition in February and the human sacrifice in March?

He turned to the yellow folder next to the workscreen, leafing through its contents. About a dozen handwritten flyers, and another six typed on an old-fashioned typewriter not linked to the national electronic network. The flyers had been discovered under a panel in a truck whose driver had been killed at a roadside stop.

The flyers repeated scurrilous rumors about abuses in Anacosta Ploreville. Paragon read the various accusations while muttering rejoinders under his breath. Decent Plore women and children forced to view pornographic art exhibitions ("no appreciation for culture"); ever-rising prices for shoddier goods ("no tolerance for sacrifice"); the heavier ADF presence in Ploreville ("if you didn't commit sedition, we wouldn't need to do that"); a Plore storekeeper had been robbed by police with no recourse; authorities had built a new tax office on what had been a popular soccer field; obituaries that the official Plore newspaper refused to print due to the deceased's valiant civil war record. "Better as compost," Paragon said to the last item, although his aide was unsure whether the commander meant the obituary or the deceased, or both.

The analysts from the Suburban Crimes Unit, which dealt with Deplorables, had told him the paper was standard printer paper, which could not be traced aside from it being generally sold in Anacosta Ploreville. Whoever had bothered to painstakingly handwrite the broadsheets clearly sought to avoid ADF scrutiny. "The handwriting is quite archaic," said one analyst, "probably that of an elderly woman, at least seventy years old. Cursive was not taught in schools after about 2040."

"We can't interrogate every old woman in Ploreville," snapped Paragon. "Have you tested these papers for fingerprints?" Every DJR citizen and Plore had eye and finger prints stored in the massive ADF databases.

"Not yet, Commander. We just acquired these."

"Well, go do it then. And don't report to me that you've been handling them."

Just before lunch, one of Paragon's internal informants entered via the back entrance to the Resolution Command vault so that the secretaries and junior analysts might not recognize her. The Antifan Defense Forces routinely monitored Social Crediteers, whether through their household appliance or armband feeds, but as Paragon knew, sometimes senior ADF officers themselves deserved scrutiny.

The informant showed Paragon a sheaf of photographs of a grainy figure parking a car at a school and walking into a shabby brick rambler several blocks away. "South Rockville, December fourteenth and December twenty-ninth," said the officer.

"What would he be doing in that Plore neighborhood?" Paragon asked. "Who lives in that house?"

"Zionists of the Jewish persuasion, sir. There is a seventy-two-year old rabbi, named Robert Goldberg; his daughter, Devorah; his son-in-law, Isaac Bernstein; and five children."

Paragon clicked his tongue with distaste. "Breeding like rabbits." He shuffled through the photographs. "What a shame we can't do an appliance feed from Plore houses." He suddenly thought: *Rosen is 275, I am 290. I can authorize a tap on his armband.* It had never occurred to him before. Given that Rosen was deputy director, he would need to secure the assent of Gemma Carpenter, the senior counterintelligence officer, but he would tell her that he feared Rosen had fallen under the sway of Christian proselytizers. Judaism had unfortunately escaped notice by the DJR's lawmakers, but Paragon was not particularly squeamish about details. Jews, Christians, whatever. Once the officer had left, he called Gemma. If these Jewish rumors were correct, Rosen was a backsliding heretic unfit to live, let alone lead the ADF.

That same morning, hundreds of miles to the north, David was hunting in the woods with several men from the roundup. His knife had been restored to him, and it was too important and lethal a tool to keep sheathed. For now, the villagers seemed to expect him to stay, another wandering Plore who might be waiting for spring, but whom inertia might keep with them. Sometimes that happened, and it was all right as long as the newcomer earned his keep. They quietly noted he continued to sleep in Aunt Lucy's house even after one might have expected him to move into the single men's trailer.

While he waited for Lucy to arrange his passage to Anacosta, David tried to stay useful, lest the community consider him a layabout. He chopped wood, but soon realized, ruefully, that he had no really useful skills other than wielding the knife. Nor did the brewery seem to need another set of hands at the vats. So there he was, marching into the barren woods on that Friday morning with three other men, including the surly Seth. The sky was a pallid gray under thick cloud cover, a depressing reminder that spring was several months off.

The group mostly hoped to find Nutritious Food Animal No. 1. Nutes slept during the daytime in underground dens, and even though the men's thin-soled boots crunched on the snow cover, the sluggish nute had not evolved sufficiently to develop alertness or speed against predators. All of the men, including David, carried large hunting knives. Seth bore a high-tech crossbow, legal for Plores, with aluminum arrows; all respected his prowess with the weapon. If one of the men managed to spot an elusive deer at a distance, Seth would bring it down, for sure.

"This is the hungry time of year," Lucy had told David. "Folks will be grateful for anything you bring back." The villagers had pooled their funds to celebrate Christmas decently, and the memory of roast chicken and white rice would have to sustain them until spring.

You killed a nute when you were on your own, David reminded himself. You can do it again. He tramped dutifully behind the others, his eyes scanning the woods and the ground for a nute coppet before he fell into one.

It was relatively safe for David to leave the sanctuary of the roundup, at least in the company of the other men. If police, or even Antifans saw their group, David would just appear to be another scraggly Plore hunter, especially with his dark sunglasses, hunter's cap and now longer beard. He normally would have shaved it off, but it was a helpful disguise. Just in case, he carried another man's ID in his pocket, since Mike Potter of Massena was a wanted man. But it was a cold, gray afternoon, and no one who didn't need to be out in the woods was around.

One of the men, peering through binoculars, saw a deer a few hundred yards away. Seth aimed, and brought it down. They cheered, tied the dead animal to two thin tree trunks, and carried it back into the roundup. "Too bad it was a doe," said one of the men.

"No choice," Seth grunted.

The butcher took the carcass from the hunters, who then began heading out again.

"Wait, are we going back out?" David asked. After two hours in the woods, he was thoroughly chilled and dispirited by his hanger-on status. He thought longingly of Lucy's space heater, or possibly of the armchair next to the library shelves.

Seth looked at him superciliously, his brown hair flopping over his left eye. "Hey, town boy, how much eating you think we're going to get from one deer? Maybe you can catch us a few nutes, hey? Talk fancy to them and invite them to a dance?"

David narrowed his eyes. He was a former Antifan commander. He wouldn't allow himself to be bested by some backwoods rube. "If I had your toy, man, it would be a lot easier." The foursome trudged back into the woods. David was determined to earn his keep before the day ended. But it was slightly troubling that for all his efforts to be just humble Mike Potter from Massena, Seth and presumably others could detect that David's background was not quite as humble as theirs—in fact, more like Lucy's. But I too am a Plore, David reminded himself. I belong here too.

About an hour later, David saw some movement out of the corner of his eye. He realized it was a nute coppet. The others were slightly ahead of him, and they did not see him edging stealthily toward the coppet. He plunged his knife into the coppet, producing a cacophony of squeals and squeaks. He stabbed right and left in a frenzy, the nutes trapped in the nest. One streaked past David, but another knife-wielding man speared it. The men counted five dead nutes, a respectable haul. They placed the creatures in a large canvas bag that David carried over his shoulder back to the roundup. This time they had harvested enough game to stay at home the rest of the day.

"Come and watch some TV with us?" Seth asked him, a new note of respect in his voice, and generously added, "You brought us some luck with the doe."

Not wanting to offend Seth, David accepted the offer, even though he just wanted to return to Lucy's house. The foursome watched a wrestling competition and drank the roundup-brewed beer, which they called Our Swill. David knew something about wrestling, so by the time the men parted for dinner, he had bolstered his political capital with them.

"There is no going back," Lucy argued. "If we ever destroy the DJR, we cannot afford a republic, let alone a democracy, ever again. We will have to seize power in the name of the Deplorables. We failed the first time, because we did not realize it was a struggle to the death until it was too late."

David and Lucy sat at her kitchen table, over candlelight, after a dinner of nute stew and potatoes from the cellar. The candlelight was not for romantic reasons, but because the roundup's monthly electric allotment was precious. Even though it was early in the month, or perhaps because it was so early, or because she needed to set a good example, Lucy avoided using electricity after dinner, except for the electric heater, which she turned off at bedtime. They wore several layers of jackets against the cold. The candlelight shadow made Lucy's pale skin look less papery and more translucent; her passion animated her features. From what she had told him about her background, David guessed she was probably about twenty years older than him. Yet despite all the hardship she had endured, she seemed perhaps only fifty, not sixty.

Both agreed that the DJR's foundations were brittle—socialism had crippled its economic power and ideology had required excluding half the population from the national project. The slavery of low Social Crediteers in the Economic Zone camps, and the menial labor of the Plores throughout the country created the impression of productivity, but no one outside the DJR wanted to buy its manufactures. The obsession of the universities with Diversity, and the small number of students who knew enough about real math and science to make technological advances, ensured the DJR would slip further behind the US and Canada, and even the Texas Republic. But the DJR could still stumble along for decades to come. Lucy quoted Adam Smith, "'There's a lot of ruin in a nation.'

"When it rots, we may be able to push it over," said Lucy, "and at least control our own territory and be left alone."

"But why would Social Crediteers want to join us then?" asked David. "If you only want a Deplorable-ruled version of the DJR, you give them no reason to rebel against Anacosta."

"I don't want the Social Crediteers to join us. I want them to starve and die in their Cities. Or we kill them when the day comes. They have a poisonous ideology—dividing us by race and class, and using it to justify their tyranny. And they really believe it. The Soviets had to parrot their ideology, but once they were free to drop it, they did. They knew among themselves, in private, it was rotten. I do not believe any of the Social Crediteers want liberty, not anymore, not even for themselves. We can't win them over."

"And you don't want liberty for the Plores either?" David challenged her. "Because if you don't want a democracy or a republic, and yet you seem to think we will live as free people, how do we do that?"

"We have our roundup here…among the other villages. We live at peace with each other. We produce, we trade. We could have businesses if we were allowed to, if we weren't treated like nutes in a coppet. Yes, you need a government to represent us to other governments, I suppose, but really, what would a free people need from Anacosta, or Washington? Or even an Albany?" she said, referring to the former capital of New York State. "If Washington hadn't made itself the arbiter of everything, controlling it wouldn't have mattered. The Blues could have captured it, and it would have meant nothing to the rest of the country. But power was centralized there."

"Roads? A military?"

"We could build our own roads," she said intensely, "through cooperative efforts. We just need our own banks to fund capital projects. And a military? Why do we need marching troops? Or a navy? Does any other country wish to conquer us? It's not the eighteenth century, you know."

"The DJR is a protectorate of China."

"That's different," she snapped. "The DJR couldn't feed itself, so it turned to the Chinese for aid. If we were free to produce and trade with each other, we wouldn't need to feed off of wealthier countries. If we don't want to coerce other countries, and no other country would invade us, what is the purpose of a military? It would only seek aggression to justify itself and demand weapons and equipment."

"How would we enforce laws against fraud and other crimes?"

"At the smallest level of government necessary. Police forces based locally. Maybe a sophisticated crime lab in a city, and maybe an appellate court, but did we need a Department of Education? A Department of Labor? How much did the former federal government do that couldn't have been pushed down to local levels? Of course smaller levels of government could cooperate with each other, but neither would have the power to compel the other." Lucy looked at David defiantly.

"In other words, you'd dismantle the country even further. It's bad enough that the world's most powerful country broke up into three—no, really four entities if you count the states that joined Canada. You talk about the eighteenth century not being relevant, but you'd just as soon return us to the fourteenth century and leave us at the mercy of every other country."

"What would you suggest, Mike?"

"We would need to reunify with the United States. They still have rule of law. People live there normally, like they used to here. Without going back to medieval townships and guilds."

"Mike, how do you know what's going on in the United States? We've been cut off from them for almost forty years. For all we know, they're forcing women to have babies and lynching black people, just like the DJR tells us. How do you know?"

"We live on the Canadian border. Sometimes we can see their TV news in Massena or get ahold of a Canadian newspaper. The truckers and the fishermen talk. I imagine it's kind of similar to how Canada operates." He had an idea. "What about Canada? Would you accept a new DJR in a Canadian mold?"

"Mike, I have no idea what that would mean. I just want to be an American again." She got up, reached into the cupboard, and extracted the cork of a half bottle of wine while standing at the counter. Her blonde-gray hair was loose, tumbling down her back. A small gray wool hat topped her head for warmth. Two small juice glasses materialized. "Let's have a drink."

"Where'd you get this?" he asked. Most wine, even Diversity-grown, was too expensive for Plores. And this bottle was French.

"I've been saving it," she said.

"For this?" he laughed. "For me?"

"Yes. Years ago I was working in an office in downtown Syracuse. The office was managing internet connections for the GVN for the Say Lawrence region. My boss liked me, and gave me this bottle at Saturnalia one year. My husband and I were going to drink it for an anniversary, but we never got around to it. And then he was sick. So he told me, 'Save it for your next man. Don't stay a widow forever.'" The St. Lawrence region, like all place-names for Christian saints, had been renamed in 2067.

"Lucy, I'm not your next man. I'm married. I love my wife."

"Mike, you don't have to marry me. But I'm very lonely." She took a deliberate sip while staring intently into his eyes. "It's not easy being the roundup leader. It's a lot of responsibility and you can't start sleeping with men left and right or you lose your authority."

"What about Seth?"

"That's what I mean. He's no better or worse than any of the other men. He was willing to be a little more comfortable by living here with me instead of in the single men's trailers. But people didn't like it. They didn't understand why I was favoring him."

"And it's better if you favor me? Won't that upset people too?"

"No," she said firmly. "Because you're not from here. And there's something different about you. They might see you as more...suitable for me." David told Lucy about what Seth had said to him, before he had found the nute coppet.

"Yes," she nodded, "that's what I mean."

"So I'd be a suitable consort for the roundup queen?" Even in the candlelight, he saw her flush.

"It's my age, isn't it?" she demanded. "You don't want to sleep with me because I'm sixty years old? There, I said it. I'm twenty-five years older than you."

"I wouldn't have guessed," he lied. Of course, his ID card was a lie as well, and Lucy was only seventeen years his senior. He wished he could tell her the truth. "Lucy, if I wasn't married, I'd sleep with you in a minute."

"Sorry to have troubled you," she said, tired, staring into the dying flame. "I promise I won't keep you from leaving. I promise you'll leave as soon as it's safe and I've worked out your transport.

"It's not just sex, even though I want another body next to mine. I couldn't have had this conversation about the future with anyone else here. They either assume it'll be like this forever, and so it's pointless to pretend otherwise, or they want to start shooting up Syracuse tomorrow even if that'll be the death of us instantly." She pulled herself to her feet with what David recognized as a huge effort.

"It's not fair to ask a married man to cheat on his wife, even if she's in prison. Please don't hold it against me." She headed into the bedroom. "Good night, Mike."

During the night, he awoke to the sound of the soft sobbing from the other room. There was no proper door between the kitchen and her bedroom, only a curtain Lucy had hastily installed when he had arrived. He steeled himself against temptation, forcing himself to think of Malia, of his two sons, even of the stern face of his religious brother, Daniel. Soon he fell asleep again.

PART FOUR

THE PORTLAND TOWER

"We are beyond thinking."
—Paragon

Chapter 34
Latest Sensation
(Saturday, January 30, 2094)

Malia raised her hands before the cameras, greeting her adoring audience as the pulsing rock beat died down. Tens of thousands of vetted Social Crediteers whooped joyfully in the cavernous Anacosta Bowl. Malia stepped into the spotlight, and opened her arms wide, the large flowing sleeves of her gold-threaded gown spreading like the wings of a giant plumed bird. Her brown curls, grown long again, tumbled over her shoulders, and her eyes opened wide. "I have returned to you, Mother Earth!" she called out. "Hello, Anacosta!" Wild cheering.

"We love you, Malia!" they called out, whistling and applauding. In another setting, they would have on command beaten her to death.

A fat person of indeterminate gender fainted in the front row. Medics wearing white uniforms brought a stretcher and staggered off with the victim.

Malia had the routine down well, after speaking to increasingly larger and important audiences, starting with schoolchildren. Once she had been shy, but after the zoo speech, she no longer cared what others thought, which liberated her. And now, she was performing for her life, to buy time so that David, or the United States, might rescue her. Tonight Diversity Channel One was broadcasting her performance, as she once again pledged her loyalty to the government and renounced her crimes, but this time before the entire country.

"Let me tell you my Diversity story," she always began, spinning a lurid tale of plantation-owning, slave-whipping ancestors, Confederate raiders and Ku Klux Klan night riders, and then her great-grandmother who sought to prevent integration of the local schools. She at least knew from her files that her great-grandmother, Diane, had been a kindergartener in Lynchburg in the 1960s, not that one needed to be fussy about dates or ages, since history transcended mere facts.

"Then the Antifans came to rescue me!" she declared—she knew that much was true, even if "rescue" was not exactly the right word—and then told them about learning about Diversity in the orphanage, and knowledge management at college, and the False Knowledge Depository. "Then I was deceived by my husband, the traitor, into fleeing the country for the fascist Red regime."

Malia told her rapt listeners that many Americans she met in Oklahoma and even in St. Louis had secretly told her they longed for Diversity. She had insisted on writing her own speech, although Knowledge Tower experts had painstakingly edited and supplied "facts" for her narrative. The only time she balked was when the experts inserted, "the patriarchal god of the white supremacists is false. Only Mother Earth is true." She claimed she did not wish to insult the Deplorables, but in fact she was fearful of committing blasphemy.

She urged everyone to sign up for the truth serum—this was Paragon's February campaign. "Vaccinate yourselves against falsehood!" she called out to their cheers. "Protect yourself against being subject to doubts about Diversity! Become one with the Great Mother!"

"We want truth!" the audience howled. "Protect us from the Big Lie!" In the lobby, white coated medics were standing at tables to inject the serum into volunteers. Eventually, everyone would be forced to comply, but those enterprising Crediteers who proffered an arm during the intermission would get an extra five social credit points for the year, and a coupon for a pizza. Eventually it would be required of every Social Crediteer, with no extra points gained, so it paid to volunteer early.

Malia then recounted the kindness of the government to her, speaking of her love for Exterra, whom she introduced as "the love of my life, a valiant Antifan soldier on the forefront of the fight for Diversity since her early youth." A photograph of Exterra then appeared on the screens along the side, and everyone gasped at her strong, proud, and moon shadowed face. Malia praised her tutors, including the sputtering Dr. Gu.

"How full of joy I am," preached Malia, "as I am driven through Anacosta, to see the happy faces of our Social Crediteers, of all races, ethnic backgrounds, and genders, striving together to achieve Diversity in our lifetime. I did not appreciate this when I was younger. I was so selfish and ungrateful. Upon my return, my tutors taught me to be ashamed of my whiteness. I had accepted it, but just saw it as a physical trait, having nothing to do with my behavior or my character. You now know my family's racist past. But until now, I had never truly grappled with my responsibility for white supremacy, even as the DJR nurtured and raised me. I beg those of you who have learned more than me, those whom I may have offended by acting in whiteness, to educate me, to forgive me. I have done you all wrong!" At this point, she would always fall to the floor, cheered by the now-ecstatic audience. Fifteen long seconds later, Exterra—wearing a long blue gown that became her flowing blonde hair—came running onto the stage, lifted Malia to her feet, and kissed her passionately as the audience screamed, "We love you, Malia! We forgive you, Malia! We love you, Exterra!"

The commentator noted solemnly for the at-home audience, "Exterra Boyd, 185, is a captain in the Antifan Defense Forces who has taken a personal interest in the rehabilitation of Malia Jenness. Their love story is the perfect outcome to the long process of betterment that Malia has undergone. It is now time for Doctor Bob Waters, our emcee, to ask Malia questions that have been submitted by attendees in advance."

The stagehands brought two contemporary-style armchairs and a small table onto the stage, placing on the latter two glasses of water and a small vase containing a single rose. Malia sat in one chair, facing Doctor Bob. Doctor Bob, 260, a celebrity in his own right because of his nationally aired advice show and PhD in Diverse psychology, was skilled in the art of the Diversity confessional. Had he known more about truncheons and brain-cell scrambling devices, he could have served in the ADF himself. But his mellifluous voice, soft eyes, and seductive manner succeeded in eliciting confessions from his guests without a resort to force. He was a well-toned black man in his early sixties in a sharp loden green suit.

"How do you feel right now, Malia Jenness?" asked Doctor Bob, leaning forward.

Malia gave a deep, dramatic breath. "So loved, Doctor Bob! I don't feel I deserve such love."

When asked her about her husband by Doctor Bob, Malia—as was typically the case at this point of her performance—would brush aside a tear, saying, "I loved my husband, before I realized how he had plotted to destroy my life in the DJR and kidnap me into fascism. I must have been under a spell. No, I don't resent the ADF for apprehending us and killing him. He resisted arrest, you know, and so the ADF had no choice. Now that I know how cruelly he misled me, I don't mourn him at all."

Asked about her children, she smiled demurely, saying, "I hope the ADF will be able to bring my sons to me here in the DJR soon. Perhaps the US will release them from its custody." And about Rex, "I know she was turning toward Diversity even as we lived in Oklahoma. I am confident she will come to me soon. Rex, if you can hear me, come to your mother!" The emcee never mentioned that Rex had been separated from her mother for ten years even before they left the DJR, let alone why.

Malia's performances had grown so convincing that, two weeks ago, the ADF had released her from Beaufort and moved her to an apartment in the nearby Portland Tower. She was on the sixty-third floor, in an apartment situated at the end of a curved corridor so that a detail of Antifan guards could monitor the entrance without intruding on the other elite tenants. They surveilled her windows twenty-four hours a day from the adjoining tower. She only left the apartment under guard, but the plainclothes ADF troops could plausibly be explained as due to her new celebrity. The authorities had claimed that they feared Malia was at risk of kidnapping by American special forces who might have breached Anacosta. Often Exterra accompanied her so that the celebrity magazines could breathlessly gush about Malia's "beautiful Diverse-faced partner." Most nights, Exterra stayed in Malia's apartment, so she was not alone even in bed.

A trustworthy Social Credit housekeeper came each day to clean and cook for

Malia. When Malia left Beaufort, the ADF had given her a brand-new armband and a Social Credit score of 160.

"And in six months we'll decide whether it goes up or down," Exterra told her, "so you might even be a 185 like me soon! We gave you the ten bisexual points too. No need to thank me!" Thank you? Malia thought, I hate you. But she had to acknowledge that Exterra's interest in her—and Steve Rosen's intervention—had probably saved her life. Oddly, her jailers had not yet reinserted the tracking chip, the chip that was inserted behind the right ear of all adult Social Crediteers. Perhaps they felt a chip would be pointless when she was so thoroughly monitored.

Malia felt overwhelming guilt. She was publicly damning her devoted husband, who might not be dead. She dreaded her sons being kidnapped as she had been, and imprisoned like her in the DJR. Perhaps the Resolution Command was plotting against them even now, although she knew that Daniel and Fern understood the danger and would protect her sons with their lives. She could not even ask Exterra, because that would reveal she was dissembling in public, or even worse, convince Exterrra and Paragon that she "wanted" them kidnapped and brought to the DJR. At least Kevin had not succeeded in kidnapping Rex. This gave her some comfort.

She had only agreed to become a Diversity motivational speaker to escape Beaufort and make it easier for the United States or David—were he alive—to rescue her. But she now doubted it would be any easier for him to pluck her from this high tower than from Beaufort itself, or vanquish her phalanx of Antifans. Staying alive longer would help, as Steve Rosen had pointed out. Staying alive as a coward and a traitor to truth, she glumly thought.

Paragon had demanded she undergo the truth serum test before he let her leave Beaufort. Having experienced a less sophisticated version of the test at the Economic Zone camp four years earlier, and failed miserably at deceiving the examiners, Malia knew she could not pass this one either. But she had underestimated Exterra, who approached the Beaufort examiners beforehand.

"I am the partner and aide of Paragon," she said, "and he needs Malia Jenness to pass this test so that she can serve Diversity on the outside. Do you understand?"

The examiners did not dare ask Paragon himself to confirm this. It was easier for them to sign the paperwork attesting to Malia Jenness's devotion to Diversity, and end her exam early, even though she had sobbed with pain and vomited again.

After the performance, Malia slumped in an armchair in the dressing room, exhausted and drawn. She drank ice water from a glass. A dish of candies went untouched. She had promised Doctor Bob to appear on his show in a few months to report on her further progress to the nation.

Sitting on the vanity bench before the mirror, facing her, Exterra enthused, "Malia, you were so inspiring! The entire country was watching you. The ratings were the highest for any program in five years! Even the Plores were required to watch."

Malia started. Had David's family watched her humiliation from Ploreville? She could not reveal her distress. "I'm so honored," she said soberly. "I hope the Plores will learn from my example that resistance is useless."

"Oh, even better! All the Social Crediteers will realize why we are making all these sacrifices for Diversity. Now that you've told them the truth about the United States, they will work even harder to achieve true Diversity here. It was shocking to hear about how the Diverse People are kept in the ghettos. You have more credibility than anyone else in the DJR right now."

"I don't know about that," said Paragon, who appeared behind Exterra in the doorway. He wore a black suit and a tie covered in an abstract pattern. He handed Malia a bouquet of roses, which in Anacosta, in January, were extremely expensive. "Malia needs to continue working on her betterment. But well done, Malia. You struck a blow against our enemies tonight."

Malia said weakly, "Thank you, Commander."

"The *Post* wants to interview you—would you give them ten minutes of your time?" Paragon asked. Malia saw an anxious-looking female reporter and a photographer hovering in the hallway behind Exterra. She knew it was not a request, but a command.

"Of course," she said. Tomorrow the interview would be splashed across the front page of the country's premier paper of record. And it would make its way to the United States via third country reportage. She wondered whether the story of her repentance, now so widely aired, would give US officials an excuse not to press for her rescue, but it was too late to turn back.

The rounduprs grumbled about the interruption to their Saturday night viewing habits. On Saturday night, the big-screen TV in the trailer usually showed movies, unless a major sporting event preempted it. Tonight, the Knowledge Tower had decreed that every television channel in the DJR would air Malia Jenness's confession at the Anacosta Bowl.

"Nobody has to watch it," said Lucy. "But the TV needs to be set to show it. I don't want trouble with Syracuse. You can play video games or read or look at your phones for two hours or go to bed early. But in this case, we're obeying the law." Most of the rounduprs had a cell phone, which they paid for monthly, in return for the authorities' monitoring of their use.

"Crazy Social Credit shit," Seth said, representing the consensus view in the roundup. But even the Seths were swept up in the general frenzy stirred up by the national media, and at nine o'clock the trailer seats were full and curious rounduprs stood along the back wall of the trailer as well. Someone was heating up cider on the stove. It was rare for Plores and Crediteers to intersect—their lives ran parallel to each other, overlapping only in the workplace. For a brief evening, the country was united in front of the TV.

"If she insults us," said several of the rounduprs, "I'm leaving and going to bed."

David not only intended to watch, but had shown up early to seize a prime viewing spot, on the blue sofa right in front of the screen. He barely noticed when Lucy seated herself next to him; he rested his right arm on the worn armroll, tense with anticipation. This would be his first sight of Malia since August. At least she is alive, he said, so I have not wasted my time and energy in coming back to the DJR. Maybe she will give me some clues as to what to do next, where to go in Anacosta, how to free her and bring her home. In his impatience to rescue Malia, he had not planned very precisely on how he would accomplish his mission once he reached Anacosta.

"Thank you," he said to a woman who handed him a mug of steaming cider.

Upon seeing Malia stride onto the stage, David's first reaction was, she has gotten thin again. She now had 160 Social Credit points, and since the emcee had said she was no longer at Beaufort, her weight loss presumably reflected a lack of appetite, not deprivation. Only he recognized the desperation in her eyes that to strangers looked like a believer's frenzy. He listened calmly to her lies about the United States. They wrote her script, he reminded himself.

The rounduprs were mostly silent. Parochially, they listened for insults to Plores and to their God, but heard neither.

"You think they're on drugs?" he heard one young man behind him ask his girlfriend, hearing the screams of rapture from the audience.

"No," his girlfriend answered, "they just want to share in the experience. And now that they all have to take the truth serum—maybe they're just convincing themselves they believe this stuff. So they can pass the test."

"You think that this Malia means what she says?" he pressed.

"No," the girlfriend said. "They're forcing her to do this. She doesn't look happy at all, does she? Even her smile looks scared."

Yes, David thought, she is not doing this freely. This is not her personality—this is not the quiet, dignified Malia I married and still love. Maybe they have drugged her. He shuddered to see this bizarre tattooed creature called Exterra thrust herself on his wife. If only he could leap onto that stage—only a few hundred miles away—and rescue Malia!

Then the unctuous Doctor Bob began interviewing Malia, and David heard his wife clearly state that she didn't blame the ADF for killing him and couldn't mourn him at all because of how he had deceived her. Now he realized that Malia thought he was dead. She is only complying with the government because she feels she has no options, he thought. It was only when she said she hoped her sons would join her that anger began to build within him: She didn't need to say that. She's only giving the ADF an excuse to kidnap them too.

Finally, Doctor Bob asked, "What's next for you, Malia Jenness? How do you see your Diverse future unfolding?"

"Doctor Bob, I will serve wherever the DJR most needs me. I will continue to bring the message of Diversity to the country—to schoolchildren, workers, Diverse People, or even the Plores. The Plores need to hear our message. We should not assume they are lost to Diversity. Many are intelligent enough to learn from us about Diversity. Please help me help the Plores!" The crowd roared with approval, leaping to their feet in the final standing ovation.

A few rows behind him, Seth stumbled to his feet. "Fuck you, lady!" he shouted at the screen as he stormed out of the trailer.

David bent over. He felt sick. Lucy's arm encircled his shoulders. "Mike, are you all right?"

When he lifted his head to face her, his eyes were brimming with tears. He insisted on waiting until the trailer was empty before he allowed her to lead him outside and back to their house. Lucy did not dare ask questions. Their boots crunched on the snow, and with each step, David felt his heart break as well.

Chapter 35
Staying Awhile
(Saturday, January 30–March 2094)

David thrashed and turned under the blankets. Hours after the broadcast, his mind was still racing. First, he bitterly pondered Malia's betrayal, and her confession that she didn't mourn him at all. Then he reminded himself, *they have coerced her, she thinks I am dead and that she has no options at all.* Shortly afterward, he asked himself, *how could she have even hinted that she wanted the ADF to kidnap our children? Why on earth even give them that idea? And how could she let that hideous mutilated female lay hands on her? Has she just given up hope and at least thinks she could have our children brought to her?* The emotions and arguments eventually faded, only to jump again, swirling in his thoughts.

Unable to sleep, he quietly rose, and sat at the kitchen table with a cup of tea. The moonlight spilled over him, making it unnecessary to light a candle, which he feared might awaken Lucy in the next room.

What now? he asked himself. *Is there even any chance I could rescue her? Would she even want to be rescued now? Perhaps they are all pretending I am dead, only to encourage me to walk into their trap? Perhaps I should have stayed in Oklahoma, begging the government and the AIA to demand Malia's return. I was too impatient. I have brought this on myself.* Then: *how can I blame Malia for trying to lure me into a trap? She would never do such a thing.*

"That's quite a sigh," said Lucy, as she entered the kitchen, tying the cord of her bathrobe more tightly. Over the bathrobe she wore her stylish dark green wool coat to keep her warm in the unheated house. "Forty years old," she had admitted, when David complimented her on the coat. "The only relic remaining from my prewar days. But quality lasts."

"I couldn't sleep," he said, stating the obvious.

"Well, now I can't either," she retorted. "The disturbance in the atmosphere is almost tangible."

She stood at the stove, reheating water to brew herself a cup of tea. David watched once again her blonde-gray hair spilling down her back. It was indeed her loveliest feature. From behind, standing straight and tall, she looked twenty years younger.

Then she sat across from him. "All right, why were you so upset tonight? I didn't realize you were missing our Saturday night movie so much."

"It was like…" David tried to appeal to what he felt was historical precedent, but lacked the specific knowledge to cite any. "I felt sorry for her."

"There's a long tradition of heretics who lied to save their lives," Lucy said. "Galileo recanted. Sabbatai Zevi declared he was not the Messiah after all when the sultan threatened to execute him. The Communists in the show trials praised Stalin and confessed to bizarre crimes hoping to avoid being shot. Of course, it was futile, since the regime could not afford to let them live. The Red Guards in China made their victims confess to unspeakable crimes, or just to the crime of being civilized. And what do you think our precious ADF does all the time? How many times do we see knowledge criminals berating themselves in our non-free press? The ones we don't hear from didn't survive. And even before the DJR got underway, our cancel culture sniffed out thought crimes from the weak-minded. Their lives weren't even at stake, but they tripped over each other to apologize so they didn't lose their jobs and their friends. That's all it took. So pathetic.

"Mike, I have the good fortune of being old enough and educated enough to know this is a common theme in history. Wherever people have been unfree, at least in modern times, when the phrase 'consent of the people' came into use, the rulers have compelled the ruled to assent to their unfreedom, by citing the will of the collective. At least in the old days, you knew the tyrant would die eventually.

"It's not enough just to obey—they need to demonstrate that they have the people on their side. Anyone who gets out of line needs to be brought back into the fold and paraded to the sheep as having returned."

The torrent of words overwhelmed David. He looked at Lucy's animated face in the moonlight.

"There's nothing unusual about what we saw tonight," she argued. "Just another dumb Social Crediteer who's trying to save her neck."

"Don't say that," he begged her. "Please, don't call her dumb."

"Why, Mike? She'd have you killed in a moment. Did you hear what she said about Plores at the end? What's this woman to you?"

David raised his haggard face to hers. "She's my wife," he said.

A few mornings later, he was sitting in the root cellar again, poking at the vegetable pile, not because the Antifans had returned, but because Lucy had asked him to inspect the roundup's arsenal. "If we've got a real live Antifan among us, I'm going to put you to work," she said. She promised not to reveal his secret; if anyone asked about David's new responsibilities, she would say she had decided to take advantage of his security guard background.

"But you are a Plore?" she pressed, to confirm. The ADF had not advertised that Malia's Antifan traitor husband had been a Plore, and Lucy was uncertain. She would not allow a Social Crediteer to stay among her people.

"I swear by God," he said. "Everything I told you was true, other than that my family was from Ohio, not New York. My father died fighting for our side, somewhere, and my little brother died in an Antifan transit camp. You can trust me." She quizzed him on his family and youth in Anacosta, and David suspected that the information he provided would be vetted—discreetly, he hoped—with contacts in Ploreville.

As he moved the vegetables to the other side of the cellar, a battery-operated lamp trained on the floor, he uncovered about a dozen firearms, most concealed in nothing more than a plastic bag or a wooden box. Three AR-15 rifles, seven handguns of varying calibers, and two revolvers. All of them were decades old. The firearms industry in the DJR had evaporated when the civil war ended and private firearm ownership was made a capital offense. The ADF purchased most of its weapons from China, including the electronic firearms.

He clucked regretfully at the rusted mechanisms and tarnished barrels, and did his best to apply oil with some rags. Lucy gave him some thin brushes to push through the barrels, which he thought would return some of them to operability. He wondered if they could build an underground firing range. The drones that hovered overhead made outdoor use of the weapons extremely dangerous. We just need a few metal boxes to store these weapons, he thought. We have to have some here. It did not occur to him that he had made a seamless transition from "they" to "we." "Where's the ammo?" he called up through the trapdoor when Lucy came over to check on him.

"Under a shed in the woods," she said, "in canisters and some wooden boxes."

"We're going to need it," he told her later. Lucy nodded her assent to the underground firing range. Several rounduprs who worked construction in Syracuse and understood basic civil engineering could build the range. If asked about their cement purchases, the rounduprs would say they planned to build a storage shed. "I have a strong back," David said. "I can help, they just need to tell me what to do."

Lucy looked at him admiringly. "The legend is that a Plore will come from far away and lead us against the Social Credit. Even before you told me the truth, I wondered if you were him."

"I don't know about that. There's nothing special about me, other than I escaped the DJR, and was stupid enough to come back. What can one man do?"

"You can give us hope," Lucy urged. "Most of us are discouraged and beaten down. You're a Plore but you've never been defeated. You're an Antifan. You've handled weapons and killed enemies, but never a Plore. You can tell us the truth about the United States, and what's going on in the world. We can't afford ignorance. This is the most hope I've had in thirty-five years."

"You're not going to tell everyone in the roundup who I really am, are you? How many weeks would it be before it leaked to the ADF? They'd kill you all, you know."

"No, of course not," said Lucy. "I mostly trust everyone, but there's a hundred and fifty of us now. I can't vouch for everyone these days. And even if someone meant to keep the secret, they might be so excited they couldn't help but tell another Plore from another roundup."

That gave David an idea. "Are there other Plores from nearby roundups we could recruit? We won't get very far on our own." David remembered Tom, who had spoken passionately at the Candor Inn. He thought that with some training and discipline, Tom might serve credibly.

Lucy said, "There are some I would trust. We have council meetings. I will sound my counterparts out...discreetly. Individually."

So by the beginning of March, David found himself in command of a group of fifty Plores, mostly men, but some younger women who had shown Lucy's fierceness and also skill at handling both firearms and knives. Brute strength was helpful, but likely to backfire without brains, courage, and judgment. David measured each applicant against those criteria, knowing a bad guess on his part might kill them all. As far as the fighters were concerned, their leader was still Mike Potter from Massena, credible because of his security guard experience. They practiced shooting in the underground range, and used the spent cartridges to manufacture their own makeshift ammunition. The ammunition had been stored carefully, and more than David had expected was hidden away, but it would not last long at this rate.

Each evening, the rounduprs returned from their jobs in Syracuse bringing back whatever they could buy or find on their lunch hours or after work without drawing undue attention, items that back in the roundup could be used to create weapons or tools or possibly a refurbishing machine to manufacture ammunition. They brought home a motley assortment of items hidden in tote bags and backpacks: scraps of metal; glass; medical supplies; innocuous self-defense tools such as pepper spray that a Social Crediteer was permitted to use to defend herself against a Street Person. They built a workbench with a milling machine to manufacture makeshift but working rifles, an arduous process. Some of the rounduprs recollected their fathers constructing rifles shortly after the war ended, before that became too dangerous, and they pooled their knowledge. The first ugly rifle that worked was a cause for celebration. "They will get better and better," promised David. But they still had to be hidden in the metal boxes in a cellar and conveyed through a tunnel into the shooting range.

They scoured recycling dumpsters in local towns, or the woods for junk. Rounduprs did online searches that, on the surface, and infrequently made, amid a plethora of random searches, would look innocent, perhaps for a child's school assignment, but contained nuggets of queries ultimately aimed at chemistry and self-defense. Small amounts of gunpowder filtered into the roundup from Canadian sources; Lucy knew all the truckers and David didn't ask questions. Yet Lucy did not ask the truckers about smuggling David to Anacosta.

All this cost money, and David directed the roundup under Lucy's guidance to come up with ways to raise money. They had sputtered along, earning just enough to live, but now they needed to earn enough to fight, an expensive proposition. When spring came, the roundup would reopen its market along the highway, at which they sold knitted goods, tools, and produce and hot meals, and cans of Saratoga Beer. They decided to increase the poultry flock, a field in which some rounduprs were very knowledgeable. "We could sell some of this in Anacosta Ploreville," said David, "there's more money there."

Lucy reminded him, "We could use some of the truckers to deliver our goods to other Plorevilles." It was technically illegal, but no one in the Economic Tower would bother to investigate as long as the deliveries were made on schedule from the Economic Zone camps. The truckers would demand a fee for their assistance, but it would enlarge the roundup's market well beyond the county. A small committee formed to generate ideas for raising money, and another committee formed to implement the ideas.

Lucy assured him that everyone in the roundup supported the self-defense scheme, even though David continued to worry. One informant would destroy them all. The doubters were won over, at least temporarily and cautiously, by the promise of more prosperity. The men from other roundups still didn't know everything that went on in Lucy's roundup. About ten of David's band came from two neighboring roundups, and one was Tom, whose face shone with relief when he once again met David, and pumped his hand gratefully.

"I knew you were special," he said to an embarrassed David. "When I heard what you did to Battista, I said, I hope he's OK and escapes. And then I thought, what if he manages to stay around here and help us fight those bastards."

But if Tom was hankering for an early fight, he was bound to be disappointed.

"Our purpose," David told his band in the woods, "is not to wage a war against the government. Not yet. We have to learn to defend ourselves and eventually carve out territory that won't be worth Syracuse's while to come after. By the time they know we're resisting, it will be much harder for them to wipe us out."

"Who made you the leader?" Seth confronted him one early afternoon.

David looked at him coolly. "Hey, buddy, you had years to do this before I got here. What happened?" The other members of the band fixed Seth with an irritable stare. And after that, Seth quietly settled into his role as a chief lieutenant.

As for David, it was easier to tackle the immediate, tangible problems in the roundup than to press Lucy on arranging his travel to Anacosta. He admitted to himself that he had no idea what he would do when he arrived in Ploreville, how he would find Malia, let alone whether she still loved him, or wanted to be rescued by him. For all he knew, she would shriek with revulsion at the sight of him and her Antifan guards would surround and capture him.

Nor did Lucy ask about his plans. So months passed, the snow turned gray and then melted into little blackened piles, little blades of grass poked out from the ground, and the rounduprs heard birdsong again. They had survived another winter, and hope sprang forth with the tender green shoots from the trees.

Chapter 36
Diplomats
(Tuesday–Wednesday, March 16–17, 2094)

Daniel Harris and Chris Mendoza hurried up the stone steps of the National Security Council in St. Louis on a blustery March morning, buoyed by the sudden willingness of bureaucrats to meet with them. Daniel was wearing a new blue suit and a new black wool coat finer than anything he'd ever owned before. His face was tense. Chris wore a rumpled brown suit that sufficed for most Capettone meetings, but had splurged on a new blue and green patterned tie. Daniel had been reluctant to leave Fern alone with the boys, but Chris had lined up dependable armed friends who promised to guard the Harris homes 24-7 while Daniel was gone. Only then had Daniel agreed to accompany Chris. Chris was relieved, since it would have looked odd if David Harris's only relative in the United States was refusing to petition St. Louis in person for his rescue.

Driving through Tulsa and heading for the Missouri border, they confessed their fears to each other. "The signal has been dead for two weeks," Chris said, referring to the chip he had embedded in David's bedroll so they would have some indication of his location. "I don't think he would have lingered there. He'd push forward if he could." Before expiring, the signal had stayed pulsing from upstate New York for four months, which had already been troubling.

"Not a good sign," Daniel, steady at the wheel, agreed. Had the ADF found David, the propaganda mills would have gleefully broadcast his apprehension and execution. But David could simply have met a bad end in the woods with a wild animal, or a criminal. For all of David's lethality, Daniel knew his brother was unaccustomed to the rigors of the wilderness.

Daniel had persistently stayed in touch with their congressman about Malia, and the local MAGA coterie had supplemented his efforts with letters and visits. As far as St. Louis was concerned, David Harris was still an inpatient at a psychiatric hospital in Stillwater. Fortunately, St. Louis was insufficiently curious about Harris to confirm his whereabouts, the hospital director was in on the secret, and the MAGAns were counting on the US government's indifference to disguise the fact that David had returned to the DJR, violating various border agreements with the DJR.

Finally, after many calls, Congressman Glass's office had contacted Daniel to say that a meeting had been set up with the National Security Council and that AIA officers would attend. "We can lay all our cards on the table now," said Chris.

Daniel and Chris were ushered through hushed carpeted hallways. As befitted the offices housing the executive staff for the president of the United States, the discreetly lush premises featured murals, mahogany furniture, shaded lamps rather than fluorescent lights, and expensively upholstered chairs. In a conference room, they were greeted by John Gaines, the handsome thirtyish NSC director for DJR Affairs, a State Department officer on rotation to NSC. Gaines had been spending a lot of time in Toronto at the US-DJR negotiations until they had broken off when news of Malia's zoo speech surfaced. Gaines found the Harris business to be an irritating impediment to his diplomatic labors. He had agreed to meet with David Harris's brother as a personal favor to Congressman Glass, whose vote would be critical on an administration pet project next week.

"Good morning, Mr. Harris," Gaines said, offering a cool manicured hand. Chris introduced himself as a former colleague of David Harris and a family friend.

Several AIA officers entered the room, including Vernal, wearing a bright blue suit. The young woman and man with her turned out to be analysts there to lend their DJR expertise when asked.

When the pleasantries were over and they had assembled around the conference table, Gaines asked, "Exactly what are you asking from us, Mr. Harris?"

"We would like to see some effort by our government to rescue my sister-in-law from Anacosta. She was kidnapped in Oklahoma last August and has been in the hands of the Antifan Defense Forces ever since."

"But," Gaines said smoothly, "she seemed a very willing participant in that spectacle the DJR broadcast in January. How do you know she is still being held against her will?" The DJR had smugly circulated recordings of the Anacosta Bowl performance, including in the United States.

"She never believed that nonsense. You heard about her speech when they put her in a cage at the zoo. Those were her true feelings. She would never say those lies about her husband, my brother, if they hadn't forced her to. If she believed all that, she would never have fled across the border into the US in the first place. She was always grateful to be free and in the United States."

"Maybe she's changed her mind?"

"If she changed her mind, it was only under duress," said Daniel sharply. "The DJR authorities would not hesitate to have her killed if she didn't cooperate."

"Is that true?" Gaines addressed the analysts.

The young woman said, "There are no constraints on what the DJR and the ADF in particular can do to prisoners. Mrs. Harris clearly believes that her husband is dead and she likely believes she has no choice but to submit. The DJR is probably thrilled to have such a propaganda victory handed to them."

"Mrs. Harris is not an American citizen," Gaines then reminded his visitors.

"She is the wife of an American citizen and the mother of two citizens," Chris broke in.

"And her husband is unable to come here to plead her case himself? He did survive the Oklahoma assault."

"We are here to ask for help with David Harris as well," said Chris. "He is also in the DJR, we believe in upstate New York."

Gaines was taken aback. "Isn't he in the hospital? Didn't he have a mental breakdown?"

"No," said Daniel. "He went into the DJR to rescue Malia back in November. We didn't expect to hear from him—we had no way to communicate across the border. But a chip we placed in his gear last showed him in the middle of New York–Schuylkill as of two weeks ago."

Gaines flushed angrily. "Why did he do such a stupid thing? How did he think he could possibly rescue his wife from the ADF?"

"Because," said Daniel firmly, "we were getting no support from this government"—he cast a quick look at Vernal—"and we couldn't sit back and do nothing. You all kept telling us, 'We've got these negotiations going on with the DJR; we can't jeopardize these negotiations by asking for Malia Harris,' and eventually we just got tired of waiting."

Vernal interrupted, "Mr. Harris, we did get a proof of life from the ADF, if you remember, once we confirmed she was in deejer hands."

"Yes, but nothing happened after that."

Vernal cast an impatient look at the ceiling. "Mr. Harris, if you think the AIA is in a position to launch an aerial attack against Beaufort Tower and recapture Malia, you're being unrealistic."

"We didn't give any indication to the DJR that Malia's fate mattered to us. No wonder she's given up," said Daniel.

Chris said, "Now that the talks have broken off, are you able to help us? We need to locate David and we need to show the DJR that we haven't forgotten Malia Harris."

Gaines fixed the pair with an irritated look. "You've only made things worse by allowing David Harris to run back into the DJR. Now instead of just rescuing Malia Harris—which the passage of time might have resolved—we've got the challenge of extricating someone whom the DJR would never allow to leave. He is in far more danger than is his wife."

"And we can't allow the DJR to know he's in the country," Chris reminded him. "Right now we've managed to convince the DJR he's in the hospital. If they even thought he was in New York, they would turn over every rock until they found him."

Gaines said icily, "We don't plan to discuss Mr. Harris with the DJR. But what do you mean, 'We've managed to convince the DJR?' Since when are a group of Oklahomans conducting diplomacy with a hostile government?" From the condescension with which he invested "Oklahomans," it was clear that Gaines was not from Oklahoma, or any place like it. He in fact had grown up in the St. Louis suburbs, the child of Washington bureaucrat parents who had fled it after the civil war for the new capital.

Chris said, "They sent out some spies into the Harrises' neighborhood checking on him. I engaged them in conversation and mentioned that David Harris had had to go to a psychiatric hospital. They seemed to take what I said at face value."

Now Vernal was aggrieved. "Why didn't you let us know you were approached by the ADF?"

"What good would it have done?" Daniel countered. It really had never occurred to them to relay the story of the encounter with the fake workman to the AIA, not that they would have known how to approach the agency in the absence of David and Malia. Nor had AIA had reached out to him or Fern after the kidnapping.

"We will continue to ask about Malia Harris," said Gaines, "but the DJR authorities will claim that she is happy to be back in the country, and nothing she has said publicly suggests otherwise. They will also remind us that Mrs. Harris is not a citizen of ours, but of theirs. Our leverage is very limited.

"As for Mr. Harris, if you don't want us to reveal to the Diversans that he is within their borders, I don't know what we can do on his behalf. We don't have the wherewithal to locate him behind DJR lines, do we, Vernal?" Gaines waited for the acknowledgement of incapacity from the AIA representatives. "So since he got himself into this quandary, I am afraid he will have to get himself out of it.

"But from what we all know about his resourcefulness, I am sure Mr. Harris will figure out a way to rescue himself, and possibly even Mrs. Harris." Gaines said this in a tone that implied he really couldn't care less what the Harrises did next. "Perhaps we will be pleasantly surprised." He stood up, signaling the meeting was over.

Gaines strode off confidently toward his next meeting, leaving Vernal awkwardly with Daniel and Chris, all unsure where to go next. She hesitated, then said, "Mr. Harris, we haven't forgotten Malia and David. If there is an opportunity to rescue them, the AIA will not refuse." Her words sounded empty to the two men, but they thanked her anyway. You never knew.

As Daniel and Chris left the fine building to grab a sandwich before heading home to Oklahoma City, Chris said, referring to Gaines, "That is how a diplomat tells you to go fuck yourself." The wind whipped up briefly between the stone buildings.

"What now?" asked Daniel, close to despair.

"We will come up with a plan."

Chapter 37
Comedy And Tragedy
(Saturday, March 20, 2094)

A film crew was following Malia around in her apartment. Garbed in a plush red robe, Malia was starring in her own influencer video to promote various furnishings and products, including the robe. "It's made of environmentally sustainable eco-bamboo!" she prated into the camera. The Economic Tower had suggested Malia promote some of its latest furniture lines, and Paragon had agreed. She had no say in how the Antifans directed her, and frankly, she no longer cared whether she was speaking to retired schoolteachers or opening a new shopping mall or electronically signing copies of her memoir, *I, Malia, Liberated.*

Malia had read the drafts by the ghostwriter detachedly, as if she were reading a novel about someone else altogether, and that enabled her to approve them quickly. Not about you, she told herself, about some imaginary character named Malia whose ancestors rode with the Klan, and who, every night in Oklahoma, had secretly prayed to Mother Earth after her traitor husband went to bed. She took enough antidepressants each morning to survive the day; the Antifans raised no objection to her extensive pharmaceutical orders. If she had no engagements scheduled, she spent the day in bed, sleeping or staring at the wall, but even then she could not cry. The appliance audio surveillance in the apartment was running 24-7, as it did in any other Social Crediteer's home. Strangely, she had been happier at Beaufort, when she could be mostly herself. Even with Health Meat.

The one engagement she had dreaded was when she spoke to an auditorium of deathly silent Plores compelled to attend in return for food packages. She stumbled guiltily through her lines. No one applauded. "You didn't try very hard to win them over," Paragon rebuked her afterward.

Malia concluded the taping by beckoning the crew toward the politically correct signage hanging in her living room, above the eco-fabric sofa. "Love the Earth. Hate Racism. Embrace Truth Serum." You could buy the signs, carved in bamboo or mahogany, for an exorbitant sum, or, if you were a poor Social Crediteer, on plywood painted a sunny yellow by workers in the Economic Zones.

"How you live tells people what your values are," she told the camera. "I may have a large apartment, but is my furniture sustainable? Is my food grown in a way that respects Mother Earth? Do people of color and differently abled farmers earn a good living from my choices? Under socialism, it is possible." The bookshelves were empty, a sure sign of a virtuous Social Crediteer. Chefs had created the teriyaki tofu dish on Malia's counter. "It just takes a few minutes to cook it!" she beseeched her audience. "And it costs hardly anything at all! If you get tofu in your Healthy Eating bag, spend a few more cents on the teriyaki sauce and you'll have a delicious, earth-friendly dinner! I recommend you add whatever vegetables are in season."

When the crew left, Malia ate the tofu. Inspecting the contents of her walk-in closet, she decided to wear a slinky black pantsuit that evening. Paragon and Exterra were finally going to take her to the comedy club. Make me laugh, please, she thought. She remembered, I last laughed in Oklahoma City, before we went to Dallas. Emmett placed the toy pail on his head and rode around the kitchen on a broomstick, pretending to be a knight. Sadness filled her, partly out of guilt at her petty behavior in Dallas before the Antifans struck, of all weekends. She recollected David's joyous laugh when he had said, "and the mother of my sons!" and her angry reaction. She should have been ecstatic at the thought that she was the mother of two beautiful sons, not to mention her daughter, she reproved herself.

She turned around with the outfit in her hands and gasped. Paragon stood in the doorway to the closet. Of course he and Exterra could enter her apartment any time they wanted, and they almost never rang the doorbell. Sometimes she was warned of their approach because she could hear them bantering with the Antifan guards outside her door. But she had never seen him in her bedroom before. He was in the black suit that he preferred for civilian outings—it was the closest thing to an Antifan uniform that one could approximate outside of Beaufort. A white button-down shirt open at the neck lay flat beneath the jacket.

"I am sorry to disturb you," he said, not sorry at all.

"Is Exterra here?" she asked, but knowing the answer.

"She'll join us at the club. Go ahead and dress, I'll sit here and watch." He settled in the dusty rose armchair in a corner of the room next to the window.

"I think not," Malia said. This was the first time in many months that she had defied him.

"Modesty is a false virtue, you know. Fascists used it to oppress women." He placed an ankle on the opposite knee and leaned back.

"Oh, I'm not oppressed at all," she lied, and took the pantsuit into the bathroom. The door opened briefly, the red robe sailed out and landed on the wide bed, and then she locked the door. He laughed, with a note of irritation. But he watched intently when Malia came out, sat at the vanity, and began freshening the makeup left on her face from the videotaping. If she stared into the mirror, she did not need to look at his attentive face focused on hers. And she couldn't deny Khalid Ma was a handsome man and for the first time he was treating her as a normal woman, not some disgusting knowledge criminal. And lately he had been addressing her as Malia, which she found slightly ominous, rather than the almost comforting Prisoner Jenness.

"Malia, have you given any thought to your Diverse future?"

It was the same question Doctor Bob had asked her, and she had palmed it off with a ludicrous appeal to the "sensible" Plores. I have no Diverse future, she wanted to say, only one in a free country, with my husband, who might still be alive, or at least with my children. The most likely Diverse future, she thought, is a boot stamping across my face, forever.

"I thought I was living my Diverse future," she said, trying to hit the right note of flirtatiousness and plausibility. "A celebrity with a lot of Social Credit." She accidentally plastered the mascara brush across her cheek and reached for the solvent. Perhaps Paragon would not believe her sincerity about Diversity, but he would take on face value Malia's desire to live comfortably.

"That's your day job. What about your night job?"

"What do you mean?" Malia parried, feebly, fearfully. She made the mistake of turning to look at him. His dark eyes were intense. He would not be deterred. Malia became acutely conscious of the large bed behind her with the hanging rose-patterned curtains.

"No woman should be alone at night. Even one such as yourself, devoted to Diversity."

Malia could not tell him that she still believed, after all the videos and obituaries they had thrust at her, that David was possibly alive. Maybe, paradoxically, because of all the "evidence." Alive enough, at least in her mind, for her not to surrender to Paragon's overtures, not yet.

"I am satisfied with Exterra. You know that I'll get an extra forty points starting in August, once I've filed as a lesbian."

"You're no lesbian," Paragon said. "You're only saying that because you're afraid of me. In the end, I have to approve your Social Credit score, and I know you need a man. And what makes you think Exterra is still satisfied with you?"

Malia paused guiltily, not having considered this before. She had been taking Exterra's pleasure in her for granted, and had reciprocated with a somewhat perverse satisfaction in making the Antifan soldierette seek to arouse her rather than vice versa. In the face of the compulsion that had forced her to Exterra's bed, Malia had cultivated an aloofness that was her only means of resistance, although it had not discouraged Exterra. In no other sphere did Malia hold the upper hand over the Antifans. But now Malia realized that perhaps Paragon was intimating that Exterra was tiring of her, and she would do well to find another protector.

"Look at me," he told her, meeting her own dark eyes with his. "You could do much worse than me. Much worse."

"I know nothing about you. Who are you, really? Where are you from? What is your Diversity story?"

His abrupt response was, "Let's go, we're going to be late." This told Malia that Paragon was by no means as assured as he pretended, and while the swagger might be partly genuine, it was also a shield. But against what? What was he hiding? She tucked that away in a corner of her mind, knowing it might prove useful someday. In the car, she allowed him to casually drape his arm over her shoulders. The weight of his arm and the sensation were not unpleasant.

The Daffy Club occupied a cozy basement space off lower Connecticut Avenue. Comedy was a delicate business under Diversity, but the Knowledge Tower carefully vetted scripts and restricted patronage to Social Crediteers whose ideological credentials showed they could handle politically risqué jokes. Malia and Paragon arrived just before the early evening show began. The electronic easel proclaimed, "Nhoj Eelston Tonight! 8 and 10 p.m." Waitrons in black tuxes scurried among tables bearing drinks and plates; light fixtures on the cellar walls cast shadows on the elite Anacostans in the club. Attending a comedy club was among the most daring things they could attempt, since one could not just stay in receiving mode.

Aside from a contented grunt from Paragon at the sight of the newly correct name Nhoj, the mood at their table was frosty. Exterra greeted them curtly, after having been kept waiting, and she was already suspicious of Paragon's having insisted on picking Malia up by himself at her apartment. Malia's Antifan escorts sat at a nearby table.

They peered at their armband phones to look at the menu. "Rib eye, rare," said Paragon, "and an iced tea." Malia echoed him, "But medium and a gin and tonic, please." Exterra ordered chicken.

"Nhoj Eelston, Diverse folx!" proclaimed the announcer. A slight curly-haired imp bounced onto the stage.

"Last time I was here, at the Daffy—great place, isn't this? Let's have some applause for the waitrons—my name was John, but now I've become Nhoj. No, that's not Nose, folx, although I considered changing my name to Dick! Big Dick!" *(applause and laughs)*.

"Just so you don't have any doubts about my love for Diversity, I just got my truth serum shot yesterday *(applause)*. It didn't hurt that the vaccinator was a dedicated young man with a nice butt! We've got a date set up for tomorrow night, and I hope he'll be shooting stuff in me somewhere else!" *(applause, laughter)*. A similar joke about a just-departed boyfriend met with a few groans.

"Hey, that didn't seem like a very enthusiastic response! There wouldn't be any homophones in here, would there? That's a homophobe with a phone! *(dutiful laughter)*. Maybe a few Plores snuck in here? Nah, nobody seems to be eating any mud! *(laughter)*. You all seem like good Social Credit folx…Anyone hear about the Plores who were walking through the woods?" Deplorable jokes were standard material in a Diversity comedian's repertoire, since they were funnier than other, carefully curated, jokes. The audience knew its cue and laughter was safe.

"They come across a pile of dog shit. One of them says to the other, 'I think that's dog shit.' 'Does it smell like dog shit?' asks the second. The first bends down to smell it, 'Yes.' 'Does it feel like dog shit?' The one picks up a piece and sure enough it feels like shit and he nods. 'Does it taste like dog shit?' The first takes a lick. 'Yeah, it's dog shit.' The second Plore breathes a big sigh of relief, 'I'm so glad we didn't step in it'" *(uproarious laughter)*.

"A woman walked up to a little old Plore rocking in a chair on his porch. 'I couldn't help noticing how happy you look,' she said. 'What's your secret for a long happy life?' 'I smoke three packs of cigarettes a day,' he said. 'I also drink a case of whiskey a week, eat fatty foods, and never exercise.' 'That's amazing,' the woman said. 'How old are you?' 'Twenty-six,' he said" *(laughter)*.

Nhoj then told a few jokes at the expense of the United States, President Hannigan, and his wife. "A Christian calls up the White House in St. Louis and tells the receptionist: 'I'd like to become the next president of the United States.' The receptionist: 'What are you, an idiot?' Christian: 'Why, is it required?'"

Paragon smiled at a few of the jokes, Exterra giggled despite herself, and Malia manufactured a chuckle at each punch line, which became easier after the third round of drinks. Nhoj followed with a joke about President Hannigan and the three Plore wives.

Nhoj finally relented, saying, "You've been a great audience. Wish me luck tomorrow night when I get a real great injection from my handsome vaccinator!" The crowd gave Nhoj an amiable send-off.

"What did you think of that, Malia?" Exterra seemed to have forgotten her earlier pique at Paragon and Malia, and now hung on Malia's response.

"Very funny," Malia conceded.

"See, we can laugh in the DJR! I'm glad you're developing a Diverse sense of humor."

To Malia's shock, Paragon dropped Exterra off at the Avalon and said he would take Malia home. Exterra, flushed, looked as if she wanted to say something spiteful, but held her tongue and stalked into the building. Paragon instructed the driver to head for the Portland Tower. Paragon followed her into the apartment. "I want no interruptions," he instructed the guards. "Including by Captain Boyd. Unless it's a national emergency or the building's on fire."

The door closed behind them. "Make us some tea, Malia," Paragon said.

Startled, Malia complied, bustling around the kitchen so she need not look at him. She was grateful for what she considered a reprieve from what she assumed was Paragon's intended business tonight. It was a little embarrassing that she didn't know her own kitchen well enough to find the tea bags. The Social Credit housekeeper came at ten and left by six, with Malia's dinner stowed in the fridge, her laundry folded, and her medications awaiting on her night table. Paragon said, "Check the cabinet above the sink," and indeed, the tea bags were sitting there. "California Haze, please."

She poured them both tea. His large hands cupped the mug, from which steam rose, twirling.

"I don't drink alcohol, if you haven't noticed," Paragon said. "Islam forbids it." And before she could question it, he added, "and Mother Earth doesn't command it, so I need not drink."

"So you're a Muslim by tradition."

"Yes, I believe I just said so. Just as you are a Christian by tradition but have now come home to Mother Earth, as you were raised. It is all form, not function. The function is the same across all our denominations within Mother Earth."

"I don't think Exterra is very pleased with us tonight."

He gave a short dismissive nod of his head. "What she wants is not of interest to me. What I want is of interest to me. I want to lead the DJR so that we can impose real Diversity in this country, with Social Crediteers striving to improve. There is so much more we could do to bring Diversity here. We need to bring the Plores under heel—their very existence mocks us. They read books! They go to their churches! They have more freedom than our Social Crediteers do. We have become too soft.

"That stupid comedian mocked the Plores, but it is dangerous to disparage your enemy. If I had the power, I would break that treaty tomorrow. The Plores would slave for us, instead of us for them. We don't need to pay them. If they refuse to work, we will send them to incubation farms. A few might be worthy of becoming Social Crediteers. The US has become weak…they will not go to war to defend the treaty." His face shone with conviction.

Malia was grateful that Paragon did not seem to be in an amorous mood after all. "No, the US wants peace," she ventured.

"Yes," he said, finally looking at her again. "Or they are just cowards. It is often much the same thing. And you are doubtless wondering, what does all this have to do with you, Malia Jenness?"

She looked at him helplessly. Her tea was cooling rapidly.

"Marriage is too important to waste. As a senior Antifan commander, I know it would be better if I forwent marriage altogether. It stinks of fascism and backwardness."

"Exterra loves you."

"If I married Exterra, what would that do for me? We came together because she showed her dedication to Diversity and she was desperate to enter my bed. She even tattooed her face when I demanded it. How could I not sleep with her then? It was also convenient." Now he was stalking around her living room, talking half to himself.

"But then when you are in the public spotlight, and you are the leader of the Diversity Justice Republic, every choice you make matters. Your clothes, your words, your furniture, your wife. You said it well in your video today—I approved the speech, you know—'How you live tells people what your values are.'"

How telling, Malia thought. Furniture, words, wife, all lumped together in one acquisitive steaming mess. But this makes no sense. He can't be proposing to me. Malia Jenness, with her marriage to the most notorious Plore-Antifan ever, her Plore relatives, her American sons. Surely she would be the least suitable consort for an arch–Antifan Diversity ruler ever.

"Malia Ma," he finally smiled at her, stopping in his tracks to turn around and face her. "How does that sound to you?"

Awful, she thought. Like a long cat's meow, or a baby's cry. She stammered, "Are you proposing to me? After all these months, when you punished me as a heretic, how can you think I would be an appropriate wife for someone such as you? Would the ADF even let you marry me? Don't you have to go through an approval process? I can't imagine they would ever permit it."

"No one in the ADF will say no when I take for myself the wife of the traitor Antifan, who I myself brought back to Diversity. Only I, Khalid Ma, could have engineered the raid into Oklahoma—and you see how little the US has protested, because even the Americans know you belong here, not with them." By now, he had pulled his chair around to hers. Malia thought briefly of how they had sat just this way in the interrogation room. "Only I could have killed the traitor, and bedded his wife. Of course what a shame he is not alive to witness it, but the Plores will see it for themselves."

Not yet, buddy, she thought, but knowing she would not be able to fight him off if he sought to claim his reward tonight. It dawned on her that Paragon was not planning to ask her permission to marry her. He was informing her of her fate. "In the National Diversity Cathedral, perhaps. St. John Beaufort can be our household saint." Every Social Crediteer couple chose a patron saint from the MED pantheon, receiving an idol to place in a specially constructed nook in their home.

Now she was curious—his words were not those of a North American, but someone schooled in a more savage culture where the victor seized the loser's women and power was all. The shrouds of a civilized veneer were falling around his feet, revealing something much more primeval.

"Tell me your Diversity story," she begged, if only to postpone the moment at which he would presumably carry her into her bedroom. "If you want to marry me, you owe it to me to tell me something about yourself and your rise through Diversity to lead the nation."

"I was born in China," he began, solemnly, "the child of two great cultures, one the Islamic, and the other, the Sinic..."

Chapter 38
Deeper And Deeper
(Monday, April 5 to Sunday, April 18, 2094)

Warren Welcome stocked his store's freezer display case with the shrink-wrapped chicken parts from the new, mysterious supplier in upstate New York–Schuylkill. The trucker had unloaded the regular produce from the Economic Zone: boxes of Healthy Pride Flake cereal in bright LGBTQIA colors, rainbow macaroni and cheese, and Derrida crackers. You needed to accept whatever the trucker was delivering, because the more accommodating stores were visited earlier in the run, gas and time permitting, and they got the better produce. Welcome regretted having to choose the Derrida crackers, because they were of lesser quality than the alternative, Poorwhite Crackers, but he knew his clientele would shun the latter just on account of the slyly condescending name. Their choices were few, but they exercised them vigorously within narrow boundaries. And whoever Derrida was, his sins were distant and obscure, and they could ignore the insult, whatever it might be.

"I've got something good for you," said the trucker. "Fresh poultry from a Plore farm up there." He beckoned Welcome out to the truck so the store owner could check for himself.

"It's illegal," said Welcome mournfully. Legally he was only permitted to accept groceries from Economic Zone camps and local Ploreville gardeners. But the chicken looked good.

"Maybe," conceded the trucker. "But who's going to know? You can mark it up a little more than a normal Zone chicken and it still won't sit around very long. Just give it some crappy name like Antiracism Chicken so everyone'll think it's from the Zone." He paused. "I need to move it fast, just in case I get pulled over. Do you want it or not?"

So Welcome was stocking his freezer case with the illegal chicken. He taped a sign over the case, "Proud Heritage Incan Chicken," just in case.

"What's an In-can chicken?" asked the first customer who saw the full freezer. "It's not in a can at all." But she bought several packages for her large family's dinner. By evening it was all gone, even at a premium price, and Welcome had earned a tidy profit.

Not bad, he thought. It was worth taking a chance every once in a while. If the product sold quickly, it was unlikely inspectors would arrive in time to stumble across it. He went down into the basement after closing to place orders for later in the week. Most of the basement was full of dry goods and a half century of boxes and odd household items, though neatly shelved. Welcome had moved Felicia's paisley upholstered rocking chair down here after she died. In a corner under a barred window was Welcome's old wooden secretary, atop which sat his workscreen, where he did his accounts. Half an hour later, with the sun casting restless farewell rays through the window, Welcome thought he heard a sound. He swiveled quickly in his prewar vinyl office chair.

"Dad? Are you there?"

"Down here," he called up, his heart leaping joyfully at hearing Jeff's voice. He was glad he'd told his youngest son to keep a key to the shop—and to the family house next door—even after Jeff went Social Credit. "You'll always be my son, and this will always be your home, whatever they tell you in the City," he had instructed Jeff on that last day before he reported to the Knowledge Tower to embark on his new life. Welcome knew it had reassured him. Some Plore families cut off ties completely with a child who went Social Credit, but Welcome wouldn't ever have dreamed of doing the Social Credit's work for them. That's what they wanted you to do.

Jeff sank down to sit on the second to bottom step. He had walked all the way from Anacosta, because it was best to minimize his visits to Ploreville, and you were less likely to attract monitors if you avoided the buses. His legs were tired, especially after the full shift in the Euthanasia Palace. This week he was working days.

But Welcome only noticed his son's stricken face and his cheeks shining with tears.

"Son, what is the matter?" he asked, fearfully.

Jeff stripped off the black armband, rose, and carried it into a back storeroom, carefully closing the door, which in itself alarmed Welcome. Then he returned to the bottom of the staircase.

"Dad, they've told me I have to start giving the poison pills to the patients."

"But you told me that they weren't going to force you to do that." Welcome had been proud of Jeff's refusal to kill the patients. "You said they even respected you more for it."

"That was then, this is now. We have a new supervisor. They've told me—it's a they, by the way, a nonbinary—that it's unfair not to do my share of the work. And they said my attitude was non-Diverse and maybe even heresy, because I don't understand that the earth's resources are finite and we can't keep everyone alive forever. It's selfish and individualistic to want to stay alive when you are a drain on the society, and they said I was aiding and abetting it.

"They said, 'Since you were a Plore, you need to show us that you've really opened your heart to your betterment. This doesn't look good, and it makes us look like we have backsliders here. If you have this attitude, the patients will pick up on it and they might resist the doctor's orders.'"

Jeff was openly weeping now. "Dad, I wish I had never gone Social Credit."

"And if you still refuse?" Welcome's voice was harsh, not because he was angry at his son, but because he hated the evil government so much, like any upright Plore, but maybe even more so these days, he couldn't keep the hatred out of his voice. I need to watch my tone, he told himself, it might get me in trouble.

"I asked. The Social Tower would fire me. But then I would lose my apartment. At that point, the Economic Tower could send me to a Zone camp, or maybe they would let me be a street person. They won't find you another job under these circumstances. But I'm afraid because we're Plores, and he…they mentioned they could refer the case to Beaufort as a knowledge crime. It's a knowledge crime to deny Mother Earth and insist that everyone has a right to live when the environment is suffering. You know they hate us to begin with."

Welcome paced back and forth, from the desk to the boiler and back again. He switched on the small lamp above the desk, since twilight was closing.

"Daddy, I was thinking of killing myself instead."

Shocked, Welcome stared open-mouthed at Jeff. "No!"

"What else can I do? You raised us to do the right thing. Thou shalt not kill."

"Killing yourself is killing too."

"Then what do I do, Daddy?" Jeff cried out. "I'm trapped."

Welcome contemplated his youngest son. Those dark round eyes, now despairing, were the same ones that had twinkled merrily in Jeff's chubby toddler face. He always marveled, looking at his sons, that once upon a time, they had been helpless babies who trusted him and Felicia to feed, diaper, clothe, and safeguard them. Even if you were a Plore, you could shelter your children from the harsh society outside. But then would come a time, it always did, when you launched them into the world, and their hopes and dreams collided with the fences of the giant concentration camp called the DJR. And of his three sons, Jeff had been the softest, the most tender, the one who liked books.

Welcome sat next to Jeff on the stairs.

"You got a vacation coming up?"

Jeff was surprised by the question. "Yes, I was gonna take two weeks later this month. That would be about a year since I started there."

"Can you hold them off for a few more weeks? Say you understand that Diversity needs you, ask to speak with one of their fake psychologists to feel better about this in your mind? What do they call those people?"

"Diversity counselors. They're the ones who keep you in line, the soft way. The commissar keeps you in line the hard way. But if he gets involved, you're already in trouble. They said if I didn't behave, they'd refer my case to the commissar. Then I might end up at Beaufort."

"Don't do anything crazy. Just hold them off a while. I'll figure out something."

Jeff thought, how are you going to do anything? You're just a Plore, even worse, a black Plore. You run a grocery store in Ploreville. You may be a big deal in this neighborhood, but once you cross the river, you're no better than a Street Person. Maybe worse, because the Social Crediteers have to pretend to respect the Street People.

On the other hand, he trusted his father, and he could trust no one else.

"All right," he said, sniffling a little, as if he were still the eight-year-old who had ended the softball game by striking out and needed some comforting.

"Stay for dinner," said Welcome. "You'll still be able to catch the last bus to the tunnel." He was afraid of casting off his son into the dark night until he could be absolutely certain that Jeff would do no harm to himself. Not to mention that he, Warren Welcome, was lonely.

Jeff agreed to stay for dinner. All that awaited him in his small apartment had been a sad soybake, the remains of last week's Healthy Eating bag, which was supposed to have lasted him seven days but was almost gone now after five. Father and son locked up the store and disappeared into the house next door with a single package of the Incan chicken that Warren had saved for himself. As Jeff watched the Raptors baseball game in the living room, his armband resting on the coffee table, Welcome pan-fried the chicken with some kale. An idea began to form in his mind as he watched the chicken brown and sizzle in the skillet. But he would not tell Jeff until he had figured it all out, and he would not tell Jeff everything.

Two weeks later, Jeff was riding on a Diversity Scenibus through the Yramaland countryside, en route to the Finger Lakes of New York–Schuylkill. Travel was still a novelty for Jeff, and one of the few advantages a low Social Crediteer held over a Plore. Still, even a Social Crediteer had limited funds, and Jeff had balked at the price of a round-trip ticket to Buffalo, after the carbon offset surcharge. Two hundred twenty dollars.

"Never mind," said Warren. "I'll pay for it." Warren couldn't travel past Yramaland, but as a hardworking widower he could save money and they couldn't keep him from spending it.

Jeff wasn't sure why his father was so insistent that he take this trip. Yes, he agreed that he needed a change of scenery, but why upstate New York–Schuylkill instead of a Shenandoah cabin or Myrtle Beach?

"It's beautiful," said Warren. He showed Jeff photographs on his phone, including of the bungalow resort where he had made reservations for his son. "If they let me travel that far, I'd go myself. You have to go for me. It will take your mind off your worries. It's Plore-owned, so they have books you can read, in the woods." He saw his son off at the bus depot, embracing him deeply. I'm only going away for two weeks,

Jeff thought wryly.

Jeff stared out the window at the rolling Lenilenape-Sylvania countryside, farmed by Plore cooperatives under the control of the Economic Tower. The bus was full of under-100 Social Crediteers enjoying a holiday; Jeff regretted that he was six points short of a more elevated crowd and a train ride. His 94 Social Credit score reflected the totality of his menial job, his complexion, and Healthy Eating. He knew he needed to volunteer more to get over 100, or get a promotion, maybe by killing more patients.

His assigned seatmate was a middle-aged white woman with frizzy hair whose flabby arms shook with tattoos that had not aged well. She snacked on fish paste sandwiches and cookies. Her carbuds leaked with saccharine but loud diverso-pop music. The bus driver, a low Social Crediteer himself, dutifully played the month's mandated movie, an action thriller about Muslims defeating Crusaders while learning about feminism from a Mother Earth priestess who had mysteriously arisen in the Levant, possibly after having taken a seriously wrong turn.

"There's going to be a rest stop just before Ithaca," his father told him. "In Marathon. That's where you get off. Just take your suitpod and don't come back. Someone from the bungalow colony will meet you at the entrance to the rest stop."

Weird, Jeff thought. Then why did he have a ticket to Buffalo, 150 miles past Ithaca, on the Canadian border?

"It's cheaper to buy a ticket to Buffalo than to Ithaca," explained Warren. Since economic rationality was rare in the DJR, Jeff did not question his father.

At the Marathon rest stop, Jeff lifted his suitpod from the compartment above his seat, and headed for the Social Credit entrance. The rest stop was a utilitarian fiberglass building with vegan sandwich and gift shops, a Mother Earth prayer room, and a unisex washroom that smelled of urine. Women wrung out cloth baby diapers in the sinks, their armbands stashed on metal shelves above the sink, while men used the urinals behind them unselfconsciously. Modesty was bad, Jeff had learned, but habits were hard to break; he used a stall, even though the toilet was clogged.

Afterward, he waited outside the door with his suitpod. His seatmate waddled by, barking, "You'll miss the bus if you don't hurry."

He told her, "Plans changed. My family's meeting me here, don't let the driver wait for me."

"La-de-da, we've got family!" the woman sneered, but boarded the bus without further comment.

Jeff waited patiently, only wondering slightly whether the employee from the bungalow colony had remembered to pick him up. What would he do when the employee failed to arrive? Expecting an official looking employee, perhaps a middle-aged man in a uniform, Jeff was surprised when a petite black-haired girl tapped him on the shoulder from below. "Are you Jeffrey Welcome?"

He looked down to his right. "Yes, that's me." He noticed she was not wearing an armband. She seemed to be around his own age.

She led him to a battered white pickup truck and he placed his suitpod in the bed.

"Don't worry, the truck probably won't break down before we get there. And I can fix it if I need to."

They climbed into the cab, and headed into the surrounding countryside.

"I'm Rachel," said the girl. "Rachel Miller."

"Hi, Rachel. How long have you been working for the bungalow colony?"

She gave him an odd look. "My family has lived in the roundup since the war ended. My grandfather fought in the Knickerbocker Militia. He tried to escape with the family into Ohio but they were turned back, so they came home. And that's our story."

That wasn't quite what Jeff expected to hear, but he didn't press. Maybe the colony was a family business. The truck entered a park with a battered sign that said, "Taugahannock Falls State Park." The truck jounced over a rutted gravel road. "It hasn't been graded in years," Rachel complained. They eventually stopped at a wooded expanse. "Come see this gorgeous view. There's no hurry, we've got hours before dinner." They trudged through the woods for several minutes, before arriving at a panoramic deep gorge with a pounding high waterfall.

Jeff felt the mist on his face from the waterfall. How beautiful, he thought. He steadied himself on the rusted metal railing and stared up at the rocky wall a hundred feet across from them on the other side. The few country outings he'd taken with his family were tame excursions to local lakes. Sometimes they rented a rowboat or picnicked along the shore.

"Give me your armband," Rachel demanded.

"What?"

"You're going to toss it into the gorge. It's your enemy."

"I can't throw out the armband!" he exclaimed.

"Yes, you can. We're going to re-Plorify you."

"What are you talking about?"

"Your father said you needed to get away from Anacosta. You went Social Credit and it didn't work out. If you want to go on to Ithaca and get on the next bus back to Anacosta, be my guest. But you won't be staying in my roundup with your social credit. If you throw out the armband, you can live with us and have a job and not have to deal with Social Crediteers. They'll think you committed suicide by jumping into the gorge."

"I thought—I thought I was just taking a short vacation," he stammered.

"He wasn't going to tell you the truth, was he? You wouldn't have dared do it. But look how easy it will be for you to slip away from their clutches. You were last seen at the rest stop in Marathon. The armband was last traced to this gorge. It won't be recovered. They'll draw their own conclusions."

"You forgot one thing," he said, a little smugly now. "The chip."

"I haven't forgotten that. That's next. We're going to toss that into the gorge as well."

"What? How you're gonna do that?" His hand reached up to cup his right ear protectively, as if she were already springing at him with a knife.

"No big deal. It's near the surface. I'm the roundup medic. I do minor surgery all the time. I have the kit here." She raised a small brown case that she had brought with them from the truck. Jeff had naively assumed it was a girl's purse, albeit an ugly one, with makeup, a comb, her phone.

This is happening too fast, thought Jeff. His father had planned all this, and he trusted his father. But it was a capital crime to remove the chip and what if the ADF chased him up here? On the other hand, if he returned to Anacosta, they would force him to kill old, sick, and handicapped people. If they resisted the pills, he would have to hold them down while a doctor injected them with the sedative and then the killing dose. He had begun to consider committing suicide to avoid becoming a killer, so death itself, even by Antifans, would not be an unwelcome alternative. And the Euthanasia Palace knew of his distress, so would not be surprised by a suicide. Nor would they bother to recover his body in the water far below.

"And I would live in your—roundup?"

"Yes, that's the arrangement. You'd have to have a job—not in Syracuse, that's too dangerous—but we've got chickens, tinkers, teachers, brewers, handymen, you'd find something useful to do. We have books and a TV, and decent people. All Plores. The views of Cayuga Lake are beautiful."

"Are there any downsides?" he asked. Would he ever see his father again?

"Well, we're a little hungry in the winter, and you'd be a Plore again."

"I'm hungry now," he admitted, "and the Plore part sounds pretty good, actually."

He removed his armband and handed it to Rachel.

"Why don't you toss it into the gorge? It'll go farther if you do it. We don't want to risk it falling short and landing on a ledge."

He held the armband in his hands, turning it over as if he expected to see a message, whether "Do It!" or "Don't do it!" like those old black fortune-telling balls. But the heavy black cloth implanted with sensors said nothing. Rachel was right, it was his enemy. It tracked his every move, his every utterance, every choice he made of movie, video, reading, purchases. "I guess I can't save the phone," he said.

"Only if you want the police to show up at the roundup in a week looking for you. You can get another phone."

He wound up his old pitching motion, and the armband went sailing in a beautiful, almost leisurely arc, over the side of the gorge. "Congratulations," said Rachel. "Now for that chip." A few minutes later, the chip soared over the gorge and disappeared as well. A cloth bandage placed by Rachel's deft hands neatly covered the wound. Rachel had not lied about her skills. It hadn't hurt much.

Back in the roundup, a Plore identity card belonging to a Bruce Williams awaited him. As Lucy had told David, "We're not amateurs." By evening, Jeff had a clean bed in the men's trailer and had eaten chicken and rice in the dining hall. "And you have to meet Aunt Lucy and Mike Marino. They're like our mayors. They'll want to check you out."

Warren Welcome turned on the workscreen at the end of the following day, eager for some good news. All day, while he sold potatoes, beets, and crackers in a daze, he wondered how Jeff was faring, and how he had taken the news that he was going to be a Plore again. An innocent-looking coded message, ostensibly from a supplier, reassured Welcome that Jeff had reached the bungalow colony safely.

Arranging the escape hadn't been easy. Welcome had convinced the truck driver to negotiate with the chicken-raising Plore village on his behalf. Wouldn't a prosperous chicken plant always need an extra pair of hands? He had asked the driver about the roundup, and liked the answers. "Hard working people. Very tidy and organized. They keep to themselves." However, the trucker refused to transport Jeff to the chicken village. "Are you kidding? They got sensors along the highways. If the police pick up his armband or the chip, they'll pull me over instantly. That won't help your son at all. No Soko in my truck."

But then, almost instantly, Welcome said, "You're right—he's Social Credit. Why can't he just take a bus up there?" A few days later, on the trucker's next trip to Anacosta, the deal was sealed. A hundred dollars for the accommodating trucker, two hundred for the accommodating village, and another $200 for the bus ticket, but Welcome didn't grudge the money at all. His son would not be a killer, at least not of people. Chickens were another matter.

Chapter 39
A Little Bit Of Home
(Tuesday, April 20, 2094)

"Look!" Lucy entered the smallest trailer, where she and David worked side by side on quiet days at adjoining tables. She handed him a sheet of paper with handwriting on both sides. "We just got a bulletin from Anacosta. It's been a long time since we've seen one of these."

David turned off the antique cassette player on which he was listening to a local Plore band, Blue Hellions, while drawing up lists of innocuous metal parts to melt down for the roundup's armorer. Old cassette tapes, often recorded over with current music, circulated almost freely in rural areas, although the authorities would confiscate them when found on trucks or in flea markets. No Social Crediteer dared touch them. "A bulletin?"

"Yes, uncensored news direct from Plorevilles up and down the coast. Folks write out news by hand and truckers hand carry it through. It's even more dangerous than hiding passengers, but it's easier to hide sheets of paper."

David scanned the contents of the newsletter. He would have puzzled over the vaguely familiar handwriting had not the initial item alarmed him so much. "St. Paul Lutheran Threatened by Authorities." That was the church his mother attended, and to which he had accompanied her, braving the disdain of his Antifan supervisors. "Pastor Denman refused to allow the church to host a pornographic art show, after which the City cut off utilities to the church. The City is now demanding that the church host a camp for Plore children, which will include mutual sexual exploration and Mother Earth arts and crafts under the direction of the Knowledge Tower Suburban Education Unit. Pastor Denman has been told by the ADF that continued resistance will lead to the permanent closure of his church."

"Oh my God," David said. "My mother and my sisters attend there. The pastor married Malia and me, in secret. He's brave, too brave for his own good." The remaining articles were about food shortages; gangs of Social Crediteers who had been ambushing lone Plores in the City and beating them up; the narrowing range of acceptable GVN options for Plores; a Plore baby turned away from a hospital for lack of money only to die of an intestinal blockage hours later at home.

Just to avoid leaving the reader entirely depressed, a final story noted the happiness among Plores in Anacosta when news arrived of the hanging of a pro-freedom banner from a highway south of Syracuse a month ago.

"Hey, they're writing about our banner!" David exclaimed.

"Really!" Lucy grabbed the paper back from him. Her eyes gleamed with pride. "Imagine, they heard about it in Anacosta!" She and David fist-bumped. Around 4:00 a.m. on a cold March morning, a small band led by Seth had driven to an overpass under which Social Crediteers in cars and Plores in vans passed en route to jobs in Syracuse each morning. In just two minutes, they had unfurled a giant banner—thirty feet wide by ten feet tall—that read, "Demand Liberty." Colorful red splashes daubed the sides of the banner. Then the band sped back into the night.

By 8:00 a.m., horrified authorities had removed the banner, but the deed was so shocking that ADF headquarters in Anacosta learned about it immediately, and truckers who had seen the banner for themselves speedily brought the news south.

The roundup band hung more banners on roadways around the City and the message was spray-painted in alleys and on storefronts in Syracuse itself, including the main staircase to the library at Syracuse Diverse University. David and Lucy halted the campaign after several weeks only because they knew the longer it continued, the more likely the authorities would accumulate enough evidence to target their roundup, or that a vandal would be caught in the act and taken to Anacosta as a knowledge criminal. They reasoned the message had been aired, and thousands had witnessed it, and they would take a breather while they pondered their next steps.

The news item related, "We also have a report from an eyewitness." That eyewitness, who had been riding in a van with other just-released detainees from the Say Lawrence Incubation Farm back to Anacosta, had seen another banner in the Syracuse area, and a spray-painted message in back of a gas station where the van had stopped for a rest break. Even though he was a Social Crediteer, the eyewitness had shared the astounding story with a Plore coworker, who had relayed it to others in Ploreville.

Lucy said, reverently, "After all these years, I finally feel as if we are doing something again. We are stirring."

"And no one harmed," David reminded her, gently. The moment they used violence against Social Crediteers, let alone opened fire, the stakes would rise exponentially.

"Yes, we need to start cautiously," she agreed. If it was just vandalism, the authorities might lose interest after a few weeks.

David took the paper back from Lucy, running his fingers over the smooth fiber. The paper was identical to normal copier or printer paper, nothing special. Maybe stolen from someone's office in the City. Blank, it was harmless. But that handwriting...

"My mother writes like that," he mused. "She was taught handwriting in school, before the civil war began."

"Could your mother have written this?"

"No…I don't think so. They watch my whole family like hawks these days. I can't imagine that she would have dared, or that my sisters would let her get involved. It must be another elderly person. There are a million Plores in the inner Anacosta region, you know. It would be silly to think that my mother, of all those people…" His voice trailed off. "She couldn't stand the government, she hated where I worked, but she wouldn't do something this dangerous."

A knock on the trailer door.

"Come in," called David. But he cast a quick glance at the pistol on the open shelf below his desktop. He took no chances, even though Lucy's watchmen still were posted at the outskirts of the roundup.

A young black man with a medium complexion and short Afro stood in the doorway. "Hi, I'm Bruce Williams. Or I am now," he explained hastily. For his own safety, he would go by Bruce from now on. His identity card bore the name of a white man who had disappeared years earlier as a teenager; fortunately the Plore cards did not mention race since the government preferred to assume that every Plore was an unregenerate white supremacist.

"Hi, Bruce," Lucy responded. Then to David, "This is the newest member of our roundup. He just arrived from Anacosta for an extended stay. He's agreed to teach history to our students and serve as an assistant medic for Rachel."

"That's great," said David. The proper study of history was essential for the youth to understand their predicament and the way forward, and it was risky to only have one medic. "Have you had any medical training?"

Jeff looked embarrassed. "I learned some basic things while working at the Euthanasia Palace, but they were about to force me to kill patients, so that's why I ran away from Anacosta."

"But you're a Plore?"

"Yes, and then I went Social Credit because they told me they'd let me go to college, but then they broke their promise and stuck me at the Euthanasia Palace. I read a lot before I went Social Credit, so I can teach history, promise."

"Where in Ploreville are you from?" David, frowning, was curious. The young man looked slightly familiar, as had the handwriting.

"North Daniel Street, sir, near Washington Boulevard. My father runs the Welcome grocery."

"I think I know you, young man."

"Sir, I know you too." And they both laughed, Jeff with relief because he wasn't sure whether he could openly acknowledge that he knew David's real identity. Jeff had recognized Mrs. Harris's renegade Antifan son almost immediately, which explained the "sir." Nor had David forgotten his mother's grocer, although he hadn't seen Jeff in a decade.

"Lucy, Bruce and I are long acquainted."

"So he knows everything?" Lucy asked pointedly. They nodded, and she said to Jeff, "This is a secret. Our people do not know David's background. They think he is a security guard from Massena named Mike. He was Mike Potter before he got that name into trouble, so now it's Marino. You must keep this secret, not just for his own safety, but for the whole roundup's. Can we trust you?"

"Yes, absolutely," said Jeff. But he blinked hard. For a quiet place in the countryside, a lot was happening.

Lucy left them alone to chat, casting a glance at the bed in the corner, or really, a mattress on a low wooden frame. David had moved out of her house a month ago, without rancor, after coming home one day to see Seth exiting Lucy's house with a smirk. He realized it was unfair to saddle Lucy with his constant presence if he was unwilling to sleep with her. Lucy hadn't objected. The only downside was that if the Antifans returned at night, it would be harder to hide in the cellar in time. But they were digging more tunnels.

"Tell me what's happening in Ploreville," he urged Jeff. "Good and bad. Have you seen my family? My mother?"

"Sir, I took your mother to see your wife at the zoo."

"Stop it with the 'sir.' I'm just Mike here. What did you just say?" He demanded Jeff tell him the whole story. Then Jeff relayed all the Ploreville gossip, and what his father the grocer was doing to help the cause. "Your mother helps give shelter to the travelers the truckers bring." David's jaw tightened. Of course his mother would help the grocer.

David showed Jeff the bulletin. "Do you know if she writes these?"

"No, but they did arrest two ladies last week for writing these newsletters and took them to Beaufort. As far as I know, they're still there."

David knew that if his mother was associating with these ladies, let alone conspiring with them to write the newsletters, she was in the Antifan target sights. He realized that he needed to go to Anacosta, even if Malia's ultimate intentions and loyalty were uncertain. It was time to move on. He could not arrive in Anacosta only to attend his mother's funeral, but it guiltily occurred to him that would be a fitting, or karmic punishment for having lied to the rounduprs about traveling to his mother's deathbed in Frederick.

Another knock at the door. It was Seth. "The guys are here from North Roundup." David was leading the group in combat arms training, at least the rough countryside version. The to-do list included a possible raid on a police station or some other edifice of Diverse authority, but not anytime soon. David wasn't quite ready to share the extent of the roundup's seditious activity with Jeff, not yet, so he said, "Thanks Seth, I'll be there in a moment." He solemnly shook Jeff's hand, and steered him in the direction of the classroom trailer where the new teacher would meet his students later that day.

Two days later, while giving Jeff the same tour that Lucy had given him, he showed the young man a giant open-air metal shed in which tinkerers were building unmanned aerial vehicles designed with bomb hatches from which leaflets instead of explosives would drop over Syracuse or Rochester. A young woman and two older men hunched over worktables hammering metal and inserting screws and wires into the makeshift but operational devices. "When they are finished, they will each be seven by five feet," said David. "We'll call it the Deplorable Air Force." Everyone chuckled, but grimly.

Jeff was relieved to hear that these UAVs would kill no one, but was troubled, wondering what his father would think if he knew that his son was now living among Plore rebels poised to stir trouble and bring down the wrath of the ADF. On the other hand, he knew his father was doing his best to thwart the authorities by running the Anacosta depot of the Plore Underground, so maybe he would approve after all. Did his father know that David Harris, now Michael Marino, was in charge? Or was it sheer coincidence that the roundup to which his father had sent him was run by the great Plore Antifan, albeit incognito?

Marcus Vanover was entering his fifth week in this backwater called Syracuse, and coming no closer to identifying the knowledge criminals who were spray-painting subversive slogans and had hung a banner over Highway 83 at rush hour back in March. That was his official mission, at least in the Beaufort records.

His real mission was to track down David Harris, whom Paragon was sure was still somewhere in New York–Schuylkill. Paragon had told him, "Here's your chance to capture that Earth-damned Plore, so don't disappoint me." Marcus Vanover's Antifan career was on the line, and yet David Harris had vanished into thin air.

The Syracuse ADF—three officers and eleven troops who were regular sworn Antifan officers, not mere militia—had taken over the Battista case from the incompetent militia, but the trail was cold. The flurry of excitement that had rippled through their numbers when they learned a real Beaufort officer was coming to direct their efforts had died down once Vanover had rated them for their laziness and stupidity. Vanover felt that if this crowd were genuine Antifans, they would be in a larger city, if not in Anacosta. He disliked that the eleven included four women, whose influence he felt corroded the martial spirit required by the Antifan mission. The men spent more time chatting up the women than beating up knowledge criminals, he groused, and the vaunted Antifan spirit seemed to evaporate the farther one traveled from Beaufort. Even worse, the group had actually considered its job done when the banner was destroyed, and store owners threatened with fines until they erased the criminal graffiti.

So Vanover scowled as he moved through the former commercial office building in which the ADF was housed, and would have kicked a cat had one been available.

Vanover felt kindlier toward Lieutenant Loki Greene, who had been transferred from the militia to a more prestigious assignment as a sworn officer with Syracuse ADF. Clean Pig, as David had nicknamed him, trotted obediently behind Vanover, eager to learn from this actual member of Beaufort's mysterious Resolution Command. The lean, muscular Antifan with the smoky eyes resembled what Clean Pig had always imagined as the ideal Antifan. And even though he loved his wife, sometimes Greene fantasized about being taken by this strapping Antifan.

While entertaining no such fantasies about his subordinate, Vanover knew that Loki Greene was the only local, living Antifan who had actually seen David Harris, and was familiar with the Plore communities that might be harboring him. Vanover had ordered the ADF to reissue bulletins for Potter and Jocelyn Carter throughout the region. He had briefly wondered whether the bulletin ought to be issued in the name of Potter or Harris. On one hand, locals might fear harboring a man of Harris's stature. On the other, it might well give local Plores hope as word spread of the legendary Plore Antifan, and it suggested that chinks existed in the Antifan armor. In the end, they used "Mike Potter."

"How do we flush these Plores out?" he asked Greene. "We can't raid every roundup and, when we do raids, we find nothing."

"It's about time for a cull," Greene said.

"A what?"

"The cull, sir. Every few years we require all Deplorables in the region to report for two days to the local cull center—around here it might be Ithaca or Syracuse or Binghamton. They bring camping gear to the fairgrounds and we check their registration cards and documents. We make sure the fingerprints and eyeprints match our records. We enter children born since the last cull into our systems. Nothing in the treaty forbids it."

"What happens if it rains?"

"Then it rains," said Greene simply. "The more respectable Plores bring large tents or awnings. And the rest swill around in the mud like the pigs they are. But it's really quite festive. The Plores are happy to see each other, so no one complains. We give them free beer after they register. They dance and sing in the evenings."

"So how does this help us find Harris?"

"If any Plore is found outside their cull during those two days, they are subject to ten years' imprisonment. We send heat-seeking drones over the area to detect any illegal movement, and we can send the helicopters or police vans in within minutes of a positive finding. If the finding is a Social Crediteer, which we can determine immediately because of the armband signals, we ignore it and move on. We advise Social Crediteers to stay in Cities or at home during the culls, to avoid confusion."

"Are you saying that if Harris is in the area, he won't dare to come to the cull so we can isolate him out in the countryside?"

"Yes, Captain." Despite the Oklahoma City fiasco, Vanover had been promoted when he had pointed out to Paragon and Okuro that he couldn't exercise the authority to perform his mission if he were subordinate to the captain in charge of the Syracuse ADF. Now the captain was sulking in Vanover's shadow.

"How do you manage to register so many Plores in two days?"

"We bring in Social Crediteers from the area to help. They get five social credit points if they register a thousand Plores. Some don't want to have anything to do with Plores, but you'd be amazed what five credit points can do for their motivation."

"That's an idea," Vanover said.

Chapter 40
The Cull
(Monday, May 10, 2094)

"This is a problem," said Lucy, pressing her lips together as they sat over tea in her kitchen. Even though David no longer lived under her roof, they often met at her table for political conversations or planning meetings where they did not wish to be disturbed. David and Lucy didn't care if the rounduprs thought they were having an affair, it wasn't their business. David believed he had mostly convinced Lucy that a better future awaited an America that hadn't killed its Social Crediteers, and Lucy had awakened David to the Plore readiness to begin striking blows for their freedom.

Lucy showed David the announcement on her phone screen. "Suburban Cull, June 11–13, Diverse Year 39. Central New York Containment Area. Binghamton, Ithaca, Syracuse. Check djr.nys.registration for your location." The authorities thoughtfully scheduled culls for the weekends, so that Plores would not have to miss work and upset production deadlines. "Suburban" was the polite, governmental term for Deplorables.

The phlegmatic acceptance of the local Plores to the cull announcement had astounded David. "You mean you didn't have culls in Anacosta?" Lucy demanded.

"Not the same way. You had to go to the local city hall or some other official building and re-register and have your identification checked, sure. And you had to do it within one month, and bring your babies to be registered, but no way would they herd us into a field like sheep."

"You probably didn't even have a field large enough in the City."

"Good point." David had never considered how the tasteful culls of Anacosta might play out in more hardscrabble rural areas.

"What are you going to do during the cull?"

"Me? I guess I'll just stay here and putter about."

"It doesn't work that way." Lucy explained to David about the heat-seeking drones and the militia elements that would roust anyone not obeying the Call to the Cull. "Two of our people—both elderly—refused to go last time. They'd just had it—they remembered better times. And now they're spending the rest of their lives in Elmira."

"I'll think of something," said David, pleasantly. "What if I spent two days down in the cellar?"

"Won't help. They can find heat sources from a hundred feet below the ground. Otherwise we'd all be in the cellars. And of course, they'd check their records and realize Lucy Gawser from the 2091 cull hadn't registered this time, and there's no death certificate. So once you've registered with them, and you haven't been reported dead, you're trapped. Mike Marino has a death certificate, so your card isn't going to do you much good. And even if he weren't dead, or you said it was a mistake, you can't go, because the fingerprints won't match.

"Whatever you do, you'll have to take Bruce Williams with you. He won't have the same fingerprints as the real Bruce Williams. It'll trigger an alert. He stands out around here already. We know who the real black Plores are around here, all twenty of them, and so does the ADF. And your photo is posted all around the area now. Syracuse isn't forgetting your case."

David took a walk around the surrounding woods to clear his head. He then went in search of Jeff, but when he found him deep in conversation with Rachel over a bandaged plaster leg, decided not to interrupt them. Finally, he arrived at the UAV shed, where he presided over the final assembly of the twentieth drone. East Roundup had fifteen under construction, and Cayuga Roundup another dozen. As the fleets increased, so did the expanse of the metal roofs sheltering them from ADF aerial surveillance. Gary, the self-described "broken old man" whom David had met that night at the Candor Inn, turned out to have been a UAV hobbyist in his youth, and had leaped at the opportunity to help the cause.

"The Deplorable Air Force! That's a good one!" he had cackled, the dirty red MAGA hat dipping with each bob of his amused head. "Never thought I'd end up a general in the air force!"

Shortly after dawn on Friday morning, June 11, caravans of Plores began heading to their assigned culls. Some piled into work trucks or old cars; enterprising roundups such as Lucy's rented school buses. The authorities also graciously provided buses that ferried Plores to various culls for a fee, although they were scarcer on the return trip. And a few loners trudged along the roadside, turning around when they heard a vehicle to extend a pleading thumb to passing vehicles to hitch a ride. Most of the vehicles hauled trailers with food and other supplies for the long weekend. The day was starting sultry, so many Plores decided to head to their cull early to avoid the worst heat, and grab one of the better sites at the field, which meant away from the entrances, the drainage ditches, and on inclines away from puddles. If you registered early, you still couldn't leave until Sunday, but at least you could avoid the worst lines and relax with your friends after your official business was concluded. The drones would only start their rounds at dawn on Saturday.

Lucy's roundup was assigned to a field just outside Syracuse City, as it had been last time. "Lots of snide little college students doing the processing on their summer vacations. One of our guys complained, and this little Hindu missy waved her armband at him and said, 'Well, if you'd been willing to be chipped, you wouldn't be doing this, so it's all your fault!'"

"Did he smack her?" David asked sarcastically, but he knew the answer.

"It's not all bad. I'm going to be meeting several times with other roundup heads. The cull is great cover for plotting against the Soko under their noses. What a shame that you won't be there, though."

On Friday, David and Jeff headed out of the roundup on one of the two buses that Lucy had rented. Both were dressed a little more neatly than one might have expected from rural Plores heading to a campground, with button-down cotton shirts and clean jeans. David had shaved off his beard and grown out and dyed his blond curls so they were now a distinctive wavy chestnut brown reaching to his shoulders. It was a relatively easy way to counter the many posters of Mike Potter that were playing on electronic billboards in the City. He had debated painting a scar on his face—Potter's Wanted posters had no scar. On the other hand, people would stare at his face more than they would otherwise and maybe the resemblance would occur to them. He forwent the scar. Both men wore dark sunglasses and baseball caps.

At a fork in the road, the pair hopped off and darted into the underbrush along the road, much as David had traveled from Syracuse last November. They hiked several miles, emerged onto the highway and hitched a ride with a garden truck going directly to Syracuse. David once again gazed on the towers that he had last seen in November. Again, they jumped off ten minutes before they reached the entrance to that cull field, located at the former New York State Fairgrounds on the western shore of Onondaga Lake. The others on the truck bed stared at them.

"We're not there yet," warned an older white-bearded man.

"We've got an errand to run first!" called David. "Thanks for the ride."

As the two men walked away, their heavy backpacks shifting, Jeff complained, "I have no idea what we're doing, Mike. Are you going to tell me what the plan is? Where are we going to hide during the cull?" They were starting to round the southern edge of Onondaga Lake. The water treatment plant for the City loomed to their right, and the entertainment complex Diversity Fun Palace DJR was ahead.

David grinned at him. He wasn't going to tell Jeff everything, partly because the more Jeff knew, the more fear he would show, endangering them. "I'll tell you some of it, and the rest later. We are going to hide in plain sight in Syracuse.

"The drones will only fly over Plore areas. They will not fly over the Cities or the inner suburbs. Of course they would pick up our body heat if we stayed in the roundup. But if we spend the weekend hanging out among Social Crediteers, especially in large groups, no drone will spot us. I doubt there is enough drone coverage for them to start picking out the Plores from the Soko."

"But we have no armbands! They'll spot us immediately!"

David stopped and looked directly at the younger man, almost offended. "Do you think I'm an idiot? Do you not think I've planned for that?" Jeff mumbled an apology.

Half an hour later, they took shelter under an underpass just beyond the humming hive of Diversity Fun Palace DJR, as they were rounding the southeast corner of the lake and heading north. The palace would normally have been a good place to hide out among Social Crediteers, but David had suspected that with the Plores off at the cull, it would be quieter than usual, if only because Plore employees would not be available to staff the food stands or video arcades. And indoor facilities and malls had more security than did outdoor venues such as parks.

"See what I have here," said David. He opened his backpack, heavier than Jeff's, and showed him two black armbands that, unless inspected carefully, would look like any other Social Crediteer's. They were just black acrylic cloth, with none of the electronic surveillance–enabling features of an actual Social Credit armband. But a casual observer would not realize this. "And they have phones!" He unzipped the side of one armband and pulled out a genuine screenphone in a camouflage frame, on which innocuous texts had already been loaded.

"And I'm glad we have food with us, because we wouldn't be able to purchase anything with these armbands." David's ingenuity had its limits. Only Plores still used cash. Although they could also pay with phones, use of the phones to purchase anything would have revealed a Plore wandering outside a cull. David had stuffed a small battery-operated hot plate in his backpack and he still had a few of the Canadian meal packets he'd brought from the United States.

"And even better, almost no one will think you're a Plore. A black guy is automatically assumed to be Social Credit. That's the best disguise of all. And I'm your kamrat, right?" In his innocence, Jeff didn't think much of the emphasis that David laid on "kamrat."

"Yes, that's brilliant," said Jeff.

"So whatever I do, just play along, all right?"

"Got it. Where are we going to sleep?"

"We're going to camp above the lake. There are some campgrounds, but they're never full. Social Crediteers don't care for the outdoors. They like to celebrate the environment in the abstract. We'll rough it for two nights and then head back with the rest of the Plores. Have I missed anything?"

The following morning, they washed at the hand pump as best they could. David was counting on the usual Plore camp minders being at the cull, so the park would lack the staff to check whether the sites were occupied by registered users. They had waited until sundown to claim a site, by which time the registered users, all lower Social Crediteers, had arrived—the men heard the noises of children and barking dogs through the trees. Now we're outlaws, David thought to himself, almost cheerfully, as he scrubbed his bare torso. Here I am, an American pretending to be a Plore pretending to be a Social Crediteer. It's all a game. This was how he kept his own fear at bay—he had not left the roundup since November—and while he resolved to keep up a brave front for Jeff, it was not easy, not with his face plastered all over Syracuse.

"We'll walk up and down the promenade tomorrow," said David, "and sit on the benches in the sunshine, just some Social Credit guys enjoying the spectacle." The fair weather promised healthy crowds, and even though Onondaga State Park was open to all, the Mother Earth pavilion at one end with the giant idol made Plores uncomfortable. David also had known that a coronavirus pilgrimage play would be performed on Saturday, which meant larger crowds than usual. The national Coronavirus Liberation Day holiday had been observed the previous Monday, but festive events were continuing throughout the weekend as the country celebrated the imposition of political controls during the coronavirus pandemic of 2020–22. Larger crowds were safer and better than smaller ones for David and Jeff this weekend; they hoped to be lost in the swirl, and as long as they wore black armbands, few would notice them.

Around midafternoon, the two men joined the crowd, wearing matching berry colored polo shirts and creased chinos, with brand new sneakers. Their black armbands sported the logo, "DiversUp," sewn in, which might have been taken for a progressive government contracting company. Nobody would have thought them high Social Crediteers, although everyone knew that Jeff would have the additional 40 points that came with his complexion. With his hair curling on the nape of his neck, and the chin stubble, David might have been a low-level media executive, perhaps with WSYR radio, or something else creative. They were eating sandwiches brought from home, which suggested low Social Credit, but dressed neatly, meaning they aspired to greater things, or possibly were a gay couple.

The crowds were thick. They overheard a man say, "Can you imagine what a zoo it would be if the damn Plores were here today?" and a woman, perhaps his partner, respond, "Yes, and they smell too. I can tell them a mile away." Laughter faded as they were borne away by the crowd. David and Jeff dared not exchange looks.

A megaphone cut through the general hubbub, "Make way, Diverse folx! Make way! The pilgrimage is beginning!" David and Jeff inched down the bench so an elderly female couple could sit down. A group of teenage girls arranged themselves on the ground in front of the bench, folding their long pale legs beneath them like ungainly swans. The spaces along the promenade filled in quickly, as the concessions would close for the next half hour and few wished to show lack of interest in the event.

"Diverse folx, the New York–Schuylkill Region and City of Syracuse bring you the coronavirus liberation pilgrimage, performed by the Syracuse-Cortland Diverse Actors Collective with special appearances by the Syracuse City Cult of the Mask, and with a delegation from the Central New York Health Workers Collective!" Wild cheers erupted. David extended his arm around Jeff's shoulders, much to the younger man's alarm.

Several Chinese dragons began the pilgrimage, to symbolize the critical role played by the People's Republic of China in the recovery from coronavirus, including the political infrastructure that had reined in the American instinct to cherish dangerous, deadly liberty. Next came dancing coronavirus spores, leaping at the crowd with fierce faces, causing children to shriek. Actors dressed as healthcare workers in white carried a giant, twenty-foot-long papier-mâché needle, presumably the life-giving vaccine. Women from the local League of Karen, charged with the venerated Cult of the Mask, all 120 or above, bore a giant paper mask thirty feet wide down the promenade, the ear loops encircling their reverent bearers like harnesses.

Then pranced two dozen white actors, dressed in flannel shirts or singlets, drinking from bottles or beer cans, gesticulating and gamboling, making apelike noises. Beautiful long-haired young women carried signs alongside that read, "The Ignorant Killers" and "They Mocked the Mask and the Vaccine!" The crowd booed. David joined them, and, nudged sharply in his side by David's elbow, so did Jeff. That's us, David thought. No occasion lost to remind the Social Crediteers who their enemies are. Otherwise they might realize their high Social Credit masters are their real enemies. This is why we cannot fall into the trap of making the Social Crediteers our enemies as well, even though it is tempting and would be easy. We can only win by taking the high road. Diverse music played throughout the spectacle, loud, profane, and designed to stir anger. The girls rose from the ground and danced awkwardly.

High school students carried aloft effigies of the villains from the early part of the century, most of whom were no longer recognizable to the poorly educated crowds, except the crowds knew that white supremacist and capitalist villains would always exist and seek to destroy the DJR. The audience booed the signs borne by the next group of students: "President Trump!" "President DeSantis!" "Billionaire Musk!" "MAGA Maggots!" Then came the heroes, including papier-mâché statues of St. John Beaufort, and Omicron, god of Science, borne on the shoulders of athletes. As a former Antifan, David still had a grudging respect for the founder of the ADF, and those cheers came from him a little more willingly. Health-care workers then prodded forward with large needles another group of fake Deplorables, who went from downcast and sickly to vibrant and healthy as they passed down the promenade. Some collapsed and pretended to be dead, at which everyone applauded, but then the deceased performers leaped up and rejoined the pilgrimage before it moved too far ahead.

Oh shit, thought David. The next group, unexpectedly, was the local ADF detachment, including militias, and he was horrified to see Marcus Vanover at their head. You could not miss that strapping, rigid figure, the epitome of ADF discipline. Two privates carried a sign before them that read "Diverse Power Heals the Community." Don't look at me, Jeff, he silently begged his companion, and fortunately Jeff kept his eyes trained on the marchers. What is Marcus Vanover doing here? Was the disgrace in Oklahoma City sufficient to merit exile to Syracuse, or does he have another reason for being in upstate New York–Schuylkill? Vanover marched by without having given any indication he recognized David.

The crowd dutifully applauded the float of local notables. The pilgrimage concluded with a flatbed truck bearing another giant needle, pointing at the sky. It looked like a space rocket from olden times. The loudspeaker announced, "The truth serum is the new Healing Vaccine. Come to the pavilion for your healing dose! Cure yourself from the Big Lie! Five extra social credit points this week only!"

Loud rap music now thumped in the background. "Thank you, Diverse folx! The Mother Earth service will begin shortly at the Pantheon!" The crowd began heading in that direction, not too speedily. There was no advantage to speed; the closer-in seats would be occupied by dignitaries and the League of Karen and the outskirts of the crowd would allow you to gossip unmolested by ushers while still appearing pious. The middle ground would be policed scrupulously.

"Wasn't that lovely?" One of the elderly ladies sharing the bench demanded of them. "We used to belong to the league when we had more energy."

"That was awesome, gwei!" said David, code-switching into Social Crediteer speak including a dash of Chinese, which meant, "Correct!" He normally would have said, "Sure was, ma'am."

Jeff caught on. "Really showed those white supremacists, didn't it? It makes me so angry that they spread the disease and killed Diverse People." Don't overdo it, Jeff, David thought.

"Hey, look at that!" someone said.

All heads turned upward at the sight of several dozen white drones swooping in gracious formation several hundred feet above. Careful listeners heard an almost imperceptible grinding sound as well.

"Birds?" the second lady offered. Her eyesight was failing. In five years she would be invited to appear at the Euthanasia Palace in Rochester.

"It's the finale for the show!" others cried out. "Koza!" *cool.* They watched almost silently, open-mouthed, as the hatches of the drones opened and what seemed to be confetti began drifting to the ground. The drones would drop several thousand leaflets in and around the park, but with even more spattering Diversity Fun Palace DJR and downtown Syracuse.

A minute later, the first gliding leaflets, whipped one way and the other in the breeze, began to shower on the Social Crediteers. Curious, the attendees picked them up, only to drop them in horror. They hurried and even ran down the promenade to the Mother Earth service, as if demonstrated fealty to the deity would protect them from association with the heretical slogans, but the leaflets continued to pursue them relentlessly.

"NO MAN IS A NUMBER"

"DEMAND LIBERTY"

"CHINA GAVE US CORONA"

"JESUS IS KING"

"THE VACCINE IS THE BIG LIE"

David recognized all the messages, since the entire roundup had participated in coming up with ideas and scribbling them on the sheets of paper. He said to Jeff, "Let's get back to the campground right now."

The loudspeaker announced, with increasing urgency. "All Diverse folx are requested to disperse. The Mother Earth service concluding Coronavirus Liberation Week will take place tomorrow at three p.m. instead. All Diverse folx please disperse now! Please return tomorrow."

With the service canceled, the Antifans marched back up the promenade, minutes after David and Jeff had safely disappeared up the trail with the handful of others staying at the campsites. The cleaners would descend on the park shortly but the staff was shorthanded due to the cull, so visitors would find continue to find stray leaflets for at least another week in unexpected places.

The one-way drones would land in several large fields south and west of Syracuse, programmed to explode safely thirty minutes after landing. The authorities might find piles of metal and plastic debris, and might suspect these were the drones that had dropped propaganda on Syracuse City, but would have no way of tracing them back to the pilot, or pilots. If the authorities arrived early, they might be injured or killed, but "We can't help collateral damage," David had smiled.

Back at the roundup, Gary destroyed the control panel, dumped it into the latrine, and then fed the chickens and cleaned their pens. At East Roundup, the other aged general destroyed his control panel. Then both waited calmly for the militia and police to come, which they finally did late Saturday night; Gary had safely stowed his treasured MAGA hat under a trailer. The two had discussed driving out of the containment area, but they knew that trigger-happy militia checkpoints would likely detect and pull over any rare Plore vehicle on the road and it was marginally safer to try to ride out the cull in their roundups. Fortunately, the militia unit that arrested the men never even considered these elderly men could have engineered the seditious drone flyover earlier that day.

"My wife left me here!" Gary sobbed. "We had an argument."

"Then why didn't you get on a bus, you stupid old Plore?" the militia taunted him. "Fucking idiot." Just to amuse themselves, they ordered the one woman among them to beat him with her baton. Then they dragged him off to the van, where he was reunited with the other general, and they were processed for Elmira at the barracks in Syracuse. A judge would sign some paperwork, but no trial was necessary, as it was obvious the men were Plores and were absent from the cull. The punishment was applied administratively.

As dark fell, David and Jeff sat at their campfire, eating Canadian foil packet dinners. They would save their exultation for their return to the roundup, because even in this campsite, you never knew who might be listening. "Soko territory," David grunted when Jeff made a reference to the glorious drone invasion. But when David lifted his face from the fireside, Jeff saw the wide grin spread across the former Antifan's face, and smiled back.

They awoke in their lean-to the next morning to a steady dreary rain. David calculated that they were safer hiding at the campsite than venturing down to the promenade again, where someone might wonder why two men were sitting in the rain at the now-notorious site, and Antifans and police might be scouring it for remaining evidence or leaflets. The rain let up shortly after noon, and they even attended the packed Mother Earth service, after which it was safe to head back to the roundup. A few texts and an hour later, they met their roundup bus shortly off the main road, boarded it, and heard the news from the cull.

When they arrived back at the roundup, David went immediately to Lucy's house and prepared dinner for both of them. Lucy walked in the door half an hour later from the other bus, looking a little worn and grimy after the weekend. She took a quick shower, and reappeared at the table wearing a terry cloth robe, her hair damp, her face shining.

"No problems for anyone," she reported to David. "And we saw the drones!" They fist-bumped and embraced. As they sat down to dinner, Lucy told David about the Council of Roundup Leaders meeting. "Thanks to you, we are more optimistic than we've been in years," she said. "Some people even saw the drones flying over Onondaga Lake. It was magnificent, once we knew what was happening. I have to admit, more than a few thought it was a Social Credit attack against the cull field, but then there was cheering, and of course those from around here knew they were ours."

"We should do something to honor Gary and Brendan," said David. They were sober at the thought of the sacrifice of the two old men who had insisted on staying behind to fly the drones. Gary had left a note that would be cryptic to Antifans, saying, "No regrets. It was worth it."

David told Lucy about the consternation that had ensued at the promenade when the Social Crediteers realized what the leaflets contained, and how this had embarrassed the Antifans.

Her peals of laughter warmed David's heart. "After all these years! I love it!"

He explained his concern at seeing Vanover among them. "Maybe it's just a coincidence, but I don't like it. We parted on very bad terms and the ADF is looking for me, under some name.

"I've got to move on soon. My mother is in danger in Anacosta. I need to help her. You all have gotten off to a good start, you won't need me any longer."

"I think you do need to move on to Anacosta," Lucy said. "We saw all those posters of you in Syracuse. It's only a matter of time before one of our Plores decides to collect on the reward they're offering. Or an informant hears about what you're doing. And have you seen this?" She thrust her phone at David. He scanned the screen.

"Malia engaged to the Great Paragon. Wedding scheduled for Holy Halloween. Nuptials symbolize the victory of Diversity over Fascism as traitor's widow falls for handsome Antifan commander." The photo was of his own wife, her dark brown curls tumbling once again over her shoulders, smiling shyly in the arms of a swarthy Antifan commander, her head resting against his medaled chest. Now David recognized the man, the one who had gladly sacrificed his own sister to further his ambitions, two decades ago when they, both young cadets, had been serving on the execution squad. He shuddered at the thought of his wife in the lustful clutches of this monster. Malia's happiness would mean nothing to such a man.

David's head dropped onto his folded arms on the table, where he cried.

"Stop that," said Lucy. "Collect yourself. You are finally going to rescue your wife and your mother. We have kept you too long from your own mission. I will make the arrangements with our most reliable trucker. You'll be in Anacosta in two weeks or less."

David raised his head again, looking at Lucy, who insisted, "But you must promise to come back and help us afterward. You must swear not to forget us." And David swore that he would return to liberate the Deplorables, just as the legend had foretold.

Chapter 41
Shame!
(Tuesday, June 15, 2094)

Marjory Harris lay awake shortly before 4:00 a.m., that odd hour before the early summer dawn would begin to paint the edges of the sky, and during which the opportunity for a decent night's sleep was receding, the realization of which only exacerbated one's anxiety. She rarely slept well these days. Her mind raced with problems that, had she lived in a normal time, would not have troubled her. But really, times had never been normal, not since her youth. The most recent affront was the news, trumpeted all over the DJR, that her daughter-in-law Malia was about to become the bride of that brutish Antifan commander. The media was portraying it as the final victory of Social Credit over the renegade Antifan, and more broadly, over the Deplorables and the fascist United States that he had represented. It occurred to Marjory that if the DJR cause was going well, it would not need to exult in a marital announcement between two people, one largely unknown beyond Beaufort, and the other presumably a widow and now free to marry. Yet this insight gave her little comfort.

But was Malia indeed a widow? Marjory had never been quite convinced of David's death, and the cryptic news Welcome had conveyed when she last visited the grocery store only sharpened her doubts.

"I don't think your son is dead," Welcome had said.

"What do you mean?" she pressed.

He shook his head, sorry at having even revealed this much. What he knew came from an equally cryptic note smuggled from Jeff in upstate New York via the accommodating poultry trucker: "I saw our friend DH."

"It was only a dream," he lied. "Your son was buying blueberries and potatoes. He placed them on the counter, but walked out without taking them." He hoped Marjory would not put much stock in a dream. He knew the ADF was paying increased attention to the Harrises, and indeed, all their Plore associates in recent months, and he did not want to give her information that, were she arrested, could be pressed out of her at Beaufort, with dire consequences for David and, not to mention, for himself. Marjory shrugged, picked up the potato sitting on the fourth bin, and said, "Really, Sunday?" It was unusual for a traveler to arrive in Ploreville on a Sunday.

Welcome said, shrewdly, "Yes, I dreamed that Sunday night." He was no longer certain that his store was free from surveillance, not since a break-in last week in which nothing had been taken. Who would break into a grocery store and take nothing from the shelves? Or from the basement?

So at this hour between night and day, Marjory pondered the meaning of Welcome's dream. Should she try to reach out to Malia and prevent her from committing a great sin, that of bigamy? And how could this be done, without provoking the interest of the ADF? Suddenly, her door flew open, and Emma stood there in a bathrobe, frightened. "Mom, there are police cars outside!" The red flashing lights of the cars had awakened her when they stopped, and she had roused Larry. Marjory would not have seen or heard the vehicles absent a siren, because her room was in the back of the ground floor.

They heard the pounding on the door and saw shadows outside Marjory's window as officers moved to the rear of the house to prevent an escape. "ADF! ADF! Open up!"

His hands trembling, Larry unlocked the door and half a dozen Antifan officers swarmed into the hallway and the parlor, the same one where Marjory had met with her knitting, reading, and plotting confederates until her daughters had begged her to stop last month.

"We have a warrant to arrest Marjory Harris. Where is she?" The warrants were ceremonial. No one bothered to ask to see a warrant and no one bothered to show them to victims.

"The treaty…" Larry began, unwisely raising the most lingering sore point for any Antifan.

"One more fucking word about that fucking treaty, and you're coming with us as well," snapped the captain in charge, a sinewy young black man with a buzz cut and a permanent sneer on his lips.

Emma escorted Marjory, wearing her frayed pink terry bathrobe over her nightgown, into the parlor from the kitchen. They had known this moment was coming, Emma acknowledged, and they had tried to keep Marjory out of trouble, and thought they had finally succeeded in saving her from herself. But informants rarely relayed information in real time.

"Good, you're coming with us," said the captain.

"Wait! Can't she get dressed at least?"

"No need. We got clothes at Beaufort. Let's go."

"What did she do?" Emma pleaded. Maybe an answer would give them some clue about what to tell a lawyer in the morning.

The captain quickly strode over and slapped her hard. She staggered backward, and Larry steadied her. In another time and place he would have retaliated with a hard punch, but not here, not now.

"Don't play games with us, Plore bitch. You know what she's been up to."

Two women Antifans hustled her out the door, but Marjory tested their patience since she wasn't as spry as most of their victims. Marjory turned from their grip and called back, "God keep you! I'll see you soon." Her countenance was serene and confident.

"I love you, Mom!" Emma called back. Then Marjory was gone.

"God!" the captain snorted, as if she had mentioned some Aztec deity. "That won't help her now." He instructed the remaining four troops to search the house for evidence. Emma frantically considered whether Marjory had left anything incriminating around.

"Paper, sir," said one young Asian man, holding a ream of the computer paper Marjory used for writing her bulletins. "Blank." Emma was relieved that he either ignored the pens or Marjory had stashed them somewhere else.

"Take it, that's the same kind of paper they used for their illegal newspapers. They should outlaw paper. An honest person got no need to write anything on paper."

Emma and Larry sat dully on the sofa as the Antifans rifled through Marjory's bedroom, silently grateful the teenagers were hiding upstairs in their rooms, along with the cats. The captain strutted past them, contemptuously taking in the tidy, respectably shabby furniture. Bougie, or bourgeois, he sniffed, remembering his lessons at the academy in suburban Deplorable anti-culture. A landscape of a wheaten field puzzled him. He couldn't figure out what it was. Why would they have a painting of emptiness? He immediately forgot it.

His eye was drawn to a small sentimental porcelain statuette of a mother and a father seated on armchairs reading from a thick Bible to four tiny blond china children. For Marjory, the statuette, no more than five inches wide by five high, symbolized the harmonious family life they had mostly been denied—by the time she and her four surviving children had settled in Ploreville, her husband was dead and her oldest son almost grown. It was over a hundred years old, because it had been handed down to her and Elijah by her grandmother, who had received it as a wedding gift herself. It had survived the painful wanderings from Ohio and through the Antifan transit camp and to Ploreville, packed in crumpled newsprint in a soft canvas bag.

The statuette's innocence and purity angered the captain. He had grown up with a single mother on the chaotic "family" floors of Baltimore's Inner Harbor Hostel among strangers, some of them actively seeking his corruption, in a haze of marijuana smoke and indolence. He had no idea who his father was, and neither did his mother. His mother might have qualified for an apartment had she chosen to work, which would have given her the extra 30 social credit points she needed, but she preferred to spend her days watching TV and videos and chatting with other idlers in the hallways. Under the Reparations Act, she was exempt from work.

The boy spent as much time outside the building as possible, whether playing hooky from school or playing basketball and skateboarding in the local park, which was how he came to the attention of the ADF scouts who prowled the city parks and schools. The boy's combination of athleticism and surliness made him an appealing candidate for the Antifan Defense School. The school taught him how to read. He lapped up the ideology of BIPOC oppression and Diversity. Yes, he agreed, his problems were due to the lingering effects of fascism and white supremacism that the DJR was seeking to eradicate, against continued opposition from the US and Plores and other internal enemies. He learned to loathe Plores. He came to visit his mother in Baltimore after completing his first year at the school, proud in his black trainee uniform with the bright green piping, but she had died in her sleep a few nights earlier and had been immediately cremated, like trash.

Never again would he set foot in a hostel, he vowed. Now he boasted a 220 social credit score and a secure perch in the Suburban Control Unit that policed the Plores. He lived with his two girlfriends in a fifty-third-story apartment at an excellent tower.

He hurled the statuette against the far wall above the door to the kitchen. It shattered into a hundred shards that fell across the back wall of the room, while Emma and Larry stared in horror. He was pleased to hear their gasps. The couple had infuriatingly maintained their dignity, even when he had slapped Emma. He liked raids in which he and his squad could provoke fear and trembling. Were these Plores not the sworn enemies of the Diverse People? Every encounter with them should serve to remind them who was in charge, his instructors had emphasized. And this family was perhaps the most notorious Plore family in all the DJR, given their association with the traitor Antifan.

Above their heads, they heard the boots of the troops now searching the upstairs rooms. The thirteen-year-old boy and his older brother—who was almost a man— were shoved downstairs to wait. They must have found nothing out of order in Marjory's room if they were now upstairs, thought Emma, and she was confident they would find nothing upstairs. The captain, having satisfied his bullying urge, went upstairs, sending an almost beardless youngster to stand in the front hallway. The younger son sat down next to them, hunched over, on the sofa, and the older boy slumped in the rose armchair in the corner, next to the pile of china shards.

Leaving Larry on the sofa, Emma dared to wander over to the front window. It was daylight, just barely. "Look, Larry!" she said softly, not wanting to alert the sentry.

Larry stared at her, in the stupor of a man whose house has been invaded and wife beaten by secret police who were still rampaging through his belongings. He had expected this for months, and as often happens in these cases, his fears had faded just before the dreaded event actually happened. He joined his wife at the window and they peered out the curtains.

The car with Marjory had long ago left for Beaufort, and three other Antifan black vans still squatted in front of the house with their drivers waiting attentively. You never knew how many prisoners you would eventually need to take away.

But on the sidewalk across the street and in the street itself stood over a hundred neighbors, in various states of dress and undress. Their numbers grew by the minute. They were mostly silent, either because of the early hour, or to underscore their witness. Some were carrying candles, and others held flashlights pointed upward. Emma recognized the gray bouffant hairdo of Marjory's elderly friend and coconspirator, Mrs. Kennedy, surrounded by her daughter and grandchildren.

"Isn't that wonderful?" said Emma softly, her face shining.

"For all the good that will do us," Larry muttered, but it gave him a smidgen of cheer. He needed to show up at the bus depot in an hour, or miss a day of work and a day of pay. The very good excuse, that the ADF had awakened them in the middle of the night and dragged off his mother-in-law and detained them while they searched the house, wouldn't matter—if anything it could get him fired for his unsavory connections.

The Antifans tramped downstairs. "You're lucky," snarled the captain. "We didn't find anything seditious, just these games." They were the boxes of perfectly legal video games and the platform that the older boy, now employed in the City as a barista at a coffee shop, had purchased with his first earnings. He had been very proud that he could now buy his own games and not have to beg his parents for money. "We'll be taking them with us for examination."

The boy soared from the armchair. "You can't steal them!" he cried, impelled by the pure convictions of right and wrong that children assume until life teaches otherwise.

The captain signaled tersely, and one of the squad members punched the boy in the face. Blood spurted. He cried, out of shock, not because he was a coward. Ploreville had protected him until now, and only now he was realizing the extent of his community's degradation.

"How old is he?" the captain demanded. "Sixteen? If he was a little older, we'd take him with us too for that crack. We'd make him fuck his grandma in front of us. You'd better teach him how to behave respectfully around Diverse Authority before it's too late.

"All of you belong in jail. It's a disgrace that they've let you racists roam free this long. But it won't go on much longer. Paragon will destroy you all." It wasn't clear whether the captain was referring to all Plores, Ploreville Anacosta, or just this notorious stiff-necked family.

They marched out again, with the captain throwing back, "We'll be keeping an eye on you. And don't expect to see your hag mother again."

The family was less shocked by the vindictiveness than by what they heard next as the squad marched down the stairs and sidewalk to their vans. Their Plore neighbors were shouting, "Shame! Shame! Shame!" It became one single chant, as the crowd took advantage of its numbers and the dawn shadows to hide among each other.

As foul-tempered as the captain was, he recognized when he and his squad were outnumbered and an unexpected crowd could become an unpredictable mob. He was tempted to call in riot police, but he didn't want to wait for them, although it would be pleasurable to watch women and children sprawling under the ADF batons and water cannons. It had never occurred to him that almost two hundred Plores would dare convene and mock him in the street after a raid, and he was a little afraid, as bullies are when suddenly the tables are turned. *They might lynch me. That's what racists do, right?*

"Let's get the fuck out of here," he told his men, trying to maintain his bravado. He called in the riot troops from the safety of his van, but by the time they had arrived, sirens warning of their advance, the mob had dispersed to their homes, for breakfast. The video games would eventually find their way to an ADF break room in the SCU, after proper fumigation.

At the edge of the crowd, Warren Welcome, observing the scene in his discreet way, decided he would send a coded message to St. Louis, subject line: David Harris's mother arrested by ADF; first Plore protest in years follows. No, Marjory had not known the extent of Welcome's activities, and now Welcome was relieved he had not drawn her further into his network.

Larry apologized, dressed, and was off to work. He was glad he could spend the day driving up and down the streets of Ploreville, focusing on pleasantries, correct fares, and traffic laws, which were the most rational and just laws in the DJR.

Christine hurried over as soon as Emma called. She was shocked to see the red stripe across her sister's cheek.

"We can call a lawyer," said Emma. "But it won't do much good. We need to contact Malia."

"Malia! But she's gone over to them!" Christine sputtered.

"No. No more so than Mom has gone over to them. She feels she has no choice. She is engaged to this Paragon, who the ADF commander said would destroy us all. This will give her a chance to strike a blow at him, and I know she loves Mom. Remember the looks Mom said they gave each other at the zoo?"

"But how can we reach her? The ADF won't let any messages through from us."

"Every tower has its Plore staff, and if they don't have Plores, Plores deliver to them." Emma would send the question throughout Ploreville and, by midday, she would learn the name of a Plore who worked as a janitor at the Portland Tower. Even though the tower had assured the ADF when it was seeking a secure apartment for Malia that it hired no Plores, they had forgotten about the wizened old man without an armband who trudged along the hallways with his carpet sweeper. He had worked there since before the Portland Tower's no-Plore regulation had been implemented, and had been grandfathered in. His granddaughter lived with her family about six blocks from Emma and Larry.

Suddenly there was an outburst from the boy, almost a man, who had been simmering in his fresh hatred since the departure of the ADF troops, and had not left his chair. The adults had almost forgotten him. His face twisted, in a way that appalled his mother and aunt, because they had never seen him so agitated.

"If Uncle David was here, they would have never done this!"

Two days earlier, two hundred miles north, Seth had met with an old friend of his in a bar that made the Candor Inn look like a country club. The friend had moved in years ago with a girl from another roundup, way over toward Corning, so Seth rarely saw him these days. The romance had long evaporated, but the friend had stayed in Corning.

Impulsively, Seth had reached out to his old friend. He wanted to unburden himself, but not to anyone from his roundup, and not anywhere a militia member or Social Crediteer might enter. The nameless bar was perfect. It was dark even at the brightest time of day, and almost empty shortly after noon. A table fan whirred in the corner. A scowling man cleaned out a beer keg behind the bar. A middle-aged couple silently ate their lunch. The men nursed beer steins and sandwiches over heavy wooden tables with furtive graffiti carved in their corners.

"How long's she been cheating on you, man?"

"Not exactly cheating," Seth admitted. "But we had a thing going, then this guy shows up from almost nowhere last fall, and she's been sleeping with him too for a while, I'm sure."

"How do you show up from almost nowhere these days?"

"He said he was from Massena. He said he was going to visit his dying mother in Anacosta, but he never left. He's been trying to organize us to..." Seth's voice dropped, "resist the Sokos."

"Resist the Social Credit? How do you do that, man? Hit them with brooms? Smack them with one of your chickens?" News of the poultry farm's success had reached outlying communities.

"I can't say exactly," Seth hurriedly backtracked. "But we were just doing our own thing, getting by, and he's stirred everything up." Guiltily, he realized he had gone too far. All Seth really cared about was Lucy, who had awakened in him a tender side. It had been easier to pretend to brusqueness and toughness, since the roundup needed protectors, and he needed a reputation, but he had been lonely. Even though Lucy was twenty-five years his senior, he had been falling in love with her, but she had almost immediately spurned him, Seth, when the well-spoken blond man from the border town showed up. Even when she invited Seth back into her bed, he suspected he was still sharing it with Mike as well. Unable to resist, he sometimes knocked on her door when he saw the lights on in her kitchen. The couple would look up at him, and even though they were engaged in innocent tea drinking and chatting, he felt unwelcome.

And then, only five nights ago, he had entered, not too late in the evening, without knocking, and David walked out from the bedroom, a towel around his waist, but otherwise naked. "Who's that?" he heard Lucy call out from the bedroom, a note of irritation in her voice.

"Just Seth," David called back. Then, to Seth, almost gently, "Seth, don't just walk in like that. You got to respect our *loneship*," or *privacy*. "There's plenty of girls in the roundup who'd love to hang out with you—why don't you court them?"

Humiliated, Seth had stormed out, but David was right. Yet this was the first time he had actually caught them in the act he had feared, or as close as possible without a complete disgrace, and it had spurred him to reach out to the only person on earth— outside the roundup—who would listen to him and give him good advice. It had been three years since they had last met for a beer, but Seth was relieved that his friend didn't hold it against him.

His friend said, "Seth—what does this guy have over you? You're good-looking, you're *snake*," or *fit*, "and you're feeding the roundup with your crossbow…"

"I was," Seth said gloomily, thinking of the bustling poultry farm.

"Still, is he better-looking than you? What did you say, tall and blond?"

"I didn't say," Seth responded. "He's about my height, and blond, with a short beard now and light eyes. He's a little older than me, but pretty snake too."

"I don't see what he's got on you."

"Lucy's highborn, and this guy isn't an ordinary Plore. I don't care, I really don't think he's from Massena. He talks fancy. She went to college, you know, during the war, before Plores were kicked out. How can I compete with that?

"And she likes the idea that we're going to rise up against the Social Credit. That's the problem with older people, they remember the old days, and they think they're going to get them back. But it'll be on our backs, the younger guys, who fight and die. Easy for her to say, but they love to talk about it together. Not thinking about who pays the bill for their fakedreams."

"You bet," agreed his friend. "I got a good job, working in the glass factory, and they need me to fix all the things that go wrong. Social Credit wouldn't recognize a wrench if they got hit with one." He ordered them a fourth round of beers, and reassured Seth, "Don't worry, man, this is on my side," or my treat. "I see you're down, and how often do we get together?"

"What should I do?" said Seth. "What if they get married?"

"Nah," said the friend. "He came in a cloud, he'll get antsy and move on again. Just be patient."

Seth nodded. "You won't tell anyone else about him, will you? It's a secret he's in our roundup. I don't want him to be arrested. He's not a bad guy, just showed up where he wasn't needed. Promise you won't share it out?"

The friend's pale blue eyes glinted in the darkness. "Man, how can you even ask? Of course this is all secret. Let's shake hands over it." His wiry forearm met Seth's, in the childhood gesture they had always bonded over when hiding a prank from the grown-ups, and their joined fists bobbed down to the table and then back up again.

"Thank you, man," Seth said. "I'll just wait this out. This kind of guy won't stay forever, you're right. I don't want to lose my chance to marry the roundup leader by getting jealous over nothing. In the end, she'll realize that I'm for keeps."

"That's the right spirit, man," smiled his old friend. "Don't lose your cool." He paid for their meal with bills pulled from a thick wallet.

Chapter 42
Coffee Shop
(Wednesday–Thursday, June 16–17, 2094)

Malia stretched her legs out over the ottoman as she scribbled notes on the latest draft for next Monday's advice column, "Malia's Social Credit Corner." The editors and censors sent her three questions twice a week. She would pen some proposed replies and they would send her the final copy, which rarely resembled hers. Most of the time she could guess the appropriate answers, and she knew it was a test of her ideological fidelity, so Malia tried not to give away her own preferences. Crafting a suitable response was actually an intellectually challenging exercise, so she didn't mind, except for appearing to commend behavior she considered immoral and even depraved. Today they had sent her three proposed questions.

Q. My elderly mother has started to lose her memory. Since she can't enjoy life as much as she used to, and it is frankly a burden to take care of her, would it be all right if I discreetly notified the Social Tower that she may be a good candidate for the Euthanasia Palace? Wouldn't this also be appropriate from an environmental perspective? Katherine, 130. *(Shame on you, thought Malia, but she knew her answer would have to be couched more ambiguously.)*

Q. I have gotten to know a Plore guy about my age at my workplace. He is very kind and we have good chemistry. But I know that Plores are very dangerous. Should I continue to date him? Keniasha, 95. *(Yes, you should be happy, thought Malia, but she would counsel unhappiness.)*

Q. I work at a restaurant that is only for 150 and above. The food there is much better than what I receive in my Healthy Eating bag at the hostel. Sometimes I sneak a bite of the leftovers that come back to the kitchen. Is this wrong? I am helping Mother Earth by not wasting her bounty. Cory, 80. *(Steal directly from the restaurant coldbox too, Malia wanted to tell him.)*

Malia was finally alone in the apartment. The housekeeper had left for the day, after tending the congratulatory bouquets that had arrived by the dozens since the announcement last week of Malia's engagement to Paragon. Her Antifan guards had taken some back home and to Beaufort with them, and others bedecked the already majestic Portland Tower lobby. The air inside the apartment was almost nauseatingly fragrant this week.

For all his bravado, Paragon didn't dare take any bouquets back to the apartment he still shared with Exterra. If that kept Paragon from insisting on sharing her bed, Malia was fine with that. That night he had declared his intention to marry her, she had kept him up for three hours explaining his Diversity journey, and he left without assaulting her, probably exhausted. Imagine, coming all the way here from China, she thought, fascinated. She knew so little about China that, for all she knew, you could reach it by digging deep enough into the earth's crust and out again. "So it was just you and two brothers," she had said.

"No, I had a sister, Patigul," he corrected her. "A half sister."

"Is she in China too now?"

He had said abruptly, "Yes, she's not here," and changed the subject.

Sometimes she found it odd to think of Paragon as a suitor, let alone a fiancé. He was scrupulously correct in her company. He had informed her that their wedding date would be Saturday, October 30. "The Knowledge Tower is planning the arrangements," he said. "Everything must be done in an ideologically sound manner and convey the right message to the entire DJR. You will hear from the Knowledge Tower about your dress and other details."

Romantic, Malia thought sarcastically. "Arrangements" sounds like a funeral. Maybe it is. Mine.

"I hope you don't expect any children from me. You do realize I will turn forty next year?"

"It doesn't matter," he said. "Children are unnecessary and costly for the earth. I will have my pick of Diverse successors when the time comes. And if I change my mind, we have excellent scientists who will help you conceive." Lab rat, thought Malia.

"What will happen to Exterra?"

"I told her she could become my secondary wife. This is very common in China and non-Western cultures, so we should celebrate that we have such options. And it is perfectly legal here. She accepts this, because she has no other choice. It is better to be Paragon's secondary wife than someone else's main wife, or no wife at all. We will have a house, finally, so you don't have to worry about crowding each other."

Maybe I should write a question to my own column, she thought. But where to start? Dear Malia, I am an American being held hostage by the ADF. A handsome but evil commander insists on marrying me, even though I am already married. But I don't really believe what they say about my husband being dead. Should I go ahead with the marriage? Signed, Malia, 160.

The doorbell rang, and she jumped. Paragon and Exterra never bothered to ring, and only the housekeeper announced her arrival with the doorbell. She looked up at the screen above the door but didn't recognize the caller.

When she opened the door, she greeted the hunched old man who traversed the corridors with his carpet sweeper and duster, sometimes humming to himself. Incongruously, he carried a large bouquet of giant purple and pink flowers.

"Amba-mam Malia," he greeted her respectfully, even though he was a Plore, and Plores did not use these Social Credit salutations. "I bring you these flowers from the cleaning staff of the Portland Tower in felicitations of your engagement."

"Why, that's very kind," said Malia, "please bring it in." The Antifan behind the man briefly waved his security wand, with which all packages were scanned for unwholesome objects, as if to reassure Malia he had screened the gift.

The janitor placed the pot carefully on the counter, and then said, "There is something wrong with the bottom of the pot, Amba-mam, I am very sorry. This was careless of us. You should take a close look to make sure it will not leak onto your kitchen counter." He lifted the pot with both hands, and Malia, curiously, saw a small paper sticking to the bottom. The Antifan guard stood in the doorway, so she dared not comment further and draw attention to the pot.

"Yes, thank you, I'll place a plate under it. Please tell the staff I am very grateful for their Diverse generosity." A few seconds later, he and the guard were gone and the door closed behind them. Malia extracted the damp paper, which turned out to be a small envelope. The card inside the envelope read:

**Meet me at Portland Revolution Coffee Shop, June 17,
around 4 p.m. Emma Davidadaughter**

Who is Emma Davidadaughter? Malia puzzled. Then she realized it was her sister-in-law Emma, using a false surname with the -daughter suffix that only highly woke Social Credit women sported, so no one would suspect the name belonged to a Plore woman who was plotting to sneak into the City. And Emma Marjorydaughter would only have led investigators directly to her in-laws had the note been intercepted, so Emma had cleverly inserted David's name into the surname as a hint for Malia. But why would Emma take such a risk just to meet her for coffee? Did she have news about David?

She opened the door and told the guards she would be going to the coffee shop tomorrow afternoon. She was required to give them twelve-hours' notice of any excursion so that sufficient coverage of her trip could be obtained, and unsuitable venues denied her. But she often went to Portland Revolution when she needed to escape the apartment and work on her column, or another article for a women's magazine, so it would attract no suspicion. It was a perfect choice; the Plore janitor must have recommended it to Emma.

By 3:30 p.m. the following afternoon, Malia was seated at her favorite blond eco-wood table in the front corner, under a poster of the muscled New Woman, 210, who had won the national women's marathon last year, and a wooden board declaring, "It Is Time to Birth the Beloved Community." Her Antifan escort would typically sit outside on the other side of the large glass pane, enjoying the sunshine for once instead of the dark corridor outside her apartment. Another Antifan paced in the back alley.

As usual, she set up her workscreen, purchased a cup of coffee and a pastry for herself, as well as for her escorts, and arrayed several sheets of paper with notes alongside them. She pretended to work, but could not concentrate. Just as a precaution, as David had taught her, she swept her arm casually beneath the table to make sure there would be no listening device. She had never bothered to check for one here before, because she had never met with anyone in Portland Revolution.

To her shock, for the first time ever, she felt a rounded bump. Of course they would place one here. They know this is your preferred table. She moved several tables away. The Antifan looked at Malia, who pantomimed, with a hand shading her eyes, her need for less sunshine spilling onto her workscreen. He shrugged, and seated himself again.

Almost exactly at four, Emma entered, hesitatingly. Emma was wearing a black cloth armband on her left arm, presumably a fake for her illegal venture into the City. Malia waved her over to the new table, and they hugged, briefly, so as not to attract attention. The Antifan's back was turned to her, as he stared out into the street. It would be hard for him to peer into the café and see the pair talking in the dark interior.

"If anyone asks," whispered Malia, "You live on the thirty-fourth floor of the Portland Tower. We've gotten to know each other since I've moved in. Let me treat you to something," she added, loudly, knowing that Emma lacked the real armband needed to make a purchase here. Emma's mouth watered looking at the showcase, and she did not refuse.

Once they were seated, Emma said, softly, "My mother was arrested two days ago. They came early in the morning, before dawn, and took her away in her bathrobe."

Malia raised her hand to her mouth. "Oh no!" Would Marjory be granted a VIP cell because of her relationship to David, or her age? Would they spare an old woman the Red Room? She doubted it, and the memory of the execution corridor cells flooded back. But she couldn't tell Emma what Marjory might be encountering at Beaufort.

"That's why I've come to see you. You can help."

"Me? I'm a prisoner myself!"

"You're the fiancée of Paragon. The whole country knows. He's the number three at Beaufort. If you asked him to have her released, couldn't he do it?"

"He could, if he wanted to. That's a big if. He's not a normal man," said Malia. "He's not marrying me for love, you know. He hates our family."

"Would he release Mom if you threatened to break off the engagement?"

"Probably not. And he won't let me break off the engagement. I'm telling you, this isn't a normal relationship. This is political, not personal."

"Can't you try?"

"What will I tell him when he asks me how I know your mother was arrested?"

Emma's shoulders and face sagged in one sudden, sad movement. "I don't know, Malia. Can't you try?"

Malia promised Emma that she would try. A few minutes later, Emma slipped out into the bright afternoon to walk ten blocks to a Diversity bus. The Antifan paid her no notice, turning his face happily to the warm descending sun. En route to the bus stop, Emma would dash behind a building, stuff the armband into a cloth tote bag, and pay her fare with the Plore phone. Even Plores could ride a Diversity bus and, at this time of day, it would be plausible that Emma was a janitor or a veterinary technician or an office drone returning to Ploreville.

Malia sat for a little while longer at the table, digesting the situation, while her coffee grew cold. Since she did not even have Paragon's phone number, and she had no time to waste, she said "Exterra" into her armband. The two women had not spoken since the announcement of the engagement. Was Exterra angry with her for seizing the primary wife spot? Or would Exterra be relieved that Paragon would marry her, Exterra, at all? Did Exterra assume that Malia would still be at her disposal after the marriage? Sometimes she asked Paragon how Exterra was doing, and he had responded coolly, "She is entirely accepting. She has no alternative," which did not exactly answer Malia's question and certainly did not reassure her. Exterra, who was probably still at work, did not answer the phone, so Malia left a brief message.

Chapter 43
The Conqueror
(Friday, June 18, 2094)

Malia had never contacted Paragon directly, let alone wanted to, and, still behaving like a prisoner, she passively awaited others to show at her doorstep. Since his declaration of their engagement, he had paid her several impromptu visits, usually in the evening. They might watch a political program on TV, or he might talk about his ambitions, or he might quiz her on her activities or on Diversity topics, alert to any signs of her backsliding. He never laid a hand on her. He even avoided shaking her hand or embracing her in greeting or farewell. On one hand, it was a relief that he had refrained from assaulting her, but as a woman, it confused her. It was beginning to become slightly insulting. Am I still contaminated? she wondered. Was he waiting for her to make the first move? Perhaps he was asexual, but hid it well? Did she smell of the basement at Beaufort?

When she commented on his gentlemanly behavior, he had said, sourly, "I have other options, you know. But you will be pleased when we are finally in bed together."

In their first official event as an engaged couple, they had attended the glittering opening of the new Climate Protection Museum on the Mall. Cameras clicked incessantly around them. In the car en route to the museum, Paragon enthused, "Old museums were about preserving heritage, things, the past. They wanted visitors to know, to learn, to think. We are beyond thinking. Our new museums are designed to make Diversans feel, to love the DJR, to hate fascism. Museums are an important part of programming humanity. It is easier to monitor and calibrate when the subject is literally standing in front of you, rather than lying in their bed looking at a device. Measure their heartbeat, their brain waves, and you will know how loyal they are to Diversity. We have sensors installed behind key paintings and exhibits."

Around eight o'clock, to her relief, Paragon showed up in her living room, in his ADF uniform as he had come directly from Beaufort. Exterra had dutifully relayed her message. She made her request, without hesitating.

"How do you know that the birthing parent of your traitor husband is at

Beaufort?" he asked sharply.

It was no use. Malia had been unable to come up with a convincing lie on short notice.

"My sister-in-law found me at the coffee shop and begged me to help," Malia said simply.

"How did she know you would be there?"

"I don't know," Malia said, but her eyes found it difficult to meet his black stare.

"Mother Earth, these damn Plores know everything. You should have turned her away. Are you on our side or theirs?"

"Khalid," she agonized, daring to call him by his first name, "she is my sister-in-law."

"Was. Your connection with Plores ought to be completely severed now. The traitor husband is dead, or will be soon."

"Will be soon?" Malia stammered. "What do you mean, 'will be soon'? You've been telling me for a year he's dead." Her hands felt cold and clammy.

"We found out he's wandering up in New York–Schuylkill. An informant came to us with the intelligence we need to finally corner him. Maybe he thinks he's going to rescue you. But he's mistaken. Either he'll be dead by Sunday morning or we'll be finishing him off at Beaufort. I have to decide whether it's worth keeping him alive a few more days just to watch him undergo torture. It's a difficult choice for me.

"He's been hanging out with Plores for a little too long. In the end, they can't resist the bounty money. Their character is notably weak."

"You've been lying to me for a year!"

"I wouldn't call it lying. It was simply the correct narrative." He smiled at her, in feline triumph.

She jumped at him in wordless, screaming fury, trying to reach his face with her small fists. Laughing contemptuously, he gripped her wrists and pulled her close. The Antifan guard opened the door without knocking. "Commander, do you need help? Is anything wrong?"

"Corporal, I never need help. I have the situation under control. Please leave." The corporal apologized, and closed the door behind him.

"You bastard!" she screamed at him. "You monster!" She tried to stomp on his black leather shoes, twisting back and forth in her desperate attempts to hit him. He gripped her wrists tightly so her hands flopped back and forth supinely.

"Isn't this useless on your part?" he asked. "Dead now, dead tomorrow, what does it matter?"

He loosed her, and she ran for the door, opening it just to face the unmoving, unsmiling bulk of the Antifan corporal. She slammed the door in his face and turned toward Paragon.

"I hate you! I hate your crappy Diversity—it's all about your power and your control and it has nothing to do with white supremacists or the fucking Mother Earth dirt-worshiping cult. You're the supremacist! If you lived in a decent country, you'd be in jail…" This time he strode quickly toward her, placing a hand over her mouth to stop the heretical accusations, because even a corporal could report them to the Knowledge Crimes Unit, but she broke loose to say, "This country is sick. People deserve to be free! The DJR is evil—I meant it then and I mean it now!"

He thrust her down savagely in the armchair in which she had been jotting her notes for the column yesterday afternoon. She stared up at his face, which was furious and smug.

"Shut up," he hissed. "If it weren't for Steve Rosen, who's a heretic himself, you'd be dead already. If I weren't playing a long game here, I'd just have you executed tonight. I need you for my next moves. I don't know how you managed to foil the truth serum earlier this year but you clearly haven't been truthful." She wondered, how is Steve Rosen a heretic?

"And you want me to let that hag mother go? Why on earth should I do you any favors now?"

"Because you still need me. I don't have to play along with this wedding game. Yes, you can kill me, but you can't force me to say 'I do' on October 30. If you let Marjory Harris out of Beaufort, I'll behave." She thought, now that I know David is alive, it doesn't matter. He will rescue me in time. Or Khalid is speaking the truth, and they will find and kill David. Then I don't care what he does to me, and I will have to survive somehow. And if he stays alive, and they force me to marry Khalid, it won't be a real marriage anyway, just pagan nonsense, and against my will, so no real sin. All this was running through her lively mind, to the point that she almost failed to notice that Paragon was looking at her with newfound respect.

"That's the deal?" he said, almost affably. "You know, I don't have to say yes, and I could just plow through and do what I want, but it's easier if you play along. The Plore hag means nothing to me, only her son. If I let her go home, will you comply?" The bulletin network had been silenced for now.

"Yes," said Malia sincerely.

Paragon reached for his phone, and Malia watched from the armchair as he called Montoya, and explained that Marjory wasn't needed for the Resolution Command's investigation. "She didn't seem to know much when we interrogated her. She seems to be on the verge of senility. I'd rather focus on the other Plore women." Montoya was objecting, to which Paragon responded with reasonable counterarguments. "If we need her again, we know where she lives. She's not running away." Finally, Paragon hung up the phone, and turning to Malia, said, "She'll be released tomorrow afternoon. I have to fill out paperwork first."

"Thank you," she said, a small smile breaking out between her tear-stained cheeks.

He responded to her smile with a short crooked one. "Stand up," he said. "I have one more condition." To her shock, he placed his lips on hers as his hands roamed her lower back and buttocks. She froze, but she could not deny the electric ripple that ran through her body, which rose to meet his. Oh no, she thought. He kissed her mouth deeply, then elsewhere on her face, and his hands reached under her blouse and brassiere, kneading her breasts. "High time," he said. "Let's see if you deserve to be the partner of Paragon." He steered her into the bedroom. Her knees were shaky. Before he did anything else, he returned to the front door and instructed the corporal to order them dinner and champagne from the restaurant downstairs. "Just bring it in when it arrives. Ignore any loud noises of pleasure you may hear from the bedroom."

"Yes, sir!" the corporal breathed, awed.

Paragon undressed and signaled to her to do the same. She had never seen him unclothed, and was surprised at his unblemished tan skin—he lacked the typical Antifan tattoos. Her eyes traveled grudgingly over his well-muscled back and thighs. Reluctantly, she shed her black slacks and short magenta blouse, the same outfit she had worn to the coffee shop. She could not bring herself to remove her underwear. *This is not right, you're married to David, David is still alive. Now you know. But Marjory can't be allowed to die in a Beaufort cell...What is right?*

"What are you waiting for?" he asked her harshly, his dark eyes flashing.

She burst into tears, and he lifted her bodily and carried her to the bed, where he removed the remaining clothes himself, almost tenderly. Then he applied his mouth to her body where it would elicit the loudest groans, the most helpless cries of pleasure. He was right, he knew his business, but it seemed entirely business on his part. His bristly black hair scratched her breasts and chin. He did not demand that she reciprocate, but explored her body as if it were a machine that needed to be examined to ensure peak performance and he was proceeding according to some manual. He uttered no sweet nothings in her ear. In her detachment, Malia noticed that Paragon turned around every minute or so, grinning, as if he were afraid the corporal actually might be standing at the door with the champagne. After a few minutes, he completed the act. Then they lay together atop the bedspread, Paragon pulling her into his rough embrace. "That wasn't bad, was it?" he smirked.

Oh my David...but he won't ever know this happened.

They brought the food and champagne into the bedroom and, naked, ate their dinner. Paragon poured them champagne and, at his directive, they toasted to the victory of Diversity. He didn't seem to care that Malia must be lying. "You might as well tell me the truth when we're alone together here," he said, "since I now know your heart is fascist to the core. I now realize that it gives me special pleasure to control someone like you. Think and say what you want, at least in the privacy of my house, but in the end you will always do what I want." *That's what you think,* she countered him silently.

As he dressed again to leave, he said, "That footage will come in handy when your traitor husband comes to Beaufort. I've decided we'll prolong his regrets and not kill him on the spot."

"Footage?" she asked uncomprehendingly, from the bed.

"The footage of our sexual congress just now. Our cameras are always operating in this room, just this room, but maybe you didn't realize it. I'm going to have our video editors make it into a very exciting movie that I plan to show your traitor husband when we have him in chains at Beaufort. That'll be the last thing he sees before we beat him to death." He grinned at Malia. "The last scene in the movie will be us toasting Diversity with champagne. Thank you for your excellent cooperation."

Aghast, Malia screamed like a wild animal. It was pointless leaping at Paragon again and her skin crawled at the thought of any contact with him ever again. She had been deceived into an astounding betrayal of David, beyond mere adultery, one that would make her beloved's final moments on earth one of complete despair.

"Monster!" she called Paragon again, but that word seemed inadequate to the task, and unfair to actual monsters. She buried herself under the covers, and shielded her face from the sight of him as he departed, whistling.

Hours later, she finally slept, and when she saw the table with the food scraps and champagne bottle in the Saturday sunshine, she would have wondered whether the whole episode was just a nightmare, except for her body aching in unexpected places. The enormity of her betrayal weighed heavily on Malia.

I must pray, and try my best to warn him. They are going to attack wherever David is hiding, and I can do nothing to protect him, except beg God to show mercy on us. With a sense of purpose, she showered, removing the stink of Paragon from her body, and dressed modestly and neatly. She kneeled all morning, with some hesitancy recalling the Christian prayers, and then mouthing her own. Let them film her—she no longer needed to deceive Paragon. In the afternoon, she took a long walk around the Portland Tower grounds, continuing to pray silently, the Antifan guards trailing her. It was all she could do. She felt powerful guilt, knowing that Marjory would rather have died at Beaufort than allowed Malia to prostitute herself to Paragon in return for her release, but that thought had not occurred to Malia at the time of her surrender, and by the time Paragon had decided he would take Malia, she would not have been able to fend him off...and if she were honest, she admitted to herself she really had not wanted to, not at the time.

She had been expected to attend the Beltane celebration in the Gardens tonight, another test of her fidelity to Diversity, but she would tell the guards she was ill. In any case, her attendance would not have served to deceive Paragon, not now. Her Beltane had taken place last night.

Sometime during the afternoon, a black van deposited Marjory at Emma's house. The Antifans thrust her onto the sidewalk, and went speeding off through the mostly empty streets. Marjory, with no visible injuries, and in her same nightgown, slippers, and bathrobe, carefully walked up the steps to the door herself and rang the doorbell.

Chapter 44
Setting Sun
(Sunday, June 20, 2094)

The sun had risen like a glowing orange ball in the morning, and now the ball, having waited out the rotation of the earth below, and the frenetic daytime activity of its inhabitants, was steadily sinking on pillowy white clouds. The orb descended calmly behind a clump of trees. A small gap in the middle of the greenery became an incandescent red square. Behind the greenery was Cayuga Lake. Even the lowliest Plore could relish the beautiful scenery. David lay back on his elbows, surveying it all.

Lucy sat down next to him, bent over, and gave him a tender kiss. David drew her down toward him and, lying on their sides, they faced each other, his gray eyes scanning her light blue ones. In the dying sunlight, he did not really see her wrinkles, not anymore.

"It's not like you to be watching the sunrises and sunsets," she teased him. She had dimly sensed him rising just before dawn, him slightly pulling on the blankets they shared, because he was not an early riser. "Next you'll be writing poems." In the back of her mind, she worried, was he going to sneak out of her house and head down the road, never to return? She had to remind herself, David's trucker ride to Anacosta was in five days. He had no reason to disappear now.

"No," he said. "I'm just restless. I'm not sure why."

David was growing apprehensive about the journey. The roundup, however narrowly bound, had become his mission, and his home. People relied on him. He had no idea what to expect in Anacosta. For all he knew, the trucker would deliver him into the hands of the Antifans. Malia's loyalty was unknown and how he would find and retrieve her remained a mystery.

This is what you came here for, he reproved himself. See your mission through. But the mission had changed during these eight months among his Plore brethren.

"You don't have to leave, you know," she smiled at him. "I'm not kicking you out."

"That I know. But I didn't return to the DJR just to hide. I have two sons back home who need their father, and hopefully will get their mother back as well. I can't stop trying to reunite us."

A shadow fell across Lucy's face in the twilight. Yes, she felt no guilt in hoping David could forget Malia, but she did not want to deprive these two faceless boys—because he had no photo to show her—of their father. David had eventually gone to Lucy's bed, seeking consolation, angered by another interview of Malia in which his wife denounced him yet again. I may not survive, he had told himself, what does it matter? Malia will never know. I want Lucy to be happy. More recently, he had added, unfairly, to his running commentary, and now that she is the fiancée of that Antifan, the score is even.

"You won't forget us, will you?" she asked him, again. Crickets chirped as the dusk gathered.

"No. I will come back, somehow. Malia and I vowed we would help people trapped in the DJR, not just Plores, but we forgot. I tried to escape the DJR when I was in Oklahoma, and it chased me back here. I learned my lesson."

"Tell me more about Oklahoma," she begged, her hand resting on his shoulder. "It sounds like the old days here. But you all moved on, and we moved—backward." She liked to hear about life in the United States. Economically, the United States had not advanced much beyond what Lucy had known in her youth, but the separation and treaty had at least allowed it to preserve its citizens' rights.

"It's like a fairy tale," she sighed after he had told her about the supermarkets and the medical devices and the police who were respected and protected the citizenry and the movies they watched at home. "Do you really think there's a chance this could all come back to us?"

"If it doesn't, I'll rescue you and bring you to Oklahoma."

"David, don't tease an old woman." He couldn't be quite sure, but he thought he glimpsed a tear on her cheek in the growing darkness. He felt ashamed of his lighthearted comment, although who knew whether he himself would ever see Oklahoma again. Soon they rose silently and returned to the house.

One of Lucy's three watchmen, posted to the east of the roundup, yawned. It was Monday morning, 0315, the stillest time of the night, and he had to fight to stay awake. Sometimes he wondered what the point of the watch was; surely the Antifans had given up on tracking Mike Marino, or whoever he was, and if they just wanted to arrest the banner vandals, daytime would serve just as well. But he was a conscientious man and, overall, it was an easy job. He drank another gulp of tea from his insulated canister.

That was his last swallow, ever. The Antifan sniper dispatched him with a silent electronic round and the watchman toppled forward into the dirt, his canister flying. To the south and north of the roundup, the other watchmen met the same fate. More than a hundred Antifans—most from Beaufort—crept steadily through the forest from the three directions against the sleeping rounduprs. Marcus Vanover and Loki Greene, determined to take the credit for the capture of David Harris, followed quickly behind the initial scouts. In command of the operation was Paragon's deputy, Deputy Commander Okuro, and the white tattoos won instant respect from the local militia who filled out the ranks.

The chickens and cows gave the alert instead. As the Antifans torched the feed sheds and the poultry coops, they had not anticipated the combined noise of the frightened animals, and the high-pitched poultry chatter and the deep lowing gave the villagers a few extra seconds of warning. David disappeared down the trapdoor in the kitchen closet that led to a newly built tunnel that would take him outside. The others would try to run into the woods, or down to the lake, or take their chances with the Antifans, whom they expected would limit their abuse to beatings, since the treaty allowed no more.

Five Antifans burst into Lucy's house, filling its coziness with their black-uniformed mass.

She looked up from the bed, wearing her pink nylon nightgown and robe that she had pulled on in haste. "What do you want?"

"You know what we want," snapped Marcus Vanover. "Stand aside."

Her hesitation angered him, and he grabbed her arm and threw her to the wall. Lucy gave a small cry, more of surprise than pain. "Move the bed," he ordered the men. "Pull the carpet away. There's a trapdoor." Lucy had bought the green carpet with her share of the roundup's chicken proceeds. Having learned from the informant's report that Lucy and Harris were sleeping together, and were doubtless in bed together before the raid, he was convinced that Harris was nearby. The sight of two pillows side by side on this widow's bed confirmed his suspicion.

Vanover stayed upstairs while the men disappeared down the trapdoor with their torches. One of them emerged about fifteen seconds later, almost sheepishly. "Captain, nobody's down here."

"What do you mean?"

"There's some vegetables, an oilcan, and blankets, but no one hiding, sir. There's a tunnel."

"Go down the tunnel, then!"

"Captain, it's very narrow."

"Sergeant, are you refusing to obey an order? Go chase the damn bastard into the tunnel! Corner him like the rat he is!"

Vanover looked quickly behind him at the doorway. Other troops were herding the rounduprs out into the square. Nothing heroic in rounding up these pathetic grandmothers and children. He, Marcus Vanover, would kill David Harris in that tunnel. He jumped with the sergeant through the trapdoor down into the cellar, although he should have left a guard with the old woman. But that would cost precious time, which might allow the quarry to escape, as would calling for a sniffer dog to track Harris's scent. What could that old Plore bitch crumpled on the floor behind him do to him, Marcus Vanover?

As Vanover landed catlike on the floor of the cellar, Lucy leaped forward, slammed down the trapdoor and closed the metal lock, and ran out, the men now trapped in the cellar. They would find that the tunnel dead-ended forty feet away. She reached for her cell phone and texted a simple "46" to David, which meant "I'm out of the house."

A hundred feet away, David emerged under the trailer in which he worked with Lucy. He crawled out behind the trailer, which backed close to another trailer, and no Antifan or roundupr had ventured in the narrow alley between them. A water pipe ran up to the roof, and David shimmied up it, and crawled rapidly to a small metal overhang covering about seven feet by three. He saw Lucy's text. Backing into the crawl space, he twisted his body, finding the second cell phone inside, taped to the roof two feet above his head. On his back, he tapped a second code. The oilcan in Lucy's cellar exploded with a great roar, engulfing the cellar in flames, fueled by blankets. The ceiling of the cellar shuddered, then caved in, the house falling into the hole. David flattened himself against the trailer roof, which shook with the impact.

He turned around again in the crawl space, now on his belly, facing the opening, listening to the screams from the rounduprs, and curses and shouts from the Antifans. Smoke and heat from the flames rose around him, and shimmered in his line of vision across the trailer roof. He prayed that his own trailer did not catch fire. Hearing a steady droning sound, he realized that observation craft were above, and he did not dare leave his hiding place. He prayed fervently for Lucy: "Please, God, don't let them take her to Syracuse."

He saw Lucy on the roof of the schoolroom trailer, about forty yards away from his hideaway, outlined by the red and orange fires consuming the roundup. He could tell it was her from the way she moved, and the long hair flying against the flames, but he couldn't make out her features in the dark just before dawn, not at that distance. She raised one of the ghost rifles from the cache underneath the schoolhouse trailer, and fired repeatedly at a knot of Antifans below her. They fired back, missing her, as she stepped back and dropped behind the water tank. Two troopers scaled the same ladder she had mounted to the roof. David watched her pick off the first one before the second replied in kind. Lucy faltered, dropped the weapon, spun around once, and then fell to the ground, her hair flowing above her body. Oh my God, David thought, burying his face in his folded arms. Lucy! Braver than me, I've been hiding like a nute in a coppet. It gnawed at him that he had slain no Antifans so far.

The dawn was rising. Then a sound he had not heard in twenty years overwhelmed him. It was the rumbling roar of a firing squad. But unlike at Beaufort, the sound did not stop to recur at a dignified interval of five or ten minutes. It resounded continuously for an endless thirty seconds, amid screams. *It's a massacre!* David shivered.

The screams faded, then ended. David heard the jovial shouts of the Antifans. He strained to hear a roundupr's voice, any roundupr. But he heard none. Even after the trucks roared off, David was afraid to move. The Antifans might well have left sentries behind. An hour passed. The sun rolled up into the sky.

Only then he heard a familiar female voice below. "Hello? Anyone? Oh my God, oh my God."

David wriggled out and saw Rachel wandering between the metal frames of the burned trailers and the smoky collapsed piles of the wooden houses. No one else seemed to be around. Then as she edged toward the main square, David heard her scream vibrate against the silence. He cast a quick look around, saw no one else, and leaped down to the ground. Just in case, he carried an old Glock. He was more afraid of encountering an Antifan unarmed than of the penalty for carrying a firearm, since he would be executed either way. He would die on his own terms.

"Rachel!" he called.

She spun around and cried, "Mike! Thank God!" They hugged in relief.

"They're all dead," she said, stunned. "Gone." A faint putrid smell was beginning to rise with the summer heat.

"Bruce?"

"No, not Bruce." She extracted her phone and called his name. In seconds, she said, "It's safe now. You can come up." Turning to David, she said, "We ran to the lake and we hid under the rowboats. Until we couldn't bear the heat anymore and the sounds had died down. I came up here first to check because I figured it was safer for me than for him."

"Let's get Lucy. I know where she is," said David. Rachel didn't want to be alone, so she followed him to the schoolhouse trailer, where they found Lucy, lying in her bloodied pink nightgown, on the ground just where David knew she would be. David kneeled silently next to Lucy's body for a few seconds, regarding her calm ashen face, eyes closed, its skin drained of blood. You can do this, he told himself, and then, extending his arms underneath her body, he lifted and placed her over his left shoulder. *God bless you, Deplorable heroine, who spent your life fighting for right, and went out fighting. You will not be forgotten.*

The Antifans had removed their few dead and wounded, but David was gratified to see scraps of black cloth and dashes of blood that were not Lucy's. She had shed Antifan blood before she died, and David imagined her saying, "I'm glad I took some of them with me."

They cautiously entered the central square. Almost every roundupr lay there, on their sides, or backs, splayed wide or crumpled, riddled with the holes created by the Antifans' electronic guns. Blood spattered the ruins of the closest wooden houses and the dirt around them. Almost everyone wore the clothes they had been sleeping in.

He saw the woman who managed the poultry coops, staring almost peacefully into the sun. Her young son, clinging to her in death. The modest self-taught preacher who ministered to everyone regardless of their denomination. The mentally challenged young man with the wide blue eyes who spent his days walking around the roundup asking every worker if he needed help until he found someone who did. The couple who had sat behind him the night Malia confessed on TV. They had held hands that night and they were holding hands this morning as gunfire had raked over them. David had known every single one of these people by name and they had trusted him.

The Antifans came here to find me, he realized painfully. But for me, no one here would have died. When they couldn't find me, they executed the whole roundup. Never since the civil war had the DJR security forces dared to murder Deplorables in cold blood. They had respected the treaty, however grudgingly. As a senior ADF commander, David would have known about any violations, and he had to concede the Antifans had behaved correctly, if severely, toward the defeated Plores.

He had made four circuits around the gruesome assembly, calling out, futilely, "Hello? Can you hear me? If you're alive, call out!" when Jeff stumbled up to him, his face aghast. Jeff turned from him and vomited along the edge of the first corpses. Raising his head, he said despairingly to David, "The smell…"

"Is anyone else still alive?" David asked him.

"I don't know," Jeff said faintly. "Rachel's checking the trailers." He staggered off to sit under the oak tree between the ruins of Lucy's house and its neighbor.

Rachel emerged into the square carrying a small boy, perhaps three years old. "Found him under a bed in the Peterson trailer. What's your name, honey?" she asked him, despite knowing it full well. The toddler buried his head in her shoulder, too traumatized to even cry.

To their collective shock, next to appear was Seth.

"Hid in the woods," he said. A branch had scraped his face, but otherwise he seemed unharmed. His voice and legs were unsteady. "My God," he said, surveying the carnage. "We're going to have to bury all these folks. We don't even have a backhoe."

Rachel placed the little boy next to Jeff under the tree and went in search of more rounduprs. She found Stacey Kelleher, who had been shot in her own bed, in a trailer on the outskirts of the roundup, and was barely alive. She worked as a barista in Syracuse. Rachel dressed the wound, but the authorities would not send an ambulance to this roundup, not today. If Stacey survived into the evening, the others would take her to the Plore hospital in Syracuse under cover of dark.

Unless someone else emerged from the woods, that was it. Six survivors, only four in any shape to bury the rest, and that was counting Jeff, who had gone into a shell. They all looked at David for guidance.

"We'll need to dig mass graves," he said. "We won't be able to dig that many individual plots. Maybe at some point we can bury everyone properly.

"But first," David said, "Let's take photos." He pulled out his phone.

"Take pictures?" Seth was outraged. "What for?"

"Because once we bury these folks, no one will believe this happened. I am going to bring these photos to Anacosta, and somehow, we will send them to people who can do something with this information. Maybe even in the US."

Seth looked at David incredulously. Who would ever want to see these photos? Who could he ever show them to other than DJR functionaries? All the photos would do was incriminate David when the authorities finally arrested him. But David marched resolutely around the corpses, snapping photos, sometimes kneeling for a better angle, ignoring the stench.

Several hours later, they had dug a pathetic trench perhaps six feet deep by eight feet wide. They wrapped about a dozen rounduprs in sheets Rachel brought from the ruins, and placed them gently into the grave. "We have to say prayers over them," Rachel said, pulling out a Bible. She read Psalm 123: "The Lord is my shepherd, I shall not want..."

David said, as he had memorized years ago, "Our Father, who art in heaven, hallowed be Thy name, Thy kingdom come, Thy will be done on earth as it is in heaven...Forgive us our trespasses as we forgive those who trespass against us; and lead us not into temptation, but deliver us from evil...Amen." But he would not forgive the Antifans their trespasses today, even as he hoped to be delivered from their evil.

By noon, the sun was blazing, and they sat, already exhausted, under the tree's shade with their sandwiches scavenged from the food from the remaining houses. They had run out of sheets. They watched the surviving chickens pecking around the houses. David was tense, waiting for Seth to accuse him of having indirectly caused the massacre. But Seth was uncharacteristically silent. The toddler burrowed into Rachel's lap. "Well, I wasn't planning on becoming a mom so soon," she joked feebly.

Shortly after, as they were about to begin digging again, a ten-man delegation came from the neighboring roundup, having been summoned by Rachel. They brought two backhoes on trailers drawn by trucks, and more sheets. Tom from the Candor Inn was among them, and he placed his ham-like hand on David's shoulder in quiet condolence. David was struck by the newfound strength in Tom's face. The flabby, defeated flesh he had pitied on that first night had firmed with purpose in recent months. David was cheered to see such concrete evidence that the beaten down Plores had begun to organize. But looking around, he could not help asking, "To what end?"

The neighbors stared grimly at the murdered victims. No one said the obvious, mentioned the smell, appealed to God, or fulminated against the Antifans. What could anyone say? By evening, the bodies had been placed gently in one of three yawning gravesites, as many as possible in a sheet or blanket. David let Lucy lie under a sheet under a tree as long as he could. Then Rachel said gently to him, "Lucy," and he reluctantly wrapped her cool body in the sheet, tied it gently at the bottom, and carried her to the grave where she would lie with her beloved rounduprs.

Seeing him with Lucy, the men and Rachel paused their work. The backhoes stopped. "She was a heroine," David said. "I watched her fire on the Antifans from the roof of the school trailer. She wounded or killed several, I could tell." His was the closest to an eyewitness account that anyone would ever have, and the story would gain detail and impact in the years ahead. Then he whispered in her ear, "You were right. We must wipe them out. We will have our vengeance." Finally, he laid her in the grave atop other shrouded victims.

Seth watched, knowing he would not have lifted or carried Lucy's body with such love, not without thinking of his own clothes. He loved her, and I just loved myself, Seth thought, with a rare flash of introspection as he rested on the shovel handle next to the gravesite. He had tried to tell himself that the raid had had nothing to do with his drunken revelations to the man who was not really his friend. *They could have found Mike anyway, there are so many informants out there. We weren't really keeping his presence here a secret.*

Yet Seth could not ignore that the Antifans had spared his life. The squad, recognizing him from the informant's description, and checking his ID, had shoved him into the presence of Okuro, saying, "This is the man who told our informant the traitor was here. Should we let him go?"

Okuro looked him up and down, scornfully, whether because he was a Plore, or because he had betrayed his comrades, and even if that was useful to the Antifans, it only confirmed the Social Crediteers' view of Plores as dishonorable weaklings. "Let him run into the woods and hide, like the small food animal," he decreed. The squad pushed him, stumbling, toward the nearest thicket, and the leader said, "Run, you piece of crap." He ran, they shot at the ground around him, laughing, and then returned to the fray.

When Seth could run no farther, he hid in a clump of bushes, which turned out to contain poison ivy once dawn came and he could make out the leaves. Clutching his knees with his arms, he cried silently, fearing that the Antifans would come back for him. Hours after the last sounds faded, he dared to emerge and return to the roundup, where he found the others.

Chapter 45
Onward
(Sunday–Thursday, June 20–24, 2094)

By the time the burials were completed, and scripture read one more time, and fresh dirt shoveled over the graves in neat mounds, Tom's group had agreed to take in the survivors from Lucy's roundup, as well as the chickens pecking morosely around them. But not David.

"It's too dangerous," argued one man, and others nodded. "The ADF's looking for him. Look what happened here. We can't risk it."

Tom looked troubled. His comrades were right, and yet it was wrong to abandon the man who had done so much for them, even if fate had turned against them, only temporarily, for sure. Why had they eagerly followed Mike's guidance if they were not willing to make sacrifices? Had anyone really thought that the Antifans would accept with equanimity the Plores sending leaflet-dropping drones against them, or painting slogans on buildings? And who else could have led them forward, except for a man sought by Antifans?

If we throw each other to the wolves when times become tough, Tom thought, we will not deserve to be free men again. At the same time, they could not be cavalier with the lives of the two hundred people, including dozens of children, in his own roundup.

An idea occurred to him. "Mike can stay in the lean-to north of here." The shed was halfway between their roundups. "And I'll stay with him, until his ride comes on Thursday. We can take turns watching."

"I'll stay with you too," Seth interrupted.

David was grateful for their support. The contents of his backpack had long scattered, his bedroll had been destroyed in the explosion, and he was unprepared to live on his own in the woods, even in summertime. Nor did he know whether the truck driver would show up on Thursday as scheduled. And Antifan helicopters were occasionally circling overhead, spying on the survivors, perhaps hoping to find Harris after all, or just as a reminder.

On Thursday morning, David stood just off the main road that intersected with the gravel one leading to the roundup. On a normal visit, the truck driver—whose rig could not navigate the winding gravel road—would stop here at eleven o'clock, and the rounduprs would help him load chicken into the truck. Behind him were Tom and Seth, as well as Rachel and Jeff, who had come to see him off. David was touched at the send-off.

The driver came on time. He was surprised to see the group waiting for him. "Hey, where's the chicken?" he asked.

"No more chicken," David said. "The ADF came by and destroyed the whole roundup."

"Nothing to do with the chicken?" the driver asked, alarmed that the scheme might have been uncovered by the authorities.

"Not about chicken at all. But we won't be selling it again for a while. I'm here for my ride to Anacosta—Lu- Lucy arranged it."

"OK, she didn't answer the text I sent yesterday so I wasn't sure this was still on. Glad I came by, since you guys paid a lot for this ride." The driver beckoned David into the cab and showed him the hiding place accessed by a drop hole under the seat. "We gotta get going, it'll look weird if we sit here much longer."

"Just a second," said David. He jumped off the back, leaving his satchel behind, and embraced his friends one more time.

"Man, don't forget us," Tom urged him. "A thousand guys are waiting for you to return."

"We need you," Seth admitted. "If you need us, send us word. We'll come fast as greased lightning." David's heart was warmed by the classic Plore phrase.

"Tell my dad…" Jeff hesitated.

"I'll tell him you're doing fine. That you're both doing fine." David smiled down at the petite dark-haired young woman.

Rachel said, "We'll be OK, Mike. We'll pray for you, and you for us." At some point during the stay in the woods, David had told them the truth about who he was and where he was going. How could he have kept this secret any longer to this small group once they had experienced the worst together? But they still called him Mike.

"Hey, kamrat, you want me to pick you up next week instead?" the driver called out irritably.

"I'm coming!" David waved one last time to the group, leaped into the cab, and followed the driver's instructions. For eight hours he would crouch eight feet under the driver's seat in a small compartment with a small vent to the outside, and an extension under which he could stretch his legs if needed. It was technically only six hours to Anacosta, but the driver made several stops along the way, mostly to the small collective farms under the purview of the Economic Tower, picking up eggs, milk, and produce. The driver sighed regretfully at the loss of the lucrative chicken. He hoped the problem was not chicken-related, because he didn't want to lose his job, and he definitely didn't want to go to jail. But his imagination was fortunately insufficient to figure out what the problem might be if it weren't chicken-related.

That evening, Marjory set out to do some shopping, carrying the reusable cloth bag that had been mandated for environmental reasons. Warren Welcome had just called to say he had acquired blueberries, and as one of his favorite customers, Mrs. Harris should have the opportunity to buy them before they disappeared.

"I'm keeping the store open a little later tonight," said Welcome. "You won't have to fight the crowds. You might want to bring one of your daughters to help you walk home with the groceries." A little odd, thought Marjory. Even though the two days at Beaufort had been relatively gentle, and she felt as strong as ever, perhaps others saw it differently.

Ploreville by evening was not a halcyon sight, and as Marjory walked with Emma to the grocery, even before nightfall, they saw girls standing on street corners waiting for customers. Before sunset, the customer might be a Plore man walking home from work. After dark, even Social Crediteers drove over the Potowmack, at least the ones exalted enough to own their own cars, looking for some action on what they considered "the low side." You could do to a Plore girl what a Social Crediteer might report to her building's commissar as misogynist behavior, at least if you had cash. For enough money, a Plore girl would even call them 'amba-sah' in the throes of their lust. Years ago, Marjory had despised these girls, but she and Emma knew times were tough, and not all these girls had families to depend on, and sometimes they were raising children on their own.

Welcome was waiting for them, and locked the door behind them.

"These must be some blueberries," Emma joked.

Welcome said, "I've got something even better than blueberries for you. Come this way." He led them down into his basement, carefully helping Marjory down each step.

They turned right at the bottom step, and saw a scruffy, blond-bearded man in work clothes rise awkwardly from a mattress in the corner. Marjory recognized him first.

"David!" she gasped. Emma's eyes widened as she cried out. Then they hurried to him, Marjory more haltingly, and his arms circled them in a great hug.

"Momma!" he said, what he had called her when he was a little boy, and more rarely afterward. It what he had cried when they forced him, a fifteen-year-old half child, to go to the Antifan Defense School and he didn't want to go, but he knew he must. It was what he had called her the last time she had seen him, when he had brought Malia's cats over to her house, lying that he and Malia were taking a trip to the West Coast and would be back in two weeks.

"Em!" They laughed, and cried, and hugged again.

Welcome brought three folding chairs from a corner of the basement and discreetly withdrew. The trio exchanged news about the family, quickly, fleetingly, as if they might be interrupted and arrested at any moment.

"I'm back to rescue Malia," he admitted, as they looked at him with dismay.

"You were safe in the US!" Emma said. "What about your sons?" She took out a recent photo of Emmett and George that had arrived in the mail only last week from Daniel and showed it to David.

"I couldn't leave her in the hands of the Antifans," he replied, "although they seem to be treating her all right now. It wasn't the case when I crossed the border back in November. Then I saw her on TV calling me a traitor and saying I'd deceived her..." He buried his head in his hands.

Marjory touched his shoulder. "She's not on their side. She's just trying to stay alive."

"I went to see Malia a few weeks ago when Mom was in Beaufort," Emma told him. His head jerked upward as his eyes stared with horror at learning his mother had been jailed in that sinister tower. He could not have known. "And she did what she needed to do to get Mom released."

Concerned, he turned to Marjory. "What happened to you there? How did they treat you?"

"Well, David, I am here," she smiled archly at him. She didn't want to worry her son, not now. "They let me sit and rest in a cell for two days and just called me names. Maybe you still carry a little cachet around there."

"She's waiting for me, I know," said David. "I heard about the zoo. I know you went to see her and you took a big risk to do it. I know she gave a speech about freedom in front of the crowd..." Cloistered in Ploreville, the women had not known about the speech, and they begged him for more information. Of course, neither had the City at large heard about the speech.

"So brave," sighed Marjory. "And she sat in that wooden chair, really like a martyr from the olden days. You must rescue her, David, and soon, before they force her to marry that awful savage." The country had learned yesterday that the wedding would take place at the College of the Earthloving Priests in Lenilenape-Sylvania, formerly Pennsylvania, and now named for the tribe from whom the evil Quaker Penn had stolen the land.

"I will find her and I will bring her home," he said firmly, just as he had told Malia he would find her daughter and bring her home, and hadn't he done exactly that?

It was dark by the time the women left via the back basement door, with more kisses and hugs that none of them wanted to break off. Who knew when they would next meet or if they would meet again? Welcome helped David drag the mattress into the back room, away from the ground-level windows. Burglaries happened, and a trespasser might well seek to profit from reporting a mysterious basement occupant to the authorities. A small toilet and sink in the room made it resemble a prison cell, except the room's inhabitants were generally traveling to freedom, much as David was.

"I have something to show you," David told Welcome. Before he turned on the phone, he reassured Welcome that his son had been one of the very few survivors of the massacre. Welcome stared at the photographs of the bodies and the burned buildings. "Would you not consider this a violation of the treaty?"

"This has never happened before," Welcome murmured.

"Can we get this to St. Louis?" David asked. He knew that if Welcome was a member of the ring that spirited Plore travelers up and down the East Coast, he might have a suggestion or know of someone who could help him convey the news to the United States.

"Yes," said Welcome. "They can scan the photos for the metadata and they will be able to pinpoint the exact location where these were taken." Silently thanking God that his own son had survived, against all odds, Welcome took the phone and downloaded the photos to his own hard drives. In another day, the photos would be with his handlers in St. Louis. But he didn't plan on telling David this, not yet. Also, he knew two Plores on the cleaning staff of the Texan embassy, even though the government generally preferred to send low credit spies in the guise of janitors to work at embassies. Welcome would send the phone to the embassy tomorrow with one of the cleaners, who would pass it to the helpful junior officer who was so interested in the human rights situation in the DJR.

"You won't need this phone again," said Welcome. "It's dangerous if they're looking for you. They can determine who took photographs in the vicinity of your roundup on that day, you know. I'll get you a new phone, in your next name, and we'll destroy this one, forthwith." He would not tell David about the Texan embassy.

Under Welcome's supervision, David dyed his hair and beard brown again, in the sink in the back room. Welcome showed him the new false papers that he had prepared for him and the hazel contact lenses he would use. The ID card just awaited a photograph, which Welcome snapped of him in the back room, and affixed to the card as David watched respectfully. Clearly Welcome was accustomed to this task. As Lucy had said, "We're not amateurs." His new card read:

SMITH, MICHAEL VERNON
DOB: MAY 5, 2052, ANACOSTA
PLACE OF RESIDENCE AT LAST REGISTRATION CULL:
    FREDERICK, MD
ID: 65945677433104
HAIR: BROWN EYES: HAZEL
PARENTS: (1) CHARLOTTE RUTHERFORD; (2) FINN SMITH
CARD EXPIRATION DATE: APRIL 30, 2099

"You just went through the Frederick cull in April," said Welcome, "so you have a legitimate document here. "The real Smith died in the hospital last month of pneumonia. His wife passed this card on to us and we paid her a tidy sum. Like a life insurance policy." He gave a short rueful laugh. "We'll load your photo onto the phone, just don't buy anything with it. Use cash."

After they finished their business, Welcome relaxed in the office chair and David on the stairs, both cautiously enjoying the other's company in the near-dark. Welcome wouldn't dare let David enter his own house next door. As the night grew long, David told him how Jeff had become a medic and a teacher, and about Rachel. He described how he and Jeff had escaped the cull, making sure to praise Jeff's courage. Welcome nodded, content enough. Finally, the grocer began talking about his other two sons, including the oldest, who washed windows, and the middle one, who was a self-driving car dispatcher and helped in the grocery.

"In the United States they would have been professors and lawyers. From what you told me, Jeff could have been a doctor there. But here..." He shook his head regretfully. "You're lucky if you can eat."

Then he talked about how he had fought with the Reds in the civil war, a young man in his early twenties, fresh from college with an economics degree. "My father was a supporter of MAGA. He believed in exercising his rights, whether to carry a concealed firearm or to speak his mind about politics. He said we'd fought for three hundred years to exercise our rights and damned if he wasn't going to do just that. He was afraid of the communists who pretended they were on our side—black people's—but just wanted to take control of the country using us as stepping stones. They assumed we were on their side, but then they took over our neighborhood—we lived in Richmond—and moved another family into our house, to share it. Not a good family. They took drugs and fought and punched holes in the wall. But they were now our betters. The next week my father and I went to West Virginia to join the Reds. That was in April 2053. He didn't come back. I did."

David's inquisitive look prompted Welcome to say more. "The Antifans ambushed our squad near Charleston. Most of us got away, but not my father. We came back, and they had strung him up on a tree, like a lynching, except weren't we Reds the lynching side? They put a sign on him, 'Ungrateful...' well, 'N-word.' *That* was the pro–Black Lives Matter side. So I vowed that I would never forget, and I would never forgive, and I would do whatever I had to do to respect my father's memory. So that's why I help with the travelers. His name was Harold Welcome, and I named my oldest son for him."

"I lost my father too in the war," said David. "But we never got his body back. Maybe it was just as well."

Welcome went to a small cabinet and extracted a bottle of prewar cognac. "Expensive stuff," he said, "but let's toast to our fathers." A few minutes later, the men clinked small shot glasses together, and David said, "To our fathers."

"To liberty and to the MAGA," Welcome responded evenly. "Let's be worthy of them."

Welcome would not tell David about the former comrade in arms who showed up in Anacosta briefly around 2060, recruited him into the service of the AIA, and wired his house for communications with St. Louis. The down payment for the grocery had come from St. Louis in the guise of a bequest from an imaginary aunt in Missouri.

"Time for bed, young man," Welcome said, slightly ironically. "In the morning, we'll figure out how we're going to rescue your wife."

David woke briefly around 4:00 a.m., on the mattress in the windowless basement room, in complete darkness. Random thoughts buzzed through his brain. Less than a week ago, he thought, I lay next to Lucy, and she was alive, and the roundup hummed like a beehive. All of that is now gone. Now I owe them all a great debt; they paid in blood. There is no way Malia and I can return to Oklahoma and live the way we did until last year. Perhaps I waited too long to leave the roundup. Maybe Malia no longer wants to be with me or our sons. Maybe the roundup would all be alive today if I had left earlier. What's done is done. They will go down in history—a free history—as heroes. Someday.

He tensed at the sound of a creak in the unfamiliar basement beyond, but nothing followed. Seeking the reassurance of its cool plastic, he reached for the firearm in the space between the mattress and the wall. Good, it was still there. He fell asleep again.

PART FIVE

FOXHALL ROAD

"The urge to save humanity is almost always a false front for the urge to rule. Power is what all messiahs really seek: not the chance to serve."
—H.L. Mencken

Chapter 46
The Wall
(Wednesday, June 30, 2094)

The four women and one man waited for Paragon and Malia at the table in a conference room at the Knowledge Tower. They were honored to have been assigned the responsibility of ensuring that the upcoming nuptials of Paragon to the repentant renegade Malia met the highest standards of Diverse hygiene. Mother Earth—a faceless swirl of robes—surveyed the room from a painting hanging prominently on the wall over the group's leader.

The coordinator of the wedding plans, A, 170, in charge of the Diverse Ceremonies Unit, was gaunt, freckle-faced, and perpetually angry. She wore the badge of a knowledge warrior, on which a robed black woman wielded a sword. Praised for her devotion to inclusion and equity, she lavished abuse on her subordinates. She had recently changed her embarrassingly Christian first name, Veronica, to Acinoreva, in the mass Name Taking that year. "We must lead the way in devotion to Diversity," she had lectured the few holdouts. They called her Acid-oreva behind her back.

The second woman, B, 200, represented the Mother Earth Cherishing and Exaltation Unit. Her tasks were to ensure that the wedding ceremony showed due respect to Mother Earth, and to select the right assortment of participants, as well as the correct liturgy. She was African-Diversan, about thirty, wearing an exquisite red dress with a high carbon offset, and very high heels that caused her buttocks to sway when she walked. Her plump red-lipsticked lips and severe wide eyes gave her the look of a South Pacific idol. Her enemy was white supremacism, which she could find in anyone who opposed her. She wore the badge of Black Lives Matter.

The third woman, C, 174, was in charge of the catering. She was urging a gourmet vegan feast for appearance's sake. She was white, with a broad chest that made her resemble a pigeon, wearing a severe professional suit to broadcast her status. Her main professional triumph had been marrying the African-Diversan chief of music at the Knowledge Tower. She wore a rainbow badge.

The fourth woman, D, 156, would oversee the media attending the event. She was blonde, round-faced, quick to complain and to remind everyone her pronouns were she/her, as if any doubt existed. She left as early as possible each day, citing her responsibilities as a birthing and chest-feeding parent. She wore a badge that proclaimed, "Ally."

The man, E, 172, presided over the facilities and the construction. He was short, multiracial, curly-haired, and outclassed by the fervid women. He just wanted to do his job. The ideology washed over him, given his preoccupation with joists and piping, but his sly sense of humor could not be entirely suppressed. His badge was the most neutral of the lot, of the DJR flag with the green earth against a black background, and he wore it out of duty or prudence.

While they waited for the famous couple, Acinoreva sputtered, "This Commander Ma must be crazy. Did you see the movie he wants to show at the ceremony?"

"The one where he rapes Malia?" asked C. "That is so misogynist!"

The man, E, wondered if they would show it to him, just so he could confirm its misogyny for himself.

"Typical white supremacist behavior," sniffed B.

"But isn't he a person of color?" inquired D. "I've never met him before, but I've heard he's a Muslim of Chinese origin." She pronounced it Moo-slim.

"You know," B said disdainfully, "that white supremacist behavior is not always a function of white skin. That is an unsophisticated view. Many black people exhibit white supremacist behaviors, particularly those who remained in the US, or are secretly disloyal to Diversity. Antiquated notions about hard work or time are often a sign of white supremacist leanings…"

"Well, they're already late," noted the man, "and we're on time, so we'll have to work harder on our Diverse behaviors." He giggled, ignoring B's scowls.

"Are we really going to permit that to be shown on all the media channels? I think it would undermine the holy and sacred spirit of the event." That was D.

"The Antifans are brutes!" Acinoreva nearly shouted. "The masculinist orientation of Beaufort remains an obstacle to Diverse supremacy."

"They've objected to the vegan feast," C said soberly.

A fey young man in a polka-dotted jacket ushered Paragon and Malia into the room. Malia wore her trademark red gown—long gowns were back in fashion— against which her dark curls tumbled enticingly, and Paragon his Antifan uniform. The women were jealous of Malia, who had usurped a role that rightfully should belong to a woman who truly loved Diversity. That said, they also feared her for her connection to the Antifan traitor and her life in the forbidden United States. Some looked at her only discreetly, sideways. Something disturbing shimmered about her.

Malia sat demurely at the table next to Paragon, hands folded on the table before her.

"Commander Ma, Communicator Malia, thank you for your presence today," Acinoreva said formally. Each representative would explain their plans for the great event. They all vaguely knew that Captain Boyd would also be united with the Commander and Malia that day, but she was a pale absent shadow next to the powerful physicality of the couple sitting in front of them.

"We must have meat," Paragon told C. "Many guests will be traveling a long way and some will be representing the People's Republic of China. They must be fed a hearty meal that will not seem lacking in hospitality and offend our friends." C dutifully wrote down, "Chateaubriand."

"We must have an imam in attendance with the archbishop," he told B. "And our patron saints will be St. John Beaufort and Omicron. No, we do not need a female patron saint. And why not two?" Each newly married couple or group in the DJR chose a patron saint, and the plaster statue given them by the priest would occupy a place of honor in their new home. B gulped and acquiesced, her fleshy lips trembling.

"The movie, Commander…" Acinoreva began.

"Yes? What about the film?" He stared at her, his dark eyes challenging her. The bitter Acinoreva felt a fluttering in her half-dead vitals, but she plowed on resolutely.

"It is inappropriate for a sacred wedding ceremony. It is misogynist since you clearly take Communicator Malia against her will. We have no objection to the nudity, of course."

"I beg to differ," Paragon said coldly. "Much the same happens at any Beltane celebration, as I am sure we all attended earlier this month. So we didn't have a collective in attendance at the time, but now we will. I hope you are not too dense to recognize the symbolism of the retaking our fascist runaway for Diversity. This is a truly Diverse message of which you should all be proud."

Malia finally spoke up, listlessly. "It was not against my will."

Paragon gave her a catlike look of satisfaction. "You see? The movie stays."

In the self-driving car afterward, Malia said acidly to Paragon. "I'm glad you found a use for the movie, since you haven't managed to capture my husband." They were driving to the house the ADF had just given to Paragon on the occasion of his upcoming marriage, on Foxhall Road. The Avalon apartment would no longer suffice.

Paragon glared at her, resentful at having been reminded of his subordinates' failure, and of the loss of Vanover. By themselves, in the self-driving car, they were honest, if cruel, to each other. "It is just a matter of time. He is trapped here in the DJR. Eventually we will capture him."

She had already asked him how she could marry him, Paragon, when they both— and hundreds of Antifans—now knew her husband was still alive, even if they could not acknowledge the fact publicly.

"Who cares?" Paragon said. "Really, we should have moved beyond marriage years ago."

I will be rescued before your farce of a wedding takes place, she retorted silently.

But she said this as much to reassure herself as to snipe at Paragon.

The car pulled up in front of a rambling two-story twentieth-century colonial house on a three-acre plot, a luxury in Anacosta. Almost no one lived in a house in Anacosta these days, let alone on such expansive grounds. The lemon-yellow frame house, long unoccupied, sat in a state of disrepair. A covered porch ran along the front. Malia could envision herself relaxing on the porch, with another stiff drink, surveying the lush lawn and maybe glimpsing the Potowmack in the winter. Not that she intended to hang around that long.

An Antifan sentry saluted Paragon, who reciprocated. "Malia, let me show you our new home." Malia followed him into the dusty central foyer. They both sneezed.

"Look, here's the nook for our saints." Eventually, they climbed the stairs and toured the empty bedrooms. Paragon would have a suite to himself in the center of the floor. Malia's would be to the left, and Exterra's to the right, with adjoining doors from Paragon's own rooms. Malia was grateful for the promise of privacy, although she admonished herself again, there will be no wedding.

Her bedroom featured a large picture window looking toward the river. In the winter, she would actually be able to see the Potowmack, Paragon told her. Her eyes lighted on a crew of about two dozen workers in the distance. They were building a brick wall. To Malia they looked like a swarm of busy ants.

Paragon stood behind her. "They are building a very high wall around the whole property so we will have privacy."

Malia felt a moment of panic at the thought of being enclosed behind the brick wall. "How high will it be?"

"Twenty feet," Paragon said. "But we have three acres, so it won't be too claustrophobic. You won't need to leave much once we are married. Perhaps for a doctor's visit. You will be kept very safe here, I promise."

"Why shouldn't I leave? Am I going to be a prisoner here, behind these walls? Won't I be a free woman once we're married?" she demanded.

Paragon didn't respond, not at first. He stared out of the window, behind her, and placed his hands on her shoulders. She tried to whirl around, to confront him, but he held her tight, his arms across her upper chest, forcing the back of her head to lie against the pad of his front shoulder. His rough armband scraped against her cheek.

"I will not let you contaminate Diversity," he said. But the strange thought occurred to him, unprompted, nor will I let Diversity contaminate you. As they had walked through the house, Malia in her red robe had again reminded him of Patigul. Of course, Patigul once married had insisted on binding her own straight dark hair in a turban, so...was it the way Malia glided from room to room?

"I'll kill myself if you keep me here as a prisoner," Malia said desperately.

"That may be," he said, releasing her. "I will not grieve overlong. Your purpose here will have been achieved."

"The Diverse People love me! They want to hear from me! How can you keep me from them?"

"They do not know of your hypocrisy. It would be better for them not to hear your lies at all. Your career will come to an end after our marriage. You can tend a garden here at the house. I am fond of tomatoes. Or learn to cook. Or breed one more time. The Diverse People are fickle and stupid. They will forget you."

Several hundred yards away, David stood up, stretching, his aching back welcoming the movement. His trowel rested on the low table, next to the vat of gray composite. He drank deeply from his canteen. Today he had learned how to lay bricks; in his journey as a wandering Plore he had learned skills that had eluded him in decades as a Beaufort commander or as a refugee in Oklahoma. The other men on the crew, all Plores, all with outsized hands that came from decades of practicing their trade, tolerated his lack of productivity once they realized he was brand-new. "You'll get faster," they reassured him, and they were generous with advice.

When Welcome said he had another new arrival to Anacosta who needed work, his associate who ran a job clearinghouse that helped supply Plore labor to the City said, "You know that old house up near Potowmack Boulevard? The one that used to belong to the billionaire they put in jail for knowledge crime? The Antifan commander— you know, the one who's going to marry David Harris's widow—is building a giant compound up on Foxhall, with a brick wall around three acres. They can't get enough bricklayers. Is your new guy up for that?"

Welcome said his new guy was definitely up for that.

David looked intently at the large yellow house in the distance. Malia might be there right now, or she might not, but that was her intended prison, he knew. Was she looking in their direction? Was she despairing, or content as the intended wife of Paragon? So much, including his life, depended on her reaction when he finally saw her again.

He would have to figure out how to access the house when she was present. It would not be easy—the Social Credit crew chief, 94, scrutinized them like a hawk, at least early in the job. The crew moved in unison to their breaks, including the toilet huts, and back again, almost as if chained together by their ankles. At the end of the day, under the stern gaze of a uniformed Antifan, the thirty men and two women were counted off before boarding one of two vans; one went directly to the tunnel that connected the City with Virginia. The other van went to South Rockville, where David was renting a room in a boardinghouse, far away from where Arlington Plores and the informants among them might recognize him.

When David had reported to the crew chief, the stringy little Social Crediteer scrutinized him, and ordered him to extend his smooth hands so that he could inspect them, as he had David's registration card.

"You've never done this work before? What kind of work have you done?"

"Security guard, sir."

"You're not going to be sitting around eating donuts, you know. This is hard work."

"I understand, sir."

"Hopefully you're smart enough to learn fast. I never know with Plores."

"Yes, sir, I'll do my best."

The crew chief found David's, or Mike's, demeanor sufficiently obsequious and his athletic build at least suggesting he was capable of physical labor. And the crew chief couldn't be fussy, since he needed bricklayers badly. His own boss, who reported to a 150-point Social Crediteer at the Social Tower, which oversaw housing, was under severe pressure by the ADF to finish Paragon's brick wall by the time of the wedding, and the discord had rippled downward to the anxious crew chief. On his own, he was promising $100 to any of his workers who could recruit a bricklayer who would stay at least two weeks on the job. It was worth it.

Chapter 47
The Treaty
(Wednesday, July 7, 2094)

"I have some good news for you, but it is somewhat grisly," said Gaines. The National Security Council director for DJR policy looked uncertainly at Rex, who had insisted on accompanying her step-uncle and Chris Mendoza to St. Louis this time. This time he was treating his visitors with less condescension.

"I'm a grown woman," Rex said loftily in his direction. She crossed her legs, and leaned back to take a full view of the impressive room with the murals and the rich furniture. Even though she and her mother had been received by then president Tomlinson in such a room when they had first arrived in the United States, her memory was hazy. Today, in her blue print dress and matching jacket, she felt grown up and sophisticated. If she finished her political science degree, could she work here? She imagined herself sitting at the head of the table, directing various subordinates to give their reports...about what? Walking on the gleaming parquet floors to the meeting room, she had compared herself with the poised young women striding by, and thought, Nobody could tell I was from Oklahoma, or grew up in the DJR. I could fit in here.

Chris figured that St. Louis wouldn't have summoned them just to humiliate them a second time, so he was optimistic that they would make progress on this visit. Vernal faced the Oklahomans across the table with two different analysts.

Gaines dimmed the lights with a quick touch on the table, and a screen descended at the front of the room. "We have broken off the talks with Anacosta after receiving these photographs. The AIA has verified them as having been taken near Ithaca, upstate New York, probably several weeks ago at most." The talks had resumed in April, with Malia's zoo speech forgotten.

Before flashing them onto the screen, he remembered to say, "These were taken by Mr. Harris. They do not involve Mrs. Harris at all. We have confirmed that Mrs. Harris is alive and well in Anacosta."

Aside from the AIA officers, who had pored over them many times already, the group took a few seconds to absorb the images.

"Oh!" cried Rex, raising her hands. Daniel crossed himself. Chris stared, his mouth open.

Gaines signaled to the AIA officers.

"We estimate that over 150 people, all Red Deplorables, were massacred by the Antifan Defense Forces in a village near Ithaca," Vernal began. "David Harris had been living among them, according to our agent in Anacosta, to whom he gave the online photographs."

"Where is he now?" Chris asked.

Vernal said, "Our agent says Harris is in Anacosta and is working to find and recover Malia before her wedding to Commander Ma."

"Can the AIA help in any way?" Chris asked impatiently. "If we have an agent in Anacosta, surely you can do something now?"

Gaines said, "We have just démarched the Diversan government to release Malia Harris, noting that she was a US person before her kidnapping, if not a citizen, and the US has an ongoing interest in her welfare and human rights. The photographs, and the complaint about the apparent violation of the treaty have been forwarded to the Treaty Commission. I do not see how the Commission can dismiss this evidence. If the DJR has been found to violate the treaty, then we can consider further steps to call for the recovery of David and Malia Harris."

"How long will the Commission take to make a decision?" Daniel asked.

"The Commission meets twice yearly, with the next meeting to be held in Mexico City in November."

"No!" said Daniel, "By then it will be too late. The wedding is scheduled for October 30th."

"What does that matter?" said Gaines casually, "It's not a real wedding, is it? She's still married to David Harris.

"And as much as I hate to admit it, since I am a diplomat by profession, it is not diplomacy that will help you at this point, but our intelligence services. Now that the talks are stalled, and the Commission is likely to rule against the DJR, the administration has no objection to your receiving assistance from the AIA. But that is between you and the AIA and must remain secret."

Vernal nodded across the table. "If David can find Malia, we might be able to exfiltrate them from Anacosta. Come back with me to headquarters before you leave town, and we'll talk about what might be doable." She was gratified that the government would now be able to help the Harris family. Malia's kidnapping still weighed on her conscience.

"First, let's have lunch," Gaines said, to their surprise. He smiled at Rex, "and why don't you tell me about what you're studying at college? You know, we have some internships for bright young students such as yourself." As they walked down the high-ceilinged hallway to the cafeteria, Daniel, walking alongside Chris and Vernal, gazed glumly on Gaines and Rex chatting in front of them, Rex's high heels clipping briskly on the marble floors, and her tendrils of dark hair, so much like Malia's, starting to escape her professional bun. By the time the trio climbed into Vernal's self-driving van for the trip to AIA, Gaines had given Rex his business card, shaken her hand a little longer than Daniel liked seeing, and urged her to contact him.

A few hours later, Emma opened her door to find a round-faced older man with a double chin in a fedora and heavy black suit, far too heavy for the warm summer evening, on her doorstep. She didn't recognize him from the neighborhood, but he wore no armband, which was reassuring, as were his twinkling blue eyes. He wheeled a suitpod clearly labeled "Healey Vacuum Parts," so she assumed he was a salesman, and was about to gently turn him away, when he said quietly,

"I am not really a salesman. Are you Emma McArdle?"

She nodded. Nothing that happened to the Harris family was ever strange, not anymore.

"May I come in?" he asked. "Please pretend you want to look at vacuum parts."

Emma knew that Antifans kept surveillance trained on her front door, not all the time, but often enough that discretion was advised. For all she knew, they could read her lips from a distance, if not those of her visitors, whose backs were turned to surveillance.

"Yes, our vacuum is broken," she said loudly. "Perhaps you have a part we could use to fix it. It's so expensive to hire repairons these days." She ushered him in, calling Marjory to join them.

He didn't look like any of the Plores they knew. Emma wondered what the white strings hanging over his belt could be, and should she warn him that his outfit was askew? And why did he not remove his hat, when the weather was so warm? But he willingly sat on their sofa, and while he turned down the lemonade, he was happy to drink water.

Then once they were ready to hear him, he told them, "The suitpod is filled with old vacuum parts, just in case I was stopped by the police. If they interrogated me about what one does with the vacuum parts, I would be at a great loss to answer." He reached into the interior pocket of his jacket, "But here's what I was instructed to give you."

Emma extracted a black and gilt card on heavyweight stock from the white envelope he gave her.

COMMANDER KHALID MA, ANTIFAN DEFENSE FORCES, 290

INVITES YOU TO HIS WEDDING

WITH MS. MALIA JENNESS, 160,

AND CAPTAIN EXTERRA BOYD, 185

SATURDAY, OCTOBER 30, 2094 (DY 39)
4 O'CLOCK P.M. TO LATE
RECEPTION AND DINNER TO FOLLOW

THE COLLEGE OF THE EARTHLOVING PRIESTS
YARROW AVENUE, BRYN MAWR, LENILENAPE-SYLVANIA
OFFICIANT:
THE RIGHT HONORABLE ARCHBISHOP OF ANACOSTA
WITH ASSISTANCE FROM IMAM FAROUZ SHIMADI

TOTAL SECURITY WILL BE IMPOSED

"UNITED IN LOVE FOR DIVERSITY,
WE SHALL ACCOMPLISH ALL THINGS
AND DESTROY OUR ENEMIES,"
—THE BOOK OF INTERSECTIONAL JOY

Marjory gasped, and Emma flung it to the floor.

"How dare you bring this to us?" Marjory said. "Of all people, us! What is the idea?"

"My friend said you would be angry," the visitor said, "at first. But it is not an invitation for you to attend this travesty of a wedding, at least not in the traditional sense. Look on the back side."

Emma picked up the invitation and saw a smaller white envelope affixed to the back of the card. She pulled out a folded sheet of paper, covered in small handwritten notes presumably about the wedding and a map, presumably of the college itself.

"Why are you giving this to us?" Now she was curious.

"Because he said that you knew someone who would want this information, to do a good deed, but my friend had no idea how to reach him. He thought that if anyone knew how to find this person, you would. He told me nothing else. I don't live around here, I live in South Rockville, and I have a long journey home from here."

"Who is your friend?" Marjory asked. South Rockville and Arlington Plorevilles rarely intersected, and she realized that this stranger had no idea who the Harrises were, or whom he was visiting. Or he was putting on an excellent act.

"I am not at liberty to say, but he is a good man, and believes in God. His conscience troubles him in the work he does, and that is all I will tell you." His round face shone with sweat in the heat. "You can trust him, but he will understand if you cannot give it to the intended recipient."

A few minutes later, Rabbi Goldberg was back on the sidewalk, where he slowly extracted his billfold, deliberately, ostentatiously counting its contents, as if he were pleased to have made a good sale to these ladies in need of vacuum parts. Just in case an Antifan surveillant was tracking his movements. Then he trudged off, wheeling the suitpod toward the bus, which would take him to the tunnel. From the Kennedy Center depot at which Marjory had met Jeff Welcome last year, he would board another bus whose last stop was near his house. A trip that might have taken an hour by car would take almost three hours by enforced public transportation.

Rabbi Goldberg might have saved himself a great deal of time had he known the intended recipient of the wedding information was living only seven blocks away from the rabbi's home, in a boardinghouse favored by itinerant working Plores.

Chapter 48
Reunions
(Wednesday, July 28, 2094)

Malia awoke late, around eleven, and pushed a button. Five minutes later, the robot emerged from the delivery elevator with her breakfast tray, and deposited it on the small bistro table near the window. Whirring softly, it retreated back into the elevator. The elevator door closed. Malia leaned back on her pillows and shut her eyes again.

Malia knew she was alone in the house, other than the Plore cook with whom Paragon had forbidden contact and, on some days, renovation and painting crews. Thus the robot servant—the latest technology—had been installed, since to Paragon's irritation, the ADF had failed to deliver an appropriate low Social Credit servant. Nobody suitable for the job was eligible to take self-driving cars to the remote location and Diversity buses came nowhere near Potowmack Boulevard. The Plore cook rode the bus to the house each morning with the bricklayers. On Sundays Malia suffered because one of the Antifan guards prepared her meals, including one day even a horrid quinoa paste sandwich.

During the day, Malia was forbidden from leaving her suite, although no one, let alone Paragon, had explicitly told her this. When she had tried the door handle on her first morning in the house, two weeks ago, she found the door was locked despite her jiggles. But after the workers left for the day, the door mysteriously unlocked, and she was free to venture elsewhere in the house. Except that several Antifans were guarding the house at night and they camped out in the unfinished living room among the white-draped furniture. When she came upon a black-clad foursome lounging on their bedrolls, laughing coarsely among themselves, they looked at her, appraisingly, almost insolently. Her status as Paragon's intended bride—or at least one of them—did not seem to impress them unduly. She knew they were there to keep her from leaving as much as they were there to protect her or Paragon's house. One soldier was always standing guard underneath her window.

"Lady Paragon," one said, "it might be best if you stayed upstairs."

"I need some fresh air," she said, moving toward the front porch she had admired on that first day. She was not afraid of them, not anymore, not after that nightmare in the Beaufort basement. They did not stop her, but two of the soldiers accompanied her outside and sat on the steps a few feet away from her while she breathed the cool night air. When she finally came back inside, they followed.

She fled back to the suite, which at least had a large viewing screen, and various exercise equipment. She had complete access to the GVN. But she was a prisoner, even more isolated than when she had occupied a Beaufort cell, where at least she could hear the murmurs of the guards, or undergo interrogations, or host Exterra's visits. The sumptuousness of her surroundings had varied, and her Social Credit score had risen to support the pretense that she was willingly in Anacosta, but she had always been a prisoner. The "Malia's Social Credit Corner" column continued to run in the *Anacosta Post*, but Malia hadn't seen a draft in several weeks. Presumably the Knowledge Tower found it easier to produce the column without her.

Paragon and Exterra were still living at the Avalon, and she had not seen either for several weeks. She glimpsed them in the gossip news feed occasionally, attending a gallery opening or the Celebration of Total Vaccination when the truth serum campaign reached the goal of 95 percent of adult Anacostans inoculated. She read a short news item that Paragon had traveled to Las Vegas to meet some Chinese associates. Las Vegas was on the border with the United States, and its casinos and brothels were maintained for select foreign visitors, mostly Asians, but also rich Americans herded across and back in carefully monitored tour groups.

One day costumers came to the house to fit her for what they called her wedding gown. It was long and black, but edged in gold, and featured an anarchist symbol, also in gold leaf, on the front and back.

"Beautiful," enthused the lead costumer, a sharp-faced middle-aged woman. "Not in a lookist way, of course, but as a symbol of our love for Diversity."

Like a crow, Malia silently retorted. But even a crow chooses where it may fly. Each day, when she stared out her picture window, to which she had dragged an armchair, she saw the brick wall rising around her. The section nearest her was five feet high. If she were standing before it today, she would just barely be able to peek over it. In another week, it would be a foot higher, she knew. Panic swelled within her chest at the thought of the prison growing steadily around her, like waves above a capsizing boat. She had not panicked in the Beaufort execution hallway, but here she felt even more desperate. She clasped her hands together in prayer, and then sat on the floor to meditate, which gave her comfort.

The Plore cook regaled the bricklayers with descriptions of the interior of the house while they waited for the van to pick them up one morning. A squat, rawboned woman of about seventy, she had beefy hands herself, muscled with the wielding of the cast-iron skillet and the metal whisks of her trade. She had retired a few years ago from the kitchen of the restaurant in the Azteca Tower—"I'm really good at burritos," she bragged, "not that I was supposed to be making them, not being Spanish"—but then her grandson had been severely injured in a construction accident, and she needed to return to labor for their household to continue receiving the minimum income check from the government.

"And then the kitchen has a dumbwaiter—that's what we used to call them, before they forbade that word—which the robot rides up to the lady's room. I put the meals on a tray and the robot brings it to her."

The brown-haired man with the short beard and golden-brown eyes listened intently. The cook liked him, because she had a fancy for well-spoken handsome men, even if it was no longer reciprocated, and this gentleman treated her respectfully. He reminded her of the son who had died a few years ago.

"How tall is the dumbwaiter?" he asked. "How do you operate it?"

"Oh, it's between five and six feet tall," the cook responded. "This robot is programmed to visit the lady with her meals at eleven a.m. and five p.m., and it leaves extra for snacking. That's her schedule, she's not an early riser."

David chuckled to himself, knowing this all too well.

"So when the robot enters the dumbwaiter, and the time comes, the elevator takes it upstairs automatically. The robot puts the old tray inside its shelf, puts down the new one, and goes back downstairs. It's the latest technology. Before I leave, I make sure the supper is prepared."

"You've never seen the lady yourself?"

"No, no, it's forbidden. She mustn't associate with us Plores, says the Paragon. She's all alone in that room, locked in during the day. Maybe she comes out at night when none of us workers are around, but then the soldiers are watching."

"Does she eat the food you make for her?" David wondered whether he could gauge Malia's state of mind from her appetite.

"What do you think?" the woman demanded indignantly. "Fifty-five years of cooking in Kentucky, and then Anacosta, in kitchens all over, and you think she wouldn't eat my food?"

"No, I'm sorry," David said gently. "Of course, your food is good. I just think if she's all alone in that room maybe she doesn't want to eat. Maybe she's sad."

"Sometimes she doesn't finish her meals," admitted the cook. "I try my best, I feel sorry for her." The van pulled up.

David exchanged looks with Seth and Tom.

The pair had shown up one night last week at David's boardinghouse in Rockville. He had been lying on the thin cot in his narrow room with the crack along the wall, metal folding chair, and cheap wooden dresser, a castoff from some City sale. He would read his phone until he felt sleepy, then go down the hall to the washroom, and turn off the light by ten. All in all, he would have rather lounged in the more comfortable parlor, but he tried to keep to himself and maintain a low profile, since there were always boarders, especially the few women, primed to gossip and flirtation, who might easily create "a business."

A knock on the door. David tensed, but the landlady called out, "Mr. Smith? You have friends downstairs." Who could this be, he wondered, maybe Warren Welcome coming to warn him of something? She would not have said "friends" if they were police, and police would not have waited politely downstairs, not with a hardened criminal such as himself. He pulled on his shirt and with some trepidation went downstairs.

"Oh man!" he said when he saw them, shaking his head, a wide smile spreading across his face like sunshine after rain. Seth and Tom laughed happily at his surprise. They embraced him as if they were long lost brothers. "Old kameraten," he said sideways to the landlady.

They couldn't talk in the parlor, not with the suspicious bald electrician in the corner reading his phone and two women in the window seat giggling about something. "Let's take a walk," David suggested, "and catch up." The summer sun was setting, and children were finishing their play as the trio strode through the neighborhood, avoiding the main avenues where police and sometimes Antifans were posted.

"We had to come and help," explained Seth. "Nothing's doing up in Cayuga now," by which David knew he meant "the resistance."

"We kept wondering what was going on with you," Tom chimed in. "And you got to need some help. We see that wedding is still on."

"And it shouldn't be," declared Seth.

"Since you mention it," said David, "I was planning to attend the wedding. I'm sure they wouldn't mind a few extra guests." Let any casual listener think they were discussing the nuptials of an ex-girlfriend. "Where are you staying?"

"Nowhere yet," said Tom. "We just came from seeing your friend in Arlington. You think your place has room for us?"

When they returned to the boardinghouse, they immediately sought out the landlady.

"I have one extra room you two can share—I'll pull in a mattress and some blankets. It's $220 a week for the room, payable up front. When another room opens up, one of you's gotta take that, I'm only letting you share because there's nothing else and you know Mr. Smith. What kind of work do you do? You gotta work, I'm not taking loafers."

"They're bricklayers too," said David. "And they'll be working tomorrow morning with me. Our boss is desperate for help."

The landlady nodded, satisfied so far. Tom was a builder by trade, and it was easy to see him as a bricklayer. Seth she wasn't too sure about but he didn't look citified. "And you're from this containment area? You're not here illegally?"

"Not at all, ma'am," said Tom reassuringly. "Look, here is my card and my kamrat will show you his too." Warren Welcome had given Tom and Seth the identification cards they would need to survive in Anacosta, and new phones whose records matched their official data.

"That's all right," said the landlady, "If Mr. Smith vouches for you, that's enough."

They were also armed, having resolved that it was worth risking capital punishment to help their friend. In the night, David showed them the underground cache he had dug where he hid his weapon, encased in a cloth bag, and the two Plores placed theirs in the basement hole too. They swore fealty to each other over the hole, not that the gesture was really necessary, but it reassured them that the final act was beginning and they were doing something important.

A week later, the opportunity came. The crew chief broke up the bricklayer squad into smaller units dispatched to different parts of the wall, now six feet high. David, Tom, Seth, and another man were working on the section closest to the main entrance of the property. Three stood on ladders, methodically laying cement on the bricks and then placing bricks from a six-foot-high hoisted basket onto the cement. The fourth refilled baskets with bricks and vats of cement, and then cranked them up to the men laying the bricks. Every hour or so they switched with him.

It was close to 4:00 p.m. David was stationed on the ground. The fourth in their group, a weathered man in his midfifties, was humming to himself as he listened to music from his earpods while laying the bricks. He kept to himself, which the trio preferred, so they always asked him to join them when the crew was divided into smaller squads. Some of the other men were chattier, and possibly nosier. You could never tell who might be an informant, but David hazarded that a real informant would be more attentive to their conversation than was this worker immersed in his music all day.

The grocery delivery truck showed up on schedule. Seth shouted down to him, "Quicksnatch!" a Plore slang term which meant nothing related to bricks, except it was their code indicating that he had seen the van approaching over the wall. David sprinted over to the gap in the wall. The Antifan guards would already have checked the driver's credentials about two hundred feet closer to the main road, from the little guardhouse shack.

The small two-axle box truck lumbered by at the requested fifteen miles per hour. David, lurking behind the edge of the brick wall near the roadway, recognized the painted slogan, "Virtue Foods, Owned by the City of Anacosta." He instantly leaped onto the back of the truck, plastering himself face front against the metal doors and clutching onto the metal lever, careful not to pull it down and release the door. The doors were black, and David had worn black jeans and T-shirt that day to avoid standing out against the truck. The truck continued jolting up the driveway, giving David confidence he had not been seen. He could not have risked running the hundred yards between his brick duties and the house—the Antifan sniper posted on the roof would have detected him immediately. As it was, David had had to gamble that the sniper would not have been training his sights in the direction of the main entrance when he leaped onto the truck, but he knew one sniper could not be looking everywhere at once.

The truck curled up next to the kitchen entrance, and the Plore cook came out, wiping her hands on the apron, to receive the deliveries. She did not show surprise to see David. "Good," she said, "Help me bring in the groceries." The driver normally would unload the boxes and bags next to the entrance, leaving the elderly woman to carry them in herself. He was on a tight schedule and if he didn't complete the run in time, they would dock his pay. Since the woman didn't seem alarmed by David, the driver decided not to worry either, and quickly resumed his journey.

David brought in the last heavy box, silently lest the Antifan guard at the foot of the staircase hear his voice. The cook indicated with her elbow the dumbwaiter. She pressed the lowest brown button on the right of the device, and the doors opened. In a few seconds, David had inserted himself inside the box, and then she closed the door. He had paid the cook a handsome sum to let him make the ascent, after he vowed that the lady in the room upstairs loved him, and whatever happened, he would swear secrecy on the cook's role, pretending he had deceived her.

"How would you know the Paragon's lady?" she demanded when he followed her home one afternoon, offering the money if she would only look the other way and let him help her bring the groceries into the house, which was welcome assistance, money aside, what with her aching joints. And she desperately needed the money, what with the electric bill sharply higher due to the Treasure Earthly Resources campaign that had just been imposed on Ploreville, and which in practice meant a steep hike in utilities. The treaty did not forbid charging Plores exorbitant sums for utilities. Many Plores were now doing without electricity except at stated evening hours, which during the hot Anacosta summers meant homes became brutal heat boxes. Plore families were sleeping on roofs and in parks, like in the very old days, well before the DJR.

"I was the gardener's assistant when we were kids growing up together," he lied, "when she was at the orphanage. We spoke true to each other, but then she went to college, and I stayed behind."

"Spoke true to each other" was Plore lingo for "pledging troth." That was a plausible story, by Plore standards, and the cook was touched at the thought of the teenage romance. She knew from the media stories that the Paragon's lady had grown up in an orphanage. And the cook trusted David, perhaps because of that dead son he resembled, who had been a kind and religious man.

"Here's the $200 I promised you. We must keep this a secret."

Malia was meditating, once again, on the red eco–yoga mat. "Ommm…" she chanted. "Om, om, om…" She was visualizing herself in the Hickory Hills, where she and David had hiked, David carrying Emmett on his back. She zoomed in mentally on an anthill she recalled, taking the time to draw in her mind's eye the pattern of red ants scurrying around, each programmed with its own task to serve their queen. She thrust away a disturbing thought that these red ants swarmed in Anacosta, serving Paragon and the other Social Crediteers. When she reached that exquisite moment at which she forgot she was in this yellow prison in Anacosta, she heard a strange set of thumps in the background.

Startled out of her reverie, she scrambled to her feet. At first, she feared that Paragon might be visiting, and was moving around on the other side of the wall separating their suites. Or possibly workmen? But she would have heard their voices, and their tramping up the broad staircase, at the bottom of which the Antifan soldier stood guard. She looked wildly around. Then she heard a deep, familiar voice on the other side of the dumbwaiter.

"Malia? Malia?"

"Oh my God!" She ran over to the dumbwaiter and pressed the manual release button.

And there standing before her was her husband, her David. His hair was brown, and his eyes were a strange hazel-green, but it was her David, wearing all black, covered with dust from his day of labor. They had been separated almost a year ago now.

"Don't faint," he grinned at her, stepping forth from the dumbwaiter and encircling her in his arms. "So I'm a little late." He stepped back, inspected the room quickly for surveillance devices, and saw none, while she stared open-mouthed at him, crying and smiling at once. She turned on the TV for background noise to mask their conversation, and he asked, "Where's your armband?" She reassured him that no armband was spying on her—Paragon gave her one on the rare occasions when she was permitted to leave the compound. She could not make phone calls without one, though, so she was indeed a prisoner.

They said nothing for close to a minute, hugging as they both silently cried. Then, in a hushed voice, David said, "I hope you never doubted I'd come rescue you."

"Today?" she whispered, knowing how close the guard stood to her room. "How?"

He hated to disappoint her. "Not yet," he said, flinching at her crestfallen face. "But now you know that sick wedding will not take place, or at least it will not succeed. I am here in Anacosta, I have friends who will help, and if we have to kidnap you from that accursed college, and die doing it, we will do it. Not that I plan on any of us dying.

"Remember I once told you, do you think I would not have a plan? Haven't I always told you that I always have a plan?"

She nodded, remembering when he had first outlined for her in virtually those same words, five years ago, how they would find and recover her daughter.

"It is better that you don't know what the plan will be," said David, but he didn't want to admit to her that he himself wasn't sure what the plan was. Their lips met and they kissed deeply, tenderly, again and again.

"Oh my God," she said. She asked about Rex, and David told her quickly how he had confronted them in the airport and brought Rex home, where she was continuing her studies. A flood of relief washed over Malia.

Her hands roamed over him, as if she still could not believe he stood before her in the flesh. They finally drew apart. "They told me you had died in Oklahoma," she said, "in the raid. Until recently, when Paragon admitted you had survived, I thought you were dead and I was alone." He drew her into his embrace again.

"We need to be able to communicate," said David. "I can send messages to you through the cook, but not often. She's a good woman, but won't take too many risks. She thinks we met at your orphanage when I worked on the gardening crew. That's the story, just in case you actually talk to her."

"I have an idea. I'll start writing my newspaper column again. It's a twice a week column. They took it away from me, but I can get it back. If you read the first letter of every other paragraph, in reverse order from the bottom, it will be a message to you. I can't promise this will work, but you can access that column, right?"

"Yes, in the *Anacosta Compost*," said David wryly. "It's very painful to read. Did you really write that balagan?" "Balagan" was a Plore word that meant nonsense, but it was widely understood.

"Yes and no. They always edited it a lot to get the right level of wokeness. It's hard to sound that stupid, so I was at a disadvantage. But I'll try to be so woke that they won't have to edit it and mess up my messages."

She told him, before he had to ask about Paragon, about the movie. Just in case he were captured and found himself watching it at Beaufort, he should never doubt her loyalty. She had been tricked, she told him. David grimaced, whether because of the lurid details, or the ever-present reality that he might still die horribly at Beaufort, or the confession she had slept with Paragon, or all three. Not that the last surprised him. If anything, he had envisioned them in near-constant lovemaking, so this was a partial relief. And he would not say anything about Lucy, not yet.

"I have to go," David said, hating himself for not leaping from the window with Malia in his arms and leaving the whole cursed building behind them. But they would be mowed down in seconds if he gave in to that impulse. "Send only the most important messages, not in every column. Because we are taking great risks by doing this at all."

They embraced one last time, for now. "I love you," she said, her natural reticence blown away by David's powerful demonstration of loyalty to her. Who else would have dared come to her here? In a cramped dumbwaiter?

"I will always love you," he said, "and we will escape this evil place and be back in Oklahoma soon with our sons. Our plan is in motion."

"I know we will do it," Malia responded, whispering. "I will keep praying."

In a half minute he was back, half-crouched, in the dumbwaiter, and Malia sent him downstairs. She sank down onto her knees on the yoga mat, overcome by the great proof of God's love for them, that He had enabled this reunion, even if it were their last.

The Plore cook, hearing the thud of the machine landing in the corner of the kitchen, released David from the box. He saw Malia's supper on the counter—a pasta verdicchio, a small salad, a white dinner roll, a slice of chocolate cake. A glass of white wine. A bag of pretzels, perhaps for a bedtime snack. The robot stood serenely in another corner, waiting for its assignment. The cook loaded the meal into the robot, and it waddled into the dumbwaiter. David watched with amazement.

It was the end of the workday, and the pair walked down the driveway together, calmly, toward the vans. David returned to his workmates just as they were finishing for the day, and only the fourth man gave him a peculiar look. "They called him away to the house," explained Tom, to which the music-loving bricklayer only grunted.

The cook had planned to tell any who confronted them that she had asked the crew chief to spare the worker, with his technical knowledge, to help her repair the coldbox that seemed to not be working very well. The shift change at three o'clock meant no Antifan on the new shift would wonder how he had accessed the building. The Antifans, who recognized her, figured the workman next to her must have been attending to something in the kitchen. A drywall crew was laboring in the hallway, so the guards might possibly just have assumed this man was from the crew. To them, most Plores looked alike.

As the van headed back to Rockville, David wished he really did have a plan, as he had reassured Malia. All he had were the notes and invitation that his mother had sent him via Welcome. And a few vague ideas that needed to gel sooner rather than later. He was grateful for Tom and Seth's presence, but he didn't want to throw their lives away in a futile rescue attempt either.

Chapter 49
Working Woman
(Sunday, August 8, 2094)

"Happy anniversary, Malia," Paragon greeted her as he entered her suite, unannounced, but not entirely unwelcome, at twilight, after the summer sun had mostly set. She hoped to gain some information that she could convey to David as promised. For that, she needed her column back, and for that, she needed to appeal to Paragon. She had begun to fear that Paragon might not even appear until just before their wedding, rendering the whole column communication effort worthless. And even if it were Paragon, she was relieved to have some company after weeks of unrelenting tedium, except for David's own visit, the thrill of which had begun to fade as she realized that here she was, still a prisoner.

Malia looked at him uncomprehendingly, because she knew her wedding anniversary was October 9. She had undressed early, and was wearing her pink bathrobe prior to taking a long eco-bubble bath, one of her few pleasures. He was in black slacks and a black jacket with a blue buttoned shirt underneath; he was never a casual dresser, she had learned.

"Surely you must remember the momentous occasion a year ago tonight that brought you back home?"

I hate you, she thought, realizing with a great jolt of sadness that she had not seen her sons in over a year, and likely neither could remember her now. Only the memory of David standing in this room a few days ago kept her from screaming with despair. Now she had hope, but hope also fueled her revulsion and hate.

"Yes," she murmured, her eyes lowered, because otherwise he would see her anger, "so much has happened since then."

"Indeed...here you are, not just back in the DJR, no longer a menial 70-point apartment servant, but about to become the wife of the most powerful man in the country. A remarkable ascent. And everyone thinks you have now embraced Diversity."

"I didn't realize a coup had happened this week," she retorted acidly, "and you were now in charge. Nobody tells me anything here."

He laughed, almost genially. "You may be right about the coup. I'll tell you later. First, let's have dinner." He called out, and two Antifan guards brought in a trolley with covered platters. They covered the small round table with a snowy tablecloth, then laid on it a small red rose in a glass vase, china, silverware, and linen napkins, before saluting Paragon and withdrawing. The tureens and platters remained on the adjoining trolley.

"Let me change into something respectable," she said, heading into her closet. She placed the bubble bath container on the dresser and scanned the rack.

"I don't see the need," he responded, but followed her into the closet. He picked a yellow ankle-length sheath with a zippered front. "Yellow's a good color for you." He watched her dress.

As they sat at the table, Paragon lifted the silver domes and inspected the dishes underneath each. He introduced each ladleful, "Chicken curry, non–culturally appropriative. Steak au poivre, non-appropriative. Not that I worry about the French. Sautéed spinach." He poured the red wine, not Diversity-grown, into their glasses. "We must toast to your anniversary of liberation."

Malia reluctantly drank to her kidnapping. She needed to turn the conversation around to the wedding. Fortunately, it was entirely plausible that a bride might want to learn more about her wedding, especially less than three months before the event that she had barely been notified about. "Shouldn't we talk about the wedding?" she asked.

"Why? Everything is planned. You have your gown, right?"

"Aren't we going to have to rehearse?"

"We'll go up to Lenilenape a few days before the ceremony. That will be plenty of time. You just need to do what you're told—the priests will direct you."

"Is it ridiculous for me to be curious about a wedding in which I happen to be the bride? Or *a* bride?"

"Very well, what do you want to know, my fascist sweetheart?" Paragon smiled loftily at Malia.

He relayed to her the details of the ceremony, beginning with the loathsome movie, and culminating in the cup ceremony in which the bridal trio would drain their goblets in unison. "Mine will contain juice but yours can contain wine, which will come from grapes cultivated by Diverse hands at our finest vineyard." Then the archbishop of Anacosta and chief imam would proclaim them married "under the brow of our Great Earth Mother," and a giant projection of Her visage would rise behind them, ending the ceremony.

"What about our security? I haven't been outside Anacosta since I…returned here. I heard that there was a robbery on 81 a week or two ago. Are the roads safe?" She was careful to use the word "robbery" so she would not imply any political motives, and thus remind Paragon that Malia might well be hoping for a last-minute rescue.

"How do you know about that?" Paragon quizzed her, his air of superiority jarred.

"I heard the guards discussing it downstairs a few nights ago," she said. It might just have been a strong-arm robbery in which a band of desperate Plores stopped a self-driving car and accosted the couple, hoping for some valuables, even just food. But since Social Crediteers did not carry cash, and it would be difficult to pawn any jewelry or electronics belonging to the couple, even in Ploreville, it was possible the attack was a politically motivated strike. The masked bandits had roughed up the man and woman and vanished into the night with little loot.

"The roads are completely safe," Paragon assured her, reminding himself to ensure a sufficient number of vehicles and protectors guarded their wedding convoy to Lenilenape. "Pay no attention to baseless rumors.

"And don't get your hopes up about any last-minute rescue at the college. We have unprecedented security in three rings around the College of the Earthloving Priests. No Plores will be permitted within the rings. We have complete control of the skies above the college, thanks to our drone fleet. If David Harris tries to rescue you, he will be killed instantly. I almost hope he tries."

"I am resigned to becoming your wife," said Malia, "or one of them. I was not always happy in Oklahoma, I must confess." She was inching her way toward mollifying Paragon, the better to ask him to restore her column.

"Of course not," said Paragon. "What a desolate wasteland. I saw it for myself on Beltane last year, when you failed to appear as ordered. Very materialistic and shallow. Obsessed with hypermasculine sport. And I'm sure he could not satisfy you in the way a real Antifan can."

She ignored that comment, and asked him about her column. "Seriously, I'm terribly bored. Remember, I did graduate from Justice—on campus—with a degree in knowledge management. Can't I use it for Diversity?"

"Let the Knowledge Tower write it. It's really beneath you. I thought you'd be grateful I reassigned it to the Tower. Why do you want to bother with that nonsense?"

"Because," she pouted, "I'm lonely and bored and I'd like something to do. And readers like it. I was getting lots of fan mail."

"Fine. Now that I think about it, maybe you can write some columns about the need to inoculate children with the truth serum. We're getting some holdouts, and I don't want to send them all to incubation farms, it's not economically viable. We've threatened the parents with loss of Social Credit status, but some don't seem to care. They just swallow the disinformation about strokes and paralysis. You can be helpful to me here. We'll give you information and you can write it up."

"Is it true?" she asked him.

"Our information? Well, it's true to the narrative, my dear Malia. So what if a few hundred people have bad reactions? Either they'll get better, or we'll send them to the Euthanasia Palace. But I don't want it getting out that we've been sending children to the Euthanasia Palace, that will only make the parents more stubborn still.

"Look, do you want the column back or not?"

"Yes, thank you, Khalid. It will give me something productive to do."

"Good. Now in return, you can do something productive for me."

Damn, he's got me. I need this column.

He led her into the dark cave of his bedroom adjoining her suite, switching on the lights with a wave of the hand. She was already familiar with the suite, which was several times the size of hers. When a cleaning crew came to clean her room twice a week, the guard would usher her into Paragon's suite to prevent her from mingling with the Plores. "Lady Ma, this way please." They were scrupulously respectful, at least in daytime.

The first time they confined her in Paragon's suite, she had stepped into the lower level, a brown-carpeted living room area with sofas and armchairs and metal-trimmed glass tables, perhaps for him to entertain close friends. The door closed behind her, firmly. A large TV screen hung above a credenza on her right. A kitchenette lay ahead on the other side of the room.

Then to her left, she saw a short wide flight of carpeted stairs leading to a spacious bedroom area under a giant skylight. The suite was otherwise windowless. She climbed up the stairs, almost as a petitioner approaching a throne, looking around at the massive walnut furniture. The drawers were mostly empty, as was the walk-in closet that was almost the size of her bedroom. On the other side of the room was a door that she assumed must lead to Exterra's suite; she opened it and explored the room. It was a mirror image of her own, but the window looked out toward the City rather than to the Potowmack, and it boasted a small terrace. No sign indicated that Exterra had ever visited the room let alone slept there.

She returned to Paragon's quarters, climbed onto the great bed covered in a pattern of round earth symbols, and reached for the signaler that commanded the skylight covers. Paragon had a choice of designs, ranging from stars and planets to abstract patterns, Chinese paintings and erotica, and then finally, a photograph of a youngish woman in a turban with haunting dark kohl-rimmed eyes. Malia lay on her back, staring at the photo above. A former partner? Or was this the mysterious sister in China whom Paragon refused to discuss? She didn't look Chinese at all.

"Lady Ma," said the Antifan at the foot of the bed. She had fallen asleep under the mysterious gaze. "Your room is ready again." Presumably he would not chastise her for sleeping on the Great Paragon's bed, when he must have assumed she was accustomed to lying in it. She quickly scrambled off the bed, switching the skylight to its default open window, through which the sun was shining.

They undressed, Paragon removing his armband and placing it on the mahogany dresser. He unzipped her dress in one sharp movement, and had her step out of it, and she then allowed him to press himself against her. His mouth trapped hers, and his tongue plunged into her mouth. She kept her eyes closed so that he would not see her hatred.

"The bed," he said, as he steered her to its vast expanse and pushed her down on it. They crawled awkwardly to the center, where she wrapped her legs around his back at his command and he did what he wanted.

He took her a second time, more leisurely, but still, his hands this time were more driven by his excitement and curiosity than hers. But Malia liked that, because it put her under no obligation to confess that he had pleased her. Finally, she lay in his arms against the soft large luxury eco-pillows. The sky loomed large above them, since he liked sex under skylights. This skylight was larger than the one at the Avalon. It was relatively dark in this quiet corner of Anacosta. Hundreds, thousands of years ago, his nomadic forebears had copulated under open skies in the Gobi Desert, or in their grass yurts through which glints of moonlight darted to stripe a breast or a backside.

"Am I a better lover than your fascist Plore?"

No, she wished she could spit out at him. Instead, she looked at him coyly, pretending at embarrassment. "Oh, I don't know," she giggled. "Maybe a little."

"The College of the Priests is quite beautiful," he said, his arm curling around her back and his hand playing with a long breast. He lifted it and raised it to his mouth, as she whimpered. "Part of it was donated by a racist plutocrat, Rockefeller. It used to be a college for elite women, and it trained many devoted activists for Diversity. When the revolution was won, we took the college from them and made it a college for our priests. But they were happy to give it to us, I understand."

"I'm a little frightened to be leaving Anacosta," Malia lied. "I feel safe here, behind these walls."

"I knew you would," he said. "That's why I had them built, for you. But you will travel in an armed convoy and the entire college is at our disposal. Only Social Crediteers will be allowed within the security rings and, in the final week, no one will be able to stay within the inner ring unless they are connected with our wedding or are priests at the College."

An armed convoy, she thought. In his few minutes with her, David had hinted of growing Plore unrest to the north, and his involvement in inciting it, but she would not have imagined it would have reached the point at which Paragon might fear it would strike against him personally.

"I suppose it will be impossible for my husband to rescue me from my wedding," she teased him, dangerously.

His dark eyes narrowed at her, causing her to briefly fear she might have aroused his suspicions.

"We control the skies around Lenilenape with our drone fleet, and the ground, of course. Every vehicle entering the grounds will be searched and sniffed by dogs. Your traitor husband, wherever he is, will get nowhere near our wedding." Paragon wondered where David Harris had gone. Since the ADF had destroyed the rebellious clusters in the Cayuga region, authorities had detected no sign of Harris. If Harris was planning to infiltrate the college, defying hundreds of armed Antifans to rescue Malia, he was welcome to sacrifice his life doing so.

"Maybe I shouldn't be telling you this. This is tightly held information."

"Khalid, who I am going to tell? The guard downstairs? The robot?"

"Fair enough, you've convinced me," he laughed, pulling her back under him. Rain began to spatter on the skylight.

Afterward, he took the signaler and switched among various channels, Malia noting he flipped quickly past movies, preferring the news. "Look," he said, stopping at Diversity News Tonight, "the children who have been moved to our new children's village in Delaware. We are opening them all over the country. Children who graduate from the village will be offered choice slots at our finest universities, and be guaranteed a good future. We have terminated the rights of the parents and the state will be their parent."

"Aren't the parents reluctant to give them up?"

"Yes, if they are backward. This first crop is coming from the children of parents who have failed their truth serum tests. We now know they are secret fascists. If they wish to avoid Beaufort, or the incubation farm, we give them this choice. Most are happy to cooperate."

Thanks for reminding me why I hate you, she thought. You people have taken all my children from me too.

"The plan is to eventually make collective child production and rearing the norm. Our birthrates have been going down; I suppose that's the price of realizing that parenthood simply passes on privilege in most societies. The solution is to industrialize the production of citizens. We will supply DNA-laden sperm and egg matter to grow the children in factories. We can probably just pay Plore women to be the surrogates—we do that already for our New Women and gay citizens, but not on an industrial basis. I envision huge factories, full of Plore women bearing Social Credit babies. Maybe we will open it to low social credit women, give them a point boost for a few years if they show dedication to birthing for the collective." He sounded pleased with his own ingenuity.

Malia wondered whether this plan was fully in motion, or Paragon was just confiding his depraved ambitions to her. "Are you already doing this?"

"Once our wedding is over, I will have a freer hand."

The following Thursday, David scrolled down the *Anacosta Post* as the van headed back to Rockville from the work site. It comforted him to occasionally look in the direction of the house as he worked, knowing Malia was perhaps reciprocating his gaze, yet it was agonizing to still not know how he would engineer her rescue. So close, yet still so far away. When approached, Warren Welcome had confessed he had no ideas. "They won't permit Plores in the vicinity of the college that week—otherwise we could infiltrate through the serving or the work crews. Everyone will be vetted very carefully.

I will see if we can do anything, but I am not optimistic."

The walls now reached seven feet high, but Paragon had decreed they must rise to twenty feet. Heavy equipment was being brought in to facilitate the work at greater heights.

"We'll be working through Christmas," enthused one of the men. Steady labor was welcome as the government placed Plore food rations and utilities under pressure. These workers knew they would be able to buy gifts for their children and even a cardboard tree—it was forbidden to kill a tree to decorate a home for the heretical holiday and all but essential use of plastic was banned.

David ignored the jouncing of the bus and the banter of his colleagues, as he found Malia's column and checked the first letters of alternative paragraphs, his eyes laboriously trailing up the column's paragraphs.

"THREE RNGS SECRITY"

Chapter 50
Check And Checkmate
(Thursday, September 9, 2094)

Steve regretted having accepted Paragon's invitation to visit the Resolution Command. As deputy director, he knew he should have been gratified to hear about the various operations the command carried out across the continent and the world. Although some of these efforts seemed unsavory and maybe even pointlessly sadistic, Steve conceded it was better for the ADF to be on the offensive rather on the receiving end of other countries' tricks. The US president probably had no idea what was causing his constant headaches; several billionaires had disappeared in succession, with none realizing the kidnappers to which they paid ransom worked for the cash-strapped DJR; and the eager Diversity Movements in various US cities reported to Beaufort, and received funds and training in political organization in return.

"Very impressive, Khalid," Steve said, when the tour had ended, and he was finally sitting opposite Paragon's desk. Steve was conscious that his chair was a few inches lower than Paragon's, and he instantly realized he had fallen for one of the oldest tricks in the book. I'll give him a few more minutes, and then I'll excuse myself. "Nice vase you've got there. Chinese?"

"Thank you, Steve," said Paragon formally. "Yes, a gift from our grateful friends in the People's Republic." He would never mention his family here. Not that they were coming to the wedding, nor would he have invited them with the movie he planned to show and the double brides. Maybe in accordance with Chinese tradition, Malia should have been the wife, and that annoying Exterra only the concubine, but it was too late now. And the ghost of Patigul stood between him and his mother, even now, widening a gap between them with the years. His mother only thought he had not protected his sister, which was bad enough, but Paragon knew how much worse the truth was, and that he could never share it with her.

"I don't want to keep you much longer, Steve, you've been very generous with your time this morning. But I did want to run some other business by you." Paragon reached for a large manila envelope to his right, checked its contents, and then passed it across the desk to Steve. "Can you explain what these are?"

Steve opened the folder calmly, but Paragon took pleasure in the deputy director's almost instantaneous flush and shaking hands.

"Taken in Rockville over the last ten months," Paragon said. "You seem to visit this Plore house quite often."

"How dare you? What business is it of yours that I have some Plore friends? It's not illegal."

"No," Paragon said a touch regretfully, "in of itself, not technically illegal. Not that it looks good for a senior ADF officer to socialize with Plores. But don't you know that the house is occupied by active Jewish Zionists?"

"They are Jewish. And so what? Plores are not forbidden to worship according to their traditional faiths."

"No, *they* are not." Paragon let that pronoun sink in.

"Are you accusing me of engaging in illegal worship?"

"Of heresy, Steve. You've been engaging in Jewish religious rituals for at least the last year, and maybe much longer."

"Only Christian proselytization is banned."

"Steve, if you had bothered to read the Basic Law in question…" Khalid pulled up the Basic Law on his workscreen, which he had prepared in advance. "It says, 'Social Credit citizens must conduct all worship in Mother Earth Diversity settings. Worship in a MED Christian, Jewish, Hindu, Muslim, or other branch is permitted as long as the officiating priest is an affiliate of the DJR Priestly Convocation.'" Harris had been allowed to skirt this rule by claiming to be accompanying his mother to church, but such tolerance had evaporated in the wake of his escape.

Paragon allowed himself a touch of humor. "I doubt your rabbi is a graduate of the College of the Priests."

"You have no proof that I engaged in illegal worship, only that I visited this house to see my friends."

"Steve, would I leave such details unchecked?" Paragon tapped a button, and to his horror, Steve recognized the sounds of the Shabbat worship at Rabbi Goldberg's, with the two dozen men mumbling prayers at their own individual pace, so it sounded like a pebbly oceanic roar.

"So they're worshiping. What does that have to do with me?"

"Patience, Steve." A few seconds later, he heard himself invited to deliver the morning's d'var Torah, or Torah lesson, and listened to his own thoughtful commentary on Abraham's sending of Ishmael and his mother, Hagar, into the wilderness. He had been proud of that talk—it proved that even after all these years, he was capable of more than shooting a firearm or wielding a baton. He only regretted having to keep this triumph secret from his deeply Diverse wife.

"We have other tapes of you engaged in heresy as well. Did you think that your armband was safe from a feed? Be glad that we didn't catch you in the act of drinking the blood of Mother Earth's babies."

Steve lunged across the desk. Paragon jumped up and took a few steps back, his hands up. Both men knew that Resolution Command officers on the other side of the door were listening to the sudden raised voices, even if the words were inaudible, and the scraping of the chairs. They sat down again. Steve's shoulders slumped and his voice was tired.

"All right, Khalid, what do you want?" He figured if Paragon had just meant to destroy him, he could have called Gemma Carpenter's officers to arrest him outright and avoided confronting him directly.

"Steve, you've given a lot to Diversity and to the ADF. It wouldn't be fair to send you to prison let alone the firing squad over this error in judgment. And, true, you weren't spouting Christianity. But those of us leading the ADF have to set a good example for our troops and our country…"

"Khalid, cut the crap. I'm not the one who decided to save my career by sending my sister to the firing squad."

Paragon's eyes narrowed. "But that was setting a good example. In the old corrupt days, I would have arranged to have her life spared, because she was connected to the ADF through me. We would have hired a lawyer who would have said, 'Oh, she has four young children, she just made a mistake.' But would that have been the right example for Diversity? She was running an illegal mosque and they were calling Mother Earth a heresy. I have no regrets.

"Anyway, it was twenty years ago. Hardly relevant now."

"It helped your career," said Steve pointedly. "Everyone was very impressed you chose to serve on the squad to kill your own sister." The last thing Patigul had seen before they blindfolded her was her brother's implacable face as he cradled his rifle.

"Do you want to hear my suggestion to save your neck?" Paragon asked acidly. "Or should I just call Gemma?" He raised his armband closer to his mouth to speak her name. Steve nodded.

"Very well," said Paragon. "You're close to retirement. You could have retired already, with thirty-six years in ADF uniform. So why not move up the departure date? There's a lovely community awaiting you in Orlando City, 150 plus, you can golf, swim, spend more time with your wife. There's a Ploreville, so they'll wait on you hand and foot."

"Are you in that much of a hurry to become deputy director, Khalid?"

Paragon laughed shortly. "Ah, Steve, it's so hard to fool you. Yes, I want to impose Diversity, faster than we are doing now. We could do so much more. We have gotten sluggish, lazy, too comfortable. We have settled for so little."

"What do you want to do, Khalid? What are we not doing now?"

"When we first begin testing the truth serum takers, I want to make sure that we actually punish or kill those who do not love Diversity. I want to start breeding factories to offset our population shortages and orphanages. That will be good for the parents too, so they can spend more time helping society and be less preoccupied with giving selfish advantages to their children. We need to scrap that treaty and chip the Plores and take away their books and churches. Do you know, they actually have books in Ploreville? Oh yes, you would know, the Zionists are very tiresomely attached to their books." Paragon smiled maliciously at him. "The Plores should all be forced to go to the Zones, where we need menial workers. Maybe a few can become Social Crediteers."

Steve half-listened to the torrent of words. *He is a madman, the worst thing I could do is make way so he could destroy the DJR as a functioning country. But what choice do I have? If I say no, I will be explaining myself this afternoon to Gemma Carpenter and Vlad, and they will have me executed. I may never even see Vicki or our daughters again.*

Steve waited for the diatribe to end. "All right, Khalid, when do you want me to put in my retirement request? Tomorrow?"

"Oh, well, nothing that immediate. That might raise suspicions about your visit today, especially with that temper you just exhibited. I'm glad you're being so reasonable, though. Why jeopardize your life when a very pleasant retirement awaits? You were going to retire eventually, and I was going to become deputy director anyway, so why drag things out?

"As you know, I have a very important wedding coming up. Once I have taken David Harris's wife, who I personally recovered, as my own, the entire DJR will recognize my leadership. The event will be the most purely Diverse, inspirational event since the founding of the country. I will be the most famous man in the DJR, and my path to ultimate leadership will be open. The country will demand it."

"I'm afraid you won't be able to find any footage of Vlad in a Christian service. He may not take so kindly to being pushed aside."

"He's already due for retirement," said Paragon breezily. "He's now been director, what, for almost three years? It will be obvious who should take the reins. But I can be patient for a little while longer, while I exert leadership over the whole ADF, not just this command. Everyone will respond to true Diverse leadership. The Antifan spirit will become profound again.

"So, Steve, my suggestion is you put your retirement request in sometime next week, to become effective in early November, and then it'll be obvious to everyone who needs to replace you."

"Aren't you going to have a honeymoon with your brides?"

Paragon laughed curtly. "No, I can't afford to leave Anacosta at this time. Don't think you'll be able to launch a coup while I'm on a beach somewhere."

That was not what Steve had intended, but he could see how Paragon might project that perspective on the situation.

As he departed the room, he asked, "How does it feel to marry someone who must hate you?"

Paragon, who had walked him to the doorway, smiled in that feline way of his. "In this case, it feels exquisite."

His eyes trained on Steve's less-than-erect back as the deputy director headed toward the staircase back up to the executive suite, Paragon thought to himself, If Patigul had to die for Diversity, everyone else should get it good and hard. Let her sacrifice mean something.

Leaving the Resolution Command, a dazed Steve barely noticed, but still correctly returned, the crisp salutes of its officers. He glimpsed Captain Boyd through the clear glass of her office, her half-dark half-pale face bent over her workscreen. He felt sorry for her, clearly poised to be the second wife after the celebrity Malia, but perhaps she and Paragon would have a more normal marital relationship than they would with Malia. Yet Paragon had said to him only a week ago about Captain Boyd, "She is trivial-minded. I am tired of her, but must keep my promises."

Back at his desk, Steve berated himself for his naivete. How could he think that he could make dozens of visits to Rockville without attracting the attention of a rival at Beaufort? How could he have assumed that Paragon, with his overweening ambition, would not have seized any opportunity to vault into Steve's position?

Then, what to do? Steve stared dully at his statue of St. John Beaufort. He recollected the 115th Psalm: "They have mouths but speak not; eyes have they but they see not."

The easiest thing to do would be to swallow hard, take Paragon's deal, and ease gently into retirement. Vicki would urge him to take it, after castigating him for his recklessness. But Steve knew that every day, on the golf course or on his veranda, it would stick in his craw that he had not resisted Paragon, just to stay alive. It would be a complete abdication of the Antifan spirit. He still believed in the Antifan spirit. Another option would be to take Vicki and his daughters on a trip to Mexico, from which they would simply not return. But they would be penniless, in a foreign country. Maybe they could make their way to the United States.

Could he arrange for Paragon to be killed without implicating himself? Nobody knew he had a motive to assassinate Paragon, not yet. But how would one find and hire an assassin? In Steve's experience with criminal matters, such ventures usually ended badly for all involved.

What if the wedding crashed and burned? Would that be sufficiently humiliating to sideline Paragon and stymie his ambitions? Would Paragon forget about Steve Rosen once the deputy director job became a practical impossibility?

What could he, Steve Rosen, do to ensure this wedding blew up in Paragon's face? The black and gilt invitation was lying on his desk—Vicki had been urging him to bring it home, since it would be the event of the season and she wanted to show it to her friends—and they wouldn't be able to decline. He ran his index finger along the edges, mulling the possibilities. Perhaps David Harris would suddenly appear and rescue Malia. Knowing David Harris, Steve found it hard to believe that if he were in the DJR, the former Antifan commander would refrain from a rescue attempt. But he had no idea where Harris was, or how even a David Harris would manage such a feat. If it were successful, however, Paragon's ambitions would definitely implode.

Montoya entered the office. "Rosen, where have you been all morning?"

"Getting a tour of the Resolution Command. Khalid runs a lot of schemes out of there. Some of them will give me nightmares tonight."

Montoya marked the invitation lying on the desk. "And this wedding is the biggest scheme of all. I guess we're going to have to witness this spectacle. I shouldn't complain—three years ago we asked Khalid to bring back Harris and his wife, and we got it." His tone was faintly rueful.

"Sure did. You think Harris could show up?"

"I hope he tries. That would be the end of him. That hall will have more Antifans per capita than any square inch in the DJR except this building."

At that point, Steve remembered that in a corner of Montoya's office, in a small cabinet, sat the confidential red alert phone that, if picked up, would ring in St. Louis, in the office of the secretary of defense. He determined to work late that night. He would say, "This is Blue Heron," his code name, so St. Louis would know this was the real deal.

Chapter 51
No Picnic
(Sunday–Sunday, September 5–12, 2094)

"You could maybe get within a few miles of the college, but what good would that do?" Welcome lamented. The two men were sitting on sacks of flour in the windowless workroom in the grocery basement, the door closed, with only a small lamp illuminating them, even though it was the middle of a sunny late summer day. The air was stale. David was used to it by now, they met like this almost every Sunday now. Sometimes David took the van to Arlington Ploreville from Paragon's estate at the end of a workday, but it was riskier.

Welcome showed David a drawing that Marjory Harris had given him of the Athena Chapel in which the wedding would take place. The building featured several turrets and large iron doors with leaf carvings, and was constructed around a giant Romanesque arch.

"Memorize this, because I'm going to destroy it later," Welcome said. David pored over the drawing of the chapel, with little armed stick figures positioned in the balcony and at various intervals throughout the building. "If this is an honest effort to give us information, it's from someone who is ADF and who is privy to high-level security information." Answering David's unasked question, he added, "Or someone who is trying to trap us. But this looks credible.

"Here are the other entrances to the building," he said, pointing to various nooks and side doors. "All guarded twenty-four hours a day by ADF starting five days before the wedding. That's when the workers will arrive. They'll be living in tents on the campus, on the old playing fields, where the Beltane takes place." He pointed to a site to the north of the chapel. "No Plore workers allowed."

David said, "Here's today's column. She says that her suite will be above the Goddess Arch, on the other side of the campus, and she is sharing it with...the Antifan freak, the other bride." He almost choked on "bride."

"I hope they're getting along these days," Welcome joked, allowing his desiccated sense of humor a brief airing.

"I don't think that's funny. Do you think we should try to rescue her from the suite or from the hall itself?"

"They'll be more distracted at the wedding itself, and maybe even more relaxed, thinking the need for security is about to end and their job is over. Maybe during that movie?" The population had been titillated with revelations about the lurid movie, which would guarantee an abundant viewing audience nationwide. For that movie alone, David vowed, I will gladly kill Paragon.

"Here's your next assignment," Welcome said. "Next Sunday. The Men's Bible Study Club of St. Luke's in Hagerstown is having their annual picnic, well, actually their first annual picnic, at Tanisha Nkokwo Park in Frederick. Still Anacosta containment region, just barely. You're going to ask for Oren Olliver."

"How'm I supposed to get there?"

"We'll drive my van. I'm delivering something to a Social Credit friend in Frederick." Welcome had recently plowed his profits into the giant carbon offset needed to buy the van, ownership of which had been approved by Arlington city hall. The acquaintance would confirm online that Welcome was making a legitimate catering delivery, and Welcome would follow through, at a loss. The acquaintance was fine with getting virtually free food, assuming Welcome just wanted to have an excuse to drive the van into the countryside. Welcome sometimes went outside just to admire the "Welcome Grocery: Say Hello to Good Food" painted on its side.

"So you're going to the picnic too?"

"I don't think so. I'd stand out like a...well, black Plore. I'll wait for you in the parking lot. I'll give you a tray of deviled eggs so you look like you belong."

Welcome stood up, stretching. "Your mother and sister will be here shortly." The sisters alternated weeks, because while it made sense one of them would be accompanying Marjory, two would attract attention. While they visited, Welcome packed their wire wheeled shopping cart with groceries, so no one would wonder why the Harrises spent a lot of time in the shop but always emerged hands-free. Just for the Harrises, and against his conscience, Welcome had decided to temporarily open the store on Sunday—David's only free day—and close on Monday, at least for now. Not only could the family visit, but he could meet with David.

"I've got to see how things are going upstairs," Welcome said, trudging up the staircase to make sure his middle son wasn't besieged by customers. David edged out into the relative comfort of the basement to wait for his mother and sister, grateful for the reprieve.

A week later, David steered the van onto 270 as they headed for northwestern Yramaland. Welcome was rusty behind a wheel, and so gladly accepted David's offer to drive. Both were looking forward to a change of scenery. They had to stop at the mid-Montgomery County checkpoint, but the policewomen quickly found the authorization for Welcome's delivery in Frederick, and didn't ask to see David's identification, so they were detained less than five minutes. "I can't much drive anymore—poor eyesight," Welcome explained to the matronly policewomen, one of whom clucked sympathetically. "So I've got my own driver!"

If the policewomen could have seen David's tense eyes behind his sunglasses, their antennae would have jumped, but they couldn't. The gun was still in the basement of the boardinghouse, because Welcome would not risk it being found in his van. David relaxed again as they headed toward Frederick, made the delivery, and headed for the state park. "Nice that you've got a boy to help you," the Social Crediteer had jested. Once in the parking lot, Welcome handed David the deviled egg tray, pointed him in the right direction, and reclined the seat to take a nap.

It was National Security Day holiday weekend, again, and the park was busy with holiday picnickers, mostly Plores but also some Social Crediteers who were easy to pick out, not just because of their armbands. They must have been high-end Social Crediteers because they owned cars to drive all the way out to this park, or they were local seigneurs ruling over Plore masses from their comfy positions in the Frederick County government apparatus. To David's surprise, the park did not segregate the two castes, and it was actually first come first serve for the pavilions when you reserved online.

David stopped briefly to tie his sneakers and collect himself at a small concrete apron featuring a resin tribute to the park namesake, Tanisha Nkokwo (2010–2052), Liberator of Frederick. Nkokwo's stern and resolute face was carved in the resin block, wearing an anarchist newsboy cap and a checkered scarf, with a word bubble containing her best-known quote, "The Diverse People Must Enjoy Leisure After the Revolution." Hey, the revolution's back, David thought, as he continued down the gravel path. At a distance, he saw men playing softball, but couldn't tell whether they were Social Credit or Plores.

David found the correct pavilion and banner a few minutes' walk down the main gravel path. "Say Luke's Men's Club Annual Picnic" read the blue letters on the white background. About twenty men milled about, some sitting at picnic tables, others lounging on the grass or under a large oak tree. David was impressed at the social engineering by whoever had realized a group of young men would not attract undue attention if gathering under a "men's club" banner. Only Plores could get away with any "men's club."

"Is Oren here?" he asked the grim-faced woman tending an electric grill.

The stout thirtyish woman with a square face and graying hair escaping from a messy bun scrutinized him, then jerked her finger behind her, "He's standing next to the coldbox in the blue T-shirt—put the eggs on the picnic table here," and went back to her soyaburgers, since meat was not permitted in state parks. "This battery's almost out. Damn, who charged this thing?"

David approached several men next to the portable coldbox, which was full of sodas and beer. Oren, a tall, wiry man in his midthirties, with close-cropped dark hair and bright brown eyes, had been expecting David, and recognized him immediately, breaking forth from the cluster to greet him with a strong handshake and a clasp to the shoulder. "Our distinguished visitor," he smiled. "Oren Olliver, at your service."

"Da— Mike Marino," said David, flushing at his near error as he basked in the warmth of this admirer.

"No fret-fret," Oren said, after David was introduced briefly to the other men in the small circle, and he ushered David aside. "I know who you are, and it is an honor to meet you. The other men know you as Mike Marino who escaped from Cayuga, but that's it for now. We've been doing some interesting things ourselves, and your project may be the best opportunity to join forces and make a splash." Welcome had told David that Oren's band had waylaid the Social Credit car on 81.

"Be careful with your splash. You know what happened to our community up in Cayuga."

Oren nodded soberly, but added, "What can you do? Bow your head and die slowly?" They looked at each other, understanding. "Someone has to take the first step. I honestly think they are killing themselves with their craziness. And eventually the tree will rot from within, and we will knock it over and bring this country back to a republic, if not actually united again with the US.

"All I ask is that if you manage to rescue your wife, and escape back to the US, you won't forget us. The US needs to help us. That's all we want in return for helping you. You can stay there if you make it back, I wouldn't blame you. By the way, just so you know, St. Luke's doesn't actually have a men's Bible club. So don't ask anyone questions about catechism.

"We'll talk more shortly. First, let's get something to eat."

"I'm a little afraid of your cook," said David.

"That's my sister, Rebecca. She's the toughest man here. We might bring her along—she'll show no mercy. Absolutely hates Social Credit."

David was hungry, so was glad to eat the soyaburger, a deviled egg, and some potato salad. He took a can of Translove beer. Unless things had changed, he knew that the ADF never bugged outdoor venues far from the City. Yet, force of habit made him pretend to drop the cardboard fork so he could scan underneath the picnic table.

Then the men gathered in a large group to sing hymns. Oren motioned David to the middle of the gathering, where they were surrounded. Oren occasionally hummed, while the others sang, led by a prim-looking middle-aged man with a goatee. It was not a melodious group.

"That's Marvin. He looks like a librarian but he's a watchmaker by profession and a bombmaker by necessity. He's going to come up with something very powerful as a wedding gift.

"About fifteen of us have sworn to participate. We will lay down our lives for you and your wife, if needed, but we don't plan to die, at least not without killing some Antifan snoutfaces first. If we succeed, we will put Social Credit on notice, and it will inspire others. It won't end there. But how we're going to get into the college, past all those perimeter checks, I don't know."

David said, "This was bothering me too, but I had an idea today while driving up here from Anacosta. If we knew the companies that were sending workers to the college, we could intercept them on the road, take the armbands, impersonate the workers till the wedding. I mean, we couldn't do the food prep job…"

"That might kill some of the bastards prematurely," Oren joked, with an elbow pointed in the direction of Rebecca, who was wrapping leftovers on the picnic table. Another man would help her wheel the trash to the central composting pit; Social Crediteers usually hired a park employee to dispose of their trash. "But yes…that's an idea."

"Ha!" David rejoined, now a little sorry for the hardworking sister, whose heart was in the right place. "But maybe the facilities crew, repairons—we need some handy guys with skill sets for that one—you got musicians?"

"Can't you tell how badly we sing? But what would we do with the real Social Crediteers?"

David shook his head. "They're not doing anything wrong. Some of the guys can take them off to the woods for a week and keep them in a shed. Let them go afterward, no hard feelings."

"Uh, you haven't thought of something, kamrat."

David bristled at the condescension. "Haven't thought of what?"

"You get to run away when this is all over. Back to Iowa, or wherever it is you live. Our guys stay behind, get pointed out by the Soko musicians, and that'll be the end of them."

The St. Luke's picnickers were belting out a lusty "What a Friend We Have in Jesus," when they realized two police officers were standing grimly on the sidelines.

"Uh-oh," David heard a fellow say behind them.

"Who has the permit here?" demanded the white male officer.

Rebecca strode forward. "I do—here it is." She thrust her phone screen at him.

"You can't sing those songs here. You're creating a disturbance. There's been a complaint." The second officer, an older black woman, indicated a group of young Social Crediteers holding wineglasses under a fancy green cloth pavilion. A shriek erupted from one of the Social Crediteers, perhaps a drunken young woman laughing at a joke.

"You can share your fake Jesus doctrines when you're by yourselves," admonished the white male officer, "but not in the hearing of DJR citizens. You're lucky we don't arrest you outright." Spreading Christianity was a capital crime, although the treaty also allowed Plores to worship freely among themselves, which presented a delicate balance at times such as this.

Rebecca swelled up, like a toad, hissing. "You want us to suck Mother Earth, officer?" She took a step closer to him, and he raised his armband-clad forearm warningly. The black officer placed her hand on her taser gun. "Talk about fake doctrines!"

"Rebecca," said Oren softly, "lay off, it's copa," or copacetic, all right. He placed his arm around her and walked her away from the officers, calling back, "It's under control, officers, thank you for the warning. She's not well." Nobody else was eager for a confrontation, including the police, and the gaggle broke up. The men awkwardly rose and resumed their conversations. Oren steered Rebecca to a corner of the grounds and David watched him speaking with her intently, probably along the lines of, don't draw attention to us. We've got a mission. We can't jeopardize it by antagonizing the police. What if they file a report about us? The stout woman, almost as tall as her brother, stared resentfully at the ground.

When David entered the park, he had been temporarily gratified by the sight of Social Crediteers and Plores sharing the space. Maybe it's possible to live together, he had told himself. The clash corrected his naive interpretation, reminding him who made the rules, and who obeyed, and who delivered the insults and who swallowed them.

David and Oren moved to a picnic table, talking intently in low voices, clumps of the men deliberately surrounding them to shield them from the view of other parties, and keeping up loud conversations that drowned out theirs. But the Social Crediteers couldn't complain about that. Rebecca brought them slices of chocolate cake and another two beers. "Sure," she snarled genially when David thanked her.

"You can't be the commander in this operation," Oren insisted. "I know you've got the experience, but you're going to be focused on rescuing your wife. Which is the right thing to do. But I'm responsible for my men."

You can't be the commander? Which one of us was an Antifan for twenty years and a commander for ten? "That's why you'd be a good deputy," said David. "Because you know your troops. But have you ever broken into a building and used force to break up an illegal meeting? Do you know how to secure a building? Which guards you want to take out? What do you propose doing?"

"I would overpower the guards and take their weapons," said Oren, "while we toss Marvin's bombs into the orchestra seats from the balcony. You grab your wife and run for it. We'll carjack the chauffeured cars and drive home."

"Kamrat, you forgot something," David smiled, enjoying his revenge. "They carry electronic firearms registered only to themselves. Our men will not be able to fire those weapons."

Oren was silent. They were manufacturing guns in their community, one by one, but faced the same challenges Lucy's roundup had in finding ammo and safe concealed places for shooting practice. And they would have to smuggle them into the college and the chapel if they couldn't count on firing the Antifan weapons.

"Let's say I know the enemy," David reminded him. "I know the protocols for guarding an event like this. They will all be focused on the stage, not on who's sneaking up on them. We will be in the building when the event begins, so they will assume anyone in the building has been vetted. The armbands on workmen will reassure them.

"Oren, let me ask you something. How many men have you killed in your life?"

"None yet," the younger man admitted.

Talking big, though, David thought resentfully. He was tempted to ask whether at least Rebecca had killed anyone.

"Do you want to know how many I've killed? At the command of the DJR, dozens. Since the night my wife was kidnapped last year, another dozen. I sliced an Antifan militia commander into ribbons last year. Again, I'm not proud of it, but the experience will come in handy here. Are you sure that, when the moment comes, you'll be capable of knifing an Antifan? Breaking his neck, when he is possibly stronger than you? Can you call yourself battle-tested?"

"You've convinced me," Oren said, humbled. "I place myself and my men under your command."

Some of the men hovering nearby realized belatedly—and Oren would swear them to secrecy one by one on the drive home—that they were now in the service of the legendary Plore Antifan himself. Rather than frightening them, the news gave them added confidence and pride.

PART SIX

THE COLLEGE OF THE EARTHLOVING PRIESTS

*"Woe unto them that call
evil good and good evil,
Who present darkness as light,
And light as darkness,
Who present bitter as sweet,
and sweet as bitter!"*
Isaiah 5:20

Chapter 52
Great Goddess Arch
(Monday, October 25, 2094)

The Antifan-driven car, escorted by three black vans in front and three behind, each brimming with armed guards, bore the brides to their wedding in Lenilenape-Sylvania. Malia gazed upon the red, yellow, and orange colors of the Yramaland countryside. She had forgotten how starved she was for a view other than one of the ever-rising wall. The black armband, newly restored to her for the excursion, felt stiff and papery along her arm. Paragon would join them in several days.

This was the first time Malia and Exterra had seen each other since the night at the comedy club in March. Malia had lived in seclusion, and neither had sought out the other. Exterra was satisfied to have Paragon to herself at night. After the evening at the comedy club, Paragon had reassured her that his courtship of Malia Jenness was entirely political, and since they slept together at the Avalon each night, Exterra had no reason to distrust him. Exterra was confident that after the wedding, even though Paragon had regretfully told her that he would have to designate Malia as the senior wife, for political reasons, he would always favor her. "You have marked Diversity on your face, how can I not be faithful to you?

"She remains a fascist," Paragon said of Malia to Exterra. "How can I trust my deepest secrets and heart to such a creature? We cannot let her roam around Anacosta, so this will keep her under guard without having her in a cell in Beaufort. The US cannot complain, since she is not a prisoner, correct? Would a prisoner be allowed to marry one of the leaders of the DJR?"

"Khalid, you are so brilliant," gushed the relieved Exterra.

Thus, Exterra was showing more amiability during the ride than Malia had expected. Paragon had charged her with "keeping an eye" on Malia, although how Malia could escape with the college bristling with Antifans, Exterra had no idea. Exterra herself had no intention of spending the next week in lockdown in their suite. But to humor Paragon, she wore her Antifan uniform for the ride, as if she were indeed on duty. Malia wore the long red robe with the velvet sash that had become her trademark. The color suited Malia's dark hair and eyes, but Exterra triumphantly told herself, she looks thin and anxious. *I am almost ten years her junior, no wonder Khalid comes to me at night, not to her.*

"What are you doing, Malia?" Exterra asked curiously after, Malia's hunger for scenery finally sated, the senior wife to-be turned to her armband. She seemed to be working on a document.

"My column," said Malia shortly. "Khalid has given me permission to begin writing it again."

"I can see you might want something useful to do. At least you can pretend to serve Diversity."

Malia gave a crooked smile, as she crafted a response that would tell David the movie would be shown first, before the ceremony began. The chronology galled her, since it meant the lascivious audience would watch her nuptials fresh from viewing her humiliation on the screen. Still, it wasn't very much information, and she hoped to learn something more useful at the college.

Welcome had received a list from the vacuum salesman (who was now repairing the grocer's chronically temperamental machine) of the workers' names and their social credit numbers, the routes they would travel, and their expected time of arrival at the college. His eyes landed on one line, a dozen stagehands, eleven men and one woman, coming from Baltimore, courtesy of the Baltimore City Council. "The fear alone is a good sign," David said to Welcome, referring to what was the exacting scrutiny of the workforce. "Five years ago, no one would have thought any such event in Lenilenape could be threatened."

"I'd rather they were less fearful and more careless."

More alarming was the news that Marjory and Emma Harris were being held at Beaufort. "Hostages for good behavior," David explained to Welcome on that weeknight when he had returned with the Arlington Ploreville van from work. Tom and Seth had left the bricklaying crew and were now training with Oren's band outside of Hagerstown. "At least *you're* reliable," the scrawny crew chief had sniffed at him. But David would soon disappear himself.

"Well, Commander, are you going to behave?" asked Welcome.

The two men laughed gruffly. "Not a chance," said David. "My mom and sister wouldn't want me to." At night, with less bravado, he hoped that Beaufort would not actually kill them if he succeeded in rescuing Malia and himself. Hostages were most useful as deterrence, but killing them usually was an unsatisfying revenge.

The ride was uneventful, and three hours after they departed Anacosta, the caravan arrived at the college. Three women in long hooded black robes bedecked with a jeweled green earth insignia greeted them outside the Great Goddess Arch, although on closer inspection Malia realized the one on the right bulged an Adam's apple. The hoods were lined with green velvet. What a beautiful setting, Malia thought, looking around her at the stone buildings, none very high, with all so serene and quiet that even individual birdcalls were heard.

"I am Aleta Hekatedaughter, 290, Great Priestess of the College," said the petite blonde woman in the middle. "Welcome, Communicator Malia, Captain Exterra, to the College of the Earthloving Priests and to the embrace of Her Motherness.

"This is Ceridwen Sagedaughter, 270, my deputy," and indicating the New Woman, "This is Melusine Lilithdaughter, 300, our political commissar. We are honored to have been chosen for the celebration of your marriage with Commander Ma." It was a sore point that Ma was not a Strict Pagan, but the ADF had assured the Great Priestess that at least both Malia and Exterra belonged to Strict Paganism. It also troubled Aleta Hekatedaughter that Malia had practiced Christianity, quite willingly, while living in the United States. However, the ADF had sent the College a "Confirmation of Diverse Faith Fealty," assuring it that Malia had proven convincingly, citing her truth serum test, that her traitor husband had forced her to live as a Christian and bear him two sons under patriarchy, and that she had secretly prayed to the Earth Mother throughout her exile.

"We would not have freed her let alone allowed her to marry Commander Ma," said the Knowledge Tower liaison pointedly, "were she still a heretic." Since neither the Tower nor the Great Priestess actually had the final say in who should marry Commander Ma, all found it preferable to believe that Malia had truly reformed.

Malia started as the clock tower chimed eleven.

"Ah yes," said Aleta. "We are so accustomed to the peals of the clock tower that organize our hours of worship and service to the Mother. Would you like a tour of the College before we repair to lunch, or..." diplomatically adding, "are you too tired from your journey?"

"We're quite tired... Exterra began, but Malia interrupted, "Yes, Your Reverence, *I* for one would love to see your college. I have heard so much about the beautiful grounds and the holy air that envelops one here, I cannot go another hour without experiencing them for myself." Malia was subtly adopting the demeanor and the words of the priests before her, because she knew it would reassure them. Exterra, on the other hand, retreated into her Antifan shell.

The party trailed through the Great Goddess Arch, with Ceridwen pointing above to the "VIP suite where you shall both stay," and onto a gravel path. The clock tower soared on their right in a narrow building with slate steps. "Titania Hall, over two hundred years old." As they walked along the paths toward the dormitories, the priests came out of the buildings to show obeisance to the exalted visitors, all but the oldest kneeling on the grass. They wore humbler versions of the dark robe of the Great Priestesses, but all sported the same round green symbol on the front and back.

Malia won the goodwill of the priests by raising her clasped hands to the crowds, and calling out the traditional, "Earth greetings to you all!" She had asked the Knowledge Tower what greetings would be appropriate at the College, which had pleased the wedding organizers. The crowds called in unison as the party trailed down the paths, "May Mother Earth sustain you!" to which she cheerfully replied, "And may She destroy our enemies."

They crossed the Goddess Green, and entered the Athena Great Hall where the feast would be laid after the wedding. "The dais will be here, and forty round tables with ten feasters at each," said Melusine in her deep voice. Malia was awed by the high stained-glass windows and the pennants, each bearing the name of a MED saint. While much smaller than the National Diversity Cathedral, its dark woods and hushed interior conveyed a somber, intense feel. Once this room had been a library, a storehouse of knowledge. A ten-foot-high idol of Athena stood in the far corner, approached by a set of triangular stairs in the corner surrounded by various offerings of food, drink, and precious cloths.

"Our novices are always petitioning for her favor," smiled Aleta. "And, I must confess, sometimes their teachers. There has been a statue of Athena here for well over a hundred years, even when the students were Christian, because even then, they yearned for truth."

Eventually, they came to the far end of the campus and the chapel, which Malia instantly recognized from her searches on the GVN that morning.

"I would like to see inside," said Malia, "since I am imagining what the wedding will be like."

"A truly astounding event it will be," agreed Aleta. "Of course."

They entered a small dark wooden lobby, and then into the great vault of the chapel. Giant tapestries depicting gods loomed around them. "It seats six hundred," said Melusine, "and will be full on the wedding day." The most architecturally inclined of the group, she pointed out the arches and the two balconies, and noted the seats were carpeted in fine cloth of moss, harvested from the Piedmont and worked by Diverse Social Crediteers of good character.

"So will guests also be sitting in the balconies?" asked Malia.

Aleta looked a little pained. "In the mezzanine, yes, our priests will sit. But not in the uppermost balcony"—she pointed upward—"because that is where our Antifan protectors must stand, due to the threats that I am told fascists have recently made. However, I have insisted that they be discreet—no more than three or four soldiers will guard the balcony. There will be ample security around the building itself, so we need few soldiers inside. Especially since so many of the guests will be Antifan in any case."

Melusine interrupted, "It's just as well, because that balcony is not as structurally sound as it might be. We meant to have it repaired a few years ago, but as long as we don't use it often, we prefer to use the funds for instructional purposes."

"You should be grateful to the ADF for protecting us," Exterra burst out, resentful at having had to trail the lying Malia, the obvious fascist, around the campus, and to see the love of the priests for her famous rival.

"Of course we are grateful to the ADF," Aleta said smoothly, "but we don't want to risk anyone's safety. Safety is a gift from the Earth Mother, you know."

"Threats from fascists?" Malia cried, visibly alarmed. "I had no idea! What kind of threats?"

"Nothing concrete," Aleta reassured her, "There is some restlessness to the southwest. A gang of Plore bandits is roaming around the area, and on the other side of the Lenilenape border in Yramaland, but nobody really thinks they would try to interfere with this ceremony. Our security is too tight, and they are just wild bandits. Please do not worry."

"The ADF is imposing total security on the site," Melusine said. "There will be three rings of security reaching to the town and no Plores will be permitted entry starting today and through the wedding day itself."

"If the ADF is in command, I have no fears," Malia declared.

The group climbed the side staircase to explore the stage, above which was a giant tapestry of the Earth Mother Herself. The stage was dominated by a long altar, draped in green.

"The two of you and Commander Ma will stand behind the altar, facing the guests," said Melusine. "The archbishop will be facing you, and the imam Their Holiness will stand here. Priestesses Aleta and Ceridwen will flank you as her attendants. The three ceremonial cups will be placed on the altar for you to drink from. And the movie screen will come down in front of the tapestry at the beginning of the ceremony, and retract afterward."

Malia insisted on walking around backstage, peeking into the dressing rooms, and marking the route from those rooms to the stage. The recessional would exit the front doors and the party would be taken in golf carts to Athena Hall. Malia noted the nearest exits, and opened the doors, to the bemusement of the priests. Exterra tensed. "What on earth are you doing, Malia?"

"I'm slightly claustrophobic," Malia apologized to the priests, "and even if I am not outdoors, I feel more comfortable if I know the outdoors is near—the presence of Mother Earth steadies me." She ignored Exterra's contemptuous smirk, but the Antifan then remembered how Malia had dashed out, ridiculously, from the Avalon on the Harvest Holiday.

The nearest exit from the stage led directly into the side driveway, and another into the alley behind the chapel from which fields could be seen. That alley led directly to a paved driveway that intersected with the main road. The fields would be covered with tents for the soon-arriving workers. Behind the fields two self-driving cars and a truck ambled down a quiet road. This was a fine Social Credit neighborhood just within the bounds of the City of Philadelphia.

"Thank you," said Malia. "What a lovely campus."

After the gracious vegetarian lunch, the brides were escorted to their suite. The large room featured a high fireplace and mantel with a telescreen, lushly upholstered sofas and chairs, and two adjoining bedrooms with baths. An altar stood in the back corner, with a stack of hernals on an adjoining table. "For your devotions," said Aleta. "Three presidents have stayed in this suite. Normally the archbishop herself would stay here but we have put her in another guest room.

"You have the afternoon to rest and relax. In the evening, after dinner, we have arranged for you to meet with some of our most promising students, and in the morning, we will have a Mother service to celebrate your visit. I believe your first rehearsal is the day after, on Wednesday, and the archbishop herself will rehearse with you on Thursday. I have assigned novices to attend to your every need around the clock." Downstairs on the staircases, women Antifan soldiers were positioning themselves for the duration.

Once they were finally left to themselves, Exterra began to complain. Her bed in her adjoining bedroom was poorly made up, she had detected dust along the edge of the dresser, and how could Malia shamelessly pretend to be a devotee of the Earth Mother and playact herself in front of the crowd of priests when everyone in Anacosta knew she was dissembling?

"You misunderstand me," Malia said frostily. "I am resigned to being the *senior* wife of Paragon. My husband is dead. I have returned to Anacosta, my home, and now embrace again the religion of my youth. When I was in the US, I pretended to be a Christian, so as not to anger my husband. If I must marry Paragon to prove my goodwill and loyalty to Diversity, so I shall."

"You're only going to be the senior wife because they need to keep a close eye on you. Khalid loves me best."

"Your jealousy is all too apparent," Malia spat back. "Why don't you have the girls bring you something to drink?" The novices quickly ran to bring ice cream and wine and, within the hour, Exterra was snoring lightly on her bed. Malia finished the ice cream and turned to her column, overjoyed to have a quiet moment to inform David of the most convenient exits for an escaping bride and her rescuer. Nor did she overlook the salient fact that only three or four Antifans would be in the upper balcony on the wedding day.

She dispatched the column to the Knowledge Tower editors before Exterra awoke and could demand to see it. She had learned to write to the specifications of the Knowledge Tower so perfectly that they rarely reworked her sentences, but now all she really cared about was that they left the first word of each paragraph alone. To her, that was the sign of a beautifully written column, even if she had just advised some desperate woman to volunteer to work in an Economic Zone concentration camp to forget a failed relationship.

Malia then stood at the window overlooking the interior grounds of the College. Now that the distinguished visitors were safely ensconced in their private suite, the priests were released to throng the lawns again. In their black gowns with the green circle on front and back, they proceeded from Introductory Earth Theory to Goddesses of Yore to Sexual Pleasure and the Priestly Profession to Climate Change and Mother Earth to Church History 101: The Covidian Demise of the Christian Churches. Malia watched the dark figures flowing around the lawns, sometimes pulling together in a clump, then breaking off. Occasionally a pair of Antifan soldiers passed by, and disappeared under the arch.

She stared, troubled, into the filmy glass window, which really did need a good cleaning. Somehow, David was planning to rescue her from this stronghold, stiffening rapidly with black Antifan uniforms like egg whites into a meringue. She knew that even if he had to do it himself, he would, but at what cost?

She suddenly remembered that in his final message to her, sent on the breakfast tray and rolled up in the paper napkin with the silverware, David had written, "Find Gaia Annadaughter, she is a friend." All Malia knew was that Gaia Annadaughter lived at the college, but she had no idea who the woman was, or how she would help her.

She poked her head out of the room. The startled novices jumped up from watching a movie on their screens.

"Would you please arrange for me to see Gaia Annadaughter?" she requested.

The novices looked confused. "She's only one of the janitors," said the elder. "She's really nothing. Are you sure, amba-mam?"

"Please," Malia stated, more firmly. "Perhaps she can come by tonight after dinner?"

The younger girl was dispatched in search of Gaia Annadaughter. Malia knew well that the humblest people were often the most useful operatives. They were least noticed, and most despised, which gave them the obscurity and the incentive needed to succeed in their missions. Malia knew that her own low status, as a 70, had enabled her to lurk in the background, collecting valuable intelligence on the Economic Tower bureaucrats. She also knew well that arrogance usually masked a weakness that could be exploited, but she had not figured out what Paragon's was, unless it was the secret about the sister. Malia hoped that she would not have the time to learn what lay behind the secret and that it would all be immaterial in a few days.

Chapter 53
Gaia Annadaughter
(Monday, October 25, 2094)

Malia had forgotten about the post-dinner meeting with the promising novices. By the time she and Exterra returned to their suite, it was 9:30. She feared that Gaia Annadaughter would not come tonight, and then she began to fret that Exterra's presence would prevent her from speaking freely with Gaia. At the very least she knew Exterra would report their meeting to Paragon.

Fortunately, Exterra had decided that whatever rules applied to the hapless Malia did not apply to her, the Antifan captain. While returning to the suite, Exterra had encountered some old acquaintances from Beaufort who had invited her to a drinking party that night, which she had every intention of attending. She suspected that after the wedding, her own latitude would shrink as Paragon ascended. If she had to resign from the ADF, so be it, Paragon had hinted as much, but for now she would enjoy her last few nights of freedom. And she would underscore to Malia that the soon-to-be senior wife was the real prisoner. She idly wondered whether she would soon prove her worth and superiority over Malia by bearing Paragon a child—a son, of course—because Paragon was like that, Diversity or no Diversity. Surely Malia was too old to have another child, and she had already greedily spawned three, even if they were in the United States.

Exterra had disappeared into the night—the sentries would not force her to stay in the suite—and Malia paced back and forth, hoping the opportunity would not go wasted. The glass lamps on the walls automatically dimmed, to preserve electricity after 10:00 p.m.

About ten minutes later, she was delighted to hear a timid knock.

"Come in," she called. The door creaked open.

Malia had expected to see a younger, hearty woman, given the presumed physical demands of the janitorial job, but at least not this tiny hunchbacked creature who was at least seventy. Her straight gray hair half-covered her wrinkled face. Instead of a robe, the woman wore a practical black smock with pockets over cotton pants and a frayed armband.

"Are you Gaia Annadaughter?"

"No," the woman responded. "But I was her friend. They said I should come to you instead."

"Come in," said Malia, alarmed by the "was." "Please close the door."

The janitor was shaking, so Malia sat her down in an armchair, poured her a glass of wine, and gave her ginger cookies from the generous refreshment bar the College had laid out for her and Exterra. Malia noted that the woman ate with a good appetite, even greedily, so she fed her a large slice of chocolate cake as well. Hungry, I know what that's like, they won't feed the low Social Credit enough, even when they do the hard work.

When the woman seemed to have relaxed, Malia said, gently, "Please tell me who you are, and where Gaia Annadaughter is. I was told to ask for her when I came here."

"I am Sohan Maweidaughter, 70, amba-mam." Malia did a quick accounting—lowest menial labor score: 30; probably 10 Asian points, 5 female cisgender, 20 Healthy Eating points, if they even did that here. Extra points here and there for obeisance at various services or volunteer activities. "I worked very closely with Gaia and we shared a room in the basement of Owlet Hall. Our main responsibility is to keep the hall tidy for the students and to run errands for them.

"I am sorry to tell you that Gaia died three weeks ago."

Sohan's tone was more somber than Malia would have expected from someone just having to tell her that a stranger whom she had sought to meet had expired. Yes, it was unfortunate that Gaia had died, if only because her life had doubtless been difficult, and her loss furthermore would likely complicate the rescue attempt. But Sohan sounded truly sympathetic, as if Malia had known Gaia personally.

"Gaia was sorry to have missed you. When we heard about the wedding, she swore me to secrecy. She said, "' Malia Jenness is my niece. I want to live long enough to see her in person. Perhaps she will be willing to see her old aunt.' But by then she was coughing, much weaker every day, and they were pressing her to go to the infirmary and accept the death pills. I was doing her work as well as mine."

"I have no aunt named Gaia."

"She was not always Gaia," Sohan replied calmly.

Malia quickly ushered Sohan into her bedroom, urging her to sit on the accent chair while she herself perched on the bed. When she had met David over four years ago, he had combed the files for evidence of her relatives. She knew that the Antifans had brought her to a transit camp in Charlottesville with her grandmother Annabel—yes, close enough to Anna. Annabel had a daughter named Jennifer who was assumed to have died in the house fire, but no body was ever found. David could find nothing about Malia's mother, not until they got to the United States, where government records confirmed that a twenty-seven-year-old woman named Katherine Jenness from Lynchburg, Virginia, had died in a skirmish in Tennessee with Antifans in 2058. Yet

Jennifer never surfaced, whether on the DJR or US side.

"Only close to her deathbed, did she tell me her story. She was once named Jennifer, and she was from Virginia. The Antifans came to their house, killed her grandmother, and burned the house down. They had left her for dead, outside the house on a cold winter night. Fascists came sometime during the night and took her to the hospital behind their lines for treatment. While she was recovering there, the Antifans took the town, in February 2059.

"She went mad at the sight of Antifans, and they put her in a psychiatric hospital for several years. When she had accepted Diversity, and was pronounced cured, she took the name Gaia Annadaughter to show her loyalty. Then they gave her a job cleaning the wards and a Social Credit armband. So then she eventually made her way here, because she was a hard worker and she did not cause trouble. She came to the College in 2072 and we became good friends. And for the last twenty-two years, we had just done our jobs, living quietly in the basement and picking up our rations from the commissary each night.

"So I was very surprised when she told me that she was your aunt. Gaia truly hoped she would see you again. She tried to send you messages in Anacosta, once we saw your TV show and realized you were alive and in the DJR again, but they must never have reached you."

Malia thought painfully of all the fan mail she had received after her confession at the Anacosta Bowl. Overwhelmed by the torrent of emails, and sickened by their gushing restatements of her surrender, Malia had skimmed through only a small portion of it. But she also knew that the ADF had scrutinized all her emails and would most likely have erased any from someone claiming to be her relative.

"Sohan, I have a friend on the outside who said I should find Gaia Annadaughter and she would help me. How they knew this, I have no idea. I do not want to be married to Paragon—I know you must find this strange. But he is evil. What would Gaia have done to help me?"

The old woman gave her a shrewd look. "What would you want her to have done, amba-mam?"

Malia could not admit that any rescue attempt was underway. She mostly trusted this stranger, and she mostly believed her story, but what if she was wrong, and Sohan was an ADF plant? Exterra's convenient absence also made Malia wonder whether Sohan might be sounding her out on any rescue efforts. And really, what could one janitor do? But the revelation about Gaia refusing the death pills gave her an idea.

"I would like to have death pills to kill myself rather than go through with this marriage. Can you get me these pills? I would keep them in my robe, and I probably would never use them, but it would give me courage knowing I had this option."

Sohan's eyes lowered. "I would hate to give Gaia's niece these death pills after Gaia herself fought them."

"Perhaps it will not be for me after all," Malia said, not quite knowing what she was saying.

Sohan nodded. Even if Malia poisoned Paragon, the obscure Sohan would almost certainly escape scrutiny. She brought out of her pocket a small eco-plastic container, which she handed to Malia. "Here, you can have mine. Cyanide papier. It dissolves in liquid instantly, they said.

"They gave them to me last week, because I could not finish cleaning the rooms that day, I was so weak and tired. The next day, I managed to finish, but it is a struggle every day. My new partner is much younger, but she resents having to do my work for me. I can't blame her.

"I can always say I lost them or threw them out. They will be happy to give me another set."

"And," said Malia, "since I will probably not use these in the end, all I ask is that if you see an opportunity to help me, please take it. I don't know what that will look like. Maybe my husband will come and rescue me, but of course we haven't been in touch."

"We janitors are everywhere, and yet we are invisible. Sometimes we can help. I will try to keep an eye out," Sohan promised her. With her crafty intuition honed by forty years among conniving young woman and their superiors, she suspected Malia knew more than she let on, but approved of her circumspection. The forces ranged against them were powerful. It was unlikely they would allow Sohan anywhere near the chapel that day, and she would be on lockdown with all but a few privileged priests who would sing the liturgy from the balcony.

Malia knew Exterra might come back at any moment, but she kept Sohan in her room, asking about her Diversity story and, more important, a lifetime's worth of questions about Gaia, what she had looked like, what she had said about her family, and how she managed to tolerate living among the Earthloving priests when she hated the Antifans and everything they stood for.

"She was good at lying," said Sohan. "She pretended to be loyal and Earthloving, but she secretly believed in Christ. I would not turn her in for that, because to me, Mother Earth Diversity is all about finding your own god. She called him Jesus, so what? She was a good person, despite everything she had suffered, and she found comfort in her Jesus, who she said had suffered too."

Malia was moved. "Yes, that is exactly so. He took on the sins of the world, and suffered for our sake."

Sohan looked dubious. "Well, perhaps. Gaia said they nailed him to a cross, and he died so. I do not understand how a real god could allow this to happen to him."

"It's a little more complicated than that," Malia smiled.

"It is dangerous to talk about this Son of God, especially here. I should be going now."

"Yes," said Malia. "Thank you for sharing all this with me. I am sorry I did not come here earlier; I would have helped her." They rose, and as Malia's hand touched the doorknob, she turned and asked, "How exactly did she die? She didn't take the pills in the end?"

"No, I heard a great choking in the night, I went over to her bed, and held her hand, and she called out, 'Lord Jesus! I see you!' and then I knew it was over. Fortunately, no one heard her cry those words, since we are alone in the basement. I didn't want to disturb anyone until morning, not for a mere janitor, they would have yelled at me, so I prayed my own prayers by her bedside until dawn and never left her alone."

Malia's fingers left the doorknob, and she embraced Sohan. "On behalf of my family, the one that I never really knew, I thank you. God bless you."

As she did that, they heard a crashing sound in the living room as a glass shattered. Exterra had returned, drunk, with two other Antifan women and a man, and they had flung themselves on the sofa and chairs, prepared to continue the party, since some of the young ladies had complained about the ruckus they were making in the garden behind the social hall. Malia had hoped to give Sohan more food to take back to her room, but it was impossible now.

Malia angrily confronted the foursome, but the louche group instead fixed their unsteady gazes on Sohan, who had followed her out of the bedroom.

"Hey, what's that dwarf doing in her bedroom?" laughed the young man. In another setting, it would have been a knowledge crime to insult a disabled person, but Antifans were generally exempt from such scrutiny.

"Malia, you cheating on Khalid with a dwarf?" sneered Exterra. Her raucous laughter filled the room, and the two other women joined in. "That's Malia for you, getting her kicks on with low social credit freaks. That's where she started, you know."

"She was bringing some clean linens for the bed," said Malia stiffly. Meanwhile, Sohan tried to slip out of the suite, her eyes brimming with tears—less because of the Antifans' stinging insults than because of Malia's thanks and warm embrace. She was accustomed to calculated rudeness and words spoken in disgust rather than drunkenness.

Exterra sharply told Sohan, "Go into my room and make that bed properly. Whoever did it was incompetent."

"Yes, amba-mam," Sohan said, and disappeared into Exterra's room.

Malia then turned to the three other Antifans and said, "Out of here. All of you. Except that one—" she pointed at Exterra, "whose mutilated face I will have to stare at the rest of my life. Get out!"

Exterra gasped. "Can you believe what she said? Malia, Khalid will punish you for that! You…"

"I doubt it. I'm sure he thinks the same thing every time he looks at you."

Malia turned to the other three. "Out. Now." They sidled out, a little bit ashamed, but more concerned about whether Commander Ma would find out about their insolence to his senior wife and punish them instead.

Sohan emerged, whispered, "Good night, amba-sehm," the polite plural, and disappeared into the night. Malia went to bed, locking the door to her room.

Several hours later, Sohan, crouching on the concrete floor of the utility room in the basement of Owlet Hall, cast a curse spell on Exterra Boyd. She had picked several blonde hairs off the pillow, which was enough. She regretted not having had the foresight to ask Malia for a hair or some other personal effect so that she might have cast a power spell to help Gaia's niece. But enough of Malia's presence still hovered around Sohan that the elderly woman, by staring at a photograph of the celebrity on her armband screen, was able to generate a goodwill charm for her. That will have to do, Sohan thought, and may be enough so that she does not consider taking the pills herself.

Chapter 54
Blood Is Shed
(Tuesday, October 26, 2094)

Shortly after dawn, David and six other men, including Oren, Tom, and Seth, stood just off the side of the road, black balaclavas in hand for the moment when the group would intercept the small bus coming from Baltimore. Some held shiny objects in their right hands that would explode on impact. David, Tom, and Seth held their weapons and all the others concealed their newly manufactured guns. All wore black jeans and jackets, the customary uniform of stagehands that also would serve as quasi-Antifan costuming for the initial interception.

They stayed just far enough off the road not to be casually visible to other drivers, although only a few cars flashed by, most of them self-driving cars with occupants absorbed in their important tasks rather than viewing the familiar drab scenery between Baltimore and Philadelphia. Most travelers going between cities on the East Coast relied on trains, since intercity car travel was prohibitively expensive, even for high Social Crediteers.

Just ten minutes ago, two women from Oren's town, standing on an overpass to the south, had phoned to confirm that the bus labeled "Baltimore Official Work Unit" had passed by them. Another pair of watchers would call when the bus reached a spot five minutes away.

It was an unusually cool morning, and the men stamped about, not too loudly, but trying to generate some warmth before the sun rose fully. David had spent the last week with Oren's group, and now knew all the men by name and backstory. He felt he could trust them. Oren had sworn them to the mission and vouched for them. But only to Tom and Seth could David admit trepidation. "This is it, guys," he muttered to them during that last five minutes. "No going back now. Thank you for coming with me this far." *I have brought several dozen people into this plot, and not all of them will survive the week.*

"We're all-in," Tom assured him. The tired, pouchy-faced man from the Candor Inn had toughened since last November. The three men each balled a fist and bumped them together.

"Us too," said the other kameraten, so the trio from Cayuga made way for more fists.

"To success," said David.

"To bashing in a few Soko soyboys," rejoined one small wiry man.

"Not if we don't have to," cautioned David, but he suspected it was a losing cause. And if beating up Social Crediteers motivated these men, so be it.

"It's coming," said another man with binoculars who was looking downhill towards the approaching bus. They pulled on their black balaclavas.

The two men entrusted with the grenades tossed them, almost gently, so they exploded a few hundred feet ahead of the bus, which needed to stay drivable and intact. The bus skidded to a stop, and the two vans pulled alongside it, concealing it from other traffic. David leaped toward the door, and signaled the driver to open it. When the driver hesitated, David shot through the plastic, which was not bulletproof, and the driver hastily opened the door.

"ADF undercover unit!" David shouted. "Hand over all armbands!" He stared over the dozen blank or frightened faces of a low credit group in black jeans and long-sleeved black shirts, the uniform of the stagehand union from Baltimore. Some of the workers had been asleep, so were groggy. Most of them began fumbling with the straps of their black armbands.

The dozen Social Credit workmen were accustomed to heeding authority, the black worn by David and the men who followed him was certifiably Antifan, and the band had the advantage of surprise. The men—and one woman—started handing over their armbands obediently. Then one of the brighter or more alert men realized that none of the attackers wore armbands themselves. "Hey, you're not Antifans!" He cried, "Emergency!" into his armband to summon help.

David sprang over—no time to order anyone else to the job—and punched the man straight in the face. While the man slumped to the floor, unconscious, David grabbed the armband, and when the emergency operator came on, he said, calmly, "Sorry, wrong number," and ended the call. Meanwhile, his men had collected the armbands, and the dozen workers, including the driver, were quickly ushered off the bus and into Oren's vans. The transfer would not have been visible to anyone driving by, since the van entrances faced the woods. Standing beside the vans, David called out, "Nobody's going to get hurt if you cooperate!"

Two of the band carried out the unconscious worker, who was bleeding from his nose and lip, and laid him on the floor of one of the vans, which sped off to the agreed-upon meeting place fifteen minutes away.

Tom got behind the wheel of the workers' bus and, with David and Seth, followed the vans. The assault and the transfer of the workers into the vans had taken only three minutes. David nodded to himself with satisfaction. They had practiced the routines endlessly during the past week, not overlooking the complicating possibilities of more resistance.

At the isolated meeting spot near Havre de Grace, another six of Oren's followers were waiting for them. David checked off the names and social credit numbers on his list of the Baltimore workers, efficiently assigning each to one of his band, careful to match physical descriptions as much as possible, even though there was nothing to be done about the reality that two of the stagehands were African-Diversan and none of the Plores were. Rebecca was going to have to impersonate the one woman, a small swarthy Latinx named Araceli Perez, 100. The first six stagehands he processed were moved into one van, which shot off toward the hideout with two armed Plores as guards and a third as driver. The phones of the twelve fake stagehands had been given to the van drivers, for safekeeping in the roundup. Discovery of any of these Plore phones on the college grounds would doom them all.

Three more workers had boarded the second van, and the man whom David had punched was laid on his back across the second bench to the rear, with two more guards in the last seat, from which they could keep an eye on the hostages. Araceli and a final man were left.

Araceli spat at David and Oren, and furiously said, "You dirty Plores! You fucking white supremacists! You won't get away with this. You can't defeat Diverse Power!"

Oren contemplated her briefly, his eyes glinting. Then he grabbed the meek man beside her, raised his gun, and shot the man in the head before the victim even had time to react to the weapon. The final worker slithered, dead, to the ground. Araceli's red-painted mouth opened in horror, and she breathed faintly. "Ay!"

"See that, bitch?" Oren said. "Open your hole again like that, and I'll kill another friend of yours." He would not kill a woman, not unless he had to, but executing the innocent man in her stead—so innocent he died without realizing it—was equally effective. It demonstrated that these Plores were armed, and they were ruthless, and that even verbal resistance would have deadly consequences. Oren shoved her, weeping, into the van, and it too sped off. Everyone in the van had seen and heard the killing, and it would cow them, at least temporarily.

Even David was shocked. He had not expected a killing, not so soon, not after a verbal challenge from one woman. He had hoped to fend off Oren's willingness to execute the workers, even though he recognized that Oren's concern about what would happen after their release was warranted. It was not something he wanted to worry about, not yet. But David's opposition was enough to at least postpone the ultimate decision, and David ruefully recognized that if the mission succeeded, he wouldn't be the one around to make the final call.

He and Oren dragged the body into a thicket, which would have to do, because time was fleeting. They rubbed sanitizer on their hands to wipe out the bloodstains. David and the others boarded the bus, which quickly drove off. Tom steered deftly, having had some experience driving a bus in Syracuse. Everyone logged onto their new armbands, acquainting themselves with their new identities. David showed everyone how to erase the existing passwords and create new ones.

"Hey," said one man, "my fake partner is asking how the trip is going. Do I respond? Also, I didn't know I was going to be gay."

"Wait till we get there. Read some of your guy's messages to him so you know what to sound like when you write back. And tell your loved ones you won't be able to write much for the next few days because of the tight security and the busy schedule."

"You're all going to be playacting," David reminded them. "Learn your part. And everyone, learn everyone else's new names. Don't call anyone by their real names." David realized with some trepidation that he was going to have to impersonate Bradley Earthlover, 118. That was the dead man. David hoped that this wasn't a bad omen for him. Bradley had a wife who had already sent a loving message, which made David feel even worse. "We're so proud of you," she had gushed, "helping with the Diverse event of the century…"

The Lenilenape-Sylvania border loomed ahead, a nerve-racking moment since the patrols would pull vehicles aside at random to make identity checks. Fortunately, and maybe because the wedding was well publicized to law enforcement and the participants made known to authorities beforehand, the bus sailed through. The group cheered on the other side. An hour later, they were pulling up to the checkpoint at the College of the Earthloving Priests, or more precisely, into a very long line of wedding workers who apparently had all been told to arrive at the same time. Harried Knowledge Tower clerical workers with some College employees did the actual check-in, but the ADF troops stood nearby, ready to react if problems arose. The crush made the anxious workers less likely to grill the arrivals.

Tom grunted, "Baltimore stagehand crew," and an Antifan came on board to tap each of their armbands with his electronic wand. All the armbands worked perfectly. The Antifan gave Rebecca a somewhat perplexed look. "You don't look Latinx," he said.

"That was my sperm parent," Rebecca responded. "My birthing parent was very blonde." She had been rehearsing this line for two hours now. The Antifan shrugged. "Free to go," he told Tom as he jumped off the bus. The College worker gave Tom a map that showed where he needed to park and another map that pinpointed their tents on the playing field where they would stay. "Here's the commissary for your meals."

"Thank you," said Tom, adding, "Mother Earth be with you," as a friendly salute. She beamed in response, "And may She destroy our enemies!"

They started to roll away, but the Antifan waved them down. Uh-oh, thought David.

"Is Bradley Earthlover, 118, on the bus? They're looking for the crew chief."

"That's me," said David reluctantly. Trust Oren to kill the crew chief, and of course that would now be me. They had been unable to plan for that. So much for a low profile. Bradley seemed to have changed his last name in recent months, presumably in obedience to the call to eradicate lingering religious or fascist names. David wondered what Bradley's previous surname had been. Maybe you'd better scroll through the armband and find out before someone asks you.

"When you get settled in, report to the facilities desk in Athena Chapel with the other crew chiefs," the Antifan ordered.

"Yes, amba-sah," said David. They rolled forward again, this time uninterrupted, toward the playing fields, where in June the priests coupled in Beltane worship. But today, the fields were full of insulated white tents, which from above looked like clouds.

More than 150 miles to the west, the vans drove past Oren's town. Deep in the woods, they pulled up at a ranch house in a clearing. The guards told their terrified prisoners to remove their blindfolds. They stood around, dazed, blinking at the sun like birds.

"Nobody's going to be hurt if you cooperate. After the wedding, we'll let you go," promised the new leader, a rawboned middle-aged grocery employee named Quinn. David and Oren had taken anyone with construction or handyman experience for the fake stage crew. This left behind those who were less skilled, less successful, and more resentful.

After what had happened to Bradley Earthlover, nobody seemed inclined to argue. They obediently filed down into the cellar from the outside entrance, including the man David had punched, who was groggy, and bloodied, but finally mobile. The door shut on them. Two men had already gone into the house to bar the inside staircase to the cellar.

Quinn went into the shabby kitchen with peeling wallpaper and found Rachel and Jeff Welcome making cheese sandwiches at a butcher block table, as for a house party. "Showing some Plore hospitality, I see."

"Gotta feed them," said Rachel.

"They'll be better behaved if they're not starved," Jeff added.

We'll see, Quinn thought. "One Soko probably needs some medical attention. You can look at him when you bring the food down. Another guy we left dead in the roundaway."

"What'd he do?" asked Jeff.

"Nothing. Oren shot him when the little Spanish lady mouthed off at him. He never even knew what happened, just fell down."

Jeff pressed his lips together. This crowd made him nervous. David had brought the couple down from Cayuga because he thought their medic skills might come in handy. Jeff and Rachel had watched the training all week, as they had dedicated themselves to outfitting the basement for a dozen hostages, like innkeepers in a modest but hygienic lodge. They had made sure the toilet and the sink were working and towels were available. Jeff wondered who owned the house, which was spare but not dilapidated. Their job was by far the most benign. They did not touch the firearms, and just attended to what would be the welfare of the temporary guests.

The intense but calm presence of David had reassured Jeff and Rachel. With David around, Oren was more subdued, and the other men took their cue from the businesslike pair. David was deadly serious, making sure the attackers knew their plans inside out, and barking angrily at careless errors. "You'll get us killed doing that! What the hell are you thinking?" By the time the two-week training period ended, David was finally satisfied.

"You're just used to Anacosta," Rachel teased Jeff when he had complained about the coarseness of the gang. "You Anacosta types are like princes, you know, among us ordinary folk."

"No," he said, staring at the ceiling in their bed the morning the men had all gone off to waylay the stagehands. "Something's off about them. It's about revenge. I feel like I'm living with pirates. For Mike, it's all about the mission."

"Well, what other mission would these guys have? They don't have Mike's reason for doing this mission. They're not going to risk getting killed just to get some fresh air."

"I just hope that no one gets killed, period. It might be safer to be storming that college with Mike than stay here with a bunch of Social Credit hostages and crazy Plores. I can't explain it, Rachel, but I get a bad vibe from them."

"If it's all about anger and revenge, it means they aren't completely under control. If one small thing goes wrong, they might lose it..."

He had texted his father, discreetly, on the first evening on the clean phone he was sharing with Rachel. "Rough situation here. This could go south quickly. Can you get me out of here?"

The reply, when it finally came, was bleak. You're on your own. A few minutes later, more gently, follow your woman's lead. She knows the deal.

Rachel leaned over and gave Jeff a fortifying hug. "Come on, let's get moving. They might be here in two hours."

"Rachel, is it so terrible that I'm hoping they change their minds and forget about this whole business?" The dark-haired young woman gave him a tolerant but slightly condescending smile, and headed for the chair where she had placed her jeans and sweatshirt. She cared deeply for Jeff, who was a tender and caring lover, and did everything he could to make her happy, but sometimes she thought, he's too gentle for us country Plores, someday he's going to get hurt.

Jeff thought, despairingly, that life in Anacosta Ploreville had been kind and easy, by comparison with everything that had followed. Once he had plunged into Social Credit life, each promised refuge had become a nightmare. The Euthanasia Palace, of course, and then the kindly roundup by the shores of Cayuga Lake had suddenly transformed into another kind of nightmare. Now, the preternatural calm of this remote Yramaland spot itself bespoke trouble to come. He pulled himself heavily out of the bed and began to dress.

Chapter 55
Rehearsals
(Wednesday, October 27, 2094)

"My wives!" Paragon announced as he entered the suite above the arch. Exterra squealed, ran to him, and embraced him. To her irritation, he immediately looked over her shoulder at Malia, who was sitting with stiff dignity in an armchair, perusing the proof version of what would be her final column in the *Anacosta Post*, relieved that all her clues had survived the Tower censors. The astute reader—and only one reader—would glean that chauffeured cars would line up in the side driveway of Athena Chapel during the wedding so the most elite guests who were not staying for the reception would not be inconvenienced, and could depart quickly after the ceremony.

The atmosphere in the arch suite had been chilly for several days, with the women barely speaking, and Exterra praying loudly and ostentatiously at the Mother Earth altar. "May You implant in me a child for Diversity!" Despite her apprehension, Malia still could not resist a twisted smile at that plea: It doesn't work that way, honey.

"Malia, aren't you happy to see me?" Paragon's tone was triumphant, almost sugary. In two days would come the glorious ceremony in which all DJR eyes would fasten on his victory over fascism, in the form of Malia's subjugation. The following Monday he expected to see the official notification of Steve Rosen's resignation in the daily Beaufort bulletin.

I am happy to see you because it brings us one day closer to my rescue and your doom, Malia thought. Aloud, she said, "How providential Mother Earth was to bring you here safely."

"Indeed! Shall we go for a stroll before the rehearsal?"

A few minutes later, the priests—heading to their classes or to the refectory for lunch—watched the trio heading past Titania Hall toward Merlin Green. "How beautiful the brides!" they said in their stilted language that all learned as novices. "How Diversity is praised!" The trees were in full autumnal glory, reds, yellows, and some surviving green. The air was cool but all were comfortable. Paragon wore his uniform, on his right Malia one of her toastier red gowns, and on his left Exterra, who had switched into a navy blue gown with a plunging neckline.

"It compliments half your face," Malia had greeted her that morning.

Several uniformed Antifans followed at a respectful distance, but sufficient to keep the curious priests at bay. As the entourage passed Owlet Hall, with its tall narrow windows, a small Asian janitor sweeping the porch peered at them. Malia nodded in her direction, and reached into her robe pocket and felt the small eco-plastic canister resting in its depths.

Malia's patience was wearing thin, but she reminded herself this was not necessarily betraying her intentions to her jailers. Had she displayed a calm countenance, they might have suspected she expected a reprieve or even a rescue. Her irritation, properly calibrated, might be explained as the helpless response of a prisoner with no way out of the closing trap. So she doled out her snippy remarks sparingly, as if she could not quite bear to keep them contained.

As they were approaching the bottom of the hill, where lay the newly named Omicron Institute for Settled Science, home of cutting-edge Diversity research aimed at narrative-confirmation, Paragon turned to Exterra, and requested she meet them at the Athena Chapel. "Go ahead," he said. "I must speak with Malia alone."

Exterra turned and flounced away, followed by two of the four Antifan guards. Paragon dismissed them all, and when the group had safely retreated, he indicated a rounded stone bench. "Shall we sit?"

Malia inclined her head in reluctant compliance and sat. Paragon seated himself next to her, not quite touching her. The bench, which had initially been inscribed with the name "MOON," perhaps a benefactor of the old college, now read, "Love Mother Earth's MOON." Paragon had chosen the spot well, since they were concealed from casual passersby.

"You must think I am quite the monster," he began.

"Are you expecting me to argue with you?"

"You aren't doing badly, you know. In a few days, you will be the senior wife of the third most important man in the DJR…sorry, I meant person…and a few weeks later, the second. In a matter of time, the first. Think of where you were only five years ago. Could you have dreamed this would all happen to you? Is it not like what they called a fairy tale?"

"I could not have dreamed I would have a loving, kind husband and three children, live in a free country, and be kidnapped from all of them and returned to slavery."

"Don't be so petty. I wish to acquaint you with my thought processes and my plans. If you are to be my senior wife, I must share them with you. I do not believe Exterra is capable of comprehending them but you are intellectually capable of sharing my ambitions. I believe that your new luxurious lifestyle will disabuse you of any love for the United States even if you currently harbor remnants of fascist thought."

Remnants? Malia laughed to herself. "Tell me, Khalid," she said. In a week, if all went well, she would relay all this to her AIA handlers.

"You know I had a half sister, in addition to my two full brothers. Her name was Patigul."

Malia nodded.

"I have not been forthcoming about her, because…well, it is not the proudest moment of my life. She was full Uighur, a devout Muslim. My father was Chinese, but hers was Uighur. We came to the DJR when my father was dispatched to help the new country institute a social credit and socialist system. Then he and my mother returned to China, but Patigul and I stayed here. She married another Muslim, just a menial laborer, and they had four children, paying the carbon offsets each year. I did not know she was practicing Islam apart from the Mother Earth Diversity Church, and that she was in contact with dissidents overseas who were instructing them in old-fashioned heretical practices." His swarthy face flushed with the humiliation of the remembrance, either of Patigul's poor marriage or her illegal Muslim practice, or both.

"I was a junior ADF officer when they told me that she and her husband had been arrested for knowledge crime. She was imprisoned in Beaufort and they were to be executed, because she would not repent. I went to her and begged her to recant, for the sake of my career. And of course, for her children. The authorities would have forgiven her, eventually, after a prison term. But she would not bend. If she had truly loved me, she would have done what I asked.

"So when the moment came for her execution, I volunteered to participate on the firing squad. It was not pleasant, since I had loved her so much. But my whole life was at stake. Had I not volunteered, the scandal would have destroyed my hopes of advancement."

"Uh…how long ago was this?" she asked, for lack of anything better to say.

"Twenty years ago this month. To think she could have risen with me, had she only been more cooperative. I hope you will be more reasonable than she was.

"After Patigul died, I resolved that I would be unyielding for Diversity. I would make everyone in the DJR suffer for what they did to us, but it would be for the cause. There is no point in continuing in a haphazard, half-hearted way—what would be the point of her sacrifice? Why should we just bumble along, pretending to be Diverse, when Diversity would always be out of reach because we did not have the courage of our principles? Her sacrifice would not be in vain.

"So it is entirely due to Patigul that I have innovated in Diversity. The incubation farms, the truth serum, no-carbon-footprint working from home, names that celebrate Diversity. Soon the dismantling of the family unit. Eventually the destruction of the Plores. We have enslaved them, but they still live and we know they resist Diverse Power." Paragon's face took on a dreamy cast, as if he had almost forgotten Malia was listening. "We have not even begun. When I become director, I will push aside the whole rotten apparatus and we will strive for total Diversity."

Why me, Malia wanted to scream. Why take me along on this depraved journey?

"You remind me of Patigul. She resisted Diverse Power when she could have profited by it. I do not consider myself a bad Muslim just because I worship within the MED doctrine. Allah is Mother Earth and Mother Earth is Allah.

"After the incident at the zoo, where you shouted heresy at the visitors, and it bounced off against their stupid brains, I realized there was something special about you. You were a pure representation of what we struggle against. Shooting you would have been a waste. When we made the movie, I realized that you had not truly converted to Diversity, and that indeed, you could not. It was not in your nature. But you could not be allowed to wander loose, or tell the US what you have learned about us and fight us from afar. So I decided to marry you regardless, and keep you safe. Not kill you, as we killed Patigul. But keep you apart from Diversity, so it neither taints you nor you taint it."

"I want to go home," said Malia firmly. "My sons…my daughter."

"No, that will not be. Have a child for me. Now let's go over to the rehearsal." He leaned over and kissed her on the cheek.

As they stood up, Paragon concluded, "I will not make the same mistake I did with Patigul. I should have protected her too."

Meanwhile, Malia rolled the little plastic cylinder in her hand, in her deep robe pocket, as she had throughout the whole walk. It was becoming a nervous tic. "Khalid, what happened to Patigul's children?"

Paragon said firmly, "I did not ask, and I did not care."

"Shouldn't you? Weren't they your nieces and nephews?"

"Family ties are less consequential than ideological unity. I needed to set an example. But they were not punished for their parents' sins." He strode ahead of her, impatiently.

David's crew was scrambling to learn the ropes, some literally, of the Athena Chapel stage. The two electricians in his crew were handling the lighting board, Rebecca the props—including the great ceremonial cups, the wine, and the juice for Paragon—and the youngest man would be responsible for video, including the evil movie, which would place him adjacent to the top balcony. The young Plore needed to run the movie well for the rehearsal, and then, perhaps, not so expertly, during the actual wedding. Nobody seemed to think it odd that some of the stage crew needed to check out the balconies in the almost empty hall, and they jogged up and downstairs without any challenge. Others, including Oren, would be arranging the holy altar, and ensuring the chairs for the most esteemed witnesses were placed in the most auspicious locations as decreed by Melusine's astrological charts.

The six-foot-tall priest with the bounteous artificial cleavage had taken a special interest in David, much to his alarm. *As if I have nothing else to worry about.* On late Tuesday afternoon, Melusine had spent half an hour instructing him in private on the arrangements, while running her fleshy hand along his thigh as he sat there. Play your role, he told himself urgently, since his real instincts hovered somewhere between "Mention your loving wife, not the one who is getting married on this stage," and "Deck this Soko freak." The morning's adrenalin still coursed through him.

He sat there, pretending to be frozen, as the powerful hand kneaded his thighs, first one, then the other. His body was responding, helplessly, Melusine noted with satisfaction.

"Do you love Mother Earth, Bradley?" cooed Melusine. "How would you like to worship in my private quarters? We'll have a special meal, only the best, and then..."

He had just stammered, "Amba-mam..." when several priestly functionaries arrived, breathless, with some crisis for her to handle. Melusine followed quickly in their wake, ignoring David.

Now, a day later, he had been bent over the curtain tracks trying to loosen a stuck cord and, scrambling back up to his feet, was taken aback to find her looming over him.

"Hello, handsome 118," Melusine cooed in a deep voice. "I've been waiting for your visit."

"Amba-mam, we have been very busy here. I can't leave my crew while we are preparing for the great wedding. Also, I wasn't sure it would be permitted."

"It is permitted, since I am in charge here. When the wedding is over, come to the reception, and you may sit near my table and I will feed you from my plate. Then we shall spend the night in my quarters. We will worship together. I will send you home in my personal car."

"Yes, amba-mam." Thank God not before the wedding, David breathed with relief. After the wedding ceremony, Melusine would have to find a new date. But now he began to understand the special subservience of the low Social Crediteer, which Malia had lived until he rescued her five years ago. Hated by the Plores and despised and exploited by their Soko betters, low Social Crediteers dared not object to the latter's demands. Melusine would not have deigned to touch a Plore, but Bradley Earthlover, 118, married or not, was fair game.

At that moment, Paragon and Malia arrived for the rehearsal; Paragon strode down the center aisle with Malia trailing behind. Exterra emerged, having been sulking in her dressing room. Several Antifans arranged themselves behind the stage; David, ducking behind the curtains just in time, noted their placement. He had provided the crew with black baseball caps that said "Crew" in white block lettering. The main reason was to conceal his own face from Antifans who might recognize him, but overall the wearing of the caps and only black created the impression of an antlike crew whose humanity was submerged into their task.

The stairs creaked as David climbed up to the first balcony and checked on the lighting crew. "Got it, Brad," they reassured him.

So he climbed up to the second balcony, which was dark and narrow. The movie projectionist said, "I've been practicing, Brad. It'll be fine." David nodded. No Antifan guards were here today for the rehearsal, but David knew several would be posted on the day of the wedding. He had asked whether some extra supplies could be stored up here, and they had refused, citing the security presence, so he confirmed Malia's information.

The building had been thoroughly searched on Wednesday morning, and nothing unusual found, which David had learned in the course of his duties as the stage crew chief. The next search, the morning of the wedding, would be more rushed and more cursory, he knew, since the Antifans would be reassured by the earlier scrutiny. His crew would arrive earlier than anyone else, which would spare them the body searches that the guests and other workers would endure at the hands of the Antifans. Just in case, they had discovered a sacristy where long-forgotten vestments were kept. The crew stashed some important items for the wedding far underneath dusty dark green chasubles, probably dating back to the seventies. The Antifans would likely give the closet a perfunctory look—the old vestments were heavy—sneeze loudly, and recall they had already searched it on Wednesday.

David decided to watch the rehearsal from the top balcony. It was perfectly plausible that the stage crew chief would want to observe his crew's performance from a distance. His arms crossed, he stood far enough back in the balcony that Malia would not recognize him, not easily. Watching Ma, David recognized his old colleague. But no one would have guessed this man, now filled out in full maturity, would ever become number three at Beaufort.

The processional began. Several young novices dressed in white danced down the aisle, then two sober lines of two dozen green clad priests singing "Herm of Joy at Earthly Uniting." Next came the provost of the College, then Aleta. Finally, Paragon, Malia, and Exterra, in that order. Melusine and Ceridwen brought up the rear. The bridal trio and the MED functionaries and archbishop mounted the stage as the chorus proceeded upstairs to the main balcony with the dancing novices. Melusine announced, "And now for the celebratory documentary, showing the triumph of Diversity over fascism, in the form of Commander Ma's taking of Communicator Malia." The film showed uneventfully. Exterra's mouth opened wordlessly, and she was so overcome that she did not even notice a small trail of drool pooling in the corner of her lips.

David refused to watch, closing his eyes in the darkened auditorium. *Even if I die on Saturday,* David told himself, *I will kill this Ma first, and tell him why.* Aleta then pronounced, "And so be it to the enemies of our Mother Earth! We will now read from the Books of Dworkin and of Intersectional Joy.

The complete destruction of traditional marriage is the path to liberation. Each of us, yea, shall find our partner, or partners, and define our bonds how so shall we will. The nuclear family must go. The overpopulation of the earth must end. If womyn only bear children in full will, the earth shall breathe a sigh of great relief.

Mother Earth casts her benevolence over the trees, the rivers, the fields, the animals, and the people, all equal before her. Let the trees and the flowers populate the earth, and let humankind stand aside in shame.

As the empty words swirled around them, Paragon absentmindedly considered how he would rearrange the deputy director's office.

Accompanied by the musicians, the chorus trilled in their sopranos the "Chorale for Earth Marriage no. 3," by the famed Diverse composer Abuwekeza Shonkalezi, born Ken Jones.

"And at this point Your Reverence," Melusine said, addressing the archbishop, "conducts the actual ceremony."

Cecelia Mountainspring, 320, stepped forward. She was still the same squat creature whom Malia had last seen at the Earth Weekend five years earlier. Fortunately, the archbishop neither remembered that Malia had escaped her deportation to the Economic Zone, nor possibly the event at all. She did not wear her regalia for the rehearsal. Instead she was encased in eco-nylon pants and sweater, like any high Social Credit mother.

"I shall relate the liturgy, as I do for any marriage celebrants. There are some differences here, because you are three. At some point, I ask you, Commander Ma, if you wish to take both of your brides to treat with equal honor and love. You, presumably, will assent, saying, "Ayah, I shall, may Mother Earth witness." Then, Communicator Malia, I ask for your assent to take Commander Ma and Captain Boyd as loving spouses to treat with honor and love. You also respond, "Ayah, I shall, may Mother Earth witness." Then, Captain Boyd, the same for you. The obligation to your spouses is identical, regardless of your or their gender or status.

"However, Commander Ma has indicated he wishes to select a first and a second wife. In recognition of his critical service to the Republic, we have permitted this minor amendment to our marital laws. At this point, I will turn to you, Commander, and say, "Please pledge to your first spouse," and you will say to Malia, "I name you my first spouse." Then Malia drinks, you turn to Captain Boyd, lift your cup, and drink first to Malia, and then to Captain Boyd, in sequence. Then Captain Boyd drinks as the second wife. Then you raise your goblets together, so they touch, in harmony. Is this all clear?"

The three nodded.

"At that point, I pronounce you married under Mother Earth, in the Diversity Justice Republic, a union that no one shall rend asunder, unless you want to, in the year 2094 or Diverse Year 39. Priestess Melusine, what comes next?"

"Your Reverence, the image of Her Holiness Mother Earth is then flashed against the black wall behind the altar. Lighting! Hey, lighting, wake up!"

With a shudder, the image of a breasted, faceless Mother Earth appeared and then steadied on the wall.

"The chorus will then sing 'Exalted Be Her Forever,' and we will do the recessional in the reverse order of the processional. Golf carts will be waiting outside to bring all the wedding celebrants to the feasting hall," said Melusine.

"I was disturbed to learn that the vegan feast was replaced with beefsteak," the archbishop intoned disapprovingly.

Paragon became alert and conciliatory. "Only because our great benefactors from the People's Republic of China will be attending, Your Reverence. I was reluctant to forgo the vegan feast—I am fond of cauliflower steak myself—but we cannot risk an international incident. Our Chinese friends are very sensitive to any indication that we are disparaging them. They always are lavish and meat-giving when they host us, and any perception that we do not value their friendship sufficiently might cause an international incident that would be harmful to the DJR."

"Well, we cannot have that, Commander Ma, can we?" the aging archbishop smiled, not immune to the commander's hint of roguish charm. Paragon winked at her.

They practiced the ceremony twice more before heading to lunch, which meant broadcasting the awful movie twice more. At one point, when Paragon and Exterra were exchanging their vows, and their eyes were safely focused on each other, Malia quickly looked up at the oddly familiar figure in the balcony to confirm it indeed was David. Imagining the balcony and stage ringed with Antifans, and the getaway doors guarded by them, Malia still had no idea how David planned to engineer their escape, and had no idea how he had inserted himself onto the stage crew. She hoped he would not be betrayed by the crew, whom she took to be legitimate Social Credit stagehands. How can one man, even this man, defeat the heart of the Diverse Power, which will be filling this room, she asked herself? What could she do to help him?

Chapter 56
Nutes Running Everywhere
(Friday, October 29, 2094)

Jeff had started sleeping in one of the vans. "I can't sleep, what with all them moving around and talking in the basement," he told Rachel.

"I can't hear them at all," she countered. "You're just imagining it."

"It's like mice in the walls or the basement. You know they're down there. What if they burn down the house just to escape?"

"That wouldn't be very smart of them. Anyway, they don't have matches and I feel perfectly safe," Rachel said. Jeff looked glumly at her. Rachel was so beautiful, he thought, even in her ragged long-sleeved blue T-shirt and the jeans that needed washing. When she tossed her head, a sheaf of straight black hair bounced backward, her face alive with the excitement of doing something for the cause, at last. Jeff reminded himself that Rachel had lost her parents, her brother, and several other relatives in the Antifan massacre, and sometimes he could tell she was thinking of them, and would try to comfort her. Of course she would be more resolute than him, with his family safe in Anacosta, he sighed.

Unarmed, they were never alone in the house. One or two watchmen in the kitchen were always guarding the indoor door to the basement, and two others outside in front of the cellar door behind which the eleven prisoners were contained. Three times a day, the kitchen door opened and Jeff would go halfway down the stairs, and pass down plates with sandwiches, a hot dish casserole, or scrambled eggs that the inmates would divide among themselves. Once they even baked cookies for the prisoners. Then he would sit at the top of the staircase waiting for them to finish before taking back the dishes and the trash in a separate bag. As good Sokos, the prisoners insisted on having two extra bags for recycling. If that's all being a Social Crediteer involved, Jeff thought mournfully to himself, I'd have stayed with them.

Into the second day, the prisoners had yelled and hurled threats at them from the basement. But this made no impression on their jailers, and when Rachel canceled dinner on the second night due to their rowdiness, this sufficed to guarantee better behavior afterward. A Committee of Unjustly Detained Loyal Diversans (CUDLOD), represented by Araceli and two of the men, confronted Jeff. "Just because we are prisoners does not mean we should violate the laws of Mother Earth. We need a box for compost and a copy of the MED Main Hernal for worship."

"What's the difference between the two?" Jeff had uncharacteristically retorted.

"Be glad you have a toilet and a sink and a place to lie down," Rachel said. "Don't make this harder on yourselves, you'll be back home in a few days." Rachel's reasonable, almost maternal tone had a calming effect on the Sokos. Each indeed had a mattress and a blanket, which was no small sacrifice for these deprived hosts.

The din had subsided into sullen grumbling by Thursday. The sound of boots tramping overhead reminded the prisoners that armed Plores stood ready to kill them should they rebel. Still, the presence of the dark-skinned Jeff on the other side was especially galling to them. First tentatively, then more aggressively, they baited him while he waited for their plates and debris at the top of the stairs.

"How did a Diverse person like you fall in with this gang?" was a genuinely curious and reasonable question, so Jeff didn't mind answering it.

"My family is Plore, since the war," he said. "I went Social Credit but then they forced me to go to a Euthanasia Palace and kill innocent people. So I ran away and became a Plore again." When Rachel heard this, she screeched, "How could you tell them this? Do you want the ADF to track you down here? After all we did to keep your secret?"

But then she grimly reassured herself, they won't likely be freed to tell anyone else. In her casual discussions with the local guards, outside the house, they were all coming to the tacit realization—as yet unvoiced openly—that the eleven prisoners, if released, would only lead the ADF to their hiding place, or to identifying them. But no one dared do anything, not yet, without David and Oren's authorization.

The infuriated response of the prisoners to Jeff's answer depressed him further.

"So you think it's all right to have useless people sit around and take from the collective and Mother Earth when they can no longer work?" Araceli challenged him.

"Lots of people who don't work live in the pens, like Solar City in Anacosta," he said. "And everyone else works to feed and house them. And the Street People don't work at all."

"That's different!" a black man a few years older than Jeff said. "The Diverse People are entitled to the support of the country after hundreds of years of oppression." Jeff thought, even the Street People were publicly fed, and provided tents by the City in which they lived. When walking around the City, Jeff had often encountered those long despondent multiracial lines of beggars as they awaited their morning or evening allotment of food. The Street People served a purpose for the government, reminding low Social Crediteers what would happen to them should they resist the State and reassuring them that others were even worse off. Once Jeff had rescued a low Social Credit girl from a pair of Street Men who were trying to drag her into an alley.

When they were finished eating, one of the prisoners would bring him the box with the dishes, leaving it a few steps below where Jeff waited, and then the bags of trash and recyclables, and return to the bottom of the staircase. Jeff would place the box and bags at the top of the staircase once the Soko had returned to the bottom of the stairs, and knock three times. A guard would open it and Jeff would return the dishes under the protection of his rifle. No one dared rush him with the barrel pointing above his shoulder at the crowd below.

They taunted him, unwisely, with "You know it's a capital crime to own a gun? What do you think is going to happen to all of you when this is over?" The man whom David had punched, whose face now bore purplish yellow bruises, said sharply, "Stop talking that way." Jeff realized that this was the smartest Soko in the bunch, who not only had immediately realized the gang were not Antifans at all, but that it would not be in the crew's interest to remind their captors of the likely consequences of releasing them.

This man looked like a workingman Plore himself. He was powerfully built, more than the average undernourished low Social Crediteer, with glinting green eyes, buzz-cut brown hair, and a face that was rugged even before it met David's fist. He had been a longshoreman on the Baltimore docks, graduated to operating a crane, and then seized an opportunity on the City of Baltimore's official stagehand crew. The crew's duties largely consisted of moving podiums and calibrating flattering lighting for officials' speeches, but the man liked the idea of working indoors, and his 100 social credit score did not suffer with the change. He was a committed Marxist, and the crew's political commissar, sharing nuggets of anti-capitalist insight in their moments of backstage leisure. In his off hours, he was penning a play called, "Earth over Love over Money," that he was sure he could convince the City to stage. So he had powerful arms, a hatred for fascists, and an instinct for dramatic plotting that made him stand out in this otherwise dispirited group of prisoners. Jeff and Rachel were especially leery of him, and when Jeff relayed how the man had cut off the remarks about Plores owning guns, she frowned silently.

One morning the prisoners claimed the toilet was broken. "I can fix it," said a man. "Just pass me some tools." But those metal wrenches and screwdrivers would be weapons in the wrong hands; even if Jeff was gentlemanly, he was not naive, and neither was Rachel.

"I'll fix it," said Rachel, who was handy with tools. The Sokos were instructed to move back to the far corner of the basement while one of the guards trained his rifle on them and Rachel disappeared into the bathroom. She immediately flushed it. And ran the faucet in the sink.

"Nothing wrong with this toilet," she said sharply, before returning upstairs. The prisoners glowered, their ruse detected by these ignorant Plores. "And if anything does go wrong, we won't bother to fix it now. You can just use buckets."

On Friday morning, Jeff and Rachel sat at the kitchen table, peeling potatoes. Rachel was going to bake them with cheese in two large casserole dishes. Harry, a thirtyish concrete hauler, balding with sharp blue eyes and a short brown beard, sat in the corner, his rifle laid across his lap, watching a GVN video on his phone. The bolt was drawn across the door to the basement. It was always possible that a prisoner had crept up the staircase and was listening behind the door, so the trio kept quiet, with the conversation mostly limited to mundane household topics.

"Tomorrow's the wedding," Harry ventured at one point, looking up from the news feed. The couple nodded, and kept peeling and chopping. The unsaid theme was, "What do we do next?"

"Guess they'll come back up here," Rachel said. "Not Mike. Oren will know what to do."

Would they just release the prisoners, jump into vans, and flee to Cayuga? That was plausible. But this was Oren's hometown, and if he and the others planned to continue staying here, how could they just allow the prisoners to walk into the nearest militia or police station and lead them directly back here? The most humane thing they could do would be to drive their prisoners, blindfolded, back to near Baltimore, push them out to find their own way home, and then speed pell-mell back home. Still, it was likely that, as a totality, the Sokos would give enough scraps of information to the ADF that would allow the ADF to track them down here regardless.

The two heavy unbreakable glass casserole dishes came piping hot from the oven. "Wouldn't mind some of that," said Harry, sniffing audibly. "Wish my wife cooked like you did."

"I've got more for us," Rachel reassured him. "Don't worry." Harry smiled and reinserted his earbuds.

With Harry looming behind him, Jeff took one and then another casserole dish down to the inmates, first throwing some dish towels down for them to handle the dishes safely. He passed down two jugs of water. The first day, Araceli had asked, "Is this eco-water? We only drink eco-water." Eco-water was recycled sewage, and perfectly healthy, or so they said.

"It's from the tap. You decide what you're going to do when you get thirsty," Jeff had said.

Today, he sat on a slightly higher step, listening to rustling behind and below him as the prisoners ate collectively and wordlessly out of the casserole dishes with eco-plastic spoons. They knew from the passage of light and dark, glimpsed in the small reinforced windows of the cellar, that four days had passed and the wedding they should have worked—the expected highlight of their careers—would take place tomorrow. The smell also tells you, Jeff thought wryly to himself. The prisoners had been given their changes of clothes, after Rachel and Jeff had searched the suitpods for weapons or communications devices, shaken out the clothes for contraband, and then dispatched them downstairs in cloth bags. Still, after several days, eleven mostly unwashed bodies in a confined space began to emit a sweetly stale odor.

One more day, Jeff told himself. Then Oren'll come back and tell us what to do. It'll work out somehow. He needed to remind himself that the operation was coming to an end, because the mood today was decidedly surly as the inmates baited him. His blackness enraged them, including the two African-Diversans in the group. You'd think I ran away from their plantation, he thought grimly. Well, he told himself, you kind of did.

"As a Diverse person"—they were strangely reluctant to say "black,"—"you should have shown more gratitude to the DJR for helping your people."

"They didn't help me at all," Jeff said curtly, finding the "your people" vaguely offensive. "What did the DJR ever do for African-Diversans other than making us your pity objects so you could climb over us and take power? If you respect Diversity, why don't you respect diversity enough to include the Plores?"

They stared at him with horror. He waited impatiently for the dishes.

Finally, the political commissar approached him with the two casserole dishes and the spoons. In the kitchen, Rachel would count the spoons to make sure none were being cached by the prisoners. Relieved, Jeff stood up to take the thick glass dishes, *one more meal over*, and as he rose from the step, he realized, too late, the glass casserole dishes were being flung directly at his face, calculated to catch him unawares as he steadied himself on the staircase. Blinded by the dishes and covered in the remains of the casserole, Jeff tripped and fell forward on the staircase.

The man grabbed his arm and hurled him down the stairs, capitalizing on Jeff's downward momentum. Jeff landed at the bottom, groaning, and clutching his bloodied face. His left arm had sustained the impact of the concrete floor at the bottom of the staircase, and it was broken. As he lay there, he thought dully, did I hear him call me the N-word, or did I just imagine it?

In his haze, Jeff heard three knocks at the door, the signal for Harry to open it, but Harry wouldn't know it wasn't Jeff knocking. He tried to call out, but only mustered a moan. The door slammed open into Harry's face. The commissar ran from the house with the rifle Harry had dropped, followed by five other inmates. Jeff heard the door slam shut on the remaining five. An anguished cry came from one victim who'd been kneed in the groin by Harry; the Soko had fallen down the stairs, taking the others with him, two of whom landed on top of Jeff, amid the smashed non-breakable glass. Jeff heard Harry slam the bolt shut to the basement, and rapid footsteps across the ceiling as Harry chased after the escapees. Then all went dark.

Harry caught up with one of the escapees. The man pushed him aside with the animal desperation of one who knew his life hung in the balance, and fled into the surrounding woodland. The other guards were now on the chase.

Gunfire rattled through the quiet compound, felling several of the slower escapees. Two managed to crawl a few yards, then collapsed, dead. Another picked himself up, and stumbled toward the fields ahead, a hand pressing against his right thigh.

Harry shouted into his phone, to the others on the network, "They've escaped! Heading toward Paxton Road!" He jumped into a van with one armed man, and the other guard leaped into the second van parked at the house, the one Jeff had been sleeping in. The escapees would eventually reach Paxton Road, so, with reinforcements, the guards could intercept them. Past Paxton were fields, and one mile beyond that, the one Social Credit house on this side of the town, occupied by a frail retired judge in her nineties with blood on her hands.

Rachel ran downstairs when she heard the uproar. She had been making the bed. She saw immediately what had happened. "Bruce! Bruce!" she called. The groaning on the other side of the door alarmed her—was Jeff down there? She heard more than one voice, but she did not hear his. Had he gone running out the door to chase the escapees? She saw both vans were missing.

She had no idea what to do. Even if Jeff were in the basement, she did not dare open the door. She called Harry. "What happened?"

He told her, briefly, as his eyes scanned the road ahead for the Sokos. "Stay there and wait for reinforcements," Harry ordered, as the van jolted down Paxton Road. "Yes, he's down there, but so are five of them, you can't open the door. He'll be copa till we get back. They won't commit a hate crime against him. I pushed them all down the stairs. Holy crap, there's one!"

The connection ended as Harry ran over the escapee with the van. The other Plore guard leaped out and finished off the man with a quick rifle shot. Farther down Paxton Road, he saw the injured man emerging from the bushes and trying to make a quick painful dash into the fields. This Plore guard was a good shot, and before the escapee could plunge into the fields beyond, he too was downed.

This left two escapees still on the loose, including the political commissar.

The vans pulled back so each was poised at an end of the road. Unless the escapees made a huge detour, they would be within the sights of one van or the other.

Another half dozen men arrived with a pair of German shepherds, who picked up the scent from the house, and, barking, surged into the fields, their handlers behind them. One man picked up a call, listened briefly, and then said, "Good work, son." His twelve-year-old son had gotten a drone for Christmas, an expensive toy, but it was paying off today, as it navigated the sky above the fields between Paxton Road and the judge's house. The man called the dog handlers, who were already heading in the direction where the drone had spotted movement. The dogs ran down one escapee about twenty yards before the judge's house. He was dispatched quickly.

The political commissar managed to stagger into the judge's yard. A house this nice, this tidy, with a garden, and signs that proclaimed, "We Love Mother Earth" and "Science is Settled" signaled that he had reached safe Social Credit territory. He had dropped the gun in the fields, not wanting to be found with it, and not knowing how to use it, although he was familiar with guns as a props master, where they were usually wielded by the Deplorable villain of a drama. Breathing hard, he knocked on the door, and then pushed it open as a square-faced middle-aged housekeeper, visibly terrified, opened it. He edged into the house.

"I'm 100," he reassured her. "I've been kidnapped by Plores. I escaped. They're going to disrupt the big Antifan wedding. We were going there to be stage hands…"

"Where's your armband?" she asked, suspiciously.

"They took it, so they can pretend to be us and infiltrate the wedding!" He knew he must have sounded like a madman, and the housekeeper's eyes were wide. "Please call the police, immediately!

"Wait, are you a Plore?" he asked, noticing her bare arms, but of course many people took their bands off at home, which was permissible.

"Are you mocking?" she said. "Of course not, bless Mother Earth!" She pointed to a black armband on the table. "That's mine!"

"Call the police," he said urgently.

A reedy voice sounded on the intercom, "Marla, what's going on down there? Who's visiting? I told you I don't want any strangers in the house and no men!"

"Don't worry," Marla said to the desperate man. "Just hide under the dining room table and she won't see you. She's mostly blind." He obeyed. "I'm calling our militia number right now."

She picked up the armband and spoke the number of her husband into the phone, not the emergency number at all, and spoke quickly before the commissar realized it. "Here at the judge's house. You've gotta come quickly. We've got a Social Crediteer, says he is, who was kidnapped by the Plores. He's hiding from them." She called out to the man hiding under the dining room table. "Are you the only one who got loose?"

"No, they're shooting all the others who ran out of the house with me. They've all got guns, the Plore bastards. We're being held hostage in the house on the other side of the fields. There's others in the basement, most likely." The man began to calm down, believing luck was on his side and safety was nigh.

"They'll be here in five minutes from the town," Marla assured him. "Wait, I think I see some Plores out there, with dogs." The man gasped frantically. Who would arrive first, the Plores or the militia?

"Hurry, come into the kitchen," said Marla. "I can hide you in the pantry. They won't dare come into the judge's house, but if they do, they won't get far before the militia arrive." The man scrambled out from beneath the antique dining table and she locked him in the pantry.

Then she opened the door and let the Plore men in, silently leading them to the pantry. Unlocking the door, she then stood back in a corner of the tidy kitchen, wiping her hands on her white smock. The last thing the betrayed and cowering man saw were stern-faced men in the narrow doorway. One quick shot to the head finished him off. Dogs barked outside, then quieted.

"Marla, what on Mother's Earth is going on downstairs?" the shrill voice broke forth on the intercom.

"Nothing, amba-mam, just a delivery," Marla spoke into the intercom. Even though Marla was a Plore, and Plores avoided uttering the humiliating Social Credit honorifics, the ninety-year-old judge liked to hear the proof that once she had been the senior judge in the entire county, sentencing Red sympathizers and Plores to prison or death even before the civil war. Deplorables had called her "Judge Bloodyhantz," a play on her surname, Hantz. "I'll be right upstairs, amba-mam."

To the men, she said, "The judge can't walk on her own anymore, she won't come downstairs. We can remove him before anyone knows he was here." The van drove up, the four men carried the heavy body out and placed it on the van floor, and the group quickly returned to the house where Jeff and the remaining five prisoners lay in a tangle on the floor of the basement. The day's business was not yet over.

Marla placed the judge's armband back on the dining room table. Returning to the pantry, she busily scrubbed the blood off the tile floor, congratulating herself for having convinced the man to hide in the pantry, the domain of the Plore menial. Her husband had given her a quick, silent salute, and a proud smile, as he and his band departed the judge's house. That's my girl.

Chapter 57
Do What You Have To Do
(Friday, October 29, 2094)

Jeff drifted in and out of consciousness alongside the cinderblock wall where he had dragged himself after landing at the bottom of the staircase. Sometimes the sharp pain in his left arm woke him up. Once he thought he heard Rachel calling, "Bruce! Are you all right?" to which he replied, probably in a whisper rather than the bracing shout he imagined, "Yes...I'm all right." At first he thought he was alone, but then realized he was locked down here with the remaining Sokos, who were nursing lesser injuries. Dimly, he knew some had escaped, since the basement was quieter and smelled less than before. The other men must have gone after the escapees, otherwise they would have rescued him by now. He couldn't see out his right eye and the left was turned to the wall. Oh God, he thought, if they want to kill me now, nothing will stop them.

One of the less-injured Sokos kicked him feebly in the back, but they otherwise left him alone. They don't want to be charged with a hate crime, he suddenly realized. They searched his pockets for his cell phone, with which they would have called for help, but fortunately he'd deliberately left it upstairs with Rachel.

He must have slept for a few minutes, waking to the sound of the prisoners wielding a wooden chair against the cellar door to try to burst it open. The chair splintered quickly. They dismantled a cabinet and slammed the wooden shelves against the door, but they were only made of particleboard, and the hatch held. They must have known the guards were away, since no one reacted to their efforts from the outside, but they would be returning, either successful or failed at apprehending their fellow crew members, and in either case in a foul mood, and the time for escape was dwindling. They couldn't count on one of their crew fellows having managed to alert the authorities, and indeed nobody seemed to be coming to rescue them. An old oil burner sat, unused for decades, in a corner; they desperately tried to remove some parts, pulling and pushing, but the machinery was rusted and they had no tools except their own hands.

Then they had the idea of using themselves as a battering ram. Two men at a time held the arms and supported the back of the strongest in the crooks of their arms while he slammed his feet against the hatch. After several minutes, they switched places. Eventually, they heard a creak of loosening metal, and they cheered. This encouraged them to keep slamming at the hatch from inside with energy. About ten minutes later, to their glee, the hatch popped open, wood splintering, and they scrambled out, boosting Araceli first and then clambering after her.

Unaccustomed to sunlight after three days in the cellar, they could barely see, until Araceli shrieked, "Ay!"

Surrounding them in a half-circle about thirty feet away were their guards, and their armed and grim-faced reinforcements from the town, every available Plore man in on the kidnapping plot, and a smattering of women, totaling about two dozen in all. Rachel, having heard the kicking, had fearfully run out of the kitchen to await the returnees. Relieved to see reinforcements arrive, she directed the crowd here and then ran back into the kitchen, unbolted the door, grabbed her first-aid kit and hurried downstairs to take care of Jeff.

The locals would have arrived earlier, but the guards who had pursued and killed the escapees had had to take the time to bury the bodies where they lay, including the political commissar's, in the field near the judge's house. They alerted others, who came from their jobs at the Diversity Warehouse outlet, the grocery store, the hospital, the gravel pits, the kitchens of the roadside Social Credit Only–Eating House and Rest Stop, their own small shops, the Anacosta Self-Driving Car Repair Facility, the cryptocurrency telesales center, and the juvenile detention house. Only those who could conjure up a plausible excuse for leaving in the middle of the day—otherwise it would have been known to the authorities that dozens of Plores had abandoned their work stations, which would have automatically excited suspicion—ran for the homestead, but even then, it took some of them half an hour to arrive. It was now about 2:45 in the afternoon and the sun had disappeared behind clouds, creating a sudden chill.

They were waiting for instructions from Oren, but the fake stage crew was preoccupied with preparations for the wedding, and the text when it finally came was cryptic:

"Do what you have to do."

"Stand back!" ordered the de facto leader, a bald and grizzled night-shift veteran of the juvenile detention house, which was divided into a Plore wing and a Social Credit one, with only Social Crediteers guarding their own. The Sokos were tentatively moving toward the fringes of the circle, but shrank back at the yell.

"We're taking you back to Baltimore," he announced, to the prisoners' visible relief. "You've caused us a lot of trouble, and we don't want to get arrested by the Diverse Power."

"See! I knew!" Araceli cackled.

"But we're going to take you back separately," he cautioned, "so we don't attract attention on the way. And we have to blindfold you, so you can't tell the police how you got here."

"Yes, yes!" the prisoners chorused agreeably, gleefully planning how they would report immediately to the police. No one asked what had happened to their comrades.

The Plores blindfolded each of the five, and led them in separate directions into the nearby woods. "The vans are waiting for you on Paxton Road, through these woods. I'll make sure you don't trip," said one guard to his charge.

"Wait!" said the juvenile prison officer. He pointed to the lone African-Diversan left in the group and whispered to Harry. Harry nodded and disappeared into the house. "Kamrat, you stay here for a moment, OK?"

Rachel was tending to Jeff in the kitchen, having maneuvered him up the stairs. She put his broken arm in a splint, and was removing glass shards from around his injured right eye with a set of medical tweezers. "Ouch!" he cried, but he was now able to open his eye partially. Rachel placed an antibiotic lotion and bandage on the eye and was dabbing a wet towel on Jeff's face to remove blood, and salving the bruises when Harry burst into the kitchen. "Bruce, we need you."

Rachel looked up. "How can you need Bruce at this point? If you need a medic, I'll come."

"We don't need a medic, not yet. We need the opposite of a medic right now."

They both stared at him, uncomprehending.

"Someone's got to execute the black guy. We're not going to do it. Just in case. If Bruce does it, then at least he wouldn't get charged with a hate crime."

"I'm not killing anyone," said Jeff, somewhat indistinctly through his battered mouth.

"Fuck you," said Harry angrily. "You let everyone else do the killing for you. If you'd been more careful, this whole mess wouldn't have happened today. Finally, you've got to get some skin in the game." Rachel quietly thought, this is the real issue; they see the gentleness, and they hate it. If we were all this kind, they would have destroyed us by now. The times are too brutal for this man to survive, unless he learns to conform.

"I'll do it," she said, rising to her feet.

"No..." protested Jeff, somewhat lackadaisically.

Harry shrugged. "Go ahead, let your woman do the dirty work for you. Come on, Rachel..." They headed back out the door.

Jeff shuddered. That was one of the worst insults one Plore man could levy at another. He was even more dejected now than when he had been lying at the foot of the stairs agonized that the prisoners had fooled him. He stiffly rose to his feet and called out, "Wait, wait, I'm coming." Then he staggered through the door, his partial blindness causing him to brush the broken left arm against the doorway, sending jagged pains through his whole body, and limped after the pair.

"The van's only a few hundred feet ahead," the woman promised the blindfolded Araceli. She and her husband, bearing the family's new ghost firearm, equipped with a silencer, had escorted her into the woods, crunching dried leaves underfoot. Araceli became tenser and quieter. Her air of triumph, at having cowed these ignorant Plores, at having survived, had evaporated.

"Are you sure?" she asked faintly.

"Of course," said the woman. "You'll be driven back to Baltimore. But we're not driving downtown, you'll have to figure out your way home from wherever we drop you off."

This sufficed to bring Araceli to the secluded spot where the woman said, "Kneel down."

"Why?" asked the frightened Araceli.

"Because that'll make it easier," the man finally spoke.

"For me?"

"No, for us." The man pushed her down to the damp, leaf-matted ground, where she wept and cursed them. His wife aimed carefully, two-handed, at the back of her head.

Araceli's last words were "I hate..." and then the gun fired. She jerked extravagantly and then lay, finally silenced.

They buried her in a shallow grave a few feet away, piled logs on top so that animals would not disturb it, which might reveal the body to searchers, and then trudged home.

The woman was sober at having committed her first murder, and faintly regretful, thinking of church services on Sunday and possibly an afterlife burning in hell, although very few people, even Plores, believed in hell these days, not when you could experience it so much more conveniently on earth. "Travis, d'you think this was all necessary?"

"What?" he asked gruffly.

"All this death and killing just so some Social Crediteer doesn't have to marry this ADF commander. I get that this Mike Smith is a big deal, the most famous Plore ever, and if he rescues his wife, it'll be a huge win for us, but a lot of people are dead now because of this. Yeah, they're Soko, but they're human beings too. It's not like he was saving his wife's life."

Travis, who was walking ahead of his wife, shrugged, the shoulder lines of which she could see through his thin jacket. I'll have to find some flannel to line it with ahead of the winter, she thought absentmindedly.

"If we say no when our people need us, we'll never shake off the Soko," he reminded her. "Didn't they massacre Mike's whole roundup in Cayuga? They don't care about the treaty anymore. We could be next. At least we're giving our people a reason to still have hope." Still, he was grateful their children were almost grown.

"Let's just hope that wedding *torks*"—*self-destructs*—"or yeah, this might be for nothing," said his wife. She wondered whether they would have to pack up their roundup and flee into the Cayuga territory after the wedding, their entire life left behind.

The local Plores, the ones who had not disappeared into the woods with their victims, were hanging back, waiting for the denouement before they could head home and start preparing dinner. They eyed Jeff, his left arm in a sling, his eye bandaged with a white cloth, limping steadily toward Rachel, Harry, and the kneeling last Soko in the center of what had been the half circle. They got him bad, several thought to themselves. Let him do the final deed.

Harry was about to hand Rachel the handgun when they saw Jeff approaching.

"I just want to say," said Jeff, turning to the assemblage, his back to Rachel and Harry and the Soko, "that I don't want to do this. We can't be worse than the Social Credit. We have to try to be good Christians. I know we are better than this..."

"Are you going to tell that to the ADF when they show up tomorrow?" a man jeered at him. "They won't be Christians!"

The kneeling, blindfolded Soko recognized Jeff's voice and cried out, "Brother! Don't hurt me! I'll join your group! We're all one people, we're all Diversans!"

The catcalls picked up, fueled by fear that Jeff might cave.

"No, we're not! We're not Diversans, we're Americans!"

"Last week, you hated our guts! You'd bring the ADF here in a minute if you could!"

"Either do it or give the gun to your girlfriend!"

"You'd do it if he were white!" That one stung.

Jeff made one final plea to the near-mob. "We could spare his life. We'd watch him carefully and make sure he didn't betray us...If we do this, what does that say about us? What does it say about our cause?" But his voice lacked conviction.

"Bruce, you gonna do it or not?" Rachel's voice was impatient and tired. "Dozens of people are counting on you not to get us all killed."

"All right," he said, hobbling over to them. She handed him the firearm. He had never fired at another human being, nor in anger, only in target practice at Lucy's roundup range. He moved his fingers hesitatingly around the grip and touched the trigger lightly.

"You're not left-handed, right?" asked Harry with some solicitude, giving him one last excuse to bow out.

"No," he said, moving slowly behind the Soko. He raised the barrel. There was no safety, since this was a model where you just pulled the trigger steadily, beyond the initial catch. "I'm sorry it's got to be this way. Maybe you got a last prayer, brother?"

"Oh man!" wailed the Soko. "I got a mother! I got sisters!" And then his voice turned hateful. "You fucking crackers! The ADF's gonna get you! Black cracker too! I'm gonna be a saint in the MED when it's all over!"

Jeff's hand shook, but at that distance, he couldn't miss the target. The gun clicked, silenced, and the last of the Sokos fell into the dust in the yard. Rachel checked his pulse, nodded upward, and a small clutch of the locals bore the body off on a stretcher into the woods. Rachel and Harry took a small shovel and covered the blood spatters. The rest of the crowd dispersed, soberly.

After nightfall, a van brought Jeff and Rachel, packed into a cardboard box with air holes behind the driver and surrounded by cargo, to the border with Lenilenape-Sylvania. They waited along the side of the road for a truck, passage secured at the last minute, that took them back to New York–Schuylkill and the Syracuse area by dawn. Two motorcycles arrived to bring them back to Tom's roundup, where they had lived since the massacre that summer.

The rounduprs were surprised by how taciturn Jeff and Rachel were, but the couple didn't want to frighten anyone, and even more, didn't want to give them an excuse to kick them out. This was now home. "They let us leave a day early, since Jeff broke his arm falling down the stairs," said Rachel. "No, we haven't heard about what's going on at the wedding." The next morning they were back at their duties, Rachel wrapping bandages, reorganizing vials, and treating an ingrown toenail, and Jeff teaching history, as if the bizarre week had never happened.

Chapter 58
Last Night Of Their Lives
(Friday, October 29, 2094)

Holding his warm eco-foam enviropod, David chose to leave the crowded eating tent and sit in the twilight on the hillock that rose above the worker tent city. He craved some quiet and time to think after four days of rushing, yelling, commotion, mini-crises and other dramas that accompanied the presentation of the most monumental DJR event in years, let alone the effort to disrupt it. The ground was cold and hard, but he wore a warm cloth jacket with a faux sheepskin lining, and a heavy gray cotton scarf.

He surveyed the tent city, whose artificial tube lights were now flickering on. From above it resembled a humming space station. He identified his own crew's compound—three adjoining insulated plastic tents—along the far right of the field. To their north were musicians, whose late night practicing serenaded the crew members to sleep, and on the other two sides, florists and pastry cooks. The main kitchen staff and waitstaff totaled about a hundred. A total of three hundred Social Credit workers would serve about twice as many guests. David turned around to look toward the main campus, where Malia was presumably eating her own dinner with Paragon and Exterra. Was she thinking of him? Had she noticed him, despite his best efforts to keep his presence secret? David had not wanted to burden Malia with knowing he was on the premises, fearing that she would not be able to keep the secret, that her face would glow with relief, and Paragon would extract the knowledge from her, or even that she would talk in her sleep.

As he ate the tofu walnut stew, he calculated that everything was going as well as could be expected. His makeshift crew had performed so well that no one suspected a group of impostor Plores had infiltrated the sacred College grounds. Plore workers were more efficient and less lazy than Social Crediteers, so even though his crew was inexperienced, they compensated by learning their roles quickly and energetically. His crew had rehearsed both their official responsibilities and their actual plan, the latter in secret, of course, after the chapel had emptied for the day. Some of their weapons were already buried deep in the sacristy on the third floor, and the others would come in with the crew members who planned to arrive well before the security forces took their positions.

The only close call had happened that afternoon during the mandatory Mother Earth service for the workers. David had separated the crew into several small groups, figuring that any unfamiliarity with the service would be less noticeable on the parts of one or two Plores than if all were seated together. Since no security presence monitored the entry of the worshipers, the service also allowed the crew members to bring in weapons and hide some under their seats to be retrieved early tomorrow. David knew that the final ADF search would come at 1:00 p.m., before guests were admitted to the chapel, but his crew would retrieve their stashed weapons before the search began, and no one would search them at 8:00 a.m.

Rebecca and Oren sat together, next to a clump of nattering female sous cooks. When everyone rose for the Four Minute Hate, and the usual effigies of US and Plore enemies were paraded around for the requisite hissing, booing, and epithets, the sister and brother were noticeably ill-at-ease, and under pressure made the mistake of shouting curses that were culturally Plore—"Dambags! Cornsuckers!"—rather than the elaborate vetted library of safe Social Credit insults. When they sat down, one of the women curiously asked them, "What was you shouting there? You sounded like some of the Plores I work with."

Oren said, "Yeah, we picked up some of the things our coworkers say. There's a lot of Plore workers in our building. Might as well mix it up a bit, right?"

"Uh-huh," said the woman, a little guardedly. Who would interact with Plores to the point of adopting their jargot?

"Look, mind your own business!" Rebecca snarled, to the alarm of the sous cooks. Oren grabbed her arm, and said quickly to the others, "She's neurodiverse, please understand."

"OK, OK," said the woman, and the incident should have been over, but Oren sensed the women were sneaking looks at them occasionally. The brother and sister tried to behave normally, but it was hard when you didn't know any of the lyrics to the herms and had to hum while pretending to mouth the lyrics. If they had known a Mother Earth service would be forced upon them, David would have made them practice the liturgy as well.

"Where you from?" the sous cook asked, sotto voce, as Great Priestess Aleta raised the Chalice of Joy, trilling, "Mother Earth, your masses revere you!" The priests on the stage passed the chalice among themselves, each reciting a blessing after sipping the Diversity-grown wine.

"That's none of your business either!"

"Araceli, please," Oren urged. To the woman, he said, "I'm sorry she's so rude, she can't help herself. She fell off a platform a few years ago when we were doing a show...

Baltimore. We're with the stagehand crew here."

"Don't Baltimore folks know any herms? You guys don't go to a lot of services, do you?"

Sensing that Rebecca was a few seconds away from escalating the confrontation, Oren squeezed her arm, and regretfully said, "No, I'm afraid we're not very good churchgoers."

"Churchgoers?"

Uh-oh, a Plore word, thought Oren. "You know, goers to Mother Earth Church." The correct Soko equivalent would have been "earth praisers."

Fortunately, the service ended shortly afterward, and Oren and Rebecca filed out the opposite way from the sous cooks in a long line of subdued workers. Hopefully they won't remember us in a minute, Oren thought, and please, God, don't let any of them be informants. Thank goodness we're gone tomorrow. One way or another.

"Hey, Mike," Oren said, emerging from the darkness below with his own enviropod. "Mind if I join you?"

"Sure," David said, pointing to the ground next to him. Oren sat down heavily. They temporarily shut down their armband feeds, which the former Antifan had taught the crew to do. Just in case.

"That was a close call you and Rebecca had at the service. Nobody that nosy was sitting by us."

"You think we got a problem?" Oren asked.

"No, I don't think so, everyone here's now focused on tomorrow. I'd worry more if this was the beginning of the week. I'm more worried about what happens to you guys after the operation. That Baltimore crew won't be going back to Baltimore. Don't forget to leave the armbands behind so they can't track you home."

"Bloodbath," Oren grunted unsentimentally. "I'm not surprised we had to get rid of them, but I'm sorry it had to be such a balagan. We were lucky that guy who you punched didn't get the best of us in the end." David had heard the whole depressing story.

"We'll probably have to move up into Cayuga," said Oren.

"If the ADF doesn't track you down, you might want to lie low for a while. No sudden movement. Just do your *waydown,* *normal thing.* "The resistance isn't going away."

Oren looked pensive. "I don't want to go back to normal. Years pass too quickly, and then you're too old and tired to try to change the system. I want to avenge my family."

David hadn't wanted to press, but he was curious as to what had brought Oren into the resistance. "Exactly who are you avenging, Oren?"

"Rebecca and I had two other brothers. One of them went to jail about ten years ago for punching a Soko who started a fight with him. The law only went one way, the

Soko went free. Then he was killed in a prison fight. Our other brother started hanging around the weed joint." The authorities established public hangouts for drug users, ostensibly in the name of public safety, but it was a way to pacify and enfeeble Plores, especially younger men, who could often be enticed into providing information in return for extra supply. "He started on fentanyl, overdosed, and that was that. By that time his wife and kids had left him and gone back to Anacosta where her family lives.

"We're using their house for the operation. My sister-in-law doesn't know, she thinks Rebecca and I are just taking care of the house while she's gone."

David had noticed the children's rooms, decorated with scrawled drawings of Bible scenes and school artwork, but had been afraid to ask whose they were.

"He was a good mechanic until the drugs took over. He brought me into his shop, and I was handling most of the repairs while he was spacing out in the weed house.

"So, you see," Oren told David, "there's no time to waste. I just hope both Rebecca and I make it home, because our family doesn't have a whole lot of avengers left. I don't know if you understand how much we hate the Social Credit."

Except for the last four years, David had spent almost his entire life in the DJR, and resented being treated like an outsider. "My father was killed by them. My mother and sister are sitting in ADF headquarters to guarantee my good behavior. I hope they won't be killed on my account."

"I'm sorry," Oren apologized. "We've all got cause to hate them."

Oren had not been entirely honest with David about his motivations, but how could one say, "I'm also doing this operation to become the most famous Plore in the DJR after you. When you come back, if you come back, which I doubt, you will have to reckon with me as an equal."

As the two men trudged down the hill to the camp, now looking forward to the warm tent, David began worrying again about his mother and Emma. Once he had decided to move forward with the rescue operation, he had refused to allow himself to be distracted by thoughts of Marjory and Emma languishing at Beaufort. Knowing the ADF, he surmised they were being decently treated if only due to Marjory's age and their David Harris connection in which St. Louis had an interest. He hoped that once the wedding operation ended, they would be released, since executing them might only create further unrest among the Plores. But he couldn't assume it.

Back in the tent, the crew stayed up late, all knowing it might well be the last night of their lives. Rebecca produced a dusty bottle of cognac, said, "I've been holding on to it for too long," and poured everyone a small glass of the liqueur. Laughing, they toasted to "a successful wedding!" and the "happiness of the bride, I mean brides!" No eavesdropper would have suspected them of anything more than relief at the prospect of the long week ending and of returning to their apartments and families. Just in case, they avoided using Plore jargot.

David raised his hand to quiet them, and he said, seriously, if quietly, "Thank you all. Whatever happens tomorrow, I am grateful for your support and your fellowship and your courage. I cannot say more. This great effort will never be forgotten."

"To the best crew chief a man ever had!" Tom raised his glass, his eyes brimming with tears. They cheered loudly enough for the pastry cooks, who needed to rise earliest of all, to grumble among themselves.

This might be our last night alive, Marjory and Emma fretted in their VIP cell at Beaufort, although neither dared say it to the other. They were grateful that they were allowed to remain together. Every other day, they were permitted to walk in the prisoners' courtyard. They ate enough calories, although they dreaded the Health Meat as much as Malia had. The ADF interrogators had been brusque, but unable to admit that David was alive, could not ask the Harris women questions about whether they had met with David in recent weeks. The women with a clear conscience could say they knew of no plans to rescue Malia, and the vitals reading devices confirmed they were telling the truth. The interrogations had ceased once the ADF lost interest in what the women knew.

Marjory and Emma wanted to pray but knew the guards in the anteroom would yell at them. So instead, they held hands and prayed silently, for Malia, and for David. The telescreen had broadcast news coverage of the wedding, flashing photos of Paragon, Malia, and Exterra across the screen, and treating viewers to a tour of the lovely College. It aired the entire thanksgiving service that David and his crew had been forced to attend. The women tried to turn off the coverage, but the ADF wanted to revel in their shame at Malia's defection and ensured they missed no detail. They thought to themselves, how will he get into that college? How can he rescue Malia against the might of several hundred Antifans gathered in that pagan chapel? Will they survive? They barely remembered to ask themselves, will *we* survive?

The shift commander came by to visit them personally. He stood in the doorway and said, almost reassuringly, "We don't expect any trouble tomorrow. If the wedding is uneventful, you will sleep tomorrow night in your own home. Good night."

After he left, Marjory and Emma gave each other despairing looks. If they made it home tomorrow, it would mean that Malia had been married against her will to Paragon. If David succeeded in rescuing Malia, they might be executed in revenge. And what if he tried to rescue her, but failed? Then they might all be dead by tomorrow night—the worst of both worlds.

"God has not forgotten us," Marjory whispered to Emma, quoting Psalm 91. "Under His wings you will find refuge; His faithfulness will be your shield and rampart." Emma nodded.

They looked up at the screen. A full-screen photo of Malia, looking demure and serious at the same time, faced them at that moment. I've got this, she seemed to be telling them, or so they preferred to believe, because the caption read, "Communicator

Malia, 160, Senior Wife of Commander Ma, ADF Hero." By tomorrow, her social credit score would rise to two-thirds of Paragon's, or 194. No Diversan could imagine she was unwilling to marry Commander Ma, except possibly for those few who had heard her speech at the zoo.

Chapter 59
Don't Blink
(Saturday, October 30, 2094)

The seats were filling with the guests, or the spectators. Malia heard their steady, droning buzz as she sat in the dressing room, submitting to the makeup artists. "Hold your eyes open, amba-mam, don't blink," ordered the pink-haired young woman.

Her makeup done, Exterra, gowned in robin's egg blue, left her dressing room to peek from behind curtains at the assemblage. To her delight, she recognized some of her favorite celebrities in the crowd. In the second row sat both Director Montoya and Carolina Cruz with Deputy Director Steve Rosen and Vicki Rosen, bodyguards behind them. The Rosens looked anxious, which Exterra attributed to Paragon's clever outflanking of Rosen. This might be the last elite event the Rosens attended before moving to Orlando, Exterra guessed, and no doubt they were saddened at their imminent demotion. About a third of the audience was black-uniformed, with Knowledge and Economic Tower elites filling out their ranks. The Antifans not expressly charged with protection had been required to leave their weapons in their cars or in lockers in the lobby.

Paragon, in dress uniform, first exchanged Antifan salutes with Montoya and Rosen, and took Carolina and Vicki's hands in his with a gallant flourish. He moved up and down the aisles, greeting the guests. He waved graciously to non-Antifan guests who sat in the middle of the assemblage. Unlike in a normal MED service, none of the elite guests were wearing pink pussy hats today.

"A great day for Diverse Power!" more than one guest bleated at him, to which he smiled and nodded.

"Diversity!" cheered others.

"It's like a royal wedding!" gushed one Knowledge Tower female, who then briefly wondered whether she had spoken inappropriately, since royalty was presumably racist. A few of her colleagues had spoken disparagingly in hushed tones of Paragon's choice of two white women as his brides, but she knew they probably were jealous of her invitation.

A hundred and fifty miles away, in Anacosta, Marjory and Emma were watching from a Beaufort viewing room. A camera was trained on their faces so that photos could later run in Ploreville's *Suburban Record*, under a caption such as, "Traitor's Birth Parent and Sibling Watch His Widow Marry Antifan Hero." Rows of Antifans sat behind them, arms crossed.

In Ploreville, Warren Welcome sat in front of his telescreen with a beer on the coaster on the side table. His late wife had been fanatical about coasters, and he still honored her wishes. For all he knew, the day would end with Antifans on his doorstep to drag him off to Beaufort.

Twenty minutes later, the little girls and the priestly cantarias, or singers, proceeded down the aisles, as they had practiced for days. The heads then turned as Paragon strode down the aisle, followed by Malia, her eyes demurely fixed on the back of his leather dress jacket, and then Exterra, who sneaked glances around her to capture the admiration of the guests. She knew her former comrades in the Pittsburgh gang were watching, envying her triumph. The trio climbed the stairs to the stage and sat in a series of upholstered metal thrones emblazoned with earth symbols. Malia's hand itched to return to her pocket, in which the deadly canister lay, its cap loosened just enough to keep the pills inside.

I will use them, Malia thought. There will be a death today, to mar this evil celebration. But she was not entirely sure yet whose life she would claim.

Before them sat three ceremonial cups, bearing the insignia of anarchism, Paragon's personal emblem. At the end of the ceremony, the thrones would be removed, and the trio would stand before the cups to drink their sacred contents. Malia's eyes flickered over the cups.

Upstairs, David's crew stealthily removed the remaining firearms from the sacristy, as the Antifan troops in the balcony focused their attention on the stage and the guests below. The troops trusted their comrades to guard the stairwells and entrances from any ill-intentioned intruders. But the black-clad crew members darting around in their sneakers and black caps were no more noteworthy to them than the gray pipes that ran through the building.

"On behalf of the College of the Earthloving Priests and the Archbishop of Anacosta herself, I welcome you!" Aleta raised her draped arms in greeting, and a hush fell over the assembly. The service began with heartfelt prayer and thanks to Mother Earth.

Malia looked downward at her lap, for all appearances, a humble devotee. Only about fifty feet away, David peered out from behind the curtains, the trusty handgun hidden underneath the loose T-shirt and the black jersey sweatshirt. His faithful knife was secreted in a side pocket on his denim slacks with an extra magazine. He knew exactly where his men and Rebecca were waiting for their cue. He uttered a quick prayer: Lord, we are in your hands. Help me rescue Malia. Bring us home safely. Destroy this sewer, may it be Your will. In the name of Jesus Christ, amen.

Eventually, Aleta, somewhat hesitantly, announced, "And it is now time for the most excellent holy movie showing the recovery for Diversity of Communicator Malia."

Despite her best efforts, Malia emitted an anxious sigh. Paragon smiled down at her from the height of his throne. "And now they will all see," he whispered to her. "You can never return to normal again."

After this movie is shown, Malia thought, I will kill myself. Or him.

The four screens came down, one above the trio's heads, and two smaller ones to the sides so guests seated along the walls could also watch. A fourth screen descended over the hall facing the wedding party, so they could enjoy the movie as well. The hall darkened, and silenced.

"The Taking of Communicator Malia for Diversity," read the screen. Malia's fingers opened the vial in her pocket, and she extracted a pill.

Paragon appeared on the screen. "Let this be a lesson for all the Diversity Justice Republic. There is no escape from Diversity. It is an iron rule that the Diverse must crowd out the racist and the phobic. Thousands of Experts have confirmed this Diversity Truth. Malia Jenness was ungrateful to the Diverse People who raised and educated her. She listened to a traitor, a mere Plore, who seduced her, and went with him across the border into the fascist United States. The Antifan Defense Forces could not accept this betrayal. We sent our forces into Oklahoma to kill the traitor and recover Malia, and we succeeded. But her heart remained impure..."

Malia glanced sidelong at Paragon and Exterra in the darkness. Exterra's face— the pale side was the side Malia saw, as if the moon had risen—was aglow with the revelation of Diverse Truth, and her pouty mouth pursed as she stared at her beloved's image. Paragon was also absorbed by the movie, or more precisely, the images of himself, instructing the people as a leader should. No matter how many times they had viewed the film in rehearsal, it still engrossed him.

Malia's hand crept at the level of the table toward Paragon's cup. It rose slowly, from the side facing her. She dropped the pill into the cup and the hand retreated slowly back to her lap, so he should see no sudden movement.

"And now," a grinning Paragon told the rapt audience, "you shall see how I conquered her." The first frames of the video, in her apartment, showed Paragon embracing her as he said, "High time. Let's see if you deserve to be the partner of Paragon."

David gritted his teeth. This was the first time he had forced himself to actually view the film, despite all the runnings in rehearsal. Malia seemed willing enough to melt into Paragon's arms. Had he done all this, risked so many lives, for someone who cared so little for him that she would willingly give herself to this savage? Of course, he was not watching the footage, which had been excised, of Malia condemning Diversity beforehand, or bargaining with Paragon to release Marjory from jail in return for cooperation. Malia had explained this to him when they met in the house on Foxhall Road, but it was hard to remember that faced with the actual movie.

The film froze in mid-frame, and the screen went dark. The lights switched on again.

Rising from his chair, Paragon cried out, "What incompetence is this? Start the film again, immediately!" He pointed indignantly toward the balcony.

A hubbub rose from the audience. "Bring back the movie!" Technicians ran up to the video booth where loud angry voices could be heard.

Malia's face shone like the sun breaking out of the clouds. She was given a reprieve, whether by chance or design she knew not. Paragon swore that the guilty parties would find themselves in Beaufort tomorrow. How many times had the film run uneventfully in rehearsal? This was clearly sabotage of some sort, but he could not admit that, not yet. As long as the wedding concluded with his marriage to Malia, he would emerge victorious, he told himself.

After ten minutes of futile efforts to recover the video, and the realization that even the backup file had somehow been corrupted, the decision was made to repair the video while the ceremony continued. "We will view the video at the conclusion of the ceremony," Aleta primly notified the disappointed crowd. The cantarias burst out into joyous song, like birds in springtime, and the archbishop ascended onto the stage.

Melusine herself was on stage, but her deputy, a small mustachioed wizard in a conical cap of the male priesthood, berated David and demanded he punish the incompetents and the miscreants. "I'm not going upstairs, amba-sah," David told him calmly. "I need to supervise here. I have several crew members doing their best to fix the problem. We will see the video." Reassured, the wizard sidled off. We'll see the video in hell, David promised. And that's my last amba-sah, ever.

"Commander Ma, do you agree to take both of your brides to treat with equal honor and love?"

"Ayah, I shall, may Mother Earth witness."

"Communicator Malia, do you take Commander Ma and Captain Boyd as loving spouses to treat with equal honor and love?"

"Ayah, I shall, may Mother Earth witness."

Exterra listened and assented to the same request.

"And now for the cup ceremony," the archbishop whispered to the trio. Aloud, she told Paragon, "Commander, please pledge to your designated first spouse."

Paragon lifted his cup high before the crowd, which raised its hands in recognition. Malia's sweaty hands were clasped before her. Oh my God, have I truly done this? Should I stop him from drinking? But no, no turning back. Perhaps the pills were placebos and Sohan gave me them just to make me feel better, and they will not harm him at all…

She waited for him to say, "I name you my first spouse." But the words did not come, or at least not for her. Because to her shock, Paragon turned from her and handed his cup to Exterra. "I wish to name Captain Boyd as my first spouse." He took Exterra's cup for his own, which was not the protocol, but which some saw as a gesture of his great affection for her.

A great murmur rose from the crowd. Exterra broke down in joyous tears. Khalid would not embarrass her on this stage before the most important citizens of the Diversity Justice Republic! *He saw me poison his cup,* Malia realized, *and since he would neither die, nor interrupt the wedding, he will kill Exterra.*

Exterra raised the cup to her lips and drained it, frowning slightly as she tasted the strangely sour juice rather than the expected wine. But she was overjoyed at Khalid having chosen her after all. Beaufort must have permitted him to change his mind at the last minute. Malia would be subordinate to her, forever.

Paragon drank, and then turned to Malia and sipped again. His angry black eyes met hers. *I know what you have done, and here is what you have done.* He could have demanded a new pouring, but it would have been an additional flaw in the ceremony after the interrupted video. Everything needed to proceed smoothly from this point, and he gambled that perhaps Exterra would live. He did not know exactly what Malia had placed in his cup, perhaps a drug to impede his sexual performance on the wedding night, or to nauseate him at the feast, but he did not think she would dare kill him. Still, he could not take the risk. Malia sipped from her cup.

In another ten seconds, the archbishop would declare the marriage valid under the laws of the Diversity Justice Republic. In the right balcony, Seth and Tom crept toward the Antifan soldier whose back was turned to them. At the last second, their footsteps creaked on the old wooden floor, and the soldier whirled around.

To their left, the other two Antifan soldiers were pushed over the balcony into the crowd, landing on guests thirty feet below. Crew members tossed small objects over the balcony after the soldiers. The remaining Antifan in the balcony fired his weapon, grazing Tom in the shoulder, but, his anger roused, Seth shoved him over the ledge into the crowd before he could fire again. *This is for Lucy, this is for the whole roundup, this is when the Antifans chased me into the forest and that commander with the tattoo called me an animal.* He and Tom then hurled their bomblets into the crowd below, Tom using his good left arm.

Shouts and cries filled the chapel as the bombs exploded: "Mother! Mother Earth!" and even a stray "Jesus!" from someone who had hidden his faith until now or who was perhaps elderly. Antifans ran to get their weapons from the lobby, but one of the bombs had detonated in front of the main door, and piles of smoking debris now barred them from that exit. Paragon ran to his dressing room to grab his firearm. The bodyguards hustled Vicki Rosen, Montoya, and Carolina out the secret entrance beneath the stage; Steve Rosen had already left the auditorium.

On the stage, Exterra, choking, slid to the floor, and died, almost unnoticed in the chaos. Only Malia stared in shock at that half-moon face, on which angry blisters had erupted.

A huge groaning, creaking sound erupted around them, amid the cries from the wounded. It lasted a full ten seconds as people looked wildly around them for the source of the strange noise. The rickety balcony, weakened by the explosions underneath it, collapsed in slow motion on top of the cantarias in the mezzanine, which then collapsed onto those guests who still sat petrified in the rear of the orchestra. Wooden beams and metal buttresses slammed guests in the head. Those who fled for the back exits were killed and injured by debris, or trampled.

As the balcony fell, the Plore crew members who had seized it from the Antifans fell with it, the individual fighters almost gliding in formation over the audience as their arms and legs waved in the air. Several of them, landing on killed or injured guests, were able to stumble to their feet and run for the stage, where the designated exit was for the attackers. Tom made it outside. Two fighters lay motionless amid the crowd. Seth scrambled to his feet, his ankle sprained, but not in time. Antifans who had returned to the auditorium with firearms picked him off, seeing that he was armed. Seth leaped into the air with the force of the multiple electronic bullets fired at once by several soldiers, and fell forever.

David ran out of the wings as the balcony collapsed, and grabbed Malia's hand. "Let's go!"

"Stop!" Paragon had returned with his weapon, determined not to let David Harris win this time. "I'll kill you both first." He glanced over at the dead Exterra. On Monday he would use this disaster to exterminate the Plores, the treaty be damned, he vowed.

David thrust Malia toward the stage door, and spun around, his own weapon now in hand. His shot knocked the gun out of Paragon's hand. As the commander bent down to retrieve it, David and Malia disappeared backstage around the corner. The frustrated Paragon fired through the curtain separating him from the couple. The electronic beam of the heat-seeking Antifan gun burned a charred black wound through the curtain and hit Malia in the side just below her rib cage. Another shot caught her in the right leg a step or two later. She staggered. David lifted her, and propelled them both out of the building through the side door.

A very young Antifan soldier rose in front of them, aiming, wasting time by shouting, "Halt!" David shot him first. He jumped over the Antifan's body, half-carrying Malia with him.

Paragon had just turned the corner around the curtains, in pursuit, when Rebecca emerged behind him. Eager to kill Malia's defiler—she had watched the movie every time, growing angrier each day—she aimed with a shaky hand, and fired, poorly, hitting Paragon in the arm. He turned, more annoyed than angry, fired back, and hit her in the chest. Her large frame crumpled to the ground, but her sacrifice gave Malia and David the seconds they needed to escape.

"This way, sir." A tall gray-haired chauffeur opened the door of a luxurious sedan for Malia and David. He was wearing the special event mask required of servants of the elite. If you had a masked driver like this, and a car like this, you were among the most august in the country. David had been told by Welcome to expect the car and driver, and he and Malia collapsed into the back seat. He threw her armband into the gutter.

David thought, Thank goodness that Paragon had not yet had the chip reinserted into her head, which would have allowed the ADF to track her whereabouts. "After the wedding; it will be my special gift to you," Paragon had told Malia.

The car sped off, racing past milling Antifan troops who had no idea what to do in the chaos, and would not stop cars clearly belonging to their superiors.

"My men..." David said.

"There are two other cars waiting for your fighters," said the chauffeur. "Anyone who can make it out that door will be rescued, if they do so quickly." David had emphasized to the group the need to reach the stage exit as quickly as possible after the explosions. He had not realized the balcony would collapse, and while it had served their ends, it had most likely caused the deaths of several crew members.

Glancing backward, David saw with horror that two uniformed Antifans sat in the row behind them. He reached for his belt.

"Commander Harris, don't you recognize me anymore?" It was Sergeant Candiss Yardley, who had served on David's squad. And sitting next to her was Captain Conor Chung. Both had been relegated to prison guard duty after David's disappearance and their brilliant careers had stalled. In spite of the dire circumstances, both beamed at him.

He laughed, tiredly and with great relief. "Never thought I'd see you guys again!"

"We're happy to help, Commander," said Chung.

The chauffeur pulled off his mask, and looked at David and Malia in the rearview mirror. "This isn't my normal job, Harris." It was Steve Rosen. "And don't call him Commander, he ran away from the job."

"Oh for God's sake, Steve..." But Steve was smiling at him too.

They stopped a few miles down the road behind an abandoned gas station. Night had fallen. Steve made David put on the chauffeur's uniform, including the mask, and take the wheel. The uniform was too big for David, even over his clothes, but nobody would notice as long as he sat. Steve was wearing his uniform underneath. He traded places with David, and made a brief phone call back to Beaufort.

"Deputy Director, she's bleeding badly," said Yardley. She raised a hand covered in fresh blood.

Chung grabbed a first-aid kit under the seat and began cleaning the wounds and covering them with duct tape and clean white bandages. Yardley and Rosen kept pressure on her leg at his direction, with Chung saying, "No tourniquets, it'll kill the tissue. Just pressure." His efforts would stanch the bleeding for a short while, but Malia was already drifting out of consciousness. David realized to his horror that he might have "saved" Malia only to watch her die in front of him, in this Antifan car. He cast several glances behind him at her blanketed form, and then was afraid to look again.

The car continued racing down the expressway, heading for 95.

"Where are we going?" David asked, mechanically, speeding.

"Delaware," said Steve behind him. "We're going to get you out of here."

Malia was huddled under several blankets on Rosen and Yardley's laps while Chung returned to the rear seat. Chung and Rosen pressed fresh bandages on top of the ones that had soaked through with blood.

"Sir," Chung said, "I'm not sure she's going to make it."

They pulled to a halt at the Delaware border stop. The sensors had picked up five passengers, but only three armbands.

Steve rolled down the window.

"Sir, you have two unauthorized passengers in the car," said the young Antifan guard at the checkpoint.

"Do you know who I am?" Steve showed his credentials. "We are getting the hell out of that catastrophe of a wedding in Lenilenape. Did you receive the alerts, Private?"

"Yes, sir," said the Antifan, gulping as he realized he had stopped the deputy director's car. His eyes trailed over the middle seat, with a blanketed body lying across Rosen and Yardley's laps. "Is anything else wrong?"

"My wife is bleeding badly. She was injured in the attack and her armband has gone missing. I want to get her to Wilmington as fast as possible." The Antifan Orthopedic Specialty Hospital was in Wilmington, so it was plausible the car would be heading there and not to Philadelphia.

"Should we call an ambulance for you, sir?"

"No Mother Earth dammit, it'll take another ten minutes. This is desperate! Let us go or you'll be in the brig on Monday!" Since the young Antifan had no doubt he was in fact interacting with the angry ADF deputy director, he relented and, rather than call a supervisor, let the car speed off. If Rosen's wife died because of his own decision to hold the car for a supervisor on account of two armbands, his own career would be ruined.

They soon were approaching the towers of Wilmington City. "Downtown. Riverfront. MED Cathedral," read the road sign. It was now dark, and the lights twinkled. It was a much smaller City than Anacosta, with the towers rising to fifty, but not eighty, stories high. Its Ploreville faced the City across Brandywine Creek. But aside from the hospital, this City was entirely unexciting. Soon they had left Wilmington behind, heading for the state park at the upper reaches of Delaware Bay.

Malia groaned and, turning over, vomited over Steve's feet.

"Malia, say something!" David demanded. He knew it was important that she stay conscious.

"I love you, David." But then she passed out. Chung leaned over the back seat and injected another blood thickener packet into her arm. But it was only postponing the inevitable.

Marjory and Emma watched the first Antifans falling from the balcony, not quite understanding until the explosions began. They dared do no more than look excitedly into each other's eyes. The coverage halted and most of the Antifans ran from the room to report to their offices.

The deputy commander of the Financial Crimes Unit who had been left behind at Beaufort and charged with monitoring the Harrises as they watched the wedding, materialized in front of them, his lips pressed together angrily. Anyone who knew David Harris was still alive, and he did, would have realized Harris was responsible, somehow, for the catastrophe.

"Let's go," he ordered. Marched downstairs, the two women found themselves in the execution hall, placed in separate cells. Normally all the cells would have been occupied since the Saturday night killing schedule was about to begin. But two cells had been reserved for the Harris women, just in case. Just as Malia had not quite known at first where she lay, neither did they.

"Don't separate us, please," begged Marjory.

The commander gave them a contemptuous look. "You can see each other in your Christian heaven," he sneered, and departed as the door clanged behind Marjory.

"Momma, I love you!" Emma called as they pushed her into a cell farther down the hall.

An hour or so later, they began to hear the screams and the rolls of gunfire at regular intervals and, with dread, realized where they had been taken. But no one came for them.

Ambulances were arriving at the college from downtown Philadelphia City, Wilmington, and as far away as Baltimore City to save the wounded. When the carnage was finally cleared after midnight, more than a hundred guests and priests had died and as many again brought to hospitals for treatment. It had not yet dawned on the authorities that the stage crew had been entirely kidnapped and replaced by insurgents. They assumed a few criminals had infiltrated into the building that morning by pretending to be stagehands. Only when the Baltimore crew members failed to check in or report for work on Monday would the ADF begin to discern the extent of the deception. Even then they still had no idea where the real crew members had gone—they had disappeared without a trace. One dead Cayugan and one Yramalander were discovered with actual crew member armbands, which was not quite enough, not yet, to implicate their hometowns.

Warren Welcome busied himself in his kitchen, frying some eggs, and humming

"Sweet Caroline." He had just received a text from Jeff that briefly said, "Home safe and sound." The only blemish on Welcome's happiness was the thought that occurred to him: *Now three generations of our family have known war.*

Chapter 60
Beach At Night
(Saturday, October 30, 2094)

The car screeched into the parking lot alongside the beach, spraying gravel. An ambulance was already waiting with the red earth symbol on a white background. David started when he recognized the white Beaufort medical uniforms, but he was also relieved. If Steve had summoned them, he would trust the pair, a man and a woman, who laid Malia on a stretcher and bore her into the ambulance. He paced helplessly, with Yardley and Chung waiting sympathetically nearby.

"To the beach," Steve said curtly, pointing.

"But..." David waved helplessly in the direction of the ambulance.

"You're not leaving without her, I promise. They're going to stabilize her and our chief surgeon—of the whole ADF—is waiting on the boat to operate on her."

Looking behind him anxiously, David followed Steve and the other two Antifans through the reeds and onto a sandy, hardpacked autumnal beach. The remnants of a purple and pink sunset lingered above the jetty that stuck out into the upper reaches of Delaware Bay. Somewhere below the bay was the Atlantic Ocean, and escape.

A small aluminum rescue boat approached from where it had been waiting under the jetty. An aluminum dock was released, inched toward the beach, and stopped when it latched on to the sand. It was the DRS *Victory*, or the Diversity Rescue Ship *Victory*.

"Do you see that vessel farther out?" Steve pointed to a larger vessel, with dimmed lights, farther down into the bay. "That's the DHS *Gain of Function*. The most advanced hospital ship in the ADF Navy, on the East Coast at least. Our surgeon is on board."

"And then what?" asked David.

"And then we transport you both to another ship that will take you farther into international waters and home. Not sure of the route, but you won't be landing again in the DJR."

"What ship?"

"Be patient. I won't leave the beach until you and your wife are on board the *Gain of Function*."

The medical technicians came loping past them with the stretcher, with Malia lying pale and unconscious, and an IV tube attached. They moved her onto the rescue ship and into the berth, and sat alongside her, one technician holding the IV. David started in her direction, but Steve stopped him.

"They'll get you on the next trip. The boat can only handle three, plus the pilot."

"But…"

"The sooner she gets to that ship, the sooner her life is saved. Do you want to capsize it by crowding on board?"

David shook his head, but cast an anguished look in her direction. He felt calmer than he had in the car, however, now that medical personnel were in charge, even if they were Antifans.

The aluminum deck retreated into the underside of the boat, the pilot revved up the engine, and soon the small craft was chugging into the upper bay toward the *Gain of Function*. Two minutes later they watched it draw up alongside, and Malia's stretcher was fastened to some rigging that pulled it up to the deck, where other personnel met them.

"One more passenger in your party," said Steve, as the headlights of another ambulance shone on them from the parking lot. "I wasn't sure they were going to make it."

A minute later, another stretcher was borne past him.

"Momma!" he cried.

Unlike Malia, Marjory was conscious, and reached her hand to David. He clasped it with both hands, marveling at how frail it felt and how it shone like veined marble in the rising moonlight. "David," she said faintly. "I'm coming with you and Malia. If you don't mind."

"Mind? Are you all right? What have they done to you?"

"Nothing," she said. "We can talk later." She fell back on the stretcher as the rescue boat headed back toward the beach.

"Your sister decided to stay here, with her family," said Steve. "But she had a choice, mind you. I've ordered that she be released, so she should be home now."

"Steve…I can't thank you enough. I know we wouldn't have made it here tonight without you." David did not want to refer to the behind-the-scenes help he now realized Steve had provided, not with Yardley and Chung standing by. The pair had been willing to help Steve exfiltrate him and Malia, as a debt owed to a beloved commander, but the wedding had now claimed so many Antifan lives that Steve could not afford to be implicated in the disaster.

"Harris, I'm getting tired of you and your wife complicating my life. It's easier to expedite your trip home. Just don't come back, please." Steve thought to himself, I am doing what I can to atone for some of my sins. This is a small start.

"Tell Khalid Ma not to kidnap her again, and I'll stay away." But David knew he would be returning to the DJR, whether Steve liked it or not.

"Commander Ma's ADF career is over," said Steve. "I fought in the ADF for a progressive future, one that embraced all, and promoted equity and reduced suffering…but not that. We are taking the reins back tomorrow. The DJR can do better. We must do better."

David was dubious that such a future was achievable, not under the iron fist of the ADF, not in a society that controlled reading and viewing, working and leisure, and divided the population into high and low Social Credit and despised Plores, rather than uniting them. Did not Steve realize that any socialist government inevitably must coerce its population, and ban free discussion and economic activity, just to survive? But he would not argue with Steve on this chilly beach, with reeds waving in the night breeze. Let Steve find out for himself.

"And Harris, one more thing. I am helping you and Malia get home, because you didn't ask to come back and your sons need you. Your bandit friends got a head start tonight to disappear. But starting Monday morning, when I return to the office, we will track them down and destroy them. The ops center"—at Beaufort—"is telling me that sixty-three ADF personnel are dead, so far, and an equal number of other Crediteers. Wilmington and Philadelphia intensive care units are overflowing. We cannot allow that to go unpunished. We owe that to our colleagues, and we owe it to Diverse Power. Just in case you think I'm going soft, or that the DJR is going to tolerate this insurrection."

David understood. "Thanks for the head start, Steve. But if the DJR doesn't change, and doesn't understand a society can't be held together by slavery, it won't last. I hope you can do something to fix that before it's too late."

Steve rolled his eyes. "Oh, before you leave us forever, Harris, hand over that weapon."

"Which weapon?"

"The one that could get you into a lot of trouble in this country if I cared to follow up," Steve said. He held out his hand.

"In gratitude for your help, Steve," said David as he pulled out the firearm and placed it flat in Steve's palm. He was more sentimental about the knife anyway.

The rescue boat returned, and the deck crunched again into the sand. The medical technicians disembarked, and helped install Marjory's stretcher. The elderly woman, sedated, now slept peacefully. With only one meditech needed for Marjory, David was asked to board the boat.

David shook hands with and embraced both Yardley and Chung. "Thank you. I know you've paid a price because we worked together. I hope your situation will improve."

"Commander, we're honored," said Yardley. "Perhaps we'll see you another time, when relations between our countries are better." Chung nodded vigorously.

"Harris, I wish you and Malia all the best," said Steve. "Tell the Americans that some Diversans want to work with them to build better relations, would you?"

"I will tell them they can trust you. Thanks for everything, and good luck to you too."

They Antifan-saluted each other, one last time. The salute felt strange to David, after five years, but also satisfying, in a closure kind of way. David followed the tech and Marjory into the vessel, and settled himself next to his mother. A few seconds later, the boat pushed out from shore again. David watched the figures on the beach until they became black dots and then receded entirely from view. By then, the two-story hospital ship was looming above them in the dark. *We aren't away from the DJR yet,* he reminded himself, and now he, Malia, and even Marjory were entirely at the deejers' mercy, out from under the umbrella of Steve Rosen's protection. Yet none of the Antifans had patted him down, and he was still armed with the knife, just in case.

Tom and Oren, who was carrying Rebecca's heavy body over his shoulder, climbed into a car waiting outside the stage entrance, waved into it by an anxious-looking Social Credit driver. *Can we trust him,* Oren wondered, but it was either that or carjack one of the other vehicles awaiting their distinguished owners. *Some of whom wouldn't be needing a ride home anyway.*

The terrified Soko driver, who had been hired at Steve Rosen's direction, couldn't be sure that the mysterious paperwork on his phone would reassure police. And there was no hiding that his passengers were Plores who had escaped from the carnage at the college, and therefore could be assumed to be assailants. He had not expected to be driving Plores until the last moment, and he was sure it was illegal. And there was a dead woman behind him and he was superstitious. Seeing the man's anxiety, Oren became equally jittery. *If we are stopped,* Oren thought, *I will shoot all but Tom and take over the wheel myself.*

"Is she still alive?" Tom asked Oren.

Oren shook his head. "Not leaving her in that place. We'll bury her decently, at home." Unsaid, but realized by both men, was that if Rebecca's body remained onsite, with or near Araceli's armband, it would quickly unravel their entire subterfuge, and Oren's band would immediately be apprehended, if not killed outright. It was almost certain some casualties would be retaken with their false armbands, and the deception realized, even though all had been instructed to ditch the armbands when the assault began. *We'll head into Cayuga,* Oren decided.

Either the driver lost his nerve entirely, or this was the original plan, because he drove behind an abandoned store just outside Downingtown, and told his passengers, "One of you drives home from here. I'm outta here. I'm gonna take a bus."

"Are you sure?" Oren asked, but he wasn't going to argue with the man.

As they drove into the night, no one seemed to be pursuing them, and Oren and

Tom began to relax, just a little. They planned to cross into Yramaland, and back into the Anacosta containment area, west of Gettysburg, near Thurmont. It was far enough from populated areas to have isolated crossings, yet not very close to the Economic Zone camps at the frontier, and then they would be in Oren's backyard. A trucker would bring Tom and Seth to Cayuga tomorrow afternoon, but now, Tom realized, it would just be himself. Same price, though.

"He was hotheaded," said Tom, meaning Seth. "But he had a good heart. He wanted to do the right thing. He became focused after they destroyed his roundup. He found a purpose."

Oren's thoughts turned to Rebecca. "I'm the last sibling in our family. The Antifans have now destroyed all of us, except me."

"So you're going to still fight."

"Yes, our parents are gone, and I have no wife or kids, not that it would matter anymore. Aren't you going to fight?" Oren challenged him.

"If Mike returns. I don't know how we'll do it otherwise. They'll destroy us forthwith."

Oren said, "Mike won't return. We don't even know if he'll make it out of the country tonight. If you lived in America, would you come back here to face off against Antifans? Again?"

Tom's jaw set firmly. "If Mike escapes, he'll return. He promised us."

Oren shrugged: You have no choice but to fight. We have laid down a gauntlet tonight, and we will be joining you in Cayuga. To hell with containment areas. To hell with those ID cards. We go off the grid and we will feed ourselves. He did not press Tom, whom Oren sensed was mentally and physically exhausted rather than cowardly. "My shoulder hurts," Tom admitted.

They crossed the containment line without incident under cover of dark and were back in the house by midnight. Despite the lateness of the hour, Oren dug a grave for Rebecca in the woods, the house caretaker steering them away from the other fresh graves. The moonlight spilled over Oren and the caretaker as they dug for hours, Tom apologizing for his inability to help. He helped them place Rebecca's body in a sheet and fold it around her.

"She ain't gonna want to lie with Sokos, that's for sure," said Oren, roughening his language and voice as he began grappling with the reality that his beloved, if eccentric, sister, was gone. "I told Mike she was the best man in the group, and you know, she was, except of course she was all woman…She took such good care of me after she got divorced. She cared a lot."

Tom placed his good arm around Oren's shoulder, and led him into the house. "Let's have a drink." An hour later, the third car arrived with the final four survivors. A nurse came by to treat Tom's graze, and set a broken arm and a broken foot, caused by the falls from the balcony. She gave the broken arm man a sedative, because he was distraught. "I can't believe we did that! I didn't think so many people would die!" Oren sighed, it was worse here, from what they're telling me.

In the morning, the people of the town gathered, and resolved to move en masse to Cayuga, and resettle Lucy's roundup. Tom would bring the news back with him to Cayuga so they could prepare for an influx of a hundred newcomers over the next few weeks. And that was how the Cayuga resistance truly began, in a village that eventually grew into the redoubt called Lucyna.

Chapter 61

DHS *Gain Of Function*
(Saturday–Sunday October 30–31, 2094)

"Happy Halloween," a crew member said perfunctorily as he walked by carrying a metal box.

David looked up from the deck chair in which he was waiting for news of Malia. It must have been past midnight and now it was October 31, Halloween. For a moment he wondered whether the "Happy" or the "Halloween" was an insult, given that all knew he was on tenterhooks awaiting news about Malia's surgery. Whether or not Malia would survive was very much in doubt, and he was known to be a Christian. So what was "Happy Halloween" supposed to mean? But he forced himself to conclude that the greeting was simply a routine DJR pleasantry, and sank back in the chair.

Exhausted, and lulled by the gentle waves, he had catnapped repeatedly all evening. He saw the lights behind the curtains in the operating room, and as long as the lights were on and activity could be glimpsed behind the curtains, there was still hope.

Restless, he rose and, clutching at the rail, stared into the dark water, which merged at the horizon with the dark night. Malia too was hovering between earth and sky, he thought, in that murky no-man's-land between life and death. A kind nurse had come out to update him, twice, so far. "The doctor has removed the bullets. One bullet penetrated her colon. The team is siphoning off the bleeding and they will stitch the wound internally."

"Will she..."

"I hope so. Pray to Mother Earth for a favorable outcome."

They even have to ruin this moment with the idolatry, David thought irritably, but then he told himself, they mean nothing ill by it. I'm tired of fighting and killing tonight, let it go. Let it all go, except for Malia.

The captain, a middle-aged African-Diversan, in the white uniform with green trim of the Antifan Defense Forces Navy, had come off the bridge to greet David during the long evening. "Mr. Harris, we are waiting for the other vessel. It is about forty nautical miles to the south. When it approaches, in about three hours, we will meet with it just outside of DJR waters, in international waters, and transfer you and your party."

"Whose ship is it?"

"I am not entirely sure myself. This whole affair has been kept secret, even from me and my crew. But they are a friendly party and you need fear nothing."

How could it be less friendly than an Antifan Navy vessel, David chided himself. Probably an AIA ship, rescuing me and Malia in a covert operation, finally, now that they need take no risks. He was relieved that no one on board the *Gain of Function* seemed to be angry at him for his history, his desertion, or for orchestrating what easily had been the worst casualty event in the entire history of the ADF. If it were not for Steve Rosen, they could easily kill us and throw our bodies overboard. He quickly patted his shin pocket. Then he remembered that while the other Antifans were watching the transfer of Marjory to the *Victory*, Steve had discreetly passed him a folded-up square of paper, indicating he should read it later. David now unwrapped it.

In Steve's handwriting were the words, "Amazing Antifan spirit, my friend. Don't do it again." David grinned, and then tossed the note overboard, for Steve's protection.

And then he remembered his mother. The captain brought him to the small cabin where his mother lay, attended by a woman crew member in the corridor outside.

"She has been resting quietly," the crew member assured David. "I brought her some water and crackers earlier since her stomach is unsettled."

With his hand on the doorknob, David looked questioningly at the woman. She nodded.

He thanked the captain and the crew member, closed the door behind him, and listened to the steady breathing of his mother. As if she could sense his presence, Marjory awoke, and smiled to see him. He seated himself on a rattan high-backed chair next to her bed, and reached out for her hand, which felt cool.

"Remember once you said you wanted to take a cruise?" he reminded her.

"Yes, we were such inland people. And then the war came and there were no cruises for the likes of us. But better late than never."

He told her about the ship coming to rescue them from the Antifans and take them to the United States, although he admitted he didn't know exactly who was rescuing them.

"In a few days, you'll see Daniel and your grandchildren."

"How is Malia?"

"I don't know. The surgery seems to be going all right. The nurse wasn't promising anything, though."

"If she doesn't make it…"

"Mom!" he said, agonized. If Malia didn't survive, it would be his fault, when he could have left her alone, persecuted in the DJR, but very much alive, and awaiting a bilateral accord.

"I'm sorry, we'll pray, and perhaps God will be kind to us, finally, after having endured so much." So they prayed for several minutes, reciting psalms.

When they finished, David asked, "Are you injured at all? Did they mistreat you?"

"No, dear, they didn't lay a hand on me, or on your sister. But they forced us to watch the wedding, and when it blew up—that was spectacular, David, your father would have enjoyed that so much—they marched us down to the basement and put us in these cells. And then we had to listen to prisoners being dragged down the hall and then we realized they were being shot. It was nightmarish. I will never forget that."

David held his head in his hands. "Oh, Momma, I'm sorry. That's the worst place in the whole tower."

"After about an hour, they came for your sister and me, and we were afraid it was our turn."

"Oh my God!"

"But they said they were releasing us. When they were processing us in the office, they said, you can go to the United States if you want, but you have to decide now. A ship is waiting to take you to the US with your son.

"Emma chose to stay—that was right, she needs to be with Larry and her children. I...I have been a burden to them. I have caused them trouble because I cannot just sit there and let the Diversity...the Diversity forces...continue to trample us. I remember... better days."

"You weren't a burden, Mom! Never!"

"Anyway," she smiled at him, "I want to live in a free country again before I die. And you're right, see my new grandsons. And my granddaughter. She's very pretty, I bet.

"David, I'm tired. I'll let you go and check on Malia."

"All right, Mom, rest for a while. The other ship will be here in a few hours, the captain said."

Suddenly, she looked hard at him. The soft fuzzy edges of her exhaustion crystallized for a moment.

"David..."

"What, Momma?"

"Did you ever work on that floor?"

"What floor, Mom?" He delayed, but he knew what she meant.

"The floor where they kept Emma and me tonight."

He hesitated, wondering whether he should lie. But he was tired of lying, and of the year he had spent deceiving everyone, constantly switching names, evading the cull by pretending to be a Social Crediteer, pretending he was a regular Plore, pretending he was a low Social Credit stagehand who was already dead, always pretending. If you couldn't be honest with your beloved mother, could you be honest with anyone, anymore?

"Yes, Mom. I worked that floor for a year, many years ago. They made me. I drank a lot to forget what I saw and did."

She turned to the wall.

"Momma, please forgive me. It wasn't my choice."

"Of course I forgive you," she said, still facing the wall. The unspoken statement was: But forgiveness is not mine, it is God's to give, or those whom you wronged.

"Momma, please look at me. Please say it's all right."

With some effort, she twisted around, and smiled faintly at him. "David, it's all right. I'll always love you. Go check on Malia."

"I'll see you in a few hours," David promised her. She said a quiet "Yes," and closed her eyes.

Outside in the corridor, the crew member caught his arm as he was about to brush past. "I heard you and your mother pray," she said.

"Are you going to tell the authorities?" he whispered harshly. "They know we're Plores, they know we're Christians. Can't you just let us pray in peace?"

"I wish I could have joined you," she said, her brown eyes brimming with tears. "It was very beautiful." She had pressed her ear to the thin cabin door to hear better.

David was taken aback. It was much more dangerous for this young woman to confess her desire to pray as a Christian than for him and his mother to have prayed privately in the cabin, when freedom was so near. They had completely forgotten in the silent cabin, with the gentle thrum of the engine and the soft hushing waves beneath them, about the crew member in the corridor.

"Does your god forgive sins?" she asked, very quietly but intently. "Not the sins of littering, not the sin of living as long as you want. But the sins that are about how you treat other people?" These sins were of no interest to the Mother Earth Diversity Church. David knew this young woman was troubled by something she had done, or had been done to her, but did not want to press. I am not a pastor, he thought.

"Yes, He forgives these sins, if you have faith in Him. And His Son died for our sins, so we are forgiven and can start fresh."

The young woman beamed at him, and David smiled back, a little crookedly, before mounting the stairs to the deck to the hospital area. The nurse came out to meet him. "Mr. Harris, the surgeon has finished. Would you like to see her? But she is still asleep."

They ushered him into the recovery room, and he gazed upon Malia's white face, hoping she would awaken as Marjory had, but she did not.

"Her vital signs are close to normal," the nurse assured him. "It is a good sign that she has no fever. The scar will be very unpleasant, but someday it will fade."

"I'll take any scar as long as she lives," David said. He stepped over to the hospital bed and kissed Malia's forehead, very gently. "Is the surgeon available? I would like to thank him for saving my wife's life."

The nurse shook her head. "They has gone to sleep. They does not wish to meet you."

The nurse urged him to get some rest, "We have a bunk prepared for you," but David would take no chances. The surgeon's disdain for him was a reminder that, despite the politeness and professionalism of the crew, and even the secret Christian yearnings of one crew member, he was still on board an enemy vessel. One angry Antifan sailor loyal to Paragon could still kill him. He had to stay awake and alert until the mystery ship arrived and they could safely board. He owed that to Malia and Marjory. Again he patted the side shin pocket.

The nurse arranged for a crew member to bring him breakfast. It was shortly after 0300. As he was finishing the toast and eggs, and downing coffee outside Malia's room, watching off the starboard side, he realized a thin white line on the horizon was actually a ship. The DHS *Gain of Function*'s engines started, and it began moving toward the boundary between DJR and international waters. Black waters churned before them as they steamed toward the other vessel.

But the ships were not racers, and distances were deceiving. It was another hour before the mystery ship came close enough so that David could see it was a giant yacht, two and a half stories high, including the bridge. Several people were standing on the deck, waving, but at that distance and in the dark he couldn't recognize anyone. They didn't seem to be in uniform, or no uniform that David recognized. And then he saw the ship's name, Private Ship (PS) *Mar-a-Lago*, Pensacola.

The ship pulled alongside, and the crew members from each linked them together with a giant grinding noise and a bump that almost caused David to fall.

The captain appeared again.

"Mr. Harris, I am about to discharge my obligation to our deputy director by allowing you safe passage onto the PS *Mar-a-Lago*. I want you to know that I had to order two sailors not to kill you outright once they knew about the wedding attack. But we are exercising Diverse discipline in obeying our deputy director, who told us you would not return to the DJR."

"Thank you, Captain," said David, sincerely. He had been wise to stay alert. "I appreciate your assistance and...your discipline."

Hospital crew members transferred stretchers bearing Malia, and then Marjory, over the side of the boat onto the deck of the yacht, where the new crew reached out and took them.

"Goodbye," said the captain, indicating that David should follow his wife and mother. He did not offer his hand, and David felt it would be inappropriate, even disrespectful, to Antifan-salute this time.

He said, "Thank you, Captain," again, and turned and climbed over the edge of the *Gain of Function* onto the *Mar-a-Lago*.

The ships were detached and, in a minute, the *Gain of Function* had begun its trip back to the Wilmington City docks. David was reassured to watch the white ship with the lights grow smaller and then disappear toward the shore. The *Mar-a-Lago* engines revved up and they began heading south again, into freedom.

"My friend," said a familiar voice behind him. "So good to see you again."

"Chris!" David exclaimed, spinning around to embrace the beaming Capettone robotics director.

The two men hugged for a good half minute, laughing joyfully. Chris thought, he looks worn, and gaunt, but alert.

"How…how did you do this?" David asked, waving at the yacht.

"Mr. Baxter Berry donated his yacht to the cause. The AIA was authorized to help rescue you and Malia from the DJR, but the government was unwilling to take the lead, and show its hand—you know, we still need that access to the Port of Los Angeles, right? so they turned to us, the MAGA. Mr. Berry said he had lost interest in sailing, and I arranged to buy it from him on behalf of the Oklahoma MAGA Party. To Mr. Berry's credit, he sold it to us at a very reasonable price, since I think he felt badly over having let you go. We'll find uses for it, no worries.

"We sailed from Bermuda, and we are heading back there. It is the nearest non-DJR port. Your wife needs to be in a hospital, and perhaps your mother does too. It is a beautiful place, with palm trees, and you can relax for a few days, and communicate with your family in Oklahoma. Depending on how Malia is doing, you will be home in a week."

David wanted to tell Chris about the whole year, and his adventures in Cayuga and Anacosta, but he was suddenly incoherent. "I…so much to say…how can I thank you all?"

"You're exhausted, David. We have prepared a comfortable bed for you. Go get some sleep and we'll have plenty of time to catch up. It will take two days to reach Bermuda. We have a nurse on board who will take care of Malia and your mother. Who I very much look forward to meeting. So, sleep, my friend…"

With the adrenalin having sloughed off, David was overcome by weakness. "Yes," he agreed. He turned around, and acknowledged the cheers of the six-man crew. "Thank you all, thank you," and stumbled downstairs. The dawn began creeping over the horizon on the port side.

Chapter 62

Paragone

(Saturday, October 30, 2094)

Back in the Foxhall Road mansion, Paragon shoved a few black jackets and slacks in a suitpod. The guards at the gate had allowed him to enter the compound, but he detected a slight chill in their obedience, as if they recognized him, and were behaving correctly, but no longer revered him. The disastrous spectacle, and the blow to Diverse Power, had logically damaged Paragon's standing. Until the TV coverage stopped abruptly, the whole country had been watching the wedding, even the Plores. His wedding had led to the deaths of dozens of Antifan officers, and while officially blameless, Paragon could not escape the taint.

He was relieved that Steve Rosen apparently had not yet issued orders to arrest him, especially since he was vulnerable while at Foxhall Road. Presumably Rosen was still managing the chaotic scene at the College, which Paragon assumed was entirely of Rosen's making as he sought to prevent him, Paragon, from forcing him out of the ADF. He should not have trusted Rosen to comply. He now remembered that Rosen had left his seat when the movie began, and had not returned. Paragon had just assumed that Rosen was too fastidious to sit through the movie.

Paragon had watched that infernal David Harris flee the chapel with Malia, but he refused to believe that Harris had orchestrated the entire disaster. Nor could he conceive that Plores had killed so many Antifans, not on their own. Somehow David Harris had managed to infiltrate the low Social Credit stage crew, that much Paragon understood, but he could not have done it without the aid of a senior ally, and who else had an incentive to ruin the wedding but Steve Rosen? The pieces of the puzzle fell into place for Paragon, who assumed that Rosen would move swiftly to neutralize him. I have a few hours, no more, to escape.

He threw a few toiletries and underwear into the suitpod, and hurried down the stairs. He tried to ignore the throbbing left bicep that Rebecca had shot at in her final fury. To his relief, the self-driving car that he had commandeered at the College was still waiting. "Obama Airport," he ordered, and none of the Antifans stopped him from leaving. But neither did the gate guards salute his departure. The situation was ominous. To his regret, the celadon vase and a safe full of foreign currency would have to stay behind at Beaufort. Perhaps they would hold the vase for his triumphant return, someday.

At the check-in counter, no one stopped him from claiming his boarding pass, although he suspected that the lovely dark-haired Latinx attendant seemed a tad uncertain. When she went behind the counter to check with a supervisor, he panicked, wondering if he should turn and flee in another car, somewhere else, maybe south to Florida. But in a minute, the attendant returned with the gift bag that all superior Social Crediteers were given when they boarded a Diversair flight, and he relaxed. "We ran out, amba-sah, so I had to unlock the closet to get you one."

The flight left without incident, with a prayer over the loudspeaker to Omicron and Mother Earth. Paragon eagerly swallowed the painkillers brought by the steward. As they flew south, to cross Texas and Mexico en route to Los Angeles, Paragon's thoughts turned, angrily, to that bitch Malia Jenness. She had attempted to poison him during the ceremony, whether in conjunction with Steve Rosen, or David Harris, or both, or possibly just on her own initiative. How foolish of her to think he was oblivious to the small, mouselike movement as he watched the movie, the brilliant movie his enemies had sabotaged.

As the archbishop had droned on, Paragon had contemplated his options. He had suddenly realized Malia's treachery presented an opportunity to rid himself of Exterra. First, he would please the Diverse audience by selecting the non-heretic Antifan woman as his senior spouse, since he knew many Diversan elites resented the rise to prominence of a traitor's widow. Indeed, their gasps of shock and pleasure had gratified Paragon, and the unwitting Exterra had played her part perfectly. He decided he would fully revenge himself on Malia behind those looming walls once they returned to Anacosta, and would blame Exterra's death on Plores, as a pretext for launching a final program of extermination against them. But then the soldiers had toppled from the balcony, which groaned and collapsed, Paragon had run for his firearm, and, when he returned, David Harris was stealing his, Paragon's, remaining bride.

Paragon had purchased the airline seat next to him as well, because he did not want to risk interaction with someone known to him. He gambled that the attendance of most top elites at the wedding—including Knowledge Tower director Mitsuyama and the senior ADF ranks—would severely restrict the number of potential passengers who would recognize him, even from the media. But most of the seats in sustainable class were empty on this odd off-season Saturday night. He was hungry, so he ate, thinking regretfully of the chateaubriand that no doubt would go down the undiscerning gullets of the rescue workers. This would be the night to start drinking, he mused, but he declined the cocktails. He napped, and, when he awoke, scrolled down his armband phone for news alerts. Nothing about the wedding.

As Paragon disembarked in Los Angeles, he heard in Chinese, "Commander Ma Kang-li please proceed to the China Air lounge." It was not repeated in English, lest some Diversan overhear. He smiled, and almost relaxed, knowing he was safe.

The Chinese consul general in Los Angeles, Wu Jin-lai, greeted him just as he entered the lounge. They had last met in Las Vegas in August, where under the guise of a gambling spree, Paragon had reported on his efforts to promote ever higher levels of Diversity in the DJR. Wu was a small balding man in late middle age, whose innocuous looks and diplomatic title concealed a shrewd intelligence officer with thirty years' experience.

"You are on Chinese territory now," Wu told Paragon, "so they cannot arrest you here." Part of the protectorate agreement between the PRC and the DJR decreed that all commercial enterprises owned by China in the DJR were sovereign PRC territory. The ADF would not dare invade the lounge to arrest him. About two dozen businessmen and a handful of women sat around the hushed lounge, having concluded business deals with the Economic Tower and ready to return home. Paragon overheard some jokes about the stupid Diversans they had cheated. He heard the distant pings of the slot machines in the adjoining room.

A Diversan physician arrived to remove the bullet from Paragon's arm behind a screen in a corner of the lounge. After he bandaged the arm and left, a Chinese waitron brought a teapot and snacks to their corner.

Wu said, "I believe you overreached with this wedding, Commander Ma. Perhaps it would have been best to wait for the deputy director to retire in the fullness of time."

Paragon bristled. "Diversity was flagging, *Da Ge*, Eldest Brother. I hope the Central Committee will not punish me for imposing socialism with zeal. And I have always been attentive to your and Beijing's commands."

"Yes, the committee has no criticism of your service on our behalf. But what happened this afternoon? Do you think Deputy Director Rosen was responsible?"

"Absolutely. I had backed him into a corner. He was going to submit his resignation on Monday. I underestimated how desperate he was to retain his job."

Wu slurped his tea with noisy relish. "My sources tell me a band of Plores killed the real stage crew, and impersonated them all week with a plan to disrupt the wedding and rescue the wife. We will decide whether we tell the ADF on Monday how this happened. It might not be good to let everyone know that Plores are capable of such a deadly attack. It might create confusion among your people."

"Plores!" cried Paragon. "They couldn't have planned an attack this sophisticated."

"Led by this David Harris they did. A very dangerous man. You should have killed him a long time ago. If he comes back to the DJR, who knows what damage he might do? Hopefully he will escape with his wife tonight back to the US and never return.

You will deal with him justly when the US has embraced Diversity. Regarding that program, your efforts against the US have been highly praiseworthy. We cannot afford to let up there.

"But do not worry, Younger Brother. You will return to China tonight for consultations with the service. The timing is not bad. You will take a brief hiatus while we think about the next steps, and you can return to the DJR once the dust settles. The Diverse country needs strong leadership, and perhaps a genuine Deplorable threat will make loyal citizens demand strong leadership that only you can provide. We in Beijing will make your case, have no fear." Generous Chinese financial support to the DJR made for a government pliable to Beijing's wishes. Paragon happily thought that with Beijing behind him, his exile would be short.

Nonetheless, exhausted, Paragon slumped in his chair. He lit and inhaled a cigarette, which was legal on Chinese soil.

"And we will bring your mother and brothers to visit you in Beijing. No doubt it has been too long since you last saw them. A reunion, a reprieve, a rest, you deserve it all."

Yes, Paragon thought, I would like to see my mother again. I will explain that I could not save Patigul from her own designs. I will tell her that Diversity is very strict, unlike in China we make no exceptions for family or money. But she will ask about the children. When I return to the DJR, we will locate the children, before it is too late to please her. They are now grown, somewhere. Malia was right, they are my nieces and nephews.

Then: She has escaped. Strangely, he was not as bitter about it as he would have expected. It had been like capturing a butterfly that was no longer a real butterfly when you staked it to the display board, but just a dried-out set of wings. Or creating a fragrant potion whose sweetness dissipated when exposed to air.

"China Air Flight Twenty-Two now boarding for Beijing." The tired businessmen stood, stretched, and gathered their briefcases and workscreens.

"Ma Kang-li, it is time to go home." Wu Jin-lai rose with him and escorted him to the gate.

Half an hour later, the doors to the aircraft closed, and Paragon was finally able to close his eyes and sleep. The flight attendants brought him pillows and blankets. The nightmarish day was over and, on the bright side, he was not married to anyone. The jet streaked into the Pacific night sky, leaving Diversity behind.

Chapter 63
The Depths Of The Heart
(Tuesday, November 2, 2094)

The following afternoon, David stood on the deck, frozen in grief. The body, wrapped in canvas cloth and adorned by metal weights, lay on a makeshift bier covered by a green damask tablecloth that might have belonged to the Berrys. The yacht had stopped and the engines were cut. Four of the six crew members stood by, caps in hand. David himself wore a blue button-down shirt, a blue jacket, and a pair of tan chinos that Fern had sent with Chris from David's own wardrobe. Everything was now a little loose on him after a year of privation and manual labor. The sea breeze whipped around them, tousling David's hair. Small whitecaps dotted the blue waters below. It was still the North Atlantic in November.

As a deacon at his church, Chris was prepared to officiate. "It's not a Lutheran prayer book, but it is Protestant," he said apologetically. "I wasn't expecting this would happen."

David grunted. "Good enough." His eyes were bloodshot. He had only slept about four hours when Chris came to wake him up with the news from the nurse.

"We are here to lay to rest, in the depths of the ocean, the body of Marjory Anne Mitchell Harris, who was born in freedom in Ohio, in the United States, and who, after a lifetime of challenges and suffering in the Diversity Justice Republic, died outside its prison walls. Her last waking hours were spent in the company of her son, David, standing here, from whom she had been separated for so long. She was on her way to be reunited with her other son, and to see two grandsons and a granddaughter for the first time. One of the last things she told David was that she wanted to live in a free country again before she died. If she did not quite achieve that, she did not fail, because she died a free woman."

Chris went on to relate what David had told him about Marjory's heroism, her courage in the face of Antifan oppression, her conviction that justice would prevail someday, and her love for the Lord and her family. "She wrote illegal bulletins with news about Ploreville, and arranged to have them sent up and down the DJR so that

Plores elsewhere in the country would know what was happening…She ran illegal knitting and reading clubs to conduct anti-regime activity under the very noses of the ADF…She aided illegal travelers…"

David thought that only when he had defied the ADF and escaped to the United States with Malia and Daniel had Marjory come into her own. The show of courage by her sons had awakened a dormant passion in her to reclaim her freedom.

Chris then spoke of Marjory's childhood, her marriage to Elijah, the suffering of the civil war. "She bore five children, one of whom died in an Antifan transit camp. She raised all her surviving children to walk with God and to be respected by others."

Anguished, and knowing he had not always walked with God, David thought, the last words I said to her was my confession that I had worked the execution corridor at Beaufort, which she had just barely escaped that night. I dragged criminals who were not really criminals out of their cells and down the hall and shot them as coldly as a butcher brains a steer. Could that knowledge have been the final blow for her? Did I cause her death? I should have lied, one more time. And this year I have committed more murders still.

They recited "The Lord is my shepherd." Then a final prayer:

"We, therefore, commit the earthly remains of Marjory Harris to the deep, looking for the general Resurrection in the last day, and the life of the world to come, through our Lord Jesus Christ; at whose second coming in glorious majesty to judge the world, the sea shall give up her dead; and the corruptible bodies of those who sleep in him shall be changed, and made like unto his glorious body; according to the mighty working whereby he is able to subdue all things unto himself. Amen."

"David, do you wish to add anything before we…go ahead?" Eulogies were not a common Lutheran practice, since saving by grace counted more than deeds. Listing the deceased's praises even at this stage could be considered somewhat arrogant, a usurpation of God's role as the ultimate decider of the deceased's final destination.

"I am glad she is finally with my father after all these years. That's all."

Chris looked oddly at David, but decided David was only being considerate of the hardworking crew. And every moment they lingered in these waters meant a later arrival in Bermuda. "All right, gentlemen," Chris said to them, "we're ready."

The four crew members approached the body—David had looked on his mother's face one last time that morning before they wrapped her in the canvas shroud—and extended the board on which she rested short-end-wise over the side of the yacht. Then they tipped the end downward. The shrouded body did not move at first. Some scrap of canvas caught on the wooden plank. They increased the angle of the board, and the weight of the metal met gravity, and then she slipped quietly into the water.

David watched the canvas bob briefly just below the surface and then it sank so he could not see her anymore. And then the yacht's engines started again and they left her behind for the fish and the deep to take. After the crew had dispersed, David stood for a long time staring behind them at the waters where Marjory now lay, until the site had vanished beyond the horizon. Unseen tears streaked down his face.

As much as David mourned his mother, and he would mourn more later, he was more preoccupied with Malia. She lay in the stateroom bed, under a skylight, her long dark brown curls tumbling over the pillows, her forehead glistening with a sheen of perspiration.

He had sat with her all morning, and said a few words, hoping she would awake. But at most, she opened her glassy eyes, said, simply, "David," or "I love you," or "Are you really there?" and sank again into unconsciousness.

"My mother died," he said to her, but there was no response.

And he had cause to worry. The nurse confided that Malia now had a rising fever and a high white blood cell count. She changed the dressings and the IV bag, swabbed Malia's mouth with a wet foam stick, and emptied bedpans. "I'm sorry, Mr. Harris, I think the wound—in the torso—may be infected. There is an odorous discharge. Her leg looks all right." That had been a flesh wound. The nurse would lie awake that night wondering if she might lose both patients with whose care she had been entrusted.

"Damn," David said. He could not bring himself to look at the wound, and apologized to the nurse, who said calmly, "There is no point in you doing so, Mr. Harris, unless you plan to operate." He hoped they could arrive in Bermuda before Malia's condition worsened.

Chris said, "I've called ahead. An ambulance will meet us at the dock. Our captain will go as fast as he safely can. Tomorrow morning around ten o'clock we should arrive in Hamilton." He handed David the phone. "Do you want to try calling your brother again?" The connection had broken off almost immediately that morning, and then events had moved too quickly.

"Daniel?" David asked. A wave of relief washed over him as he heard his brother's voice.

"Here's Emmett, say hello to him. Emmett, your daddy is coming home. Say hello to him."

In the background, David heard crying.

"He doesn't want to come to the phone, David, he's confused. It'll be easier once you're actually in front of him."

"Daniel, Mom died last night. We just buried her at sea. And Malia...she's here, but she's not doing well. We have to get to Bermuda before it's too late." He started to tell Daniel about his last conversation with Marjory, but then the connection broke off. Just as well, David told himself, this topic was ill-suited for a screen. He could have called Rex as well, but procrastinated, hoping for better news and knowing she would want to speak most with her mother. He could not bear to tell Rex that her mother might not survive.

David did not leave Malia's side until midevening. The nurse brought him dinner. When he realized that he was keeping the nurse from her bed in a corner of the stateroom, he excused himself, but asked, anxiously, "Please come and get me if there's any change. Any time of the night. Promise?" The nurse promised.

David found Chris reading a book in the lounge next to a wide ceramic bowl of pretzels. He flung himself onto the circular sofa a few feet away and said, "This is a disaster. My mother is dead, my wife might be dying. Is this the reward for a year of trying to fight the ADF? Will I return—with nothing to show for my fight?"

"David, David." Chris laid the book down, and David, glancing at it, saw the title, *The History of 21st Century China*. At least Chris was broadening beyond robotics. "This is no time to lose hope. Think of the great things God has done for you this year. But you haven't told me what happened after we sent you on your journey. Please tell me what happened between then and the wedding. We know about the massacre because we got your photos, and only then was the NSC willing to let AIA help us."

It was a relief to unload the story of his travails. David hadn't realized how much he had bottled up inside of him. Only to Chris could he tell everything. He talked about the Candor Inn and how he came to the roundup on the shores of Cayuga Lake, how he had trained the fighters and about the poultry farm. He started to talk about Lucy, and saw Chris's face and realized no confession was necessary; Chris knew what had happened, and did not judge him. Then he spoke about evading the cull, and Warren Welcome, and bricklaying, and how he tricked his way into Paragon's house for his brief reunion with Malia, and how he had united with the Plores of Oren's town to infiltrate the wedding. He hesitated, and then told Chris how the Plores of the town had killed the Social Crediteers when they fought back and tried to escape, admitting the killings would have happened regardless. Only one side could have won that day.

"Chris, they are so brave. They had nothing to gain from helping me, except to strike a blow against persecution. If they are alive tomorrow, it will be a miracle. I promised to come back and help…"

"Help them do what?"

"Help them to be free again. We can make a difference. On their own, they are lost and the ADF will destroy them. We can tip the balance."

"And who do you mean by 'we,' my friend?" The tan eyes glinted at him.

David faltered, "Me. And the AIA. And the MAGA. Anyone who cares about America and wants to fight oppression…" His head sank into his hands. "I know, that sounds ridiculous. The US government doesn't see the threat, we just want some ports. And what can a few of us do? It's hard enough just keeping the US free, with all the DJR plotting against us. Forget it."

"No, it is possible," said Chris. "If there are sincere fighters waiting for leadership in New York, we may be able to help them. Money will be an issue, and how to safely communicate with them and supply them. But these are logistical problems, not scientific ones. There are always limits in science, but in logistics and politics, the limits are about how much risk you want to take and how much money you want to spend. These Plores seem to be willing to take risks."

"They have no choice," David responded. "They have been driven to the wall, more and more. It was worse this time than five years ago. If Paragon is gone, and my old friend Steve Rosen is in charge, it will be somewhat better, but Steve cannot envision a DJR without socialism, so he cannot imagine one without dictatorship, so there will be no change. There is no solution to the Plore problem other than democracy, for all."

Chris regarded him with pleasure. "My friend, you are far more politically astute than you were back in Oklahoma. At that time you just saw the Antifans as a personal problem, for you and Malia. Now you understand what the real issues at stake are. It is the same for the Filipinos, struggling to breathe free against the Chinese. If we do not fight for ourselves in the US, we will also perish as a free people."

Then seeing David's eyes glaze over slightly, Chris laughed, and said, "I apologize for my lecture. But for your mother's sake, do not give up now. We will not let her die in vain."

"Or Malia," David said.

"Malia will be all right, God willing," said Chris. "Despair is a sin against God. Despair is a monster that says to God, I have no faith in You. Let's pray for Malia's recovery, and I would like to pray for your healing too. You took no gunshots, but you are also in pain, I can tell. You have seen horrific things this year, and I know you did not tell me everything." David let Chris lay hands on his shoulders, and pray aloud, intently.

"In Jesus's name," Chris concluded, and then it was time for sleep. David lay awake for a while, recollecting all the strangers in the DJR who had helped him, at risk of their own lives. He prayed that Oren and his band were safely home in Yramaland. He prayed for Tom and Seth, but did not know whether they had survived the attack. Maybe AIA could task Warren Welcome for an update when he, David, returned home.

The next morning, David awoke, and hurried to the deck to find that Malia's fever was higher and she was delirious, tossing and turning. The nurse looked anxious. He ate a bite of a croissant and sipped black coffee, but lacked any appetite.

"Two hours now to Hamilton," Chris reassured him. The yacht cut boldly into the blue waters, as if it knew it was on a mission. They had benefited from fair weather and favorable winds throughout the journey. David returned to Malia's room to sit alongside her bed. He held her hand but, restless, she pulled it away, and he did not try again. He counted the minutes.

PART SEVEN

BERMUDA

"[The United States was] born to be a special place between the two great oceans with a unique message to carry freedom's torch. To a tired and disillusioned world, we've always been a light of hope where all things are possible."
—President Ronald Reagan, Boston, November 1, 1984

Chapter 64
Safe Harbor
(Wednesday–Saturday, November 3–6, 2094)

"Bermuda," Chris said quietly, as the yacht came within sight of land. An hour ago, he had pointed out the famous white longtails swooping by. One, with a fifteen-inch-long tail and black markings, had perched on the railing only a few feet away, resting, before flying off.

David leaned forward. "Hamilton?"

"Not yet, it's on the other side of the bay. We were excused from customs clearance in St. George due to Malia's emergency. We'll catch up with the paperwork later."

They sailed into Grassy Bay, slowing down, deferential to the other, mostly smaller yachts and sailboats. The warm autumn sun beat down on their faces. The crew began trotting around on the deck in preparation for landing. The yacht turned around the promontory and headed for Hamilton on its south side.

David went into the stateroom to check on Malia and to bring her the good news. But she was asleep. He stared despairingly at her pale, still face. They had not spoken to each other in twenty-four hours, unless you considered a stray muttered, "David," a conversation. Once, mysteriously, she had called out, "Sohan, Sohan, help," but David had no idea what that meant.

Last night the nurse had looked at him sadly, and said, "Sepsis, I'm afraid." The antibiotics had kept the infection in a holding pattern at least temporarily, but they were not quite the ones Malia needed. This morning, all the nurse said to him was, "She is no worse, but no better."

Afraid to ask her more, David had scrolled on Chris's phone for information about sepsis, all of which had alarmed him. Nor had Chris even tried to reassure him once the dreaded word was pronounced. "We're almost there," was all the scientist could tell him.

A calm, tidy harbor lined with pastel buildings rose reassuringly before them. A safe harbor, finally, after all their travails. Soon the yacht had pulled up alongside one of the wider, outlying docks, in tribute to its size. To their relief, an ambulance with two medical workers waited just beyond the dock. A black diplomatic vehicle with an American flag pulled in behind it. A few young boys sitting on a wall, perhaps skipping school, waved at them.

The ambulance crew ran with a stretcher up to the *Mar-a-Lago* and shouted to the yacht's crew. A few minutes later, the stretcher came forth with Malia and the nurse bearing the saline solution alongside her. They disappeared into the ambulance and sped off to the hospital. "We'll catch up with them at the hospital," said Chris, looking at the screen on his phone. "Rangeley Weston herself is waiting for them."

"Rangeley Weston? Capettone's Rangeley Weston?"

"Are there any other surgeons named Rangeley?"

Rangeley Weston was the chief surgical expert of Capettone. "Baxter Berry sent her here personally. You said the ADF chief surgeon himself operated on Malia, but Rangeley got into medical school without social credit points. The hospital here has given her special visiting privileges and, once she has operated on Malia, she has promised to stay for a while and give lectures to the staff. Malia could not be in better hands now."

"Chris, I hope you're right," David said.

"Good morning, Mr. Harris, Mr. Mendoza," said a trim thirtyish man in lime green shorts that went down to his knees, black knee-high socks, and laced leather shoes. David was taken aback. "I'm Jim Valdez, the assistant consul. Please don't be alarmed by my outfit, it's standard Bermudan office wear. You know, Bermuda shorts? Let's get in the car and we'll meet up with your wife at the hospital. Dr. Weston is standing by, ready to operate."

En route to the hospital, he handed David a small envelope. "An invitation from Sir Keirnan Thomason and Lady Thomason. They'll be holding a reception on Saturday night. He's a press lord and a baronet."

"What's a baronet?"

"I was afraid you'd ask that. But the personage of interest is actually Lady Thomason. She is passionately pro-liberty. She will ask you all about the Deplorables. Sir Keirnan is the bank."

Six hours later, Rangeley Watson entered the waiting room. David and Chris had been sitting mostly in silence, with brief trips to the cafeteria and to sit outside on the veranda overlooking water and palm trees.

Rangeley Watson was a tall African-American woman still wearing her surgical scrubs and black framed glasses that gave her an owlish look. "Mr. Harris," she said, "I have good news for you. Your wife is resting in the recovery room. Her leg was fine, under the circumstances. However, we diagnosed a gastrointestinal fistula that was leaking fluid into the vascular system. We drained the wound, installed a robotic suction cutaway—you can thank Chris's lab for that innovation—and I removed gangrenous tissue. She is doing as well as can be expected."

Relieved, David thanked her effusively.

"I have never before seen a wound caused by electronic gunshot. I understand this kind of weapon is only used in the DJR. The tissue around the electronic shot wound became gangrenous very quickly. She is lucky to have survived. I will bring what I have learned back to Capettone so we can develop methods for treating such wounds more effectively. We don't have those kinds of weapons in the United States, thank goodness, but you never know.

"Mr. Harris, that's for another day. I want to say that whoever operated on her before me botched the job, and in such a way that I can only think malice was at work."

"But that was the chief surgeon of the Antifan Defense Forces!" David cried out. "He would have been one of the best surgeons in all the DJR! He would have trained in China!" Even now, after all his suffering at the hands of the ADF, David still believed that the organization represented professionalism, even when brutal. He found it hard to believe that mere animus could overpower a physician's oath, and even if the physician bore him and Malia ill will, shouldn't Steve Rosen's diktat have guaranteed a competent operation?

Rangeley Watson looked grim. "If he was one of the best surgeons in the DJR, then why would he not have sutured the wound more tightly? From what I can tell, it began leaking almost immediately. He also used an inferior grade of suturing thread. The surgery was carelessly done, recklessly. In the US, he would have been sued for malpractice. I know the DJR is poorer than we are, but surely the equipment available to their elites is comparable to ours."

David recalled that the surgeon had refused to meet him after the operation on the DHS *Gain of Function*. Had the person been afraid to face him after deliberately botching the operation on Malia? And while David was certain Steve Rosen would never have considered that the chief ADF surgeon would operate so maliciously on Malia, the surgeon may have reasoned that Steve Rosen would never learn that Malia had died as a result of his malpractice, or if Rosen somehow learned of her death, he would assume it had happened despite the surgeon's best efforts.

"But will she live?" he begged Dr. Watson.

"I believe so," Rangeley Watson said encouragingly. "I have brought the newest Capettone devices with me and she will have the finest care here. This is the best hospital in Bermuda, and in the British Commonwealth outside of London, if I might say so myself. If the night goes smoothly, you will be talking with her tomorrow. I would suggest that you and Chris go and have a stroll and some dinner. I can recommend Kingston Pub—my cousins own it. Tell them I sent you. Yes, my family is from Bermuda, so I didn't need a lot of convincing to come back for a visit."

Back on the yacht, David called Daniel.

"Thank God," Daniel said at the good news. "Hopefully you will be home in time for Thanksgiving. Baxter Berry offered to fly us all out to Bermuda, but I think it would be too much to deal with Emmett and George at this time, as much as you want to see them. I really think he feels guilty about how he treated you. Don't be surprised if he offers to bring you back on board at Capettone."

The word "guilty" reminded David of what he had not yet told Daniel.

"I feel as if I killed Mom. She spent her last night on earth on the execution hallway. When I was an Antifan, I dragged innocent people to their deaths on a Saturday night. Then on Sundays I sat next to her at St. Paul's. When I was saying good night on the yacht, she asked me if I had ever worked on that hallway. I should have lied, but I've been lying for over a year, and I'd had it. And I just couldn't lie to Mom, not now, not under those circumstances."

"How did she react?"

"She turned to the wall, and I begged her to forgive me. She said of course she forgave me, but you know her. She really seemed to be saying, "I forgive you, but it is not my forgiveness you need. And now I will never forget." She gave me one last look, and then said she was tired and wanted to sleep. That was the last time we ever spoke. She was gone in the morning."

"David, I have some news that I think will comfort you. We got a letter from Christine the other day—it was dated just before the Antifans took Emma and Mom as hostages. She said Mom had just been diagnosed with lung cancer. It was pretty advanced. The Antifans didn't care about her diagnosis, but she likely wouldn't have survived long anyway, not in the DJR. I'm sorry she didn't make it to Oklahoma, where we could have tried harder to save her life. But from what Christine says, Mom may have been very far gone by the time you saw her again."

"Then why would she have come with us?" David demanded. "She could have lived longer if she'd gone home and rested comfortably instead of coming with us."

"A little longer. Maybe she did want to see *me* again. I'm her oldest child, you know. You saw her during the summer, but it's been five years since I last saw her. And maybe she wanted to see her grandchildren. And maybe she thought in the US they might be able to treat her illness."

"But why didn't she tell me she was so ill?"

"You'd just rescued her. She was tired. She thought there would be time the next day or the day after to tell you the truth. She probably thought she had more time than she did.

"David, be grateful that she passed so peacefully into the Lord's hands, on a sailing boat, free at last, not in pain. Don't berate yourself for the inevitable. If you hadn't told her the truth, she would have suspected you were lying, and that would have hurt her more. She would not have asked that question unless she knew the answer. So you passed her test, the test of integrity and ownership of your sins. She died free and in full knowledge of the truth."

The next morning, David arrived at the hospital as soon as visiting hours began. He sat, waiting, doglike in his patience, by Malia's bed, for an hour. The nurses had told him that her fever had disappeared overnight and, smiling, one added, "That is a good sign." He imagined he saw a touch of pink in Malia's cheeks.

Then her eyes opened, and she recognized him. They held hands. A nurse came in the room to check Malia's vitals and change the IV, and pronounced her as good as could be expected. Malia said she felt little pain, just some discomfort in her side and leg. The nurse said, "Please take these peels, madam." But it was just the local accent, since all she gave Malia were pills and not fruit at all.

"You know, the last time I woke up in a hospital, it was at Beaufort, and a fat drone nurse was sitting on me videotaping," Malia told him. "This is much better. Are those palm trees? Where are we?"

"Bermuda, in the middle of the Atlantic Ocean. Until the *Mar-a-Lago* picked us up, I had no idea myself where we were going." So for the next half hour, as she lay peacefully against the crisp white pillows, a light breeze refreshing them, David told her the story of their escape, the desperate drive to the Delaware beach, which she only hazily recalled, the farewells with Steve and the junior officers, the arrival of Marjory at the last minute, the journey on the DHS *Gain of Function*, the transfer to the *Mar-a-Lago*, sent by Baxter Berry ("See! I told you he wasn't a bad person, just afraid," Malia reminded him), and now her second operation. He refrained from accusing the ADF surgeon and just said, "You needed a second operation."

But Malia said, "I thought it was a dream. But I was being operated on and it hurt. There was a doctor in scrubs, and a nurse. And he said, 'You don't deserve to live after what you did to Paragon and the ADF.' Did he die?"

"I don't know what happened to Paragon but Exterra died on the stage as the balcony fell."

"I do remember seeing her lying there, now. I poisoned the drink, David. It was meant for Paragon but he realized what I had done and he pretended to make Exterra his senior wife so he could switch their cups. It was dastardly of him."

"It was dastardly of *you*," smiled David. "But she deserved it, so don't waste your time mourning her. I don't think it would have been a very happy marriage."

"How wonderful to wake up here and be safe again, and to be together, finally, after all this time." Then, "Where is your mother? Is she also in the hospital?"

David told her about Marjory's sudden passing and the dignified burial at sea. "She is now with my father." He would share the details another time.

Malia sighed, shaking her head. "Can we call home and see Emmett and George?"

"It's early there," he protested, but not energetically. How could he refuse her anything? They dialed Daniel and Fern, and soon Emmett was on the TV screen above Malia's bed. "Hi Mommy, I'm glad you're all right, Mommy. Are you coming home soon? I miss you. I won a race at school." George peered anxiously at them, and darted off, calling, "Mommy!" Malia took a sharp, painful intake of breath, and David reassured her, "He'll know his real mommy soon again." Rex soon appeared on the screen, having run over from the house as soon as Fern called, and she and Malia cried with joy to see each other, alive, and well, and importantly, free. Rex told Malia all about Nathan and how kind he was and how she would meet him soon.

Malia was discharged from the hospital on Saturday morning. They had expected to rest comfortably on board the *Mar-a-Lago* before flying back to Oklahoma City via New Orleans on Monday morning. David lay next to her all day as she slept, marveling in his good fortune, watching the planes of Malia's face rise and fall with her breath, sometimes close enough that he felt her breath on his own cheeks. He would not let her out of his sight. Chris had departed on Friday morning, and they had embraced in farewell like brothers.

The nurse came in occasionally to check on Malia and change her dressings. David apologized for his squeamishness, looking away, but the nurse said, "It's my job, please." She was visibly relieved that she had a recovering, rather than dying patient, and a batting average of .500.

A call came from Jim Valdez at the consulate on Saturday afternoon. "I'll pick you up at seven o'clock."

"What?"

"The Thomason party, remember?"

"What?" David had completely forgotten the invitation from the baronet and his lady. He found the invitation in the jacket pocket. "Jim, I just can't. I need to stay here with my wife. We've been separated for well over a year."

"You'll have the rest of your life together. You don't want to miss this party. These are important people who can help you. Can Malia make it?"

"She just got discharged from the hospital this morning! How can she go to a party?"

"What party?" Malia asked. When she found out that an actual baronet and his lady were hosting, and they were sympathetic to the cause of liberty, her natural shyness evaporated. "Yes, we must go, David! We'll bring the wheelchair and the nurse can come too."

"Jim, she wants to go," David said disbelievingly.

"Of course she does! Who doesn't want to meet a baronet, whatever they are? And the house is absolutely gorgeous, just seeing it is worth the price of admission. It sits right on a hill overlooking the water. It looks like a pink cake. Amazing windows."

The nurse was mostly disapproving, but didn't mind an outing either. "Mind you, Mrs. Harris cannot eat solids or drink alcohol." David and the nurse managed to work a loose red dress that Chris had brought from Oklahoma over Malia's head. It fell around her legs as they held her up. She was very pale, but the color still became her.

"Are you sure you want to do this?" David asked her as the 7:00 p.m. hour approached. "I can go alone, really."

"David, when will I ever again have a chance to go to a baronet's party in a pink house on the water in Bermuda with people who share our values and might help us in future?"

Jim Valdez's car pulled up to the dock.

Chapter 65
Moon Gate
(Saturday–Sunday, November 6–7, 2094)

They were driving to the party in Jim's car. "What are those towers over there?" Malia pointed at a cluster of silver towers, lights twinkling against the dark horizon, separated from the main island by a causeway. They seemed to be floating against the sky. It reminded her, disturbingly, of Anacosta.

"That's New Island, completely man-made," said Jim. "Bermuda's gotten a lot livelier since our civil war. It became a crossroads for all kinds of folks who facilitate trade and interaction with North America since there isn't really a US role anymore. St. Louis couldn't replace New York and Washington, or even Florida. Canada's too cold and Mexico's still too dangerous, and not English-speaking.

"We can meet with DJR types in Bermuda if we need to, and instead of coming to Washington, which doesn't really exist anymore, foreigners meet up here. But Bermuda is a small island. They didn't want all the traffic, and to lose their character, but London wanted the prestige and the money, so this was the compromise. A territory doesn't get to call the shots.

"North American and Commonwealth enterprises and persons live and do business on the regular islands. You'll see some of these characters at the Thomasons', by the way. A lot of money rolling around Bermuda these days."

Just as Jim had promised, the Thomason house resembled a long pink cake with ample windows opening out onto a wraparound porch overlooking the bay below. Torchlights in the garden around the house cast shadows against its walls.

"Oh how adorable!" Malia said. Her eyes, starved for color after more than a year among the dismal DJR towers, had greedily swallowed the pastel roofs and blue waters around her as they drove through Hamilton back to the yacht earlier in the day.

Sir Keirnan himself greeted them in the foyer, a thin, gray-haired man of medium height. "Sorry you had to lift the wheelchair into the house, fellows. We're just not set up for the handicapped." He indicated the large room with the windows. "Please join the party." He turned to other guests, who seemed to be distinguished businessmen and spouses of greater interest to him.

The large room was thronged with an eclectic, lively crowd. David pushed Malia's wheelchair into a corner from which she could view the room. Jim pointed out several key figures as servers brought them cocktails and hors d'oeuvres. David requested and got an apple juice for Malia.

"Lots of New Island people tonight. Lady Thomason will let anyone come, except deejers. She won't invite them. There's the consul of Azawad." He indicated a very tall man with a profile that might well have been carved in obsidian, wearing sweeping white robes and and a towering headdress. Azawad was the Salafist Islamic empire in the heart of North Africa. It loftily ignored the carping about human rights from the feeble United Nations now located in London. Slavery had been reintroduced in the great Sahel salt mines, and women were less prized than cattle. "Azawad has billions of dollars to invest from the Sahel mines, so everyone's maneuvering for that great business opportunity."

In the conversational grouping next to him was a petite blonde with saucer-blue eyes and a glittery blue gown who reminded Malia of Exterra. She was emotional about something, and her tremulous laugh rose above the conversational buzz, as she lifted her cocktail glass to her mouth again and again, without sipping.

"That's the European Union president, visiting from Brussels. Russia is pressuring the EU to withdraw support from the Baltics and Poland. It's been a hundred years since the Soviets lost those countries, and they want them back. But the EU can't place pressure on Moscow the way NATO did, so good luck there. She's talking to the Russian consul." Malia and David looked at the towering bald man with the dark beard whose stern face radiated contempt for the EU representative.

Malia recognized someone else. "David!" she said, clutching her husband's sleeve. He looked at her, alarmed. "That's Will Kendall!" Why isn't he in prison, she thought indignantly. Five years ago, she had last seen him hustled by Antifans across the tarmac at the Economic Zone camp after they had thwarted his efforts to escape via plane to Mexico to enjoy his ill-gotten gains.

"What?" David's face flushed with anger. "How did *he* get here?"

Will recognized them, and gave them an airy wave, as if to say, "No hard feelings." He wore a beautifully tailored jacket and slacks, and was engaged in conversation with a bullet-necked Mexican wearing a gold chain whose own jacket was a tad tight.

Jim mentioned a few more names, some recognizable even to Malia and David. "That's the daughter of the richest Russian oligarch...That is Zuo Wang. He won the Oscar last year for Best Actor." Malia said curiously, "For an island in the middle of the ocean, this seems like a very elite crowd. I'm surprised that countries so far away—like India and Azawad—have consuls here. This feels more like London."

"Not a coincidence," said Jim. "This is a very important posting for most diplomats. It's more like the United Nations—with business opportunities—than the UN itself is these days. I really was lucky to get the deputy slot here. But if you haven't figured it out, I don't really work for the State Department." He paused to take in their confused faces, and said, "Uh…Vernal says hello, if that helps you figure out who I really work for here."

"Oh!" they chorused.

"Really," Jim said, "if I were State Department, would I be working on a Saturday night?" He added, "This place is rich with opportunities for the attentive spy. I'll be able to file a cable tomorrow just based on what I pick up tonight. If you don't mind, I'm going to work the room for a little while. Please excuse me."

Malia said she wanted to sit on the porch overlooking the water. David was able to open two French doors to push the wheelchair through. Nobody else seemed eager to join them, so they had privacy, sitting in a companionable silence. At one point, David said, "I'll get us something else to eat. Do you want more of that tomato soup in the little cups? I'll bring back several."

Shortly after David went for food, Will Kendall joined her on the deck. Malia shrank back. Nothing would have stopped him from throwing her over the side of the balcony into the garden below, but Will seemed as genial as ever, taking David's seat.

"I'm sure you want to know why I'm here and not in some DJR dungeon," he said. "After a year at Hupachuca"—the DJR supermax criminal prison in Arizona—"they came for me and said they needed my skill set on the outside. So I'm the main DJR facilitator here in Bermuda. Acquiring all kinds of lethal things for our country, for the best price possible. I'm a little surprised to see you, though. Weren't you supposed to be married to the great Commander Ma? You and your Plore husband really live a charmed life. He should be dead."

"It isn't my country anymore," said Malia. "I'm an American." Or she would be soon.

"Who knows where the border will be in ten years?" Will smiled at her. "If Russia and China can swallow up other countries, who will stop the DJR from nibbling away at the US?

"I just wanted to thank you, because even though a year in that prison was completely un-fun, it's worked out in the end. I've got private bank accounts you wouldn't believe, and more girlfriends than I know what to do with. Much better dating in Bermuda than in the DJR."

"I was told our hostess doesn't invite deejers," said Malia. "How come you're here?"

"Always keep a bunch of passports around," said Will. "Tonight I'm Mexican, unless anyone wants to speak Spanish, in which case I will suddenly become a Canadian."

David came back on the porch, a server behind him with a tray. In a few seconds, he closed the gap between himself and Will, and growled, "Get away from my wife, you bastard, before I throw you off this balcony. In a normal country, you'd be in prison for life."

"I know, isn't that amazing? I was just thanking her for the great business opportunity you two gave me, eventually. Beautiful. I'd buy you drinks, but it's all free tonight."

Under David's malevolent gaze, Will stuttered, "Cheerio!" and disappeared back into the main room. The server laid down the tray on their table and followed him. David gave Malia his jacket, as the night was cooling off. But even Will's reappearance could not diminish the pleasure they took in looking at the bay and the twinkling lights of Hamilton harbor on the other side of the water. Malia sipped her gazpacho, and David ate small roast beef sandwiches from his plate.

"Much better stuff than I've been eating most of this year," he said. "I don't miss the nute meat." This made him think of his Plore comrades, about whose fate he had no idea. Had they made it back home? Had they evaded the wrath of the ADF? The hardscrabble hills of Yramaland and Cayuga seemed very far away at that moment. But without those kameraten, David acknowledged, Malia and I would not be here tonight.

The door to the porch swung open, and a green-gowned woman in her early sixties came to greet them. She was tidy, but not glamorous, comfortably rounded, with no-nonsense short gray hair, and calm blue eyes. A sparkling light sea green shawl covered her shoulders.

"I've been looking for you!" she said. "I'm Sarah." She was also an American, judging by the accent. David and Malia were confused, because they had no idea who this friendly Sarah was.

"I'm your hostess!" she said laughing at their perplexity. "I know, you're expecting me to speak like Queen Madeleine, aren't you," referring to the aged King George VII's aristocratic queen consort. "No, I'm an ordinary American, or was once upon a time. Keirnan and I met at Oxford, the civil war broke out back home, and it seemed safer to stay and raise our family in England. About ten years ago we relocated here. I still have my US passport, and every once in a long while, I go to Chicago, where I still have family, but honestly, it's just not the same anymore.

"Have you noticed, everything is smaller, tenser, less creative, less…just less? The world is smaller, but not in a good way. Everyone has turned inward."

Malia said, "We have nothing to compare it to, Lady Thomason…"

"Please, just Sarah. Because I'm going to call you Malia and David. We've just met, but we are already friends and we share convictions. Of course, you have nothing to compare today to. How I show my age! Jim has told me all about your adventures. You are both so brave." She motioned to a server. "Please find Mr. Valdez from the US consulate and have him join us. Thank you."

While they waited for Jim, Sarah asked David, "The Plores—what do they want?"

"They want to be left alone by the government. If they had arms, they could defend themselves and make it not worth the ADF's while to bother them. They could be ignored, since the ADF simply would not tell the Social Crediteers about the rebellion."

"The narrative is most precious to the government," explained Malia. "In other words, they would rather tolerate a band of rebels keeping to themselves as least for the moment than admit to the country that there were dissatisfied citizens."

"But they're not citizens, right?" Sarah asked. "What if the DJR gave them citizenship? Would that appease them?"

"Citizenship doesn't mean much in the DJR," said Malia. "You get a social credit score, fewer freedoms, and more monitoring. Every few years you get to approve the leaders your betters have chosen for you. It's kind of paradoxical, but in some ways the Plores are freer than the Social Crediteers."

"Could we get Social Crediteers to join an uprising?"

"Not immediately," said David, recalling his arguments with Lucy. But for the vagaries of life, Lucy could have easily switched places with this passionate woman who was about her age. Yet Lucy had always doubted that Social Crediteers were redeemable. "Once we had territory, and got the message out, some might join. Many of us believe that Social Crediteers have been indoctrinated to the point at which they are beyond saving."

"Do you? Are you really in that camp, David?"

"I don't know," said David. "When I'm optimistic, I tell myself we could make inroads and build momentum. Unless we make some headway, we'll just stay in the countryside and they'll turn their Cities into even more of a fortress. It'll be like a chess game when no one makes a real move. And then there's the West Coast—I don't have a good sense for how to even start there."

Malia asked, "I don't mean to offend you, Sarah, but why do you care so much? You have a good life here, and the DJR is just a small place on the globe. There's still a United States."

"Because I remember. The world needs the kind of United States we had a century ago. One that was willing to exercise leadership. Before they let the woke and the greedy destroy it. Now we see what the hunger for power, unchecked, has done to the rest of the world. Just look around my living room tonight.

"Russia and China have been subjugating their areas of the world. One of the saddest days for me was when China took over the Philippines and we could do nothing to help our treaty ally because we no longer had the Pacific seacoast. Russia has conquered Ukraine again, and is poised to seize back the Baltics, and other countries in eastern Europe have relinquished their NATO memberships under pressure. Even Britain is not in a position to speak for, let alone defend, what remains of the free world.

"The phrase 'free world' dates me. My parents used it, but even then it was spoken ironically. We have been on a long, slow slide back into barbarism."

David said, "We can't send troops everywhere. The old US got into trouble by trying to solve countries' problems for them." He was repeating the MAGA line.

"Of course not," Sarah replied, "but the world needs to see an example of how free people live and prosper to know it is possible and to take heart. The 'city on a hill.'" David looked confused, while Malia nodded in recognition of the phrase.

As she spoke, Jim Valdez had taken a seat at their table.

"I throw these parties because it's helpful for my friends at AIA and MI6 to meet with their sources and recruit new ones. Right, Jim?"

"It's been a good evening," Jim admitted. "I was in the car recording some of my—findings."

"And there are elements in the AIA who understand the challenge and who are willing to work with us to bring the cause of freedom to the DJR. Right, Jim?"

"Yes, Sarah, but we are not in the majority. Most of them would rather just hunker down in St. Louis and not cause problems with our prickly woke neighbors. We would take a half loaf and beg the deejers for port access. But that's not the way a great country should be."

"No, it isn't," Sarah agreed. "The United States can't play the role on the stage it needs to play. There is no example for the world, let alone an actor for good. The Chinese Communists and the Russians say democracy is the reason for our failure, and it is convenient for dictators to believe that. Look at Azawad and Guatehondura"—the former Central America, now a criminal state run by drug cartels, unabashedly selling marijuana, fentanyl, and heroin around the world.

"A strong United States would be a beacon to the world. But since our civil war, countries have learned the lesson that might makes right, but not good. And billions of people live in despair."

Malia was becoming impatient. "Sarah, are you offering to help us? Are you just lending us moral support, or more?" She was vaguely conscious of the throbbing pain in her side. The meds were wearing off again.

"Oh my dear, of course. I wouldn't invite you here just to ply you with cheap political statements. I'll be coming to visit St. Louis early in the new year and we'll plot then. And don't worry about Keirnan. I don't object to his polo team or the racetrack bets, and in turn he will gladly underwrite my new hobby. And Thomason Press Holdings might start asking a few more questions about the DJR."

"That reminds me," said Jim, pulling out his phone. "I saw this article from the *Anacosta Post* while I was in the car." He handed Malia the phone. She read it quickly and passed it to David.

"Commander Khalid Ma, 290, Attending Consultations in China with PRC Leadership," David read aloud. The wedding was mentioned only in passing. "His devotion to Diversity led him to depart Anacosta immediately after his wedding to Captain Boyd, 194, and Communicator Malia, 194, on October 30…"

"Who are nowhere to be found this week," laughed Malia. Her right side ached with the effort. She took the phone and read: "Commander Ma will stay in China for an extended period while he negotiates the latest section of the PRC-DJR treaty governing scientific and cultural research."

Mocking the tendentious style of the Post, she concluded, "Communicator Malia is alive and well in the capitalist territory of Bermuda. Captain Boyd is not alive or well at all."

"Malia and David, let me and my driver take you around the island tomorrow afternoon. Only as much as you can bear, my dear. But there is a lovely moon gate arch overlooking the water where you can sit together and hold hands. The moon gate is a romantic Bermuda tradition and you cannot leave without visiting one."

The next afternoon, on their last full day in Bermuda, Malia and David sat side by side, hand in hand before the moon gate, with her in the wheelchair, and him in a canvas folding chair that the driver retrieved from the back of the black limousine and set up before discreetly retreating. Just as Sarah had told them, the moon gate was a round brick arch around which vines twined. Through the moon gate they glimpsed the bay and several boats. The thin November sun was just beginning to descend. Sarah tapped on her phone near the car a few hundred feet away.

David pushed the wheelchair through the arch, as Sarah had instructed them to do. "It will bring you both luck. That is the tradition."

"I'm glad Sarah convinced us to come here," said Malia. "Very romantic." She smiled at him, thinking, he is thinner and harder than when we were last in Oklahoma. I see more gray hair in those blond curls. He needs a haircut. He has not told me everything that happened, to spare me. I'm not sure I want him to tell me any more. Look what he did to himself to rescue me. How will I ever repay him?

David wondered, will she ever be strong enough again to hear everything that happened to me? How much she has suffered because, once upon a time, I was an Antifan commander. My past came after us with a vengeance. But her face is still lovely. It's not just the physical features, it's the purity of her heart and her courage. No one else could have survived this ordeal with their honor intact. Every time they tried to force her back into Diversity, she bounded back.

"Remember when we argued just before the kidnapping?" David asked her. "You said you wanted to become a professor, and I teased you about the dissertation? I said you were a great mom to the dissertation. That was mean. I apologize. I've regretted saying that a million times."

"So you don't mind if I become a professor after all? Even if it means we have to leave Oklahoma? When Baxter Berry's probably going to give you your job back?"

"I don't want his job. And I don't want you to become a professor."

"No?" Malia's voice trembled. Not again! Had he learned nothing from all their suffering?

"No, we've both got more important things to do. You're going to be the country's most important DJR expert, for sure, but not in a classroom. That would be a waste of your talents. And I'm not going to sit behind a desk either. As soon as you're feeling better, we're going to take the battle back to the Sokos and the Antifans."

She understood. "Yes." They would never hide again from the challenge.

He leaned over, she leaned in, even though it hurt a little, and they kissed tenderly.

A distant horn honked, very politely, because they were in Bermuda, after all.

"That's our ride," said David.